PLAGUE OF SHADOWS

THE ALDORAN CHRONICLES
- BOOK TWO -

written by

MICHAEL WISEHART

Copyright

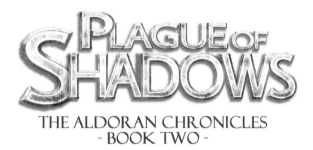

PLAGUE OF SHADOWS

THE ALDORAN CHRONICLES
- BOOK TWO -

Books by Michael Wisehart

Street Rats of Aramoor

Book 1 | Banished

Book 2 | Hurricane

The Aldoran Chronicles

Book 1 | The White Tower

Book 2 | Plague of Shadows

Map of Aldor – West

Map of Aldor - East

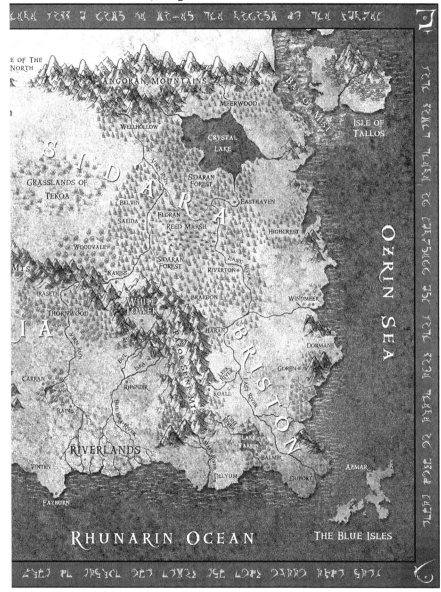

Map of Aramoor

BAY OF TORRIN

1. LUMBER YARDS	5. WILDFIRE COMPOUND	8. BAYSIDE	12. SHIPPING YARDS	16. OLD MERCHANT DISTRICT
2. THE ROCKSLIDE COMPOUND	6. LANCER BARRACKS	9. THE TEMPLE	13. THE PIT	17. THE WARRENS
3. LANCER CORPS	7. SANDSTORM COMPOUND	10. KING'S SQUARE	14. THE ROYAL PALACE	
4. THE GUILD		11. AVALANCHE COMPOUND	15. THE GRANARY	

ARAMOOR

Map of Easthaven

1.East Bridge 2.East Inn 3.Maugora's 4.Barracks
5.Sidaran Assembly Hall 6.Overlord Barl's Estate 7.Dockworks
8.Orlyn's Apothecary 9.Harbor House 10.Reloria's Sweet Shop

Chapter 1 | Joren

*J*OREN RAN AS fast as he could.

He stumbled over his own feet as he struggled to make his way down the stone encasement. His hands were too busy trying to fasten the gold clasp of his new white mantle to pay attention to where he was going. His nostrils flared as his unpracticed fingers fumbled with the pin. The needle finally slipped into place, and he released a short sigh of relief, then shifted his belt to keep his scabbard from bouncing against his leg.

"Why did the Archchancellor have to pick today of all days for a visit?" His voice followed him down the cold stone as he worked his way farther into the bowels of the White Tower. *How deep do these tunnels go?* he wondered.

The scent of oil from the torches lining both sides of the narrow passageway did little to mask the lingering stench of mildew. Occasionally, he caught a trace of rich earth—dark soil he hadn't smelled since he was a boy on his uncle's farm in northern Cylmar.

It was Joren's first week as a member of the Black Watch, and he was already off to a bad start. He wasn't sure why the new recruits had been summoned, only that his late arrival was certain to have him tossed out on his ear. He couldn't afford to lose this position. He needed the work.

Being the third son of a poor tailor, Joren had no inheritance, no chance of a position within the family business, small as it was. His older brothers had already filled those roles, which left him with nothing more than the odd bit of day labor from other merchants in town. So, when the Black Watch had arrived in Ecrin to spread word that the new High King was looking for able-bodied men from Cylmar to fill their army's ranks, Joren was one of the first to sign up.

It had only been a few weeks since the deaths of Overlord Saryn and the previous High King. Since then, Prince Dakaran had wasted no time in claiming his father's throne and declaring Cylmar as part of the New Elondrian Empire. With this announcement, men from Cylmar had flooded over the borders, looking for work.

At twenty-five years of age, Joren was already too old to find an apprenticeship with a local guild and was thankful to have the opportunity to be an armsman. It was an honest profession, one whose skills could be used for future work down the road. Best of all, he could help protect Aldor from the danger posed by these wielders. Their presence seemed to be growing.

The sounds of booted feet and clanging scabbards ahead urged his pace. "Good, I'm not too late." He couldn't have picked a worse time to have a privy run. He emerged from the tunnel and found himself at the edge of a deep chasm, with a rather impressive stone bridge leading across.

He didn't have time to stop and marvel, as the rest of his company had already made it to the other side and were passing through an enormous archway into another section of the cavern.

The doors leading into that section began to shut.

No! He ran as fast as he could across the ancient bridge, barely slipping between the monolithic doors before they closed. A low rumble reverberated off the cavern walls as they came to a stop. He turned and was surprised to find there were no guards stationed on the inside. *Strange,* he thought. *Then who shut them?* Not wanting to draw attention, he rushed over to where the other recruits were waiting and fell in line.

"You!" a woman's voice called on his left.

Joren stiffened. Was she talking to him? He turned. Several of the bulradoer stood not far from the Watch, their black hooded robes shading their faces. One of the shorter bulradoer was looking in his direction. He wasn't exactly sure what purpose the bulradoer served, but from the rumors, it was best to stay as far away from them as possible.

He cast a brief glance at the recruits beside him and finally took a step forward.

"Me?" he asked, his hand trembling as he pointed to himself.

"Yes, you. We require your assistance."

"Of course . . . *mistress,*" he said with a curt bow, not quite sure how to address her. Not that it mattered. He'd been caught and was likely about to lose his position. With a nervous gulp, he left his place in line and headed in her direction. "My name's Joren, mistress. How can I help?"

"Just stand there," she said, pointing to her right.

Joren did as she said. The bulradoer seemed to be distracted by something else, so he used the time to get a better look at the cavern. It was massive, its domed roof shrouded in darkness. He wondered how high up it went. He was also surprised by how warm it was, considering how far underground they were. The place smelled of torch tar and nothing else. None of the lingering, fetid smell of mildew he had experienced in the tunnels on his way down.

In front of him stood a circular barricade of stones, each one marked with a unique symbol. Even if he could read, he doubted he could have translated them. They looked ancient. A half dozen of the white-robed inquisitors mingled off to the side, watching as the bulradoer gathered around a large block of stone inside the ring.

Behind the bulradoer stood one of the largest trees Joren had ever seen. Easily two, maybe three times that of a normal oak. It was a sickly looking beast, its branches twisted and gnarled, like it had been plagued with an arthritic malady. It reminded Joren of his grandmother's hands, with the knuckles and joints bent awkwardly to the sides. How it had managed to grow so far underground and in the middle of a cavern, Joren couldn't guess. One thing was for sure: It didn't look alive anymore. The branches were bare, not a single hint of green in sight.

A pedestal had been placed between the tree and the rectangular block of stone. The slab was about seven feet in length and stood about three feet in height. Someone was lying on top of it, but from where Joren was standing, he couldn't quite make out who it was.

Behind the tree lay a pool of black liquid. The light from the torches reflected off the surface, giving it the distinct appearance of tar. He shivered when he noticed it was moving, as if an invisible giant was stirring it with an enormous ladle.

One of the bulradoer waved in their direction, and the woman beside him headed into the circle of stone, motioning for him to follow.

Joren scrambled to catch up. Once inside, he was better able to see the proceedings.

The female bulradoer led him through the gathering of inquisitors and around to the side of what he could now see was a marble slab with distinct black veins. The body lying on top turned out to be one of the inquisitors. To say the man was obese would have been an understatement. His bald scalp and face were covered with a web of tattooed symbols.

The inquisitor's robes were bloodstained, and judging by the hole in the front of his neck, he clearly wasn't going to be getting back up. Strangely, Joren didn't notice the pungent smell of death coming from the body. He frowned. Why was the man there? For that matter, why were any of them there?

"Is he dead?" he whispered to the woman beside him, instantly regretting the ridiculous question.

"Unfortunately," a deep voice behind him said, causing Joren to jump.

He turned to see a tall gaunt-faced man in crimson robes moving through those gathered behind him. Joren's eyes widened when he noticed the mitre on the older man's head, and he quickly bowed.

The Archchancellor studied him with sunken eyes. "Is this our volunteer, Lenara?"

"It is, Your Grace," the female bulradoer said.

"I'm Joren, sir," he said with a second bow, not quite remembering when he had volunteered.

The Archchancellor nodded and moved to the stone-cut podium at the head of the slab and opened a book that was resting on top.

Lenara motioned Joren forward, removing her hood as she did. She was at least ten to fifteen years older than he was, her curly auburn hair trailing loose down her back. She turned, and he paused when he caught her eyes. They were reddish-purple, almost raspberry, and, when viewed from a certain angle, had tiny gold flecks that seemed to draw him in. Realizing he was staring, he quickly looked away.

The other members of the bulradoer filed in behind them, taking their places around the altar, forming a circle with the Archchancellor at its head. The Archchancellor's attention was preoccupied at the moment as he flipped through the pages of the large book. He paused briefly to look at the inquisitors. "Dismiss the Watch."

One of the white-robed individuals stepped outside the stone ring, and the rest of the Tower's guards turned and left. Joren didn't know if he should feel honored or worried at being the one member allowed the privilege of staying.

The Archchancellor spoke, and Joren turned back around. He was reading from the book, but Joren had no idea what he was saying. He'd never heard the language before. He leaned over to the female bulradoer. "What's going on?" It almost looked like the Archchancellor was performing an incantation. But that would be absurd, since he was the head of the White Tower.

"Quiet," Lenara whispered, her tone stern.

"Is that magic? I . . . I thought we were here to destroy magic?"

The Archchancellor stopped his reading and looked up. "The only way to stop magic is with magic. Magic isn't tangible. It's like the wind. You can't see it, only its effects. It can't be destroyed any more than you can destroy the wind, or light." The Archchancellor raised his palm, and a ball of light suddenly appeared.

Joren nearly swallowed his tongue.

"However, it can be contained," the Archchancellor said, cupping the light between his hands, momentarily snuffing it out.

Joren's mind was racing. Suddenly, everything around him felt wrong, like he'd opened his eyes and realized he was standing on the edge of a cliff but didn't know how he'd gotten there.

The Archchancellor—the head of the White Tower—was a *wielder*? He realized the Archchancellor was still speaking and tried to focus.

". . . why it falls on the White Tower to contain this threat." He lifted his arms to those gathered around the altar. "We are the only ones equipped with the knowledge of how to battle this evil. It is a great burden we bear, having to allow our bodies to be vessels for magic's use, but it is a burden we will gladly suffer if it means saving but a single soul the pain of its existence."

The Archchancellor truly seemed anguished about having to use magic. Joren could certainly see it on his face. The gauntness in his cheeks, the bags under his eyes, even the wrinkles of his brow, all spoke to the lingering toll magic must be taking on his body.

"Whatever I can do to help, Your Eminence," he said with a slight tilt of his head. What else was he going to say, standing there surrounded by wielders? He was suddenly feeling quite alone. No wonder they had sent the rest of the recruits out.

The Archchancellor smiled. "You have no idea how relieved I am to hear you say that. You have a special quality that I could sense the moment you walked into the room."

Joren spared a quick glance at Lenara and the other bulradoer. It seemed they were all looking at him. "I do?" The man sounded sincere, but there was still this lingering doubt. Maybe it was just nerves. This was his first week, after all, and he wanted to make a good impression.

"You are a power for righteousness, my young friend. And that power comes from here." The Archchancellor placed his hand over his chest. "A pure heart. And I need that purity now to help me restore another righteous soul—one that has dedicated his life to helping the peoples of Aldor, one who has proven time and again to be a force for good against the wielders of this land, one who has given his very life to defend us all. The man who lies before you was murdered last night by the very ven'ae he sought to save."

Joren looked at the dead man lying on the slab and clenched his fists. It seemed that even the White Tower wasn't immune from the death and destruction of these rogue wielders. "What do you need me to do?"

The Archchancellor smiled. "Please," he said, motioning to the altar, "step over here and we'll begin."

Joren took a couple of steps forward, stopping in front of the slab where the large man lay. The branches from the tree were casting eerie shadows across the prostrate body.

"I will need you to help me stabilize our sleeping inquisitor."

Sleeping? The man wasn't even breathing. Nonetheless, Joren leaned over and laid his hands on the dead man's arm.

The Archchancellor cleared his throat. "That's not exactly what I had in mind. What I meant was that I will need your help in stabilizing his spirit."

"His spirit? How do I—"

"Hop up on the stone and I'll explain it to you."

Joren felt a slight twinge of unease but followed the Archchancellor's instructions anyway. The slab was cold, even through his uniform.

"That's good. Now if you could just lie down right there beside him, I'm going to use your inner strength to help stabilize our friend here. He will be a bit disoriented from his journey back to us."

Joren looked at the dead man beside him, his earlier apprehension growing as the seed of doubt took root. "What should I do?"

"Just lie back and relax. We are attempting to bring his spirit back from where it was sent. This chamber is a very special place. It holds a fissure that breaches clear through to the underworld." He pointed at the branches above him. "This is the Tree of Souls. Its roots reach down into the fissure and act as a conduit for these spirits to be brought back into the realm of the living."

Bringing souls back from the underworld? Was that even possible? This was sounding more and more like a very bad idea. He was about to say something to that effect when he felt someone take his hand. He turned. Lenara had left the circle and was now standing beside him.

She looked just as surprised by the contact as Joren, but she didn't release her grip. In fact, she tightened it. Her hand felt good in his. It was warm, comforting. Tilting his head, he looked up at the Archchancellor behind him. "Will I feel anything?"

"It will be over quickly." The Archchancellor raised his arms just like before and began to read from the book. He started chanting in the unknown tongue, and a soft breeze stirred through the cavern. It blew across Joren's face, stirring Lenara's robes.

As the chanting grew, so did the wind, growing to a roar as the gusts encircled the cavern. Over the sound, Joren thought he could hear something else. It might have been a baby crying, or possibly a young girl. It was unsettling. The weeping soon turned to wailing, and then an ear-piercing scream. And not from just one individual but thousands. Millions.

He wanted to put his hands to his ears, but his arms wouldn't move. What was happening to him? He raised his head and saw that the lower branches of the tree had wrapped themselves around his arms and legs and were working their way upward. When had that happened? He hadn't felt them. He tried to say something, but the rush of the wind and the strange chorus of voices drowned him out.

He looked at Lenara. There was a strange sadness in her eyes, but her hand continued to squeeze his. For some reason, he could still feel her touch. He was determined not to embarrass himself in front of her, so he closed his eyes and opened his mouth to take a deep breath, but as soon as he did, something clawed its way inside.

His eyes ripped open. He tried forcing his mouth shut but it wouldn't. Something was holding it in place, spreading his lips farther apart. He could hear his jawbones popping at the joints, searing pain ripping through them further still. Tears flooded his eyes, momentarily blurring his vision. His mind screamed out, but no sound came. He watched in horror as the tree's branches, having now wrapped his body like a cocoon, were forcing themselves into his open jaws. He howled silently as they pushed deeper and deeper inside, down his throat, and into his gut.

Joren tilted his head to get the Archchancellor's attention—something had gone wrong—but the Archchancellor's face held no pity, no remorse, no disgust. His focus lay solely on the book in front of him and his chanting.

Joren's body convulsed. The tree was now deep inside him. He could feel its limbs moving around in his chest and stomach as if he were in a constant state of retching and yet not able to relieve the pressure. Everything spun as the nausea took over.

Joren had seen men in pain before. Once, he saw Tallis Nareen have his entire arm ripped off at the elbow after getting it caught in one of the stone presses, but even then, he couldn't imagine the pain being more than this.

Joren looked to his right and found Lenara's raspberry-colored eyes staring back at his. Another harsh jolt of pain brought his attention back around as the screams began to fade and a single voice came into focus. It grew louder. Joren searched the faces of those standing closest but couldn't find the source.

What's happening?

The voice was growing more distinct. Almost like it was coming from . . . inside him. It seemed to be laughing.

Suddenly, the branches retracted from his mouth, and he realized he had no feeling. The pain was gone. He spared a quick glance to his side to see if Lenara was still gripping his hand. She was.

Is it over? Why can't I talk?

"Get rid of the old body," the Archchancellor said as he glanced over the podium at the slab.

Joren watched as the bulradoer struggled to hoist the inquisitor beside him off the stone. *Didn't it work? What happened?* He tried to speak but nothing came out. He tried to move; his limbs were unresponsive. He tried to look at Lenara, but even his eyes no longer obeyed. *Help! Something's wrong!* he screamed. But no one heard. Panic took over.

Suddenly, his entire body started moving on its own. He could hear someone talking, but there was no one there. Other than being able to tell it was the voice of a grown man, he had no idea who it was.

Someone please tell me what is going on!

Everything faded, and the darkness took him.

The Tree of Souls had gone still once more, as had the pool of inky shadows behind them. Closing the book, Valtor made his way to the side of the altar and looked down at his work.

The young recruit looked almost peaceful, considering the amount of blood that was seeping from his ruined mouth. It saturated the front of his white tunic and mantle.

"Heal him, Lenara."

The short bulradoer released her grip on the guard and waved her hand over his jaw. She repeated one of the first healing incantations taught to all bulradoer, and the bones snapped back into place as the lacerations knitted themselves together. The guard twitched, the fingers on his hands knotting into fists as the skin around his mouth resealed, revealing a rather sadistic grin. The guard sat up and looked at Valtor.

"Where is Ferrin? Where is my dear smith?"

Chapter 2 | Ferrin

FERRIN PULLED BACK on the reins, bringing the small band of riders to a stop. He was panting almost as much as his poor horse. Behind him, he felt Rae stir as she loosened her grip on his waist.

"Are you still alive?" he asked.

She held her hand in front of her eyes to block the sun and grunted, which for Rae typically meant yes.

Nostrils slowed alongside Ferrin, Suri still snugly wrapped in her blanket in front of him. Little more than her nose—which was red from the cold—and her eyes could be seen through the material. Ferrin couldn't tell if she was asleep or squinting against the afternoon light. She was the quietest six-year-old he'd ever seen.

Their ride through the Pass of Arnon had been a brutal one, as the heavy winds gusting down from the sheer cliffs had cut right to the bone. The pass crossed through the Razor Spine Mountains, an unforgiving range of barren rock rising to form sharp spikes, like those of their razorback namesake. It was the longest mountain range in Aldor, stretching to either side of the plains as far as the eye could see.

Ferrin inhaled deeply through his nose, enjoying the smell of freedom. He couldn't help but smile as he looked out across the sea of yellow ahead of them—the Rymiran Plains. Dried or not, it was the first grass he'd seen in months. He wanted to shout, but he didn't want to risk giving away their location. Besides, the last thing he needed was another scolding from Rae.

After taking a moment to stretch, he wiped his eyes, unsure whether the tears were from the cold, the hard ride, or the emotions of the moment. Turning in the saddle, he looked at the empty pass behind them. They had accomplished the unthinkable. They had escaped the walls of the White Tower. Now they just needed to elude the long arms that were sure to be pursuing them.

Rae peered beneath the bandages on her chest, inspecting the wounds Cheeks had inflicted while on the rack.

"How are they?" he asked.

"Same as the last time," she said curtly.

Ferrin took the hint and turned back around.

Rae's injuries were taking a long time to heal. Since using magic required the wielder's own strength, she had to be careful not to use too much. She could end up doing more harm than good.

"That's a beautiful sight," Nostrils said, staring out at the sea of wild grass before them.

Ferrin marveled at the way it rolled across the plain, like a swelling tide under an easterly wind. "It is indeed."

"What is this?"

Ferrin turned. Rae was hanging halfway off the horse, stretching to rub her hands across the top of the matted stalks. "Grass," he said, smiling at her innocent curiosity. He wondered what it must have been like growing up in a world of shadow and stone, never having witnessed anything beyond the drab walls of the Tower.

"Grass?" They were close enough to Nostrils for Rae to hand Suri a couple of pieces to play with. The little girl smiled as she waved them around. Suri had the same caramel skin and dark hair as her mother. Unlike the other warm-skinned people Ferrin knew, she also had Rae's peculiar pale-green eyes.

As much as Ferrin would have liked to take the two of them around and show them this whole new world, they didn't have the time. "I can't speak for the rest of you. Your lives are your own," he said, glancing at Nostrils. "I don't know if you have family, but if so, I would suggest you relocate them before the Tower scoops them up to use as bait. As for me, my former life is over. I'm going to make sure my sister is safe and then find a small community tucked away in the middle of nowhere, somewhere I can live out the rest of my days in peace. It's hard to rest when you're forced to sleep with one eye open."

"I'm going with you," Rae blurted out.

Ferrin turned. "Are you sure? If you have family somewhere, I may not be going in that direction."

"I don't have family," she said, staring rather wide-eyed at the field of dry grass, seemingly mesmerized with its movement. "I told you. I was born in the Tower. I've never left it."

Nostrils turned. "You've never been outside?"

"That's what I said." She looked at Ferrin. "You got me and Suri into this mess. You'd better get us out." Her lips tightened into a scowl, daring him to disagree.

"Well, I guess that settles that." Ferrin had hoped she would come with him but hadn't wanted to force her. It was her decision. She was going to need a lot of help adjusting, and he didn't like the idea of setting her and Suri loose. They'd be worse than domesticated animals released into the wild. Neither would survive long.

Ferrin looked at Nostrils. "What about you, Captain? Do you have a wife and kids waiting back home?" With as few wrinkles around the man's eyes as Nostrils had, Ferrin guessed he couldn't have been much more than ten years his senior. Other than his nose, the man's appearance was fairly average: leathery skin from days in the saddle, callused hands, and chestnut hair trimmed short enough that it didn't hang much lower than the bottom of his ears.

The former White Tower guard leaned forward in his saddle, cold leather groaning under the motion. "I've been a military man all my life. Never had much time to settle down. Unlike you, I've got no ties, so I figure one place is as good as another. Besides"—he tapped the hilt of his sword—"I reckon you could probably use another good arm with a blade, and to be honest, I wouldn't mind the company." He scratched at the week-old growth on his face. "What'd you have in mind?"

"Rhowynn first," he said, his gaze shifting north. "I need to make sure my sister is safe, and after that, Easthaven."

"Easthaven?" The captain gave him a puzzled look.

"There's a man there I need to get a message to." Ferrin's mind was drawn back to that cold, damp cell where he had left Azriel bound. The only thing the old seer had asked of him was that Ferrin find Azriel's son, Kellen. Short of dying, there was nothing that was going to stop Ferrin from doing just that.

"You're a good man, swordsmith," the captain said, "but don't you think you're taking your obligations a little too seriously? The Black Watch will be hunting us. We don't have time to go traipsing halfway across Aldor just to deliver a message." The captain twisted the reins in his hands. "Don't get me wrong. I feel sorry for the seer's situation, but we have our own safety to consider."

Ferrin nodded. "Like I said, you have no obligation to come with us, Captain. For my part, I hope you do, but I gave Azriel my word."

Nostrils nodded, though not with great enthusiasm. "Understood." He leaned back in his saddle and rubbed the back of his head. "What now?"

"We'll have to stay off the main roads. My thought was to skirt the edge of the mountains until we pass into Keldor. From there, head north up the Taloos River for Rhowynn."

Nostrils grimaced. "Even with the extra coin I was saving for when I managed to break loose of the Watch, I doubt I'll have enough to get us half that far."

Ferrin leaned over and dug around in his travel sack, fishing out the purse he'd stolen in one of the legate's chambers during their escape. "I don't believe that will be a problem," he said, and tossed the heavy pouch to the captain.

Nostrils startled as he tested its weight before pulling loose the drawstrings and looking inside. His eyes widened even further as he removed a couple of gold coins. "Where did you get this? There's more gold here than what I could earn in the next ten lifetimes as captain."

"I guess the legates enjoy a higher stipend than the guards."

"I'd say."

"What is it?" Suri asked.

"It's gold," Nostrils said. "You buy things with it."

Ferrin chuckled, as the captain had to keep pulling the little girl's hands out of the purse.

Nostrils smiled as he tightened the strings and tossed the purse to Ferrin. "I daresay we'll make Rhowynn, with enough left over to buy a small town."

The captain's comment might have been overreaching, but it was good to know they had something to fall back on. Ferrin tucked the gold back into the bottom of the sack.

Nostrils cupped his hand over his eyes and looked up. "We better get going while we still have the light."

Ferrin nodded. "We don't want to get caught out here in the open. Thornwood Forest should allow us to travel unseen through the day and hopefully let us catch a few winks at night."

"Sleep?" The captain stifled a yawn at just the mention of the word. "I'd almost forgotten what that was."

Ferrin certainly knew the feeling.

"Here," Nostrils said. "It's your turn to hold Rona." He handed

Ferrin the reins to the extra packhorse carrying their gear and supplies. They'd been trading off carrying the mare's reins for the last two days. But it was the first time anyone had attempted naming her.

"Rona?"

Nostrils smiled. "A girl I courted in my younger years. Stubborn as a two-headed sniffer."

Ferrin laughed, and the horse whinnied as though she knew they were talking about her. "Rona it is." He tightened his grip on the reins and glanced over his shoulder at Rae. "Hold on."

Rae wrapped her arms back around his waist, and Ferrin kicked his mount, sparing a quick glance behind to see if Nostrils had done the same. Even though Rae seemed to be getting the hang of riding, she was still having difficulty understanding the concept of riding *with* the animal and not *against* it. Her body bobbed up and down at the wrong times. He could only imagine the bruising her backside must be enduring. His had already gone numb, but he wasn't sure whether that was from the bouncing or the cold.

They made good time as they crossed the open plains north toward the standing tree line ahead, the soft lowlands giving way to rougher terrain the closer they got. The sun hadn't yet dropped below the western horizon by the time they reached the first of the outlining groves of mountain fir. The soft padding of the horse's hooves in the tall grass turned to crunching thuds as they rode across a blanket of pine needles and fallen cones.

So far, there had been no sign of pursuit. Ferrin hoped that whoever came after them confined their search to the main roads.

Rae and Suri seemed to be enjoying themselves despite the circumstances. Their eyes darted back and forth from one thing to the next as they attempted to touch anything and everything that came into reach. Ferrin was having a difficult time keeping from laughing.

It seemed the only two words they knew how to say were "What's that?" as they pointed at some new thing. They were particularly enthralled at the wonder of so many different-sounding birds. There was a smile of rapture on each face as they poked their ears to the wind, listening for more. Every now and then, Ferrin caught himself doing the same.

Night came early within the confines of the trees. Ferrin brought them to a stop not far from a meandering stream that wound down from the mountain's base, and they made camp. As dark as it was, Ferrin figured smoke from a small fire wouldn't be seen, and they were going to need the heat in order to make it through the night.

The snows of early winter had not yet arrived this far south, but the chill in the air was enough to set his teeth to knocking. Other than the uniforms they had taken from the dead guards, neither he nor Rae nor Suri had a proper set of clothing.

It didn't take long for them to get a small blaze going. Ferrin and Nostrils led the horses to the stream and let them slowly drink their fill. After rubbing them down for the night, they fed them some of the oats the captain had procured from the Tower's stables and a single apple each—a treat for all the hard work they had done over the last couple of days. It was the least they deserved.

Suri, who had been shadowing Ferrin around the campsite, made sure she got an apple as well. She gobbled it down as fast as the horses, not sparing even the core.

Ferrin took his seat at the fire across from the little girl. Her blanket had fallen around her legs as she amused herself with a couple of pine cones.

"Here, get some water," the captain said as he started on the food. He handed Ferrin a kettle.

Ferrin, too hungry to argue, took the pot, filled it from the stream, and hung it over the fire, anxiously awaiting whatever Nostrils had in store.

Rae tried not to appear too interested. She walked over, looked inside, grunted, then sat down beside Suri.

Nostrils went to work cutting up vegetables, roots, and strips of dried meat before tossing them into the water to boil. Occasionally, he would lift the ladle, blow, and stick his tongue to it, after which he would make a face and toss in a few more of the wild onions Ferrin had found while nosing around the stream.

Ferrin felt like his stomach was about to gnaw straight through his backbone. If the captain didn't hurry up with his tasting, he was going to stuff *him* in the pot. Suri's fascination with the pine cones and sticks petered out as the aroma wafted in her direction. She bounced up and down, pointing at the old kettle. "I want! I want!"

"It's almost ready, Suri," Nostrils said, dishing a small helping into a tin bowl for the little girl. "Let it cool first." He dished out a separate bowl for Rae.

The captain poured Ferrin a good helping, and Ferrin barely had time to nod before the first slurp of hot stew washed across his tongue, sparking to life his long-shriveled taste buds. Having dined for the last few months on nothing more than stale bread and what tasted like week-old wash water, he thought the meager meal couldn't have been better had it been served on gold dishes from the royal palace.

He swallowed, and the stew warmed his body the entire way down. He released a slow, satisfied moan as he leaned back against an old stump and continued dipping.

Nostrils seemed determined not to let Ferrin outdo him as he dished up a heaping bowl for himself and started shoveling it in.

Rae clicked her tongue with a disapproving shake of her head as she looked at the two men.

Ferrin, with his mouth stuffed to the brim, glanced over at an equally engorged Nostrils and shrugged. Without a second thought, they were back to the work of lifting spoon to mouth and back again.

Freedom had never tasted so good.

Chapter 3 | Ferrin

BY THE TIME FERRIN returned with another armload of wood to feed the fire, the meal had been cleared and Suri tucked into the blankets Rae had laid out for their bedding. He was thankful for the warmth. The sun's passing had left behind a deep chill, as patches of fog were already rolling in.

Sitting on his own bedding, Ferrin closed his eyes, taking pleasure in the simple cracks and pops coming from the timber. The smell of the smoke and warmth of the blaze took him back to his shop in Rhowynn. He missed working the smithy, almost as much as he missed Myriah.

For the thousandth time, he wondered what his sister had done when she returned home to find the front room torn apart and him gone. Had she gone to the wielder council for help? How long had it taken Harlin to sweep in and rescue her? Ferrin ground his teeth as he stared at the flames. Harlin was the reason he'd been captured in the first place, betraying Ferrin in order to get closer to his sister. His thoughts darkened as they shifted to what he would do to the man once he returned.

A twig snapped in the woods on his right, and his dream vanished. He turned to study the shadows lurking just beyond their campsite. Nostrils turned as well. An itch clawed at the back of Ferrin's mind. He couldn't shake the feeling that something was out there, watching, but after several long moments of nothing, he shrugged and turned back around.

"Tell me, Captain, how did you end up with the Black Watch?"

The light from the fire cast shadows across Nostrils's face, accentuating his most prominent feature. Ferrin realized he really didn't know anything about this man who had risked so much to help them escape. Azriel had said to trust him, and at the time, that had been good enough for Ferrin, but now he was risking more than his own life.

"Call me Myron. Some titles are best left in the past." He stared at the fire a moment before saying anything more. "When you've been an armsman as long as I have, you don't have much else to fall back on. I started out as a lancer in the Briston Corps in Duport, but after a while, one battle seemed to be no different from the next. So, I left." Myron snapped the twig he'd been fiddling with and tossed it into the flames.

"I was making my way north when I ran into a troop of Black Watch at a small village I had stopped at. Seems they had some sort of wielder infestation." Myron's eyes widened, and he quickly raised his hand. "Sorry. No offense," he said, gesturing at Ferrin and Rae, who was listening intently from her place beside Suri.

Ferrin waved the comment off, and Myron continued.

"Evidently, one of the locals had accused his neighbor of being a wizard, since for two years running the man's crops had gone bad while his neighbor's remained healthy. Of course, according to some of the other villagers, it probably had something to do with the man being about as lazy as a pack of pond turtles on a sunny day. But, as you're well aware, the Black Watch doesn't rightly care if there's sufficient proof."

Ferrin snorted. "I can certainly attest to that."

"Yes, I bet you can. The funny thing is, not only did they arrest the neighbor with the good crops, they also arrested the one with the big mouth as well." Myron chuckled. "Can't say I felt all that sorry for him, though."

Ferrin agreed. He would have loved to have seen Harlin arrested when they had come for him.

"Anyway, the one who'd turned in his neighbor tried to make a break for it." Myron shook his head. "Ain't that just like a greedy coward?" He spat at the fire and it hissed. "I wasn't about to let that fool get away after what he'd done to the other fellow, so being the clumsy oaf that I am, I stumbled out from behind my tree, clutching a piece of firewood." He shrugged again and smiled. "It wasn't my fault the man ran face-first into it, now was it?"

Ferrin smiled. He liked Myron's dry sense of humor.

Rae, stoic as always, simply grunted.

"Long and short of it is, they offered me stable work, and I accepted. The White Tower had always been known for keeping Aldor safe from magic. I figured, what better job to take than one where I got paid to make a difference?"

Ferrin could think of a few.

Myron undid his sword from his belt and laid it next to the folded blanket he was using for a pillow. "It wasn't until I was in my second year and well on my way to making captain that I was first assigned to the Hall of Inquisition. My eyes were quickly opened. Up until then, I hadn't let myself believe the rumors about what went on down in the lower parts, what they were doing to the prisoners."

"And yet, you did nothing about it," Ferrin said, suddenly feeling a twinge of anger as a rush of memories flooded his mind. Memories of his time on the rack with Cheeks, the cuttings, the stabbings, the burnings and breakings. He looked at Rae. She, too, seemed to be lost in thought as she stared at the flames, the whites of her teeth beginning to show as her lips curled.

Myron nodded. "I'm ashamed to say I turned a blind eye. I tried to find ways to justify what was happening. Even told myself the wielders were going to destroy Aldor and it was our job to stop them."

This time it was Ferrin's turn to snap a twig—more of a limb, really—as he tried to find a way to release his anger that didn't involve him leaping on top of Myron and beating him senseless.

"No one wants to think of themselves as bad," Myron said, face blank, head lowered. "I'm a hard man. Not proud of it, but not afraid to say it, either. There isn't much these eyes haven't seen, not with as many battles as I've fought. Men can do some pretty detestable things to each other in the name of war, but what I witnessed down there . . ." He visibly shuddered. "It had me too scared to even try leaving. Best thing that could have ever happened to me was talking with that seer friend of yours."

Ferrin didn't say anything. Myron sounded sincere in his shame, and it would be hard to overlook the fact that he *had* given up his previous life to join them as fugitives, but it was still difficult to hear what the man had been a part of. He remembered the unexpected shame he had seen at times in Myron's eyes compared with the other guards, but forgiving those actions was going to take more than a bowl of stew and a single shared conversation.

"How about you, smith? What's your story? Lot of rumors floating around the Tower about the man who couldn't be broken."

Ferrin leaned forward and hugged his knees. "I have a small smithy in the workers' district of Rhowynn. Or at least, I had. Not sure now. It wasn't much to brag about, but it brought in enough to get by.

"When I wasn't much older than Suri there," he said, pointing his stick at the now-snoring little girl curled up beside Rae, "I discovered I was different. My parents were dead, so my sister and I went to live with our aunt and uncle. When they discovered my ability, they sold me to a peddler named Pinon on his way to Briston." He shrugged. "I've got nothing to complain about, though. My time with Pinon taught me the ways of the world. I quickly found out that he had a gift as well. He was able to manipulate people's feelings through suggestion. He could persuade you to buy anything."

Myron shook his head. "That's a very powerful gift."

"Yes, but he was very careful about how he used it. Pinon had strict rules about what he would and wouldn't do. Don't reckon most people would have been able to resist the temptation the way he did." Ferrin knew he probably wouldn't have been able to.

"Ain't that the truth."

"I'd asked him about it once, why he didn't use it to sell more, but all he would say was that during a moment of anger, he had forced a feeling into someone's mind, and before he could take it back, the person had killed themselves. After that, he was determined never to use his gift again, except under the direst of circumstances."

Myron's eyes were as wide as the gold buttons on his uniform. "I hadn't thought about that side of it. Imagine what you could do with an ability like that. The people you could sway."

"What happened to your sister?" Rae asked abruptly, prompting both men to turn and glance across the fire.

"She came with me. She couldn't stand the thought of being separated, so when I left with Pinon, she chased us down." Ferrin smiled. "We've never been separated since." His smile faded. "Until now, of course.

"When I was old enough, Pinon used the last of his savings to purchase me an apprenticeship with a Rhowynn smithy named Ryneer. It was a perfect fit, and under his instruction I grew to love not only the work, but the metal. By the time Ryneer retired, I'd saved enough gold to purchase his business, which eventually gave me the opportunity to pay Pinon back." Ferrin grinned as he thought of the old peddler, and his life in Rhowynn. "With the new smithy up and running, Pinon was able to retire and live out the rest of his days with us." Ferrin sighed. "He died a few years back. Closest thing I ever really had to a father."

After a moment of silence, Rae spoke up. "I'm sorry."

Her reaction took him by surprise, and he smiled. "Thank you." Noticing the dour expressions on their faces, Ferrin decided to change the subject. "It didn't take long for the smithy to come into its own. Unfortunately," he said, tucking a strand of red hair behind his ear, "being the impulsive lad that I was, I decided to start experimenting with my gift. I found I could not only forge the metal into whatever I wanted with just a touch, but I could actually change the properties of the blades into something that was more durable, sometimes nigh indestructible."

Myron leaned forward. "What do you mean by 'indestructible'?"

"Most blades scratch and nick and bend depending on the type and amount of use. Some even break. Mine don't."

Myron pulled his sword partway out of its scabbard and looked at the blade. "You're telling me your blades don't even scratch?"

Ferrin just smiled, then continued his story. "Pretty soon, people started coming from all around to get a blade done by this nobody smith in the worker's district, and because I loved the attention and praise I was receiving, not to mention the extra gold, I kept it up. My sister warned me not to use my gift so openly. I thought I could hide it."

"What's your sister's name?"

Ferrin startled once more and looked at Rae. "Her name is Myriah."

"That's a lovely name," Myron said. "Sort of a womanly version of my own."

Ferrin hadn't considered it before, but they were similar—*Myron and Myriah?*

"What happened next?" Rae urged, clearly interested in the story.

"Let's see. After I had decided to ignore Myriah's warnings, I received my first big break. A commission by the High King himself."

Myron, who had been slouching on his bedroll, sat up. "No fooling?"

Ferrin nodded. "The king wanted a special pair of swords constructed. A gift, I believe. He had two stipulations, however: the blades were to be unique, unlike any I had ever made, and he wanted me to craft them in a way that spoke of dragons." Ferrin smiled, remembering the long hours spent dreaming up their design.

"Dragons?" Rae asked.

"Yes," Ferrin said, not wanting to go into a lengthy explanation of what a dragon was if she didn't know. "They were beautiful."

"I'm sure they were," Myron said.

"You can imagine the uproar that brought when the guilds realized they had been passed over in favor of a no-name smith. More unexpected, though, was that my betrayal didn't come from a competing smithy but from someone I would have called a friend." Ferrin tugged hard on his lengthening beard, letting the pain swell inside him. "*Friend* might be a little strong . . ."

Myron huffed. "There's a special place in the abyss for murderers, rapists, and those who sell out their family and friends." He paused a moment to think. "Come to think of it, there's probably a special place in there for those of us who aided the White Tower in its crimes." He shivered. "I can only hope I'm allowed a chance at redemption."

"Redemption is the best we can hope for," Ferrin said.

Myron nodded slowly, then turned to Rae. "How did you get mixed up in all of this?"

Rae gave Myron a hard stare, then grabbed her blanket, lay down beside Suri, and pulled it over her head.

Myron looked at Ferrin. "I reckon she doesn't want to talk about it."

Ferrin couldn't help but smile. He knew how long it had taken him to coax her out of her shell far enough to acknowledge his existence. He figured it would be a while before she opened up enough to discuss her undoubtedly haunted past, especially with a man. After what she'd been through, he couldn't blame her.

Myron stood and strapped his sword back around his waist. "Guess I'll take first watch."

"Wake me when you're done," Ferrin said, tossing a couple chunks of wood onto the fire and watching the sparks float into the canopy of trees overhead.

Myron nodded as he pulled on his gloves and buttoned up his overcoat. He grabbed an extra blanket out of one of the travel sacks, trudged off into the shadows, and disappeared from view.

Ferrin lay back on his blankets, listening to the popping of the flames. He wasn't sure how much sleep he was going to get. He still couldn't shake the feeling that they were being watched.

Chapter 4 | Ferrin

FERRIN WOKE WITH a start as a gloved hand pressed over his mouth.

"Shh." The look on Myron's face told Ferrin he wasn't being woken for his turn at watch. "Wake up, smith. We have a problem."

Ferrin bolted upright from his blankets. Judging by how little the fire had dimmed, he hadn't been asleep long. Their pursuers must have traveled all night to catch up. How could he have been so foolish? He should have pushed them harder.

"Where are they?" he whispered as he snatched his sword up from under his bedding and scanned the trees. "How many?"

"It's not the Watch."

Ferrin wiped the sleep from his eyes. "Then what's the problem?"

Myron held out his torch toward the western edge of the campsite. "There." The entire front row of pine was glowing with yellow dots.

"Smoke and ash!" Ferrin leaped to his feet.

Rae, with Suri still half-asleep in her arms, slipped between the two men. "What's happening?"

Ferrin turned and pointed toward the mountain face behind them. "We need to get to the rocks."

"What are they?" Rae asked.

"Wolves," Ferrin said.

"Red wolves, if you want to be exact," Myron added. "Smaller than the grey, but more vicious."

Ferrin slung a few of the travel bags over his shoulder and grabbed the horses while Myron lit another torch from the fire. The horses were prancing nervously as the deadly predators crept out of the shadow of the trees and into the campfire's light. Myron was right; they were red wolves. Ferrin had seen some before during his travels with Pinon. They always ran in packs, which made them more dangerous.

Their fur glistened as they crossed out of the trees, white fangs bared.

Slowly, Ferrin and the others backed toward the larger rock behind them. Rae hugged close to Ferrin, clinging protectively to Suri.

The wolves moved in step with them, growling as they came.

"I've never seen wolves attack a full camp before," Myron said. "Have you?"

"No. Especially not one with a fire still going."

As soon as they reached the base of the mountain, Rae tucked Suri into a shallow crevice in the rock.

Ferrin dropped the bags and handed the horses' reins to Rae. "Don't let go, whatever you do," he said. "We can't afford to lose them."

Rae hesitantly took the leather straps. She looked just as uncomfortable holding the horses as she did watching the wolves.

Ferrin raised his sword and followed Myron out to meet the creatures.

The pack stretched across the small clearing. Ferrin counted at least ten, lips pulled back as they snarled and barked. He tightened his grip on his sword. A couple of the wolves howled, sending bumps down both of his arms.

"The Black Watch aren't looking so bad right now," Ferrin said.

Myron grunted. "I was thinking the same thing." He swung his torch. "Go on! Get out of here!"

"You tell them, Captain!"

"Shut up, smith, and start using your magic to get us out of this mess!"

Ferrin grabbed for the transferal around his neck. It wasn't there. He turned and almost caught the crystal in the face as Rae threw it at him. He grabbed for it but missed. The chain landed between him and the closest wolves. "Rot!" He edged forward slowly, keeping his sword up in case the wolves attacked.

The wolves hunched, their fur bristling, but instead of attacking, they backed up. They continued to growl, but none of them so much as moved toward them.

"What's this?" Myron asked, looking just as astonished as Ferrin.

Ferrin leaned over and slowly reached out to grab the chain. He was close enough to pet one of the wolves. It snarled, but he held his ground. His fingers slipped around the chain, and he slowly pulled it back to him. He slipped it over his head and ever so carefully backed up to where Myron was standing.

"Have you ever seen wolves act like this?"

Ferrin shook his head. He could feel the stone around his neck activating, his magic coming alive. He could suddenly sense it all: the steel of the swords, the buckle of Myron's belt, the chain holding the crystal, even the gold in their travel sacks. He could feel everything. But how was that going to help them against a pack of hungry wolves?

The animals started forward once again, but this time, their focus seemed to be on Myron, as they shifted right.

"Is it just me or do these things seem to like me more than you?" Myron swung his sword, missing the most daring by a few inches.

Ferrin moved to help him. He could feel the metal in his sword come alive as he thinned the core of the blade, stretching the metal to expand its reach and compensating for the change of balance by adding a bit more to the grip and pommel. "That's better," he said as he swung at the closest wolf. He clipped the animal, causing it to yelp and back off.

"How about helping a friend out over here?" Myron said as he moved closer to Ferrin.

Ferrin reached out with his magic and touched Myron's blade, repeating the process.

The captain took a few test swings at the encroaching pack. "Oh, I like this!"

Behind them, the horses pounded the ground in fear, trying to break free and run. Ferrin could hear Rae fighting to hang on.

"Why aren't they attacking?" Myron asked, panic in his voice. "What are they waiting for?"

"Move back," Ferrin said. "We can't let them separate us from Rae and—"

"Stop it!" a high-pitched voice shouted behind them.

The entire pack froze.

Ferrin turned far enough to see Suri crawling out of the crevice Rae had placed her in. She was still clutching her blanket.

She pointed her finger at the pack, scowling deeply. "You stop scaring my mama!"

The wolves slowly began to move back, stopping just in front of the fire to watch the little girl.

Suri started forward.

"No, Suri!" Rae cried. "Come back here!" Forgetting about the horses, Rae ran for her daughter, but as soon as she did, the wolves' hackles rose again, and they started to growl.

"Stop it!" Suri said, reprimanding the animals with another cold stare and wag of her little finger. They immediately quieted. Some even sat. The largest of the pack stepped forward and pranced toward her.

Rae rushed forward in a panic. "Suri!"

Ferrin grabbed Rae and held her back. "Don't spook them." Ferrin was shaking almost as much as she was. Was he making the right decision? What if the wolf killed the little girl? Something inside told him to wait.

Suri didn't move. She stood her ground as the huge animal closed in, its face level with hers.

What in the name of the Creator is going on?

"By the powers," Myron whispered as they watched the enormous wolf stand toe to toe with the little girl and do nothing more than stare.

Suri reached for the wolf. Ferrin could feel Rae's body trembling as the little girl gently laid her hand on top of its furry head. Instead of ripping her arm from its socket, the wolf tilted its head far enough for her to scratch behind its ears.

Realizing he'd been holding his breath the whole time, Ferrin exhaled.

The little girl giggled as she continued to rub the wolf's head a moment longer, then she took a step back. "Now go home. Shoo," she said with a wave of her hand. The wolf turned, and the pack followed him back down the small rise and into the trees beyond, disappearing into the night. No one moved as the little girl playfully skipped back to where Ferrin stood holding her mother.

Rae broke free of Ferrin's grip and threw her arms around her daughter. "Are you all right? Why did you do that? You could have been killed!"

"No." Suri shook her head adamantly. "They weren't going to hurt us, Mama."

"And how do you know?"

"They told me."

"What do you mean, they told you?"

"The big one said they'd been told to keep us here but not to hurt us."

"You could hear them talking, child?" Myron asked as he knelt beside her.

Suri looked up at him. "Can't you?"

The others shared an awkward glance.

Rae released Suri, turned, and punched Ferrin in the chest. "Don't ever do that again! Don't ever try to keep me from my daughter." She turned and marched Suri back up to where the horses were surprisingly still standing. Whatever Suri had done had somehow calmed them down as well.

It took Ferrin a moment to catch his breath from the unexpected punch. Once he did, he turned to Myron. "Pack your gear. We need to get out of here."

Chapter 5 | Amarysia

AMARYSIA EMERGED FROM the queen's chambers and gently closed the door, not wanting to disturb Ellise after she had finally managed to doze off. The queen was one of the strongest women Amarysia knew, but since the death of her husband, she had taken to spending more and more time alone in her chambers.

Amarysia couldn't blame her. Ayrion's death had her wanting to do the same. The halls felt emptier with him gone. She used to enjoy moving about the palace, hopeful for the chance to see him, even at a distance. She missed their talks, their walks through the gardens. Sometimes, she would watch him when he wasn't looking. He was always so serious, giving out his orders, making sure his men were holding the standards he expected of them.

"We need to quit meeting like this," a voice behind her said, causing her to jump, recognition twisting her stomach. She turned and found Prince Dakaran decked in his finest. He grabbed her hand and pressed it to his lips, holding it for an uncomfortable amount of time.

"You must forgive me," he said. "Where are my manners?" Instead of releasing her hand, he cupped his over it. "You have suffered a great loss. The entire kingdom has. If you ever find yourself in need of someone to talk to, I want you to know you can come to me."

She retracted her hand, then curtsied. "Thank you, Your Highness—"

"Actually," he interrupted, "it's Your *Majesty*."

Amarysia bit her tongue and curtsied once again. "Of course . . . Your Majesty, my apologies."

"Think nothing of it," he said with a glib wave of his hand.

His smile was as repulsive as it was unwelcome. How did so many women find him charming? He turned and walked away, leaving her to pull herself together before making her way back to her own chambers.

She shut the door behind her and flipped the latch, taking a moment to lean back against the wood and gather her thoughts. Her feet hurt from standing for the last couple of hours while waiting on the queen. With a heavy sigh, she pushed off the door and crossed the room, retrieving her brush on the way to her bed. Brushing her hair was one of the best ways she knew to calm her nerves. Something about the way the bristles tugged softly on her scalp soothed her spirit.

The fire in the hearth to her left was warm and relaxing. She let it soothe her nerves as she tried to slowly release the pain of loss that had taken root. Then she noticed the vase of wilted flowers sitting on the mantel and started crying. They had been a gift from Ayrion on his last day before heading to war. She didn't have the heart to toss them out, even though the petals had all but fallen off and the stems were hanging over the sides like willow branches.

She forced herself to look away, to try thinking of something else. She needed to see how Sedge was doing. It had been a week since she'd delivered any supplies to her brother. But with the changes that were happening in the palace at present, and having to be there for the queen, she was finding it difficult to get any free time to herself.

Laying her brush on the table beside her bed, she slipped out of her dress—making sure to drape it over the chair to keep it from wrinkling—then quickly hopped into bed and crawled under the heavy blankets.

She had just begun to doze when she was startled awake by what might have been a knock at the door. She waited a moment to see whether the knocking returned or if it had been the start of another restless dream.

She heard it again. Three short knocks.

"Just a moment," she said, uncurling from her pillow and crawling out from under her heavy comforter. She shivered as her bare feet hit the floor. She grabbed her robe from its spot on the chest at the foot of her bed and put it on. Lighting one of the candles from her dresser, she headed across the room.

"Who is it?"

"I have a summons from Her Majesty Queen Ellise," came the response from the other side. It sounded like one of the palace messengers, but Amarysia couldn't understand why she would be getting a summons. She wondered if the queen had fallen into another fit of tears and needed further comforting. Amarysia wouldn't have minded indulging in a little more herself. Holding up the candle, she unlocked the door and pulled back on the latch.

She'd barely managed to turn the handle when the door burst open and she was shoved backward into the room. A hand pressed against her mouth to keep her from crying out as the glint of steel reflected off a knife that went to her throat. The intruder kicked the door shut, hood pulled tight around their face.

Amarysia's mind raced as she tried to make sense of what was going on. She thought it was a woman's voice she'd heard, but maybe she had been wrong. The hand clamped around her mouth was strong. Was it Dakaran? She trembled at the thought. Surely he wouldn't be so bold as to take her right in the palace with the queen so near. Then again, this was Dakaran, and with Ayrion gone, there was no telling what he might do.

She thought about fighting back and making a run for the door, then changed her mind as the edge of the blade pressed tighter. Any attempt at escaping now would end with her throat being slit. She didn't want to suffer the indignity of being molested, but her instinct for preservation snuffed out any thoughts of trying to run or sacrificing herself as a martyr on the malefactor's blade.

"What happened to Ayri?"

Amarysia blinked in confusion. "What?"

"What happened to Ayrion? Don't make me ask again, hussy."

Kira? Relief flooded in. At least she knew she wasn't about to get raped before having her throat slit. The clan chief would just slit her throat and be done with it.

Kira released the knife from Amarysia's neck and pulled back the hood from the black cloak. "Can I let go of your mouth, or will you do something stupid?" Kira looked down at her costume. "I just had these scrubbed this week, and I don't want to stain them with your insides if I don't have to."

Amarysia glanced at Kira's clothes and almost laughed. The fierce clan chief appeared to be wearing one of the maids' uniforms: a long grey dress with a white apron over the top, and a white bonnet to hold in her hair.

"What are you doing here?" Amarysia asked, attempting to keep her voice civil, considering Kira was walking the tip of her blade across the back of her fingers. "How did you get past the guards?"

Kira walked over to snoop through the items on Amarysia's dresser. "That's easy. Ayri and I used to sneak into the palace all the time when we were kids. There's an old access tunnel behind the—" She stopped and turned around. "Wait, why am I telling you this? Next thing I know, you'll be running off to tell the queen and have it sealed up." Kira pointed her knife at Amarysia. "Quit trying to change the subject. I want to know what happened to Ayri. There've been rumors all over the city. Rumors of his—" The chieftain couldn't bring herself to say it, so she turned and started pacing in front of the fire. "And . . . And I needed to see for myself."

Amarysia was more than a little surprised. Had living in the Warrens kept Kira oblivious to what was happening in the outside world? For the first time, she was starting to understand the depth of this woman's feelings for Ayrion. And found herself jealous. Kira had gotten to know him as a child while living on the streets. They had depended on each other. Those bonds were strong. The woman's presence was proof enough of that.

"The rumors are true," she said, tears welling at the corners of her eyes. She didn't want to send the knife-wielding woman into a fit of rage, but Kira deserved to know the truth.

Kira stopped pacing, but her dagger never did. It continued to spin around in her well-trained hands. "How'd he die? Was it a good death?"

Was it a good death? "Of course it wasn't a good death! No death that takes Ayrion away from me is good! What kind of stupid question is that? What's wrong with you?"

The knife stopped twirling. Kira was about as calm as a stampede of naked Northmen as she ran at her, crossing the room with the grace of a drakkar on the hunt. Even in her apron and bonnet, she was intimidating.

Amarysia stood her ground. The candle in her hand might have been shaking from fear, but she kept her face from showing it.

Kira stopped just short of plowing her over. She took a moment to look her in the eyes. "I see there is some fight in you yet, hussy. That's good. You'll need it. Now, you listen to me, and you listen good!" The tip of her blade pointed accusingly. "Ayrion was a warrior. And men like him deserve the honor of dying with sword in hand, not sucking their gums from a seat in front of the fire."

Amarysia's hands were balled tight as she fought back the urge to head-butt Kira in the nose. "You have no idea what Ayrion wanted!" she fired back. "Sure, he was a warrior, but he was so much more. He was a good man. He wanted a family, a home, like a *normal* person." She hoped Kira caught the jibe. "And I would have given it to him." Amarysia was unable to hold back the tears as a flood of emotions washed over her—things she had been too afraid to tell Ayrion when he was alive.

"I would have given him a home, given him children, given him my heart, but now—" She sobbed. "It's all been taken away. Ayrion is gone, and I never even got a chance to tell him how I felt."

Kira groaned and took a step back. "Stop your crying. It's giving me a headache. It's been a long time since Ayrion and I—" She sighed. "I'm sure he knew how you felt. Men are more observant than we often give them credit for. Well, some of them, anyway. I just figured if anyone would know what happened to him, it would be you." Kira walked back over to the hearth and held out her hands. "Did Ayri tell you about our meeting after your little excursion into the Warrens?"

"What meeting?"

"He probably didn't want you to worry."

She wondered why he hadn't told her.

"Ayrion had talked with the king about the disappearances and wanted to tell me what they had arranged. While he was there, I came on to him." Kira paused, no doubt wanting to spur a reaction.

Amarysia didn't give her one.

"Anyway, I told him no one would ever have to know. It would just be between me and him." She didn't say anything further.

Knife or no knife, Amarysia was about ready to jump on the woman. "Well, go on! Tell me, then! You seem bent on destroying what good memories I have left."

Kira smiled. "He refused me, didn't even have the courtesy to think about it first. Just said *no*." She huffed. It was a rather contrived effort at being upset. "Any guy who can turn this down," she said, running a hand over her body, "is either celibate, married, or seriously not right in the head."

Amarysia found herself smiling. Had she misjudged the gruff woman? Was there a softer side under that rigid exterior?

"Now stop your bawling and tell me what happened."

Amarysia stiffened. *Guess not.*

She spent the better part of an hour relaying everything she had learned about Ayrion's death: where, how, the circumstances surrounding it, the conflict with Cylmar's overlord, the horrific creatures, even her conversation with the queen about how close Ayrion had been with her husband. She left nothing out.

Kira slunk onto the adjacent divan, leaning forward to let her elbows rest on her knees. "I don't know what to think," she finally said, breaking the silence. "I still can't believe he's gone. And with the death of the High King, I dread what will happen to this kingdom. How someone as upright as Rhydan could have sired a half-wit, no-account drunk like Dakaran, I'll never know."

Amarysia almost smiled. Kira certainly had no problem speaking her mind.

"I've also heard rumors that Dakaran plans to get rid of the High Guard and replace them with guards from the White Tower."

Amarysia's attention perked. "I've heard nothing of that. Are you sure?"

"About as sure as I can be with anything regarding that twit."

"It wouldn't surprise me. But I doubt the queen would allow it."

"Aren't you the naïve one. Dakaran has already taken the throne. There's little the Queen Mother can do. If I were you, I'd be looking for new accommodations."

"I can't leave the queen. If what you say is true, she'll need me now more than ever."

Kira stood. "There may come a time when you don't have a choice." She pulled a ring from her finger. "Use this to get into the Warrens if you need to."

Amarysia took the ring and followed Kira to the door.

"I guess we in the Warrens truly are on our own. I can't expect Dakaran to honor his father's word and look into the disappearances." Kira pulled her hood back over her head, covering her bonnet. "I wish you well," she said as she cracked the door and peeked into the corridor. Turning, she offered a sweeping bow. "Until we meet again . . . hussy." She slipped through the crack in the door, letting the latch click shut behind her.

Amarysia locked the door and walked back to her bed, spinning Kira's ring, a single emerald surrounded by rubies, in her hand as she did. She was too agitated to sleep now. She fastened the ring to one of her favorite gold necklaces for safekeeping. It was too big and gaudy to wear on her finger as Kira did, but she wanted to make sure she had it at all times.

Chapter 6 | Kira

K IRA CREPT DOWN THE hall, relieved to be out of that room. She didn't think she could have taken another minute of Amarysia sobbing over Ayrion. She glanced down at her right hand and the High Guard ring Ayrion had given her in case of an emergency. Her own eyes started to burn. *Stop it!* There was nothing more annoying than watching someone cry. Unless, of course, she was the one making them do it. She smiled.

She rounded the corner and headed down one of the rarely used service stairwells to the first floor. She knew her way around the palace, having spent a good deal of time there as a teen with Ayrion and Dakaran. She had told the hussy that she had snuck in through a secret entrance, but in truth, she had pretty much walked in.

The Warrens had several of their members working inside the palace as maids, cooks, stable hands, and even groundskeepers. A way to keep their ears open to the latest happenings, most importantly to know when and where another raid might occur. She prided herself on the ingenuity of the idea and wondered why no past chieftains had thought to do the same.

Once outside, she made her way across the courtyard to the stables where Heflin, one of the stablemen on duty, was grooming her horse. His knowledge of horses had helped him become the most recent Warrens member to garner a position inside the palace walls.

"That was quick," Heflin said, dropping the horse brush in a pocket on the front of his leather apron. He held the reins out as she approached.

She took the straps. "Wasn't much to say."

He chuckled.

"What?"

"I still can't get used to seeing you in a . . . a dress."

Kira glanced at her maid's outfit and sneered. "It's not a dress, you nitwit. It's a costume. Now, where's my jacket?"

"I put it in your saddlebag. I wouldn't wear it, though, until you're over the bridge. I have this," he said, holding out a long cloak.

Kira took it with a snort and wrapped it around her shoulders. *Does he think I'm an idiot?* She placed her left foot in the stirrup and swung herself over. The horse tossed its head, and she instinctively grabbed the reins. She didn't like horses, preferring instead to walk or run. Horses were too bulky to take through confined spaces like the Maze. But she had no desire to make the trip to the Warrens on foot at this hour.

With a flick of the reins, the mare left the stables in the direction of the upper courtyard, its hooves echoing off the stone. The noise grated on her as she bounced stiffly in the saddle.

The south bailey was empty this time of night, apart from a few well-placed guards. They watched her as she passed. She crossed the bridge spanning the Shemoa River, and the guards on duty there merely nodded. They didn't appear as concerned with keeping people from leaving the palace as they did with stopping those trying to enter. Earlier, she had been forced to climb off her horse and submit to an inspection before the guards had let her in.

Her legs prickled in the frigid air, like a hundred tiny needles were being stuck through the skin. The evening breeze coming in off the bay was relentless. Why women wore dresses was beyond her. They were so constrictive. She had to hike hers almost past her knees to sit comfortably in the saddle, which left her legs bare to the open air. Next time, she was going to have to bring a pair of long stockings.

She turned down the second street on her right and found Po waiting right where she'd left him.

"That was quick, Red."

"Not quick enough," she said, directing him into a small alley on the left, where she planned on changing outfits. She wasn't about to show up in the Warrens wearing an apron. She hopped off her horse and grabbed her clothes from the saddlebag. Her teeth were already starting to chatter. "Tell me if you see anyone coming." She quickly untied the apron and stuffed it in the saddlebag, then unbuttoned her dress and let it drop on the ground at her feet.

Her hands shook as she pulled on her top and yanked up her breeches. The cold leather caused her to yelp. Lastly, she flung on her red overcoat and walked around to where Po was sitting on his horse, keeping an eye on the road.

"Where's my sword?"

He unhooked it from his saddle and handed it down to her.

She strapped it around her waist. "Don't think I didn't catch you peeking," she said, trying to sound annoyed.

Po coughed. "I did no such thing."

She smiled, finding his embarrassment amusing. Po had been in love with her since he was old enough to even know what it meant. When he'd first arrived in Wildfire—the street tribe she had run as a kid before joining the Warrens—she had taken him under her wing. He was six years her junior, not that age would have stopped her. If she wanted something, she took it. But as much as Po wanted their relationship to move beyond the bounds of friendship, she just couldn't see him as anything more than a little brother. Not that she hadn't tried. And as many times as she had told him to find someone else, he never did.

She swung up on her horse, and they headed south around Bayside. They made it as far as Flint Street when a man rode out of one of the nearby alleys. She reached for her sword, but before she had it halfway drawn, the man pulled back his hood. It was Kerson.

"Chief, we have news."

Kira stopped her horse and let the big man move alongside. "What news?"

"More kidnappers have been spotted."

Finally, she thought. "Where?"

"South, near the water."

"Take me there."

Po turned. "Red, shouldn't we let the others handle it? There's no need for the chief to go lurking through the streets at night."

What he meant was there's no need for '*you*' to go. Po was protective of her, sometimes too protective, and Kira wasn't about to lose this advantage. She had made a promise to Ayri. Reevie had been missing for weeks and was most likely dead, but the last thing she'd told Ayri was that she would find him.

She looked at Kerson. "Well, what are you waiting for? You heard my orders. Take me there."

Kerson glanced at Po, then shrugged and turned his horse around. Kira had been surprised by Kerson's loyalty. Ever since she had spared his life during the Right of Oktar, he had remained faithful to her wishes. She hadn't honestly expected him to stay true to his word, even with the severe ramifications, but he had. In fact, besides Po, he was turning out to be one of the only other members she actually trusted.

They continued south around Bayside, Kerson's enormous frame in the lead. His horse seemed to be having a difficult time. And no wonder. The animal was far too small, leaving Kerson's feet to scrape the ground as they went.

The star-filled sky added light to the road ahead. The streets were all but vacant. They passed a few stragglers on King's Way, undoubtedly making their way home from one of the local taverns, but the farther south they rode, the fewer people they saw. They passed a couple of patrollers making their rounds, but even their presence had vanished by the time they reached the north side of the shipping district.

In the past, the kidnappers had been seen moving their freight by water, so as they continued south around the boatyards, Kira kept waiting for Kerson to turn in, but he never did.

"Where are we going?" Kira called ahead.

Kerson slowed, letting her catch up. "They were spotted moving along the Tansian River just west of the Maze. They appeared to be heading southwest toward the abandoned warehouse district."

The warehouse district? She couldn't help but note the irony. If the kidnappers had taken Reevie, they would have marched him right past his former home in the Granary. Where better to hide a boat than a set of docks no longer in use?

They continued around the northern shipyard. The brothels seemed to be the only buildings with lights on in the windows, calling weary sailors after a long and lonely voyage at sea. Those lights typically stayed on all night.

They crossed the bridge leading over the Tansian, where the river widened into the bay, and took Mora into the old warehouse district. They tied their horses off behind a deserted building near the inner wall and went the rest of the way on foot. Kira was glad to finally be off her beast. Her backside was sore from the constant bludgeoning it had taken in the saddle. She rubbed at the tender area but stopped when she caught both men watching.

Fog as thick as porridge slithered in off the bay, forcing them to keep a cautious eye on where they placed their feet. The roads this far south had holes large enough to get lost in.

So far, Kira hadn't heard the first hint of anyone being there besides them. Were they too late? Maybe the kidnappers had taken another route. This was the first time since Ayri's departure that the kidnappers had been spotted. She was going to be upset if they lost them again.

She felt like she was walking through a graveyard, and the crumbling buildings were tombstones marking the place where the bustle of life had once been, a remembrance to a thriving community now forgotten.

They were nearing the outer wall that separated the warehouses from the docks when Kerson signaled for them to stop. They moved forward to the edge of the building and peeked around the corner. Up ahead, three individuals stood watch at the gate, peering out at the bay. Kira couldn't see who they were.

One of the three took a step back as a patch of fog opened, giving Kira a clear look at her face. It was Gwen, one of her best trackers, which meant the other two were probably Griff and Preece. The three seemed to do everything together.

Gwen was taller than Kira, well built with short brown hair and watchful eyes. She was quiet as a mouse and had a nose like a bloodhound. Turning, she spotted Kira and the others and waved them over.

Kira reached the gateway and looked out at the empty docks. "Where are they?"

"We followed them here," Gwen said. Griff and Preece nodded in turn. "They had a boat waiting." She pointed off to the right. "They took it north up the coast."

"Then why are you standing here?" Kira asked.

Gwen huffed. "'Cause Griff said we were to wait for instructions."

Griff cleared his throat. "I thought it'd be best if we waited for you." He was the taller of the two men and stronger built. But having thick arms to swing a blade wasn't everything. You needed a head filled with something besides sap.

"I've already given instructions!" Kira hissed. "Brainless! From now on, I'm leaving Gwen in charge. And if I find that either of you has given her a hard time about it, I'll castrate the both of you."

Both Griff and Preece nodded. "Yes, Chief."

"Now move! We need to catch up with that boat."

The six of them ran down the levee toward the abandoned docks below. They kept a longboat there at all times, mostly used for raiding the larger cargo ships coming back from Briston. Briston ships tended to have a fair supply of root vegetables and herbs, not to mention apples from some of the best orchards in Aldor.

Kira stepped into the boat, trying to hide the shaking in her legs. She had always feared water, and not just because she couldn't swim. There was very little that frightened her, but floating on top of something when she couldn't see what was underneath did.

She slipped and grabbed Preece on her way to the bow. Preece wasn't much taller than Gwen, and nearly as slender, but he was handy with a sword and light on his feet. He caught her, holding on to her jacket until she found her place at the front. Gwen took a seat next to her while Po sat at the back with Preece, leaving Kerson and Griff in the middle with the oars.

"Hurry," Kira said, coaxing the men to pick up their speed. Her knuckles were white where she gripped the edge of the boat.

Griff, as tall as he was, looked like a stalk of wheat when sitting next to Kerson. Then again, a rock troll might not have fared much better. It took entirely far too long for the two to find their rhythm. Kerson's heavy strokes had the boat nearly spinning in circles as Griff struggled to keep up. It took Po counting out the beat before they got it. Once they did, the boat lurched forward through the waves.

Other than having a couple of white sails floating farther out in the deep, which they spotted as the patches of fog came and went, the bay seemed to be devoid of life. They passed a number of ships anchored against the north docks, their cargo either already offloaded or waiting for first light. She could see a couple of the Watch walking the decks. Those who happened to see their boat stopped and waited for them to row on by before continuing their rounds. The last of the big schooners shrank into the distance as their boat moved up the coast.

"Faster," she urged. "They've got to be here somewhere." They should have caught up by now. With a boatload of prisoners, they couldn't have been going all that fast. Had they missed them in between the sailboats?

The two men picked up speed, and the boat pushed ahead. They followed along the low barrier wall on their right, which kept the water from flooding Bayside and the residents living there.

The mist thinned as they reached the inlet where the Shemoa poured into the sea. The cliffs on the far side grew as they made their way up the river. It wouldn't be long before they reached the bridge connecting the palace to Aramoor.

"Where are they?" she grumbled, doing her best to keep from looking down into the water's depths.

"We've got to switch," Griff said, panting like a dog that had chased its tail for the last hour. Po and Preece quickly swapped places with the other two, and the boat started forward once more.

"There!" Gwen said, pointing to something along the opposite bank. "Do you see it?"

Kira scanned the far side, finally spotting a small craft moving along the face of the cliff. "That's got to be them. Row, before we lose them."

The other boat was bigger than theirs and packed to the brim. She could see a couple of black-robed individuals mixed in with the rest. Where were they heading? There was nothing out there but water.

The bridge was just ahead, its massive columns rising up from deep below the water's surface. It looked even bigger from underneath. As they passed by one of the columns, she craned her neck to see the top. She imagined it collapsing, enormous carriage-sized stones dropping all around them. Shaking her head, she released the terrifying image and turned to see how far the other boat had gone.

"Stop," she whispered back to the others. "Stop rowing."

The oars came out of the water as everyone turned to see what was happening.

Kira scanned the other side of the river, but there was no sign of the boat. "Where'd they go?"

"They were right there," Gwen said, pointing to a spot along the western shore just shy of the last pier.

Their boat was being pulled backward in the current now that the oars were no longer moving. Kerson reached out and grabbed one of the footings and maneuvered the craft alongside.

"What do we do?" Po asked, sweat streaking down his brow.

Kira didn't see any other choice. She pointed to the cliff face. "We need to get over there."

Po and Preece started rowing once again.

"Keep your eyes open," Kira said, more to Gwen than the others, since she was up at the front with her watching.

Once on the other side, they slowly rowed along the outer rock. Kira bit her lip in frustration. "How could an entire boat filled with people just vanish?" No sooner had the words escaped her lips than they rounded a small outcropping and found a hidden channel leading into the mountainside. The way the rocks had formed on the outside hid the entrance; no one on the river would have spotted it unless they were directly against the cliff face, risking damage to their boat.

This has to be it, she thought as she directed them to turn around.

"Don't you want to see what's in there?" Po asked.

"Absolutely," she said with a smile. "But not with only the five of you watching my backside. It's time we wake the clans."

Chapter 7 | Kira

"**Q**UIET DOWN!" Kira shouted at the crowd gathered around the platform in the main assembly chamber. "I can't hear myself think." She glanced at Kerson, who was standing just right of the stage, his massive frame stretching his shirt and vest to the point of ripping. "Kerson, kill the next person who opens their mouth without being recognized by the council."

Kerson drew his two-handed axe and stepped onto the bottom level of the three-tiered platform so he could see everyone—or more importantly, so everyone could see him. There were five seats, including one for the head of each of the four Warren clans: two on the first level, two on the second, and one at the top, where Kira sat as chief.

The assembly hall had never been so quiet.

Every eye nervously watched Kerson as he deliberately scanned the room, looking for someone to kill. Kira smiled. She could have heard her stomach growl. In fact, she did. *When was the last time I ate?* She pushed the thought aside.

"Once more for your thick skulls, we have found the kidnappers' lair, and I intend to lead a company of our finest into their nest and burn them out."

A man near the front cautiously raised his hand, unwilling to speak out with Kerson standing so close.

Shilvan, one of the clan heads seated on the second level, pointed at the man. "Speak."

"Why should we risk our necks for Aramoor's citizens? We owe them nothing."

More than a few grunted, heads bobbing in agreement. The four leaders of the clans said nothing. They turned stiffly in their seats as if waiting for her to answer.

"I'll tell you why," Kira said, scooting to the edge of her high-backed chair. "Because I gave my word." She looked around the room. All four clans were represented, everyone wearing their clan's color, whether by sash, headband, belt, or vest. The assembly room felt smaller somehow. She remembered how intimidated she had been the first time she had been allowed admittance. The banners hanging from the walls representing the four Warren clans, the pillars lining the outside with their bracketed torches, the men and women gathered around with a fierceness in their eyes that would have had most soiling themselves. Kira, on the other hand, had determined right from the start that she would sit in the top seat or die trying. Ten years later, here she was.

"We might be some of the most cutthroat sons of faeries in Aramoor," she said, "but at least we have our word. You ain't worth a hock of spit if your word means nothing. Putting that aside," she said with a wave of her hand, "who have these cloaked men taken?"

No one answered.

"Have they stolen the good citizens of Aramoor out of their beds? No! They've taken the homeless, the street kids, the castaways that no one cares about or will notice. You ask me why we should care. That's why!"

The room was quiet. Faces turned with quizzical looks, many shrugging in confusion.

She shook her head. She was surrounded by idiots. "You," she said, pointing at the man who had asked the question. "Tillweed, or Willis, or whatever your flaming name is."

The man gulped. "Tillis, Chief."

"Were you born here, Tillis?"

The man glanced around the assembly hall. "In this room?"

She growled, having half a mind to order Kerson to kill him for being stupid. "No! Were you born in the *Warrens*?"

"No, Chief."

"Where were you born?"

"I was born in the Maze."

Perfect. "So, it's safe to assume that one or both of your parents are dead?"

Tillis nodded slowly, clearly trying to figure out where this was going.

"Where did you live before coming to the Warrens?"

"In the tribes," he said. "Rockslide, if it matters."

Kira sneered. She hated Rockslide. Her former tribe had been at war with them for years. She looked out across the rest of the gathering. "How many others started out on the streets before coming here?"

Almost every hand went up.

"That," she said, smacking the arm of her chair, "is why this is important. What if these men had come five years ago, or ten? How many of you would they have taken?"

Heads slowly rose as understanding sparked in their eyes.

"These abductors are taking our future. What happens if there's no one left to fill our ranks, no new generations for us to depend on? These kidnappers are stealing our people!"

The crowd moved, anxiously shifting from one foot to the next, some reaching for their weapons.

"We run these streets!" she shouted, hopping to her feet. "Are we going to let these Defiler-loving sons of goats walk into our home and steal from us?"

"NO!" they shouted back, raising blades and clubs in the air. Even a few of the clan heads were on their feet.

"Good! Because tomorrow night, we do what we do best. We slit their throats and feed their corpses to the river!"

Each clan chose ten of their best to represent the Warrens. Kira, not having an official clan of her own since her rise to chief, volunteered Po and Kerson to be her escorts. She would have been hard pressed to leave them behind. Po, because of how he felt about her. And Kerson, because of his oath of fealty.

It took all the next day to get them organized, armed, and moved down to the lower docks without alerting any of the city patrols. It had also taken some heavy negotiating to rent enough longboats and skiffs to transport everyone up the bay.

They waited for cover of darkness before pushing off. The five longboats were larger than the one they'd used the night before, which helped ease the nervous tension in her stomach at having to once again leave the security of dry land. Each boat seated at least ten: eight in the middle, including two sets of oarsmen, a lookout at the front, and one at the stern running the tiller to keep them on course. The longer boats also came with the added blessing of not having to mix clan members. Each clan had their own boat.

Instead of moving directly up the coast, they rowed farther out into the bay before angling north toward the river. As much as Kira hated being this far from shore, she didn't want the ships in port to think they were a raiding party. A sight like that would have had the watchmen ringing the bells for sure.

The thickening fog and calm water helped them glide along at a steady pace without the worry of being seen. Apart from the regular lapping of the oars, the bay was eerily silent. Kira kept a close watch from the bow of the lead boat as they approached the cliffs on the other side. She focused on what lay ahead, doing her best to swallow the rising fear at what might be lurking beneath their boat. The stone supports for the bridge loomed out of the fog on their right. They were getting close.

By the time they reached the other side, her knuckles were white from clinging to the sides. She directed the helmsmen with hand signals, and they steered the boats over against the rock. She hoped they didn't run into the kidnappers on their way in. She'd much rather surprise them inside than have to engage them in battle over the water.

They slowed as they reached the outcropping of rock that blocked the hidden tunnel into the mountainside. The passageway behind the rocks was only large enough for a single craft. Kira's boat was the first in. They drew in the oars to squeeze through, and everyone ducked, as the tunnel entrance wasn't much more than a foot or two above the bow.

Her hands trembled slightly as they floated through the blackness ahead.

"Draw your swords," she whispered back to the others, unable to see anyone behind her. "Pass it on." She could hear the ring of steel on down the line. By now, all five boats had to be inside. She could barely make out a faint circle of light behind her from where they had entered.

Without torches to light the way, the path ahead was lost to darkness. Kira reached up to feel her way along the rock, keeping the boat moving forward. The lap of the water against the boat and tunnel were the only sounds she heard. Soon enough, the echo of the water grew distant as the passage widened to the point where she could no longer touch the rock. She wondered how deep the channel was.

A faint light marked a split in the passageway ahead. The light was coming from the left branch. Voices echoed in the distance. Not the kind of voices from a pleasant conversation, but from what sounded like cries of agony. The repeating echoes gave her some idea as to the size of the cavern they were floating through. By the sound of it, the roof had risen out of reach.

They made it to the edge of the split and found a small inlet with a docking area that had been cut out of the stone. Torches lined the upper walls, lighting a hewn walkway that circled half the inlet. Rope ladders hung from the shelf every ten to twelve feet down to the water, where several boats were already tied against the sides. From the water to the top of the cavern was at least thirty feet. The walkway led around to a tunnel at the front of the inlet with a single guard standing watch.

Kira's boat was the first in, the others still coming up behind. She turned and whispered to Griff on the third seat. "Can you hit that guard from here?"

Griff studied the distance. "I think so."

"You think so, or you know so? You miss, and we lose any chance at surprising them."

He looked once again and nodded. "I can do it."

Some of the other boats were floating up beside them as Griff nocked an arrow and stood. "Don't anyone move," he whispered, drawing the string to his cheek. Kira held her breath, doing her best to keep the boat steady. Griff held the arrow for what felt like forever. She was about to tell him to shoot already when his fingers finally released the string, and the arrow flew from the bow with a thrum.

The lone guard groaned and stumbled backward against the wall. She smiled, then the guard moved. He pushed himself up from the wall and stumbled for the open tunnel. Before Griff could nock a second arrow, there was another thrum from one of the boats farther down, and the guard groaned once more, this time slumping into a sitting position with his head drooping forward.

Kira spotted Gwen two boats down, hooking her bow back around her shoulders.

They stowed the oars and moved the boats into place alongside the remaining hanging ladders. Kira's boat, along with two others, took the left side, while the other two took the right. She grabbed for the ladder, but Po insisted he and Kerson go first. Their way of keeping her safe. She finally agreed, standing back to let them head up the wall in front of her. She had to admit it looked kind of fun.

It was an interesting experience, climbing up something that swayed back and forth. A quick glance over her shoulder had her clinging to the rungs. She hoped the rope held. She hated to think what might be swimming in those dark waters below.

Before she could turn back around, Kerson grabbed her arm and yanked her up onto the walkway. She bit down on her tongue to keep from berating him. A quick punch to the arm let him know she didn't appreciate being manhandled.

Once at the top, she started around the shelf toward the tunnel entrance as the rest of her crew made their way up the wall and around the walkway on the other side. They met at the entrance. Whoever these kidnappers were, they had quite the setup. If it wasn't so hard to access, or if not for the fact that she would have to cross the water to get to it, she wouldn't have minded making this place an extension of the Warrens. A fallback in case the underground was ever taken.

Griff and Gwen retrieved their arrows from the dead guard and nocked them once more.

Torches lined both sides of the stone corridor ahead. Kira drew her sword and dagger and motioned them forward, cries of pain urging them to go faster. She stopped at each new corner and peered around the side before pressing on. By the time they reached the last turn, she could hear other voices besides those begging for mercy.

She moved to the edge to peek around the corner when someone walked around the other side. She dropped her sword, catching the side of the blade with the top of her foot to keep it from clanging, and grabbed the man's mouth, yanking him up against the wall. She planted her dagger in his chest and watched his eyes glaze over. It was an instinctual reaction, one she could have kicked herself for. They could have used him to find out who was inside.

It wasn't until Kerson had lowered the man to the ground that she noticed what he was wearing: a white mantle with a crest showing a sword piercing a rising sun. He was one of the White Tower's guards, a flaming member of the Black Watch. What did the White Tower have to do with kidnapping vagabonds from the streets of Aramoor?

A voice in the back of her mind whispered she needed to get out of there. If the Black Watch was involved, this was bigger than they realized. She forced the warning aside. She'd made a promise to Ayri. If Reevie was here, she was going to find him.

Po handed her her sword, and she tried once more to get a look around the corner. The tunnel opened into what looked like a long room or wide corridor, larger than the one they were in. Cages—stacked three high—lined the walls on either side. They were filled with people. More of the Tower's guards paraded in front of the pens, some stopping long enough to toss in what looked like pieces of bread. Those inside nearly tore each other apart trying to get to the food. The guards stood back and laughed, while others wearing black robes studied the cages and their occupants and scribbled on pads of parchment.

What in the Pits of Aran'gal was going on down here?

Kira tried to find Reevie amongst those huddled inside the cages, but they were too far away to get a good look at their faces. Another set of screams came from somewhere on the right, sending chills up her arms. Whoever it was, they were being tortured. Kira didn't much care for torture, but there were times when she had found it necessary. She couldn't imagine what required the torturing of a bunch of Aramoor's destitute. Only the truly depraved would be caught up in whatever was going on down here. She had come to rescue Reevie, but now she just wanted to kill whoever was doing this.

The Warrens' fighters pressed in behind her, clearly just as anxious to get on with the killing as she was. With each new cry, they shoved her a little closer to the edge. They needed to get a better idea of what they were up against, but there was no way to do so without being seen. All they could hope for was the element of surprise.

She raised her sword and gave the signal.

Kerson released a roar that nearly had her jumping out of her skin, and they charged.

Kira tightened her grip as she flew out of the tunnel just behind Kerson and Po, doing her best not to get trampled by the rest of the clansmen as they poured into the chamber. Griff, Gwen, and Preece were directly behind her.

For a brief moment, the guards and the black-clad scribes froze, the nearest of them cut down before the rest even thought to reach for weapons.

By the time Kira passed the first set of cages, she could see they weren't in a single room but a large tunnel. The left side of the tunnel stopped at a set of wide stairs, leading up to an open chamber at the top, while the right side ended about twenty feet down, just past the last of the cages.

Kira stuck her sword through the back of a woman in black robes as the woman flung her papers into the air and tried to run. Pulling it free, Kira turned and blocked a guard's swing for her head. She raised her dagger to finish him off but was beaten to it by a couple of clansmen as they raced past on their way to the stairs, both sticking the man in the gut on the way.

The prisoners huddled at the backs of their cages, crying out in fear. She scanned the first three on her side, but there was no sign of Reevie.

"Bloody vomit! Kira! Behind you!"

Kira spun. A short man in ripped clothing stood at the front of one of the cages on her left, pointing at the stairs. It was hard to tell who it was, as covered as his face was in dirt and bruising. But she recognized the voice.

Reevie.

"Watch out! There's more!"

She turned. Men in white uniforms emptied down the stairs from the rooms above like worker ants bursting from a freshly poked mound. Where had they all come from? Were they living down here?

She didn't have time to worry about Reevie. "On me!" she shouted to her fighters, and charged the stairs. Po and Kerson rushed past her and hit the front line seconds before she did. Kerson took three men down with one powerful swing of his axe. Arrows buzzed past as Griff and Gwen unloaded from somewhere behind them.

Kira ducked, barely missing catching a guard's sword with her neck. While she was down, she buried her dagger in his gut. He collapsed on the steps, tripping the man behind him, who fell forward and landed perfectly on the tip of her sword.

"My thanks," she said, pulling it out and swinging at the next. Po shouted and stumbled back a step, blood on his arm. She deflected the next sword, kicked the man in between his legs, and slit his neck when he dropped to his knees.

The press of the Tower's guards was forcing them back, but her fighters continued to cut through them with vengeance.

A guard on her left landed a lucky strike on her shoulder. She yelled at the stab of pain and grabbed the wound. Kerson roared and buried his axe halfway through the man's torso, soaking Kira and those nearby in blood. She cautiously moved her arm, feeling out the injury. The cut hadn't been deep enough to stop her; it just hurt like the blazes. Just another scar to add to her collection.

She killed another guard with a quick lunge and thrust, then turned and shouted at those behind to free the prisoners. If they couldn't stop the Black Watch here, they could at least get Reevie and the others out of the cages and back down the tunnel toward the boats.

A wave of heat suddenly rose behind them, followed by screams. She turned. Four of her people, along with some of the prisoners, lay sprawled next to the cages. Each had been burned to the point of being unrecognizable.

What just happened? Kira pulled back from the fighting. The prisoners were retreating from the opposite end of the tunnel where a single robed individual stood with arms raised. His hood was back. She couldn't tell what he was saying.

Kira had a bad feeling.

Griff and Gwen turned to the newcomer, aimed, and released their arrows. They veered into the wall as if hitting an invisible shield.

"Wielder!" Kira cried, grabbing Po and yanking him back down the stairs. "We need you!" They had barely made it through the clan lines when the lone wielder sent another wave of fire at the two archers. Gwen and Preece managed to dive into the tunnel they had come from, leaving Griff scrambling in the opposite direction. Part of the flames hit his side, and he screamed.

Gwen charged out of the tunnel and jumped on Griff, trying to extinguish the fire with her own body.

"Po!" Kira slowed as they passed Griff and Gwen.

The wielder raised his hands once more, but nothing happened. He looked down, then tried again. Nothing. His eyes bulged, and he dashed down another smaller tunnel on the left. Kira ran after him, threw her dagger, and caught him in the leg. He went down screaming, crawling as fast as he could toward a large metal door at the end.

Kira and Po caught up. "Stop!" Kira ordered, Po lowering his blade in the man's path. The wielder reluctantly stopped.

The torch on the wall revealed a well-groomed beard, short brown hair, and eyes to match. His chin, though strong, was trembling. "What have you done to me?"

Po kept his sword close as Kira knelt beside the man. "Not so tough without your magic, are you?" she said with a smile.

The wielder bared his teeth like a cornered animal, pressing his back against the left wall.

Behind them, Kira could hear the ongoing clash of steel, punctuated by the occasional roar from Kerson. At least she knew he was still alive.

"What did you do?" the man demanded. "Where's my magic?"

She simply smiled.

The wielder looked up at Po, then back at Kira, not understanding what had happened.

"Now, you'll answer my questions, or I'll make sure you never talk again. Why is the White Tower kidnapping homeless vagabonds and street urchins? What is this place? And why in the flaming Pits would the Tower be working with wielders?"

The man sneered but didn't open his mouth.

"Talk, you faer—"

The wielder leaped forward, impaling himself on Po's blade.

Kira didn't move, her mouth open in shock. "Did you see that?"

Po looked just as stunned as she was as he stared at the man hanging from the tip of his sword. "I didn't do it, Red. It was him." He pulled his sword out of the dead man's throat and let him drop.

"I know. Pits! If I hadn't seen it, I wouldn't have believed it." She got back to her feet. "What the blazes is going on down here? Come on!" She looked at the metal door once more, then turned, and they both ran back toward the fighting.

By the time they reached Griff and Gwen, the majority of the Tower's guards were dead or dying. Kerson and some of the others made sure of it as they went from one to the next, stabbing those still moving.

"Keep some alive!" she shouted. "We need answers!"

"I can help you with that, Kira."

She turned as Reevie pushed his way to her side.

"Move," Reevie said, waving Gwen back so he could get a good look at Griff. Gwen and Preece had been trying to do what they could, but neither had any experience with burns like this. Reevie, though, had extensive knowledge of medicine and healing.

"What are you doing here, Kira?" Reevie asked. "How did you find this place?"

"Will he make it?" Gwen asked, looking more concerned than Kira
had seen her before.

The right side of Griff's body had been badly burned. Reevie poked
at the darkest areas where Griff's clothes had melted into his skin. The
smell turned Kira's stomach, and she attempted to breathe through her
mouth.

"It's bad," Reevie said after his initial examination. "We need to get
him to the orphanage. I have herbs and salves we can use, but there's no
guarantee."

Gwen looked at Kira with pleading in her eyes.

Kira nodded. "Fine. But I need to talk with Reevie first. Take as
many boats as you need and get these people out of here. We have other
wounded that need help, and our dead need to be taken as well. I don't
want anyone to know who was here." She stood and glanced around at
the fallen. "We'll be along shortly. I want to have a look around before
we go."

Under Gwen's supervision they began carting the homeless and
wounded back down the tunnels toward the docks.

At least a quarter of Kira's fighters had been killed.

Po, Kerson, Reevie, and a couple of clansmen stayed behind to help.

She watched the procession of clansmen head through the tunnel
before turning to Reevie. "We need to talk."

Chapter 8 | Kira

"WE'VE BEEN LOOKING for you for weeks," Kira said as she and Reevie walked alongside the empty cages, trying not to step on the dead as they went. Reevie limped along, his clothes worn, his face and hands scuffed and dirty. His face was gaunt and his eyes sunken from lack of nourishment and sleep. It was the first time she'd seen him with a beard, the same light-brown color as his hair. It made him look older, more rugged.

"Even Ayri helped," she said. "Went all the way to the king on your behalf."

Reevie stopped. "Ayrion was looking for me? Where is he?" He turned and scanned the room as if hoping to see the man in black come strolling in. Kira fought back a sudden swell of emotion. She had rehearsed what she would say more than once if she found him, never getting it right. Then again, how was she ever to get *telling Reevie his best friend was dead* right?

"He's not here," she said, and directed them to a bare spot on the steps to sit down. "How much do you know of the recent battle with Cylmar?"

"What battle?"

That answers that question. "The Battle of Belbridge."

Reevie shook his head. "I knew things didn't look good. Is that where Ayrion is?"

She wasn't sure how to answer, so she didn't. "Before Ayri left to fight the Cylmarans, he spent every night looking for you. And he made me promise to keep looking while he was gone."

Reevie smiled.

Kira didn't know what had come between Ayri and Reevie, probably the same thing that had come between her and Ayri—the fact that he had chosen the king over them. Ayrion had always been meant for great things. Anyone could have seen that, but it was still hard to watch him leave, knowing the rest of them had been left behind.

Reevie must have noticed her doleful expression, because his smile faded. "What aren't you telling me?"

She took a deep breath and continued. "Ayrion didn't make it back from the battle."

Reevie's brow lowered. "What do you mean? Where'd he go?"

"He didn't go anywhere. He just didn't make it back."

"I don't understand."

She clenched her fists. "He's dead, Reevie. His entire unit was killed trying to save the king."

Reevie didn't say anything. He simply stared at her as if she wasn't there, his face blank, focusing on nothing. Finally, he lowered his head, probably not wanting to cry in front of her.

The silence grew more awkward by the moment. Finally, Kira stood and left him to his tears as she started up the stairs. She hated watching people cry, especially people she cared about.

"How did it happen?" he asked before she reached the top.

She turned. "I'm not really sure. From the pieces I've gathered, it sounds like Cylmar cast their lot in with wielders, and they brought an army of hor'hounds down on top of them. But if I know Ayri, he didn't go down without taking every last flaming one of them with him." Her eyes burned. *Curse you, Ayri.* She turned to hide wiping them.

"Did you see the body?"

"What?"

"Did you see Ayrion's body? Did they have a ceremony?"

"No. They had one for the king, though."

Reevie seemed to perk, and he wiped his eyes. "Then you don't know for sure that he's dead."

Kira grunted. "He didn't come back, Reevie. He's dead." *Typical Reevie,* she thought. Not wanting to argue the matter, she continued to the top. "What do you know about this place? Why are the Tower's guards rounding up vagabonds? And why in the flaming Pits were they working with a wielder?"

She could hear Reevie limping up the stairs behind her. The open room at the top was empty. It seemed to be nothing more than a large junction that connected three separate corridors. The first was the steps that led down to the cages, the second a narrow stairwell on the other side of the room leading up to some unknown location, and the third a hallway branching off to the right. A couple of tables lined the left wall, filled with papers and writing utensils. She marched over to get a better look.

"They were documenting the experiments," Reevie said as he scuffled along behind her.

"What experiments?" Po asked as he and Kerson reached the top of the stairs and glanced warily around the room before poking their noses in the other passageways.

Kira continued perusing the sheets of paper on the tables. There was little to see but scheduling. Each calendar day had little markings that looked like some form of shorthand. She had no idea what they were recording. The squiggles didn't make any sense.

"He experimented on *us*," Reevie said.

Kira laid the parchments back on the table and turned. "Who was experimenting on you? The wielder we killed?"

"No. Although he helped." Reevie plopped down on one of the chairs at the nearest table. "It was the Archchancellor."

"Valtor? Valtor was down here experimenting on people? What was he doing?"

Reevie stared blankly at the wall behind her. His hands were shaking, and the look on his face was more than unsettling.

"Does it have something to do with that metal door we found on the other side of the cages?"

Reevie nodded. "I heard them call it T'Ross Mauktor."

Kira leaned back and rested against the front of one of the tables. "Call what? The door?"

"No. The room. I overheard them say it means *room of a thousand nightmares*."

"Let's go take a look."

"Are you sure that's wise?" Po asked. "A thousand nightmares doesn't sound like a place we need to be visiting."

"I want to know why the Archchancellor of the White Tower would be secretly kidnapping Aramoor's discarded." Kira smiled. "Besides, I didn't think you were scared of anything, Po."

"Not scared," he said, straightening his shoulders. "Just cautious."

"We should go before more guards show up," Kerson said in his low, gruff voice as he started down the stairs leading to the cages below. Even he sounded wary.

He wasn't wrong. She certainly didn't want to get caught down there if Valtor made an appearance. But, at the moment, her curiosity was stronger than her sense of self-preservation.

"Come on," she said to Reevie, pushing off the table and starting for the stairs. "We'll take a quick look and then be on our way."

"I'm not going in there," Reevie said as he followed her across the

room. "Few of those they took in came back alive. And those that did . . ."

Kira stopped and waited for him to catch up.

Reevie shook his head. "They didn't come back the same."

"What do you mean?" She let him put an arm on her shoulder for support as they headed down the stairs and between the cages toward the back.

"I mean they came back something else."

Po turned. "What's that supposed to mean?"

Reevie pulled her to a stop beside the entrance to the tunnel that led back to the docks. "I'm not going in there," he said. "I'll wait for you here."

She sighed. "Fine." She looked at the two additional clansmen who had remained to guard her. "You two stay with him," she said, nodding at Reevie. "Po and Kerson will come with me."

The clansmen smiled in relief.

Kira took the left corridor, passing the dead wielder on the way. She still couldn't get over the sight of him leaping onto Po's sword.

She stopped just outside the door and took a moment to study it. The light from one of the nearby torches showed a fair amount of rust, probably from their closeness to the water. The entire place felt moist. She drew her sword and looked at Kerson.

"Open it. Let's see what they were up to down here."

Kerson moved to the front and grabbed ahold of the lever, pulling it back. The door gave an eerie whine as it cracked open. With a firm grip on his axe, he grabbed the handle and pushed.

The chamber beyond was much larger than the others they'd seen. Torches had been placed on some of the stone pillars, giving ample light. She didn't see much in the way of a thousand nightmares, but she did see a number of shelves, cabinets, and long tables, with half-used candles lining each.

"Kill me," a voice said, causing all three to freeze. It sounded like it had come from one of the two tables near the center of the room. She glanced at the other two, and Po shook his head, clearly not wanting to go any farther.

She shrugged off the fear and continued forward, motioning for them to follow. They did, rather reluctantly. Their earlier desire of keeping her safe by volunteering to go first apparently didn't apply to this room. She started for the two tables in the middle, her eyes darting about the shelves in case there were more wielders lurking about.

They passed a cauldron on the left that was every bit as large as a hogshead. It seemed to be built right into the floor.

"Please, kill me." The words were barely understandable.

Behind the tables was an empty podium, and behind it—at the back of the room—was a door with some very strange noises coming from it. She kept her eye on the door as she reached the two tables. On the right was a metal table in the shape of a person's body, and on the left, a wooden table where a man lay bound hand and foot.

Kira pulled her dagger and began sawing at the leather straps holding the man's left wrist. "Cut the other side," she told Po.

Po nodded, and he and Kerson walked around the table to get at the other bindings. "Creator help us!" Po jumped back, tripping over his own feet and landing against a set of shelves. He quickly drew an *X* on his chest and spat off to the side.

Kerson ran for the exit, shouting something about the place being cursed.

"What in the flaming Pits is wrong with you two?" Kira left off cutting the strap on the man's ankle and walked around the table to see what was going on. She froze, the breath catching in her throat. She hadn't noticed it at first because of the darker shadows on the right side of the man's body, but he was missing an arm. In its place was something that could only be described as a scorpion's pincer—large, with a hard shell that ended in a hooked claw.

The claw moved, and she jumped back, knocking Po into the shelves behind them once again.

"Please kill me," the man said.

"We need to get out of here, Red. This is the Defiler's work." Po didn't wait to see if she agreed and started for the metal door.

Kira told herself to follow, but she was too mesmerized by what was lying on the table in front of her. She noticed the right side of the man's face had begun to change as well. A thick crustacean-type shell covered most of what she could see. How far down did the changes go? His clothes were probably hiding the rest.

Giving the table plenty of room, she moved back around to the other side where he was still human looking.

"Have mercy," he said, his voice coming out somewhat garbled.

"What happened to you?"

"Something's wrong inside me. Pain. Nothing but pain. Kill me. Kill me!"

Kira inched her way closer to the table, keeping a close eye on his other side in case he broke free. The man turned his head for the first time and looked at her with his one remaining human eye. "Please."

Her hands were shaking. She took a deep breath and released it, then took another, building her courage. She took one final gulp, stepped forward, and plunged her dagger into the man's chest.

His head reared, and he released an awful hissing noise that had her scrambling back against the metal table behind her. She held her hand over her ears until the hissing and convulsions stopped. Cautiously, she made her way back over to the table. The man's eye was still open. He blinked, tears streaming down one side.

"Thank . . ." The breath left his body, and his eye closed.

She removed her dagger and ran for the door, passing the cauldron on the way. For a brief moment, she thought about stopping, but her legs didn't agree. Po and Kerson were waiting for her just outside, neither willing to step foot in the room again.

"Time to go," she said.

She got no argument from them as they raced down the hallway and back out into the main room.

"What was that noise?" Reevie asked, looking nearly as frightened as the two clansmen guarding him.

"You don't want to know," she said, grabbing him under his right arm and half dragging him down the tunnel toward the docks. "We need to get out of here."

Chapter 9 | Jair

J AIR COULDN'T STOP COUGHING. He waved his hand in front
of his face, driving back the dust as he walked alongside the old
tinker wagon. His skin and clothes were beginning to change color as the
reddish dirt from the dry roadbed clung to him. He pulled his coat tighter
to keep the dust from staining his blue shirt, but also to fight against the
chill. The sun might have been shining, but the wind coming off the
grasslands to the north was anything but warm.

It had been a couple of weeks since he had first awoken to unfamiliar
surroundings with people he didn't know, and discovered he was a
stranger to himself. As his strength had returned, the older couple that
had found him had taken to the open road. With nowhere else to go, he
had no other choice but to tag along. Whatever the woman, Zynora, had
done to bring him back from the brink of death had also cut down on the
time for healing considerably.

Jair forced himself to walk as much as his body would allow. Zynora
had told him the fresh air would do him good. He coughed and covered

his face as dust from the road enveloped him once again. Somehow, he didn't think this was what she'd had in mind.

"How much farther?" He looked up at the front of the wagon and chuckled at Tameel's relaxed position—feet propped up on the footboard, head back against the wagon. If Jair didn't know better, he'd have thought the old man had fallen asleep. Wouldn't have been the first time.

"Well, let's see," Tameel said with a deep yawn, not bothering to so much as shift his weight. "We left Hedgemont beginning of the week. Crossed into Sidara a good day or so back, so . . ." He scratched the top of his white head. "I reckon we'll reach Woodvale before supper. Nice little town, Woodvale."

He transferred the reins to one hand and struggled to close the front of his coat with the other. "Friendly people," he continued. "You'll find most of these small communities right neighborly, if a bit on the poor side."

Jair noted that the last observation seemed to dampen the man's normally cheerful disposition. Having spent the better part of the past week pestering the older couple with questions about who he was, where they'd found him, what side they thought he had fought on, and who had won, Jair had been forced to concede that for now it was best to lay low, heal, and try to regain his memories.

Tameel and Zynora had taught him all they could about the subtle art of trading as they headed for their eastern coastal routes. Just because he didn't know who he was didn't mean he couldn't pull his own weight. At least, that's what Tameel had said.

"Jair, come give me a hand with these weapons," Zynora said from the back of the wagon. "They're too heavy for an old woman like me to carry."

Jair laughed. Zynora was as strong as an ox, but he didn't mind helping wherever he could, especially if it meant a break from the dust and gnats.

"Be right there," he said. It had taken him a while to get used to the name Jair. Even though he had no memory of his own, the name didn't feel like his. Zynora figured the memory loss was caused by the trauma and the amount of blood he had lost before they had found him. He hoped it would return in time, but for now, he needed to focus on regaining his strength. What better way to do that than to accompany the only people he knew on their peddling expedition through the five kingdoms?

Other than his lack of strength, his body seemed to be functioning normally. He didn't think he'd lost any range of movement, and he had no problem speaking and was pleased to discover he still remembered how to read.

When asked, Tameel and Zynora had both refused to take him back to where they had found him, no matter how much he begged. All they would say was they had recovered his body while looking for survivors, but he felt there had to be more to it.

They did eventually tell him that they believed he was one of the Upaka because of the unique lack of color in his eyes. Apparently, his people lived in the uninhabited regions of Keldor and were best known for their killing. Not exactly a great start.

The only possessions he had from his former life were a black stallion they'd found wandering near where he had been discovered, a pair of beautifully designed swords, a long black leather coat—which they had paid a skilled leather worker to patch since it had three holes in the back—and a single black onyx ring with a strange white symbol at the center that they'd found on a chain around his neck.

One thing was clear. He distinctly had an affinity for all things black.

He opened the still-moving wagon's back door and hopped up on the step. "What do you need moved?"

"Those right there," she said, pointing to a pile of swords and scabbards in the corner. They had been selling off some of the collected weapons in each new town they rode through.

Jair spent most of his days with Tameel, learning how to make *the*

Sell. "It's not their job to know if they need it or not," Tameel kept trying to explain, "it's yours. They *always* need it. They just don't know it yet."

"Where do you want them?" he asked, stepping inside to lift the weapons.

"In the front." She pointed to an empty spot behind a large chest where she had cleared out a few rolls of cloth to sell. Clearly, his presence was not a complete waste of rations, since it turned out that warriors with an affinity for black were quite skilled at heavy lifting and manual labor, even while recovering their strength.

Jair spent his evenings studying the ways of the Dar'Rhivanni with Zynora as she educated him on the finer points of what it meant to be one of the nomadic traders. Her first order of business had been to find him a suitable name. After a number of unsuccessful attempts, she finally settled on Jair—one of the Rhivanni's four founding ancestors, who just so happened to be the father of the Dar clan to which Zynora and Tameel belonged. Jair was said to have possessed a remarkable inner strength and been a man of few words. But according to Dar legend, when those words were uttered, hurricanes formed, rivers dried up, and mountains split in twain.

Jair thought it an honor to be named after such a revered figure.

However, in the quiet confines of the wagon, Zynora enjoyed calling him Grey Eyes. It was a simple label but one that expressed her fondness for their adopted stray.

As Tameel had predicted, it was indeed pushing evening when they caught their first glimpse of the small town of Woodvale. The early-winter sky was a bright tapestry of color as they followed the dirt road leading into town.

Woodvale was good to its name—a small valley cut out of the

surrounding forest. The town was quaint, much like the others they had passed through. One- and two-story buildings sided with simple wood planks lined both sides of the street. There were a few shops at the center, interspersed between local residences.

People stopped to stare at the colorful wagon, then went back to whatever they were doing, some shaking their heads. Jair never knew from one town to the next how they would be received. Some were happy to see the tinkers, even friendly—others, not so much.

Tameel kept the wagon rolling, not stopping until they reached the far end of town, where he pulled off the road onto a back trail in a thick grove of trees, which eventually led them to the front of a small inn. By the time Tameel had steered the wagon around to the far side of the stable, the stars had already begun to make their presence known.

"I'm going to see if Blithe has any food to spare," Tameel said as he climbed down from the front seat and handed Jair the reins. "I might need your help."

Jair hopped down, tied off the horses, and hurried to catch up.

Zynora stuck her head out of the back and called after them, "Be sure to ask him about some extra oats for the horses."

Tameel waved in acknowledgement.

The sign over the door read THE SMOKIN' PIG. Appropriate, Jair decided, since the first scent wafting toward him was that of burnt bacon. The inn was a modest stone-and-cedar two-story structure, with decayed plaster and a steep thatched roof. A narrow balcony lined the face of the second floor, acting as an awning to keep the weather off those sitting on the porch. Horses were tied to both sides of the entrance, signaling a rather large gathering inside.

"Appears quite busy for a Fourthday," Tameel said as he stepped up on the porch.

After a courtesy whack of their boots on the front side of the entrance, they stepped inside and promptly shut the door to keep the cold air out. As expected, the inn was nearly filled, standing room only. Pipe smoke hung in the air like a thick fog, dulling colors and stinging eyes. At the back of the room, a not-so-talented older gentleman struggled with his langeleik on a makeshift stage. A few of the tipsier patrons sang along to a round of "Bart the Fool" with about as much accuracy as the instrumentalist's fingers on the strings.

Jair wondered how he had known the instrument's name. It seemed a strange thing to remember when he couldn't even recall his own.

He followed Tameel as the old man shuffled along the edge of the room, heading for the kitchen. Jair couldn't help but notice more than one sideways glance as they passed. Tinkers were never the most celebrated of guests, but there was still a healthy respect for their services, if for no other reason than it was widely believed that to treat a tinker ill would bring a full year's bad luck.

They stopped just outside the kitchen and waited as the innkeeper— Blithe, Tameel had called him—slaved away in front of a large brick oven. To say Blithe was a big man would be like calling the Sidaran Forest a mere stand of trees, or the Ozrin Sea a good-sized swimming hole. The man was as wide as he was tall, though Tameel said he was as gentle as a lamb, unless of course you messed with his family. Or his cooking.

Again, Jair was left puzzling why he could remember names like the Sidaran Forest or the Ozrin Sea but not the ones that mattered most. He hoped the others came back as well. The sooner the better.

The two watched the innkeeper slice a fresh loaf. Tameel waited for him to finish laying the cheese garnish around the sides of the platter before clearing his throat. When that didn't work, he resorted to calling the man's name.

Blithe looked up from his work, still flipping out the cheese wedges with hands that seemed to act on their own. For a moment, it looked like he was trying to determine who they were, but then recognition settled in and he halted his arranging. He motioned with his head to the far side of the room. "This isn't a good time, Tameel."

Jair followed Tameel's example and slowly turned his head. The last two tables in the far corner were filled with armed men in white mantles, a couple of whom were banging their tankards on their tables and shouting for more ale, taking clear advantage of the young maids trying to serve them.

Some of the armsmen were looking in their direction.

"Yes, I see what you mean," Tameel said. "I'll find a more appropriate time." He turned to Jair. "We need to go."

"Come see me in the morning," Blithe said. "They should be sleeping off the ale by then."

Tameel nodded and started retracing his steps, Jair on his heels. They were only halfway across the room when Jair caught movement on his left. Two of the white-robed men had left their seats and were shoving their way through the crowd. "Where are you going, tinkers? Come have a drink with us."

The room quieted as Tameel made a break for the door. Jair's stomach knotted as he sensed the old man's fear. Despite their words, whoever these men were, they didn't seem to care for the Rhivanni.

Once outside, Tameel hobbled as fast as he could across the lawn toward their wagon, passing the stable on the way.

"Jair. Quick. Untie the horses!"

"Why? What's going on?" he asked as he ran to obey. "Who were those men?"

"What's wrong, Tameel?" Zynora asked from the back of the wagon. "The Black Watch. They're inside!"

Chapter 10 | Jair

J AIR SCRAMBLED UP into the front seat with the reins. "What's
the Black Watch?"

"Later!" Tameel hissed. "We've got to get out of here."

A group of men approached from the inn, each wearing a similar
white mantle, each with a sword at his waist. Something about them
stirred the briefest flash of memory, and he realized his hands were
shaking. For some reason, still unknown to him, these men filled him
with a deep sense of hatred.

Patrons of The Smokin' Pig filed out the front door to see what was
happening.

Jair stood up in the wagon seat and scanned the grounds, quickly
weighing their options. Apart from the road leading back into town, they
were surrounded by trees. Even if they managed to get the wagon rolling,
how far would they get?

He heard Tameel at the back, ordering Zynora to get inside and hide.

The white-robed guards stopped a few feet shy of the stable.

"We have orders to take all Rhivanni vermin in for questioning," a man at the front of the group said. His disheveled hair hung over his shoulders, and week-old growth covered his angular face. He took a step forward and laid his hand on the hilt of his sword as if daring them to defy his orders.

"We've broken no laws," Tameel said, keeping his head lowered. "We don't want any trouble. We'll just be on our way."

The guard stepped forward and grabbed Tameel by the arm. "You're not going anywhere."

Jair lowered his head as well, but not for the same reason as Tameel. He didn't want the guards to see his eyes. Zynora had told him that his people were even more disliked than the Rhivanni.

He hopped down and slowly walked to the back of the wagon, stopping in the shadows to keep his face hidden. "Let him go," he said quietly.

The guard looked up. "What did you say, tinker?"

Tameel looked at him and shook his head. Jair ignored him. "I said, let him go."

Zynora climbed down from the back of the wagon and stood beside him. "Jair, don't provoke them," she whispered. "It's not worth it." She put her hand on his arm. "It'll be all right."

All right? These men were threatening to take all three of them in for some kind of questioning.

By now, the entire inn had emptied, the patrons murmuring amongst themselves as they watched the proceedings, most still clinging to their drinks.

The guard handed Tameel off to one of the men behind him, then turned to Zynora. "I see by your headdress that you're a practitioner of the Kojzu. It's been a long time since we've had the pleasure of putting one of you through purging," he said with a smile that made Jair's skin crawl.

Jair took a moment to study the men. There were eight guards. The man at the front was obviously the leader. *Take him out first and unbalance the rest.* They each had a sword strapped to the left side of their waist, except the second man on the right, who had his strapped to the opposite. *Left-handed.* The white mantles could be intimidating, but in reality, they were also constricting. *Limited movement.*

The third from the left is missing an eye. The man holding Tameel has a limp in his right leg. And three of them have definitely had too much to drink.

Behind him, the wagon was only a few steps away. He needed to get Zynora inside.

As if hearing Jair's thoughts, Zynora edged toward the back door.

"Where are you going, wrinkles?" the guard asked. "I have something special I want to show you." He motioned toward the stable. "Bring it out!"

The barn doors swung open, and two more men in white robes led some*thing* out. Whatever it was released a loud shriek that shook Jair to his core. *What in the name of darkness is that?*

"Sniffer!" Tameel cried in fear.

The onlookers in front of the inn scattered in all directions, some heading back inside, others running into the woods.

The creature in front of the barn was grotesquely misshapen, most of its body mercifully covered by a black hooded cape that had been shredded at the ends. Even hunched, it stood at least two feet over the tallest of them. Its fingers, if you could call them that, were at least three times the length of a normal man's, with talon-like nails that curved ever so slightly downward. Its body, from what Jair could see at the front opening, was mere sinew wrapped in layers of moist, discolored skin. The arms reaching out from under the folds of the cloak, much like its fingers, were disproportionate to its body, twice the length of a human's.

It gripped two enormous swords, each blade gradually widening at the end, pulling their balance forward.

The creature pulled its hood back with a disfigured finger, and Jair's breath caught in his throat. The sniffer's head was human in shape, though larger and deformed. The back of its skull was covered with moss-like patches of long hair, which hung like rain-soaked willow branches down its back.

Its head lurched upward and convulsed, giving it the distinct appearance of an animal searching for a scent, which was odd, considering it lacked a nose. Where one should have been, there were two gaping holes. It almost looked like the skull of some monster after worms and decay had consumed the soft tissue.

Keeping an eye on the creature, Jair picked up a hand-sized log from the wood pile stacked next to the wagon. He felt like the village idiot, standing against ten armed men and a creature fresh out of his worst nightmare with nothing more than a piece of firewood. It wasn't like he could ask them to wait while he went inside and grabbed a proper sword.

"Too much of a coward to face me yourself?" Jair asked the guard, hoping to play on the man's pride and draw him out.

The guard grinned. "Hold your positions," he said to those behind. "This one's mine." He drew his sword, the ring of metal filling the cold evening air. The man didn't even bother to raise the blade.

Jair shifted his stance, his body twisting slightly to put his strong arm forward. What was he doing? This was insane.

He took a deep breath as he left the wagon to meet the guard. The man lunged, swinging for his head. Jair felt his arm move as if on its own. Lifting the wood, he caught the blade, showering them both with splintered pieces of kindling. *What was that?* He reared back to throw what was left of the log at the man, and suddenly everything around him shifted, and he was somehow back beside the wagon, still holding his piece of firewood.

"Hold your positions," he heard the man saying. "This one's mine."

Jair looked around. *What just happened?*

The man charged all over again, but this time, Jair already knew what he was going to do, and instead of using the wood to block the guard's blade, he struck the inside of the man's sword arm before he could complete his swing. The impact violently compressed the guard's muscle, forcing his hand to open and his sword to fall.

Before the blade hit the ground, Jair snapped the log across the guard's leg. His left knee shattered with a sickening crunch. The guard opened his mouth to scream, but Jair thrust the butt end of the wood straight up into the man's jaw with enough force to snap his neck. The guard dropped, twitched, and went still.

Jair looked down at his shaking hands. Where had that cold precision come from? Was this part of his Upakan training coming to the surface?

The remaining guards stared in awe.

Behind him, the wagon door creaked. "Jair, catch!"

Jair turned. He dropped the stick of wood and snatched the two blades out of the air. *His* blades, or so he'd been told. And he believed it, because right now they felt less like swords and more like extensions of his own arms.

He held the unique weapons out in front of him. It wasn't their perfect balance in his hands or the exquisitely crafted dragons that embellished the forward crossguards that drew his attention. It was the iridescent blades themselves, each one black as midnight and smooth as wet glass. They were both deadly and beautiful.

Jair turned, realizing the guards' bewildered expressions had changed to fear . . . even recognition. A few of them murmured something about a "guardian protector."

The name brought with it a flash of memory. A man in plated armor wearing a crown. It vanished as soon as it appeared. *Who was that?*

The sniffer's head shot upward, its jaws parting to the point of seeming dislocation as it released an ear-piercing screech that made everyone jump, including the guards. It screamed again and ran straight at Jair.

Chapter 11 | Jair

JAIR THREW ONE OF his blades, responding to an instinct that moved faster than thought. He felt the throw before he released the weapon: the force of exertion, the turn of wrist, the position of arm, and when to release for the blade to make two complete revolutions before hitting its mark. He had no idea how he knew. He just did. What was happening to him? Was he controlling it, or was it controlling him?

The blade plunged straight into the sniffer's chest, stopping at the hilt. The creature slowed only long enough to pull the sword out and drop it at his feet. Dark blood oozed from the hole in its chest, but the wound didn't seem to slow the creature. It released another shrill and charged.

Jair gaped. Another vision struck, and he spun to the right, raising his sword at the same time to block the sniffer's heavy swing. Their blades connected, and he was shocked by the lack of impact. The blow should have thrown him from his feet, but there had hardly been any force behind it.

Back and forth he parried and blocked, dodging one blow only to be set upon by another. The creature was fast, and Jair was already down a sword. The strange flashes of premonition continued to dance through his mind, making it seem as though he were fighting two sniffers at once, nearly overwhelming his senses. Pushing everything aside, he struggled to concentrate on the visions, to understand them. The creature was going to swing right, so he moved to the left. It was going to lunge, so he spun to the side and deflected.

The sniffer howled in rage as Jair managed to stay just out of reach.

He knew he couldn't keep this up. His body was already weakening. His movements, so crisp a few minutes before, were growing sluggish. His hands barely held their grip, and his arms were growing heavier by the moment. He had to do something, and fast.

Jair pivoted to block a fierce strike to his side but missed the secondary strike from the creature's elbow. The force knocked the wind from his lungs and sent him flailing to the ground, where he rolled to a stop. He winced, trying to catch his breath, and the sniffer reeled in glee, momentarily dropping its guard.

If they can't walk, they can't fight! a voice in his head said. Not able to take the time to place where he'd heard it from, he struggled to his knees, waiting for the creature to make the first move. He didn't have to wait long. The sniffer came for him. It raised one of its giant swords and swung, clearly intending to split Jair in two.

Jair waited till the last moment, then rolled, bruising his ribs and arms on roots and rocks as the sniffer's blade was buried in the ground where he'd just been. Jair turned and swung with everything he had. The sword struck the creature just below the knee, cutting straight through one leg and most of the second.

The creature howled and toppled backward, the fresh stump flailing as it grasped at its remaining ruined knee.

Jair flipped back to his feet and swung for the creature's neck. His blade bit flesh, and an eerie whine escaped the sniffer's lips as its head rolled away from its body. What was left of the creature went still.

Keeping a close eye on it, he quickly retrieved his other sword.

The guards, who had moved to the front of the barn to get out of the way, drew their swords. Even the one holding Tameel seemed to decide the old man wasn't worth the trouble and pushed him out of the way to draw his own.

"We heard you were dead," one of the guards hissed as they spread out to flank him.

He didn't give them the chance.

Their white mantles didn't remain white for long. Whatever had been controlling him up until this point took over, and he tore into them, spinning and sidestepping, lunging and whirling. As tired as he was, his arms didn't let up, removing swords, hands, arms, heads. By the time he was finished, he could hardly breathe. His hands fell to his sides, still gripping his swords, and he suddenly realized that he was more scared of himself than he had been of them.

The surrounding woods were silent except for an old hoot owl somewhere in the distance. He saw Tameel and Zynora, noting their ashen faces and that they made no attempt to approach him. He didn't blame them. He was covered in blood. He could feel it dripping from his face and hands. What had he done? What was happening to him? It seemed the biggest monster had survived.

"By the Defiler's beard!"

Jair spun and almost threw his sword when Blithe stepped out from behind an old oak, eyes ready to pop out of his head. "They were right. You *are* the Guardian Protector. What are you doing in Woodvale?" he asked.

Jair had no idea how to respond. What was a Guardian Protector? He scanned the morbidly efficient pile of corpses at his feet and wondered if maybe he didn't want to know.

"We found him left for dead at the last battle," Zynora said softly. "He lost his memory. He doesn't know who he is."

Blithe looked at the sniffer and its masters. "Appears he didn't forget everything."

Jair focused on the edge of the black blades in his hands, trying to recall something, anything. Any memory that might give him an answer to who he was and how he was capable of such destruction.

"I'm right glad to be livin' here in Sidara and as far away from those sorts of troubles as possible," the innkeeper said, rubbing his beard nervously. He looked at the cluster of blood-smeared body parts littering the ground around him. "Then again, I guess I don't live far enough away."

There was a moment of silence before Tameel finally spoke up. "We need to hide the bodies," he said as he nudged one of the Black Watch guards with his boot.

"I can handle that," Blithe said. "You three need to stay off the main roads wherever possible. The Tower's presence is growing stronger in these parts, and with all the strange things happening around here, there aren't too many who oppose it. And now that Dakaran has taken his father's throne, I have a feeling that things are going to get a whole lot worse."

"How do you mean?" Zynora asked.

"Well, word has it, soon as Dakaran was crowned High King, his first order of business was to dismantle the High Guard and replace them with these pigs." He spat on the closest white-cloaked corpse. "So, if he really is the Guardian Protector, you'd best stay hidden, 'cause anyone found with him is as good as dead."

Jair sighed. He wiped the blood from his swords on one of the guard's robes before turning around. "He's right. If I am this Guardian, then there might be others who will recognize me. It would be safer for the two of you if you went on without me."

Zynora balled her fists and planted them on either side of her waist. "At the moment, you don't know your front side from your back. And if you think I went to all the trouble of healing you just to let you go wandering about the countryside and getting yourself killed because you didn't remember no better than to eat the yellow berries instead of the purple ones . . . well, you got another thing coming."

Jair almost smiled. The tone of her voice said he wasn't being given an option.

Zynora turned and started for the back of the wagon. "Blithe's right. We need to get moving before people start asking questions."

"That's a good idea, wife," Tameel said, then looked at the innkeeper. "You sure you don't need us to help you with this?"

Blithe pulled his cloak a bit tighter. "Nah, Molly and I'll take care of it. The way these sacks of dung treated my girls, I'll be more than happy to dig their graves. You just get yourselves down the road."

"We can't thank you enough, my friend," Tameel said, stepping forward to shake the man's hand. "If there's anything you need—"

"Gettin' rid of scum like this is thanks enough. You just make sure to keep our Guardian there protected. Day might come when we'll need him again."

Jair raised his head. "This might sound like an odd question, but do you know my name?"

Blithe gave him a blank look.

Jair tried again. "The Guardian Protector . . . what was his name?"

Blithe blew out his lips and shook his head. "Don't rightly know; never actually thought about it before. We only know you as the Guardian Protector. Actually," he said, crossing his thick arms, "I believe the white riders might have mentioned it earlier. Let me think. Arnon . . . or Roan—"

"Ayrion," a woman said as she approached from the inn, carrying a large basket. She was short with dark curly hair, a button nose, and a full apron to match Blithe's. By her age and the way Blithe put his arm around her, she was the innkeeper's wife. "They said the Guardian's name was Ayrion. I remembered thinking it was a pretty name." She chuckled.

"Ayrion," Jair repeated the name to himself, hoping it would spark a memory. Unfortunately, it didn't. "I'm in your debt, madam. Until now, I didn't have that much."

"Here you go," Blithe said, taking the basket from his wife and handing it to Tameel. "I had Molly put together some leftovers for you. They should last you a day or two, I reckon. You headin' toward Easthaven?"

Tameel accepted the basket with an appreciative smile. "We have a place up north where we can take shelter for a while, at least until this blows over. Maybe with some rest, Jai . . . or Ayrion's memories will return." With that, he limped back to the wagon and handed the supplies up to Zynora.

Ayrion followed him to the wagon, rather disappointed that hearing his name hadn't somehow returned his memories. At least they knew what to call him now. He untied the horses while Blithe helped Tameel up to the wagon's seat. Zynora met him at the front with a damp rag. "Here. Clean yourself up."

Ayrion nodded and climbed up beside Tameel. He could worry about changing his clothes later. Best if they got underway. He'd just finished wiping his face and hands with the rag when Zynora opened the front hatch behind the seat and handed him a woolen scarf and some gloves. "Here. This should keep you warm tonight," she said before leaning over to place a woolen cap on top of Tameel's head. "And this should hopefully hold in what little brains you have left, old man."

Tameel shook his head, then winked at Ayrion.

Ayrion smiled at the old couple's affections. He wondered if he had someone like that waiting for him back in Aramoor.

Tameel waved at Blithe and Molly, then slapped the reins and turned the green-and-gold tinker wagon around, following the path back to the main road.

Chapter 12 | Kellen

KELLEN LIFTED HIS HANDS to his mouth and blew, hoping to coax some warmth back into them. He was actually thankful for the colder weather. The winter gusts helped dampen the stench of rot, at least from the human remains. The spiders were a different matter altogether. He rubbed his hands together, then loaded another body onto the hauler.

Kellen stopped every time he passed within sight of Nilla's grave, eyes filled with tears. He had chosen a quiet spot overlooking the rambling stream behind their cottage. His hands shook from more than the cold as the image of his wife being laid in the soft dirt returned to haunt him. The way she had looked up at him before she died. The pain in her eyes from what the spiders had done to her flooded the thin wall he had built in his mind to protect himself. He began to cry.

He felt a hand on his shoulder and turned to find Reloria standing beside him, wiping away tears of her own as she swiped the long gold feather from her teal hat out of her eyes.

"You let it out, dear," she said. "Best not to hold it in."

Kellen dried his eyes. "I can't stop thinking about it. Every time I close my eyes, I see her face."

Reloria nodded. "I remember when my late husband passed," she said, handing him a piece of sugar candy from her purse.

He ate it, letting the mint flavor ease a little of the tension.

"The feelings will always be there, but trust me, they will get easier with time."

Kellen wasn't sure he wanted them to. He didn't want to ever forget.

It had been a couple of days since they had returned to the old homestead after their battle with the Tallosians and the spiders, and still no word from Ty or Breen. He was getting worried. Was Ty in worse shape than the wizard had thought? Had the arachnobe's poison been too much for Nyalis to handle? Kellen tried not to worry and to trust the wizard could do what he said, but it was difficult.

Overlord Barl had insisted after Nilla's burial that Kellen and Adarra return to his estate for their own safety. It was obvious that it would be quite a while before the battleground—which was their home—would be cleared and cleaned enough for habitation.

Kellen had sat with Ambassador Lanmiere and Overlord Barl until the wee hours of the morning each night, discussing at length the threat they now seemed to be facing, how the new king's policies and the explosion of power from the White Tower would affect Easthaven and the rest of Sidara.

They spoke of the people's fear of magic. Kellen addressed the most common fallacies that fed that fear. He even told them of Easthaven's Wielder Council. There wasn't much sense in hiding it now, especially after what the overlord had just endured. He did keep the location of the Harbor Houses a secret, though, for the sake of the council as well as those they were continuing to protect.

Overlord Barl and Lyessa had been by earlier to see how progress was coming before leaving for a meeting. Something to do with expanding the barracks. Lyessa had stayed to help Adarra and Fraya mop up spider guts inside the house. Not an easy task. A number of the walls and a good deal of the furniture would need replacing.

Eventually, Lyessa and Fraya had left to check up on the one individual who was not present: Aiden Raycrest, Lyessa's former fiancé. Fraya had managed to heal the deepest of the young man's wounds, but it had taken a lot out of her, as close to death as he had been.

Adarra said she felt as though she owed Aiden, since it was his failed attempt at saving their lives that had nearly cost him his. Still, Kellen found it hard to forgive Aiden for having tried to give his son up to the witch.

Kellen wheeled the two-handled hauler to the western edge of the property, where they had dug an enormous pit for burning and burial. "Here's another load," he called down to Veldon, who was busy using his magic to burn the corpses.

Veldon wiped the sweat from his balding head. "Feoldor! Grab those bodies, won't you?" He turned and unleashed another wash of flames onto the grisly pile of rotting cadavers.

"Yeah, yeah, yeah, hold your horses!" Feoldor grumbled, turning to look at the bodies and body parts Kellen was dumping beside the pit. He lifted his hands, and the air shifted beneath the corpses, lifting them off the ground. He rotated his arms toward the fire, and the rotting heap of flesh moved with it. Feoldor dropped his arms, and the bodies fell into the flames, scattering ashes and sending puffs of smoke into the canopy above.

"I'm starting to smell them again, Feoldor!" Reloria shouted from somewhere back near the house. "Can you do something about that?"

"Fire and ash! I can't do everything," Feoldor said. "I know I'm good, but I'm not the Creator!"

Kellen pushed his hauler back to the next pile of corpses in front of the cottage, passing Reloria on the way.

"Ain't that the truth!" she muttered, adding a Northman's axe to the pile of scavenged weapons. She shook her head, nearly losing her gaudy lavender hat in the process. "I swear I don't know what I'm going to do with that man. All his fussing is leaving me with a sour taste in my mouth."

Kellen smiled as he stopped the pushcart beside the next load and wiped his face with a rag. Even in the cold early-winter air, he was still managing to work up quite a sweat. He was thankful for the work, however, thankful for anything to keep him from sitting around thinking about everything he'd lost: the warmth of Nilla's presence as they slept, the comfort and security of having her close by, the way she could cheer him up with a single smile, always there to offer her love and support. She was their family's foundation. And now she was gone.

Kellen shook his head to drive away the painful memories as he leaned over and grabbed another dead Tallosian and tossed him on the back of the hauler.

After a couple more trips to the fire and back, Kellen took a break and sat on the half-empty hauler for a moment, clearing his thoughts as he watched Orlyn busy himself with vines that had at one time draped a good portion of their house. Very little of the vines had survived the spiders' onslaught. Only a few strands still remained; the rest lay in pieces around the house, leaving nothing to hide the destruction the spiders had wreaked.

Orlyn held his rune-covered staff firmly in his right hand. The crystal at the top emanated a pale-green light, which he pointed at the cottage. The vines slithered across the top of the roof like long, emaciated garden snakes, producing a slight hiss as they worked their way across the wooden shingles and thatching, then crawled down the front of his house, stopping just shy of the stone foundation. Kellen found himself almost smiling as the curtain of green filled out across the front as though nothing had ever happened.

"Have you heard anything concerning Ty or Breen?" he asked the apothecary as Orlyn added some winter daisies amidst the vines.

Orlyn took a step back, admiring his handiwork, then turned. "Communication through the forest has been slow, and so far, nothing about the boys. But then, there probably wouldn't be with Sheeva hiding them."

Kellen nodded. He had asked the assassin to go along for that very reason. Standing, he stuffed his sweat rag back into his pocket and continued loading the dead. As he lifted another one the lifeless Tallosians for burial, he wondered if somewhere up north, someone was doing the same to his son.

Chapter 13 | Breen

BREEN'S FOOT TAPPED the dried leaves as he anxiously watched the slow rise and fall of his brother's chest. How long was he going to sleep? How long till they knew something?

Ty lay on a soft pad of green undergrowth somewhere deep within the heart of Meerwood. They weren't related by birth, but it didn't matter. This strange white-haired boy was just as much family to him as Adarra, and Breen would protect him no matter the cost. He was the oldest, after all. The responsibility of keeping them safe fell on his shoulders.

But he had failed.

His mother used to say everything happens for a reason. He could see her in the kitchen, using her rolling pin to emphasize her words. "The Creator doesn't make mistakes, Breen."

Tears burned his eyes. He wanted to believe her. He wanted to know why the Creator had let this happen. He wiped a run from his nose.

What little sky he could see through the trees was filled with stars.

Breen soaked in the beauty of the ancient woodlands, trying to distract himself from the emotions churning inside. He had grown up hearing the stories of Meerwood—the forbidden forest—and the dark magic that lurked within.

Instead of the death spoken of in the stories, Breen felt a renewed sense of spirit. Apart from battling the painful memories of their conflict with the Northmen and the spiders, he was oddly enough at peace. Safe. For once, he didn't need to constantly look over his shoulder to see if anyone was following.

Even Sheeva, with her unwavering watchfulness and utter lack of emotion, appeared to be finding it difficult to remain vigilant. He had even spotted the short white-haired assassin relaxing beside a small pool earlier that morning. He didn't think she had slept at all the previous night. The eyelids covering her piercing amber eyes were beginning to droop. For someone who was endlessly expecting an enemy to attack at every corner, it was amusing to watch her remain on guard in a place where there was nothing but tranquility.

Ty mumbled something in his sleep, then went quiet. It wasn't the first time. Breen wondered what kind of restless dreams his brother was having.

It had only been a couple of days since the wizard had saved them from Mangora and her spiders. Nyalis claimed that the arachnobe's poison pumping through Ty's veins could not be extracted by natural means. Not even Fraya, with her gift of healing, could have saved him. So, Nyalis had taken Ty to a place where the wizard could safely draw out the poison himself. Apparently, that meant traveling to Meerwood.

Breen had insisted he be allowed to come along, and a word from Breen's father had Sheeva accompanying them. But when Lyessa announced that she intended to join the party as well, Overlord Barl declared it would only be over his dead body. Her father eventually won.

In the end, the only other person to join them was Gilly. The dwarf had used his gift as a voda to convey them up the East River with unnatural speed. Breen had never witnessed Gilly's magic for himself before, other than seeing Gilly manipulate water in a cup. But that was nothing compared to their trip upriver. The rush of the wind against his face as their boat soared across the water had been invigorating. Sheeva had cloaked them with invisibility as they traveled north, another aspect to the woman's gift that Breen hadn't known she could do.

It had been a strange feeling, being invisible. Everything felt slightly off. Colors were faded and dull, and sounds seemed distant, as if he were looking at the world through a piece of tinted glass.

Once they had reached the northern shore of Crystal Lake, they had left Gilly with the boat and headed into the southernmost part of Meerwood.

Nyalis had set up some sort of protective barrier around that part of the forest, saying it would block all forms of dark magic. Breen had little choice but to take the wizard's word for it. He knew little about magic, personally, other than his singular gift. But give him a sturdy bow, a full quiver, and a brace of knives, and he'd be right at home.

Breen sat down by the fire and picked up a piece of the wood they had stacked. He inhaled and smiled. *Cedar.* He tossed it onto the fire, sending orange sparks floating skyward. His mind wandered to his mother once more. He could almost see her hovering just over the flames. He blinked, and the image was gone.

He lifted the bow lying next to him. It had been one of the Tallosians'. His own had broken during their fight, and this one was the only replacement available. The Northman's bow might have been longer, but the workmanship was shoddy at best. He could pull the string with hardly any effort. Unfortunately, it was the best he could find, but it didn't come close to replacing the one he had lost.

He laid the bow down and glanced at Ty once again, watching the rhythmic movement of his chest. Nyalis had worked into the wee hours of the previous night, drawing the poison from Ty's body, using several different potions and tinctures, along with some rather lengthy incantations he'd read from books he had produced from the pockets of his baggy robes. Any normal human would have succumbed to the poison long since, but whatever it was that gave Ty his power had somehow kept him holding on long enough for Nyalis to complete his work.

Ty's fever had broken earlier that morning. His breathing was growing stronger, and the color in his cheeks was returning as well. A good sign. He had slept through the day, tossing and turning occasionally but never opening his eyes.

Growing tired of staring at his brother, Breen grabbed his cup, emptied out the few remaining drops of watered-down ale, and set it in front of a tree about ten feet from the fire. He walked back to his bedding and sat down. Reaching into his jacket pocket, he pulled out three marbles, spinning the clear balls in his hand before holding one up to admire its symmetry.

He turned and took a moment to study the cup, releasing his magic and letting it fill him. The cup seemed to draw closer the more he focused. He could feel the breeze and the dampness in the air, and judge how much their effect would offset his throw, then adjust accordingly. He'd been using his gift since he was old enough for his father to explain it.

Pinching one of the marbles between his thumb and pointer finger, Breen took a deep breath and tossed.

He heard the clack of the marble hitting the tin and smiled.

He held up the second marble, this time focusing on the tree behind the cup, letting his magic pick the spot with the right angle and speed to be effective. Again, he took a breath and tossed, putting more force behind this throw than the last, since pine bark didn't produce the same amount of bounce that a more solid object would.

The marble flew from his fingers and hit the tree in the exact spot he'd been aiming for and ricocheted backward, clacking twice as it bounced off the first marble already in the cup.

This time, Breen closed his eyes altogether, imagining the cup from memory. Not bothering to take a breath, he simply tossed the marble in the air and waited.

Nothing.

Had he missed? He opened his eyes and found Sheeva standing beside the cup and holding the little ball with a devious grin.

"You're a good man, Master Breen."

Breen started and turned as Nyalis walked up and joined him beside the fire, planting his staff between his legs. The wizard had vanished for most of the day, supposedly off to do some more research. Breen never could figure out where he went. He'd be there one moment, then gone the next.

"I don't believe you've moved beyond eyeshot of him since we've been here."

"He's my brother," Breen said.

Nyalis leaned forward, resting his elbows on his knees. "I'd always wondered what it would be like to have a brother, or sister for that matter. Alas, I was an only child." He chuckled. "My parents said I cured them of wanting more."

Breen returned the wizard's smile. The old man had a calming way about him, not at all what he would have expected from a wizard. Then again, it could just be this place. Who knew what kind of magic Nyalis had floating around? Breen almost shivered, but despite their being as far north as they were, the temperature inside the forest was surprisingly comfortable. Snow would be arriving soon, and yet Breen found that his simple leather coat was more than enough to battle the slight bite to the evening air. In fact, he found the crispness rather refreshing.

Nyalis pulled his robes close to his body. "These old bones don't stand up to the weather as they used to. Age is a funny thing. They say it brings wisdom, but the trade-off, well . . ." He chuckled. "I think I could do with a little less wisdom."

"I bow to your age . . . and wisdom," Breen said. "But speaking for myself, I wouldn't mind possessing a little bit more."

The wizard studied him with a careful eye. "You have more than you know," he said, then turned back to the fire. They both sat in silence, watching the flames as they performed their merry dance across the glowing embers.

"Your brother has a lot of growing to do and so little time to do it, I'm afraid."

Breen shifted his gaze to Ty's bedroll and watched the flickering light cast shadows across his brother's sleeping face. "I will be there to help him."

Nyalis turned his head. "Yes, I believe you will." On the other side of the fire, Sheeva stirred, settling herself against a pine and momentarily diverting his thoughts. "There is a darkness growing in Aldor," he said, leaning on his staff. "And it knows of your existence."

Breen felt his muscles tense as a profound discomfort settled into his bones.

"When your family thwarted the witch's attempt at your brother, you revealed yourselves as a threat to the Tower's plans. That threat will not be allowed to remain. I fear you will not be ready to stand against what is coming."

"Well, that's encouraging," Breen said dryly, but in truth, he'd been wondering the same thing. How could their small band of wielders fight against something as powerful as the White Tower? Even with Ty?

"It's when you find yourself surrounded by darkness that a single light can shine the brightest. When good men stand against the tide—"

Sheeva grumbled something from the other side of the fire.

"—and good women as well," Nyalis offered apologetically, catching a glint of Sheeva's piercing gaze, "there is always hope."

A soft moan from Ty's side of the fire had everyone turning as a pair of azure eyes finally blinked open.

"Ah, I see our young faeling has made his way back to the land of the living."

Breen was off his seat and at his brother's side before Ty had a chance to lift his head. "How do you feel? Can you move?"

Ty slowly raised one arm and then the other. "I think so." His voice was weak.

A nod from Nyalis and Breen helped his brother to a sitting position.

Ty smacked his lips and glanced around the small campsite. "I'm hungry."

Breen smiled. Apparently, he wasn't too sick to eat.

After feeding his brother some of the broth left over from supper, Breen went on to explain everything that had happened since their battle with Mangora. He did his best not to break down in front of Ty, but the pain on his brother's face as he recalled their mother's death mirrored his own. Tears streamed Ty's cheeks, and Breen put a hand on his shoulder, trying and failing to hold back his own.

"Tell me about your magic, Ty," Nyalis said curiously as Ty wiped his eyes for the third or fourth time. "How has it developed?"

"What do you mean?"

"What can you do with it?"

Ty shook his head. "I'm not sure."

"Have you been practicing? Strengthening it?"

"No. Not really. I've mostly kept it hidden."

Nyalis looked a little perplexed. "And why would you do that?"

Ty looked stunned. "Because I don't want to end up getting arrested."

Nyalis leaned back against the old stump he'd been sitting in front of and sighed. "I thought you would have been a lot further along by now. I'm surprised you managed to change your hair at all, if that's the case."

Ty felt the top of his head. "Change my hair?"

"Yes. I set it to change back once you had performed a feat of magic strong enough to show me you were ready to begin your training."

"My training?"

"We'll discuss it later."

"I shot fire from my hands," Ty said.

"Nearly killed himself doing it," Breen added in his defense. "He can also talk to animals."

"Can he now?" the wizard said.

"And make you see things that aren't there."

Nyalis leaned forward. "Is this true?" he asked Ty.

Ty shrugged, looking embarrassed. "I guess."

"Tell me about it."

Ty went on to explain what had happened during Performance Night at the East Inn some weeks back. Nyalis listened intently, asking a question here, making a suggestion there, clearly trying to determine the extent of Ty's capabilities.

"Mentalism is a very dangerous piece of magic," Nyalis said. "It was a trait most used by you-know-who."

Breen shivered.

"Being able to plant and extract thoughts is a powerful gift to possess." He stared at Ty a moment longer, making Breen uncomfortable. "Perhaps you are not as far gone as I believed. Still, we have a lot of work to do if we are to get you ready."

Ty looked at Breen. "Ready for what?"

"For what is coming."

Could the wizard have been more cryptic? Breen wondered. "What is coming?"

"A discussion for another day," Nyalis said, leaving them once again without answers.

"Here's a question," Breen said. "What's the difference between a wielder, a witch, a bulradoer, and a wizard? Oh, and a faeling," he added with a quick wink at Ty.

Nyalis paused to think. "That is a complicated question, my young friend. I'll see if I can find an easy way to explain. The one thing that all of these have in common is they must first be wielders. Those who are not can't use magic. Wielders are born with magic. Most have only a single gift that requires a transferal to use. A few, like your family, have innate magic that doesn't require a crystal."

"Sheeva doesn't need a transferal either," Breen said. "Is hers innate as well?"

Sheeva leaned from her perch against the giant pine, showing interest.

Nyalis shook his head. "No. The Night Walkers are something entirely different, which I won't explain at this time."

"Night Walkers?" Breen looked at Sheeva, and she sneered.

Nyalis smiled. "That is for her to explain if she so desires. For the others, as long as you were born with magic, you are capable of learning other forms of magic, like weaves, incantations, potions, and runes. Most magic can be categorized as either elemental, mental, or arcane." Nyalis seemed to catch himself. "But that's a lesson for another time."

Breen sighed in relief. He hadn't realized how complicated magic could be.

"A bulradoer," Nyalis continued, "is simply a wielder who has learned some rudimentary forms of magic and uses those gifts for the White Tower's purposes. They like to think that they are something akin to wizards." He snorted, *loudly*. "But they'd barely rank as a second-year apprentice. A true wizard spends a lifetime learning their craft, building and excelling in all forms of magic. And there was no better place for learning than the Wizard's Keep of Aero'set."

Nyalis stared at the fire in thought. After an uncomfortable couple of minutes of silence, Breen finally cleared his throat, and Nyalis looked up. "Oh, where was I?"

"The Wizard's Keep?"

"Forget the keep," Ty cut in. "I want to know what a faeling is."

Nyalis smiled. "Yes, I guess you would. A faeling is someone born from the union of a human and a faerie."

Ty's eyes widened. "I'm a . . . faerie?"

"Half-faerie."

Breen swallowed the dread he felt rising in his chest. The Fae were feared and hated even more than wielders. They had tried to subdue mankind, many setting themselves up as gods to be revered and worshipped. But they were long gone—pushed back by the wizards in the last age. Was this Nyalis's idea of a joke?

"Your father was Fae and your mother human."

"Who are they?"

The wizard shifted uncomfortably against the old log. "I'm afraid I don't have the answer to that. I found your mother in a cabin in the Northern Heights. She died giving birth to you. And I never saw your father."

Ty lowered his head, and Breen decided it would be best to change the subject. "What about Mangora? Is she a bulradoer?"

"Mangora and Valtor are something more. They have spent their lives trying to accumulate magic. Though they are much stronger than the average bulradoer, they are a far cry from being true wizards. But don't underestimate them. Each is dangerous in their own right, as you have seen."

The conversation stretched on into the night. Ty peppered Nyalis with questions about the Fae and wizards. Nyalis answered, but often the answers were vague, and Breen wasn't sure if that was for Ty's sake or theirs. Ty's body was still very weak, and he fought with every ounce of strength he possessed to keep his eyes open. Breen found the losing battle rather amusing. After helping Ty back into his blankets, he watched over him until his brother had drifted off to sleep.

"I'll take first watch," he told Sheeva before she could disappear back into the trees.

Sheeva nodded and resumed her seat, flipping one of her blades into the air and catching it as it came down. Her bright amber eyes remained alert.

"Neither of you will be required to keep watch," Nyalis said, standing with the help of his staff. "These woods are protected. You are safe here. I suggest both of you get some rest for your journey home." Before either of them had a chance to protest, the wizard raised his hand and mumbled something under his breath.

Breen felt like stones had suddenly been glued to his eyelids. He tried to force them open, but it was a hopeless battle, and everything quickly faded into darkness.

Breen's eyes fluttered open, and he shook his head to clear the cobwebs. The conversation with Nyalis flooded back into his mind, and he hopped out of his bedroll. The sun was out and warm. By how high it was overhead, it was nearly midday. He didn't even remember crawling into his blanket.

He turned at the sound of movement behind him. It was Sheeva leaping from her covers, knives in hand, and knocking over a sealed jug of something that Nyalis had evidently laid out for them.

"What happened?" she asked.

Breen snorted. "What do you think? The wizard did one of his hand-whirly things on us." He yawned and stretched. "Got to admit, though, I feel pretty good." He picked up the jug, pulled out the stopper, and poured himself a cup. He tested the warm liquid with the tip of his tongue. It appeared to be some sort of raspberry tea. Tipping the cup, he took a healthy swallow. He turned to see if Ty wanted some and spat half his mouthful across the fire.

"Where's Ty?" His brother's bedding was empty. "Ty!"

No answer.

"Where's that old man when you need him?" Sheeva asked, looking at the spot where Nyalis had sat the night before.

Had Nyalis taken Ty somewhere? Had Ty wandered off in his sleep? What if Nyalis had taken Ty to that wizard school and left them to fend for themselves? Breen was halfway into the woods, bow in hand, when Sheeva called him back.

"Here," she said, holding out a small piece of parchment. "I found this."

Breen unfolded the paper and read it aloud, twice. "*Breen, don't worry about me. I'm with Nyalis. He needed to talk to me about something important. Not really sure where we're going, but he said that you and Sheeva should go home. I'll be back when we're finished.*"

Breen looked at Sheeva. "It's his handwriting, but I'll be hanged if I leave here without him."

Chapter 14 | Ty

TY'S EYES FLUTTERED OPEN, and he was overwhelmed by the rush of light.

Slowly, shapes and colors took form. Turning his head, he discovered he was lying on a plush carpet of soft grass under a canopy of willow trees. The air smelled of jasmine and honey. And even though the light was bright enough to see by, the sky was blanketed in stars, their presence overpowered by . . . *two moons*?

Ty sat up. *Where am I?*

Behind him stood a stone archway, surrounded by a few worn pillars and a crumbling wall, clearly all that remained of some ancient structure. Whatever it had been, it was very, very old.

Ty stood, surprised to find he had the strength to. After the spider's bite, he was lucky just to be alive.

Beyond the garden paradise rose an impenetrable wall of trees, like the bulwark to a great city, trees so thick he couldn't see past the first few rows. A meandering stream separated the forest wall from the garden. It encircled the entire enclave like a moat but, although moving, didn't seem to be going anywhere. It sang merrily, calming his spirit, reminding him in some small way of the brook behind his house. It had been his mother's favorite spot to read right before sunset. She'd sit underneath the old oak and watch the colors fill the sky.

His chest tightened as he considered the fact that his mother would never sit there again. He clenched his fists and felt his magic spark to life, igniting the flames inside him, their heat threatening to overwhelm everything else.

He took a deep breath to calm the rage. It took several moments of concentrated effort, but he was able to get his emotions under control, and the flames faded to embers. Wiping his eyes, he turned to the ruins behind him, hoping to drive the memories away by focusing on something else. Anything else.

Near the center of the structure was a white-marble dais. It stood out from the rest of the building, not so much because of the white marble but because it appeared untouched by the time that had ravaged everything else. It had steps on all four sides, leading to a raised platform on which was an onyx basin.

Ty stared at the basin. Were his eyes playing tricks on him, or was the bowl really floating in the air? He stepped through the stone portico leading into the ruins and started up the steps toward the peculiar floating bowl. He could see his image reflecting in its slick curvature. Strange symbols were etched around the rim, an ancient language he knew nothing about and certainly had no way of reading. Perhaps it told what this place was, or maybe it was a prayer to the Creator. The dais did have the look of an altar of sorts. Cautiously, he swung his hand underneath the bowl and once over the top. His eyes weren't lying. It *was* floating. He leaned forward and glanced over the rim.

The inside was filled with a silvery liquid, its surface smooth enough to make it look almost solid. He reached out with his finger.

"I wouldn't do that if I were you."

Ty whirled, jerking his hand from the basin. Nyalis stood at the edge of the ruins, just beyond the stone archway. "Where are we?" Ty asked, leaving the platform.

The wizard raised his arms. "Y'tarra. It's been a very long time since anyone besides myself has set foot in this place."

"Ee . . . what?"

"Y'tarra. The *In-Between*."

Ty looked around. "In between what?"

Nyalis chuckled. "Y'tarra is located between the realm of man and the realm of Fae. It's a sanctuary for wielders strong enough to find it."

Ty looked up at the swirls of color and the two moons. "How did we get here?"

Nyalis stepped over to the side of the portico and patted one of the stone blocks. "A very ancient portal. They were created by the first Wizard Order millennia ago as a safe haven from the faerie, back before the Faerie Wars. A number of them still exist, if you know where to look. Meerwood happens to be home to one."

"If this place is between our realm and the faerie realm, does that mean . . ." Ty nervously scanned the outer trees. "There are faeries here as well?"

"Not many," he said, and started into the ruins toward Ty. "I've spotted a few over the years, but they don't bother me, and I don't bother them."

"Where does that go?" Ty asked, pointing to a small path behind Nyalis that led into the forest on the other side of the stream.

Nyalis turned. "Ah, many different places."

"The realm of the Fae?"

"No, thank goodness. But enough about the faerie realm. We have other things to discuss."

"Like why everyone on this side of the Angorans is trying to kill me?"

Nyalis's brow furrowed as he seemed to consider the question.

"Control!" he finally said with a wave of his staff.

"Control?" Ty scratched his head. Maybe the wizard had misunderstood him.

"Why do people do anything? It's about control. People need to feel like they are in control, whether it's merely control over their own lives or control over the lives of others. For the most part, humanity is content with maintaining the illusion of control. They get up in the morning, go to work, earn a wage, support their family, raise their kids. And in doing so, they feel they have maintained some semblance of control."

"What does that have to do with people trying to kill me?"

"I'm getting to that," Nyalis said. "Men seek power for a multitude of reasons. But in the end, it comes down to one thing: They are looking to control an outcome. People see the world differently. That's part of being human. Your experiences in life shape your perception, and there are those who want to turn their perceptions into reality, whether for good or evil. Unfortunately, reality is never that simple."

Ty was having a hard time following the wizard. He still didn't understand what *control* had to do with the White Tower wanting to grab him.

"For example," Nyalis continued, "when someone says the ven'ae need to be destroyed because magic is evil, most truly believe what they are doing is right." He shivered, holding firmly to his staff. "Many unspeakable atrocities have been committed under the guise of the *greater good*."

"Why can't they see magic isn't evil?" Ty asked. "And that those of us born with it didn't choose to be like that? Seems pretty simple to me."

"Because, my boy, as long as no one is there to challenge their misguided beliefs, they will continue."

"But that still doesn't answer why the Tower is hunting me."

"Those in power don't like it when someone shifts that balance. And that is why they hunt you, my young friend. You are the weight that upsets the scales of their *control*. They've had a noose around the neck of Aldor for quite some time, and they can't risk anyone cutting the knot."

Ty thought he was beginning to understand. And if what the wizard said was true, it was indeed troubling. The Tower was afraid of him. Well, maybe not *afraid*, but certainly worried, which still seemed ridiculous to Ty. He was just one person. What did they have to be worried about? Maybe it wasn't really *him* they were concerned with as much as the wielders rallying around him. If the White Tower's goal was to control all of Aldor, then they certainly couldn't allow wielders to speak out against the atrocities taking place inside the Tower. But if the truth came out, what would people do about it? Would enough be swayed to make a difference?

Ty released a heavy sigh and sat on the dais step. His life was spinning out of control. The whole world was spinning out of control. A couple of weeks before, the only worries he had were finishing his chores, killing fresh game, and playing his flute for Performance Night. How had things come this far?

"I wish I'd never been born with magic," he said softly.

Nyalis shuffled over to join him, groaning as he lowered himself onto the step. "Magic does come with its fair share of risks. You, more than others, because of the nature of your gifts. You have power, Ty. It might be weak and untested, but you have the potential within you to be much, much more. There are those, especially within the Tower, who want that power for themselves. To control and use it to further their own ambitions."

"What can I do?"

"You have the same options as the rest of us: run, hide . . . or fight."

Ty saw his mother lying on the kitchen floor, body ravaged by spiders, the way she had looked up at him, using her dying breath to tell him she loved him. The anger inside stirred once more, and he gritted his teeth. "I want to fight."

Nyalis turned. He seemed surprised by Ty's answer, or maybe it was the eagerness in his voice. Truth was, Ty had never wanted anything more in his life.

"But I'm about as useless as a three-legged donkey. If it wasn't for the sacrifice of others, I'd be digesting in the belly of one of those spiders right now." He raised his hands and looked at them. "What good is it to have power if I can't use it?" He bit down on his tongue. "Even Lyessa had to save my life."

Nyalis smiled. "Nothing wrong with having a strong woman watching your backside, my boy."

It was Ty's turn to look surprised.

The wizard lowered his head, looking a little sheepish. "That didn't exactly come out how I intended." He pursed his lips. "Or did it?" He looked Ty in the eyes. "You might feel helpless now, but trust me, you have the ability to become a powerful force in this world, for good—or for evil."

Ty didn't want to be a powerful force. He'd be just as happy being a gamekeeper like his father. He was fine with living a simple, quiet life, and with settling down and raising a family. But it seemed the fates had something else in store.

Nyalis tapped Ty's shoulder. "This mark is a symbol of your strength. There are some who are born with the ability to do magic, although most will never know it, or recognize it for what it is. And then there's you—one of the Marked Ones."

"Marked Ones?" Ty remembered seeing a book in Mangora's shop that talked about the Marked Ones.

"Yes, as we discussed earlier. You weren't just born *with* magic. You were born *of* magic."

"Because my father was a faerie?"

"Yes—"

"But weren't the faeries evil? Didn't they try to enslave humans?" Ty gulped. "Does that mean I have evil in me as well?"

Nyalis laughed. "Son, everyone has evil in them. We are all capable of it. As for the faeries, yes. Many of them did terrible things. But some did not. Some of them even helped the humans fight back. So, you see, even you have misguided preconceptions."

Ty nodded. He supposed he did. Every text he'd ever read or story he'd ever heard said that the Fae were monsters who came to enslave humanity. Still, knowing that some of the faeries weren't as bad as the books made them out to be didn't make him feel any better. Not only did he have to worry about people fearing him because of his magic, now he had to worry about them finding out he was half *faerie*.

Unfortunately, it didn't seem like he had much of a choice. Like Nyalis said, he only had three options: run, hide, or fight. And if he chose to fight, he needed someone to show him how. "How can I learn to use my abilities?"

Nyalis laid a hand on Ty's shoulder and smiled. "That, my boy, is what I brought you here to discuss."

Ty sat up. "You did?"

"Centuries ago, there were great schools of magic." Nyalis waved his hand out in front of them, and the ruins disappeared, along with the garden, the stream, even the brightly lit night sky. Ty was no longer sitting on the steps of the dais but moving down a long corridor, young men and women in colored robes scurrying around him. Some acknowledged him with a nod or a smile; most continued on, seemingly unaware of his presence. "These were places where the people could come and learn how to use their gifts for the betterment of all. In these schools, wielders came together to study their craft and expand their knowledge, hoping to one day claim the title of wizard or sorceress."

Ty tried to look at his hands, but they wouldn't move. He looked down and realized he had a beard. *What's happening?* It was as though he were looking through someone else's eyes. Was this a memory he was seeing? Could Nyalis make others see things like Ty could? He didn't really care. He was too caught up in the revelry of the magic.

"However," Nyalis continued, "most of those schools were

destroyed during the Great Purge. A few of the stronger ones remained by hiding themselves away with magic. One school in particular had been built on top of a ley line of elemental magic. Tapping into that power, we were able to keep it hidden throughout the centuries."

The scene once again shifted, and Ty was no longer walking down a bustling hallway but was instead standing outside an enormous fortress. On either side of him stood a number of other robed individuals, all with their arms outstretched and pointing toward the citadel. They were all chanting—Ty as well—although he couldn't make out what was being said. A few moments later, the entire fortress vanished into thin air, not a trace left behind except a gaping hole in the mountainside where it used to be.

The image vanished, and Ty was once again sitting on the step outside the gardens, his heart racing.

"The school's name is Aero'set, and it needs to be—"

"Wait." Ty turned and looked at Nyalis. "What do you mean, 'we'? You said, '*we* were able to keep it hidden.' Are you saying *you* were around before the time of the Great Purge? That's not possible. That would mean you're at least a thousand years old."

Nyalis grinned. "A bit older. But that's a topic best saved for another day. Right now, I need your help in retrieving Aero'set."

"Me? Why do you need me? You're this all-powerful, clearly ancient wizard. Why can't you just bring it back?"

"A wizard, yes. All-powerful, hardly. The Keep of Aero'set was built by faeries during the First Age, and it requires faerie blood to retrieve it."

"Why is this place so important? There are no wizards left. Other than you, right?"

Nyalis grew solemn. "For the last two millennia, ranging as far back as the Faerie Wars, there have always been two main seats of power: the White Tower and Aero'set. If we are to have any hope of fighting back against what is coming, we are going to need the wizarding school's help."

Ty blinked. That was about the most straightforward answer Nyalis had given him yet. "Where is it?"

"Ah, well, that's the thing," Nyalis said with a half-smile.

Ty's shoulders drooped. He was getting the nagging feeling this was going to be a whole lot more complicated than he would like.

The wizard reached into his robes and pulled out a small maroon pouch and held it out for Ty.

"What's this?" Ty asked, taking the pouch and loosening the drawstrings. He upturned the purse, and a silver compass plopped into his hand. A broken compass, he amended, watching the needle spin around and around. He glanced once more at the two moons above him and shook his head. Determining which way was north seemed out of the question.

"It's time you begin your training."

Ty's head shot up. "Training?" That was what he'd been waiting to hear this entire time. "I'm ready!" This was it. He would learn how to avenge his mother. If Nyalis would train him to use his magic, he could learn to fight back. He could put an end to Mangora once and for all.

The old man laughed. "Are you indeed?"

Ty hesitated. "Yes."

"I guess we'll find out." Nyalis looked at the silver instrument in Ty's hand. "That compass will be your guide."

"To what?"

"To Aero'set, of course. What have we just been discussing?"

"I thought we were discussing my training."

"Young man, this is the start of your training. Passing these four tests and returning the keep will push you further than you've gone before. It will force you to use more than just your magic. You will have to use your noggin." Nyalis rapped his knuckles on the top of Ty's head.

"What four tests? This is the first I'm hearing about tests."

Nyalis tugged on his long whiskers. "Hmm. I suppose we didn't talk about the tests, did we?"

Ty huffed. Why did everything with this wizard have to be so complicated?

"We can talk more about that when you're ready. For now, I'm sure your family and friends are anxious for your return."

"Can I take someone with me?"

"What?"

"To return Aero'set. How many people can I bring?"

Nyalis shook his head. "None, I'm afraid. This is a task to test the bearer's worthiness, not others'."

Ty rested his elbows on his knees, suddenly feeling nervous. The farthest he'd ever been on his own was a trip into Easthaven to pick up supplies for his mother. And that had been a disaster. "When do I need to start?"

"That is up to you, lad," Nyalis said with a huff as he pulled himself up with his staff. "But I'd suggest sooner rather than later. Winter is setting in. Don't want to get caught in its grip. Oh, and whatever you do, don't lose that compass." With that, Nyalis pointed his staff at the portico, voicing some kind of incantation.

"Wait!"

Nyalis stopped and turned.

"You never told me where to start."

Nyalis shook his head. "I really am getting old. When you're ready, you can meet me here."

"In Y'tarra? I don't know—"

"No, Meerwood. I'll be here to show you where to begin."

"What should I pack?"

"I would bring a month's worth of supplies to be safe. Could take a while."

"How do you know this is even going to work? As you say, I'm only *half* faerie. Will that be enough?"

Nyalis's face grew grim. "I pray it is." He turned back to the stone archway, raised his staff, and began chanting once again.

A light flickered between the arch, so faint Ty almost didn't notice. Then a wave of light erupted, and everything between the portico shifted. Where the grass and willows had once been now stood a stand of redwood. It was like looking through a doorway into another world. In a way, he guessed it was. He was still standing in the same ruins. He could see the willows and grass and stream on either side of the portico, but when he looked directly between the archway's two sides, the garden was no longer there.

Nyalis lowered his staff, looking rather drained.

Ty walked over to get a closer look. "Do I just . . ."

Nyalis nodded. "Just step through and follow the trail. It will lead you back to the campsite."

Ty nodded, took one last look around Y'tarra, and stepped through. It was a strange sensation, like a strong tingling across every inch of his body.

The first thing he noticed was the sudden drop in temperature. He turned. Oddly enough, the same ruins he had encountered in Y'tarra were there as well, all except the dais and the floating bowl of silver liquid. The stone portico was standing right behind him, but the doorway was gone.

He looked up. The sky was still filled with stars, and whatever had been keeping Nyalis's garden lit was gone too, as he could hardly see the path ahead of him. The smell of jasmine dissipated, and in its place hung the scent of fresh pine and smoking embers. He followed the trail toward the smell of smoke. Before long, he could see light ahead, guiding his way to the campsite.

Sheeva was the first to see him. With a start, she hopped up from her seat.

Breen, who was in the middle of tossing another log on the fire, spun around. "Ty! You're back!" His brother hopped the fallen tree to meet him. "Where've you been? We thought something had happened!"

Ty felt all the air inside his body whoosh out as Breen engulfed him in a voracious hug, lifting him completely off the ground.

"I left you a note," he wheezed. "Nyalis had a few things to talk to me about."

Breen released his grip. "When you said 'a few things,' I figured it wouldn't take all that long."

"Well, it didn't." He pointed at the stars. "Look, it's not even morning yet. It only took a couple of hours. Were you afraid I was going to miss breakfast or something?" He started to chuckle but then noticed the strange look Breen exchanged with Sheeva. "What?"

"Ty, it hasn't been a couple of hours. We've been searching for you for three days."

Ty's face went blank. "Three days? That's impossible. We only talked for a couple of hours at most, and then I came back."

Breen looked even more confused than Ty. He took a seat on his bedroll and waited for Ty to do the same. "So, how do you feel?"

Ty plopped down onto his bedding and gladly accepted the mug of tea Sheeva offered, steam wafting over the rim. He blew across the top and took a small sip. "I feel fine." He let the liquid warm his insides as he rubbed his hand across the previously damaged shoulder where the arachnobe had injected its poison, the tear on his tunic now the only reminder. "The pain's gone."

"Well, that's something at least." Breen still looked confused. "So, where did you go?"

Ty scratched his head. How was he going to explain where he'd been when he wasn't exactly sure himself? He took a deep breath and gave it his best shot.

Breen's eyes started to glaze over as Ty got around to describing two different moons. He went on to explain how Nyalis had tasked him with finding some sort of ancient faerie keep, as well as the tests he would need to pass. By the time Ty was done, both his brother and Sheeva looked even more confused than before.

He waited for a volley of questions, but surprisingly, none came. Instead, his brother offered a single statement. It was the last thing Ty thought about before finally dozing off to sleep.

"Just so you know, I don't care what the wizard says. I'm going with you."

Chapter 15 | Ty

BEFORE DAWN HAD broken through the trees, Ty was up and helping Breen and Sheeva pack what gear they had for their long trip home. Once finished, they stood at the edge of Meerwood, gazing in silence at the barrier Nyalis had raised to keep out unwanted guests. Ty was the first to touch the somewhat transparent amber that stood between them and the rest of the world. It was very similar in color to Sheeva's eyes.

"Are you sure that's a good idea?" his brother asked. "Better let me go first."

Ty didn't give him the chance. Before Breen had taken a single step, Ty slid his hand through. "It doesn't hurt. It feels kind of like water." He pulled his hand back out to examine. "Dry."

Breen was the next to offer his hand, then Sheeva.

Ty tried staring through the wall to see what was on the other side. Even though partially transparent, it was like looking for fish in a brook after a rain. He could see the bottom, but not very clearly. "Do you think

Mangora's still out there?" Ty asked, hoping there wasn't a horde of spiders waiting for them on the other side.

"I doubt the wizard would let us leave if he thought she was," Breen said. "Either way, we can't stay here forever. We need to get home." Holding his breath, Breen closed his eyes and stepped through. Ty waited to see if his brother would drop dead or burst into flames. He didn't. So, Ty stepped through, with Sheeva bringing up the rear.

The water-that-wasn't-water was warm and left his skin tingling. He stepped out on the other side, and a gust of frigid air hit him in the face. He turned back around. "I want to go back inside."

His brother caught him by the arm. "Let's go."

The morning air was frosty compared to the forest, and a low-hanging fog moved across the mouth of Crystal Lake. Ty could see every breath. Nyalis must have been controlling the temperature inside the woodland for their benefit. He tried stuffing his hands inside his trouser pockets, but the effort was of little use since he kept losing his balance as they picked their way over the exposed rock at the northern tip of the lake.

It felt like they had been traveling for hours by the time they reached the western side of the basin, fog still clinging to the edge of the water in pockets.

"Hello there, pretty assassin!"

Ty and the others stopped and scanned the edge of the water where he thought the voice had come from. A small skiff with a single passenger floated out of the mist. "Gilly!"

"That's me!" the little man said, pointing to himself with a big smile. He guided the boat up to an inlet between some of the larger rocks.

"How did you know we were here?" Ty asked. "Have you seen the spiders?"

Gilly shook his head. "No spiders. I saw where you had gone in, and I knew you'd have to come back out, so I've been circling this part of the lake every day waiting for you. I told you I would keep the boat safe."

"That you did," Breen said, clapping the dwarf's small shoulders as he stepped into the boat. "And we are very grateful for it."

Once everyone was inside and seated, Gilly moved to the bow and grabbed hold of the boat's nose, his pudgy fingers curling around the wooden edge. "Are you ready?"

"Wait," Sheeva said as she took off her gloves and placed her hands on the sides of the boat. First, the white-haired assassin disappeared, then the boat, starting with where she was sitting and quickly spreading to the rest. Gilly was next to go.

Ty yelped, as he and Breen appeared to be hovering above the water. "What happened? Where's the boat?"

Breen smiled. "You were unconscious the last time we did this." He grabbed the boat and disappeared as well.

Ty was now alone, just him and the water. He smiled. Apart from walking through a doorway into another world and stepping through a golden wall of water-that-wasn't-water, this was by far one of the most interesting things he'd done on this trip. "I love magic."

"Your skin has to touch the boat," his brother said behind him.

Ty laid his hand on the edge of the craft, or at least where he thought the edge was, and the boat—along with its occupants—reappeared. But everything around him seemed to be hazy, like all the color in the world had grown tired. Had they floated back inside another patch of fog?

"We can't have everyone seeing us moving back downriver in this manner," Breen said. His brother's voice sounded strange. It seemed almost distant, as if coming from another room with a wall in between. Was this what the world was like for Sheeva when she was hidden?

"Hold on," Gilly said. "Here we go!" The little dwarf laughed as the boat lurched forward, throwing the others back in their seats. Ty looked behind them, expecting to see a sizable wake, but the water was as smooth as glass. His hair whipped behind him as he raised an arm over the side and caught the wind. They sped across the open water toward the mouth of the East River, and from there, home.

With Gilly's help, the journey back took less than half a day as opposed to the three or four days it would have taken without his help. Before Ty knew it, they were once again pulling the old skiff out of the water and back onto dry land. He was relieved to finally be free of Sheeva's invisibility and to have the colors and sounds and light back to normal. As fun as it had been to experience her magic, it was something he wouldn't have cared to endure for an extended period of time. It left him feeling almost light-headed.

The sun was beginning to set, and long shadows were creeping into the forest when they left the river's bank.

"Are you sensing anything, Ty?" Breen asked, stepping over to the trailhead to scan the trees.

Ty closed his eyes and let his magic spread out around him, penetrating deep within the woodlands. He could feel the animals slowing down for the day, making ready their nests. He could sense the flora settling in for the night, flowers' petals closing as they waited for the next day's sun to arrive. "I don't feel anything. I think the spiders have left the area, at least for now."

"Good to hear. But under the circumstances, let's keep as quiet as we can." Breen withdrew his bow and nocked a long shaft. Sheeva nodded her approval and fell in behind the others, her blades held ready at her sides. Breen took the lead.

Ty kept his senses spread like a net across the forest around them, waiting to pick up on the slightest movements. He realized that since his return from Y'tarra, his magic felt fully recharged. He wasn't sure if it had anything to do with the place itself, or if the wizard had done something to him, but he certainly felt stronger. After his fight with Mangora, where he had drained every last ounce of magic he possessed, he couldn't have sensed the toes on his feet. But now, he found he could sense at least a mile in any direction.

Quickly and quietly, they padded across dried leaves and moss, keeping to the path before them. Their pace increased the closer they got.

There was an uneasy tension on everyone's face. Ty could only imagine it had something to do with the overwhelming stench of death in the air. Had the witch and her spiders returned to finish the job?

Stepping out from around the last copse of trees, they caught their first glimpse of home. Ty could hear Breen breathe a slow sigh of relief as they spotted smoke rising from the chimney. A good sign.

Once across the small bridge that spanned the brook behind their house, Ty could see lights on inside the cottage. The house didn't look the same. Shutters were missing, shingles as well; windows were boarded up; deep grooves scored the walls where the spiders had dug in, attempting to burrow through. Oddly enough, the greenery covering their home looked completely untouched.

"Looks like we made it in time for supper," Ty pointed out, noticing for the first time the grumbling of his stomach.

"There are extra horses in the pen I don't recognize," his brother said.

All four pulled to a stop, quickly searching the surrounding yard and woods for signs of unwelcome guests.

Sheeva stepped between Ty and Breen. "Hold on to me."

Chapter 16 | Ty

TY GRABBED SHEEVA'S WRIST but tried not to hold on too tight. As soon as his hand made contact, the world of color faded once more. His own breathing sounded like hollow echoes from inside a great cavern.

Gilly already had hold of her other wrist, so Breen placed his hand on the back of her neck, causing Sheeva to flinch.

Cautiously, they started for the front of the house, stopping just outside the door to listen. The only thing Ty could hear was the echo of his own breathing. Breen finally lifted the latch to the front door and gave it a slight push. The door whined as it slid slowly open.

His father and sister were sitting at the dinner table, along with most of the wielder council.

Everyone turned and looked at the door.

Feoldor wiped his mouth with his napkin. "I thought you fixed—"

Sheeva released her magic, and everyone at the table gasped, Ty's father and Veldon hopping from their seats as Reloria squealed.

Adarra knocked Orlyn's staff off the back of his chair as she ran across the room. "Ty!" She plowed into him and wrapped her arms around his neck, nearly squeezing the life out of him. His father wasn't far behind. He couldn't reach past Adarra to get to Ty, so he hugged Breen instead.

"At least someone is thinking of me," Breen grumbled. Adarra stuck her tongue out at him and smiled.

Once the last of the hugs had been dispensed, the other members came around to greet them in turn, expressing their relief at seeing them alive, especially Ty.

While Feoldor caught the two brothers up on the council's cleanup efforts over the last few days, Gilly told Veldon of their trip on the East River. Sheeva, quiet and watchful as ever, remained in the background, happy at not being the center of attention. Although, Ty noted that his father took the time to stop and thank her for helping his boys.

"Is Fraya not here?" Breen asked, looking around the room.

Ty's father shook his head. "She and Lyessa have been helping Aiden with his recovery. He was about as close to death as one can get. Fraya said his wounds will heal, but his mind may take a while."

Ty shrugged at the news, not really caring how long it took Aiden to heal—or if he ever did—and looked around the room. It was different. Everything was still situated in the same place; however, most of their furniture had been destroyed during their fight with the spiders. The pieces that had remained mostly intact still had cuts or gouges; some bore dark stains from where blood had soaked into the wood. There were a few new pieces scattered about as well, probably donated by members of the council. Adarra's rocking chair had somehow managed to come out mostly unscathed, but the long bench Ty enjoyed lounging on was gone.

It was clear the council had spent a lot of time cleaning the inside of the place out. The spiders' stench was still present but not as overbearing as it had been. It would take a while to air out completely, considering how much of the house had been painted in the green filth.

Thankfully, the unwelcome reminder was being overpowered by a new scent. Ty took a whiff. "Something smells good," he said, glancing at the kitchen, half expecting his mother to come walking around the corner with a ladle in her hand and an apron around her waist.

But she didn't.

He felt his father's hand on his shoulder, as if he knew exactly what Ty was thinking.

"Let's eat," Orlyn said as he retook his seat at the table, "before it gets cold."

Ty joined the others as they discussed all the details of what had happened since their departure some days back. The bowls and platters had been picked clean by the time Ty managed to explain his visit to Y'tarra and the realm between realms.

"Nyalis said that I was different from other people with magic. He said I wasn't just born *with* magic. I was born *of* magic. He told me I was one of the Marked Ones."

"Marked Ones?" his father asked.

"Are you talking about that thing on your shoulder?" Breen asked.

Reloria pulled a piece of red taffy from her purse. "What thing on your shoulder?"

Ty stood, removed his coat, and rolled up his sleeve far enough to show the marks that ran from his shoulder down to his forearm.

Breen whistled. "It's grown."

"You've seen this before?" Ty's father asked.

Breen nodded. "It was only on his shoulder last I saw."

From the amount of magic Ty had released against the witch, he was surprised the mark hadn't grown all the way down to his fingers. As it was, it stopped about three or four inches above his wrist.

Adarra leaned forward to get a better look at the intricate patterns. The curves and angles and sharp points flowed beautifully together as they wrapped completely around his arm. In some places, the designs looked almost like miniature flames; in others, beautifully crafted blades; while others still gave the appearance of something similar to lizard scales. One thing was certain: while the unique patterns seemed to be stretching farther down his arm, they were also growing denser, leaving less of his skin showing.

"Some of these markings almost look like runes," Adarra said, suddenly excited. "See here, and here."

"Do they hurt?" Orlyn asked from across the table. He, along with the rest of the council, had scooted forward to get a better view.

"No," Ty admitted. "At least not right now."

Feoldor fluffed his side whiskers. "Not now?"

"It hurts when they spread, which seems to be when I use too much magic, something Nyalis told me that I need to learn how to control. Without the proper training, my magic could kill me."

The council exchanged furtive glances.

"Is Nyalis to train you, then?" his father finally asked.

Ty nodded. "I believe so." He didn't want to tell them about needing to leave home to do it. At least not yet. With everything he had put his family through, the last thing he wanted was to up and leave. Besides, he had a few things he needed to do first before he could think about going off on some quest for Nyalis. Namely, finding Mangora.

Breen saved him from having to say anything further. After taking a long pull of his mulled cider, his brother proceeded to finish their tale by describing the boat ride down the river. Gilly beamed with pride as more than a few of the members smiled and nodded their admiration down the table to him.

Ty's father laid his hand on Ty's and squeezed. "It's good to have you back home and safe." He glanced at Breen. "Both of you."

Breen cast a wary glance at Ty, and their father caught the look.

"What is it?"

Blazes, Breen! Ty could have choked his brother. Why did he have to go and do that? Ty tried thinking up a plausible reason for the look, but with the pressure of everyone sitting there staring at him, he couldn't concentrate. Wringing his hands under the table, he finally sighed. "I can't stay."

"Can't stay?" His father leaned forward, resting his arms on the table. "What do you mean, you can't stay?"

"I've been told I have to leave."

Adarra stared across the table. "Leave? Leave where?"

"What's going on?" his father asked, his expression growing more serious.

Ty pulled out the pouch Nyalis had given him and removed the silver compass, laying it on the table for everyone to see.

Those closest leaned forward to get a peek.

"Nyalis wants me to find an ancient school for wizards called Aero'set and bring it back."

"Bring it back?" Orlyn shifted in his seat, his baggy sleeves hanging loose over the side of the table. "Where is it now?"

Ty shrugged. "I don't know. Nyalis said it's important. He seems to think that without it, we won't survive what's coming."

"You mean the White Tower?" Reloria asked.

Ty shrugged again. "I'm not sure." He was getting tired of saying that. "Evidently, Aero'set is where they used to train wielders to use their gifts."

His father turned. "So, he wants you to go there to train?"

"I bet they have some powerful weapons in there for us to use," Veldon said from the other end of the table, where Ty's mother normally sat. The head of the wielder council had been rather tight-lipped up till now.

"I guess." Ty honestly hadn't considered that possibility. "Nyalis didn't say. But he did seem to think that this keep was important in our effort to defeat the White Tower."

"Is it dangerous?" Reloria asked, sticking another piece of taffy into her mouth.

Once again, Ty had to answer with uncertainty. "Possibly." He wished he could tell them more, but that was the extent of what he knew. The wizard hadn't exactly been forthcoming. Maybe Nyalis didn't know much more than that himself.

"When are you supposed to leave?" his father asked.

"Nyalis didn't say. He just told me that when I was ready, I should return to Meerwood." Ty tried to hide the uncertainty in his voice. He was eager to make the journey, bring back the lost school of magic, and start his training, but he was also just as hesitant. He couldn't imagine leaving his home, his family. They needed him now more than ever.

Ty's father pulled his long-stemmed pipe from his pocket and chewed softly on the end, something he did whenever he faced a tough decision.

The others picked up on the cue and decided it was time to call it an evening.

After the last goodbyes were said, Ty and the rest of his family began cleaning up. Ty cleared the dishes and wiped the table with a wet cloth. He didn't notice all the gouge marks and cracks in the tabletop until the dishes were moved.

He lifted the rag and looked back over his cleaning, remembering the times his mother had asked him to do it and he had spent the entire time grumbling and complaining. How often had he taken her for granted?

Ty stared at the end of the table and his mother's empty seat. His eyes burned, but the tears never came. He had held them back for so long that now, he couldn't pry them loose. He began wiping down the chairs. As long as he kept his thoughts focused on something else, it didn't hurt quite so much.

A sniff from over by the fire made him look up. His father stood from stoking the flames. There were tears in his eyes. He rested his arm on the mantel and took a puff on his pipe. "Breen. Adarra."

Adarra stepped out of the kitchen and wiped her soapy hands on her apron.

Breen appeared from the hall that led to the bedrooms. "Did you call?"

Ty's father nodded. "It's time."

Ty tensed, twisting the rag in his hands. He knew what his father was referring to.

His father led them out the front door and around the side of the house. They started for the small bridge at the back, but Ty stopped before they got there. He stood beside the well, unable to move, as though paralyzed by spider venom all over again. Just across the brook, underneath the oak where his mother spent her time reading, he saw the pile of newly turned soil and the wooden marker at its head.

He looked away. He couldn't face her. After all, he was the reason she was dead. He felt empty inside. Hollow. Void of everything except the pain. He didn't think he could survive the guilt. He didn't want to. Why couldn't he have taken her place?

"It's not your fault, son," his father said, startling Ty into raising his head. "Don't blame yourself."

"Who else can I blame?" Ty asked, more forcefully than he had intended. "I wasn't strong enough to protect her."

"None of us were."

"But it's *my* fault. Mangora was here for *me*. Mother died because of *me*." Ty wanted to cry, but the tears still wouldn't come. Rage took their place, burning him from the inside out. Sweat broke out on his forehead as he twisted and pulled on the rag to the point of tearing.

"You're right, Ty," his father said. "She did."

Ty took a step back, stunned.

"She also died for me, and for Breen, and Adarra. Your mother fought and died for those she loved. We all have a choice, son, and she made hers." His father took a step forward and laid his big hand on Ty's shoulder. "She loved you very much, Ty. Take comfort in knowing that she is now resting in the arms of the Creator, watching over us from above."

Ty felt anything but comforted. He pulled away from his father's grip and took another step back.

His father sighed. "Don't let this grief destroy you. Your mother would never have wanted that. Honor her by living your life."

Ty had another way to honor his mother—a promise he had already made that needed fulfilling.

"Come," his father said, motioning for Ty to follow him as he turned back toward the bridge.

Ty shook his head. Without saying another word, he turned and headed back inside.

Chapter 17 | Valtor

"**H**AVE YOU MADE your decision yet?" Valtor asked Dakaran as he weighed the answer in the newly crowned king's eyes. Valtor had been using his magic to soothe Dakaran's nerves all day in preparation for the upcoming meeting with Commander Tolin, but under the circumstances, sparing a little of that magic for himself might have been prudent.

After news had reached Valtor that his hidden laboratory under the palace hadn't been quite as hidden as he presumed, he'd spent the majority of the previous day combing through the bodies of his Black Watch, trying to discover who could have raided the underground dungeons. Every single one of the prisoners had been released. Or had they broken out on their own?

He shook his head. A rabble of half-starved vagabonds couldn't have overpowered an entire contingent of the Tower's guards. His men were dead, including one of his bulradoer, and not a trace of the perpetrators could be found, leaving him more than a little on edge. It was one thing to kill a group of armsmen, but quite another to take on a wielder trained in combat.

He took a deep breath and slowly released it. He couldn't think about it right now. It was a problem best saved for another time. He needed to focus on the immediate issues, and that meant getting rid of Commander Tolin. He turned and pushed another string of magic into Dakaran, watching as the king's shoulders relaxed.

Dakaran tended to let his emotions get the better of him most days, requiring additional effort on Valtor's part to mollify and shape those emotions into something that would serve both their interests. The wine didn't help. It was hard enough to keep Dakaran focused without the added effort of also keeping him sober. Drunk, his emotions required a forceful hand, and Dakaran was not firmly enough under Valtor's grasp for that. For now, his touch needed to remain light.

Valtor was surprised at Dakaran's hesitancy to relieve the commander of his duties. Neither Valtor nor Dakaran could afford to keep Tolin around. Under the king, the commander of the Elondrian Lancers was one of the most powerful positions in the kingdom. They needed to fill that position with someone they could control. Tolin wasn't that man. He had been vastly loyal to Rhydan and would certainly get in the way of Valtor's future endeavors.

Tolin had already been very outspoken in his argument against replacing the High Guard with the Black Watch, and worse, people were listening. Valtor hoped Dakaran wasn't one of them.

"I believe so," Dakaran said, spinning his goblet in his hand. He sat behind the desk where his father had spent most of his days. Valtor didn't care much for the room. He couldn't help but think of Rhydan every time he stepped inside and was exposed to everything from the shelves of books covering Elondrian military campaigns to the mounted trophies and weapons hanging on the walls. He had assumed Dakaran would have set up his own study, decorating it in a manner more befitting his lavish tastes. To Valtor's astonishment, the former prince had demanded the use of his father's study instead.

"Are you going to tell me or just leave me guessing?"

Dakaran smiled. "I'll let it be a surprise."

Valtor tightened his grip on his staff, his nails practically digging into the wood. Dakaran had grown more obstinate of late, ever since receiving his father's crown. He wore it everywhere he went, like a child showing off a new toy. Valtor only hoped the newness abated quickly, along with the defiance. If Dakaran continued along this path, Valtor's magic might not be enough to keep him in check.

A knock on the door had them both turning.

"Come," Dakaran said.

A guard wearing the white mantle of the Black Watch opened the door and stepped inside. He looked first to Valtor in front of the hearth, then at Dakaran. "Your Majesty, Commander Tolin is here to see you."

Dakaran made an effort to sit up straight. "Send him in."

Tolin stepped into the room, removed his feathered tricorn, and bowed. He was wearing his ceremonial uniform today, something he only did for official purposes. His crimson cape draped low over his left shoulder, covering his long-sleeved gold doublet. His sword hung from his waist, the gold polished to reflection. Had the man been expecting this meeting? Of course he had. Tolin wasn't a fool. Another reason why Valtor needed him gone.

The king stood behind his desk and headed for the arranged seats in front of the fire. He motioned for Tolin to join him. "Please, Commander, have a seat."

Tolin waited for Dakaran to take his seat in the high-backed chair across from him before sitting. Valtor remained where he was by the hearth, not wanting to appear too forward but at the same time acquiring a better view of Dakaran.

"I'm concerned, Commander," Dakaran said, crossing his legs as he balanced his goblet on the arm of his chair.

"Concerned, Your Majesty?"

"With the deaths of my father and the Guardian, and the fall of Cylmar, not to mention the return of creatures like the hor'hounds, we are clearly in a time of . . . transition." Dakaran lifted his goblet and took a small sip. "No one likes change. But change is inevitable."

Valtor smiled. Dakaran was using the very words Valtor had relayed to him not two days earlier. He was glad to see the new king had been listening. With Dakaran, he never knew.

Dakaran lowered the goblet back to the arm of his chair. "I am not my father, Commander. I have my own way of doing things."

Tolin nodded, sparing a brief glance at Valtor.

"I'm concerned, though."

Tolin shifted his gaze back to the king, his expression unchanged. "In what way, Your Majesty?"

"Take the disbanding of the High Guard. Ever since my proclamation, I have heard nothing but disapproval."

Tolin took a moment before answering. "Your Majesty, I understand change is inevitable. But if not tempered with moderation, change can be destructive."

Dakaran's grip on the stem of his cup tightened. "Are you saying you disagree with my decision, Commander?"

Tolin responded evenly. "I'm saying that the High Guard has been a symbol for this kingdom since the time of Torrin, and it seems callous to disband them right after such an enormous sacrifice on the battlefield."

Dakaran's brows lowered, which meant his temper was rising. Valtor pushed a little more magic into him to soothe his nerves. "And after the inexplicable failure of the High Guard to protect my father, do I not have the right to judge them accordingly? Do I not have the right to surround myself with those I can trust to keep me safe?"

Tolin looked stunned. "Of course, Your Majesty. I'm simply trying to point out how the decision could be viewed with skepticism. Your father was always open to hearing my counsel; I hope you will allow me to continue to offer it."

Dakaran's hand loosened slightly, his shoulders relaxing. "What other areas of concern would you counsel me in?"

What was Dakaran doing? Valtor took a small step forward, hoping to draw the king's attention. It didn't seem to work. Or if it did, Dakaran wasn't showing it.

Tolin rested his arm on the side of his chair. "There are those in the Elondrian Senate who believe it necessary to proffer additional aid to the White Tower through taxation. With the sudden reemergence of hor'hounds and the apparent rise in wielder activity, fear has taken hold of many. But, like your father," Tolin said, sparing another directed look at Valtor, "I would caution any decision that allows the White Tower to extend its reach. Your father kept the Tower on a short leash for a reason. If turned loose, who's to say where it would stop?"

"Preposterous!" Valtor snapped, caught off guard by the man's brazen implications. "As Archchancellor, I control the actions of the White Tower. Under the authority of the king, of course," he said with a bow to Dakaran. "The very reason we are seeing the rise of wielders and the return of such beasts is because the Tower has been forced to operate with its hands tied behind its back. How can we do our job without the resources needed to accomplish it?"

"You seem to be doing just fine without them, Chancellor," Tolin replied. "From the reports I'm getting, it seems the Tower's guards are multiplying like jackrabbits. There's hardly a backwater hamlet in all the five kingdoms that hasn't received a visit from the Black Watch. Tell me, Valtor, how is it the Tower has managed to amass such a force *without* the aid of the Crown?"

Valtor fought to keep his own emotions in check as he took another step forward and smiled. "Let me get this straight, Commander. First, we're not doing our jobs well enough, and that's why we're seeing an increase in wielder activity, and now we are doing our jobs *too* well because we are managing to make our presence known in the farthest reaches of the five kingdoms. Which is it? Seems you have a very clear bias." He chuckled. "Next, you'll be declaring we are in league with the very ven'ae we hunt down."

Tolin didn't respond, but Valtor noted with satisfaction the man was gripping his hat so hard he'd crumpled the brim.

Valtor turned to address Dakaran, infusing him with a strong sense of empathy. "Your Majesty, it is all too clear where the commander's loyalty lies. The White Tower has ever been the bastion of hope for the jun'ri. We are the only defense that stands between us and the return of magic. Without us, Aldor would fall prey to the very thing that brought us to the brink of destruction all those centuries ago. Magic cannot be allowed to run rampant. If the weeds are permitted to grow with the wheat, the entire crop could be lost."

Commander Tolin leaned forward, scrunching his hat even further. "What does growing wheat have to do with making sure the White Tower is held under strict control? Your Majesty, whether or not you reinstate the High Guard is your choice—for my part, I hope you do. But regardless, my chief concern is that in opening our coffers to the Tower, you may inadvertently be creating a different kind of beast. One that may very well turn on us all."

Valtor gritted his teeth, forcing himself to smile. The commander had certainly come out swinging. He hadn't expected such a direct assault. Then again, Tolin was a military man, and he had to know his time was drawing to a close. At least, Valtor hoped this was the case. He turned and looked at Dakaran, who was looking rather pensive in his chair, rubbing the bottom edge of his goblet.

Why wasn't Dakaran saying anything? Valtor could feel the sweat beading on his forehead. Was he standing too close to the fire? He took another couple of steps closer to the king.

Dakaran tapped the side of his goblet with his finger. "I appreciate your concern, Commander, but I disagree."

Valtor exhaled.

"I believe after what we saw with Cylmar and the rebellion they incited, Elondria is going to need a strong ally—"

"But, Your Majesty," Tolin interjected, "you make it sound as though we are in conflict with the other kingdoms. Cylmar was an unfortunate circumstance, I grant you. Overlord Saryn was a fool and his desires reckless. But those same sentiments are not shared by our neighbors. Keldor, Sidara, and Briston have ever been our allies. If there was ever a time to come together, it would be now. I would suggest a convening of the Provincial Authority."

"The Provincial Authority?" Valtor scoffed. "Your Majesty, the only way to ensure Elondria's safety is to wield a weapon powerful enough to keep any potential adversaries from attacking. The White Tower is that weapon. And in your hands, it can be used to keep the peace."

"In the king's hand?" Tolin pointed at Valtor. "Are you planning on stepping down as Archchancellor, then, and turning over power to the Crown?"

Valtor's eye twitched. Tolin was becoming more of a nuisance by the moment. "Of course not. Someone needs to be there to oversee the day-to-day activities. Unless, of course, the king wishes to take up residency in the Tower as its new head?"

"Hardly," Dakaran said. "My place is in Aramoor." He looked up at Valtor. "I'm more than happy to allow the Archchancellor to continue his role . . . with my supervision, of course," he said with a grating smile.

Valtor bit down on his tongue. *As if Dakaran has a choice in the matter.*

Dakaran took another sip of his wine and relaxed in his seat, staring at Tolin a moment longer. "As it stands, Commander, I don't believe our desires are in alignment. And I'm sure the reason for this meeting hasn't come as a complete surprise."

Tolin took a deep breath and leaned back against seat. "No, Your Majesty."

"You served my father well, but frankly, I need a commander I can trust to carry out my orders."

"Your Majesty, a wise king surrounds himself with those who aren't afraid to challenge his decisions."

Dakaran didn't respond, something Valtor found unnerving.

"If I have lost your confidence, I am truly sorry, Your Majesty. I would ask, though, that you don't take my failure out on my men. They are good soldiers of Elondria."

Dakaran appeared to mull over Tolin's request. "I will take it under advisement, Commander," he said, then stood.

Tolin quickly followed him up.

"I thank you for your service, Commander Tolin."

Tolin bowed, definite concern in his eyes. "By your leave, Your Majesty." The man sounded deflated. Valtor maintained his smile when Tolin glanced his way.

Dakaran dismissed Tolin with a nod, and Valtor watched as the former commander left the room with a little less kick in his step than when he had entered.

"Well done, Your Majesty," Valtor said, offering Dakaran a congratulatory smile. "For a moment there, I was beginning to worry you had changed your mind."

Dakaran didn't say anything. Instead, he walked back over to his father's desk and sat down, digging through a small stack of papers. Valtor waited a moment longer to see if he was going to respond. When he didn't, he finally left.

Chapter 18 | Dakaran

AFTER HIS MEETING with Tolin, Dakaran spent the rest of the morning celebrating with a fresh bottle of wine before making his way to the throne room. He had surprised even himself with his handling of the former commander. Even Valtor had left with his version of a smile on his face. Why had his advisor been so worried? Valtor's constant patronizing was beginning to grate on Dakaran's nerves. As a result, he took great pleasure in finding ways to make his advisor squirm—payback for the man's incessant whining about protocol and appearance and how Dakaran needed to curb his drinking. What was Valtor so worked up about? Being king wasn't all that difficult.

Dakaran squirmed, trying unsuccessfully to find a comfortable position on the gilded monstrosity that was the High King's throne. Finally, he grabbed a pillow from one of the servants and stuffed it under his backside. "Ah, much better. Hand me the other one."

The servant timidly offered another velvet cushion, and Dakaran wedged it into the corner and leaned back. "There, you see. That's how

I want this arranged every time."

"Yes, Your Majesty," the man said, and bowed, keeping his eyes to the floor.

Once a week, the king was to open the throne room to his people, a ritual his father had stupidly established decades before. His father claimed it gave the people reassurance, knowing the king was personally aware of their needs. Dakaran didn't see the point. Wasn't that what the Elondrian Senate was for?

This was the first session he had held since taking the crown.

Dakaran's head was already aching, and the proceedings hadn't even started. He had hoped the wine would help, but it had only dulled it slightly. He had been dreading this session all morning. If he hadn't been afraid of losing the people's support, Dakaran would have abolished the practice immediately. But even Valtor had advised against it.

Where was his advisor, anyway? Dakaran looked out across the army of attendants lining both sides of the hall—all dressed in their formal uniforms, the colors indicating their type of service within the palace.

But no Valtor.

The throne room appeared even grander from where he sat at the top of the platform than it had the times his father had dragged him to watch when he was younger. The room was three stories tall, both sides sweeping upward to a point, giving the impression that the room was a long archway. Marble pillars as green as the Sandrethin Forest in spring lined either side of the walkway from the entrance all the way to the throne itself. The floor tiles were cut from the same stone, the marble's white veins especially bright where the afternoon sun streamed in through long windows at the sides.

Dakaran could remember playing in the throne room as a child when his father had been away on business. He would climb up on the throne and pretend to order people around.

He allowed himself a grin. It was no longer just pretend.

"You," he said, pointing at one of the butlers in his royal-blue-and-white uniform. "What's your name . . . Never mind. Fetch me some more wine." His goblet was nearly empty, and the only way he was going to make it through this was if he had some way to dull the pain.

The servant bowed, grabbed a decanter from the table behind him, and rushed up the stairs. He bowed again at the top, quickly refilling Dakaran's glass, and after bowing once more, rushed back down to retake his spot in line.

A door on Dakaran's right opened, and Valtor entered, his mitre resting comfortably atop his head like a royal coronal, the tip of his staff clicking as he made his way up to the throne.

"Where have you been?" Dakaran groused. "If I've got to sit through this, then you will too. Keeping up this charade was *your* idea, after all."

"Yes, Your Majesty." Valtor stopped on the second tier to bow before approaching the final set of steps to the throne.

Dakaran held out his hand, the royal signet facing up. The Archchancellor paused to consider. Dakaran didn't relent. He stretched his arm even farther. "Appearances, my dear Archchancellor. We must keep up appearances."

Valtor pressed his lips together in a thin line. Dakaran knew his advisor hated kissing the ring. He hated to look like he was humbling himself, but Dakaran didn't care. After all, Valtor wasn't the High King. He was. The man had to be reminded who was in charge on occasion, and this was one of the more satisfying ways to get back at Valtor for his incessant pestering.

Valtor finally bent at the waist and brushed his lips across the royal crest before taking his place behind Dakaran's right shoulder.

"Is this really necessary?" Dakaran asked, already thinking of other, more enjoyable things he could be doing with his time—like sleeping, or bathing, or sneaking into town for a night of hard drinking. Really, anything else right now would have been preferable. He started to rub his temple but realized his headache had dissipated. Had the wine kicked in already? His thoughts seemed clearer.

"You are the leader of Elondria, sire. You must appear to lead. One way to do that is by allowing your subjects to believe that you are interested in what they have to say. They need to feel like you care about them."

Dakaran groaned. He hated getting lectured by his advisor, especially when he knew Valtor was right.

"Think of your subjects as sheep."

Dakaran turned. "Sheep?"

"Yes, Your Majesty. Sheep need a shepherd. Someone to gently herd them in the right direction."

"I hate sheep. They're dirty, loud, smelly creatures."

"They can also be vicious, aggressive, and deadly. There's a reason a wolf doesn't attack the flock as a whole. One on one, he's the more powerful, but if he bunches the herd into a corner and gets them frightened enough, they will trample him to death."

Dakaran shivered as he imagined a flock of sheep with bloody hooves racing toward him.

Valtor leaned against his cane, his fingers gently stroking the top of the wolf's head. "You'd be surprised how much you can get away with by simply allowing the people to believe their problems are being heard."

Valtor had a point, and it wasn't like this session would be physically tedious. He just had to sit there and pretend to care. "Fine. The sooner we get started, the sooner we'll be finished."

Valtor signaled the chamberlain, who in turn gestured for the guards to open the gold-leaf doors at the other end of the hall. Outside, a throng lined the hallway, waiting for their chance to speak with the new king.

Dakaran whimpered as the chamberlain's attendants in their crimson-and-gold uniforms organized the crowd, letting in clusters of people at a time and then sorting them by petition.

The morning seemed to drag on for days as one citizen after another was ushered before the throne to make their appeal, grievance, or accusation known.

One farmer demanded his cattle be allowed to drink from a stream that ran across his neighbor's property. Apparently, he believed he had more right to it since he had the larger herd.

A couple of bakers, outraged at a miller for raising the price of his wheat, demanded the king force a lower fee.

One man brought his daughter with him to let the king know she had been taken advantage of by some of the new white guards, and that he wanted justice.

One look at her and Dakaran couldn't help but feel jealous of the guards. She was quite the beauty.

One by one, they continued to pour into the throne room, each with their own set of grievances, each with their own demands. How had his father put up with it for so long? One merchant upset with another, guilds upset with higher taxes, farmers upset with drought, travelers upset with the growing number of highwaymen. There were even a disturbing number of people claiming there wasn't enough food.

Dakaran continued to hold his smile, although it was slipping. Each request was met with the same reply: "I will make sure to look into this matter immediately," he said, with a flourish. "Next."

More groups came and went, and pretty soon Dakaran's eyes were glossing over as what little patience he had started with ran dry. Valtor was right. They really were nothing more than dirty, annoying sheep, bleating about one grievance after another.

He considered just having the entire assembly step inside, all at once, so he could address them as a whole and explain to them how foolish they sounded and that the king had more important things to do with his time than to listen to their incessant whining. However, before he got the chance, the Queen Mother and her head lady-in-waiting, Amarysia, stepped through the gold-leaf doors.

The guards and servants all bowed as the two ladies made their way down the long chamber toward the dais. His mother looked well, her head high, but he could see the redness in her eyes. She'd been crying again.

Their gowns flowed behind them as the crowd parted. His mother's was a deep lavender with black trim. She had been leaning more toward the darker hues since his father's passing. Amarysia, who kept a step behind the queen, wore soft azure with gold trim, which accented her long blonde curls very well. She was one of the most stunning women he'd ever seen.

They made their way up the platform, stopping just before the final rise to bow in turn. "Good morning, Your Majesty," his mother offered before climbing the remaining steps to take her seat in the queen's throne to his left. Amarysia, like his own advisor, stood just off his mother's shoulder.

Dakaran forced himself to look away so as not to appear too forward. A touch on his hand brought his attention back around.

"How did you sleep, dear?" his mother asked. "I've been worried about you. It's been a heavy burden, having all this pressed upon you so suddenly."

He patted her hand. "I'm doing well, Mother. It is indeed a great burden, but the people . . ." he said, turning to gesture at the crowd waiting below. "They are in such need. We must find a way to help them through this, to *shepherd* them as best we can."

Behind him, he heard Valtor cough. Dakaran nearly laughed but caught himself in time to keep the appropriate expression of a concerned monarch on his face. "It's my duty," he continued. "And I'm willing to fulfill it for the good of the kingdom."

His mother beamed at his words. "It's good to hear you say so, Dakaran. Your father would be proud."

Dakaran tensed, a sudden pressure building in his chest as an unwanted memory flashed to the forefront of his mind—his father looking up at him, begging him for mercy. His mother squeezed his hand, and the memory vanished.

Behind his mother, Amarysia held a polite smile, but Dakaran could tell she wasn't convinced.

He twisted in his seat. "Valtor, cancel my engagements and set up another meeting here in the next day or two. I want to make sure everyone has had a chance to voice their concerns. Our people's needs should come first."

Valtor bowed his head and smiled. "Yes, Your Majesty."

The astonished, if not pleased, look on his counselor's face was almost worth the added hassle.

Chapter 19 | Barthol

THE COLD EVENING WIND whipped through the side streets of Aramoor, cutting Barthol to the bone. He stopped long enough to pull his tattered cloak tight around his large frame. His hood was raised, shielding his face from those passing as he carefully scanned the nearly empty street ahead.

For those unaccustomed to the vast expanse that was the capital city of Elondria, it was a perpetual maze, an endless supply of directional choices. But for someone born and raised in this labyrinth of back alleyways and side thoroughfares, it was home. The early-winter air kept the normal hustle and bustle down to a minimum. Even the street vendors had closed their booths early as shoppers rushed to get home while there was still light.

Satisfied that no one was coming, Barthol headed left down Beech Row. Already, he had heard three different versions of his untimely demise, each one more ridiculous than the last. Who in their right mind would believe he'd had both his arms eaten off and still managed to keep fighting? The only thing the stories had in common was that in each he had been portrayed as a hero, giving his life for king and country in the heat of glorious battle.

Of course, it was all a lie. There had been no honor in what had taken place. He'd lost everyone. His entire unit. His captain. His king. He had fought side by side with Ayrion since they were barely old enough to shave. He had considered Ayrion his closest friend. And now Ayrion, his men, the king—they were gone.

Most men, having walked off a battlefield in such a way, would have kept walking and never looked back. But Barthol had a family. More importantly, he had a very dangerous secret to share.

Having witnessed the prince's treachery, he knew he couldn't just go waltzing back into town. If Dakaran were to find out he'd survived, he'd be as good as dead, along with his entire family.

The thought of home spurred his feet. Having spent the better part of two months either on the road to battle, in the middle of battle, or on the road back from battle, Barthol was anxious to sleep in his own bed. His house wasn't exactly what you would deem stately, but it wasn't located in Cheapside, either. He had managed to work his way up within the High Guard's ranks, which afforded him, his wife, and their young daughter a comfortable living on the eastern side of King's Square.

It was nothing compared to those ghastly mansions on the west side, but for the son of a poor bosun who had grown up on the rougher side of town, it was quite the accomplishment, something that his family had been extremely proud of.

He stopped at the next corner and glanced across the street toward his house. Three stories. The main floor held the family rooms for both dining and entertaining, while the second floor housed the living quarters. He had renovated the top floor to allow a small living space for his father after Barthol's mother had passed from cholera a few years back.

His father, who had spent most of his life at sea, was unaccustomed to living alone. Now he spent his days keeping his grandchild entertained with wild stories of the deep.

The streetlamps on his block had already been lit. Barthol scanned the yards and windows of the adjacent homes, watching for any sign of movement. So far, it didn't appear that anyone had been keeping watch on the place. He had circled the block twice just to make sure. He wasn't sure why he was being so cautious. Everyone believed him dead.

He exhaled slowly, his breath frosting into the evening air, reminding him once again of how inadequate his clothing was. He had traded his armor and uniform to a peddler for a simple tunic, trousers, and an overcoat, along with enough food to last him from Belbridge to Aramoor. The peddler had certainly come out ahead in their deal, but Barthol had hardly been in a position to argue. His need had been greater than the peddler's.

Barthol took one last look around before crossing the street. He squeezed his hands to stop them from shaking. He wasn't sure if it was the cold or the excitement of seeing his family that had him so nervous, especially knowing they thought him dead and gone. He couldn't imagine what Kensey must have suffered, believing she would be forced to raise Arina and care for his father on her own.

His journey home had given him ample time to consider if it was wise to return, or whether it would have been better to let them go on believing he had died. It would probably be safer. He had thought of relocating to one of the other kingdoms and sending for them once he had found stable employment.

He shook his head. It would be far too cruel to let them continue suffering like this. Besides, he needed to tell someone about what had happened, if only to ensure that even if something were to tragically befall him, Dakaran wouldn't get away with his treachery.

Quickly, he made his way across the street to the brick wall that fronted his garden. With the help of a large oak growing just outside the wall, he reached the top and slung himself over, landing in a pile of raked leaves.

He knelt where he landed, listening for any sounds of alarm. When none came, he moved forward through the small jungle of low-hanging trees his wife had been growing for shade against the afternoon sun. While Arina was at her studies, Kensey enjoyed her quiet time outside, reading her fancy novels.

It was Kensey who had taught Barthol to read and write. He'd always complained that he had no need for such frivolities. He was a simple man who led a simple life.

He almost laughed at the thought. His early progression through the ranks had been due, in large part, to the fact that he was one of the few armsmen who *could* read and write; a necessary skill when sending and receiving orders. He had never thanked his wife for that. He would make sure it was one of the first things he did after all of this was over.

Testing the latch on the back door, he twisted it to the right. The door opened, and he slid inside. Barthol had barely managed to flip the latch back into place when he heard a high-pitched squeal behind him. Without hesitating, he leaped over the tea table and pressed his big hand over the girl's mouth to stifle the outburst.

The small parlor was dimly lit for the evening. The rest of his family were probably making ready for supper. Before he could pull back his hood, his wife and father burst into the room, halting where they stood when they saw the cloaked figure with his arm around the young girl.

"Now listen here, you ruffian," his father called out, grabbing the closest thing his hand could reach—his granddaughter's wooden flute. "I be one of the king's own, served thirty years as a fleet captain in His Majesty's navy. Why, I've killed more men than you could count on your fingers and toes. If you don't release my granddaughter this instant, I'm gonna stuff this here flute so far down your windpipe, it'll give new meaning to the phrase 'whistlin' out your stern.'"

Barthol laughed. "First of all, it was *twenty-two* years as a ship's *bosun*, and the only thing you ever killed were the rats on dry dock that found their way into the galley cheese."

No one spoke for a long moment.

"Barthol?" his father finally asked.

"Of course," he said with a smile as he removed his hood. He could feel his throat tighten. "Who else would be foolish enough to break into the house of a crazy man threatening death by flute?"

"Well, I, uh . . ." His father quickly replaced the instrument on the nearby shelf. "What's wrong with you, boy? Thought I raised you better than to go sneakin' around and scarin' us all half to death!"

His wife stood there, jaw agape. Even with tears rolling down both cheeks and her long black hair covering half her face, Kensey was the most beautiful sight he'd seen in months.

"Daddy!" Arina spun around and leaped into the air, wrapping her arms around his neck and her legs around his waist. "They said you were dead, but I knew it wasn't true. No one can kill my daddy!"

Barthol couldn't hold back the tears any longer. He buried his face in her hair and sobbed.

"You're here!" Kensey cried as she rushed across the room and wedged herself under his arm, squishing Arina in the process. "You're really here. They said you were dead. Died with the king. They called you a hero—" She stopped talking and began kissing. It felt like she was going to peel the flesh right off his face. It was wonderful!

"Slow down there, Kensey," his father said. "Give the man a chance to breathe." He laid a firm hand on Barthol's shoulder. "Supper's on the table, son. Come have a seat, and you can tell us all about it over a bowl of pork and lentils."

Barthol turned to follow his father into the dining room. With Arina wrapped hand and foot around him and Kensey smothering him with her lips, only one thought came to mind: *I need to die more often.*

Chapter 20 | Ayrion

AYRION WINCED AS THE old tinker wagon managed to find yet another pothole, sending a blistering ache running along his rather bruised backside. He grunted at the old man sitting next to him.

Tameel just smiled and shrugged, then gave the reins another whack. "Giddy up there!"

It had been three days since their encounter with the Black Watch and the disturbing creature Tameel had called a sniffer. Instead of continuing east toward Riverton, as they had planned, they had turned northward, skirting the western edge of the Sidaran Forest. Each day brought them a little closer to the foothills of the Angoran Mountains and the town of Wellhollow.

"What is Wellhollow like?" Ayrion asked, trying to take his mind off his sore undercarriage by studying the black onyx ring hanging from the chain around his neck. Clearly, it was important to him . . . but why? "Is it a large city?"

Tameel leaned back against the wagon wall, keeping his eyes on the road ahead. "I wouldn't say it was a city." He propped his feet on the toe board and relaxed his arms, the reins loosely gripped between his fingers. "More of a village, really. Maybe twice the size of Woodvale." He tugged gently on the right strap, directing the two horses back to the center of the road. The prairie grass on the left side proved tempting, though, and gradually the horses drifted back toward it. "It's a rough town, Wellhollow. Full of trappers, loggers, hunters—all sorts of mountain folk who'd much rather spend their days in the quiet of their own company than in the niceties of social life.

"Up there," he said, pointing ahead of them where the flat grasslands were eventually devoured by the curve of the horizon, "they have their own set of rules and codes to live by. Most wouldn't understand, but you spend a winter up in those mountains, and you come to realize that those rules will save your life. They don't hold much to meddlin' in each other's affairs, but if one of them ever finds some trouble, the others are pretty quick to lend a hand."

Ayrion liked the way that sounded. Could be a quiet life would suit him. If only he knew whether that was how he had *always* felt. He tucked the ring back under his shirt. No matter how many times he held it, the memories wouldn't come.

Other than finding out his name and that he was Guardian Protector to a now-dead king, Ayrion was still no closer to discovering who he was than the day he'd woken in Tameel and Zynora's cabin. If he was this Guardian, it might be safer for any of his past relations if he were to remain hidden—at least for the time being. At least until his memory returned.

So, for now, he was more than happy to relinquish his role as *Ayrion*, Guardian Protector to the Crown, and take on the role of *Ayrion*, traveling partner to a pair of crazy old tinkers. *Ayrion* couldn't be so uncommon a name that he shouldn't use it. More importantly, he hoped that in using it, it might spark some more memories.

Tameel kept the pace slow but steady, not wanting to push the horses.

There was no need to rush. The next village wasn't for another couple of days, and streams were in abundance.

The enormous stallion that Tameel and Zynora had found on the battlefield whinnied from the back of the wagon where he had been tied. He didn't seem to like it when Ayrion rode up front with Tameel.

The horse seemed to know him. Whenever Ayrion stepped out from the back, it would snort, shake its mane, and head over to nuzzle him. Ayrion found the bond between them strong, quite possibly the only true link to his past, apart from his blades.

Even bareback, he had found the black warhorse more comfortable than the hard timber of the front wagon seat. Unlike Tameel, Ayrion's backside had not quite developed enough calluses to make the time spent up there more bearable.

". . . as long as you don't say anything about that while we're there, then you'll be right as rain," Tameel said. "Yep, nothin' to worry about."

Say anything about what? Ayrion wondered. *What was he talking about? Drat! I should've been listening.*

Before Ayrion could ask him to repeat it, Zynora stuck her head out of the front opening. "Either of you care for a snack? I just pulled out some salted pork. Tryin' to make room for these extra supplies."

Ayrion looked at Tameel, who was already salivating. "I don't believe we're all that hungry up here," he said with a wink. "Thank you, though."

"What?" Tameel bellowed, almost dropping the reins. "Speak for yourself, boy!" His eyes were wide and nostrils flaring when he turned and caught the amused looks on their faces. "Oh, very funny, Ayrion. Very funny." He held out his hand for a cut of the meat. Tameel stuffed the piece between his teeth and bit down.

With each new day, Ayrion grew all the fonder of the eccentric couple. The two were like the parents—or grandparents—he couldn't remember having.

He smiled as the first hint of afternoon sun peeked through the clouds and warmed his face. With the mist still clinging to his breath, Ayrion opted to leave his colorful tinker jacket on. He tugged the woolen cap lower on his head, flattening his mop of black hair around his face.

"There should be a creek up ahead for us to water the horses," Tameel said, somehow still looking comfortable despite the rutted road. The wooden seat had been worn down at the center and its edges rounded from the use the old man had put it through over the years. "Pass through here once or twice a year when making the rounds." Tameel pulled back his cap and scratched the top of his white head. "Couple years back, we tried crossing with a caravan of wagons during one of the rainy seasons—"

"Another reason why we stopped coming through this way during the spring," Zynora said from inside the wagon as she listened through the open hatch.

"Aye," Tameel agreed. "One of the wagons overturned—"

"It was the wagon directly in front of us," Zynora interjected. She shook her head and clicked her tongue. "Could just as likely have been us."

Tameel nodded. "Killed a young mother and her child. They drowned right in front of us. Nothing we could do. The river was far deeper than they had expected, and it pulled the wagon downstream. Some of the men tried jumping in, but they couldn't get to them in time." He shook his head.

"Is it safe to cross now?" Ayrion asked, remembering it had rained a few nights back.

Tameel nodded as he jerked once on the reins to remind the horses he was still there. "After that incident, the townsfolk built a bridge for crossing. It's not much to look at, but it'll get the job done in a pinch. Nope, never have had any problems gettin' Ol' Lera here across." He affectionately patted the wagon's sideboards, which had once been a deep green before the paint had faded and started chipping.

Zynora stuck her head out. "Wish he'd rub his hands over me the way he does this old heap of wood. Might've had a few more children if he had." She ducked back inside, leaving both men embarrassed and blushing.

Up ahead, Ayrion spotted a break in the road.

"What did I tell you?" Tameel said, pointing. The bridge was just coming into view. He was right. It wasn't much to look at, barely large enough to fit a single wagon. One seemed to be getting ready to cross.

On further inspection, the wagon didn't appear to have any horses harnessed. Perhaps the owners were watering them before heading on. A group of men stood off to the right side of the bridge, just in front of the creek bed. Ayrion couldn't make an exact count, but there looked to be at least five or six, possibly more. Far too many for a single wagon. Their horses were tied to a tree behind them.

Another look at the wagon showed it had been turned sideways, almost as though it were blocking the bridge instead of waiting to move across.

Tameel pulled up on the reins, slowing the team down as they neared. It was obvious now that the dray was being used to stop passage. The men turned at their approach.

"What's going on?" Zynora asked, sticking her head out the front and spotting the gruff-looking men off to the side.

"Stay in the wagon," Tameel said.

"Aye, that be sound advice, husband." She ducked back inside but left the front hatch open.

A couple of the men in front stepped forward, revealing a young boy behind them. The boy wore a colorful array of clothing, much in the same style as the tinkers', with a gold earring dangling from his left ear. His hands were clasped tight, hugging close to his body, and he kept his head lowered, his eyes darting nervously from one man to the next.

"Looks like trouble," Ayrion said.

"Could be right."

"What be your business in these parts, tinker?" one of the men in front said, taking another step forward. He kept one hand on his belt and the other on the hilt of his sword. His round face was half hidden beneath a bush of whiskers.

Ayrion leaned back so Tameel could address the man, who was still ten to fifteen feet from the wagon.

Tameel put on his friendliest smile, the one he used when dealing with new customers, especially those who didn't care for his way of pricing. "If you wouldn't mind movin' your wagon, gentlemen, we'd like to pass."

"Well, now, I guess that all depends."

"Oh?"

The man smiled. He held up his hand and rubbed his fingers together. "On the size of your purse."

A couple of the men behind him snickered. Ayrion hoped this didn't turn into another situation like the one they had run into at Woodvale.

"Ah, I see." Tameel glanced at the rickety bridge and the road beyond. "I was under the impression that passage was free to *all* travelers."

"I guess you got the wrong impression, then."

Tameel fidgeted with the straps. "We've been travelin' this way for years, never had to pay before."

"What can I say?" The man shrugged. "Things change. Times are hard for all of us. Man's gotta earn a livin'."

The others chuckled again.

"What be your price, then?"

The man thumbed his chin. "Well, let's see. We normally charge a couple of silvers, but for a pair of fine, upstanding tinkers like yourselves, we'll make it an even four."

"Four silvers?" Tameel nearly came out of his seat. "What kind of robbery is this? I could purchase enough grain to keep my horses fed for weeks with that much coin."

Ayrion laid a hand on Tameel's arm.

The highwayman smiled, glancing over his shoulder at the bridge. "Well, we got to consider the upkeep, and that ain't cheap. Then there's a charge for protection—"

"Upkeep?" Tameel bellowed. "What upkeep?" He pointed at the dilapidated planks and fallen railings. "This old thing hasn't had a new board put on it since the day it was built. And what kind of protection could you possibly be charging us for? Is there some kind of rabid overgrown prairie gopher living under this bridge?"

The other man remained surprisingly calm, considering Tameel's outrage. "Crossing protection. Like you said, this old thing is mighty unstable. Who knows what might happen if you were to try crossing it without our help?"

Ayrion figured that must be what had happened with the young boy. Probably hadn't been able to pay the toll, so they'd planned on taking it out of his hide. Ayrion turned to the hatch and whispered inside. "Get my swords."

"No," Tameel said softly, so as not to be heard by the men. "No violence. We can do this without killing. Besides, they might hurt the boy."

"But I can—"

"No." He shook his head. "Go get the purse."

Ayrion exhaled sharply but eventually crawled into the back. Giving in to these highwaymen was a mistake. As much as he hated letting bullies like this take advantage of them, though, Tameel might be right. They had to think about the boy. Ayrion could still hear the conversation going on outside as he made his way toward one of the chests near the back.

"What about the boy?" Tameel asked.

"What about 'im? He's a rover. We don't want their kind round here, drinkin' from the same water as us honest folk."

What do they have against rovers? Ayrion wondered. From what he'd been told by Tameel and Zynora, they were much like the tinkers.

They spent their lives traveling, doing their best to stay out of others' affairs.

Ayrion grabbed the smallest of the coin purses hidden at the bottom of the chest, making sure it had only a silver or two more than what was required, and headed back to the front. Zynora pointed to where she had stashed his swords just inside the front hatch, close enough that he could reach them if he needed to. He nodded as he passed.

"Well, if you're an example of the *so-called* honest folk around here, sir," Tameel said, "I believe I'll take my chances with the child. How much for his passage?"

Ayrion crawled through the front hatch and handed Tameel the leather purse.

The man eyed the size of it and tugged on his whiskers. "Well, he has caused us a great deal of trouble, what with him kicking one of Perel's teeth loose." He pointed back to one of the men who had an arm on the boy. The man quickly began to rub his jaw. "So, I'm thinking another silver would do."

Ayrion bit down to keep from responding.

Tameel opened the drawstrings and picked out the appropriate coinage. He juggled the five silver pieces around for the bandits to see. "Here's your payment. Now let the boy go."

The man eyed Tameel's hands for a moment before turning around and nodding for them to release the boy.

"Come here, rover!"

The boy didn't move—too scared, no doubt—until one of the men standing behind him gave him a forceful shove.

The highwayman reached out and grabbed the boy by his collar and marched him around to Tameel's side of the wagon. "Hand me the coins and I'll release him."

Tameel laid the purse down on the seat beside Ayrion before leaning over and dropping the coins into the man's awaiting palm.

Surprisingly enough, the man released the boy and walked back around the horses to his wagon. He motioned for the others to help, and they pushed the wagon off the road.

"No!" the little boy shouted. "We need to go back. I need to find a healer." Tameel pulled him up onto the seat. He tried jerking out of Tameel's grasp, but Ayrion grabbed him instead and placed him on the seat between them.

"We need to go back!"

"The only place we need to go is out of here," Tameel said as he snapped the reins. "Giddy up there!"

Ayrion tensed as the wagon slowly approached the bridge. The highwaymen stood to either side, watching quietly. He kept one hand around the rover boy and the other just inside the front opening, where Zynora had placed his swords.

The boy squirmed to get out of the seat, but Ayrion held him down.

The bridge planks creaked and groaned as the heavy wagon rolled slowly across. It wasn't until they were on the other side and moving up the next hill that Ayrion finally breathed a little easier.

"Why didn't you let me take care of them?" Ayrion asked Tameel.

"Because unleashing those blades can't be the answer to all our problems. It only draws more attention. Besides, I'd be more than happy to pay a couple of silver to not have to dig half a dozen graves. By the time you got through with them, it would have taken us the rest of the night to clean up the mess."

Ayrion couldn't argue there. After what had happened back in Woodvale, he really didn't care for another dark glimpse into what he had been.

The little rover boy jerked out from under Ayrion's arm and stood. "Didn't you hear me? We need to go back!"

Tameel stopped the wagon. "Go back to what, boy? What's wrong with you?"

The rover child began to cry. "I need to get a healer. We need help!"

"There's no healer back that direction," Ayrion said, trying to calm the child down. "We just came from there. Closest town is days away."

Zynora stuck her head out the opening. "Who needs a healer?"

The boy almost jumped out of his seat and onto the horses, surprised by the voice behind him.

Clinging to Ayrion's arm, he turned around to get a look at Zynora. "We do."

"We? Who's we? The rovers? Are you Nathillian?" When the little boy's head began to bob up and down, Zynora moved back inside. "Well, get in here, child, and tell us all about it."

Chapter 21 | Ayrion

Ayrion CLIMBED INTO the back of the wagon and took a seat on an old barrel as Zynora jellied a biscuit and handed it to the boy.

"I'm Taylis," the boy said, stuffing the biscuit in his mouth, barely chewing before swallowing it down.

"I'm Zynora, and that old codger there is my husband, Tameel, and this is Ayrion."

Taylis sniffed and wiped his eyes, still working to regain his composure. "Thank you for saving me. Those men were going to do bad things to me and my family."

Zynora wiped a tuft of hair from the little boy's face. "Well, you don't have to worry about them doing anything to you now, Taylis. You're safe with us." She poured him a glass of water, and he gulped it down at an alarming rate. "What were you doing out here in the middle of nowhere all by yourself? Who needs a healer?"

Taylis drained his drink and handed it to Zynora. "People took sick a couple of days back, just after we left Belvin. The folks there told us to leave." He cocked his head. "Why are people so mean?"

Zynora placed a hand on his shoulder. "It's because they're ignorant. People fear what they don't understand."

"What happened next?" Tameel prompted.

"It started with Elder Borin, but since he's always complaining, no one paid him much mind. At least, not until some of the others started to take ill. Pretty soon, a lot of people were feeling sick. Even Mama."

"What are her symptoms?"

"Symptoms?"

"Why do you believe your mother is sick?"

"She says her stomach hurts real bad, and she's always asking me for something to drink, but when she drinks it, she vomits."

"And you say a lot of people in your group are showing the same problems?"

Taylis nodded. "That's when Mama told me to get on ol' Bleu and ride for a different town and try to find a healer." The little boy paused. "Mama doesn't usually let me ride by myself, but I'm big enough, you know."

"I'm sure you are," Zynora said. Ayrion noted the look of concern in her eyes.

"What do you think, wife?" Tameel asked.

"I won't be sure unless I see them. Could be anything from a bout of food poisoning to cholera." She looked at Taylis. "What happened next?"

"When I came to the bridge and saw those men, I tried asking them for help, but they were bad men, and they pulled me off Bleu and tried to take him. But he ran away." Taylis stopped and looked down at his worn shoes. "Bleu was my best friend." He wiped another run from his nose on his sleeve. "I don't know what me and Mama will do without him."

"It'll be all right, son," Tameel said, leaning forward to pat the boy on the knee. "Can you take us to your camp?"

The waning light through the front opening reflected in the boy's wet eyes. "Yes, sir."

"Good," Tameel said as he stood. "We are part of the Rhivanni, which is a distant relation to the Nathillian. My wife has studied the healing arts of the Kojzu, so we might be able to help."

Taylis's eyes brightened. "Really? You think you can help Mama?"

"We'll do our best," she said as she jellied another biscuit. She handed it to Taylis and turned to Tameel. "Best we get a move on. They sound to be in a bad way."

"Aye, wife, that they do."

Ayrion followed Tameel out of the wagon and climbed up on the front seat.

"Which way to your camp, Master Taylis?" Tameel asked, turning to look back inside.

The little boy stuck his head out the hatch and pointed straight ahead. "That way, about half a day's ride."

"Are you camped in the fields?"

"No, sir. We're in the woods."

Tameel grabbed the reins and spurred the horses forward. "Will you remember where when you see it?"

"Yes!" Taylis said, climbing through the hatch and planting himself between Tameel and Ayrion. "When you see a pile of painted rocks stacked by the side of road, that's where we went into the woods."

Night had fallen, and the road ahead was cut in shadow. The three-quarter moon left strips of the dead plains to sprawl in darkness, while others basked in the pale evening light. Silhouettes of distant clouds gave the effect of a giant moving puzzle with pieces waiting to be connected.

Ayrion pulled his cloak tight around his shoulders and pinched off the opening at the neck to hold in what little heat remained. He studied the side of the road, looking for the marker Taylis had told them was there. The young boy sat nestled between Ayrion and Tameel, his eyes glued to the distant tree line. Tameel had him looking for anything familiar.

"Hold on," Ayrion said. "I think I see something."

"Well, if anyone would, it'd be you," Tameel said as he slowed the horses.

Ayrion hopped off the wagon. Behind him, Taylis shouted, "That's them! That's the rocks we set! I told Mama that the one on top looked like a tortoise."

Ayrion knelt beside the pile. The rocks were painted red, blue, yellow, and green. The green one on top did indeed look like the back of a turtle shell. He climbed back up onto the front seat, and Tameel steered the old wagon off the road in the direction of the tree line.

The hatch behind them opened, and Zynora stuck her head out, allowing some of the wagon's warmth to wash across those on the front seat. She looked at the forest ahead. "They'll be far enough in to hide their campfires and song from anyone traveling this way."

"Aye," Tameel said as he gave another *thwack* of the reins, urging the horses a little faster. As the old wagon creaked along, bringing the distant trees closer, Ayrion caught the familiar song of a night owl. Its serenade floated on the wind like an ethereal call, beckoning them with the promise of rest from their weary travels. Ayrion yawned, unable to stop himself. It felt as though he hadn't slept two winks since their run-in with the Black Watch in Woodvale and the revelation of his former identity.

Ayrion knew there was something different about him. He could feel it. It revealed itself in the things he could do, the way his swords moved in his hands as though they were controlling him instead of the other way around. He wanted to know more about this Guardian Protector he was supposed to have been. What kind of man was he? Had he been respected, or feared? Was he a good man, or had he used his abilities for other purposes? Did he have family or friends who were missing him? The questions ate at him.

Tameel and Zynora had seemed to think that the Guardian had been a decent man. The former king was a good man, and he wouldn't have chosen Ayrion to be his protector otherwise. However, their knowledge was fairly limited, since tinkers tried to stay out of the affairs of others. They weren't quite as sheltered from society as they said his people, the Upaka, were, but they tended to keep to themselves as much as possible. Tameel had done his best to describe the Upaka—who they were, where they lived, why they were shunned by most of society.

Ayrion wondered how he had managed to rise to such a high position as Guardian Protector with a stigma like that attached to him.

The wagon hit a rut, jostling Ayrion from his brooding. He looked up. The tree line ahead stretched for miles, leaving only the one narrow path—just wide enough for a single wagon—as their way to enter.

Tameel slowed the horses as they passed underneath the forest canopy. The stars vanished, and the breeze died away as the trees swallowed them whole.

The lanterns swinging from the curved hooks on the sides of the wagon weren't enough to cut through the darkness ahead, so Ayrion slipped from his seat to guide the horses. Walking around to the front, he held out a lantern to light the way as he grabbed the harness and pulled them forward.

The ground was soft under his boots, leaving hardly a trace of sound. Everything around them was silent, but something tugged at the back of his mind, and he stopped to listen.

"Why are we stopping?" Taylis called down to him. "We're close. I know it." He stood, trying to see farther down the trail.

Zynora opened the front and stuck her head out, and Taylis quickly sat back down.

"Shh." Ayrion held up his hand to signal for silence.

"Quiet, son." Tameel put his hand on the boy's leg to calm him.

Everyone listened. In the distance, Ayrion thought he had heard something. There it was again, faint, like the clang of metal. "Something's wrong."

Taylis leaped from the wagon before Tameel could stop him and made a mad dash for the trail ahead.

Ayrion grabbed him by the seat of his pants.

"No! Let me go!" Taylis kicked out, trying to free himself from Ayrion's hold.

Ayrion covered the boy's mouth. "Quiet."

Tameel climbed down from the front, and Ayrion passed the boy off to him.

"Keep him here. I'll come back and get you once I check it out. It might be nothing, but better safe than not."

He ran to the back of the wagon and swung up onto the black warhorse.

The back door opened, and Zynora held out his black leather coat and swords.

Ayrion shook his head.

"Take them," she said. "You can't be too careful."

Ayrion relented and swapped his colorful tinker coat for the long black one, then strapped on the twin sheaths. Their weight on his back released a sudden flash of memory. He was sitting atop the same horse. Soldiers in black-and-silver uniforms were fighting and dying all around him. Great beasts as tall as the stallion, with bloodred eyes, mauled their way through them. He raised his sword as one of them lunged, and as swift as it had appeared, the vision was gone.

He sucked in a breath.

"Are you all right?" Zynora asked. "What happened?"

"I just had a memory."

"That's wonderful."

Ayrion frowned. "Not really." He pulled on his black gloves and leaned forward to pat the stallion's neck. "It appears we know each other after all, my strong friend."

The stallion shook his mane.

"Be careful, Grey Eyes."

Ayrion nodded and urged the large animal forward. "I'll be back," he said to Tameel as he rode past. Tameel was still struggling to keep Taylis under control. Even with the sporadic rays of moonlight seeping through the canopy overhead, Ayrion was careful not to give the stallion too much lead. It would be easy to hit a hole in the dark and cripple the horse.

Up ahead, the sounds grew more distinct: metal clanging, men shouting, women and children screaming. Throwing caution to the wind, he urged his horse faster.

An abrasive smell filled his nostrils, a smell he was growing all too acquainted with—sweet, metallic, and strong enough to taste. It was the choking smell of death.

Something strange was moving inside him. He could feel a heat rising. It was the same sensation he had experienced back at Woodvale just before his fight with the Black Watch and the sniffer. Reaching up as if on instinct, he slid one of the swords free from its sheath. With the other hand, he tightened his grip on the horse's mane and leaned forward to keep his body close to the mount.

The trail ahead ended in a large clearing, the outer rim completely encircled with wagons—wagons very similar to the one he'd been riding in for the last month, every inch of them covered with bright paints. Numerous cooking fires were spread across the center of the encampment, giving Ayrion a clear view of what was happening.

The rovers were easy to spot; they were dressed in the same colorful, baggy clothing that he, Tameel, and Zynora wore. However, there were others running through the camp, carrying old swords, axes, hammers, shovels, and whatever else they could get their hands on. Whoever these people were, they were killing everyone in sight.

Ayrion pulled his horse to a stop a few feet from the first of the wagons, and his breath caught in his throat. He was close enough to see the attackers' faces.

They weren't human. At least, he didn't think they were.

Their skin was white. Not just pale from a lack of sun, but as though they'd been bleached in a vat of lye. They were half dressed, their clothing ripped to the extent that it barely covered the areas that defined their sex. And it was no wonder. Each hand ended in a set of claws. Even stranger was the lack of hair. Some had tufts still clinging to the scalp, but most were completely bald. Even their eyebrows were gone, which made the obsidian orbs that were their eyes stand out all the more.

On his right, a Nathillian mother was trying to cover a little girl with her body while two hairless, white-skinned women—at least he thought they were women—hacked her to death with a pair of butcher knives. They threw the mother's body aside and reached for the little girl underneath.

He leaped from his mount and ran straight for them.

"Hold still!" the first said, her voice unnatural, deep, and grating, like something was talking through her.

The second seized the little girl by her shoulders and yanked her up for the first to stab. Except the first didn't appear to want to stab the girl. Instead, she opened her mouth to sink her teeth in.

Ayrion swung. The blade cut straight through the first woman's neck without a hint of resistance. It was like he'd hit nothing at all. Her bald head nodded forward as if in prayer, then fell off her shoulders.

The second woman turned with a shriek, black liquid streaming from either side of her mouth. She flung the child aside and let out an ear-piercing scream.

Ayrion held out his sword and watched as the woman threw herself onto it, ramming it all the way through her body just to reach him. He flinched as she managed a single cut to his arm before collapsing. He tilted the blade down, and her body slid free. Stepping over the women, he grabbed the child and placed her behind one of the wagon wheels and covered her with a tarp.

"Don't make a sound," he said, aware that the statement was somewhat wasted on the girl. Her face was nearly as pale as the white-skinned women, and it was clear she was too in shock to speak.

He left her in the protection of the wagon and drew his second blade. Men, women, and children in colorful garb littered the ground. The horrific black-eyed crazies were all over them. *Are they eating them?* Ayrion shivered. Most of the half-human creatures were too busy gorging to spare him a moment's notice.

He spotted a large group of the white crazies gathering on the far-left side of the camp. They were circled around what looked like one of the last remaining Nathillians. He was a big man, dressed from head to toe in thick furs, with a long-handled hatchet in each hand. By the accuracy of his blows, he knew how to use them. But there were just too many, and these people clearly had no fear of death.

Ayrion raced across the open ground toward the lone defender, trying his best to dodge the fallen bodies while lopping off the heads and arms of those feeding on them. Up ahead, the crazies pressed even harder, some fighting each other in an effort to reach the fur-covered man. The man roared and buried one hatchet in the top of a head while using the second to fend off a couple of women who were trying to sink their teeth into his arm.

Ayrion fought to reach him. He hit the rear flank of the half-human creatures and gave himself over to his swords. His arms moved the blades through the air with pinpoint accuracy, chopping down pale-skinned crazies with every swing. He had to keep telling himself that these weren't people he was killing. They were something else, something inhuman.

He cut a path all the way to the man, and together, they fought back to back against the white horde.

A bald, white-skinned boy, small enough to wiggle through the crowd, stabbed the big fur-skinned man in the side. The man yelled, and the boy's pitch-black eyes seemed to grow excited.

Ayrion turned to knock the boy away, but not before the injured man spun around and smashed the flat end of one of his hatchets across the side of the boy's face. The boy bounced off a couple of the others and hit the dirt. His head sat at a funny angle.

Even knowing what the child was, it was hard to watch, but Ayrion didn't have time to think about it. He stabbed one crazy in the neck and opened the front of another. Ayrion kept his blades swinging until there wasn't anything left to swing at.

Soon, the clearing was quiet. Deathly quiet. The stillness was unsettling.

Ayrion pulled his sword from the last victim and helped the wounded man over to one of the cooking fires. He propped him against a bench and laid his blood-soaked swords on top. "I need to stop the bleeding," he said as he turned the man over on his side. Ayrion removed his own coat and ripped off one of the sleeves from his tunic and pressed it against the man's wound. "The name's Ayrion. I'm traveling with a healer. I'm sure she can fix this up in no time."

The man gritted his teeth and nodded. "I'm Bek."

"What happened here?" Ayrion looked at the carnage and hoped Tameel was smart enough to keep Taylis away. "Who attacked your people?"

Bek grunted under the pain. "They aren't my people."

"Oh. Were you traveling with them?"

"I wasn't with them at all," Bek said as he turned and pointed at the pieces of bodies strewn in the wake of Ayrion's swords. "*Those* are my people."

"What?" Perhaps the loss of blood had affected the man's head. "Those *maniacs* are your people? They were trying to kill you."

Bek grunted, his breath shallow.

Ayrion heard the rustle of approaching steps. Grabbing one of his swords from the table, he spun, stopping just shy of Zynora's wrinkled neck.

A small wheeze escaped her lips as her eyes nearly bulged from their sockets.

"Sorry," he said. "You shouldn't . . . Why are you here? I told you to wait for me to come get you when it was safe."

She clicked her tongue at him and knelt to look at Bek's injury. "I came to tend to the wounded."

"Unarmed? What if we'd still been fighting?"

She didn't answer.

He looked back at the trailhead. "You didn't bring Taylis, did you?"

"What do you take me for? He's with Tameel back at the wagon." She pulled back the blood-soaked cloth on the trapper's side to get a better look. "Hmm. I've seen worse."

Ayrion scanned the mutilated bodies covering the rovers' camp and sighed. "I don't think I have."

Chapter 22 | Ayrion

AYRION LEFT ZYNORA to her work. Bek was in too much pain to answer questions, so Ayrion made his way around the rover camp, looking for signs of survivors, though the bodies were so mutilated, he doubted there would be any. The pungent smell of death filled his nostrils, dampened only by smoke from the cooking fires. He passed one colorfully clad body after another, watching closely for the faintest movement that might indicate life.

He found none.

After finishing a quick walkthrough, he began searching the wagons. He opened the back of a bright yellow one, and something wrapped around his leg. He jumped back, reaching for his sword. Looking down, he found himself staring into the wide, teary eyes of the little girl he had saved earlier. In all the chaos, he had forgotten about the child.

She clung to him like a tinker to his purse strings. Finally prying her loose, he knelt. "What's your name?"

The little girl pushed past his arms and attached herself to his neck.

"Marissa."

"Marissa. That's a pretty name." She started to whimper. "There's no need to cry," he said as he patted her on the back, then realized how ridiculous that statement was. There wasn't a soul in Aldor who had better reason. She buried her face against the side of his neck. "You're safe now," he said. "I won't let anything happen to you."

He could feel her relax as he scooped her up and continued his search through the wagons. Their contents were similar: cots on the sides for beds, open plank shelves for storage, sparse decorations, not too unlike Tameel and Zynora's wagon, Ol' Lera.

On both ends of the encampment, the Nathillians had set up corrals for the horses and some smaller livestock they had brought with them, including goats, pigs, and a few sheep, which were busy bleating out their fear. Ayrion couldn't blame them. One look at the horrific carnage covering the camp had him nauseous as well. He would have preferred to stick Marissa inside one of the wagons if he thought she'd actually stay, but based on the way she was clinging to his neck, he doubted it.

Heading back to where Zynora was working on Bek, Ayrion stopped to look at another group of rovers: a woman and what must have been her three children. He pushed the oldest boy off to check the ones underneath.

"What do you think you're doing?" Zynora said, heading in their direction. "Don't touch them!"

Ayrion stood and took a step back. "What's wrong?"

"These people might have cholera. How many have you touched?"

"I'm not sure."

She raised a corked bottle. "Give me your hands."

He held them out for her to inspect, but instead of looking at them, she pulled the stopper and emptied half the bottle on them.

The clear liquid burned his nose. "What is it?"

"Wipe," Zynora barked. "It's musca. Also known as snake venom. A concoction distilled specifically by the Nathillian for sealing bargains.

Trust me, not something you ever want to drink yourself."

"Is cholera really that catching?"

"Not generally. It usually comes from drinking bad water, or eating food grown from bad water. But you can't be too careful."

Ayrion nodded, making sure to wipe every inch of his hands with the strong-smelling liquid.

"Anyway, we'll need to make sure to empty and clean the water barrels, as well as get rid of any fresh fruits and vegetables." She turned and looked at the little girl. "And who do we have here?" she asked, lightly stroking the back of the girl's disheveled brown curls. She mumbled something under her breath, and her hand glowed a pale lavender, sending streaks of the faint light down into the child's body.

Marissa stiffened at first, then released a heavy sigh.

"This is Marissa," Ayrion said.

"I'm going to need to clean you as well, Marissa." It took a while, but she finally managed to coax the little girl away from Ayrion long enough to wash any open skin. "We'll have to do a more thorough cleaning later." Zynora stopped to look at the camp. "We need to burn these bodies, and quickly."

"Why didn't they put up a stronger fight?" Ayrion asked. "Was it the sickness?"

"No." Zynora shook her head. "The Nathillian don't believe in violence. They believe all manner of fighting is unjustified, one reason why they get taken advantage of so often. They believe the Great Father created them to be an example to the rest of the world of how to live in peace."

Ayrion looked down at the little girl holding tight to his leg. "A worthy goal if we lived in a world where everyone believed the same, and evil didn't exist."

Zynora shrugged. "Who am I to judge? The Dar'Rhivanni are cousins to the Nathillian. We hold to many of the same beliefs. Although if someone tries to—"

"Mama!"

Ayrion and Zynora turned.

Somehow, Taylis had gotten away from Tameel and was now running across the camp, heading straight for a red-and-gold-painted wagon near the back.

"What's he doing here?" Zynora said.

"Here," Ayrion said. "Take her." He unhooked Marissa's arms and raced after Taylis, trying to head him off before he saw something he would never forget.

Taylis tripped on one of the white-skinned people and screamed when he saw what it was. Quickly, he hopped to his feet and started running again, but not before Ayrion grabbed him.

The boy shrieked, kicking out as he fought to break free. "No! Let me go! Let me go! Mama!"

His mother's body was sitting against the front wagon wheel, surprisingly untouched. She didn't appear to have been brutalized like many of the others. As peaceful as she seemed, she must have succumbed to the illness before the townsfolk had shown up. "Your mother may have cholera, Taylis. You can't touch her." For all Ayrion knew, the boy had it too, though right now, neither he nor Marissa were showing any signs.

"I was too late," Taylis cried, head slumped forward. "I should have been faster. It's my fault. She's dead because I was too slow."

Ayrion knelt beside the boy. "None of this is your fault, Taylis. There was nothing you could have done to stop the madness that happened here. You did what your mother asked. If she hadn't sent you away, you would have died here with the others. She saved your life."

"Why did they attack us? What did they want?"

Ayrion didn't have an answer. There was no sensible reason for the slaughter, but how do you tell a grieving child that his mother died for no apparent reason?

"Let me see him," Zynora said, walking over with Marissa clinging to her skirt. As soon as they were close enough, Marissa released her grip and rushed for Ayrion's leg.

Ayrion was thankful for the interruption and let go of the boy long enough for Zynora to wash him down, picking Marissa up in the process.

"Is that musca?" Taylis asked.

Zynora nodded.

"Mama always said I was never to drink it."

Zynora smiled. "Your mother was a very wise woman." Zynora rubbed the back of Taylis's head, mumbling the same incantation she had with Marissa. Her hand glowed faintly for a moment, sending small traces of magic down through the boy. She looked up at Ayrion and nodded.

Ayrion turned at the sound of Ol' Lera rolling into camp.

"Whoa, there." Tameel pulled back on the reins, bringing the wagon to a stop on the outskirts of the clearing. "By thunder!" The old man gasped as he rose from his seat. "What in darkness happened here?" He dropped the reins and climbed down. "What are those?" Tameel asked, pointing at one of the half-naked white people.

"That's a good question," Ayrion said, walking back toward the center of camp where he had left Bek. They needed answers.

Tameel quickly tied off the horses and headed to join them.

"Can someone please explain to me why I'm not seeing a camp full of sick people but the aftermath of a flaming massacre?"

When they reached Bek, Tameel took a step forward and extended his hand, then saw Bek's were covered in blood and changed his mind. "And what is your name, sir? I hope you accept our sincerest sympathies for your loss."

The gruff-looking woodsman nodded, but there seemed to be a faraway look in his eyes—shock, most likely. "My name's Bek, and like I was telling the swordsman here, I'm not a rover. I'm from Belvin."

"Belvin. Yes, nice town, Belvin. The wife and I have traded there a time or two. The people seemed friendly enough." Tameel's smile faded when he noticed the others weren't smiling as well. "So, do we have any idea what in the flaming Pits those white-skinned monsters are?"

Zynora cleared her throat. "That would be the friendly folk from Belvin, dear."

Tameel's mouth hung open. For once the old man was without words. "Oh. Well, I, uh . . ." He glanced around at the bodies, then back at Bek. "What happened to them?"

"Start from the beginning," Zynora said, motioning for Tameel to sit on one of the benches.

Ayrion, Taylis, and Marissa joined them.

Bek laid his hatchets on the ground at his feet. "When I returned from checking my traps upriver two days back, I knew something was off. Kids weren't in school, parents weren't at work, no one was shopping in the square. In fact, most the town seemed to be staying indoors. It was like they were afraid of the light. But once the sun went down, they started coming out. And they were different."

"How so?" Tameel asked.

"The smallest thing would set them off. People who had been friends for years were suddenly enemies, parents screaming at their kids, kids yelling at their parents when they weren't yelling at each other.

"That's when I noticed other changes. Physical ones. Their eyes were darkening. Pretty soon, they were black as coal. It was like they were dead inside, a hollow shell of what they used to be, replaced with some kind of . . . darkness."

No one said a word. Ayrion was having a hard time believing what he was hearing. If not for seeing the aftermath for himself, he'd have written the man off as deranged.

"And it wasn't limited to just those in town," he said. "My wife and I live outside of Belvin, and by the time I made it home, she had begun to change as well."

"Oh, in what way?" Tameel asked.

"For one, she tried to kill me with a garden hoe when I asked her how she was feeling."

"Were there any other changes?" Zynora asked.

"At the time, no. But now look at them," he said, pointing at the nearest bodies. "They don't even look human."

"What happened to her?" Ayrion asked.

"My wife?"

He nodded.

"I knocked her out and tied her up inside the house."

"How did you end up with the rovers?"

"They were just leaving Belvin when I was returning from my traps. I passed them as they were heading out of town. Once the changes started taking place, I figured I'd come out and see if the same thing was happening to them, or if . . ." He shot Taylis and Marissa an embarrassed look. "Or if they somehow had something to do with it."

"Clearly, they didn't," Ayrion said.

"No. But when I told them what was happening, they didn't take me seriously. I'm sure I sounded like a lunatic. Besides, they were already dealing with some kind of sickness when I got here. It wasn't until the screaming started that they realized I'd been speaking the truth, but by then . . ." The big trapper shook his head.

Zynora stood and handed Taylis off to Tameel.

"Where are you going?" Tameel asked.

"I'm going to check the rest of the rovers, and then we are going to burn the bodies before going into town."

"Into town?" Tameel stood and started after her, dragging Taylis along with him. "Are you mad? Why would we be going into town? Need I remind you that's where these creatures came from?"

Ayrion held Marissa in his arms as he followed the older couple across the camp toward the far-right side, Bek just a few steps behind.

"I believe the safest course of action, dear, would be to get ourselves out of here," Tameel said, a slight tremor in his voice. "The sooner, the better. I don't want you trying to kill me in the middle of the night just because you don't like the way I snore."

"Your snoring, old man," Zynora said, "should be the least of your concerns. Now grab some of those shovels, and let's get to work."

Chapter 23 | Ferrin

ERRIN TOSSED AND TURNED for some time before realizing he wasn't going back to sleep. Finally, he got up, threw a couple more logs on the fire, and watched as the smoke trailed upward, leaving behind the fresh scent of mountain pine. Under normal circumstances, there were few things he found more relaxing than a quiet evening under the stars. Now all it did was remind him of why he was being forced to spend his nights sleeping outdoors.

Stars winked through the thick canopy of fir as the upper boughs swayed gently in the breeze. He was thankful they weren't traveling through snow, but the icy bite of the wind let him know it wasn't too far off.

Ferrin had set a strict pace, hoping to elude their pursuers, but he was careful not to push too hard. The last thing they needed was to lose the horses to exhaustion. If not for them, they'd already be in the hands of the Black Watch, marching back toward the Tower.

As it was, they had a long way to go with few places to stop and resupply, so Ferrin and Myron hunted game while Rae and Suri foraged for wild berries, roots, and nuts. Rae had to be shown which were safe to eat and which would leave you with gut rot or worse, but with winter setting in, their selection was rather limited.

Dried leaves crunched behind him, and Ferrin turned to find Myron sauntering in from where he'd been keeping watch on the outer perimeter. He knelt and warmed his hands near the flame. "Ahh, much better," he said, looking over at Ferrin. "Are we going to talk about our encounter with those wolves or go on pretending like nothing happened?"

"I was as surprised as you," Ferrin said softly, not wanting to wake Rae. He sat down on his bedding and watched Myron work the numbness from his fingers. The wolves were a topic Ferrin had purposely shied away from. After seeing Rae's reaction to Suri's magic, he didn't care to stir the flames. He wasn't sure if her anger was due to her daughter having magic or just an overall resentment of magic itself.

"She will never use it again," Rae said, startling the two men as she slipped out from under the blanket she shared with Suri. She moved a little closer to Ferrin's side of the fire, sat, and hugged her knees to her chest.

"Did you know?" Ferrin asked.

Rae shook her head.

"You had no idea your daughter could talk to animals?" Myron said, sounding skeptical.

"How would I? I've never even seen an animal before, unless you count the *men* inside the Tower."

Myron nodded. "Good point."

Something about that night had left Ferrin puzzled. "Do you have a second crystal?"

Rae looked at him like she didn't understand the question.

"You threw me your crystal during our standoff with the wolves."

"I only have one," she said, lifting the chain around her neck to confirm it. "Why?"

"Then how did Suri use magic?"

Her face tightened, apparently not liking the implication as she picked at the frayed hem of her dress. "I don't know."

"Azriel, the old seer, told me that there are some people who are born with innate gifts that don't need a transferal." Ferrin looked at the sleeping mound underneath Rae's bedding. "Suri must be one of them."

"But why is her magic different?" Rae asked. "How could she be able to do such things if I cannot?"

"From what I understand, most families tend to pass on one specific trait." Ferrin hadn't thought about it until now, but maybe that was one of the reasons the Tower wanted him so badly. Would they use him the same way they had Rae, to breed metallurgists?

"Maybe what she has wasn't passed down from your side," Myron said. "Maybe it was passed down from her father's."

Rae bared her teeth and growled.

Myron scooted back. "What did I say?"

Ferrin looked at Myron. "Suri's father was Chee—I mean, Sylas."

Myron swallowed. "Inquisitor Sylas?"

Rae turned her head, not looking at either of them.

Ferrin nodded.

"Oh. Do you think the inquisitor had this gift as well?"

Ferrin looked at Rae, but when she didn't respond, he finally shrugged. "After what Suri said the wolves were there for, I'd wager a yes."

"You know," Myron said, "with a gift like that, Suri could be of help catching game. We wouldn't be so—"

"No!" Rae spun back around. "She will not be used to fill your bellies."

Myron exchanged a nervous look with Ferrin. Even for Rae, the outburst had been harsh. "I'm sorry," he said. "I didn't mean any disrespect. I just thought her gift might help keep us alive. But if you don't want—"

"I don't. She'll not use magic again." Rae stood and marched back to her bedding, crawling in beside her daughter and pulling the covers over their heads.

Myron looked at Ferrin. "Was it something I said?"

"Don't take it personally," he said as quietly as he could so Rae wouldn't hear. "She's scared."

"I didn't mean to upset her. We really could use a gift like that."

Ferrin nodded. "Hopefully she'll come around."

The two stared at the fire for a moment, enjoying the silence.

"So," Myron said, trying to sound casual, "what's this twin sister of yours like who we're risking our lives to save? Is she married?"

Ferrin picked up a pine cone and tossed it onto the fire. "No, not married. Too busy looking out for her brother to worry about something like that."

Myron smiled. "I hope she doesn't look like you."

Ferrin laughed. "Thankfully, no."

"Think she'd be interested in a well-mannered former captain of the Black Watch?"

"I hope not," Ferrin blurted out before he could stop himself.

Myron looked a bit taken aback.

"I'm sorry. But the last thing she needs is to get caught up with a sellsword." *Especially one who was willing to pledge his allegiance to the Tower,* he thought. "That line of work doesn't exactly lend itself to home and family, always on the move, never sure if the next job is going to leave you with a sword in the chest or an arrow in the back." Besides, Myron was old enough to already be showing a little grey, not that the age difference would have mattered too much to Ferrin, but it might to Myriah.

"Guess I can't argue with you there." Myron sighed. "Do you think—"

A sharp cry from the other side of the fire had both men hopping to their feet.

Suri was sitting up in her bed, face white as a swan's neck.

Rae hugged her close and gently patted down the little girl's disheveled hair. "It was just a dream, Suri. Go back to sleep. Everything's fine."

"I'm scared, Mommy."

"There's nothing to be scared of. We won't let those Tower guards get you."

"No," the little girl said, shrugging off her mother's embrace. She pointed up at the tops of the trees behind them. "They scare me."

Everyone turned to see what the little girl was looking at. Ferrin scanned the upper branches behind them. He didn't see anything, but it didn't stop the hairs on the back of his neck from rising. What was she looking at? Was she using magic again?

"What scares you?" Rae asked. She, too, kept her eyes on the swaying boughs overhead.

Suri pointed up once again. "Those birds."

"Birds? What birds?"

Ferrin held his breath and listened but couldn't hear any birds. It was the middle of the night. Most birds were asleep.

"Maybe she saw an owl," Myron suggested.

"The birds aren't going to hurt you, Suri," Rae said, glancing at Ferrin as if to make sure what she was telling her daughter was true.

"Your mama's right, Suri," Myron said, finally turning back around. "The birds won't hurt you."

"Those are very bad birds," Suri whispered, her gaze still locked on the top of the trees. "They said they've been looking for us. They said they've been watching us."

Myron drew his sword. "I think I just felt a chill run down my back."

"You're not the only one," Ferrin said, pulled the stone knife from the back of his trousers. Something wasn't right. He was starting to feel like they *were* being watched. He had thought maybe it was the wolves again, following, but now he wasn't so sure.

A loud, throaty *caw* pierced the silence, and Rae yelped. Ferrin tensed at the unexpected shriek. Above them, an enormous raven-like creature spread its black wings from where it was perched in the shadows of one of the larger pines. Whatever it was, it looked more reptilian than bird. Its enormous wings had no feathers, only stretched skin, similar in shape to a bat. It lifted into the star-filled sky and disappeared from view.

Myron half choked as he stared up at the branches overhead where the creature had been perched. "Corax."

"What?" Ferrin asked, moving closer to the fire.

"It looked like a corax. They are the White Tower's eyes. They can track almost anything."

Ferrin grabbed his bedding. "It's time to go."

Chapter 24 | Lenara

L ENARA WOKE TO THE sound of Sylas stirring on the other side of the fire. She was still having trouble adjusting to the inquisitor's new body. She couldn't look at him without remembering how innocent the young guard, Joren, had been, or the fear in his eyes at the end.

Their campsite in the glen consisted of four firepits. Three were shared by the twenty members of the Black Watch, while the fourth—which had been placed well away from the others—was occupied by Lenara and Sylas. The distance set between their fire and the others was as much for the guards' benefit as it was for theirs.

Though they served the Tower, the Black Watch resented the bulradoer. More importantly, they feared them. Those that had been in the Tower for any given length of time were well aware of the bulradoer's power and were eager to keep a safe distance from Lenara, for which she was grateful.

Thankfully, none of the Watch chosen to accompany them were part of the new recruits, so Lenara didn't find it necessary to worry about anyone confusing Sylas with Joren, the young guard. However, that didn't stop them from keeping a distrustful eye on their new leader. And why not? He was half their age. In fact, if Valtor hadn't demanded they recognize Sylas's position, they probably would have killed him and dumped his body in the Pass of Arnon on the way out, leaving Lenara with the unfortunate duty of informing Valtor that all their work in reviving the disturbed inquisitor had been for nothing.

She didn't want to consider the consequences of that. Valtor had specifically told her that Sylas was her responsibility, so like it or not, she had to keep him alive.

As it was, the Watch seemed willing to cooperate, but from the way they grumbled to each other when they thought Sylas and Lenara weren't listening, she could tell they weren't happy about having what amounted to a green recruit ordering them around. It didn't help that Sylas was as experienced at hunting in the wild as a red-tailed rooster, and just as noisy. The man had spent the majority of his adult life inside the bowels of the White Tower. They were lucky he knew how to ride at all.

Shifting to a more comfortable position on her bedding, she poked at the fire with a long stick, moving the not-quite-burnt pieces closer to the center. Sylas grunted as he turned over. She wanted to throw a log at him. Why had Valtor chosen her for this assignment? Was she being punished? She should be tracking down the faeling, not scouring the countryside looking for some swordsmith.

She snapped the branch. She knew better than to question Valtor's orders. The Archchancellor always had a reason for everything. He was a true batmyth player. The few times she had been given the chance to sit across the board from him had ended rather quickly. It was a game of logic . . . and the man never lost. He was always ten steps ahead of his opponents. The way the pieces moved depended on the roll of the dice and the cards you were dealt. You had to know when to attack and when to retreat. No matter what Valtor did, there was always a calculated reason behind it.

Still, it didn't change the fact that she didn't want to be there. She turned and fluffed the lump out of the extra blanket she was about to use for a pillow.

"Where am I?" a voice behind her asked. She turned.

Sylas was sitting up on his bedroll.

"What are you talking about?" she said. "We're in camp."

He turned to get a better view of the small clearing, his eyes uncertain.

She turned as well. Most of the guards were asleep, though a few patrolled the perimeter, half-hidden by the trees.

After a quick sweep of the camp, Sylas turned back around, his expression odd. "I know you."

"I would hope so. We've been traveling together for the better part of a week. What's wrong with you?"

"I remember your eyes."

My eyes? Lenara scooted to the edge of her bedding. That didn't sound like Sylas. Who was she talking to? "What's your name?"

"Joren, ma'am."

Her breath caught. *Joren?* "Interesting." She leaned forward, taking time to really study his eyes. They were the same sharp brown as before but somehow softer. Which might have been from the absence of the deep scowl Sylas normally wore. In its place—bewilderment, with a hint of something else, possibly curiosity.

"What's interesting?" he asked.

"Do you know what's happened to you?"

Joren's eyes shifted as he thought. "I remember a cave. You were there. There were others as well." He ran his hand through his hair. "I remember the Archchancellor and . . . the tree." His eyes widened, and he quickly felt around his mouth. "What happened? Those branches . . ." He looked down at his chest as if trying to reassure himself that they weren't there, still wrapped around his body. "I remember the dead inquisitor. We were trying to help him, I think. There was a voice. Up here." He tapped the side of his head. "Then everything . . . stopped." He paused a moment, then looked up at Lenara. "Why can't I remember more?"

Lenara kept her face smooth, but her mind was racing. How was she going to explain this? Should she even try? Something had clearly gone wrong with Valtor's incantation. She doubted the Archchancellor had meant for the recruit's soul to remain behind. And where was Sylas? Would he return, or did he somehow get dislodged from the body? Not that she would mind seeing that happen, but if Valtor found out, he'd kill the recruit to squelch any talk of what had been done to him. And to Lenara's surprise, she didn't want to see him killed.

There was something about him. Something innocent. He reminded her of her younger sister, Viena, at least what small part of her she could still remember. It had been so long since she had a family, those memories had quite faded. But she could recall the way Viena had made her feel . . . loved.

Unlike other bulradoer, Lenara had come to the White Tower of her own accord and at an early age. Her survivor nature had encouraged her to accept the Tower's offer of fealty without argument. It didn't hurt that she had been promised the opportunity to practice magic.

"Did we help him, the inquisitor?" Joren asked.

She had to stop and think about what he was asking. "We did." *In a way.*

Joren turned and looked at the sleeping men behind him. "Is he here?"

His voice, a little too loud, caused a few of the men at the next fire over to stir in their blankets.

"He's around," she said, flicking a curl out of her eye. She was stuck facing a situation she hadn't expected. Was Sylas gone for good? Should she continue with their mission? She certainly didn't want to come back empty-handed. If she had to face Valtor and explain to him the failure of his conjuring, having the swordsmith in hand when she did would definitely lessen the blow.

On the other hand, if Sylas wasn't gone, how much should she tell Joren? She decided, for now, the best option would be to tell him as little as possible.

"I don't understand. How did we get out here? The last thing I remember, we were in—"

"What's wrong with *him*?" a voice behind her said, causing her to flinch. It was one of the night watch coming back in for a change in shift. He was a lanky man with shoulder-length disheveled hair that clung to the sides of his long face. His uniform was about as unkempt as the rest of him. The dark ring around the seat of his pants made it look like he'd spent his entire watch sitting in a pile of wet mud.

"Nothing," Lenara said, standing to face him, the top of her head barely reaching his chest.

The guard took a step back.

She glanced at Joren, who had apparently decided to stand as well. "It was a dream."

"A dream?" The guard looked at Joren. "He looks as confused as my late wife's brother. And he'd been dropped on his head as a child."

Lenara raised her hand. "*Voyestra.*" Red flame ignited from her palm, casting menacing shadows across her face. "Are you questioning me?"

The guard's eyes bulged, and he backed away. "No, ma'am." He made a swift retreat to the second fire and hopped into bed, not bothering to so much as look in their direction.

When she turned, she noticed Joren's eyes were nearly as wide as the guard's as he stared at the flames rising from her open palm.

She lowered her hand, and they vanished.

"You're . . . a wielder?"

A couple of the other guards at another fire turned to see what was happening.

"This way," she said, motioning with her head for him to follow. She left the warmth of the fire and headed for the horse pen on the outer edge of camp, her breath leaving a trail of mist behind her as she made her way to the other side of the rope corral. She shivered as she scanned the trees to make sure no one else was listening in.

Joren followed her lead and made a nervous sweep of the trees as well. "I don't understand what's going on. How did I get here? Am I going crazy?"

She put her finger to her lips. "Keep your voice down," she said, glancing past him to the other campfires. It was clear she was going to have to tell him the truth, whether she wanted to or not. She couldn't keep letting him act insane around the other guards. They might decide to take matters into their own hands and kill him anyway.

She sighed. This wasn't going to be easy. How was she going to tell the recruit that they had tried to kill him and give his body to someone else? She took a deep breath. "First of all, yes, I'm a wielder. Like the Archchancellor said, there are a few of us who are permitted to keep our powers in order to help the Tower round up the rest of the ven'ae. And second, no, you're not crazy."

"I'm not?" He didn't seem all that relieved at the news.

"This might be difficult to understand," she said, looking him in the eyes, "but you're not supposed to be here right now."

He looked at her the way the guard had been looking at him a moment ago—like she was completely insane. "I don't understand."

"The Archchancellor tried to use you as a conduit to help bring back the inquisitor's soul."

"His soul?" If Joren hadn't looked scared before, he certainly did now.

"Yes. But it didn't work. Something went wrong, and he ended up . . . inside of you." It might have been a lie, but it seemed a plausible one. Better than the truth, that's for sure.

Joren didn't bat an eye. "In me?" he said a little too loudly, looking down at his chest as if he could see Sylas staring out at him.

"Shh." She raised her hands and glanced back at the fires. *Good.* No one was moving.

"The dead man is in . . . *me?*"

She nodded. "That's why you can't remember what happened. Why you woke up not knowing where you were or how you got here." She took a step back and looked him over. "To be honest, I wasn't sure you were still in there at all. It's been days since the ritual."

"Is he gone?"

"I don't know. Perhaps. Or maybe he's still there and you managed to come to the surface while he was sleeping. Or maybe it's completely random. I have no idea. This is the first time I've ever seen this."

Joren leaned against one of the trees being used for the corral and rubbed his hands together. "At least tell me what we're doing out here."

Finally, a question she *could* answer. "We're chasing down the ones responsible for killing the inquisitor in the first place."

He nodded slowly, still looking like he'd just received the worst news of his life. Which, of course, he had. "Is there any way to fix this?"

Another question she didn't have an answer for. "I don't know. But for the sake of your own skin, you need to keep your concerns between us. The others," she said, pointing back at the camp, "have been told by the Archchancellor that you are to be obeyed. Sylas, the inquisitor who's been in control of your body, is the expedition leader. If the guards start to question your sanity, it could be the worse for you."

He nodded.

"So, for now, it's best you keep up appearances." She hoped he'd take her advice. She certainly didn't want to spend all her time keeping an eye on him to make sure he didn't say or do something stupid. She had been charged with his protection. The last thing she needed was to have to worry about their own people trying to kill him.

"How do I do that? I don't know anything about where we're going or who we're even going after."

"Just follow my lead. And speak with me before you say anything."

He nodded again.

They stared at each other for a moment until it began to feel awkward, so she faked a yawn and started back to their beds. "Get some sleep. We'll talk about it some more in the morning."

Joren looked deflated, but eventually he nodded and followed her back to the fire. He crawled into his bedding on the other side of the pit and didn't move.

She watched him briefly as he lay there looking up at the stars, then finally turned over and closed her eyes.

"Mount up! Time to go!"

Lenara woke with a start. It was still dark. It felt like she'd just fallen asleep. She turned over to see Joren stuffing his blankets into one of his saddlebags.

What was he thinking, the idiot? I told him not to do anything without seeing me first.

He turned, and one look at those eyes and she knew . . . Joren was gone.

She crawled out of her warm blanket and over to the fire, where a few of the logs were still burning. "What's going on?"

Sylas looked at her over his horse as he continued to pack his gear. "The smith has been spotted."

"Have the trackers returned?" she asked, glancing around the camp. They had brought a pair of Cylmaran scouts along for the pursuit. Both had spent years hunting large game in the lower swamplands beyond the Khezrian Wall. Their gruff exteriors and rowdy dispositions kept most of the other men at arm's length.

"*My* trackers have," Sylas said proudly as he looked up into the trees.

His trackers? Black shapes stirred on one of the upper branches. It took her a moment to realize what she was staring at . . . corax.

"Go," Sylas said to the huge reptilian birds. "Keep a close eye on them." The two hunters spread their wings with a deep-throated *caw* and lifted into the sky. Guards stared in wonder at the enormous creatures.

Lenara kept an eye on Sylas as he finished packing. That also had been unexpected. Not only was Joren still alive, but Sylas was a wielder.

Chapter 25 | Ayrion

I T HAD TAKEN MOST of the night to dispose of the bodies. They had used five of the six cooking pits to burn the remains, along with any clothing, blankets, and utensils the Nathillians might have used. They had also emptied and cleaned the water barrels and buried all the rovers' fresh fruits and vegetables, anything that might have been carrying the disease. By the time they were finished, Ayrion was ready to collapse.

Once finished, Zynora had everyone wash with boiled water and musca. Apparently, the rovers were rather fond of the drink, since each of the wagons had a barrel or two tied to the back. Afterward, they had a small service for Taylis's mother and Marissa's parents, and Bek volunteered to take the first watch in case of any other unexpected surprises while the rest of the group tried to get some rest.

As tired as he was, Ayrion couldn't seem to doze off. He lay awake in the back of Marissa's wagon, listening to the little girl as she tossed and turned beside him under the thick blankets. She had refused to sleep anywhere but her own bed, which had been made with fresh blankets from Tameel and Zynora's wagon. More than once, he had to wake her from whatever nightmare she was reliving in order to calm her down. Each time, she'd curl up against his side and fall back asleep.

Once again, he was left wondering whether there was another little girl out there who was missing her daddy, a wife who had no one to cuddle up to at night, maybe a son who no longer had his father to teach him the proper way to hold a sword. Or had his life been devoted to his work?

He crawled out from under the heavy quilt he shared with Marissa and stretched his stiff muscles. He could see the faint light of a grey dawn through the cracks in the wagon door. He quietly pulled on his boots and coat, trying not to wake the little girl as he left.

Stepping outside, he shut the door and yawned, his breath misting in front of him. The last of the campfire embers had long since expired, and the frosty morning fog slithered its way between the wagons.

Realizing he wasn't the first one up, he joined Zynora by the fire as she busied herself over a large kettle. He knelt and warmed his hands. "Morning."

"Is it?" Zynora asked, looking up at the quickly fading stars. She shook her head. "Time moves so fast when you get to my age."

Ayrion took a seat on a log placed a comfortable distance from the fire. The glen was silent. The crackling of the wood and the occasional grunt from Zynora as she stirred the kettle's contents were the only sounds he heard.

It was relaxing. After the last couple of weeks, Ayrion longed for a little peace and quiet, no matter where it came from.

He heard the familiar squeak of Ol' Lera's hinges as Tameel climbed down from the back of the green-and-gold wagon. The old man scratched at his lengthening beard and then at his stomach when he spotted Zynora toiling over the fire. He strolled over and took a seat.

The smell of a breakfast had apparently reached the outer woods, as

Bek appeared not long after, trailing through the mist like something otherworldly. He'd apparently kept watch the entire night, not waking the others. Probably still feeling guilty for what his people had done. The man seemed to glide across the ground without so much as a sound, thanks to the odd shoes he wore. Unlike Ayrion's boots, they didn't seem to have hard soles or stiff necks to support the ankles. They looked almost like tall, thick socks, stopping just below the knees.

Bek took a seat beside Ayrion and warmed his hands. "Something sure smells good," he said with a polite smile to Zynora. He noticed Ayrion looking at his feet. "You like them?"

"They're certainly unique."

"They're zabatas." He pulled one off and handed it to Ayrion for inspection.

The shoe felt more durable than Ayrion had expected but was still pliable, like it would stretch to fit the one wearing it. The body of the shoe was made from stitched hides—fur side inward—which kept the insides soft and warm. The sole was thicker, sewn from two, maybe three, pieces of leather.

"I use them for tracking. No sound and few tracks. Can't tell you how handy they've been for hunting."

Ayrion handed the soft boot back to Bek and nodded his approval. He wouldn't have minded having a pair himself.

"Breakfast will be ready shortly," Zynora said, sprinkling in some cinnamon from one of her jars.

"How far are we from Belvin?" Ayrion asked. He didn't relish the thought of visiting a place where the entire town had gone mad, but as Zynora had pointed out the night before, they needed answers. It seemed the most important question was the one everyone was too afraid to ask: *Had all this been caused by magic?* It was one thing to contract an illness that led to death; it was quite another for an entire town to lose their minds, turn into white-skinned cannibals, and go on a killing spree.

"Belvin's a good half-day ride east through the forest," Bek said, accepting a hot bowl of porridge from Zynora. He blew across the top. "It only took me a few hours, but I was riding my horse pretty hard."

"Good," Ayrion said. "We don't need to be on the roads after dark."

"Aye," Tameel agreed, stuffing another spoonful of porridge into his gob and filling his left cheek to match his right. He looked like a chipmunk hoarding nuts. "I don't want to be anywhere near that town when the sun goes down."

"You won't be," Zynora said, dishing out a bowl for herself.

"Oh? And how do you know this? Been spirit-dreaming again, have we?"

"No, you old coot, I know this because you aren't coming."

Tameel choked as he tried to swallow. "What do you mean, I'm not coming? Of course I'm coming."

"No, you're not."

Tameel looked befuddled, his bushy eyebrows lowering as he dropped his spoon back into his bowl. "And may I ask why not?"

"Because you are going to stay here with the kids. They don't need to be anywhere near Belvin."

Tameel thought a moment. "You've got a point." He started to raise his spoon but stopped. "Why are you going, then?"

"Because I'm the only healer we have, and there could still be people who need my help."

Tameel shook his head. "This whole business smells rotten, if you ask me."

Ayrion agreed with Tameel but didn't argue. Regardless of how he felt about the situation, they needed to figure out what was behind the strange madness.

After breakfast, they packed what provisions they thought they might need and were ready to leave by the time Marissa and Taylis had woken and eaten their breakfast. Behind them, the first rays of sun could be seen pushing through the trees.

"I've got to go, Marissa," Ayrion said, trying to unhook the little girl from his leg.

"I want to go too," she said, almost crying.

"I'll be back. I promise. You stay here with Master Tameel. He'll take good care of you." He looked at Tameel and mouthed, *Help*.

Tameel hustled over to the back of the tinker wagon, grabbed something from just inside the door, and returned. "Here, Marissa, look what I have for you."

Marissa relaxed her grip enough to turn her head.

Tameel held a doll, one that had been popular in all the towns they had visited. This one wore a yellow dress with a bright blue ribbon around the waist. Her hair matched Marissa's—long, wavy, and the color of chestnut.

Marissa let go of Ayrion's leg to get her hands on the new toy. She squealed and hugged it to her.

Ayrion nodded his thanks and quickly mounted before she changed her mind. He turned his horse east and joined the others as they made their way out of camp.

Behind them, Taylis chased after the horses all the way to the edge of the rovers' corral. "Be careful," he shouted. Ayrion waved at the young boy and fell in behind Bek and Zynora.

His twin blades rested snugly against his back, their weight comforting. Even without his memories, Ayrion thought he felt more like himself, knowing they were there.

By that afternoon, the forest thinned and was replaced by rows of cottages. Bek stopped at a crossroad and pointed straight ahead. "This road will take you into Belvin." He then steered his horse left onto a smaller, less-traveled road.

"If that's the case," Zynora asked, rubbing her backside with a slight wince, "then why are we going this way?"

"I need to check on my wife."

They followed Bek north as the less-traveled road wound deeper into the forest. The woods were quiet. Apart from the occasional tree-rat and a few birds flitting from one branch to another, the place seemed dead.

It wasn't long before the lane opened into a small clearing with a cabin on the left. They took the path leading off the road toward a two-story barn in back. The building wasn't much to look at, but it seemed well built, with no openings in the siding and each window having its own shutter.

Inside, four stalls lined the left wall, with a light-brown mare occupying the first. She whinnied when she saw Bek, and he patted her on the way by. "I've got feed and water," he said, directing his mount into the second stall and Zynora's into the third.

Ayrion took the last, making sure the stallion got a full bucket of oats and plenty of water. They left the horses saddled and exited the stable on their way to the house.

The front of the cabin was decorated with rows of bright violet flowers with yellow centers, which contrasted with the home's darker wood. Yellow curtains hung in the windows, adding an additional touch of color, and wooden shingles blanketed the top. There was a single stone chimney on the side. No smoke rose from its flue.

Ayrion followed Bek and Zynora to the front door, where he noticed part of the flower bed on the right had been trampled, and deep shoe prints had ground a number of the winter plants into the mud. The broken handle of a hoe lay farther down, snapped completely in half. A few feet beyond that, a trowel was stuck upside down in the yard. Must have been what Bek's wife had used in her attempt to kill him.

"Nell, I'm home," Bek said hesitantly as he lifted the latch and pushed the door open. Sunlight poured into the front room, and the door thumped to a stop against the wall.

They stood in silence as they peered into the house, Bek and Zynora waiting for their eyes to adjust to the dim light. Ayrion didn't need to wait. With his Upakan eyes, he could see just fine. The front room was quaint but clean. Vases of wilted flowers decorated the empty spaces on the table, cabinets, sill, and hearth. There were two rockers near the open hearth. The one on the right held what looked like a half-knitted sweater, and the other a whetstone.

Off to the right was an open kitchen with a dining table, a few cabinets, and a stove. A single door at the back led to what Ayrion guessed was the bedroom.

Zynora cleared her throat. "Is there a reason we're all standing out here?"

Bek mumbled something and stepped inside. "The last time I was here, my wife tried to kill me."

Ayrion heard faint noises coming from the back room, followed by what sounded like something banging against the wall. He drew one of his swords and followed the others as they headed for the back. Bek turned the knob, easing the door open. The room beyond was covered in darkness. The window on the left was shuttered; if that wasn't enough, a thick blanket had been draped over it. Ayrion whispered in Zynora's ear. "Have you ever heard of an affliction that causes people to fear the sun?"

Zynora shook her head. "I need to have a closer look at her."

Under the window, a dresser rested against the wall. The excess material hanging from the window covered the top. On the right was a second window—also covered—and a rocking chair that no doubt looked out across the backyard and the barn. And at the center of the room was the bed.

Ayrion could see Bek's wife lying on top, bound to the corner posts. As soon as she saw them, she thrashed about, fighting to break free of the cords. She looked like a green colt that had yet to be broken. She hissed as she strained against the binding, the cords taut to the point of snapping.

Ayrion tightened his grip on his sword in case they did.

Bek moved to the side of the bed and reached out to touch her. As soon as he did, she reared her head and tried to sink her teeth into his hand. He jerked away with a yelp.

"What do you think you're doing?" Zynora asked, pulling Bek back.

Ayrion stood protectively beside Zynora, poised to strike at the first sign of danger.

Nell growled as Zynora moved around the bed to examine the woman more closely. She was careful to keep out of reach.

Zynora looked across the bed at Bek. "We need light if I'm to examine her. I need to see the transformations. We might even find a clue about what is happening in the very changes themselves."

"I'll fetch a lantern," Bek said, choking on the words as he brushed fresh tears from his eyes. "But don't open the shades. I don't want to expose her to the sunlight. It hurts her."

"So, they're not just afraid of the light?" Ayrion asked, keeping an eye on the woman as she writhed on top of the sheets. "They actually feel pain from it?"

"Yes."

"That's interesting," Zynora said as she took a step closer to the bed. Nell pulled away.

"Did you see that?" she asked.

"See what?" Bek asked, moving closer.

Zynora reached her hand out slowly, and Nell curled away from the old woman's touch, releasing a sad whine as though in pain. Zynora dropped her arm, and the woman relaxed once again.

"What just happened?" Bek asked. "Why did she do that? That's the way she reacts when she gets too close to the light."

"That is curious," Zynora said, keeping her eye on the woman. "You mentioned a lamp?"

"Right." With that, the big trapper disappeared into the next room.

As soon as he left, Zynora stepped forward and once again moved her hand toward the woman, and once again Bek's wife's response was the same. The ropes tightened to the point of cutting into her wrists. Zynora looked at Ayrion. "I want to try something else. Stick *your* hand out there."

"What?" Ayrion had no intention of sticking his fingers out there to get bitten off.

"I want to see how she responds to you. Her reaction to me is clearly different from her reaction to her husband. But why? Is it because she recognizes him as the one who tied her up, or is it something as simple as he's a man and I'm a woman? The only way to figure that out is to have you try."

"How's that going to make a difference?"

"Because not only are you a man, you are also a stranger. She has no preconceived notions or resentment toward you personally, so if she attacks you the same way she did her husband, then we can at least rule out the possibility of familiarity."

"Fine," he said, completely confused but not wanting to admit it. He sheathed his blade and took a step closer. Why was he feeling so apprehensive? The woman was tied to her bed. Still, he had felt less wary facing down the monstrous sniffer back in Woodvale than he did this bound woman.

Here goes nothing, he thought as he raised his hand cautiously toward the bed. He could feel, more than see, the woman's eyes on him, a calculated stare stemming from her dark gaze. Slowly, he eased his hand forward. She didn't so much as flinch. *So far, so good.* He made it halfway to her waist and still no response. *Maybe there's something to this after all.*

The tips of his fingers grazed the side of her stomach as Bek stepped through the door. The light from the lantern lit a narrow swath from the door to the bed. Nell's reaction was swift as she lunged for Ayrion's hand, her mouth wide and snarling. His reflexes saved him losing a finger or two, but in the process, she managed to snap the binding on her right arm. Her claws tore through his neck, leaving him choking on his own blood.

He dropped to his knees, gasping, and reached for his neck, but before he could get his hand around the opening, everything around him shifted, and suddenly, he was standing beside the bed once more, reaching out.

Bek stepped into the bedroom with the lantern, and Nell snapped her binding once more, but this time, Ayrion managed to grab her arm before she could reach him.

Bek shouted and ran for the bed. Lifting the lantern, he gasped and took a step back. He didn't move, the lantern swinging back and forth in his trembling grip.

Nell had progressed even further than the villagers they had killed at the rover encampment. Her eyes were the same—black and reflective. Her skin, though, had shifted from white to the point of being somewhat translucent. Black veins could be seen beneath, marbling throughout the visible parts of her body—her face, neck, hands, and lower arms. Her lips curled, revealing sharp, pointed teeth as though they'd been filed specifically just to rip meat from bone. What was left of her hair had been shed across the bed. She truly looked more animal than human.

"Hurry," Ayrion said, still holding her free arm. "Tie her down."

Bek shoved the lamp at Zynora, nearly tripping on his own feet as he rushed to the other side of the bed to help secure his wife.

The woman was much stronger than she should have been. It took both hands to hold her back. He wondered if her strength was just another part of the physical changes that seemed to be plaguing these people.

"Careful with her nails," he warned Bek as the big trapper struggled to get the cord around her wrist. Her nails had grown considerably longer, not to mention thicker. They looked more like talons now than claws.

"What's happening to her?" Bek asked as he finished tying off the knot on the rope.

"I'm not sure," Zynora said, "but we'll do our best to find out." She lifted the lantern. "She doesn't seem to be in any pain from the light of the flame." Zynora continued to wave the lamp around in front of the woman, making sure to bathe every inch of her in its soft amber glow. "Do you have any more lamps or candles we can use to light this room?

The more light I have to work with, the better."

Bek nodded. "I have a few candles in the front and another table lamp in my workroom out back."

"Excellent," Zynora said.

Bek didn't move.

Finally, she turned the lamp on him. "The sooner the better."

Bek snapped out of his trance as the light flashed across his face. "I'll be right back." He crossed the room and stopped at the door. "You'll let me know if something"—he wrung his hands—"if something happens, won't you?"

Ayrion felt for the big man. He couldn't imagine how hard it must be for Bek to watch this happening to his wife.

Zynora lowered the lamp. "I'm sure if it does, you'll know it." She smiled. "Don't worry. Your wife's in good hands."

Bek nodded and left the room.

As soon as he did, Zynora turned to Ayrion. "We need to kill it and burn the body. I suggest using your sword to take off the head."

Chapter 26 | Ayrion

AYRION DIDN'T MOVE. Was Zynora serious? "You just told Bek his wife would be safe."

"I lied. We need to put an end to this thing while we have the chance."

"I thought you wanted to study her, to see if you could find a cure. What about your magic? You brought me back when I was half dead—"

"That thing is *all* dead."

"But how do you know you can't help her if you don't try?"

"She's too far gone. When I healed you, it nearly killed me . . . and that was just your body. Whatever's going on here is more than physical—much more."

Nell writhed in her sheets.

"Please," Ayrion begged, not wanting to think about what would happen if Bek returned to find his wife beheaded. "If things get out of hand, I'll do what needs to be done."

"We don't have time," Zynora said, pushing aside the drape to peek out the window. "The sun is getting lower. Even if I somehow managed to stop the transformation, how are you going to get us out of here? I'll be too weak to ride and so will she." Zynora shook her head. "No. It's best we do what's needed now, before he gets back."

"You said it yourself: We don't understand why these people are changing. This is our chance to find out. Maybe there's a way to stop it, even reverse it. There's an entire town of crazies out there. What if this keeps spreading?" Ayrion was growing desperate. "This was your idea, remember?"

Zynora sighed. "It was my idea to come take a look." She looked at Nell. "Well, now we have. It's time to go."

"Zynora, this might be our only chance to stop this."

Zynora shook her head. "I'm going to regret this. But," she said, pointing a bony finger at him, "if I say there's nothing more to be done, you promise me you'll do what you do best. Agreed?"

Ayrion didn't like how that sounded. Was *killing* all he was good for? He nodded reluctantly. "Agreed."

Zynora handed him the lantern and moved closer to the bed. "Hold the light up. I want to get a better look at her face."

The light accentuated Nell's twisted features as she bared her unnaturally sharp teeth and growled.

Zynora leaned over to get a better look.

"Maybe you shouldn't get so close," Ayrion said, gripping his sword with his free hand.

"Nell, can you hear me?" Zynora asked, waving her hand in front of the woman's face. "Can you understand me, dear?"

Nell watched the old woman, her dark obsidian eyes carefully tracking Zynora's every movement. She gave no indication of understanding.

"Whatever this is, it seems to obstruct the mind," Zynora said, frustrated.

Bek walked into the room, his hands, arms, and pockets filled with candles and candleholders. A single table lamp was wedged into the crook of his arm. He kicked the door shut.

Ayrion set the lamp he was holding on the dresser to help the big woodsman before he dropped everything on the floor. Quickly, they spread the candles on every spare ledge and open top they could find, until the whole room glowed with their light.

"How's it going?" Bek asked, watching Zynora work.

"Your wife doesn't seem to understand what we're saying. Although I'm very curious as to why she responds differently with me."

"Maybe it's your magic," Ayrion said.

"That's what I'm afraid of. It means this was caused by some form of dark magic. I don't know if I can undo it."

"Please," Bek begged. "You have to try."

Zynora moved to the end of the bed where Nell's bare feet had been secured and grabbed the woman's ankles.

Nell shrieked, growling and hissing as she fought to break free. The cords on her legs dug into her skin, black liquid seeping from the wounds.

"Stop," Bek said. "You're hurting her. She's bleeding."

Nell went completely still. She raised her head slowly and looked directly at Zynora. "You're too late, healer," a dark, haunting voice said from somewhere deep inside the woman.

Zynora let go of her legs, and Ayrion drew his sword partway, but Nell simply lowered her head back to the mattress and stared up at the wooden rafters overhead.

"What was that?" Bek asked, his voice trembling. "That wasn't my wife."

Zynora shook her head, jostling some of the charms that hung from her purple headband. "I'm afraid this is much worse than I thought."

Ayrion lifted the lantern back to Nell's face. "I'd say we learned something very valuable here."

"We did?" Bek asked, sounding desperate for anything to hold on to.

Ayrion swung the lantern to Zynora. "We learned that she's afraid of you. Which is a good sign. Means we're on the right path."

Zynora looked at Nell, then back at Ayrion. "This is going to be dangerous."

"Why?" Bek asked.

"Because we have no idea what this will do. It could kill her." Zynora grunted. "It could kill me."

Ayrion took a step in her direction. "I won't let it come to that."

"You won't have a choice."

"Then promise me you'll stop before it gets that far." As sympathetic as he felt for Bek's situation, Ayrion would cut Nell down in a heartbeat if he thought Zynora's life was in danger. He hoped it didn't come to that. Not to mention he was the one who had goaded Zynora into doing this in the first place. He couldn't lose her.

Zynora finally nodded and took a step closer to the bed, prompting Nell to shrink away. Zynora closed her eyes and began chanting in a tongue Ayrion didn't recognize. A light breeze moved through the room. Candles flickered in their holders, sending shadows dancing around the wood-slated walls, making it feel even more unnerving. The air was thick, pressure building, like being submerged in water, enfolded in a temporary weightlessness.

"What's happening?" Bek asked, eyes darting back and forth. "Is this normal?"

"There's nothing about this that's normal," Ayrion said, keeping his eyes on Zynora. She seemed to be in a trance.

The chanting continued, growing more forceful as the wind inside the room built. Most of the candles had blown out, their smoke rising and swirling around Ayrion's head. Zynora kept her eyes shut, her face as taut as Nell's ropes. She was clearly straining to keep focus. Ayrion wasn't sure how much more she could take. He'd never seen her perform this before. He had no idea what this was doing to her and how far she could go.

He spared a quick glance at Nell. Her body was shaking. The black veins in her face, hands, and neck were bulging. She howled at Zynora, and Ayrion kept one hand on the hilt of his blade. Bek was too busy watching his wife to see Ayrion slip the blade free. He didn't want to kill her, but he might not have a choice.

Both of Zynora's hands were now glowing.

Nell's face twisted with rage, and the dark booming voice inside her erupted in a horrific otherworldly chant of its own.

Ayrion felt as though he were in a trance, unable to do anything but watch. He listened as the two women seemingly battled each other through a mirage of strange words. This was a fight he was not equipped to handle, a fight of wills and magic, not of swords.

Zynora abruptly opened her eyes and grabbed Nell by her ankles once again. Nell reared back and screamed, this time with her own voice. She twisted and howled as the purple strands of Zynora's magic worked their way up both legs, spreading through the veins until Nell's legs were glowing.

Every hair on Ayrion's body stood on end.

Tiny strands of purple light lanced through Nell's lower torso. Ayrion thought the woman was going to snap her own limbs as she fought against the ropes.

"Stop!" Bek shouted. "You're killing her!"

Zynora's entire body shook as she held on to Nell. The old woman's legs buckled, and she went to her knees.

Ayrion raised his blade. He had to do something. Zynora looked like she was about to kill herself. As if reading his thoughts, Zynora stopped the chanting and shouted, "Give me light!"

Bek was the first to respond, frantically snatching up the nearest lamp and waving it all around.

"Not that light! The sun! Give me the sun!"

Ayrion tore across the room and ripped down the blankets covering the windows and threw open the shutters.

The late-afternoon sun shot through the window. Nell screamed as the rays engulfed her, back arching into the air. Zynora never let go, continuing to push her magic into the woman.

"You're killing her!" Bek roared.

But Zynora didn't stop. As deep as her trance was, Ayrion doubted she could even hear them.

Nell screamed again, and Bek rushed Zynora, losing all sense of reason.

Ayrion tackled him, slamming him to the floor with Ayrion on top.

"Get off me or I'll kill you too!"

"That woman's the only chance your wife has!" Ayrion shouted over the sound of the wind and the chanting. "Trust her!"

Ayrion looked up at Zynora, wondering how much longer he should let this continue. Her face was pale, sweat pouring from her brow. Why hadn't he just listened to her and killed Nell in the first place? If Zynora died, it would be his fault.

The chanting stopped, and Nell went deathly quiet. She collapsed onto the bed, and a black inky substance floated up out of her mouth. As soon as it touched sunlight, it ignited and vanished in a puff of smoke.

Ayrion crawled back to his feet and rushed to catch Zynora as her eyes rolled back into her head. She was barely breathing. He was a fool for talking her into this. Why hadn't he just listened?

Zynora opened her eyes, and Ayrion breathed a deep sigh of relief.

"How long have I been out?"

"An hour at most," he said. He held out a small tin of water and helped her sit up far enough to drink it.

When she was done, he helped her to a chair. "We need to get some

food in you."

"Yes. I need to replenish some of what I lost."

"You scared me, Zynora. I thought we were going to lose you."

She smiled. "I'm pretty tough to kill." She glanced at the bed where Nell—still bound hand and foot—was sleeping. Her skin had regained some of its color, and her nails were shorter. "Has she moved since I've been out?"

"She hasn't so much as stirred," Bek said. He hadn't left his wife's side since she'd slipped into unconsciousness. He sat on a stool beside the bed, holding her hand. "Her breathing is steady."

Zynora nodded. "That's a good sign."

"Yes," Ayrion agreed, "but we have another problem." He turned and looked out the window. "The sun is setting."

Chapter 27 | Ayrion

"WE CAN'T AFFORD TO be on the road at night," Ayrion said, peeking out the window at the fading sky. "We'll have to stay here and hope none of your neighbors decide to pay us a visit."

"Night comes early in the forest," Bek said with a nod.

"Then we better get to work."

Ayrion and Bek spent what remained of the failing twilight fortifying the cabin while Zynora rested in the chair beside Nell's bed. In the bedroom, they closed the shutters, nailed boards across the inside, and draped a heavy blanket across the window to hide the light. The glass windows in the main room had no shutters to latch, so Ayrion and Bek set up watch there. Bek secured the front door with a thick bracer.

"First time I've ever had cause to use it," he said. They did the same to the door in the kitchen, then slid an extremely heavy cabinet in front.

Once finished, they checked on the women. Nell was still sleeping.

"Can't you use more of your magic on her?" Bek asked. "The faster she heals, the faster we can get out of here. As soon as dawn arrives, we need to move."

"More magic at this point isn't going to help," Zynora said, her face still pale. She ate some soup Bek had warmed on the stove, along with dried fruit and cheese from their packs. "There comes a point when using more magic for the sake of magic is simply wasted effort. It can even harm the wielder."

Ayrion didn't think Zynora had the strength to do more, anyway. Bek didn't argue.

Something howled outside, and Ayrion slid one of his swords from its sheath. "What was that?"

Everyone stopped to listen. The howl came again, and Bek laughed.

"Oh, that. That's just a night fox." He looked up at the ceiling. "He gets up on the roof sometimes to call for a mate. Stupid thing will keep you up half the night with his whining, and the other half with his mating."

"On the roof?"

Bek laughed again. "No. He just uses the roof to call her."

Ayrion thought that seemed a dangerous way to find female company. Did it think the added height was going to increase the range of its cry? Or simply impress the female with its prowess?

"As long as he's carrying on," Bek said, "we shouldn't have to worry about something else roaming around unnoticed."

Ayrion nodded, and the two men headed back to the front window to keep watch. They sat on either side of the glass and studied the tree line on the other side of the road.

Ayrion bit off a piece of salted pork and listened to the branches beating against the side of the house. The forest was alive with song: the frogs croaking out their melodic chorus, the occasional hoot owl, the lonely night fox on the roof, barking out its mournful cry. Ayrion almost hoped some poor lady fox would take pity on the wretched animal.

"What's your story?" Bek asked, keeping his voice down. "You don't exactly strike me as someone who fancies the nomadic life."

Ayrion twisted on his seat, his black leathers creaking under the movement. "Honestly, I wish I knew." Bek passed him a funny look, so he went on to explain the injuries he'd sustained during the battle between Elondria and Cylmar and the loss of memory as a result.

Bek rubbed at the wooly growth on his face. "I've heard of that kind of thing happening before, but I've never met anyone who'd actually experienced it."

"I can't say it's all that pleasant."

"Suppose not." Bek stared out the window for a moment, then turned back around. "This might be poking my nose where it doesn't belong, but why are you traveling around the countryside with a couple of tinkers and not galloping as fast as you can back to Aramoor? Seems to me that would be the best place to start if you want to put the pieces of your life back together."

Ayrion had spent many a restless night staring up at the curved planks of the old green-and-gold tinker wagon thinking the same thing. "Yes. The answers I need are in Aramoor, and if I ever hope to move forward, that's where I'll need to go."

"Then why are you here?"

Ayrion could hear Tameel's voice in the back of his head telling him to lie, but there was something about the big trapper, a gut feeling Ayrion couldn't explain, that encouraged him not to. For some reason, he trusted the man. So, he told Bek who he was, or at least who he thought he was. He told him of the fight with the Black Watch and the sniffer in Woodvale, of the discovery of his name and identity.

"You're the Guardian Protector? *The* Guardian Protector?" Bek looked at Ayrion like he was seeing him for the first time. He sat back on his stool and wiped his forehead. "I don't know if I should be impressed or worried." He leaned forward. "What's it like, working with the king?"

"I wouldn't know."

"Oh, right. Sorry."

"So, you can see why running back to Aramoor without my memories would be about as foolish as marching men into battle without scouting the terrain. Without a single memory of my prior life, I wouldn't know who to talk to or where to even begin. If I am this Guardian, it stands to reason that most in Aramoor would recognize me. It would be hard to hide in a city where everyone you meet might know you."

"Why is that a bad thing? Isn't that the point in going back . . . to find people who knew you?"

"Yes," Ayrion said, "but from the way Tameel and Zynora said they found me, and the fact that the king somehow died while in my service, going back might not be the best thing right now. At least not until I can recover more of my memories."

"Guess that makes sense."

The bedroom door behind them opened, and Nell stepped out with Zynora's help.

"Bek," Nell said, steadying herself on the doorjamb. She had a troubled look on her face.

Bek jumped to his feet. "What's wrong?"

"They're coming."

Chapter 28 | Ayrion

A YRION STOOD AND DREW both swords. The night fox had stopped its calling. In fact, he couldn't hear anything beyond the cabin's walls. *How long had the fox been silent?*

Bek crossed the room with the speed of a panther, wrapping an arm around his wife to help her stand. "How do you know they're coming?"

"I can feel them."

"You can? Where?"

"In here," she said, pointing to her head. "It's like I can sense them."

"Animal instinct," Zynora said. "Like when you sense someone is watching you even though you don't see anyone."

"Yes," Nell said. "It's like that. But stronger."

"I think we might be dealing with vulraaks," Zynora said.

Ayrion peered out the front window. "What are vulraaks? I thought these were people from Belvin."

"They are," she said. "Or were. The term *vulraak* is from the old tongue. It means *people of the shadows*. Most of what I know of them is from very old books that've been handed down through the Rhivanni for generations. Vulraaks were created by Aerodyne and his followers back during the Wizard Wars."

"The Dark One created these things?" Bek asked. "Are you saying . . . he's back?"

"No," Zynora said. "If he were, I think we'd know it. The whole world would know it."

"How sure are you about this?" Ayrion asked, not understanding how something like this could simply show up in the middle of nowhere.

"Well, no one in the last thousand years has ever seen one."

"So, you could be wrong," Bek said, more a statement than a question.

Zynora shrugged. "I could be." She gave Nell a sympathetic look. "But I don't think so."

Bek looked at Nell. "And you feel these things?"

She nodded.

"How do we fight them?" Ayrion asked, trying to shift the conversation to what really mattered. Now wasn't the time to debate who or what they were, only how best to kill them. From what he'd seen, they were flaming tough to take down.

"There's not much written about them, except what we've already seen so far, which is that sunlight is anathema to them."

"It's also the one thing we don't have," Ayrion said.

"What do they want?" Bek asked. "Clearly, they possess some reasoning. Nell talked to us."

Nell's head shot up. "I did? What did I say?"

"Nothing important, dear," Zynora said, biting her lower lip, something Ayrion had noticed she did when in deep thought.

"From what I saw during our battle at the rover camp, these things feed on blood and flesh." Ayrion turned and look at the others. "But we also saw they can be killed."

"Can't we try to help them like you did me?" Nell asked.

"It took nearly everything I had just to bring you back," Zynora said as she walked over to the hearth on the left and grabbed a striker from the mantel. "I can't imagine what it would take to rid an entire city of such a plague, especially a city as large as Belvin." She knelt and lit the kindling.

"Won't that let them know we're here?" Bek asked.

"If they're coming like Nell says, then they already know we're here. No need to freeze to death while waiting for them to arrive. Besides, wouldn't want these things crawling down the chimney with our backs turned, now would we?"

"Hadn't thought of that." Bek helped his wife to a seat in the kitchen, as far away from the front as possible.

"Can you sense how many are out there?" Ayrion asked Nell.

Nell shook her head, hunkering down next to Zynora.

"How close are they?" Bek asked, taking his seat opposite Ayrion at the front.

There was a long moment of silence before she spoke again. "Close. I think." Ayrion could hear the frustration in her voice. "I'm sorry I don't know more. I can only sense their hunger. And what I'm feeling is getting stronger."

"That could mean they are getting closer," Ayrion said. "Or that their numbers are increasing."

Bek looked at Ayrion. "Don't like the sound of that."

Neither did Ayrion.

"I'm sorry I can't be more help," Nell said.

"It's fine, dear," Zynora said, putting her arm around the woman. "You've been plenty helpful."

"I don't want this feeling. Will it go away? They're in my head."

"I'm sure it will with time and plenty of rest."

Ayrion had been around Zynora long enough to tell when she was stretching the truth, even if only to give comfort. Zynora had no idea if it would ever go away. Right now, though, it gave them an advantage.

And they needed all the help they could get.

Ayrion didn't say it, but he felt it too. There *was* something out there. "They're here," he said. He scanned the trees but still didn't see anything. *Where are they?* The silence was unnerving.

A sharp cry pierced the night, and the sudden sensation of fear punched Ayrion in the chest. He stood. It sounded like—

"The horses!" Ayrion ran for the front door and threw the bracer open.

"What the blazes do you think you're doing?" Bek shouted.

"I've got to save the horses!"

"Are you mad? You need to save us!"

"Bolt the door behind me." Ayrion ripped both blades from their sheaths and charged around the side of the house. He heard the door slam shut behind him.

The horses' cries were wild and desperate. Ayrion didn't know why, but he could sense the stallion's pain. He had no real memories of the warhorse other than the brief glimpse of him on a rise in the middle of battle, but there was an unmistakable bond. He tightened his grip on the swords and sprinted across the open ground between the cabin and the barn. His leather coat flared open as he ran. He slowed as he neared the front. The doors were ajar, and he could see movement inside.

The moon lit the front opening, giving Ayrion's Upakan eyes plenty to see with as he raised his swords and slipped inside. Stacks of barrels and racks of tools lined the wall to his right. A stairway led up to the loft, which was packed with bales of hay.

To his left, three of the four horses were bucking in their stalls, struggling to fend off their attackers. Eyes gleamed from the shadows as the vulraaks' dark orbs reflected the moonlight. They fought to sink their teeth into the horses' meaty backsides. The mare in the first stall was down, three or four of the white-skinned creatures on top of her. Like the other half-humans he'd seen attacking the rover encampment, they were dressed in rags, their clothing shredded by dagger-like claws.

The door on the last stall flew off its hinges as the enormous warhorse kicked. The door caught a vulraak in the chest and threw it into the far wall, where it crumpled and went still. The others hissed, turning on the warhorse, until they noticed Ayrion.

Two leaped from the railing to his left and hit him in the chest. The first buried its teeth in his arm, and the second cut a wide opening across his stomach with its claws. Pain swallowed him, and he tried to scream, then everything shifted.

Another vision.

The two creatures leaped from the railing, and he spun, blade outstretched, opening both creatures right below the rib line. They landed on their own insides and didn't move.

Three more attacked from behind in a flanking pattern, displaying a higher level of cunning than he had seen at the camp. Had the vulraaks gone after the horses to draw them out? Were they trying to get rid of their only means of escape? Or did it just seem like an easy meal?

Ayrion whirled and kicked the first in the chest. He heard ribs snap, and the creature hit the ground. He removed the head of the second with his right sword while skewering the third with his left. Like the woman he had killed the previous night, the third creature didn't die right away, swinging wildly as it reached for Ayrion with its claws. Ayrion turned his shoulder to protect his chest, and the claws tore through his coat.

Pain seared his shoulder, but he managed to kick the creature back far enough to pull his blade free and then remove its head. The same black mist that had come out of Nell floated into the air and dissipated. That hadn't happened with the first group of vulraaks they had killed at the Nathillian camp. Was it because they hadn't fully transformed yet?

The first creature Ayrion had kicked was back on its feet and charging. It shrieked as it ran across the straw-covered floor. A vision took over, and Ayrion ducked to the side to miss getting hit in the face. The creature skidded to a stop in front of the last stall. The warhorse inside reared and landed a kick that caved in the side of the vulraak's skull. Its body cartwheeled across the barn and slammed into a beam on the other side.

Ayrion pulled the horse out of the stall. "Go! Get out of here!" The warhorse turned and looked him in the eyes, obviously worried.

"Go. I'll be fine."

The horse whinnied and bolted out the front.

A screech behind him had Ayrion diving to dodge another set of claws. He turned and chopped the creature's arms off at the elbow. Blood as black as scrivener's ink poured from the stumps.

The armless vulraak squealed in pain but continued forward. Ayrion had to admire its tenacity. He kicked the creature in the knee to drop it face-first into the dirt. He plunged his blade down through the back of its neck, releasing more of the black vapor into the air.

He spun, his swords up and ready, but there was no other attack. He took a moment to look around the barn. Every vulraak he found was dead. Not waiting for more to show up, he opened the other stalls, freeing Bek's and Zynora's horses. Both had sustained deep wounds but not enough to keep them from bolting out the door.

A gurgled whinny from the first stall let Ayrion know the poor mare inside was still alive. He glanced over the rail. She was on her side, her coat bloody and torn with bite marks. Blood seeped from her flared nostrils.

He opened the door and stepped inside. "Whoa, there. Shh, it's all right." She tried raising her head, one dark-brown eye watching him. He steeled himself for what he knew was coming. "It will be over soon." Lowering his sword, he slid the blade into the back of her neck, severing the spine. Her head dropped to the side, and she went still.

Ayrion took one last look around the barn, then closed the doors on the way out. The surrounding forest was silent. Was that the end of it? Maybe these had just been passing through and the rest were somewhere else.

He left the barn and headed back to the cabin, keeping his swords in hand as he moved quietly across the grass. A cold breeze rustled the bare limbs on the trees and sent a shiver down his back. Up ahead, a soft glow poured from the front window, spilling light across the flower beds.

A vision struck, and he dove to the ground, a gust of wind rustling his hair as something swooped past his head. He rolled back to his feet and spun, blades up.

An enormous vulraak rose from where it had landed and turned to face him. This creature was something new, far deadlier than anything they'd faced yet. It was at least ten feet tall and made the sniffer back in Woodvale look positively harmless. In its hands, it held a piece of wrought iron big enough to have easily cloven Ayrion in two had it made contact.

Unlike the other vulraaks, this creature's eyes were bloodred. Ayrion had thought nothing could have been more disturbing than those black, soulless eyes. He was wrong. Its bare white chest rippled with muscle, and around its neck swung a chain with a dark piece of rock attached to the end.

As Ayrion sized the creature up, he realized his hands were shaking. And it wasn't from the cold.

He crouched, waiting to see what the hulking giant would do. The vulraak didn't appear to be in a hurry. It let the tip of its sword drag across the ground, like a plow furrowing up a row, as it took up a position between Ayrion and the door. About ten feet of grass was all that stood between them.

A scraping sound announced the bracer being removed.

"Get in here, you fool!" Bek shouted from the crack in the door.

How am I supposed to do that, he wondered, *with a creature like this blocking the way?* Ayrion took a step to the right, and the vulraak lunged.

"Bolt the door!" he yelled at Bek, then jumped, sailing over the thick piece of iron swinging for his midsection. He rolled to his feet and lunged at the creature's exposed back. The vulraak turned with astonishing speed and deflected the blow, but not before Ayrion nicked the thick sinew of the creature's upper arm. Their blades touched, and sparks flew in all directions.

Ayrion pulled back and the two began circling.

"You seem a worthy opponent," the vulraak said with a booming voice. He wiped the tip of his finger through the dark blood seeping from his arm and licked it clean. "Yes, I recognize the taste of your steel. The magic is familiar. Your metallurgist is talented."

My metallurgist? What was this creature talking about? In fact, why was he talking at all?

"How is it you know my weapons? I've never seen your like before." He couldn't be sure if he had or not, but in his gut, he didn't believe so.

The vulraak smiled. "If you had, you wouldn't be alive to tell about it."

Ayrion kept his distance. "You got a name, or should I just call you . . . Whitey?"

The vulraak sneered. "I am Argon."

"Is that your human name or your . . . animal name?"

Argon growled. "You know nothing of who I am, mortal. If you did, your words would bleed deference."

"Then by all means, enlighten me."

"I'm general to the wizards of the First Order. I've been around since the coming of the Fae. Even they weren't enough to stand against me. My brethren and I have waited long for this day."

"And who are these brethren?" Ayrion asked, turning to look at the surrounding woods.

"Those that have yet to awaken."

More riddles? Ayrion tried to keep him talking, circling slowly to the left. "So, you fought in the Faerie Wars? You're looking pretty good for your age, apart from the milky skin and serious case of dead eye."

"Bold words from someone about to meet their end." Argon hissed and threw himself at Ayrion, swinging his tremendous blade like a smith's hammer, looking to smash Ayrion straight into the ground.

Ayrion dove left, rolled, and was back on his feet in time to deflect the next attack. Argon's sword swept right, giving Ayrion a clean strike at his neck. He swung, but the vulraak leaned back, and his sword missed.

Argon pivoted and swung again. Ayrion didn't have the footing to deflect the huge wedge of steel, so he resorted to the only option left and raised his sword to block the hit. With Argon's strength, the force of the blow was sure to send him flying, if not snap his arm altogether.

He held his breath as the blades hit. Remarkably, his swords absorbed the impact, leaving him with nothing more than a sharp jolt. Argon must have been surprised as well, since he took a couple of steps back instead of pressing forward.

"Tiring so soon?" Ayrion taunted, noting he had managed to circle back around to the front of the cabin, leaving Argon's back to the road.

The creature laughed. It was a terrible, dark, thunderous sound. "Hardly. But why should I have all the fun?" The giant vulraak raised his huge wedge of iron into the air. "Come!"

White bodies poured out of the dense tree line from the other side of the road.

Behind him, the cabin door opened, and Ayrion didn't hesitate. He raced for the beam of light spilling across the front walk.

Argon remained where he was, his sword raised, waiting as the others closed in around him. Ayrion slammed the door shut, and Bek threw the bracer back into place.

"Have a nice chat, did we?"

"Informative," Ayrion said, somewhat out of breath as he took up his place on the far side of the window. Something smacked the back of his head. He turned to find Zynora scowling. "What was that for?" he asked, rubbing the sore spot.

"For trying to give me a heart attack." She looked out the window at the growing throng of vulraaks in front of the cabin. "What are they waiting for?"

"They're waiting for us to realize the hopelessness of our situation," Bek said.

Ayrion had to agree. The creatures had them right where they wanted them—isolated, locked inside a wooden box. Even if they somehow managed to break through the vulraaks' ranks, where were they going to go? Ayrion had released the horses.

"Lay down your weapons and join me, and I will spare your lives," Argon called.

"And if we don't?" Ayrion shot back. The answer was obvious, but the longer he could keep Argon talking, the less time they had to spend fighting. It was a long way till dawn.

"Then we will feast well tonight!"

The vulraak horde roared with excitement.

"Give us a moment to consider your generous offer," Ayrion said, then turned to the others. "Any takers?"

Bek snorted. "On the one hand, our lives are spared. On the other, we spend the rest of them as mindless creatures running around Aldor eating people. Sounds like a fate worse than death to me."

Nell cowered against Zynora. "Don't let them take me again."

Zynora hugged the woman close. "Don't worry. We won't let that happen." She looked at Ayrion. "If these are to be our last moments, then I prefer to have them as myself and not something else."

"Then I guess we are in accord?" Ayrion stepped over to the window and shouted, "As kind as your offer is to turn us all into lifeless, bloodsucking leeches, I think we are going to have to refuse."

Argon pointed his sword at the front of the cabin and released a roar that sent the horde scurrying toward them.

Chapter 29 | Ayrion

THE WHITE, HAIRLESS CREATURES stampeded across the front lawn toward the cabin, releasing another of Ayrion's buried memories. Suddenly, Ayrion found himself staring at a wave of monstrous wolf-like creatures charging his position. He stood on a small rise, his swords drawn and bloody, the sky lit with flashes of lightning, and the howls of the oncoming horde were drowned out by a sudden clap of thunder that shook the ground. He turned to look out over the rise and found himself back inside the front room, watching Bek grab a longbow from behind the door and nock the first arrow.

Ayrion set his jaw. He felt he was so close to remembering something important, but as much as he wanted his memories to return, now wasn't the time. He glanced over his shoulder at Zynora. "Stay in the bedroom. We need someone watching that window."

The two women scampered into the back, Nell with one dagger, Zynora with two.

Bek grimaced and kicked out a small section of glass. He sighted and fired his first arrow. A squeal let them know he had hit his mark, but the creature kept running, even with the shaft sticking from its chest.

"Blazes! These things are hard to kill," Bek said.

"Aim for their heads."

"Now you tell me." Bek fired again. This time, the creature dropped with the shaft sticking from its eye. "Better!"

Ayrion could feel the familiar burning sensation building inside him. He swallowed it back. He didn't like using the magic. When he'd fought the sniffer, he'd nearly lost control. It was like a separate entity living inside him, fighting to be free.

Bek released one more arrow, then threw his bow aside and pulled out his hatchets.

They dodged shattered glass as two vulraaks dove through the window. Ayrion didn't give the creatures time to make it to their feet before he was on top of them. He beheaded the first and drove his sword through the second's mouth as it turned to attack. He chopped the arm off another as it tried to pull itself inside. The smell of their blood made him want to retch.

Bek roared as he yanked a hatchet from a vulraak's head. The creature slumped over the window frame, half in, half out, its body still jerking.

The initial rush had come at them with nothing more than their teeth and claws, but those behind were now gathering sticks, rocks, and whatever they could find to use in the attack. One of them was carrying Nell's hoe and tried grabbing Bek with it, the second time that particular tool had been used against him.

Ayrion's blades moved through the air as if some unseen force was directing them: hacking an arm here, opening a stomach there, removing the head of one while severing the backbone of another. He felt powerful. It was as though he were the right hand of death itself.

Pain flashed across his forehead, and he stumbled backward, dimly aware of the rock landing at his feet. He shook his head to focus, momentarily disoriented.

Bek shouted as the next wave of creatures fought to breach the house.

Ayrion wiped the blood away and ran to help.

In his absence, some of the vulraaks had managed to get a foothold inside the cabin. Both men were being pushed farther into the main room as the creatures climbed over their own dead to get inside.

Ayrion cut his way forward, fighting to hold ground. Body parts lay everywhere, and he was finding it hard to gain footing on floors now slick with blood. The smell was unbearable. He fought to swallow the bile that kept rising in the back of his throat.

Their one spark of hope was that Argon hadn't yet seen fit to get involved. He appeared to be enjoying watching his minions from the other side of the yard.

"How big is Belvin, anyway?" Ayrion shouted over his shoulder. "I feel like we're fighting the whole city."

"Not hardly," Bek said as he cut down a couple more of Belvin's finest. "More like one quarter of the shopping district on an Eighthday afternoon."

Ayrion decapitated and kicked the last remaining vulraak back through the window. For the moment, they had managed to thwart the breach. As long as they kept their weapons moving, they held their ground. But how much longer could they manage it before exhaustion took over? Ayrion was already sucking air with every swing.

The sound of shattered glass and snapped wood behind them had both men spinning on their heels. The planks over the bedroom window hung loose from the walls. Zynora and Nell frantically hacked at white arms trying to get in, but a fresh wave of creatures at the front kept them from being able to help.

Ayrion slid his blade through the neck of the first creature trying to get in and chopped an arm off the one beside it. He glanced over his shoulder. Zynora was wielding her daggers like a woman possessed, hacking away at anything that dared reach through. He ducked another stone and opened the front of the vulraak who'd thrown it, leaving it to join its dead comrades on the floor.

Nell shrieked. Ayrion was horrified to see Zynora was on her back, a vulraak on top of her. *How had they gotten in so fast?* Nell was backed into a corner, swinging her knife wildly at another.

Bek roared and barreled into the bedroom. The big trapper slammed both vulraaks against the wall with enough force that Ayrion almost felt sorry for the creatures.

Ayrion could feel the heat of his magic rising, boiling inside him. He feared what it could do, how it might change him. Had he controlled it before he lost his memories, or had it controlled him?

They were about to be overrun, and his heart sank as he realized he didn't have a choice. Taking a deep breath, he finally let go, giving himself completely over to it, holding nothing back.

The heat hit him like a wave, and he tore into the vulraaks, his visions taking over. He could see everything: the direction of their attack, the way they moved, the swing of their arms, the bite of their teeth. He knew what they would do before they did. His body moved as if on its own. He felt free and at the same time bound to the force controlling him. His swords whistled as they cut through the air, the dragon eyes of each crossguard sparkling as they caught the firelight.

The vulraaks fought to reach him, but he hacked them apart. He forced the creatures back to the front until they ran into the pile of their dead and couldn't retreat any farther.

They clawed and screeched and lunged to reach him, but his black steel moved with unnatural speed and accuracy. Limbs flew through the air, entrails spewed across the ground, heads bounced and rolled, and all the while black mist swirled and dissipated.

Argon roared, and the vulraaks pulled back. Those still inside managed to remove the bracer and flee through the front door.

Ayrion let his arms fall to his sides. He stared out the window, panting as he watched the last of the white creatures dash across the yard to where Argon stood waiting.

Ayrion jerked around when something squeezed his shoulder.

"Whoa, there, killer, it's just me." Bek glanced around at the dead, then back at Ayrion. "You sure have a way with unwelcome guests." He walked over and shut the door, replacing the bracer. "Why'd they stop?"

Ayrion stared out the window. "Regrouping, maybe."

"They'll be back," Zynora said as she hobbled out of the bedroom and glanced around at the mutilated bodies covering the floor. "And soon."

Chapter 30 | Ayrion

AYRION CLEANED HIS BLADES on the bits of the creatures' clothing that weren't already stained with blood. They had piled the bodies up under the window, which gave them room to maneuver and had the added benefit of slowing down any attackers trying to enter. They also re-boarded the bedroom window, stacking whatever furniture they had in front.

Outside, Argon's roar and the answering howls of the vulraaks signaled the next wave of attacks. Ayrion watched as they poured across the front lawn. His arms felt like lead; his lungs burned. He chopped the legs off the first. It continued crawling toward him, using nothing but its arms. He put an end to it with a swift thrust to the head. Pulling the blade free, he opened the chest of the next and kicked it out the window.

Bek bellowed as he swung his hatchets. Pieces of limbs, globs of blood, and strings of guts flew everywhere. He kicked a vulraak to Ayrion and was turning to the next when the front door ripped off its hinges and hit him in the face. He flew across the room and landed in a heap against the far wall, stunned but conscious, as pieces of the door rained down on him.

Argon ducked and stepped inside.

Ayrion stabbed the next vulraak in the neck, his blade slipping through the creature and catching a second behind it. He yanked his sword free and turned to face their leader. The rest of the vulraaks seemed to be holding at the window, not wanting to get in Argon's way.

Nell and Zynora worked frantically to get Bek back on his feet. Zynora's hand, which was cupped around the back of Bek's neck, was glowing a soft lavender.

Even bent, Argon's head scraped the ceiling as he turned and smiled. "It's been millennia since I've enjoyed such sport. I'd forgotten the rush of combat." He pointed at Ayrion. "I'll give you one last chance. Join us."

"And do what?" Ayrion asked, flipping a dead vulraak onto its back with his boot. "Become one of these pathetic creatures? I'll take my—"

A loud crack outside caught everyone's attention. It sounded like lightning.

It came again, louder, as if getting closer.

Ayrion looked out the front window and spotted an ugly green-and-yellow tinker wagon flying out of the darkness with a crazy white-haired specter of a man standing at the front. *Is that Tameel?* Ayrion couldn't believe his own eyes. Why was he there? For that matter, how did he know where to find them?

The team of horses thundered down the road and onto the open drive leading to the front of the house. Those vulraaks unlucky enough to find themselves in the horses' path were trampled as Tameel snapped his whip to keep them running.

Argon bellowed, and Ayrion dove to the left as the general's sword buried itself in the floorboards where he'd been standing. He rolled back to his feet and turned, ready to block the next attack.

Argon yanked his weapon free and lunged.

Zynora shouted something, and a loud boom echoed through the cabin. A gale of wind sent Ayrion tumbling across the bodies of the dead. Argon disappeared. Ayrion rolled to a stop against what was left of the front wall and staggered to his feet. *What just happened?* His ears were ringing. He felt numb.

He steadied himself, staring at the enormous hole through the cabin wall where Argon had been standing. Outside, a swath of white bodies lay plastered to the ground, from the house halfway to the road. At the end of the cleanly plowed row lay Argon. He wasn't moving. Those vulraaks still able to move rushed to protect him.

Ayrion turned around to find Zynora standing there with her arms raised. Her eyes rolled up in the back of her head and she collapsed. Bek caught her up before she hit the floor. Had she just done that? He turned back around. "We've got to get out of here." The others joined him at the front. "Stay close."

Outside, Tameel angled the wagon between the horde of vulraaks circling Argon and the cabin.

"I'll hold them back," Ayrion said, "while you get the women inside the wagon."

Bek nodded and threw Zynora's unconscious body over his shoulder.

The wagon pulled in front of what was left of Bek's home. Tameel beat at the creatures with his whip. "Get them inside! Quickly now!"

Ayrion raced to the back of the wagon, cutting down one white-skinned creature after another. Most had remained with their leader, but there were still plenty willing to risk his swords for a taste of his flesh.

Bek tossed the two women in the back, slammed the door, and turned to help Ayrion keep the vulraaks from reaching them.

"Get those horses moving!" Ayrion shouted as he ran to the front and gutted two more crazies who'd managed to get through Tameel's whips.

"I'm right behind you," Bek shouted.

Ayrion spun and, with a single stroke, took another head. "Behind you!"

Bek went down, clawed from behind. The trapper kicked the legs out from under the vulraak and, as soon the creature hit the ground, buried his hatchet in its head. Ayrion helped him to his feet, and he climbed up beside Tameel.

"What are you waiting for?!" Tameel shouted.

"Go!" Ayrion said. There was another wave coming their way. "Get out of here. I'll hold them back and meet you at the road." If he didn't manage to stop them, they'd never get the horses moving.

Tameel didn't argue. He snapped the reins. "Hyah! Move those legs! Hyah!"

The horses bolted, and the wagon lurched forward.

Thankfully, the drive leading from the road to the cabin wasn't the only way out. The cleared path continued on past the house and angled back around, rejoining the road a little farther down. If they had been forced to try turning the wagon around and leaving the same way they'd entered, the vulraaks would have had them.

Ayrion turned to meet the charge. His heart sank when he spotted Argon in the back, attempting to stand. Ayrion raised his swords. They were heavy in his hands. He danced and dodged, keeping just out of reach, letting his visions guide him. The wagon and his friends were halfway to the road. He had to hurry.

He turned to make a run for it and dropped to the ground. He felt more than saw the huge blade soar over his head.

Argon roared and spun for another swing.

Ayrion had never seen anything so big move so fast. He raised both swords and took the brunt of the hit, barely deflecting the blow. Argon swung again. And again. If not for whatever power Ayrion's blades possessed, the sheer strength of the creature would have driven him into the ground.

Argon swung and cut two vulraaks in half, trying to reach Ayrion. He clearly didn't have any qualms with killing his own if they got in his way. The rest quickly backed to a safe distance, giving their leader ample room to fight.

Ayrion's back was now to the cabin. On his left, the wagon was nearing the back entrance of the drive. If he stood any chance of surviving this, he needed to reach the front entrance and catch the wagon as it passed.

Argon swung again.

This time, instead of blocking, Ayrion ducked underneath and ran. Any vulraak stupid enough to get in his way was cut down. He could hear Argon giving chase behind him.

Ayrion's breath caught in his throat as Tameel cut the horses hard to the right, and the wagon started to tip as it veered back onto the road. Tameel never let up with his whip, and the wagon eventually righted itself once more.

Ayrion's legs were giving out, his strength nearly depleted. *"Run!"* he screamed, his coat billowing behind him as he sprinted ahead. He focused on his breathing. His heart felt like it was about to beat out of his chest, and his legs were on fire.

Behind him, Argon tore through the last of his white-skinned horde. The creature's strides far outmatched Ayrion's. With every step, he was gaining ground.

"Run, boy! Run!" Tameel shouted from the front as he struggled to keep the wagon on the road.

Bek stood and raised Tameel's crossbow. He released a bolt, and it flew past Ayrion's head.

Argon screamed. Ayrion glanced over his shoulder and noticed the arrow jutting out of Argon's chest, but he didn't slow.

Almost there. Ayrion reached the road just ahead of the horses and leaped. But instead of grabbing for the wagon's rail, he dove to the side and rolled into the ditch.

A stone the size of a man's head smashed into the side of the wagon, splitting the wood and tipping it onto two wheels. There was nothing he could do but watch as the wagon finally righted itself and flew past. "Get out of here!" he yelled at them.

Ayrion wasn't sure if Tameel had heard or not, but the wagon never slowed. Another crack of the whip echoed through the surrounding trees, and the wagon and his friends disappeared from view.

"Your friends have abandoned you," Argon said with a smile as he slowed, knowing Ayrion had nowhere to go.

Ayrion crawled out of the ditch and up onto the road, taking a moment to brush the dirt from his coat, gloves, and pants.

"I'm going to enjoy watching you die," the vulraak said.

Ayrion stopped in the center of the road and waited, nothing but moonlight between them. He felt a small sense of relief. If this was to be his end, he couldn't have asked for a more fitting one than protecting those he cared for. He almost chuckled. He was a Guardian Protector after all.

Argon swung for Ayrion's legs, and Ayrion leaped over the blade, barely high enough to clear it. He fought from one side of the road to the other, blocking, dodging, lunging, deflecting, never getting the upper hand. His breath trailed behind him as he flitted across the dirt and rock, each strike of his blades sending sparks floating into the air around him.

The rest of the vulraaks watched from the sides of the road, not willing to interfere.

Ayrion's left arm gave way, and he missed his parry, barely managing to get out of the way of the blade as it struck beside him. He wasn't going to last much longer. He could hardly breathe. His opponent was bigger and stronger and hadn't spent the last few hours fighting for his life. But Ayrion had his gifts—if only he knew how to use them. If his memories had been intact, maybe he could have found a way out of this.

Stumbling backward, Ayrion narrowly escaped losing his right leg. He swung for Argon's chest, forcing the vulraak to retreat, but only slightly. Ayrion raised his swords. His knees were wavering, and his arms could barely keep the blades high enough to block. One more hit and he was done for.

He gritted his teeth and waited.

Argon smiled. He could see it too. Ayrion didn't have anything left. Raising his huge wedge of steel, he started forward.

Ayrion attempted to lift his swords one last time.

Something flew out of the forest to his left and slammed into the monstrous vulraak, catching Argon off balance and throwing him into the ditch on the opposite side of the road.

Ayrion nearly shouted as the black warhorse pulled alongside and whinnied. He sheathed one of his swords and grabbed a handful of mane. With every ounce of strength he could muster, he pulled himself up onto its back, and the stallion took off.

"No!"

Ayrion turned. Argon was back on his feet and running. Who knew what kind of magic the ancient creature possessed? Maybe he never tired. Suddenly, as if reading Ayrion's thoughts, his horse picked up speed.

Argon was falling behind. Five yards. Ten. Fifteen. At the last moment, the vulraak leaned back and threw his enormous weapon straight at them.

Ayrion raised his sword, and the wedge of iron hit, the impact nearly ripping his sword from his hand, and flew off into the woods on the left side of the road.

Ayrion couldn't believe his luck. Clutching his sword to his chest, he laid his head against his mount's neck and stroked his mane. "I guess a good deed never goes unnoticed. Does it, my friend?"

The horse snorted.

Once he was reasonably sure he'd lost the vulraak, Ayrion slowed the stallion to a stable trot. The road behind him was empty. The stars were still out but not quite as bright, meaning the creatures would have to seek shelter soon. He doubted they had time to chase after him with dawn approaching.

At the crossroads, Ayrion turned his horse back toward the rover camp. How had the ancient creature been able to transform an entire city into a mindless horde of bloodthirsty savages? According to Bek, it hadn't taken all that long. What was to stop Argon from simply taking more cities, or entire kingdoms for that matter? Even more troubling was the fact that someone had to have released him in the first place.

Chapter 31 | Valtor

V ALTOR STOOD AGAINST the strength of the wind like one of the foreboding statues sculpted into the White Tower's ramparts and watched as the main gates opened below.

A single rider entered.

Valtor headed back inside, his crimson robes billowing out behind him. He glided down the steps to meet his guest. Both rider and mount were awaiting him in the main lobby by the time he reached the second-floor balcony. Normally, a rider's mount would be stabled with the rest of the animals, but in this instance, that would have proven detrimental to the horses and the handlers.

The guards worked to close the two massive doors, and the hollow echo of the impact filled the hall.

"My dear Mangora, I hope you have good news for me," he said, leaning over the railing as the old witch and her eight-legged pet crossed the dark marble floors below. "But since I don't see the boy, I take it you don't." He turned before she could reply and swept down the long corridor to the assembly room and his personal chambers.

The guards at the end of the hall opened the doors and bowed as he approached. With a wave of his hand, the enormous hearth on the left wall burst to life, sending shadows scurrying about the room for cover. The only other light came from the moon pouring in long windows on the opposite wall. The pale blue light contrasted sharply with the amber of the roaring fire.

Valtor moved around to the front of the long stone table and sat in the seat closest to the flame. It was larger than the other twelve, a benefit of his station. He leaned his wolf-head staff against the arm and waited.

He could hear the clicking of the arachnobe's feet against the cold stone as Mangora made her way down the long corridor. He hated spiders. Having to share a room with one large enough to saddle made his skin crawl.

Mangora stopped at the entrance, taking a moment to look around the room. "It's been a while."

"Sixteen years," he said.

"Can't say I miss the place." She slid from the creature's back, and it followed her in. The two guards at the door kept their distance. They looked relieved when Valtor gave them a nod to leave and shut the doors.

He waited for the witch to find a seat, but she chose instead to hobble over and stand in front of the hearth, aiming her bony backside at the flames. A satisfied whimper escaped her lips as she closed her eyes and drank in the warmth. "Hmm, it's the little things."

"What happened to the boy?"

Mangora kept her eyes closed and hiked her dress up to her waist. "He escaped."

Valtor gripped the arm of his chair. "You mean you let him escape."

"I didn't *let* him do anything," she said, opening her eyes. "He had help."

"From who, the local pig farmer?"

Mangora's eyes flared. "No. From the Sidaran overlord himself. Barl and his guards were at the boy's house when we arrived. They must have already been aware of his value."

Valtor considered the implications. He hadn't expected the leader of Sidara to be involved with the ven'ae. Barl had never publicly denounced wielders, but he had never been a sympathizer, either. He was somewhat of a conundrum. But clearly, if he'd been riding the fence up until this point, he was certain to have picked a side now.

"This could be a problem," he said, drumming his fingers on the table. "He'll recall the Sidaran Lancers, if he hasn't already." That was something Valtor had been hoping to prevent.

"How will this be a problem?" Mangora asked as she hobbled over to take a seat in one of the vacant chairs. "The overlord is only one man. Leaders can be replaced, as we've already seen."

"Yes, but it took years of careful planning and strategic maneuvering from the inside to do it, not an open attack."

"You managed it quite nicely with Cylmar," she said with a smirk. "I heard Overlord Saryn quite lost his head in the process. So, why not Sidara?"

"Why not Keldor and Briston while we're at it?" He pressed his thumbs against his temples. "We were able to usurp Cylmar because Overlord Saryn was a greedy son of a faerie and practically gave us the means by which to do it. Barl, on the other hand, is not a fool. If it became known that we were openly working to seek his downfall, we would have every other kingdom in Aldor uniting against us. Hence my statement: *this could be a problem.*"

"Let them unite," Mangora said, striking the table with her fist. "We will squash them like we did Cylmar."

"Maybe . . . maybe not. If we were to go to war with the other kingdoms, we could lose. Worse, it could spark a revolution within our own. Dakaran would lose the throne, and the Tower would lose the means by which to keep Elondria in line.

"Our best option is to pull back, build our defenses, and maneuver our pieces around the political board. Patience is our ally. You don't bring drastic change overnight unless you want the people to rebel." He leaned back in his seat. "Why fight for what you want right now when it's so much easier to have them hand it to you later?"

Mangora smiled.

"Still," Valtor said, looking directly at her, "I find it hard to believe that someone as capable as you, when given the chance to kill the overlord, would have found one man and his guards to be more than you and your insects could handle."

The large arachnobe shifted from its place in the corner and looked his way, firelight reflecting off its three eyes.

"There were more than just the guards to contend with. They had help from Easthaven's Wielder Council. Unlike the other councils we've dealt with in the past, this one was quite . . . resourceful. Not to mention organized. They defeated three of our bulradoer and dispatched an entire squad of Black Watch. The single surviving bulradoer tells me they have a Night Walker helping them."

Valtor's head lifted. "A Night Walker? Are you sure?"

"Of course I'm sure."

Valtor gazed at the long windows on the far wall in thought. The thin curtains draping either side of each window swayed gently as if being rustled by a soft breeze that didn't exist. He had always wondered why they did that and had concluded that they had been spelled that way at some point in the distant past. "What would a Night Walker be doing in Aldor? Their kind hasn't been seen since they abandoned their duty a thousand years ago." He traced a vein in the table's white stone. "This can't be mere coincidence."

"One more thing," she said. "The faeling has come into his power."

Valtor leaned back in his chair and sighed. "Yes, well, we knew he would."

"It appears, though, that he's been reluctant to use it. He's not aware of how powerful he could become."

"Where is he now?"

"With Nyalis."

Valtor ground his teeth. "That wizard is like a bad rash. Always popping up where you least expect."

"You would know better than anyone," she said. He didn't miss the accusation in her tone.

Valtor didn't like being reminded of his past. The tutelage he had received from Nyalis as a young man had been the best years of his life—until Nyalis left, halting Valtor's education. He had even refused to take him to Aero'set for proper training.

Nyalis had said there was too much darkness in his heart, that his desire for vengeance was too strong. The old fool hadn't faced the things Valtor had as a child. Magic wasn't banned when Nyalis was growing up. What did he know?

"Yes, if anyone would know, it would be me, which is why I told you not to underestimate him. He might be as old as the Khezrian Wall, but he is far from an invalid. The man's been around for centuries, hiding himself away in that sanctuary of his, studying, planning, scheming."

"What do you think he'll do next?"

"He will begin training the boy." Valtor balled his fists at the thought of the faeling being taken to the very place he'd been denied. "Did you at least manage to set your affairs in order before your embarrassing defeat?"

Mangora winced at the jab. "I left our little faeling a gift, one he will find most captivating."

"And how is he supposed to find this . . . gift?"

She smiled, revealing that half of her front teeth were missing. "It will find him."

Chapter 32 | Ty

D AWN SEEMED TO COME earlier that day as Ty stumbled out of bed and made his way to the kitchen to see what his mother had on the stove. It wasn't until he rounded the corner and found Adarra standing over the pot, stirring the oats, that the realization caught up with him, and all the anger, guilt, and sorrow he'd buried the previous night surfaced all over again.

"Good morning," she said when she saw him. "Get any sleep?"

"Not much," he mumbled as he grabbed a couple of bowls from the cabinet and set four places around the table.

The breakfast table was quiet, everyone staring at their bowls. Occasionally, someone would lift a spoon to their mouth and slurp. Ty noted the lack of fresh bread. Of all the things to think about, he couldn't pull himself away from the fact that there wasn't a hot loaf on the table. His mother always made bread to dip in the oats. His eyes burned. Dropping his spoon, he left the table and walked outside to saddle Waddle.

By the time the rest had finished eating, Ty had all four horses saddled and ready to go. Swinging into the saddle, he followed his family down the path to the main road. From there they headed east.

"Are you riding straight over to see Lyessa?" his father asked them. "Or will you be stopping in town first?" Overlord Barl had asked Ty's father to attend the Sidaran Assembly that afternoon.

"We'll go straight over," Breen said, no doubt hoping to catch Fraya. Adarra had mentioned that Fraya was spending a good deal of time at the overlord's home, nursing Aiden. Neither Fraya, Lyessa, nor Overlord Barl had been out to the cottage since Ty and Breen's return, so Breen thought it a good idea to let them know they were safe.

Ty was actually looking forward to seeing Lyessa, surprising as that was. He knew the battle with Mangora had altered their relationship, but he wasn't sure by how much.

Crossing Wood Lane, they parted ways with their father as he headed toward the Sidaran Assembly Hall, and the three siblings continued up River Street. Ty spared a passing glance at the alleyway where he'd first met the witch, Mangora. The very thought of her had him twisting the reins in his hands. One day, they were going to meet again, and it wasn't going to end well for her.

Orlyn was sweeping the front of his shop when they passed. Ty pulled himself from his musings long enough to wave. Orlyn acknowledged him with a bright smile and a wave of his own.

A good half hour later, the three reined in at the foot of a large stone staircase leading up to the overlord's grand estate. Lancer sentries in their green-and-gold livery took their horses and escorted them up to the entrance. Lord Barl's home seemed to be crawling with soldiers. They lined the front lawn around the garden, and others were positioned near the outbuildings. Ty spotted a few patrolling near the tree line. The overlord clearly didn't believe they were out of danger and was taking every precaution.

The day was cold. Even with the sun breaking above the tops of the trees, Ty couldn't help but shiver. He pulled his cloak tighter around his shoulders as an icy gust of wind swept across the front of the house.

He felt sorry for his sister. He knew she had to be freezing, even though she fought not to show it. She had decided to wear one of her most becoming outfits. One that revealed more than she was normally comfortable with. And the thin cloak over it was hardly enough to cut the chill.

He wasn't used to seeing Adarra like this. She had always been the reserved one, never into fancy dresses and silk lace. Not that what she was wearing would have been considered fancy by any of the girls in town.

Ty shook his head. Aiden didn't deserve her attention.

The manor's doors were opened for them, revealing a well-lit entryway. They were greeted by a tall man in a green-and-gold uniform complete with a feathered hat and white gloves. "Master Breen, Master Ty, is that really you?" Piel, the overlord's chamberlain, beamed.

Breen smiled. "It's good to see you again. I heard you took care of our family while we were away. I would like to offer you my gratitude."

"It was my pleasure, Master Breen," Piel said with a short bow before ushering them inside the foyer. "It was a breath of fresh air to have them here while they recovered. Overlord Barl, Creator bless him, is a wonderful man, but he can be quite fussy at times." He tapped the side of his angular nose and winked. The brothers chuckled.

Adarra was too busy trying to keep her teeth from chattering to join in the joke. "Is Fraya still here?" she asked.

"Yes, I believe she is. But let me direct you first to my lord's study. I'm sure he will be anxious to hear of your safe return." Without giving them a chance to object, Piel was off, headed for a long hallway tucked between two semicircular staircases.

Ty admired the enormous chandelier that always seemed to catch his attention whenever he visited the manor. It hung all the way to the second-floor railing, spreading a warm glow around the otherwise cold-looking room.

"I thought the overlord was meeting with the Sidaran Assembly," Adarra said as she tried her best to keep up with the others.

"Yes, of course, but that meeting isn't for another couple of hours yet. He's preparing now."

"I wonder why Father left so early, then," Adarra said.

Breen glanced over his shoulder. "He must be meeting with the council first."

They stopped outside a set of decoratively carved doors and waited as Piel knocked.

"Yes?" a voice asked from the other side.

"Master Breen, Master Ty, and Madam Adarra are here to see you, sir."

"Send them in."

The chamberlain opened the door.

As the overlord stood from his seat near the hearth, Ty could see papers spread across the table in front of him. "Breen, Ty, it's good to see you. We feared the worst." Barl crossed the room with a limp, and instead of taking their hands, he hugged each in turn. Fighting side by side in battle had evidently afforded its privileges. "When did you arrive?"

"A couple of nights ago," Breen said.

Barl looked at Ty. "The last I saw of you, young man, I wouldn't have laid a wager on your survival. That wizard of yours must have quite the gift." Ty smiled, and the overlord turned and headed back to the fire. "Come, tell me all about it. Lyessa and Fraya are upstairs with Aiden, but I'm sure they'll be down soon enough once Piel relays news of your arrival."

The three followed the overlord to a small sitting area in front of the hearth and took the settee across from him.

"I want to offer my strongest condolences for your loss. Your mother was one of the bravest women I know, and her dedication to her family is beyond words. She will be sorely missed."

Ty attempted and failed to hold a strong face. He was thankful that his brother was the first to speak.

"Thank you, my lord. That means more than you know."

"Yes, well . . ."

No one knew quite what to say; the silence was filled with the crackling and popping of the fire.

Barl turned to one of the guards at the door. "Have Piel bring drinks."

"Yes, Your Lordship."

Barl leaned back in his chair. "So, tell me, where did that wizard end up taking you? The last we saw, you were heading north."

Ty looked at Breen to see who would speak first, but by the time he realized Breen was waiting on him, the door to the study burst open, and Lyessa and Fraya hurried in.

Ty joined Breen and Adarra in standing to greet the new arrivals. Fraya threw her arms around Breen, and for a brief moment, Ty thought Lyessa was about to do the same to him. Instead, she stopped just short, then punched him in the arm.

"Ow! What was that for?"

"That was for not coming to see me sooner." She took a step back and stared at the top of his head.

"What are you looking at?"

"Your white hair. I'm trying to decide if I like it or not." She pursed her lips. "Hmm. I think I do. Makes you look . . . older."

"If the young ladies are quite done with their greetings," Lyessa's father said, "these two were about to regale me with the tale of their journey to Meerwood, if that's indeed where they went."

They moved to the larger sofa to accommodate Fraya and Lyessa.

"It is," Ty said as he took his seat beside Lyessa. She smelled of honeysuckle. It was intoxicating.

On the end of the sofa, Adarra's attention kept straying toward the door. A knock had her jumping in her seat. But instead of Aiden, Piel and some of the kitchen staff entered with drinks and desserts for the group.

"That's a very pretty dress, Adarra," Lyessa remarked, taking a goblet from one of the trays.

"What, this old thing?" Adarra shook her head with a nervous chuckle.

The look on Lyessa's face said she was hardly fooled. "Here, why don't you take this up to Aiden?" She handed Adarra one of the goblets. "He's still claiming to be too weak to leave the bed, so I'm sure he'd appreciate the company."

Adarra grabbed the cup. "Well, only if you think it's necessary." She stood and made a quick retreat through the door.

"And make sure he drinks the whole thing," Lyessa said with a wink to Fraya.

"I will," Adarra called back over her shoulder, hurrying into the hallway and disappearing around the corner. The two girls giggled. Even Breen chuckled.

Ty thought Adarra was acting like a complete fool. He took a sip of his spiced cider and let the warmth coat his dry throat.

Beside him, Lyessa purred as she drank hers. Ty noticed she was back to wearing her fluffy gowns again. As much as he enjoyed seeing her in them, he missed the leather trousers and top she'd worn during their battle with the Tallosians. Realizing what he was doing, he turned his head. What was he thinking, ogling the overlord's daughter right in front of the overlord? Ty forced his attention back to his drink.

After helping himself to a refill, he joined his brother in entertaining the group with the story of their journey to Meerwood. It was also another reminder of the commitment he'd made. Nyalis hadn't exactly given him a deadline to start his quest, but if he waited too long, the wizard might grow impatient.

"I don't see why you need to go running off on some insane mission to find an old magic school," Lyessa said. "You're only sixteen. Doesn't that crazy wizard know that?"

Ty's smile started to slip. "What does my age have to do with it? My magic is becoming a danger to me and to others. I need to understand how it works so I can control it. There might be answers there as to who or what I am." Not to mention, it was his best chance at finding a way to kill Mangora.

"I don't understand why we can't go with you," she said.

Ty shrugged. "The rules, evidently."

"What rules? What if something happens?"

"I don't—"

"How are you going to defend yourself? You can barely hold a sword."

"Lyessa," her father butted in. "After what we've seen him do, I'd say Ty's more than capable of defending himself."

Ty shifted in his seat. At least someone recognized his talents.

"I believe, my lord," Breen said, holding his empty glass protectively between his hands, "that it might be prudent for us to plan for the protection of Sidara in the coming days."

Ty was thankful for his brother's intervention.

"Like father, like son," Barl said with a smile. "Your father, Ambassador Lanmiere, and myself spent the better part of last week discussing that very concern. Perhaps the two of you should join us this afternoon for our meeting with the assembly. Since you are familiar with this wizard, maybe you could shed some light on what you think we might be facing."

Breen leaned forward in his seat. "We'd be happy to help in any way we can."

Ty nodded reluctantly, uncomfortable with the prospect of being asked to address the Sidaran Assembly. It was one thing to be an official member of the wielder council, but now he was being asked to address the governing body of Sidara. Did Barl expect him to reveal his identity to the assembly?

"Capital." Lyessa's father scooted to the edge of his seat. "Well, I don't want to keep you chatting with a worn-out old man like me when you have far prettier company to entertain."

"Father," Lyessa scolded. "You're not old."

Barl stood, and the others joined him.

"If you wouldn't mind, sir," Breen said, "we would like to pay our respects to Master Raycrest. We heard he was injured trying to protect our mother and sister from the Northmen, and we thought while we were here—"

"Yes, yes, of course. Good idea." Lord Barl turned to Lyessa. "Would you take them up, dear?"

"Yes, Daddy." Lyessa kissed her father on the cheek and then led them out.

Chapter 33 | Ty

L YESSA LED THEM BACK to the main foyer and up the left stairs to the second floor. Behind her, Ty took a moment to glance at the portraits decorating the wall. Each depicted a former lord or lady in various settings. The first held a bow, ready to shoot, hounds baying in the foreground while a covey of grouse flew in the back. Ty thought that if this were meant to be a realistic depiction, then the lord must have been blind. He was aiming his bow in the wrong direction.

He scanned the rest as he made his way to the top of the stairs: a lady playing a harp in a sitting room, a man holding a lavish feast, a lancer of unknown rank riding a white stallion. It was clear that Lyessa's ancestors thought very highly of themselves.

Behind him, Ty could hear Fraya and Breen whispering. He didn't turn around, but he smiled at the thought of his tough, woodsy brother being *led* around by a girl nearly half his size. The thought vanished when Ty's arm was suddenly jerked to the left as Lyessa led *him* down the next hall. At least Fraya was gentle about it.

"So, how is your betrothed?" Ty asked, attempting to walk beside her without accidentally stepping on her dress. "Relaxing comfortably, I presume?" Knowing Aiden, he was probably decked in a satin robe under silk sheets with servants waiting on his every whim. What did Adarra see in him, anyway?

"He's not my betrothed," Lyessa said, turning down the next hall.

"I thought . . ."

"Well, you thought wrong."

Ty smiled but turned his head so she wouldn't see.

"As terrible as the battle was, it did make some things very clear."

"Like?"

"Like I have no intention of marrying a man who . . ." She didn't finish, but Ty got the picture. Lyessa wouldn't be with a man who was afraid to stand his ground and fight.

They stopped outside the fourth door on the right, and Ty took a deep breath. He wasn't sure how he would respond to seeing Aiden again, especially after what he'd done to Ty. But then again, Aiden had nearly died trying to protect Ty's mother and sister from the Northmen, which was more than Ty had been able to do. Again, he bit his tongue, trying unsuccessfully to think of anything but how he had failed his mother.

Lyessa knocked, waited a moment, then peeked inside. "You decent?"

"I would hope so, with me sitting here," Adarra said from the other side of the door.

Lyessa released her hold on Ty's arm and opened the door the rest of the way. "You have some visitors, Aiden."

Ty was grateful she had relinquished his arm. Lyessa and Aiden might not still have been betrothed, but it would have looked awkward nonetheless.

He followed her in, with Breen and Fraya just behind.

Aiden smiled from his seat against some pillows at the head of his bed. "Ty. Breen. It's good to see you. We were worried."

Ty didn't respond.

Aiden was in his nightshirt, with his covers pulled to his waist. It was the most natural-looking Ty had ever seen him. No satin robe, no lace tunic, no powdered face. Just a simple white three-button shirt.

"Master Raycrest." Breen bowed slightly. "I believe we owe you a debt."

I wouldn't go that far, Ty thought.

"We wanted to see how you were doing and offer you our sincere thanks."

Aiden lowered his head. "You owe me nothing." He looked at Adarra, who was sitting quietly in a chair next to his bed. "Truly, the praise goes to your sister and your mother. If not for them, I wouldn't be here today."

Ty's mouth opened slightly. Was this the same Aiden Raycrest? Amazing what a single brush with death could do to a man.

"Not forgetting Fraya, of course," Aiden added, offering her a warm smile. "If not for her healing, my family would be mourning my passing as we speak."

Breen took a step toward the door. "We'll let you get your rest, then. We have a meeting in town to get ready for."

Ty turned and started for the door. *That wasn't as bad as—*

"Ty, could you wait a moment?"

Ty stopped just shy of the handle and slowly turned back around.

Aiden looked at Lyessa. "Do you mind if I talk with Ty privately?"

Lyessa cast a curious glance in Ty's direction before shrugging and walking to the door. She waited for Adarra and the others to step out before shutting it behind her.

Ty's stomach churned. What could Aiden possibly want to talk to him about? Was he waiting for everyone to leave so he could tell Ty what he really thought of him? Did he think Ty was trying to encroach on his arrangement with Lyessa?

"Ty, I need to ask your forgiveness."

Ty froze, his mouth agape.

Aiden folded his hands in his lap, barely managing to look at Ty. "I have nothing to blame but my own cowardice. When I tried to hand you over, I wasn't doing it to save the others. I was doing it to save . . . me."

Even though Aiden's confession wasn't anything Ty didn't already know, Ty was still left speechless. He stared at Aiden, not sure how to respond. He was making it really hard for Ty to hate him. Why wasn't Aiden saying anything? Was he waiting on Ty to say something? The silence was growing uncomfortable. "There's—"

"Can you forgive me?"

Ty stopped, the tension easing as he released a slow exhale. He hadn't realized he'd been holding his breath. "There's nothing to forgive. If it had been me, I might have done the same thing." Ty's own shame seemed to be pulling the words out of him. "There's things we all regret that are best left in the past."

Aiden studied him for a moment. "That's very noble of you to say, but somehow I doubt that in my place, you would have done the same."

Ty wanted to say something sarcastic like *You're right, I wouldn't have.* But he couldn't bring himself to do it, especially not after such a completely humbling admission. "Then your apology is accepted."

Aiden relaxed, his relief evident. "Thank you."

Ty nodded. He stood there a moment longer and, when nothing else was said, opened the door. "We'll stop by again in a day or so." He passed Adarra on his way out.

Adarra took her seat beside the bed, and Fraya stuck her head in the door. "I'll be back tomorrow to check on you." She shut the door all but a crack.

"You two go on ahead," Lyessa said with a wink to Fraya. "We'll catch up."

Gladly accepting the offer for some alone time with Ty's brother, Fraya snatched Breen's arm and guided him back toward the entry staircase. Lyessa took Ty's arm and turned them in the opposite direction.

"Where are we going?"

"I'm giving Fraya and your brother some time to talk. She's been practically beside herself with worry over the last few days. They could use a private moment. Besides, we've got some talking of our own to do, don't you think?"

"We do?"

"So, what did Aiden have to say?"

Ty thought a moment. "He wanted me to know that he wasn't going to let you go without a fight, and that as soon as he was healed, he'd demand a duel."

Lyessa stopped, her eyes as wide as her mouth as she spun him around. "He said what?"

Ty snickered. "He wanted to apologize for trying to hand me over to the witch."

Lyessa huffed and punched him in the arm, then started down the hall once more. "He actually said he was sorry?"

"I know," Ty said, catching up. "Shocked me, too."

"I'm impressed," she said. "But that's not what we need to talk about."

"It's not?"

"No." She pulled him to a stop. "We need to talk about this nonsense of you leaving."

He sighed. "There's nothing to talk about. I need to understand how these abilities work. Nyalis said he could train me, but for that to happen, I have to find this wizard's keep."

"This Nyalis character seems to have a lot of demands," she said. "Why can't you take anyone with you?" She scooted a little closer and slowly ran her finger down the side of his arm, the same arm she'd just bruised a moment ago. "I could come with you if you want." She batted her eyes.

Ty's jaw dropped. He wasn't sure what shocked him more, Aiden's apology or Lyessa's flirting. Was this the same girl who had just recently cut a man's head off in front of him? He closed his mouth with a gulp. "Nyalis was clear. I can't take anyone with me. Besides, I wouldn't want you to get hurt."

"Hurt? I was the one saving you, remember?"

A fact Ty was painfully aware of. "I know. I just—"

"I can take care of myself."

"I'm not saying you can't. Ugh. You're impossible."

She smiled as though she'd beaten him once again. He hated when she did that. It was her way of making it seem she was always right.

"Let's go see if Breen and Fraya are ready," he said, this time pulling her along.

They turned the next corner and glided down the opposite stairwell from the one they had ascended earlier and made their way across the marble-tiled floor to the front entrance.

One of the guards opened the door, and they stepped through. As soon as they saw Fraya's arms wrapped around Breen's neck at the bottom of the steps, they quickly turned their heads, trying to appear inconspicuous, and ended up facing one another.

Ty's mouth went dry as he found himself staring into Lyessa's deep-green eyes. They were bright, full of excitement. His heart was pounding. She really was one of the most beautiful girls he'd ever seen. His feelings were starting to get the better of him. How long had this been going on? It didn't seem so long ago that he'd wanted to strangle her with his bare hands, and now he wanted to wrap those hands around her.

Things were moving too fast. She was the daughter of the overlord, and he was the son of her father's gamekeeper. This whole trip to find the lost Keep of Aero'set was beginning to look more and more like the perfect solution. They needed some time apart.

Ty managed to pull himself away from Lyessa's gaze.

At the bottom of the stairs, Breen finished his goodbyes with a warm kiss.

"I'll see you at the meeting," Lyessa said, releasing Ty's arm and planting a quick peck on his cheek before he could get away.

Ty nodded, doing his best not to look too embarrassed as he walked down the steps toward his brother. He hoped Breen chalked up the redness in his cheeks to the cold.

The ride back to town was a quiet one. Ty's head was swimming with the possibilities of what lay ahead, not the least of which was their invitation to attend the Sidaran Assembly. What would the assembly do when they found out he was not only a wielder but also a faeling? Probably spend the rest of the meeting arguing which form of execution to use.

Crossing into the merchant district, Ty spotted a figure down one of the alleys, tossing a bucket of scraps from the back of one of the shops. The person was wearing a dark cloak with the hood pulled back. The figure turned and looked at him. Ty's breath caught in his throat, and his hands clenched the reins.

Mangora.

He looked again, then realized the figure was too tall to be Mangora. Whoever it was turned and walked back inside. It took Ty halfway to Wood Lane to calm down, but just thinking about the possibility of having seen her again had him wondering if anyone had been by her shop since the battle.

Ty twisted in his saddle. "I just had a crazy idea."

Breen turned, took one look at Ty, and sighed. "I'm afraid to ask."

Chapter 34 | Ty

WITH THE SIDARAN ASSEMBLY meeting still a few hours away, Ty decided to show his brother where he had first encountered the old witch. He wanted to see what all she'd left behind and if there were any clues as to where she had gone.

He had never wanted to kill someone before, but there was nothing he wanted more than to look her in the eyes and watch the spark of life fade away. He didn't like the feeling—a constant pressure in his chest, threatening to crush him—but the witch needed to die. He doubted his mother was the only person to have died because of her.

The sun was out and shining but doing little to lessen the sting from the early winter's bite. They had seen their first sign of snow two days earlier, a mere dusting, but it was a sure indication that there would be more on the way.

"Your hood," Breen said.

"What?"

He pointed to Ty's head.

"Oh." Ty lifted his hood a little higher to cover his white hair. He needed to find a cap to wear around town. Crazy stuff was becoming a nuisance. He wished he had thought to ask Nyalis to change the color back while they were in Meerwood. It would have made things much easier. But with everything that had happened, it had skipped his mind completely.

River Street was busier than usual. The closest spot for tethering their horses was outside the lamp-wright's, a few buildings up from the small lane where Mangora kept her shop. Ty didn't mind the walk.

Seeing all the people scurrying about their daily lives, completely oblivious to the danger that had recently threatened their very existence, was a calming salve to the dark emotions he was battling. It gave him hope that maybe things could be normal again. He almost laughed. He was a faeling, hunted by the White Tower, now responsible for finding and returning some ancient wizard keep. Who was he kidding? Things were never going to be normal again.

They reached the alley between the spice merchant's and the fuller's, and Ty took a moment to study it. Even in the middle of the day, the narrow street appeared to absorb the light. Above their heads, darkened windows of three-story buildings peered down on them like malevolent eyes.

Ty pulled his cloak tighter. It was cold, but the alley felt colder still. No sign hung over the door, which was no surprise. Mangora had told him the place was spelled. Only those with magic could find it, and most of those would have stayed well clear. Ty wondered how she had managed to scrape up a living all these years.

He inched closer. With each step, he could feel the hairs on his neck rising.

"This is it," he said as he stepped up onto the porch. But instead of opening the door, he stared at the tarnished copper knob. Maybe this wasn't the best idea. What if that spider was in there?

"Are we going in or what?" his brother asked.

Steeling his nerves, Ty turned the handle and gave it a slight push. The door uttered an eerie whine before catching the brass bell that hung above it. Ty jumped at the sound; his hands rose defensively in case he needed to call on his fire.

The shop was silent.

He took a step back and checked the alley, making sure they were alone, then closed his eyes and summoned his magic. It was easier this time. It only took a couple of tries before the warmth in his gut spread up through his chest and out his left arm, where it manifested in blue flame rising from his palm. The flames weren't hot, at least not to him, but they did cast a reasonable amount of light on the entryway.

"Cheerful place, isn't it?" Breen said, looking over Ty's shoulder. "After you, little brother."

"Why do I have to go first?"

"Because you're the one with the light."

Ty released a little more magic, and the flame brightened. He stepped through the door, and Breen followed him in, neither moving as they let their eyes adjust to the darkness.

Ty wrinkled his nose. "This place stinks just as bad as the last time I was here. Smells like death wrapped in fungus, with a touch of decaying old woman thrown in for good measure."

Breen chuckled.

Ty kept his ears tuned for any sign of danger as they made their way around the room. Everything appeared to be the same. The long glass cabinets that lined the wall still held all the same odd knickknacks and curios he had seen before: curved daggers with jeweled handles, gold and silver chalices trimmed with exotic stones, sealed boxes with who knew what inside, crystal vials with strangely colored liquids, glass jars with large ugly insects, some gaudy jewelry, and a few crystal orbs. Ty spotted the display of shrunken heads still hanging in the corner, which he pointed out to Breen.

"She sure has some peculiar tastes," Breen said. "Guarantee you won't find another shop like this in all of Sidara."

Ty grunted. "That's probably a good thing."

They continued on around the shop. The opposite wall held a large assortment of weaponry, including some Ty had never seen before. Breen lifted a black recurve bow and tested its pull. "Good tension." He held it out in front of him, testing its balance. "It's perfect."

The bow was beautifully made, though Ty didn't recognize the wood it had been carved from.

"I wonder if any of these have magical properties," Breen mused aloud, not seemingly expecting an answer. He did that sometimes whenever he found something especially puzzling.

The idea of these weapons being magical hadn't even crossed Ty's mind. It was an interesting thought, though. He wondered if one of them could be used to kill Mangora. It would be worth investigating, but not right now. Something else was calling to him: the small shelf of books at the back. It was one of the reasons he had come in the first place. He wanted to get his hands on something he had seen the last time he was there.

He scanned the stack of old tomes. The books, even though ancient and rather on the dusty side, showed little wear. He wondered if they had been spelled to keep them from deteriorating.

Ty thumbed through the spines. He recognized most from his last visit: *The Foresight of Divination*, *Poison: The Lost Art*, *Reshaping the World*, *Elixirs of Life*, but the book he was most interested in seeing again, *The Hidden Magic of Fae*, was not there. There was a volume he didn't remember seeing before, smaller than the others, almost small enough to fit in his hand. He read the title out loud. "*Hidden Perceptions.*" What did that have to do with magic?

He pulled the book out and blew the dust off the front cover. It seemed plain compared to the others. No decorative markings stamped into the binding. No raised designs or protective corner pieces. Just a simple kettle stitch across the spine, gold lettering for the title, and a small clasp in the shape of a hand to keep the boards closed.

Ty unhooked the clasp and opened the cover. The first page was blank. He flipped through the rest of the pages, but they were empty too.

"Why would Mangora keep an empty book on her shelf?"

"What did you say?" Breen asked, still perusing the weapons cache behind him.

"Nothing. I was just thinking out loud." He scanned the pages once again, this time from back to front.

"I think I'm going to keep this bow," Breen said.

Ty stopped about halfway through the book and looked up.

"It has a good feel in my hands. And this Tallosian bow is worse than useless."

Breen's bow had been broken during their fight with the Northmen, forcing him to make do with one of the leftovers the savages had carried. Breen hung the Tallosian bow where the black one had been. "What do you think?"

Ty shrugged. "I guess. It's just going to go to waste around here."

"Yeah, but knowing where it came from . . ."

"A bow's a bow," Ty said. "You could always try it out when we get home just to make sure it shoots straight."

Breen stared at the sleek curvature of the dark bow before finally nodding and slinging it across his shoulder along with a nearby quiver of black arrows that appeared to go with it. "Wouldn't want it to go to waste, now would we?" His smile was almost giddy. Ever the hunter.

Ty couldn't help but chuckle as he continued flipping through the pages toward the front cover. *Empty. Empty. Empty.* He flipped the last page and stopped, his eyes widening. There was something written on the page that hadn't been there before. Only two words: *They're coming . . .*

Ty was about to call out to Breen when the front bell rang.

"What do you think you're doing in here?" a voice called out.

Ty's first thought was Mangora. Without thinking, he twisted around and threw a ball of fire at the front of the shop.

"What the—" A gust of wind hit the flames, toppling items off the nearest shelves. Loose papers flew around the room as the fire was sent into the rafters and snuffed out.

"What the blazes do you think you're doing, boy? Get ahold of yourself!"

This time Ty recognized the voice. "Feoldor?"

"Who else would be stupid enough to be here?" the man growled. "Other than the two of you, obviously."

"What's wrong, son?" Orlyn asked in back of Feoldor as he tried to smooth the wrinkles from his robe. "You can't tell friend from foe?"

"Sorry, Master Orlyn, I guess I'm a little jumpy." He looked down at the book. Had it somehow known that the two men were coming? Or was it referring to something else? He opened it back up to the page. It was empty. The hairs on his neck rose again.

"Jumpy! My mama's green toe, you were!" Feoldor said in his usual charming way. "You nearly baked us in our skins. If you can't control your powers, you shouldn't be using them."

Orlyn laid a hand on Feoldor's shoulder, then grabbed one of the lanterns hanging on the wall next to the entrance. Producing a small tinderbox from his robe, he lit the wick. "Ah, much better," he said, turning back to Ty and Breen. "Now, where were we? Oh, yes, I was asking what you two were doing in here."

Breen, still wearing the black bow and quiver he had found in the back, moved alongside Ty. "Ty was just showing me where he first met the witch. We wanted to see if there were any clues as to her whereabouts or what she'd been up to."

Orlyn studied them with a careful eye. "And what have you found so far?"

"Not much," Breen said nervously. "Did you know she has shrunken heads? They're over in the corner. I'm not sure if they're real, but pretty interesting either way."

"Yes, we are aware." Orlyn followed Feoldor around to the far side of the shop as they began inspecting Mangora's wares. "You boys need to be very careful handling anything in here. No doubt most of it has been laced with dark magic. No telling what it might do to you."

Breen glanced at Ty.

"We've been careful," Ty lied as he quickly stuffed the little book he'd found inside his coat while their attention was diverted. He didn't want to leave the book behind. If what he'd seen was real and the book could somehow predict danger, he wanted to spend more time studying it. Glancing to his left, he caught his brother running his fingers across the smooth finish of the black bow, probably debating whether to put it back or not.

He didn't.

"My, what a collection." Orlyn bent over one of the counters and scanned the crystal vials and glass jars of liquid and herbs. "Look at this, Feoldor. She has *Juniprus hydrogolis*. I've only ever read of them. Never actually seen one up close. Their medicinal value is said to be incomparable. What I could do with a plant like that."

"Yes, yes, very impressive," Feoldor said, admiring the ruby-lined daggers and gem-studded jewelry. The gold practically shimmered in his eyes as he pressed his nose against the glass.

"Watch it," Orlyn warned with a nudge from his staff. "Don't let yourself get drawn in. Remember who owned this shop. I'm sure everything in here has a dark purpose. Well, most everything," the apothecary said as he went back to studying the exotic herbs. He reached for one of the glass jars. "What I could do with some of this . . ."

Feoldor slapped the old man's hand before it reached its destination. "What do you think you're doing? You just got done telling me how dangerous this stuff is."

Orlyn shook his head, looking a little embarrassed. "Of course." He cleared his throat. "You're right. How silly of me." He moved on down the aisle. "It looks like we'll have our work cut out for us," Orlyn said.

"What do you mean?" Ty was curious about what they were going to do with it all. He would have liked to continue looking through the books, but he couldn't do that with the council around.

"We'll need to inventory the shop and make sure everything is cataloged before we box it up and place it somewhere safe, away from prying hands. There's no telling what kind of damage this stuff could do."

Breen cast another wary eye in Ty's direction, and Ty felt for the book hiding in his pocket. It might not have been the smartest idea to keep it, but if it could possibly help him defeat Mangora, it would be worth it. And who knew? If the book could actually see the future, it might even help him find Nyalis's missing keep. Either way, he felt it was worth the risk. He could always put it back if something didn't feel right.

"Have either of you checked in the back or upstairs?" Orlyn asked.

Ty shook his head. "No, we'd barely made it around the room before you arrived."

"Well, no worry. We'll make a more thorough examination later this week. But for now, Feoldor and I have a meeting at the Assembly Hall. It's a rather historic day," he said, tapping his rune-covered staff on the floor in front of him. "Overlord Barl has asked the wielder council to address the Sidaran Assembly. Can you imagine that? The ruling body of Sidara wanting to talk to a group of ven'ae?"

"Yes, we've heard," Breen added.

"Oh. You have?"

"Lord Barl asked us to attend as well."

"Ah, a wise decision, especially since this all seems to be revolving around our young Master Ty here anyway." He offered Ty an encouraging pat on the back. "It might be beneficial to hear what our illustrious, and rather aloof, wizard had to say about all of this as well."

Feoldor snorted and crossed his arms. "Illustrious, my hiney. Where was the man when we needed him during our battle with the bulradoer?"

"Where do you think?" Ty mumbled under his breath. *What a stupid question.* "He was busy saving *my* life."

Everyone turned and looked at Ty.

Had he just said that out loud? He cleared his throat. "Sorry, Master Feoldor. Something about this place has me on edge."

"Understandable," Feoldor said, fluffing his side whiskers as he glanced around the shop. "This place is giving me the jitters as well."

"Let's be going, then," Orlyn said. "Don't want to linger in here any longer than necessary."

Breen was the first out of the shop, followed by Ty and the two older council members. Orlyn stepped back a few paces from the building, and after scanning the alley to make sure there was no one watching, he raised his staff and mumbled something under his breath.

Ty watched with astonishment as the front of the shop began to sparkle, very similar to the way Nyalis had constructed his protective barrier around Meerwood to keep out unwanted visitors. The shimmering in front of the old shop quickly faded and then vanished altogether.

"What was that?" Breen asked, following Orlyn up the alley.

"That was a protection spell. Something the wizard showed me before he left. It's meant to keep out vandals. It will also let me know if someone tries to get in." He passed a quick glance in Ty's direction.

Ty smiled. He was thankful he had managed to at least get the one book out before they had shown up. But there were others he still wanted to look through.

"Impressive," Breen said.

Orlyn smiled. "Yes, I had no idea I was capable of something like that. Definitely opens up a whole new world of possibilities." The tall apothecary stopped at the head of the alley and started rummaging around in one of the many interior pockets of his shapeless robe. After a while, he produced a small knit cap and handed it to Ty. "Here, this might help around town."

Ty smirked as he took the black cap and quickly put it on. It was surprisingly comfortable. More importantly, it hid his white hair. It always amazed Ty, the obscure collection of stuff the old apothecary carried around inside his robes. It was a wonder he didn't leave a trail of random items spilling out behind him wherever he went. Orlyn was truly a two-legged tinker wagon.

"There's no need to call attention to yourself if it can be helped."

"Thank you. I've been meaning to get one."

"Keep it. It was always a bit too small for my melon, anyway." Orlyn smiled and hurried after Feoldor. "We will see you two there," he said with a wave over his shoulder.

The brothers stood at the alley's entrance and watched as the two council members disappeared into the crowd. "Maybe keeping this stuff wasn't the best idea," Breen said as they walked back to where they had tethered their mounts. "I don't fancy messing with something that might be cursed."

Ty chuckled. "The only reason Orlyn said that was to keep Feoldor from snatching the jewelry. You saw the way he was looking at those ruby daggers; practically had to wipe the drool from his chin. I'm sure it's fine. Mangora was selling that stuff to anyone who walked into her shop."

Breen nodded, but the apprehension in his eyes never really left. "We still have an hour before the Sidaran Assembly meets. Let's stop at the East Inn for a bite."

Ty thought that a good idea. He grabbed Waddle and followed his brother and Acorn up Wood Lane toward River Street. He slid his hand inside his pocket when he thought Breen wasn't looking and gently caressed the spine of the small tome. Had he really seen those words, or had he just imagined it? He was anxious to find out.

Chapter 35 | Ty

T Y HAD NEVER SEEN the inside of the Assembly Hall before. It
had always been the large, mysterious white dome behind the Hall
of Justice, rising above the mansions that lined the west side of River
Street.

After wasting an hour at one of the tables of a nearly vacant East Inn,
too nervous about the upcoming meeting to eat the bowls of stew they
had ordered, the brothers finally left. They'd kept their mounts hitched
at the inn and walked the distance to the assembly building. From the
number of horses already lining the front, it had obviously been a wise
choice.

They headed up the stairs and across the white granite floors of the
atrium, making their way to a set of closed doors they'd been told would
take them into the main assembly chamber. The place was busier than
Ty had expected, men and women scurrying about like mice searching
for a way off a sinking ship.

A pair of Sidaran Lancers stood on either side of the doors, their green uniforms embroidered with the gold crest of Sidara—a large tree with deep roots fanning out in all directions. The guards all carried a sword at their waist and a halberd by their side. Those to the left of the doors held their halberds in their left hands, while those on the right held theirs in their right. Ty thought the bulky weapons would be difficult to wield indoors, especially for the two on the right who had to hold theirs using their sword arm, but it did look impressive.

Lyessa was standing to the left of the guards, waiting on them. She smiled as they approached. "I was starting to wonder if you were coming."

"Are we late?" Breen asked.

"When it comes to the assembly, a quarter of an hour early is considered late." She motioned to the guards, and they opened the doors.

The inside chamber of the Sidaran Assembly was enormous. It was easily the largest room Ty had ever seen, at least three or four times the size of the main room at the East Inn. Rows of stone benches fanned upward from the main floor in a half circle, allowing everyone within to view the stage at the front where the overlord sat.

The room was surrounded by a buttress of fluted pillars built halfway into the wall. They were wide at the base and thinned as they reached the domed ceiling. At the center of the ceiling was a glass skylight, which flooded the chamber with light. A few sporadic torches lined the outer wall, but they were obviously used more for decoration than anything.

The room was awash with color, each assembly member arrayed in their brightest apparel. They mingled about, catching up on the latest gossip. The overlord's sudden convening of the assembly seemed to be the main topic. Evidently, it wasn't usual to hold such gatherings during the colder months, but with most of the men and women of the assembly living within the city limits, it was hardly an inconvenience.

The overwhelming number of people made navigating the room look impossible, but Lyessa directed them down the steps and through the maze of bodies with very little difficulty. She clearly knew exactly where she was going. Most acknowledged her presence with a deferential nod. At one point, she took Ty's hand to keep him from bumping into an elderly woman attempting to squeeze her gown between two rows.

Once they passed, she didn't release it.

Ty found himself standing a little taller as he walked alongside her. He marveled at how much had changed over the last several weeks, beginning with that fateful night at the East Inn when she had shrewdly taunted him into his first performance. Not in his wildest dreams would he have imagined himself walking through the halls of the Sidaran Assembly, hand in hand with the overlord's daughter.

Ty was hoping they could sit somewhere near the top, but Sheeva met them halfway and led them on around to the other side of the room, where it appeared their seats were already waiting in the first row. Unlike Ty, the short assassin had no problem sporting her white hair. One look at her amber eyes had most people backing out of the way.

Up ahead, the members of the wielder council chatted amongst themselves, as it seemed no one else in the room was willing to talk to them. Orlyn smiled when he saw them coming. The tall apothecary produced a sandwich from one of his many pockets and took a bite. He offered half to Veldon, but the barrel-chested portmaster politely refused before rubbing the top of his balding head with his handkerchief, looking more nervous about being there than Orlyn.

Ty's stomach rumbled as he stared at the sandwich. He wished now he'd tried harder to finish his meal at the inn.

Miss Reloria smiled and waved as they passed her and Feoldor's seats. Feoldor, with his arms folded in front of his chest, didn't even bother lifting his head. He looked about as happy to be there as he was walking around Mangora's shop.

Ty took his seat next to a very nervous but very excited Gilly. The little dwarf had both legs curled under him on the bench. His head spun back and forth as he watched all the people mingling about. He did not like crowds, so it was hard to guess how Veldon had managed to talk him into being there. Even Ty was feeling a bit suffocated.

Ty's father sat at the end of the row next to Ambassador Lanmiere, who was no longer wearing the sling from his injury during the king's hunting expedition. Whatever they were discussing was lost to the noise of the room.

Lyessa sat next to Ty, and Breen found an empty spot awaiting him beside Fraya. Apart from the wielder council, the rest of the hall was filled with members of the ruling class. Their snobbish looks and contemptuous whispers let Ty know that he and the council didn't belong. They stuck out like a pickle in an apple barrel.

He looked down at his simple brown leather pants, faded blue top, and heavy coat, then at Lyessa's burgundy velveteen gown. One couldn't have found two more different people. Why was she so willing to let herself be seen with him?

"Order! Come to order!" a short, round man in front of the overlord's chair said. He held a large ceremonial staff in one hand, which he proceeded to whack three times on the granite flagstones. The clatter of heeled shoes and the rustle of clothing quickly enveloped the cavernous chamber as the lords and ladies hurried to find their seats.

As the last echoes of movement faded and all eyes and ears were attuned to the main floor, the chamberlain once again smacked the white stone. "This meeting of the Sidaran Assembly will now come to order." The man's nasal voice grated on Ty's nerves. "The overlord of Sidara will at this time offer an opening address in accordance with the traditions of this—"

"Oh, hang traditions!" one of the taller, more opulently dressed men said from his seat near Orlyn. Ty smiled, pleased he didn't have to listen to the little man's droning. "What in blazes is going on around here? Why has the White Tower suddenly taken such a keen interest in Easthaven? We are hearing rumors about some sort of wielder battle. And why are members of the Black Watch interrogating our citizens? There's even talk of Northmen savages boating in to rape and pillage—

"

"Don't forget about the monsters in the forest," a lady added a few rows farther up.

Ty leaned forward and looked down his row, where the only people who were not standing, shouting, or waving their arms sat in silence. He could see from the expressions on the council members' faces that they were afraid of where this might be heading. On his left, Ty's father was also leaning forward. His eyes were focused on Overlord Barl, but the look on his face said that he had something else on his mind.

His father had a gift for seeing the larger picture. He didn't let details bog him down. Ty thought he would have made a great general had he joined the corps instead of following in his father's shoes and becoming the overlord's gamekeeper. He had always been the person the council turned to when there was a problem.

The abrasive man at the front finally took his seat, and the chamberlain decided not to press the issue. Instead, giving up his ceremonial opening, he retreated to the far wall where he watched the crowd with a stern face.

Lyessa's father stood from his seat on the platform. Ty didn't envy him.

Overlord Barl raised his hands to quiet the room. "You deserve answers." His voice resounded off the inner walls as he waited for everyone to sit back down. "And I will do my best to make sure you get them."

The murmurs quieted but didn't cease altogether.

"This will undoubtedly be one of the most important assembly meetings Sidara has ever conducted. Certainly in my lifetime."

The room grew still, all eyes at the front.

"I fear there is no going back. By the time you leave here today, your perception of the world . . . will never be the same."

Chapter 36 | Ty

THE ROOM WAS SILENT, everyone at the edge of their seat. Ty needed to sneeze, but he held it in, afraid that if he did, it would start a panicked stampede. He focused on Barl to keep his mind off the sneeze. Lyessa's father looked strong. Confident. Even with the injured leg, he looked ready for battle, which was probably good, considering who he was addressing.

Barl scanned the audience. "Most of you know me well enough to know that I'm not one to equivocate, especially when it comes to matters of grave importance. So, believe me when I say that *this* is one of those times. All the way back to the arrival of the Fae, there has always been a conflict between those with magic and those without. Battles have been fought, lines divided, and the innocent made to suffer . . . on both sides."

Disgruntled murmurs rose at Barl's mention of "both sides."

"Over the last thousand years, the jun'ri have ruled Aldor while the ven'ae have been rounded up and imprisoned by the White Tower."

"As well it should be," came a stern remark from somewhere on the far left of the room, followed by a small round of applause.

The man who had been so outspoken earlier leaned forward in his seat. "You are telling us nothing we don't already know. Magic's taint can be seen all across our lands. Wielders are popping up everywhere. They're a plague on society."

Again, loud ayes filled the chamber.

Orlyn, who happened to be sitting next to the opinionated oaf, finished the first half of his sandwich, seemingly oblivious.

Ty tried reaching for his new book, but Lyessa's hand tightened on his, holding it in place.

"Are they, now?" Barl asked, taking a step forward. "Popping up everywhere? And how would you know this, Cirian? The ven'ae remain in hiding. Do you possess some secret talent for sniffing them out?"

The man next to Orlyn sneered. "I don't need a special talent. It's obvious." Those around Cirian patted the taller man on the back, encouraging his stupidity.

Feoldor looked at Lyessa. "Why do I get the feeling your father didn't tell anyone we were coming?"

Lyessa offered an embarrassed half-smile.

Great, Ty thought. *This is going to turn out well for us.*

"So, you can definitely tell the difference between a wielder and a non-wielder?" Barl asked.

"Of course!" Cirian was red in the face. "Everyone can. What do you take me for?"

"I only ask, Cirian," Barl said as he gestured to the left of the man, "because you happen to be sharing a bench with nine of them right now."

Cirian leaped from his seat—as did everyone around him—and stumbled backward, trying to get away from the wielder council members, all of which remained where they were.

Ty's hands were shaking. This was a terrible idea. What would the assembly do if Lyessa's father couldn't talk them down?

"Guards! Guards!" Cirian shouted at the top of his lungs, pointing a finger at Orlyn. "Arrest these . . . these people." He tried backing up farther but stopped when he hit the wall of assembly members behind him, all trying to do the same thing.

Barl held up his hand. "Belay that order, Captain, and kindly take your men back to the perimeter, unless I call you."

The lancers stopped halfway down the stairs, unsure what to do.

"Did you hear me, Captain?" Barl asked.

The lancer captain spared a quick glance at Cirian before raising his fist to his chest and ordering his men back to their places.

"Now listen to me, all of you!" Barl snapped, his patience clearly reaching its end. "You said you wanted answers. You all but demanded them a moment ago. Well, here you are." He gestured to Ty's row. "I have asked these men and women to help shed some light on our current situation. If it weren't for the bravery of these . . . *people*," he said with a poignant glare at Cirian, "my daughter and I would have been food for a horde of arachnobes."

Cirian straightened his coat. Ty noted he did his best not to look at them. "With all due respect, Your Lordship, but have you lost your mind? Arachnobes? Next, you're going to be telling us that Easthaven is surrounded by rock trolls, and the forest is inundated with talking trees."

A few of the assembly members laughed, that is, until a vine from somewhere inside Orlyn's robe poked its way out, slithered down the row, and wrapped itself around Cirian's hand. The assemblyman screamed as he fought to pull his arm loose. Those standing closest nearly caused a stampede as they rushed to get as far away from Cirian as possible.

"Now, now," Orlyn said to the long piece of ivy. "That's not very nice. He might need his arm." The vine released Cirian's wrist and slid back across the seat and into Orlyn's robe.

Ty shook his head. *The man's going to get us killed.*

Cirian didn't move, his hands shaking as much as his legs.

"I guess your talking-tree theory might not be too far off," Barl said.

He gave Orlyn a stern look as he attempted to calm the crowd, asking them to return to their seats.

Some returned. Most stayed where they were.

"I know you have your doubts," Barl said, signaling to a handful of guards at the back. "So, I brought you a little something to prove I haven't completely lost my mind."

Six men staggered down to the main floor, carrying something large between them, wrapped in brown canvas. From the pervasive smell, Ty knew exactly what it was, and the memories it brought had him biting down on his tongue.

Smiling, Lyessa began to poke him, but when she noticed the serious look on his face, she squeezed his hand instead.

Ty closed his eyes and swallowed, forcing down the images of his mother. When he opened them again, he concentrated on Cirian, curious how he would react when the guards revealed what was inside.

The men dropped the bulky object in the center of the floor, and it landed with a wet *pop*. Gingerly, they untied the cords holding the thick material, clearly not wanting to be standing so close to something that smelled that foul.

Those sitting on the lower rows held their noses, but all eyes were glued to the mysterious unveiling. Even Cirian stopped glaring at Orlyn long enough to see what was going on.

Once the last of the rope was undone, Barl grabbed hold of the canvas. "Ladies and gentlemen," he said with a twinkle in his eye, "I present to you your very own arachnobe." With that, he ripped back the covering, and the enormous spider's legs unrolled onto the floor.

The first three rows emptied. Cries of horror rang out as the members fought to reach the upper levels, knocking each other out of the way to get as far from the hideous creature as they could. A few of the women, as well as some of the more foppish-looking men, fainted in the aisles. Barl watched with a grim smile, and Ty couldn't help but smile as well. Nothing like proving willfully ignorant people wrong.

Feoldor laughed out loud, receiving an elbow from Reloria. Orlyn was too busy working on the second half of his sandwich to care. Lyessa tightened her grip on Ty's hand as she stared at the hideous creature.

"I'd almost forgotten how big they were."

Somehow, Ty didn't believe her.

Down the row, the rest of the council seemed to have mixed emotions as they watched the crowd's response.

"Does anyone else want to tell me that I've lost my mind?" Lyessa's father demanded.

Once they realized the creature was dead, some of the bravest of the assembly members moved to get a closer look, Cirian being one of them. Keeping his arm up to cover his nose and mouth, he stepped up beside the creature and shifted a leg with his boot. "I . . . I apologize, Your Lordship, for my rash statements."

The overlord accepted Cirian's apology with a lot more grace than Ty would have and simply nodded.

"The creature is dead," Barl said. "There's no need to panic. I figured the only way most of you would ever believe a tale so ridiculous would be to see it for yourselves. To be honest, when I was first presented with this information, I thought it utterly preposterous myself. Then, next thing I know, I'm fighting for my life against a dark witch from the White Tower, Tallosian savages, and an army of giant spiders."

"A witch from the White Tower?" Cirian looked aghast.

Barl didn't respond to Cirian's question. He did gesture to the empty rows at the front. "Please, everyone, take your seats." He motioned for the guards to take the creature away. The assembly cautiously began to file back to their benches; even those seated near the wielder council retook theirs, if not quite as close.

"Let's start from the beginning."

For the next hour, Lyessa's father laid out everything that had taken place, as best he knew it, over the last couple of months leading up to the conflict outside of Ty's home. He told of Ambassador Lanmiere's battle during his hunting trip with High King Rhydan. He talked about the coming of the Black Watch, the defeat of the Northmen, the wielder battle at the Easthaven barracks, and the eventual retreat of the witch Mangora and her spider army. Clearly, he'd spent a great deal of time with Ty's father while they were away.

Ty's palms were sweating as he recalled the events. He had tried burying the images, but being forced to listen to the details pulled them up all over again. He was practically panting by the end. Thankfully, Lyessa had let go of his hand at some point, or he might have crushed hers.

He reached for the book. Its touch seemed to calm him, to pull his thoughts back into focus. He would find Mangora and avenge his mother if it was the last thing he did. He wanted to pull the book out and take a look to see if anything new had appeared, but there were too many people around. Instead, he folded his hands in his lap and turned his attention back to the meeting.

Barl was methodical as he laid out the situation. He conveniently skipped over the part where Ty was a faeling and how this entire situation had unfolded because of the White Tower's desire to have him. He also left out Nyalis's involvement, probably not wanting to add further anxiety to an already delicate situation.

Few questions were raised during the overlord's discourse, as most people were clearly engrossed by the unbelievable account. Those few questions, whether directed at the overlord or the wielder council, were promptly answered with as much clarity as possible, trying to overcome the assembly's previous perceptions of wielders. Ty realized how difficult this must have been for them to absorb.

Cirian stood, still keeping a close eye on Orlyn and his robe. "Are you telling us that the White Tower—which has been purging magic from our land for over a thousand years—is now employing wielders of its own? If the White Tower is in league with the wielders, then why are they rounding them up?"

Before the overlord had a chance to reply, Ty's father spoke up. "The White Tower is not in league with the ven'ae. They are out to destroy us. At least, those of us who will not pledge fealty to them."

"To what end?"

"We believe they are building an army."

Heated whispers spread throughout the hall.

A lady a few rows up on the right spoke up. "If this were the case, then why have we not heard of this sooner?"

"Because you're all too stupid to see what's right in front of you," Feoldor blurted out without turning around or unfolding his arms.

Orlyn nudged him in the side. "That's not helpful."

"Well, it's true."

"The problem," Ty's father continued, giving Feoldor a harsh glare, "is that the people of Aldor have been raised on the notion that magic is evil, and that those born with magic, whether they wanted it or not, must also be evil." He pointed down the row. "Assemblyman Cirian said as much already."

"But it was magic that nearly destroyed our world over a thousand years ago," another member pointed out, this time an elderly white-haired man near the back. "Those with magic turned us into slaves, or have you forgotten what the Defiler did?"

"No one has forgotten the Dark One or what he did, but if you recall, it wasn't the jun'ri but rather the ven'ae who defeated him and his followers. In fact, if we were to apply that same logic, then I could say those born with wealth are evil."

Angry whispers spread through the room.

"There are many who use their wealth to usurp power and to drive others into fealty. They believe because they have it that it entitles them to do so. How is that any different than what you are ascribing to wielders? Just because someone is born—unwillingly, I might add—with magic doesn't mean they will use it for evil any more than those born with wealth."

Ty's father took his seat. Ty remembered having to listen to that same speech not so long ago. He also remembered how effective it had been.

Lyessa reached over and squeezed Ty's hand. "Your father is quite the orator."

Ty smiled. For a simple gamekeeper, his father was quite a remarkable man.

Cirian remained in his seat but at the very edge. "For all this talk of magic and its use, and the *supposed* misconceptions between the jun'ri and the ven'ae, we still have yet to discuss what I believe is an even greater issue. Aramoor and our new High King. Or have we forgotten his recent egregious overreach in power?"

Talk about a swift change of subject, Ty thought. Apparently, Cirian had had enough with discussing magic, which Ty was fine with. The less they talked about it, the more likely the council would make it out of there in one piece.

"Our newly appointed king has taken it upon himself to do something that hasn't been attempted since the days leading up to the Wizard Wars," Cirian continued. "How does Dakaran think he has the authority to lay claim to an entire kingdom? I don't begrudge Elondria going to war with Cylmar to protect their lands and their people. It was the right call by his father. But to then turn around and claim that Cylmar is no more and that its people and lands are now forfeit as property of the Crown is preposterous! What's to stop him from turning his eyes on us next?"

Again, the Assembly Hall was filled with worried, scared, and enraged men and women as they all voiced their opinions at the same time. It was chaos. No one person could be heard over the other, all voices mixing into an overwhelming confusion.

Overlord Barl raised his arms to quiet the audience, but it was the chamberlain who finally managed it as he whacked the butt of his staff down on the white granite.

"Quiet down!" the nasally voice yelled above the din. "The overlord of Sidara will be heard!"

The clamor lowered as heads turned back to the front.

Barl lowered his arms. "My friends, I share your concerns. You are the ruling body of Sidara, and like me, you worry about the safety of our people and our land. But where you see two separate events, I see only one. I don't believe that the growing arm of the White Tower and the unexpected actions taken by Aramoor and this High King are of themselves unrelated. In fact, I believe the two are inexplicably linked."

"What can be done about it?" one of the members called out.

"I have requested a summit with Overlords Agnar and Meyrose. I would like to hear their thoughts on the matter and discuss what actions we may take as the Provincial Authority in response to the situation. Our goal should be to prevent any further escalation from Elondria.

"But for now, I have recalled the Sidaran Lancers. I want a full battalion here in Easthaven as well as a small contingent assigned to every city throughout Sidara. I also want constant patrols on the border roads and travel stops assigned to every major thoroughfare in and out of Sidara. It also wouldn't hurt to allocate some lancers to patrol the waterways along the river."

Many of the assembly members nodded, even more so with his suggestion of a full battalion being stationed in Easthaven.

After fielding a few more questions, Overlord Barl ended the conclave with a few poignant words of encouragement and promises of swift action.

Afterward, it took nearly a quarter of an hour for Ty and the others to worm their way through the crowd of loitering officials as the assembly members shared their thoughts on the situation and the best way it should be handled. Outside the chambers, Overlord Barl pulled Ty's family aside for a quick word. Lyessa stood with Ty.

"I was wondering if you could help me with a little problem," he said to Ty's father before glancing at Ty's sister. "You too, Adarra."

Adarra's head popped up from the book she was reading. "Me?"

Ty's father smiled. "We'd be glad to help, my lord."

"Drop the *my lord*, Kellen. Any man who has fought beside me in battle, as you have, can call me Barl."

"Of course . . . Barl. What seems to be the problem?"

"I'm going to need your help with an interrogation."

Ty's attention had been wandering to his new book, but it was quickly diverted. Who could the overlord be wanting to interrogate?

"We still have the Northman that Adarra and your wife subdued during the battle. However, we can't seem to understand his dialect, and what little we can make out has me confused."

"Oh?"

"It seems he will talk to no one except the spotted warrior."

"Spotted warrior?"

Barl shrugged. "I have no idea."

I bet I could get him to talk, Ty mused. "Where is he?" He could feel the warmth of his magic building. The man might know where Mangora was.

"He's being held in the barracks prison." Barl looked at Adarra. "Do you think you could help us interpret?"

Ty clenched his fists. *Let me have five minutes with him and you won't have to interpret.*

"Depends," Adarra said, closing her book. "Do you have anything written about the Tallosian language? The more I have to work with, the better chance I'll have."

"I'll see what I can do. I think I have a book or two in my library. When you get a chance, come by and we'll see what we can find. I'll have Piel start searching."

Ty smiled. "Maybe I could be of some use as well."

Chapter 37 | Barthol

NIGHT HAD FINALLY ARRIVED, which meant Barthol was free to move about the city without the constant fear of being spotted. Even with a city as large as Aramoor, he didn't want to risk someone recognizing him and getting word back to the king. Since being back, he'd spent most of his days holed up in his home, playing with Arina, helping his wife with the housework, and enduring an endless barrage of common-sense advice from his old man. As wonderful as it had been to hold them all in his arms again, the confinement was driving him crazy. He couldn't spend the rest of his life hiding behind four walls, especially when he was holding on to a secret so large, it could start a civil war or even topple the kingdom.

The extra time spent with his family had gone a long way in helping him recover from the horrors he had endured, but each night, his wife had been forced to wake him, sweat-soaked and shaking, as he relived the battle all over again.

Kensey had begged him to talk to her about it, but how could he burden her with what he had seen and done? How could he ever explain what it felt like to watch his men, his comrades, his friends ripped apart in front of him while he was helpless to do anything about it? How could he ever make her understand that most nights he would lay his head on his pillow and fight the guilt of having survived? And then there was Ayrion—his captain and best friend—who had sacrificed himself to save Barthol. There were times Barthol wished he could have taken Ayrion's place. At least then he wouldn't feel such shame.

Barthol pressed himself up against the wall of a building at the corner of Grisdale and Elmwood and waited for a young couple to pass.

More than guilt plagued him that night. Was he doing the right thing? Maybe his father was right. Perhaps he should take his family and leave. Aramoor had been his home. But was it still? He had spent a quarter of his adult life inside the palace walls, working side by side with Ayrion. He had been able to hold his head high when he walked around town in his black High Guard uniform. Now . . . now he wasn't sure where he belonged. Aramoor would never be the same, not as long as a traitor sat on the throne.

The young couple passed, too wrapped up in each other to even know he was there. He waited until they were out of earshot before moving out of the shadows. He adjusted his hood and continued down the road, which placed him inside the northwest quarter's residential district. The roads here were clean of most debris, which meant the air smelled more of chimney smoke than rotten food. Also, the homes on the upper west side were grander than those on the eastern side where he lived, but still, nothing in comparison to the Bayside District, where the elite ruling class resided. Each of the homes in Bayside was almost a miniature palace.

When he'd been younger, and Kensey pregnant with Arina, Barthol would take his wife for long walks through the city proper. She would always insist on walking through Bayside to look at the regal manors backed against the waterfront. They enjoyed talking about what it would be like to live in one, to have such untold wealth that it required an army of servants just to keep it up.

There were times when it weighed heavy on him, knowing he'd never be able to give her such things. That's when Kensey would wrap her arms around him, lay her head against his shoulder, and say, "No matter where we live, it will be a palace as long as you're there to share it with me."

Blazes, how he loved that woman.

Barthol pulled his cloak tight against the bite of the evening air and thought through what he would say, his pace increasing the closer he got. Stopping only long enough to make sure no one was coming, he headed north on Nimbin Way, counting down the homes on the right side of the street, hoping he could remember what it looked like.

It had been a good six months since he had been to this particular house, and he wasn't sure he could remember what the outside of it looked like in the dark. The last thing he needed was to go knocking on the wrong door.

Barthol stopped and studied the waist-high wall surrounding the house in question. It was familiar. This had to be it. Taking a moment, he scanned the vacant road. The streetlamps scattered shadows from nearby trees across the walkway like long, emaciated fingers reaching out to snatch him.

Once he was certain no one was watching, he flipped back the metal latch and cringed at the loud squeak of the gate's hinges as it opened. Slipping inside, he pushed the gate shut and dropped the latch into place. He waited for what seemed like an eternity for any sign of alarm. When none came, he crept across the lawn toward the front door, sticking to the shadows of the trees as best he could.

He was within three strides of the front steps when he felt the tip of a blade press against the small of his back, and he froze.

"You've picked the wrong house to burglarize, my friend. If you pray to the Creator, now would be the appropriate time. You might be one of the largest men I've ever laid eyes on, but I promise you that my sword is no respecter of persons."

Barthol chuckled. "And if I thought for one moment you actually had something inside worth stealing, I would have been in and out before you'd have had time to pull on your flamin' underdrawers."

There was stunned silence.

"Barthol?"

The blade lowered, and the man holding it circled to the front.

Barthol pulled back his hood and watched as Commander Tolin's face went pale. Barthol smiled. "Who else would be stupid enough to creep through your wife's garden in the middle of the night?"

"Barthol Respuel!" Tolin grabbed him by the shoulders. "As I live and breathe! How's this possible? I was told no one had survived."

"Shhh!" Barthol raised his hood back into place. "Are you trying to get us both killed?"

The commander rubbed a hand through his greying hair. "I was at your funeral, you know, even said a few nice words over your grave."

"Really?"

"No. But I would have if you'd been given one."

Barthol groaned, not caring much for the joke.

"Dakaran didn't even wait for the bodies to grow cold before packing up the army and scurrying back to Aramoor. He acted like he was afraid someone was going to steal his daddy's throne while he was out." Tolin grew pensive. "So, tell me. How'd you survive? Were you one of the wounded they brought back in the wagons?"

Barthol shook his head, his arms already shivering. "Not quite. Can we talk inside? There are words that need to be said, and I'd prefer not to freeze my tail off while we did it."

Tolin sheathed his sword and motioned for Barthol to follow.

Barthol cast a wary eye at the nearby homes as he trailed the commander up the front steps. The estates on either side of Tolin's were similar in size—three stories, one stone block, the other brick, each with clay tiles and decorative molding. Definitely a step up from Barthol's home, but nothing compared to the nobles'.

Tolin held the door for him. Barthol was surprised to find the inside of the front sitting room in disarray. He remembered Tolin's wife keeping a rather fastidiously clean house. But now, there were crates scattered everywhere, some filled to overflowing, others only half full.

"Sorry about the state of things," Tolin said, shutting the door. "The wife and I are in the process of packing."

Barthol withdrew his hood. "You're moving?"

"Not much choice in the matter, I'm afraid. Not after my change in position. Can't afford to keep this place." He led Barthol to a small study at the back of the house.

"What change in position?"

"Apparently, questioning the former prince about leaving my men to rot had an automatic demotion attached to it." Tolin sighed as he shut the door behind them. "I'm no longer the commander of anything, which isn't saying much, since Dakaran has been replacing my officers with his own men anyway. All those willing to pledge fealty to Dakaran's thugs can serve the new king, and those not willing are immediately discharged without pay or reference."

"What about the High Guard?"

Tolin shook his head. "They were the first to go."

"Who's to protect the king and Queen Mother?"

"The Black Watch have been given that honor. You can't go anywhere around the palace now without seeing white uniforms." The commander knelt at the hearth and lit some kindling. "The worst thing that could have happened to Aldor was having both the king and the Guardian Protector killed in battle. I still can't believe it. I didn't think there was anything alive that could have taken Ayrion down. I guess I was wrong."

Barthol's temper flared. "Nothing could have . . . except, perhaps, treachery."

"Treachery?" Tolin stood and pointed to a nearby chair. "Start from

the beginning."

"Who's down there with you?" a woman's voice called out from the other side of the door.

Tolin raised a hand for Barthol to remain seated. He walked to the door and stuck his head out. "Just one of the palace staff wanting to know what to do with the belongings from my office, dear. Go back to bed. I'll be up shortly." Tolin waited a moment, then shut the door. "Sorry. I don't want her getting any more upset than she already is."

Barthol nodded. He could relate. Perhaps Kensey would be up to moving as well?

Tolin slid another chair beside the fire and sat. "Now, what's this about treachery? What happened on that rise?"

Barthol took a moment to gather his thoughts. He stared at the hearth, watching the flames dance across the wood as he tried to remember what had happened that day. They were memories he would have liked to forget, memories of loss so strong they had threatened to bury him. "As I recall, Ayrion and I were down to our last three or four men. The king was there as well, and with his help, we managed to finish off the rest of the hor'hounds. It was a tremendous victory. Rhydan raised his sword . . ." Barthol paused. "I remember thinking he was about to give another one of his long-winded speeches when everything went sideways."

Tolin leaned forward, worry lines on his forehead growing more pronounced.

"I remember turning to say something to Ayrion, and the next thing I know, he kicks me over the rise, and I'm rolling down the back side of the slope." Barthol rubbed his shoulder where he had slammed against rock. It hadn't fully healed. "It's the only reason I'm sitting here now. I ended up landing in a gully. My head hit a rock and I passed out. It must have kept me hidden, because by the time I came to and crawled back up the slope, the Black Watch were breaking down the command post.

"I can't swear to it, but it wouldn't take much imagining to figure out what had happened. One moment, we're shouting victory, and the next . . ." He wrung his hands, his elbows on his knees. "The only other people on that rise were the prince, the Archchancellor, and a small contingent of those white-robed sons of faeries."

Tolin shot to his feet. "This is high treason!" He paced in front of the fire. "I knew Dakaran lusted for the throne, but I can't believe he would stoop so low as to murder his own father to acquire it."

"Is everything all right, dear?" Tolin's wife called down once more.

"Everything's fine, Tirana. Go back to bed."

"Who knows how far someone like Dakaran will go?" Barthol said. "I'm still in shock at his decision to dismantle the High Guard and relieve you of duty. You'd think with changes like this, it would raise eyebrows. Where's the public outcry?"

"Everything's been done behind closed doors," Tolin said, retaking his seat. "Two days after his official inauguration, I was called to his study. He told me that with the death of the king as a blight on our campaign against Cylmar, the senate was demanding someone's head. And since the Guardian was not there to take the blame, the responsibility fell on me."

"I'd love to give them Dakaran's head on a pike." Barthol's hands were practically trembling. "We need to let the people know what's happening. That's the reason I'm here tonight. The people trust you, Tolin. They look up to you. If you were to speak out, I'm sure they'd stand by you."

Tolin lowered his head. "If only it were that simple."

"It seems pretty flaming simple to me. Dakaran has committed treason, which holds an immediate sentence of death." Barthol almost spat, but there was no place in the commander's study to do so. "I'd love to be the one holding the axe for that ceremony."

"I've heard from others, including Overcaptain Asa, that it was hinted that it would be in their best interest to leave Aramoor. Of course, Dakaran didn't come right out and openly threaten them, but his meaning was clear."

Barthol was speechless. Perhaps he was right. Maybe it would be best if they left. But still, it wasn't in his nature to give up. "What do you suggest we do?"

The commander lifted his head. "We need to be extremely careful. We can't just accuse the king of treason without proof or powerful allies willing to stand with us. I have a few contacts in the senate who'd be more than happy to get rid of Dakaran, but right now, we have nothing more than the word of a former High Guard captain who, by his own admission, was unconscious during the time of the so-called act."

Barthol stiffened. "I know what I saw, Tolin."

"I'm not suggesting otherwise, but what I'm trying to point out is that it would be your word against his, and right now, your word wouldn't be worth a tankard of watered-down mead against the High King's. Without proof, I'm not sure what we can do."

Barthol wanted to punch something. Tolin was right. His testimony alone wouldn't be enough, especially now that Dakaran was getting rid of all those still loyal to his father. He hated to admit it, but the young prig was turning out to be more conniving than he had thought possible.

"The first thing we need to do is get word to the Queen Mother," Tolin said, scooting to the edge of his seat as though he were about to stand. "She needs to know. She could be in danger."

Barthol nodded. "The queen would be a powerful ally."

"The problem is that neither of our faces would make it through the palace gates without us being immediately arrested. We need to find someone on the inside who would be close enough to relay our message."

Barthol's head lifted, a smile creeping across his hardened face. "I believe I know just the person."

Chapter 38 | Valtor

"*V OYESTRA.*"

As soon as the word left Valtor's lips, torches burst to life, scattering shadows across the thirteen red-marble pillars that surrounded the center of the chamber. The floor inside the pillars was made of white stone so smooth, it mirrored the ceiling. Not a speck of dust lay on top, as though some unseen barrier stretching between the pillars kept the area beneath untouched.

Valtor leaned on his staff as he passed between the columns toward the floating basin in the center, where the Waters of A'sterith lay waiting. The rhythmic tapping on the stone left a trail of echoes in his wake, each one chasing the next across the bare walls and vaulted ceiling, leaving a hollowed-out feeling in the pit of his stomach.

He shivered as he neared, casting a wary glance upward at the Watchers. The thirteen stone gargoyles stared down in judgment from atop their lofty perches.

Valtor shifted his gaze back to the basin and the runes etched into the onyx rim. His last encounter with Aerodyne hadn't gone so well. The memory of the pain he had endured was still fresh as he stopped in front of the bowl.

At least it was *good* news he was bringing, he thought. Of course, it was good news he'd reported the last time, but that hadn't stopped Aerodyne from leaving him kneeling in a pool of his own blood.

The Dark One's presence permeated the room. Valtor had felt it since first opening the door. It tightened around him, threatening to crush his soul, growing with each step closer to the waters. He forced himself to breathe evenly as he stretched his hand toward the basin. *"Iryseth a' Daomon."*

The silver liquid inside stirred to life, rising from the bowl and taking shape. Valtor quickly lowered his head, waiting for the hooded figure to fully coalesce.

"Speak," the voice boomed, causing him to tremble involuntarily.

He spared a quick glance at the basin. The silvery figure stood waiting. There was no face to look at, no hands to gesture with. Aerodyne was little more than spirit. "I have done as you have asked, my lord Aerodyne. Argon has been released."

The figure didn't move, which made Valtor even more nervous. Had he done something wrong?

The initial incantation for the spell had been written inside one of Aerodyne's grimoires. Valtor would have never known what it was if Aerodyne hadn't pointed him to it. He had been reluctant to attempt a spell so potentially dangerous, but when Aerodyne issued a command, you didn't refuse.

The book had labeled the spell *Plague of Shadows*. What he hadn't understood at the time was that he was awakening the long-imprisoned essence of Argon—one of Aerodyne's former generals. Aerodyne must have had a reason for it, if only Valtor knew what it was. He could only guess Aerodyne was using it to forge a way to escape his prison.

"How many times did it take you to conjure the spell?"

Valtor swallowed. "Three, my lord." His earlier attempts at releasing the enchantment around the crystal had proven ineffective. It seemed impenetrable, until he had understood that the location used was as important as the incantation itself. The spell needed hosts to infect, and without a proper supply of human bodies, the conjuring wouldn't initiate.

Once he had realized that, Valtor had given the crystal and a written transcription of the incantation to Topin. He had instructed the bulradoer to test the effects on one of the more secluded towns in Sidara, and from the bulradoer's initial report, the results were astonishing.

"Tell me everything," Aerodyne said, his voice so loud it shook the stones beneath his feet. "From the beginning."

"Yes, my lord." Valtor started by explaining what he had done in releasing the locking spell to the crystal holding Argon's essence. He then described the type of manifestation the ancient general had taken. He expounded on the vulraaks and the swiftness of their transformations. He didn't leave anything of what Topin had told him out.

The figure within the basin shifted slightly, the silvery waters sliding down the folds of his cloak.

Valtor felt sweat dripping from his brow. He clutched his staff. If not for it, he would have certainly toppled over by now. He barely had the strength to stand.

"You have done well. The first step is complete." With that, the robed figure melted back into the basin, and the water went placid once again.

Air wheezed from Valtor's chest as he breathed out a heavy sigh of relief. *First step?* What was the second?

Chapter 39 | Ayrion

IT HAD BEEN A ROUGH few days since Ayrion's showdown with Argon and their narrow escape from the vulraaks. Zynora had spent the last two days trying to heal the many cuts, gouges, lacerations, and bruises the four had sustained from their fight against the cannibalistic creatures.

The healing had been slow. Zynora was still weak from her work on Nell, not to mention the magic she had used to stop Argon. Ayrion hadn't realized she was capable of such magic. *Impulso* magic, she called it—a kind of invisible blast of power. Apparently, some of the charms she wore on her headband were made of transferal crystals. Zynora said when she was younger, she had been capable of multiple bursts without it draining her completely. But now, a single volley was enough to knock her on her backside.

She had spent most of the first day in bed, while Tameel filled her with hot soup. The rest and food had perked her up, so by the following morning, Ayrion had found her mixing a pot of fresh porridge at one of

the cook fires. Tameel sat beside her, patiently waiting with a bowl in his lap and spoon in hand.

Ayrion sat down across from the two and warmed his hands. "There's something that's been bugging me that I haven't been able to work out."

Zynora and Tameel stopped what they were doing and stared at him across the fire.

"And what would that be?" Zynora asked.

Ayrion looked at Tameel. "How did you know we were in trouble? And how did you know where to find us? The last thing we said was that we were heading into Belvin. We didn't mention anything about stopping at Bek's cabin, and we certainly didn't tell you where it was. How in Aldor did you find us?"

Tameel shared a grin with Zynora and raised his arms. "I found you with these," he said, pointing at the bronze cuffs on his forearm. "In the Rhivanni, when a couple bonds, they are given matching sidrix. Each of the sidrix is inscribed with runes that link the wearers to each other. They allow us to share our feelings." He turned and smiled at his wife. "And those feelings grow stronger the closer the armbands are to each other."

"It's a connection unlike any you'll ever experience," Zynora said. "It intensifies everything. When you can share in your husband or wife's emotions, it draws you all the closer." She laid her hand on Tameel's knee, and he in turn laid his over hers.

"Sounds rather passionate," Ayrion remarked, trying to imagine what it would be like to share another's emotions. He did seem to have a connection with his horse, but that was hardly the same.

"*Passionate* is a good word for it," Tameel said with a lecherous wink at Zynora.

"Stop it," she said, flicking his hand. She turned and went back to stirring the porridge, but her smile remained.

Ayrion left the two alone and returned to his own musings as he stared at the fire. He still wasn't sure how they had managed to survive their encounter with Argon. A couple of times, he had woken with nightmares vivid enough to have him reaching for his swords, but then he'd feel the slight squirm of Marissa as she pressed her head against his chest, and he'd lie back down.

The little girl was like a second shadow and refused to sleep unless it was within arm's reach of Ayrion. Under any other circumstance, he might have been annoyed by the child's behavior, but with all they had endured, Ayrion found that he didn't mind the extra attention. In fact, at times he preferred it, which left him wondering if perhaps there was more to him than just a killer. Did his life consist of more than war? What memories he had been able to recover didn't lead him to believe there was. Perhaps his injury was affecting the core of who he had been.

Either way, he found solace in the little girl's warmth. Affection from a child was love in its purest form. There was no judgment of past wrongs, no incrimination, no strings attached. A child's love concealed no hidden agenda, no preconceived notion concerning what they expected from the relationship. Their motives lay open and bare.

Breakfast was eaten rather slowly as the small group pondered their situation, eventually realizing they couldn't just pack up and leave. This threat was far too dangerous. Zynora described it like an untended wound. It would fester and spread, killing off whatever life it met. This infection needed to be purged, but after their last confrontation, it was pretty obvious they were going to need help, and a lot of it. Their best option was raising support from the outlying communities, since they stood the greatest chance of being affected.

As fast as it had taken over Belvin, they didn't have time to try getting help from the Sidaran capital of Easthaven. Even if it was possible, who was going to listen to a couple of tinkers? They needed to stop Argon, and the best way to do that was to warn the surrounding communities. They only hoped the plague hadn't spread beyond Belvin.

They spent the rest of the day packing supplies for two wagons, and by early the next morning, they were breaking camp and heading west out of the forest. They reached the main road where Taylis's painted rocks marked the path toward the Nathillian campsite and headed south. Before they had ridden as far as the bridge where they had first met Taylis, they turned off on a road Bek pointed out that led back into the Sidaran Forest and west toward Saeida.

It seemed a long way around to get to the small community, but since the only other route would have taken them past Belvin, they decided it was worth the extra travel time.

By late afternoon the following day, Ayrion spotted several thin lines of smoke rising from a cluster of thatched roofs over the next rise. They were nearing their destination. They passed a few wood-sided homes on their way in, following a dirt road that led them straight through the center of town. There wasn't much to see: a few simple shops; a smithy; and of course, what respectable town would be caught dead without at least one decent tavern? Where else were the poor souls of Saeida going to go to drown their sorrows? And looking at the dilapidated state the town was in, he doubted there was a shortage of sorrows to drown.

The buildings were old and worn—shingles missing, wood slats with cracks large enough to see through, fences missing teeth. The best-looking part of town was the road. Even the trees looked decrepit with their bare, twisted branches waving in the wind. Saeida appeared to be on the verge of collapse.

Not much here to save, Ayrion thought. The one thing he didn't see was a proper inn. With the sun already sinking below the tree line, their small caravan was going to need a place to stay for the night, especially since they had decided on bringing only two of the wagons, and there were now seven in their company.

The wheels jostled inside deep-rutted grooves as they made their way through town. Tameel kept their wagon in the center of the road and pulled into a vacant lot after passing the last of the buildings on the right. Bek brought the second wagon alongside. The closest shop looked to be what passed for the town chandlery.

Ayrion hopped down from the front seat and stretched, thankful to be standing on his own two feet again. He barely had time to straighten when Marissa dove off the front. He caught her in his arms, and she wrapped hers around his neck with a squeal.

"What are you trying to do, kill me?"

She giggled.

He attempted to untangle himself from her hold, but she hung on like a tick, forcing him to resort to more drastic measures: tickling.

She squealed again, laughing and begging for him to stop. Her little legs kicked against his thighs until, finally, her grip loosened, and she slid far enough to plant her feet on the ground. Her wooly hat had come halfway off in the process, so Ayrion knelt and pulled it back down over her ears, tucking the hair that had fallen in her face back under her cap. With her hand in his, they walked around to the back of the wagon to see what the others were doing.

"Place seems almost dead," Tameel said to Bek. "You don't think the plague has already reached this far, do you?"

Bek looked up the street. "Saeida's a quiet town. The people pretty much keep to themselves. I think if the plague had reached this far, there would be a lot more evidence. When the people of Belvin started changing, it was noticeable." He glanced up the street. "Keep an eye out all the same."

Ayrion looked at the buildings lining the main road. Most of the shops appeared to be closed or closing. There were a couple of people outside, but the speed of their walk indicated they didn't plan to stick around and chat.

"This town is new to me," Tameel said, tucking his white hair up under his burgundy cap. "I don't believe we've ever done any trading here before."

"While we're here," Zynora said, looking at the chandlery, "it might be prudent to see about some extra supplies. I have a feeling that medicinal herbs are going to be at the top of our list, considering the insanity we are planning."

"Aye, wife, that would be the smart thing."

Zynora put her arm around Taylis. He was quietly staring at a couple of boys tossing some rocks at an old barrel between two of the buildings. "I'll take the kids and Nell with me. You men go see about finding us some lodging. We'll meet you back at the wagons afterward to discuss how we're going to talk these good folks into risking their lives to hunt down their neighbors." She quirked a brow with a smirk.

Tameel nodded, then gestured to Bek. "Lead the way, my friend. You're the only one of us who's actually been here before."

Ayrion handed a very upset Marissa off to Zynora, then grabbed his swords from the back of the wagon. He had his arm in the first strap when he felt a hand on his shoulder.

"That might not send the best message, my friend," Bek said.

Ayrion thought about it a moment, then shrugged. "Could be right." He unhooked the straps and placed the two swords back inside. Instead, he opted for a long dagger that could be hidden beneath his black coat, and a single broadsword sheathed at his side. He closed the wagon door and looked at his horse. "Keep an eye on things while we're gone."

The stallion stomped its hoof.

Ayrion smiled. "I couldn't agree more." Whatever the bond was between him and the horse, he found it comforting. A connection to his former life. Leaving the wagons in the capable care of his horse, he ran to catch up with the others.

Chapter 40 | Zynora, Ayrion

THE BELL ABOVE THE door rang as Zynora stepped inside the chandlery and ushered the two kids in with her. Her charms swung loosely from the brightly colored band around her head, making a soft jingling as they bounced against each other.

The inside of the shop wasn't much warmer than the outside. A short potbelly stove in the corner did little more than keep the place smelling of soot. The owner wasn't around, so Zynora set about perusing the shelves.

She and her husband had done rather well for themselves, scavenging through the aftermath of the battle near Belbridge. Along with the coin they had found while rifling through the pockets of the dead, they had gathered quite the haul of weaponry to sell. But considering the chandlery's half-empty shelves, Zynora could see that having enough coin wasn't going to be the problem.

"There's some wilted plants over here," Nell said as she picked through a few items against the side wall. "Is this what you're looking for?" She was wearing one of Tameel's less-colorful caps to hide the fact that she had no hair on her head. Zynora's magic might have healed the darkness, but it hadn't given Nell her hair back.

Zynora was halfway across the shop when she heard shuffling from the back. An elderly man hobbled through an open doorway. "We don't serve your kind here," he said with a deep scowl.

Zynora ignored the prejudiced imbecile and continued shopping. It wasn't the first time she'd been told that. Although it didn't happen as much in Sidara.

The man pointed at her with his cane. "I'm talking to you, old woman."

"Old?" Zynora spun around. "You're one to talk!"

"They're with me," Nell said as she stepped out from around one of the shelves.

"I don't care who they're with. You get her and those thieving little purse snatchers out of here before I show you the backside of my cane."

Zynora's patience had reached its end. "You just try to lay a hand on me, you withered-up goat, and I'll put a curse on you that'll hump your back and shrivel your . . ." She almost finished her threat before remembering the children.

The old shopkeeper's eyes bulged, but he kept whatever vile retort he was about to offer to himself. A lot of the smaller villages they had dealings with believed that the Nathillian and the Rhivanni were worshipers of the Dark One and would put hexes on you if you got them angry enough. As ridiculous as the notion was, it did help with bartering. Who wanted to haggle with someone who might turn you into a bog toad?

Seeing they weren't going to receive decent service, Zynora led them back outside and purposely left the front door open behind them. Zynora shrugged when Nell looked at her. "The lout can clearly use some cold air to temper his attitude." She directed them back to the wagons. "I hope the men are faring better than we are."

"I told you, we don't serve rovers in here," the heavyset man behind the bar said, waving a dirty dishtowel at Tameel. "We don't want your kind soiling the decent folk of our town." Everyone in the room stopped to look in their direction.

Ayrion leaned in to Bek. "What was that about giving the wrong impression?"

Bek looked befuddled.

"Would it help to explain that I'm not actually a rover?" Tameel mumbled before finally raising his hand. "My apologies." He donned his friendliest smile. "I meant no offense." He spared a passing glance at Ayrion and Bek and turned for the door. "Good luck. I have a feeling you're going to need it." Tameel wrapped his long colorful cloak up around his shoulders and walked out the door, leaving Ayrion and Bek to face the tavern's patrons on their own.

Ayrion could see this was going to be more difficult than he'd thought. Feeling for the dagger under his black leather coat, he followed Bek through the crowded room. Sharp eyes from every table tracked them as they headed for a long piece of polished oak in the back corner, where there were still a few empty stools available. The tavern was thick with the smell of unwashed bodies, strong ale, and smoke.

On their left, a stone hearth spread light and warmth across the room as a lanky boy, maybe thirteen years of age, stood beside the fire, turning a few cuts of meat on the spit. The meat smelled wonderful compared to the rest of the room, but they weren't there to sample the food. They needed to find shelter for the night, and after seeing the people's reaction to Tameel, Ayrion couldn't help but feel they were wasting their time.

Ayrion took the free stool next to Bek, and the round-bellied owner stared at them from his side of the overly polished wood. "The name's

Abiah. What will it be?" he asked as he looked the two over. His gaze lingered on Ayrion. The taverner had probably never seen someone dressed in black leather.

"You sick?"

"What?"

He pointed at Ayrion's face.

Ayrion had forgotten about his eyes.

"No."

Abiah stared a moment longer, then looked at Bek.

Bek rested his elbows on the bar as he considered the bottles lining the shelf behind the taverner. "I'll have an ale," he said.

Abiah wiped the few strands of hair still covering the top of his head. "We only have dark."

"That's fine. I'm not choosy."

"I didn't catch your names."

"That's because we didn't give them," Ayrion said.

Abiah looked back at Ayrion and pursed his lips. "I guess you didn't. So, what will it be?"

"Make mine a cider."

The barkeep laughed, as did a couple of patrons sitting nearby.

Ayrion didn't much care. He needed to keep a clear head.

"Cider it is, then," Abiah said with a disgusted grunt. He grabbed a couple of wooden tankards and blew off the rims. Wiping the insides with the front of his apron, he walked over to a stack of tapped kegs and filled their orders. "That'll be six," he said, returning with their drinks. He waited to see their coin before releasing the drinks. When he got a look at the size of Ayrion's purse, he added, "Six . . . each."

"What kind of robbery is this?" Bek asked, coming partway out of his seat.

Ayrion laid a hand on the big trapper's arm. "It's fine." He turned back to the taverner. "But I'd say that prices like this should afford some information as well, don't you think?"

Abiah spent an uncomfortable moment staring into Ayrion's eyes before nodding toward an empty table in the back. "I'll be with you shortly."

"What was all that about?" Bek asked, following Ayrion to their table.

"We're going to need to be able to communicate with these people. Whether we get room and board or not, we still need their help in fighting those creatures."

Bek sat down across from Ayrion. "I don't know." He scanned the room. "These folks look more willing to stick a knife in *us* than the vulraaks."

Ayrion couldn't argue there. "Unfortunately, we don't have much of a choice. We can't allow Argon to wreak havoc across Sidara." Ayrion took a swallow of his cider. It had a strong aftertaste of soap, which Ayrion hoped meant that the mug had been recently cleaned.

The two watched as Abiah refilled a few more tankards before calling to the skinny kid at the spit to take over behind the bar. He weaved through the packed room, offering small bits of conversation on his way to their table. Taking a seat at the end, he leaned forward and rested his forearms on top. "So, what's all this talk about information?"

Bek spoke first. "Has there been any word from Belvin lately?"

Abiah's gaze shifted from one man to the other. "You rode all the way into Saeida to ask about Belvin? Belvin ain't but a few hours' ride to the north. Go find out for yourself."

Ayrion laid his tankard down. "So, no one has either come or gone from Belvin in the last week?"

Abiah's brows began to weigh heavy over his brown eyes. "Better be getting to your point, and fast. I have a tavern to run and don't have time to waste on a couple of crazed fools."

Bek looked at Ayrion. "They haven't made it this far yet." There was a hint of relief in his voice.

"They . . . Who's *they?*" Abiah asked.

"The vulraaks," Bek said.

"The vul—what? What flaming nonsense are you two going on about?" Abiah pushed back from the table. "I've had enough of this. Finish your drinks and be gone." He started to rise, but Ayrion and Bek both reached out, grabbed an arm, and pulled him back down.

"What's this?" he demanded.

"We're serious," Ayrion said as he glanced over Bek's shoulder at the nearby tables where heads were now turning in their direction. A single glare from Ayrion and the men went back to their own business. "We just came from Belvin. Well," he corrected, "outside of Belvin."

"I have a small place northeast of town," Bek said.

"Good for you. Now let me go."

"About a week ago, something happened to the townsfolk. They started changing."

Abiah stopped trying to pull free. "Changing? What do you mean *changing*?"

"It was small at first. They grew impatient over the littlest things. People who were quiet and timid were suddenly angry and ill-tempered. Some who'd never raised their voice against another were openly hollering and fighting in the streets—"

"Ha!" Abiah leaned back in his seat and laughed. "Sounds like Saeida after an especially long winter. So, a few people got upset; what's that got to do with anything?"

"If that's where it stopped, I wouldn't have been so concerned, but that was just the beginning."

Abiah stopped laughing.

"By the end of the week, the town had gone completely mad. The people had begun to change physically as well. They started growing fangs and claws, their eyes turned black, and their skin whitened. They wouldn't come out—"

Abiah slapped the top of the table with both hands. "What do you take me for? Do I look that gullible? This stops right here. Whatever you're sellin', I ain't buyin'.""

"I'm not trying to sell anything," Bek said desperately. "My own wife tried to kill me!"

"I can see why." Abiah stood, his belly pushing the table farther against the wall as he rose. "Now, if you two don't get out of my place, I'm going to have you thrown out."

Ayrion turned around. All eyes were on them.

"Take your rover scum and peddle your stories in some other town. You're not welcome in this one."

Ayrion stood and followed Bek to the front door. He scanned the rough faces as they passed, keeping an eye on their hands. To Ayrion's surprise, they managed to make it to the door without a scuffle. Once outside, he adjusted his coat against the cold wind whipping down the street and started for the other end of town. "Well, that could have gone better."

Ayrion and Bek joined the others and, after a quick conversation, climbed back in the wagons and left. They circled them within the tree line on the outskirts of town, using the forest as a breaker against the frigid gusts whipping across the valley between them and Saeida.

"What now?" Nell asked as they huddled in a circle around the campfire.

Tameel took a bite of his stew and sighed. "Guess we head to the next town and pray for better luck."

"I'm thinking that maybe we find you two some different clothing," Bek said as he blew across the top of his bowl before sipping the broth. "We're already fighting an uphill battle. It would be a whole lot easier if they didn't think we were another caravan of rovers. To be honest," he said, scratching his head, "I'm a little surprised by their behavior. I've never known the wood folk of Sidara to treat Nathillians this way."

"You haven't traveled very far, then," Tameel said. "It's becoming more rampant of late. With the ever-increasing presence of the Black Watch inside Sidara, more and more communities have shut their doors to strangers. Even us tinkers are finding it harder to attract customers."

Zynora nodded in agreement as she encouraged Marissa and Taylis to eat their food.

"I'm proud of my Rhivanni heritage," Tameel said, "and I won't change my appearance just to appease a group of backward fools. At the next town, perhaps Mother and I should keep the wagons out of sight and watch the kids while the three of you ride in and meet with the people."

"You can't help people who don't want to be helped," Zynora said.

Bek lowered his spoon. "Are you saying you wouldn't be willing to put on a different set of clothes if it meant saving an entire town from annihilation?"

Tameel stared at the thin soup in his bowl, then looked at Zynora. "I guess we'd be willing to do that."

"How close is the next town?" Ayrion asked, anxious to move the uncomfortable topic along. He wanted to make sure they had a plan in place before any action was taken. "Which direction should we take?"

"Northeast," Bek said, pointing off behind where Ayrion was sitting. "Estermill is another little town about a half day's journey from here. If we leave in the morning, we should be there by early afternoon."

Tameel lifted his bowl and drained what was left. "Good," he said, wiping his chin. "Estermill it is, then."

After the meal dishes were cleaned and the fire stoked, the small band of travelers turned in for the night. Tameel and Zynora slept in their wagon, and Nell took Taylis and Marissa with her. Ayrion and Bek volunteered to pitch their bedding by the fire and keep watch in case the friendly people of Saeida decided to pay them a visit.

Marissa had wanted to stay with Ayrion, but it was far too cold for her to be out in the weather.

Bek took first watch, giving Ayrion the chance to catch a few hours of sleep before his turn. He had just managed to doze off to the sound of the fire when something woke him. Sitting up, he cocked his head and listened. He thought he had heard something, or had it been another

nightmare?

There it was again. A faint cry.

Was that a wolf? He stood and walked to the edge of the camp and waited. This time, there was more than one sound, and they were growing. The hairs on his arms stood on end.

It wasn't howling. It was *screaming*!

Ayrion was already halfway to the wagon when the back door flew open and Tameel and Zynora stuck their heads out. "What's going on?"

"It's Saeida!" Bek shouted, charging back into the camp behind them. "They're under attack!"

Chapter 41 | Ayrion

NELL CLIMBED OUT OF her wagon, Marissa and Taylis clinging to either hand. "Should we run?"

"I hate to say it," Zynora said, "but we did try to warn them."

Ayrion stared out across the open valley between them and town. "There's nowhere to run. If it's the vulraaks, we have no way of knowing how many more are in the woods, or which direction they're coming from. For all we know, they could be blocking the roads out, waiting to grab anyone trying to escape."

"But we don't know that," Nell said, fear in her eyes.

"Can't you sense them?" Bek asked.

"Not like I used to," she said, readjusting Tameel's cap where it had slid sideways on her bald head.

"The vulraaks might seem like mindless brutes," Ayrion said, "but Argon isn't. And if I were him, I'd block the roadways." He turned toward the screams. "We need shelter. Out here, we have nothing but our wagons."

He grabbed his swords. "Take the supplies from the rover wagon and put them in this one," he said, pointing at Ol' Lera. "We only need the one. We'll cut the other team loose. From what I saw, the tavern looked to be the most defensible building in town. Stone walls."

"We still have the weapons we collected after the battle with Cylmar," Tameel said. "That will help."

Ayrion nodded.

"What about the children?" Nell asked, trembling so hard her husband had to hold her. "I could stay here with them in the spare wagon."

"They come with us," Zynora said, grabbing several bags from the rover wagon and handing them to Taylis and Marissa. "Put these next to the bed."

"Ayrion's right," Bek said. "We can't afford to get caught in the open. The safest thing for us to do is stay together."

"I want to fight," Taylis said, pulling a small antler-handled dagger out of the back of his pants. "I'm going to cut their heads off."

Zynora snatched the knife from him. "Where'd you get that? You and Marissa are going to stay in the wagon with Nell."

Taylis's cheeks flushed. Ayrion couldn't tell if the boy was going to lash out at her, start crying, or both.

Nell placed her arm around Taylis. "I need you to protect me and Marissa."

Taylis rolled his eyes and huffed.

Ayrion untied his warhorse and swung into the saddle. He drew a sword and kept a close watch on the surrounding woods, half expecting a crazed horde of vulraaks to come charging out at any moment.

He could feel the quiver of his horse beneath him. It was like the animal knew what was about to happen.

"Easy, there," he said as he gently stroked the horse's neck. "Save it for later."

It didn't take long before Bek was mounted and pulling alongside.

Tameel held the team steady as they left the protection of the trees, Zynora sitting beside him with a crossbow cradled in her lap.

"How are you feeling?" Ayrion asked. He hoped that if it came down to it, she would be able to unleash another one of those *impulso* blasts.

She looked at him but didn't smile. She knew what he was asking. "We'll see," she said.

Ayrion nodded and took the lead. Bek swung around to cover the rear as the small caravan picked up speed. They were nearing the first of the buildings on the outskirts of town when they saw people in their nightgowns coming out of their homes to see what was going on. This side of Saeida had evidently not been hit.

"Get to the tavern!" Ayrion shouted as they rode past. "The town is under attack!"

The screaming grew louder as the one road leading into Saeida took a sharp left turn toward the center of town, widening far enough to fit three wagons side by side. Tameel barely kept Ol' Lera on four wheels as they took the curve at full speed.

Up ahead, Ayrion could see the vulraaks coming around the corner on the far end of the street, their pale bodies gleaming in the light of the half-moon. They moved as a pack, maybe two or three deep. This looked more like a large hunting party than the full-scale attack they had faced before. The creatures didn't seem to be in a rush, either, spreading out as they ransacked the closest buildings on their way toward the center of town.

Ayrion passed the livery, noticing it was still untouched. If they managed to survive the night, they were going to need transportation. The street was filled with people, most fleeing in hysteria, a brave few attempting to fight off the nightmarish creatures.

It was a slaughter.

The lucky ones were fast enough to outrun their friends and neighbors. Those unable to keep up were cut down.

Ayrion swung his horse around the side of Ol' Lera. "Use the wagon to blockade the tavern before they get this far!"

Tameel nodded and jerked the reins to the right, steering the horses toward the front of the stone-sided building.

Ayrion pulled to a stop. He held the warhorse steady as it stomped the ground, nostrils flaring in eager anticipation. "Bek, do you think you can free the horses in the livery? Hopefully, they'll come back in the morning. If we survive the night, we're going to need as many as we can find to get these people out of here."

Bek nodded and turned his horse around, kicking it into a gallop.

Ayrion slapped his reins and chased after the wagon.

"Whoa!" Tameel shouted as he pulled the team to a stop in front of the tavern. The vulraaks were still on the far end of town, heading straight for them.

"Cut the horses free and get everyone inside!" Ayrion shouted, pulling to a stop alongside the wagon.

A wave of townsfolk flooded the street in their direction, pouring in from all sides as the vulraaks herded them forward.

"What are you going to do?" Tameel asked.

"Whatever I can." Ayrion slapped his reins and charged straight at the advancing horde. These people were never going to make it to the tavern if he didn't find a way to slow the creatures.

"Get to the tavern!" he yelled at those running down the street. Ayrion dropped the reins and drew his second blade, guiding the horse with his knees. "Take me into them, Shade," he said. It took him a moment to realize he had just called the large stallion by name. It was a slip of the tongue. A memory. Shade snorted and picked up speed.

They slammed into the front ranks, Ayrion's swords offering the vulraaks no mercy. They severed limbs, removed heads, and tore bodies apart as Shade carried them through the horde and out the back, swinging back around to go again.

The vulraaks were in a frenzy to sink their claws in him, but the enormous stallion tore through them with unyielding determination, trampling the half-human creatures under its hooves. Ayrion steered them back out, just to turn and charge through again. For the moment, they had successfully distracted the vulraaks, slowing their progression, but would it be enough?

They were still a few buildings away from the tavern, and some of the people were falling behind, those too feeble to keep up with the rest. Ayrion steered the warhorse back into the creatures at the front, struggling to hold their attention.

By the third time in, the vulraaks closed ranks around him. Shade took a deep cut to his left leg and nearly went down. Ayrion could almost feel the horse's pain. Shade kicked and screamed in defiance as Ayrion swung from one side of the horse to the other, cutting creatures apart as fast as he could.

A couple of vulraaks managed to rake Ayrion's leg, and he almost dropped one of his swords at the searing pain, but before he could bring the blade down, Shade leaped forward, tearing his way out of the pack, sides heaving. Ayrion couldn't afford to take him in again, so he jumped out of the saddle and smacked Shade's rump. "Go! Get out of here!"

Reluctantly, the horse obeyed and galloped away from the horde.

Behind him, people in their nightgowns were still pouring in from all sides of town, trying to reach the tavern. Ayrion could hear the taverner shouting to keep the doors open, encouraging those still coming to hurry.

He turned to face the creatures. There was no way he could hold off the entire onslaught, but he raised his blades anyway and drew on his magic. He could feel it rising inside him, the heat spreading from his chest to his arms as he gave himself to it. The creatures nearly trampled each other as they fought to reach him, to sink their teeth into his flesh, but with every attempt, blades as black as their blood were there to stop them.

Back and forth his arms flew as his blades cut through. He dodged and struck, weaved and cut. He killed so many of the creatures, he lost count. He could feel his strength ebbing and knew he couldn't hold out much longer—there were just too many of them. His jacket had cuts down both arms and across the front and back. He could feel each laceration.

How much farther did he have to go? How close was the tavern? He tried turning to see when a larger vulraak leaped over the others and knocked him off his feet. The creature landed on the tip of his blade and died, but the damage was already done. Quickly, he used his swords as a barrier to keep their teeth from reaching him. He kicked, snapping bones where he could.

Somewhere behind him he could hear shouting, human shouting. But he was too disoriented to determine where it was coming from. "Here! I'm here!" he yelled as he tried crawling backward toward the voices, fiercely hacking away at the only parts of the creatures available to him—their legs. The vulraaks screamed and dropped as their knobby joints were ripped open.

Ayrion yelled as a claw sank into his left thigh. The pain was sharp and swift. Then another in his right arm. He couldn't believe this was how it was going to end. He wondered if the others would keep to the mission without him, or whether they'd simply run and hide. He hoped Bek would hold them together.

A vulraak crawled under the others and lunged for Ayrion's throat. Ayrion grabbed it by the neck and squeezed, holding it off, but barely. He let go of one of his swords and grabbed a dagger inside his coat and stuck it through the creature's neck. Inky blood splattered Ayrion's face, and he gagged.

Before he could push the corpse off, the vulraaks retreated. Three or four hands grabbed him and dragged him away from the pack.

"Guess we should have listened!" a familiar voice behind him bellowed. Abiah released one of Ayrion's arms and swung an old sword at the nearest vulraak. The taverner hurled curses with every additional swing, demanding the creatures leave his town or suffer the consequences.

Bek yanked Ayrion to his feet and joined the small group of townsfolk as they fought to hold the creatures at bay. His hatchets tore into the vulraaks with impressive accuracy. The way he could use both sides of the head was amazing.

Ayrion made a quick scan of his torn jacket and pants. He winced at the deep cuts and punctures on his leg and arm. A quick glance behind him let him know they were only about twenty feet from the tinker wagon. "Retreat!" he shouted. "Get to the tavern!"

The small party of fighters broke and ran for the open door behind them.

On their right, a family of five was pressed against the wall of the next building down, trying to fend off a small pack of vulraaks. A father and older son stood in front of the others. The father had a sword, and his son had what appeared to be part of a shovel.

"That's Orin's family," Abiah shouted, spotting the fighting as well.

"Bek! Hold them back while I get that family," Ayrion said. "Abiah, you're with me."

"Fight!" Bek shouted at the other townsfolk as he turned to face the creatures once more.

The rest of the fighters turned with him, joined by a few more brave souls from inside.

Up ahead, Ayrion watched two vulraaks grab the older boy and yank him into the pack. Ayrion lost sight of him under the swarm of pale bodies. The mother screamed but the father kept swinging.

"Hurry!" Ayrion shouted at Abiah. "They aren't going to last much longer."

Chapter 42 | Ayrion

A YRION RUSHED THE small pack of vulraaks surrounding the family, taking the heads off two before Abiah had time to reach them. There were at least eight more. He released his magic and let the visions take over. Dancing between the creatures, Ayrion cut and thrust, parried and sliced. He felt invincible. The creatures couldn't touch him as he bobbed and weaved from one position to the next.

Abiah somehow kept pace, hacking away at any that fled Ayrion's blades.

Before they knew it, the rest of the vulraaks were lying dead at their feet.

Orin was too much in shock to even move. The youngest son was bleeding from a large gash on his arm, and the mother had sustained a nasty bite on her shoulder while using her body to shield her daughter.

Abiah stared at Ayrion as though he'd seen a spirit. "You scare me, swordsman."

Ayrion snatched up the injured boy. "We need to get inside." He turned to head back down the walkway but stopped. The front of the tavern was completely surrounded by vulraaks. He hoped Bek and the others were safe.

"Flaming monsters have us cornered," Abiah said.

"What are we going to do?" Orin asked, clinging to his wife and little girl.

A few of the vulraaks spotted them and broke off from the rest of the pack.

"Why did I listen to you?" Abiah groaned. "I should have stayed inside."

Ayrion scanned the building behind them. It looked like a strong wind would knock it down, but it was all they had. He put the boy down and kicked the door open. "Quick! Get inside!"

A loud boom shook the glass in the windows, and they were thrown to the ground.

Ayrion rolled to a stop a few feet away, his head spinning.

"What was that?" Abiah shouted, crawling to his hands and knees.

Ayrion almost grinned when he saw the street in front of the tavern was covered in white bodies. He stumbled to his feet and grabbed the boy. "Run!"

They charged down the walkway for the tavern door. Bek and Tameel were carrying Zynora back inside. The vulraaks that hadn't been thrown aside like autumn leaves in a brisk wind had slunk into the shadows, too afraid for the moment to pursue.

They reached the tavern, and Ayrion put the boy down.

"Why is it whenever you're around," Bek asked, "I find myself fighting for my life?"

"Just lucky, I guess."

Once everyone was inside, Abiah slammed the door shut and threw the heavy bracer into place. "That's about the stupidest thing I've ever seen!" he bellowed, turning to look at Ayrion. "The Creator didn't give you enough sense to fill a teacup. You nearly got me killed!"

"It worked, didn't it? We saved them." Ayrion bent over to get a better look at the cut on his leg. Blood was running down the inside of his pants and pooling in his right boot. A woman handed him a piece of cloth, and he pressed it against the wound. "Thank you."

"It . . . It was for your face," she said, her cheeks pale as she stared at him. "You're . . . covered in blood." Her hand trembled as she handed him a second cloth. He used that one to wipe his face and hands, then his swords.

The woman didn't move, continuing to stare. He didn't like the look in her eyes—part horror, part disgust. Was this what it was like to be a killer? If it was, he didn't want the job.

The creatures' angry screeches outside pulled him from his thoughts. They were probably getting ready to attack. The people had boarded the windows completely and stacked half the tables and furniture in front of them. Good thinking. It was going to be a long night.

Ayrion turned around so he didn't have to keep looking at the fear in the woman's eyes. "How many did we lose?" he asked Abiah.

Abiah glanced around the packed room and shook his head, releasing a hollow sigh. "Too many." He then turned to the boy Ayrion had seen sweating over the spit earlier. "Willem, go fetch me some ale; my mouth's as dry as a sand targ's backside." He smacked his lips as the freckled boy pushed his way through the crowd.

"That's your son?" Bek asked.

Abiah wiped his forehead with a cloth he'd pulled from the back of his pants. "Some days, he's mine; other days, I really wonder."

Ayrion walked over to where Orin was standing, staring blankly at the boarded-up window. "How is your family?"

Orin looked up, tears streaming down both sides of his face as he held his daughter in his arms. "My wife was hurt the worst." He pointed to the right side of the room, where some of the ladies were setting up a healing station under Zynora's careful instruction. Zynora's legs looked wobbly, but she wasn't letting it stop her. "Clara was bitten on her shoulder," Orin said. "Steffen has an ugly gash on his arm. And Tarence . . ." That was all he could say before breaking down into open sobs.

Ayrion laid a hand on the man's shoulder, then left him to his grief and rejoined Bek and Abiah near the front.

Willem returned with a single tankard and handed it to his father. Abiah downed nearly the entire thing before laying it to the side and wiping the foam from his mouth. "I think it's about time you gentlemen told us what's going on around here."

Bek crossed is arms. "Oh, so now you want to listen? Last I remember, we were being thrown out to the sound of laughter."

Abiah grunted. "Yes, well . . . what do you expect when a couple of strangers come prancing into town, claiming there's some sort of monsters coming to kill us?" He dabbed his forehead with a hand towel. "Next thing we know, we're being woken in our beds to the sound of people being eaten in the streets by a pack of white-faced lunatics. So, again, I ask you, what the blazes is going on?"

The tavern grew quiet, all eyes on Ayrion and Bek as they waited to hear the answer.

"They're called vulraaks," Zynora said, leaving her workstation to hobble over to where they were standing. She was chewing on a piece of fruit. "They used to be the good citizens of Belvin."

The room grew even quieter.

"Are you telling me those creatures out there used to be human?" Abiah asked.

"They were two weeks ago," Bek said. "I'm from Belvin. Me and my wife live a couple of miles outside of town. We watched it happen."

Bek told of how he had first noticed the changes in the townsfolk, then of his failed attempt to warn the rovers, which was where he had met Ayrion, Tameel, and Zynora.

After that, Zynora and Bek described their battle with the creatures, while Ayrion recounted his experience with their leader, Argon.

They were careful not to mention anything about Nell's transformation. There was no point to giving these people reason to fear her.

Ayrion finished with their decision to raise a force willing to fight back against this threat. "If we don't stop him, Argon could spread this disease across all of Aldor."

Zynora leaned on her cane. "These creatures are like a plague. Death would be preferable to what's in store for anyone they claim."

"It appears there's no need to go to Belvin to fight this army," Abiah said. "They're standing on our flaming doorstep."

Ayrion pointed at the door. "What you see here is just a small hunting party. There's a whole lot more where they came from."

Abiah blinked. "And you want us to just go strolling on into Belvin all willy-nilly? Are you mad?"

Ayrion smiled. "Probably."

Concerned voices filtered across the tavern. Ayrion was having a hard time selling this. He could see now why Tameel had quit allowing him to deal with the customers.

"That's right," he said, looking around at the frightened faces. "You should be afraid, but not of what's out there. You should be afraid of what's coming if we don't do something now. We have an opportunity we can't afford to squander. The vulraaks have taken Belvin, and have reached as far as Saeida, but they are restricted to traveling only while the sun is down. Because of this, their infestation will be slowed.

"We chose Saeida first because you are the closest to Belvin, which means if they are only just reaching us here now, then there's a good chance they haven't gotten any farther. But if we fail to stop them, they will continue to spread.

"We need to raise a large-enough force to go after Argon. He's the key."

"And how exactly do we go about stopping this Argon creature?" Abiah asked.

Ayrion scanned the frightened faces and realized he had backed himself into a corner. "I . . . I don't know. Yet."

Abiah thumbed his chin. "So, you want us to strap on our swords and bows and attack an army of flesh-eating monsters in order to kill a thousand-year-old general without the first idea as to how we're going to pull it off?" He looked at Bek, then back at Ayrion.

"Well, I don't know if I would have put it quite in those terms."

Abiah snorted. "Well, you've certainly got a pair; I'll give ya that."

"One of the things we need to figure out," Zynora said, using a cane for support, "is how this dark creature is creating the vulraaks. If we can determine that, it might just give us a way to destroy them."

Abiah lifted his tankard and took another swallow. "Seems pretty obvious to me." He rubbed the foam from his chin. "He's casting a dark spell on 'em."

"I doubt it's as simple as that," Bek said. "I don't think Argon merely strode into town one day and cursed everyone to turn into monsters. If it were that easy, I reckon he could've conquered Aldor when he was around the first time. From what I could tell, it looked to have started with just a few and spread from there. If everyone had gone to bed one evening and woken up cannibals, it would have been rather obvious, but it wasn't. It was more subtle than that. It began with personality changes and then moved on to physical. Although, now that I think about it, the speed of those changes seemed to vary from person to person. For example, when the—"

A woman screamed somewhere off to the right, and then another. Before long, a wave of bodies was rushing straight at them. The townsfolk stampeded like a herd of cattle away from whatever was going on near the stage at the back.

"Stop!" Ayrion yelled, but they didn't listen. He dove for an elderly woman who'd been knocked from her feet. He could hear her brittle bones snapping as her fellow citizens crushed her to the floor. He knocked three or four men off their feet to get to her.

He handed the woman to Bek and leaped up on one of the tables to get a better look. In the far corner, he could see Orin with a chair in his hand, trying to force his wife up against the wall.

"Stop it, Clara! It's me. It's Orin!"

Ayrion noticed the blood on the floor of the healing station. Two or three bodies lay in front of the small stage. He looked at Orin's wife and reached for his sword.

Her eyes were solid black.

Chapter 43 | Ayrion

AYRION SCANNED THE HEADS in front of him as the people screamed and clawed their way backward, squeezing each other to the point of suffocation. There was no way he was going to make it through. They were packed tight enough to walk across. And for a brief moment, he even considered it.

Above him, the ceiling angled upward toward the peak with thick beams running horizontal to the floor, spaced just enough that he thought he could get across. He sheathed his sword and leaped into the air, catching hold of the first. One by one, he swung across the rafters, his feet dangling just above the people's heads. But they were too busy trampling each other to even notice.

From there he could finally see what was happening.

Clara half yelled, half shrieked at Orin as he fought to keep the chair between him and her. He leaned all his weight into it as he forced her up against the wall. "What are you doing? Don't you recognize me?"

None of the other bodies on the floor were moving. Ayrion winced.

Two of them were Orin's children. The little girl Clara had been holding was on her back, her throat ripped out, and the boy was simply lying facedown in a pool of his own blood. The third was a woman Ayrion didn't recognize. She had deep claw marks on her side.

Ayrion was hanging from the second-to-last beam when it hit him. *What am I going to do when I get there?* It was one thing to blindly kill those creatures outside. He could tell himself they were no longer human, but this was someone who hadn't yet been turned. "Zynora! We need you over here!" He realized how stupid that sounded as soon as he said it. He'd just crossed the tavern by swinging from the rafters. How was she going to get there?

Ayrion grabbed the last beam, swung, and dropped in front of the crowd. He drew his sword, not sure what else to do, and started forward. A memory of Nell in her bed with Zynora telling him to cut off her head flashed through his mind. But they had found another way, he told himself. Zynora had been able to use her magic. He needed her.

Clara screeched again. She was changing faster than the others. At least, faster than Nell. Her skin was already blanching, and her hair was coming out in clumps, covering the floor around her.

Orin saw Ayrion coming. "No! Please. She didn't know what she was doing. She's my—"

Clara ripped the chair from her husband's hands and raked five claws across his chest, cutting deep into the flesh. Orin fell backward, begging the whole way down for Ayrion to spare her.

She lunged at Orin, but Ayrion tackled her before she could reach him. They rolled across the ground, and somehow, he managed to stay on top. "Clara, stop!" He knew his words were falling on deaf ears, but he was desperate.

She struggled to push him off. She was strong. Very strong. He dropped his sword to free his other hand. He had her pinned to the floor, but he couldn't keep her there on his own. "Help me!" he yelled at anyone who'd listen. No one wanted to get near her.

Orin dragged himself over to where Ayrion was holding her and grabbed one of her arms, freeing Ayrion enough to hold her feet as she tried to kick him off her.

"Zynora!"

Clara tried to bite him, and he punched her in the face. "Hold her arm tight!" he shouted at Orin, then twisted around and swung her over on her stomach. She flailed, but as long as they held her arms, she couldn't go anywhere.

Orin's grip was slipping. "I can't hold her much longer."

Ayrion knew what he had to do. It was the one thing he didn't want to. The people were already scared of him. Why was he the one everyone looked to when it came to killing? He reached for his sword, still holding her wrist as she hissed and jerked.

"No! Please!" Orin begged, weeping. "Please."

"We don't have a choice." Ayrion was afraid Orin would let go just to stop him, but he didn't. Ayrion raised his sword and stopped when he caught movement out of the corner of his eye. It was Bek. He was pushing his way along the outer front wall past the boarded windows. Zynora was right behind him.

Ayrion lowered his blade. "Hurry! We need your help."

Bek had his arm around Zynora as they rushed over to where Clara lay prostrate between the two men.

"Hold on, Orin," Ayrion said, encouraging the man not to let go. "If anyone can help, she can."

A heavy thump and a spray of blood had Orin screaming. Ayrion turned to see one of Bek's hatchets planted in the floor where Clara's head used to be. Clara went limp in his hands. He didn't move, transfixed on the fact that her head wasn't where it was supposed to be. It had rolled to the side, looking up at Zynora, who was on her knees holding the hatchet's handle. He looked at Zynora. "What did you do?"

"What needed to be done," she said, releasing her grip and letting Bek pull her to her feet.

"You could have saved her. You could have healed her."

Zynora held on to Bek's arm for balance. "I can't heal anyone right now, and unless you plan on spending the rest of the night holding her arms so she doesn't kill us all, we didn't have a choice."

Ayrion finally released the woman as Orin crawled over to his dead children and gathered them in his arms. He turned away, unable to bear the man's grief.

He made it to his feet and turned to face the people. He couldn't see much past the first couple of rows, so he hopped up on the stage.

"Listen to me!" he shouted, his sword still in his hand. "Why should we worry about keeping the vulraaks from killing you when you're just as likely to do it for them?"

The people started to quiet down as they turned to look at the stage.

He scanned the crowd. All he could see were terrified faces.

"If we're going to survive this, you need to work together. I just watched you nearly trample a woman to death in order to save yourselves. Outside, the elderly and feeble were left to the creatures while the rest of you ran for cover."

No one said a word. No one moved.

"I have half a mind to just leave you here to fend for yourselves. Why risk my life and the lives of my friends to help a community who doesn't care enough for each other to have the human decency to protect the weak!"

He looked at Bek and Zynora. Bek seemed as stunned as the crowd. Zynora simply nodded. He wondered if he'd taken it too far. He was never one for being subtle, and on top of it all, they still needed these people. He exhaled slowly, trying to release some of the anger, the rush of adrenaline surging through his veins. "Lucky for you, I'm not one to leave people behind." He lifted his sword and pointed it at them. "Now look around you."

No one moved.

"Yes, right now. Look to your left. Now look right. Look behind you.

These are the people you're fighting for. This is your town. Your family. Your friends. These are the people you are going to be entrusting with your life. We either stand together or die alone."

Before he could step down from the stage, people had begun helping up those who had been pushed down in the stampede, offering apologies and handshakes.

"What now?" someone called from over near the bar.

Ayrion stopped on the bottom step and groaned. He hadn't had a chance to think that far ahead. His only concern had been to stop the riot before they lost any more lives.

"I'll tell you what happens now," Tameel's raspy voice rang out from the other side of the room.

The crowd parted to allow the white-haired tinker through. Nell, Taylis, and Marissa shuffled along behind him.

"We lay these dead to rest with as much dignity as we can, we help our wounded, and we continue to fight."

"Are we still in danger?" another man asked on the right.

As if in answer to his question, the vulraaks began pounding on the door and boarded windows, their screeches starting up once again.

Panic set in, and the crowd started retreating toward the back of the building.

"Stop!" Ayrion shouted. He jumped back up on stage so they could see him. "You start another stampede, and I'll cut you down myself. Now pull the elderly, the women, and the children to the back. The rest of you hold your places at the front and keep that barricade protected. As long as it's up, the creatures can't get in."

"What are you waiting for?" Abiah shouted, pushing his way to the front of the stage. "Move!"

The townsfolk obeyed, gathering the women and children and those too feeble to fight and moving them to the back. The pounding and scratching continued, but other than listening to the vulraaks' unnerving cries, the people were in no immediate danger. The tavern was solidly built. Hopefully, it would hold till morning.

Ayrion smiled. "You see what happens when you work together?"

"But are we safe in here?" a man near the front asked.

"What happened to Clara?" a woman asked. "I thought we'd rescued them from those things outside."

"What if others start to change?" another said. "How do we know who we can trust? Any one of us might turn into one of those creatures."

The crowd grew uneasy, threatening to topple all the work Ayrion had just put into calming them down.

"It was the bite!" Zynora said. She was down on her knees examining Clara's body. More accurately, her head.

"You aren't going to turn into a vulraak just because you happened to be near one. We were just asking how this plague is spread. It now appears that we have our answer. See here," she said, pointing at a couple of marks on Clara's shoulder. She was bitten, whereas none of the others were.

"How do we know they won't turn as well?" someone asked.

Zynora looked at Ayrion, then back at the crowd. "We don't. Not exactly, anyway. We can only go on what we've seen. When we first fought the vulraaks, days ago, we all received multiple cuts from that battle, but as you can clearly see, none of us have changed. Of the wounded we have here, only Clara had teeth marks."

Zynora cautiously opened Clara's mouth with the tip of her dagger and lowered a lantern down to look inside. "Hah! Here's your proof. She has sacs just behind her teeth."

"Like a snake?" Abiah asked.

"Exactly like a snake," she said. "Has anyone ever died from touching a snake?"

Abiah grinned. "That's debatable."

"I mean without being struck." Zynora frowned at the taverner, and he wiped the grin off his face. "Touching a snake isn't going to kill you. In fact, there are plenty who enjoy eating venomous snakes, and it doesn't kill them. I even know of a few who've been bitten by stripers without any effect, simply because the snake's poison was never released. I'm guessing this is probably similar."

Zynora stood with Bek's help and made her way to the platform. "We will keep a close eye on our injured, but be assured, you aren't going to spontaneously turn into vulraaks. The last thing we need is for everyone to start mistrusting each other."

"As long as you stay within these walls and keep a level head," Tameel said, "you'll be safe."

The people slowly began mingling once again. A few helped Orin wrap his family in canvas tarps Abiah had been using to cover his larger casks. Zynora made sure no one touched Clara but herself. After the bodies were removed, they began the tedious work of mopping up the blood. They stored the rags along with the bodies in the tavern's cellar.

Once the dead had been seen to, Ayrion's small group gathered around the stage to talk. Abiah was included in the meeting since he, above anyone else, seemed to be the spokesperson for the town. Taylis and Marissa stood beside Nell, amusing themselves by watching the townsfolk.

"Anyone else surprised that Argon isn't here?" Bek asked.

"After his fight with Ayrion," Tameel said with a wry smile, "I have a feeling he won't be as eager to get his hands dirty."

"I doubt it has anything to do with me," Ayrion said. "I barely survived, myself. My guess is that the farther they spread, the more time he needs to spend organizing whatever it is he has in mind. Plus, I doubt he's gone to the hassle of keeping himself alive all these years just to take a chance of dying now. Why risk your neck when you can have others risk theirs?"

"Then why did he come the first time?" Bek asked.

"Probably to find out why his hunting party never returned. If I were him, I'd want firsthand knowledge of what I was up against. No better way to do that than to be in the field."

"You talk as though you've had some military training," Abiah said with a raised brow.

Ayrion smirked. "A little."

"More than a little, I'd say," Abiah said with a snort. "I've never seen anyone fight like that."

Ayrion changed the subject. "As soon as the sun begins to rise, we need to get these people out of here."

"We won't last another night holed up in here like rats," Bek said, still propping Zynora up with his arm. "Our best chance is to get to the next town, warn them, and start gathering a force large enough to fight back."

"Aye," Abiah said. "Estermill is about a half day's journey on horseback. But for a group this size on foot, it could take a day or two."

Ayrion nodded. "Have them get as much sleep as possible. At the crack of dawn, we'll take them back to the rover camp and plan our next move."

Abiah laughed. "You think a single person in here is going to close their eyes and go to sleep?"

Ayrion studied the wide-eyed faces of the Saeida townsfolk. "Guess not."

Chapter 44 | Lenara

S YLAS HAD KEPT THEM MOVING continuously since they had left the White Tower, with barely a moment's rest. The inquisitor was on a mission. He made no effort to hide his feelings and even kept Lenara up most nights, spouting off the many ways he'd make the smith and the healer pay once they caught up with them. Sylas had been humiliated, strung up on his own rack for all to see. Worse yet, he'd been murdered by the only woman he'd ever cared about, if you could call what he felt for her *caring*.

Lenara certainly didn't.

Sylas had lost something, or more accurately, something had been taken from him. His pride. And nothing short of death would stop him now.

That evening, Lenara sighed as she laid her head back on her blankets and stared up at the stars through the branches overhead. Sylas had finally dozed off after another long-winded speech about how he was going to make Ferrin and Rae pay, finally leaving her alone to her own thoughts.

She couldn't help but wonder again why she'd been saddled with accompanying Sylas in the first place, other than the fact that Valtor was clearly punishing her for her failure to retrieve the faeling child the first time. She should be the one going after him. None of the bulradoer had spent as much time studying the prophecies about his coming as she had.

She was the one who had discovered the child's arrival, the one who had brought this information to Valtor, and one of three bulradoer who had been tasked with finding him. Now, instead of being allowed to pursue this rare creature, she had to endure the insufferable rantings of a madman. The only bearable aspect to this whole journey was Joren's occasional appearance.

The young guard's presence was still a mystery. Both men's consciousnesses shared the same body, but Sylas's seemed to be the more dominant. Why? Was it solely the magic, or was it simply that Sylas was stronger? The only time Joren made an appearance was after Sylas had fallen asleep, which would seem to support her earlier theory that Sylas was the more dominant, but once his consciousness was at rest, Joren then became stronger. If that was the case, then why didn't Joren show up every night?

Lenara groaned. She hated puzzles. Grabbing her blanket, she pulled it up to her chin and closed her eyes. She had just managed to doze off when something rubbed her shoulder. She opened her eyes with a start. Sylas was kneeling beside her bedding. She didn't say anything, unsure of who she'd be addressing.

"Where are we?"

"Thornwood," she said, guessing by the confusion in his soft brown eyes that it was Joren. But she wasn't sure. "Is there something you need?" A safe-enough question no matter who she was addressing.

"How long has it been?"

"How long has what been?"

He looked around cautiously at the other guards. "Since . . . the last time."

She sat up. "It's been six days."

"Oh," he said, his smile slipping as he sat down beside her. "That long? Are we still chasing those same people?"

She nodded.

"I had a strange dream," he said. His breath steamed in front of his face as he pulled his white mantle tight around his shoulders.

"Oh?"

Joren nodded. "You were in it," he said, bringing a slight flush to her cheeks. "You were talking to me about birds."

Lenara blinked. "I was talking to you about . . . birds?"

"Yes," he said with an emphatic nod. "I was telling you that I could talk to birds."

Why would he be dreaming about . . . She raised her head. The corax. This was a new development. Some part of him was aware of what was going on. But how much?

"In my dream," he said, "I could talk to them. Even control them."

"What did it feel like?"

"I'm not sure I can explain it. It was so real. I could actually hear their thoughts in my head." The fire cast shadows across his face, honing his already sharp features. "It was as clear as the conversation we're having right now."

It was the first time she'd seen him smile. There certainly wasn't much to be jovial about, but it was nice to see, anyway. "Tell me something about yourself," she said. It had been a long time since she had sat and talked with anyone. Sylas talked *at* her. In the Tower, she spent most of her time either studying magic or researching ancient histories. She couldn't remember the last time she'd had an honest conversation with another person that didn't involve her work.

"What do you want to know?"

She shrugged. "I don't know. Where are you from?"

"Cylmar."

"What part?"

"Ecrin. It's on the western side of Lake Nari."

"Yes. I've been there before."

Joren's head lifted. "You have?"

"A couple of times when I was a little girl." Memories of her family began to resurface, memories she hadn't thought about in years. And for good reason. "My family lived in Erast."

"Erast?" A guard at another fire grunted and turned over, and Joren lowered his voice. "You're Cylmaran as well?"

She nodded. "My father traveled to Ecrin once a year to sell hides. My sister and I would usually go with him." She smiled. "I remember thinking how big the city was."

"You have a sister?" he asked. "I have two brothers. Both older."

Lenara nodded. "Her name was Viena."

"Was?"

She turned and looked at the fire, doing her best to hold back the flood of memories she had carefully dammed away over the years. "She's dead."

"I'm sorry."

"In a way, my sister is the reason I became a bulradoer."

"Really?"

"Really."

"Really what?"

Lenara turned and found herself staring into a different pair of eyes. They were no longer soft or caring, but hard and determined.

"What were we just talking about?" Sylas asked, looking quite puzzled at the fact that he was sitting with Lenara instead of sleeping in his bed.

Lenara's mind raced frantically to cover for Joren. "I was just asking whether or not you had heard anything new from the corax."

He looked up at the sky, still trying to figure out what was going on. "They say we're close. Maybe a day out. If we maintain this pace, we should overtake them somewhere around Iraseth."

"Any guess as to where the smith is going?"

Sylas turned his gaze northward and smiled. "Home."

Chapter 45 | Ferrin

"THIS LOOKS AS GOOD a place as any," Ferrin said as the four reined up in front of what might have been the nameless town's only tavern. It was hard to tell with rain coming down in sheets and no visible sign out front.

It had been nearly a week since Suri had first spotted the unnaturally large reptilian birds. They had taken a keen interest in the small group, keeping to the skies during the day and the shadows of surrounding trees at night. Whether he could see them or not, he could feel them. That sensation of dread had him pushing his small caravan all the harder.

Rae had been using her healing to keep the horses moving as they traveled night and day without sleep, adding as much distance between them and those that were following as they could. When she had collapsed from exhaustion that afternoon, Ferrin finally agreed to stop for the night.

"Here, give me your hand," he said, helping Rae dismount. Her legs and arms were shaking under their own weight. Surprisingly, she never complained. Most likely because she knew what would happen if they were caught. Still, he wondered if he was pushing them too hard.

Ferrin helped her to a bench on the covered porch and then took a step back to shake the water from his lengthening beard and matted hair. His beard was every bit as red as his hair. He'd never let it grow this long before. Leaving her on the bench, he ran back out into the rain for Suri, who was tucked up under Myron's heavy cloak.

"I'll stable the horses," Myron said, handing the little girl down to him.

Ferrin carried Suri to the porch. "We'll see you inside. I need to get them out of this rain."

Myron nodded and guided the horses around back.

"Can you walk?" Ferrin asked Rae.

She grunted as she pushed up from the bench. Her steps were unsteady, but she managed to reach him.

With Suri in one arm and Rae leaning against the other, Ferrin opened the tavern door and stepped inside. The heat was welcoming, as was the scent of cooked food. As hungry as he was, it could have been a pot of goat entrails and it would have smelled like a feast fit for the king.

A smattering of tables dotted the open floor. Every stool and barrel-top seat in front of the long bar at the back was filled. Smoke hung in the air like an early-morning fog rising above the tables.

Ferrin shut the door, and all heads turned in their direction. The room quieted, save for the periodic creak of a wooden chair, as the crowd studied the three waterlogged travelers.

He scanned the dirty, tired faces of the patrons. Quite the gruff-looking lot. "Evening," he said with as friendly a smile as he could muster.

No one replied.

A set of double doors swung open at the back, and a short, stocky woman stepped through. She wiped fallen strands of brown hair behind one ear, leaving behind white streaks of flour that blended with the splashes of grey. She patted the front of her apron and gave them an appraising look. "What's your business here?"

Ferrin cleared his throat. "We're not quite sure where *here* is."

The woman started laughing. "Son, if you don't know where you are, then you're a far sight more lost than you know."

Ferrin didn't doubt it. Having spent the last week traveling deer trails through some of the thickest woods he'd ever encountered, it was a wonder they'd managed to find any civilization at all. "We're hoping to find shelter for the evening." He sniffed the air. "And some food for our rather empty bellies."

"Well, I can't rightly say this is the best place for your missus and little girly," the woman said, "but take a seat."

Rae dug her fingers into Ferrin's arm. "I'm no one's missus," she said, and released his arm to stand on her own.

Ferrin wanted to shake his head and laugh but was afraid of her reaction if he did.

The tavern owner looked as though she wasn't sure who to address. "Well, either way, we don't have overnight accommodations, 'less you don't mind bunking in the stable with your horses." She looked at Ferrin inquiringly. "You do have horses, don't ya, son?"

"Yes, ma'am, that we do."

She nodded and wiped her hands back across the front of her apron. "I guess I could rustle up some vittles and a few spare blankets for the woman and the little one."

"Mighty kind of you, ma'am."

"No need for the *ma'am*. The name's Layna."

Ferrin nodded. "Thank you, Layna."

"Well, don't just stand there," she said, waving her arms in a shooing fashion. "Go find yourselves a table, and I'll be right with you. What are the rest of ya gawkin' at?" she asked, casting a stern gaze across the room. "Like you ain't never seen a stranger round these parts before."

Ferrin thought they probably hadn't, judging by their expressions.

He helped Rae and Suri to the table closest to the hearth, and the crowd slowly went back to their drinks or food and gossip.

Layna returned with three mugs and a pitcher with steam rising from its top. "Some cider to warm the bones," she said, filling their glasses to the brim.

"We have one more," Ferrin said. "He's seeing to our horses."

Layna cast a wary glance at the nearest tables and then leaned in a little closer. "I don't want to sound harsh, but you do have coin for this, don't you, son? You understand, of course, I can't afford charity."

"We have plenty," Rae stated as she stared desperately at the steaming drink in the woman's hand.

Ferrin coughed. "Yes . . ." he quickly added, trying not to look at Rae. "We can cover our stay and the meal."

Layna just smiled and swiped the same strand of hair back over her ear. "Well, that's good to hear. Don't want to be wasting good food on those who can't pay. Times be tough nowadays; can't be too careful."

Ferrin watched with a smile as Layna finished filling Rae's mug before finally leaving the pitcher on the table and heading back to the kitchen. She stopped at a few tables along the way to talk with customers.

"Best not to mention that we have coin to others," he said.

Rae shrugged and took a sip of her drink. "Why?"

Ferrin glanced around the room. "We never know who we can trust."

She didn't say anything more, not even a simple head-bob to let him know she understood. She simply continued to raise and lower her mug, looking over at Suri every now and then to make sure the little girl was doing fine with her own drink.

Ferrin took a deep swallow himself. The warm cider went down smooth. It was the first drink with flavor he'd tasted since his capture so many months before. Ferrin thought it was wonderful. Just the right touch of apple and cloves to tingle his throat as it went down. He finished his first glass, refilled it, then left the table and stood in front of the hearth to dry off. He moaned softly as the warmth of the flames enveloped him.

Behind him, the door opened, and Myron stepped inside, drawing all heads back to the front of the room. Spotting Ferrin by the fire, he shut the door and walked over.

"Rough-looking bunch," he said, shaking the rain from his clothes like a hound after a cold soak in the river.

"Thanks," Ferrin said with a scowl as he stared down at the new splotches of water Myron had just showered him with. "The horses stabled?"

Myron nodded. "Not much of a stable, if you ask me," he said under his breath. "Barely any hay, and certainly no oats."

Rae and Suri left the table to join them by the fire. "Here," she said, and handed Myron the mug Layna had just left. She scooted Suri between the two men to get her closer to the hearth.

Myron downed the entire helping in one gulp. "Oh, that hit the spot." He looked at Ferrin. "Did you find us a room?"

Ferrin smiled. "The stables."

Myron grimaced.

"The only place available, evidently," Ferrin said. "The owner is working on getting us a plate of whatever's on the stove."

"Right now, I wouldn't care if it was freshly caught muskrat," Myron said with an unnerving amount of sincerity. "I just want something hot and chewy."

It wasn't long before the short taverner pushed back through the swinging doors with a tray filled to overflowing. Balancing their food with the skill of a Keldoran dancer, she weaved through the tables.

The group left the warmth of the fire to settle back into their seats.

"I take it you found the stables," Layna said to Myron, handing out the plates of stewed meat layered in thick gravy. Myron nodded as he lifted his spoon, more eager to stuff his face than talk. He had nearly cleaned his plate by the time Layna had put Ferrin's down.

Myron licked his lips, and for a brief moment, Ferrin thought he was about to lick his plate as well. "I haven't tasted a better stew since my grandmother passed ten years back."

Layna smiled and took his platter. "More?"

"Do you even need to ask?"

Ferrin finished off the last bite of his own dish and wiped his mouth. "If you can keep these salvers filled till we say enough, I'll make sure there's some extra coin in it for your troubles."

Layna smiled. "I'll have you rolling out of here before I'm through." With that, she took off toward the back, this time ignoring a few of her regulars on the way.

True to her word, she had them hobbling from their seats by the time they finished what was left. Ferrin felt like he'd just made up for the last few months he'd spent starving in the Tower, eating their diet of maggoty bread and sour gruel. Unlike Myron, he'd only been able to make it through two and a half bowls before feeling an uncomfortable tightness in his stomach. He was glad he had stopped when he did; otherwise, he had a feeling he'd be losing most of it later.

By the time they finished, most of the patrons had left, though there were still two tables of men near the back, smoking their pipes, chatting quietly to themselves.

"About time we turned in," Ferrin said with a yawn as he loosened his pants straps. His last swallow of cider hadn't made it any farther down than the middle of his throat. His body felt heavy, and breathing took a little extra effort, but it was worth it.

Ferrin paid for the meal and accommodations, then followed the others out the front and around to the stable. The barn was cold and cramped but dry, and right then, that was all that truly mattered. After making sure the horses were fed, the weary travelers laid their bedding across some bales of hay near the back, keeping close together for the warmth.

"We need to set up a watch," Ferrin said to Myron as Rae and Suri snuggled under their blankets.

"I agree. Didn't care much for the look of her patrons."

"I'll take first watch, then."

"Wake me in three."

"Do me a favor and try not to snore so loud," Ferrin said with a smirk. "You'll spook the horses."

Myron tossed a handful of hay at him, then leaned his sword against the wall and crawled under his blankets.

Ferrin sat down in front of one of the stalls about six feet from where Myron, Rae, and Suri were sleeping. Without a fire to warm him, he covered himself up in his blanket and listened to the horses as they stirred in their stalls. It didn't take long before the sound of Myron's snores overpowered everything else.

Ferrin shook his head.

It was a battle to keep his eyes open as he sat there. A few hours here and there was all he had managed to claim over the last couple of weeks. In fact, he hadn't had a full night's rest since his capture in Rhowynn months earlier. He longed to be back home. To see his sister's smile. To stoke the coals of his forge and strike the hammer on the anvil.

He jerked awake. *How long was I out?* He pinched his leg to try clearing the grogginess, then glanced at his companions. Still asleep. Myron had turned over on his side, which had apparently stopped the snoring.

Something rustled off to the right near the front of the barn, and he turned, slowly. He listened, waiting to see what it was. Possibly mice.

He waited a while longer, but nothing happened.

He yawned and shook his head. *Got to stay awake.* The temperature was dropping, leaving his hands shaking and fingers numb, so he tucked them under the blanket and leaned his head back against the stable door. The rain had stopped, and the faint, pale light stemming from the window at the side let him know the clouds were breaking.

Suri fidgeted in her blankets, drawing his attention. She cuddled in a little closer under Rae's arm. He envied the warmth their bodies shared. He bit down to keep his teeth from chattering as his eyes once more began to droop.

A door hinge creaked, and this time, he came fully awake.

Faint whispers from the front of the barn had him turning his head once again, careful not to make any sudden movements and alert whoever was there that he was awake. Ferrin's sword was resting with the other weapons against the back wall on his left, between Myron and Rae. He couldn't reach them without being spotted, so he slid the stone dagger from its sheath at his waist.

He stiffened at the sound of approaching steps. A flash of movement to his left let him know that Myron was awake as well.

"Their saddlebags are empty," someone whispered.

"They must have the coin with them."

By now, the purse snatchers were close enough for Ferrin to make out their silhouettes against the moonlight. He counted six, maybe seven. Two against seven. Not good odds, especially when those two were barely able to stand from a lack of sleep. The only hope they had was the element of surprise.

Ferrin jumped to his feet, his adrenaline pumping, and shouted at the top of his lungs, hoping to startle the men long enough to gain an advantage.

It worked—perhaps a little too well. His sudden outburst scared Rae and Suri so badly, both of them screamed on top of it.

The men froze as Ferrin dove headfirst into the middle. He plunged his knife into the first man's chest as he went by. The man barely had time to cry out before Ferrin barreled into the next and opened his throat. A familiar gurgling sounded as he, too, fell.

The barn erupted into chaos. Men shouted and cursed as the sharp sting of the stone dagger pierced their flesh. The darkness was working in Ferrin's favor as the men began attacking each other, unable to see who was attacking them.

Myron flew by on Ferrin's left, barely missing Ferrin's head as he swung at one of the men. Ferrin danced to the right to keep away from the captain's sword.

A torch burst to life near the front doors, scattering shadows across the barn and revealing the gruff faces of their attackers. The flash of light almost blinded Ferrin. He covered his eyes and looked away, but not before one of the men lunged.

Ferrin dove right, slamming against a stall door, barely managing to keep from getting skewered. His fingers were having a hard time gripping the stone blade because of the cold. He spun and deflected the man's sword into the door beside him. It stuck, and Ferrin used that time to slit his attacker's forearm.

The man shouted and released his weapon, and Ferrin finished him with a quick thrust to the neck.

Four left.

Myron cried out on the other side and went down, one man holding him while the other stabbed him in the side. Two more turned to help finish him, but Ferrin grabbed the man he'd just killed and threw him into the pack. The weight knocked all four backward and away from Myron.

Myron rolled over and rammed his sword upward into the midsection of the closest man. The attacker tumbled forward and landed on top of him. Neither moved.

Ferrin rushed the three remaining men. He yanked Myron's sword from the dead man's chest and swung at the man on the left. The man raised his sword to block, and Ferrin buried the stone blade in his chest while his attention was diverted.

Two more.

He backswung on the second attacker, but the man proved decent with a blade and blocked the attempt, forcing Ferrin to jump back to keep from getting his head lopped off. The man kicked Ferrin in the side, and he stumbled backward.

Seeing their chance, the two remaining men rushed him.

He blocked the first and sidestepped the second, but they managed

to corner him against the stalls. Ferrin was a decent swordsman, but not in his weakened condition, and not against these odds. One of the men thrust, and Ferrin blocked with his sword, but while his weapon was occupied, the second swung a club at his head. Ferrin raised his arm. The club missed his head, but he heard the bone in his arm snap.

Ferrin screamed, the pain so intense his entire left side went numb. He ducked to miss a second strike, dove to the left, and tumbled over a pile of hay.

"It was a valiant effort," the man with the sword said as he raised it over his head to finish Ferrin off.

For a split second, Ferrin was almost relieved. *At least now I'll finally get some rest.*

Suddenly, a blade punched out the front of the man's shirt, and he spat blood. He had just enough time to look down at the blood-soaked tip before his eyes closed and he collapsed. Rae stood behind him, her face so calm, Ferrin found it disturbing.

The last of their attackers made a quick dash for the doors, pushing the hooded figure with the torch out of the way.

"Wait! Where are you going, you coward?!" the torch wielder shouted.

Layna.

"They're all yours," the man called back.

The taverner took one look at Ferrin and ran out the doors after him.

Ferrin started after her, but Rae grabbed his injured arm, and he nearly emptied his stomach at the pain. She spun him around and pointed at Myron. She was right. They had more important things to worry about. He followed her over to where their comrade lay bleeding beneath one of their attackers.

Ferrin pulled the dead man off, and Rae lifted Myron's shirt, laying her hands on the wound. The familiar lavender glow spread from her fingers and bore down into the open wound, lancing into the surrounding muscle. Myron gasped and then slowly exhaled. Ferrin was all too familiar with the feeling.

The light faded from Rae's hands, and she was on her feet, heading to the back of the barn where Suri was waiting, curled in a ball under her blankets.

"That . . . That was . . ." Myron stared wide-eyed at the healed wound in his side. "Incredible. I've watched her do that to you more times than I can count," he said, looking up at Ferrin. "But I never thought to experience it myself. It was like icy—"

Someone shrieked near the back, and both men turned to find Rae pushing her body weight onto the pommel of her sword to shove the blade into a body that wasn't already dead. The man moaned and went still. Ferrin and Myron watched with astonishment as she pulled the blade out of the man's back and moved to the next to repeat the process.

Ferrin glanced at Myron. Myron looked like he was going to be sick.

Ferrin cleared his throat and looked at Rae. "As soon as you finish making sure everyone's good and dead, would you mind fixing my arm?"

Rae ignored him until the last man had been thoroughly impaled, then she walked over, handed him the bloody sword like nothing had happened, and grabbed his arm.

Ferrin yelped as the icy chill rushed in. The pain eased, eventually disappearing altogether. "Much better," he said as he moved it around to make sure it worked properly.

"So much for us finally getting some sleep," Myron groused as he pulled himself up to his feet with a little help from the stall door. "Is it really so much to ask for one single night's rest?" The horse in the stall looked at him and nickered as if he agreed.

Ferrin chuckled and started sifting through the dead men's belongings. "At least we can use some of their clothes. Not much in the way of coin, though. Barely five coppers between the lot."

"Better pack our stuff and be on our way," Myron said. "As fast as Layna tore out of here, I wouldn't doubt her coming back with the rest of this sorry excuse for a town behind her."

"They're back."

Both men turned at the sound of Suri's voice. She was still curled up in her bedding, sitting with her back against the wall.

Ferrin grabbed his knife and turned to look at the doors. There was no one there. "Who's back?"

Suri raised her hand and pointed up.

Ferrin followed her gaze to a small window hidden high in the rafters.

A gruff *Caw!* rang out as the enormous bird spread its dark wings and flew off into the night.

Chapter 46 | Lyessa

"YOU HEARD ME, ladies, I want to see you spread those feet."
Lyessa glanced over her shoulder at the other two. She couldn't help but chuckle as Darryk smacked Fraya's left leg with his position stick, eliciting a wide-eyed look of embarrassment from the raven-haired young woman as the weapons master struggled to get her legs into a proper fighting stance.

Adarra, standing opposite of Fraya, nearly tripped and fell for the third time as she maneuvered into position—left leg forward, slightly bent, and right leg behind, angled outward.

"Right," Darryk said, sounding like one of her father's sergeants as he smacked his stick across the thick of his palm. "Back to your starting positions, and let's try that again, shall we?" Darryk was certainly enjoying his role. It had been a long time since he'd been a commander in the Sidaran Lancers. He was a natural leader and an even better instructor.

"Whose idea was it to do this, anyway?" Adarra griped, struggling to catch her breath.

"Yours," Fraya snorted.

From what Lyessa had learned about her new friends over the last couple of weeks, Fraya spent a great deal more time working outdoors than Adarra. Adarra tended to spend most of her free time wading through mounds of books while reclining in a firm rocker. The difference showed. Fraya was winded, but Adarra looked ready to collapse.

"You need to be able to defend yourselves," Lyessa said. "When a battle breaks out, you can't always rely on the men. And since neither of you has a lick of combat magic, it's about time you learned how to handle a proper weapon. From now on, I want you over here at least four days a week. You will learn hand-to-hand combat, and from there we will move on to weaponry and tactics."

"We aren't lancers, Lyessa," Fraya said, rolling her eyes as she attempted to perform a simple snap-kick that would have been lucky to reach her opponent's knee. "We're women. We can't be expected to fight like men."

"This is hopeless," Adarra groaned as she shuffled her back leg to move to the second position Darryk had shown them earlier. "I saw the way you fought those Northmen. It was amazing. But let's be honest," she said, stopping long enough to look at her footwork and throw her arms out in exasperation. "I could never do that."

"Yes, you can." Lyessa was having a difficult time instilling encouragement. "When I first started, I wasn't any better than you—"

"Worse, even," Darryk added with a *humph*, his eyes smiling where his mouth dared not.

"Hey!" Lyessa glared.

Darryk crossed his enormous arms over his barrel chest. "The point is, ladies," he said, "that I plan on taking what the Creator has seen fit to bless you with and turn it into something dangerous. By the time I'm done with you, if a man so much as looks at you the wrong way, you won't cower in fear. Instead, you will spend those precious moments trying to determine which of thirty-six ways you know to field-dress him and mount his head over the hearth as a trophy."

Lyessa blinked a couple of times, grimacing at the visual image, then turned and glared at him.

Darryk cleared his throat. "Forget the head-mounting. The point is, I've been tasked with giving you the tools you'll need to help keep you safe. And by thunder," he said with another smack of the position stick to his palm, "that's what I intend to do. Now move back to position!"

From the looks on their faces, Adarra and Fraya had never been as relieved to shed their clothes and crawl into a hot bath as they were at that present moment.

The steam from the tubs swirled around the room like a summer fog, clinging to Lyessa's skin, helping to ease the burn of another hard session of training.

"Lyessa!"

Lyessa turned to find her friends staring at her naked figure. She suddenly felt embarrassed. She wasn't sure why. They were as naked as she was.

Fraya pointed at her. "What happened to your . . . your—"

"Your whole body!" Adarra blurted out as she scanned Lyessa from top to bottom. Adarra was clearly not one for beating around the bush. It was actually rather refreshing. Those in Lyessa's circle rarely said what they meant. They always seemed to have a hidden agenda behind everything they did.

The two girls walked over and began a thorough examination of the damage, their fingers tracing each raised mark.

"Darryk and her father is what happened to my precious little one," Gina said, emptying a bucket of hot water into one of the three brass tubs.

Lyessa's nanny frowned at the scars.

The two girls gulped at the same time, no doubt realizing what awaited them in their training. Neither said a word as they made their way over to their respective tubs.

"Oh, don't get your knickers rolled up," Lyessa said with a smirk. "Darryk will be a whole lot easier with you than he was with me. It's the price you pay when trying to master the art of martial defense. Self-reliance doesn't come cheap. Something must be given up in return for something gained."

"Well, if it comes right down to it," Adarra said, dipping one foot into her tub and sucking in a breath, "I have no problem giving up something I clearly don't have in exchange for something that could one day save my life." Her tone held a sad touch of sarcasm.

Fraya carefully stepped into her tub and winced. "Oy, this water's hot." Her puckered lips soon relaxed as she slowly lowered herself the rest of the way in. "Oh . . . Oh, my, this is probably the most wonderful thing I've ever felt." She released a soft whimper, closed her eyes, and laid her head against the back of the tub.

Adarra's reaction was pretty much the same as Fraya's as she gripped the sides of the tub and sank into the bubbles.

The water was laced with more than just lavender. Gina always made sure it held a variety of medicinal extracts—like marigold, elderberry, and noni—that were good for soothing the muscles, treating aching joints, and softening the skin. Darryk had given her nanny the exact amounts to use after their first lesson some years back, and Lyessa had been enjoying it ever since.

She could have asked Fraya to heal the soreness with some magic, but why negate the pleasure of the hot water and scented bubbles? Leaning her head back against the edge of the tub, Lyessa closed her eyes and concentrated on clearing her mind, like Darryk had taught her to do. She focused on nothing. "*The mind controls the body,*" he would say. "*If your mind is not relaxed, how do you expect your body to be?*"

She smiled at the memory.

"I could die happy right here and now," Adarra said.

Fraya giggled.

Lyessa concentrated on her breathing as she inhaled the lavender fumes and let the tension melt away. The room was quiet. Peaceful. Something that seemed hard to come by nowadays.

"This is really nice," Adarra said. "I've never . . ." She paused a moment, long enough for Lyessa to glance her way. "I've never really had friends before. I mean, I've got my brothers, but you can't exactly talk to them the same way you can with another girl."

Fraya chuckled. "I know what you mean. It's been a long time since I've had a close friend. Ever since Mother died, I've been too busy keeping up the house and taking care of my father and the others to find time to make friends."

Lyessa could relate. "I've always been surrounded by those who see being friends with me as a way to gain station or importance. They use my acquaintance more for their own social climbing than because they actually like me." Lyessa snickered as an image of Ty popped into her head. "It's one of the things I've always liked about your brother, Adarra. He was the first person I'd ever met who didn't care that I was the overlord's daughter. He doesn't fawn over me like all the others do. Then again, he's too busy thinking up new ways to get on my nerves."

Adarra chuckled. "If it makes you feel any better, you're the only girl he treats like that."

It did, actually.

"Yep, if anyone at home ever wants to get him riled up, we just have to mention your name and watch him go."

"Hey, I give him as good as I get," she stated proudly.

"You do more than hold your own, that's for sure. Although," Adarra said, lathering her arms, "he's been acting a little odd lately."

Lyessa snorted. "When does Ty ever *not* act odd?"

"Odder than usual."

"In what way?"

"He seems more distant. Angry. He hasn't taken Mother's passing well at all, I'm afraid."

"Can you blame him?" Fraya said. "I remember when I lost my mother. Father didn't leave his room for three days. And if it wasn't for the fact that I was the only one of my siblings who knew how to cook, I'd probably have stayed in mine as well. You'll need to give him time."

Somehow, the topic had gone from upbeat to depressing. Lyessa needed to change it before her mood soured as well. "So, what about you and Breen?" she said to Fraya. "How did that ever happen? He always seemed kind of quiet. In fact, I don't think he's ever said two words to me. Don't get me wrong; he's like the epitome of what most women dream about—tall, strong, ruggedly handsome, and gentle to boot."

"The Creator knew what I needed," Fraya said softly. "His quiet nature suits me. I'm not exactly a socialite. I'd more prefer to spend an evening around the hearth than a gaudy night on the town. Just knowing he's there because he cares is fine with me."

Lyessa thought Fraya's idea of love seemed a little boring, but who was she to question what love truly was? She'd been engaged to marry someone who seemed to care more for himself than he did for her. Of course, that hadn't been *her* choosing, and she had to admit that Aiden had done a lot of growing since their battle with the Northmen, but credit for that went solely to Adarra.

"And what of our quiet bookworm?" Lyessa teased, lolling her head to the side to see if Adarra was paying attention. "A person would have to be blind not to see that a certain young gentleman has taken quite the fancy to your specific company."

Adarra's head rose slightly above the rim. "I don't know how much of that attention is because he actually cares about plain ol' me and how much is his way of trying to show remorse, or perhaps sympathy, to someone who saved his life."

"Nonsense," Fraya said. "I've seen the way he looks at you. The first time I met him, I thought he was shallow, and a bit of a prig, but I have to admit he's changed, and largely in part because of you."

"I agree," Lyessa chimed in. "He hardly resembles the man he was not two weeks back."

"When you're as wealthy as he is," Adarra said, "you aren't going to look twice at someone like me. I'm short, my hair is plain, my ears stick out, and my cheeks are freckled. Most guys wouldn't acknowledge me if I was sitting in their lap." She choked. "Not that I would ever sit in a man's lap, of course. I was just saying—"

"Quit being so hard on yourself, Adarra," Fraya said. "I think your freckles are one of your best features. They make you stand out from all the rest of the plain-faced girls."

Adarra huffed. "That's what I'm afraid of."

"My father said he asked you to try talking with that Northman you captured," Lyessa said, steering them away from what was clearly an uncomfortable subject for Adarra. "Is that wise, especially after what you went through with this particular savage?"

"I agree," Fraya said, ducking to rinse the soap from her hair. "Maybe you should reconsider. I know I wouldn't want to come face-to-face with the man who nearly killed me."

"It's not that easy," Adarra said. "I'm the only one who stands any chance of communicating with him. The Northman dialect is complex, and I've only just begun to research it. Your father was good enough to loan me a couple of books from his personal library, and I found one or two references in town, but that certainly isn't much to go on. Without my gift as a memoriae, there wouldn't be a way to decipher this amount of knowledge in time. Your father is depending on me to get some answers."

Unfortunately, Lyessa understood her father's insistence. Sometimes, you had to do things that were unpleasant. Even still, she worried this was asking too much of Adarra.

"What happens if you see him and freeze?" Fraya asked.

Adarra leaned forward and hugged her knees. "I don't know. I guess I'll find out when it happens."

Chapter 47 | Ty

"ALL RIGHT, LET'S BRING this meeting to order," Veldon said as he smacked the top of the council room table with his mug. Ty was already seated, quietly watching the others as they mingled.

Every member was in attendance. Even Gilly. Two of the seats had been removed from the table and placed against the back wall. His mother's seat was one. The other had belonged to Saleena. Two spots vacant. How many more would there be in the coming months?

If the Tower had their way, all of them. A table surrounded by empty chairs.

Ty stared at the two seats. He couldn't seem to take his eyes off them, his knuckles white as he gripped the seat of his own chair. He could feel the tears trying to claw their way out, but he fed his anger to keep them bottled up inside.

Veldon plopped down in his chair at the head and scooted forward, far enough for his midriff to press against the dull edge of the table. The flint around his neck hung loosely from its chain as he leaned forward to start the proceedings. "It has been an exciting week for the ven'ae, that's for sure." For the first time in a long time, the portmaster was smiling, and so far, he hadn't rubbed his head once with his handkerchief. A good sign.

"*Exciting* is hardly the word I'd use," Orlyn said, sitting directly across from Ty. He pulled a shiny green apple from his robe and took a bite. "Needs more oomph. *Extraordinary,* maybe. Or *miraculous.* Certainly something I would have never expected to see in my lifetime."

Veldon nodded. "I don't believe we could have had a more profitable meeting with the Sidaran Assembly had they decided to induct each of us into their ranks. To be honest, I wasn't sure what to expect when Overlord Barl extended the invitation. I was simply hoping to make it out in one piece." He smiled again. "Things are changing."

"That's what worries me," Ty's father said from the other end of the table, drawing eyes and dampening spirits. His father was known for looking at the bigger picture, and Ty was curious to see what he'd say. "I agree, of course, the outcome was encouraging, and for once, it seems we have an audience willing to listen. But change is not always a good thing. And unfortunately for us, this change means an escalation of the conflict between the ven'ae and the White Tower."

Ty groaned inside. As much as he didn't want to think about it, his father was right. He could do without that kind of change.

"Regardless," Veldon said, finally reaching for his kerchief, "what we witnessed during the assembly was historic—jun'ri assembly members sharing seats with ven'ae and listening. Granted, it took a dead arachnobe to make it happen, but it was progress."

Feoldor chuckled. "I'll never forget the horror on their pasty faces, or the way they nearly beat each other to death, running from one side of the room to the other when those hairy legs came flopping out. It was worth the risk just for that."

"I remember you not wanting to get all that close either, the first time you saw them," Reloria said with a raised brow.

"Yes, well, I, uh . . . That was different. They could have still been alive."

Normally, Ty would have smiled at the couple's playful banter, but all this talk of spiders had him thinking about the one controlling them. He stared at the table, his eyes blending the age lines in the wood together until everything was a blur. Where had she gone, and more importantly, would she be back? He had tried to use his magic to listen to the forest the same way he had when he first sensed the arachnobe, but so far, he'd been unsuccessful.

The unease he had felt when the creatures were around was gone. There had to be more clues inside her shop. If only Orlyn and Feoldor hadn't walked in on him and Breen when they had. He needed to get back in there and do some more snooping. Realizing that he was stroking the spine of the book inside his coat, he lowered his hand.

"We need to prepare for retaliation," his father said.

Veldon wiped his forehead. "I agree that we need to be ready, but having played their hand and lost, wouldn't it be more likely that the Tower would pull back and re-strategize rather than attempt another assault so quickly? Surely, they have to realize that involving Overlord Barl in this conflict has changed things. They've been lurking in the shadows for years, and now a light has been shone where none had before."

"Aye," Orlyn said, taking another bite of his apple. "They've bitten off more than they were prepared to swallow."

"After what happened with Cylmar," Ty's father said, fiddling with his pipe, not bothering to stuff it as much as spin it in his hands, "I have a feeling that secrecy is less important than it used to be. We are going to need to find a way to defend ourselves. Because when they come—and believe me, if Ty's as important to them as they say, they will be coming—I doubt it will be for just him or even the council. We could be facing a full invasion."

"Would the Tower take it that far?" Reloria asked. "It would unite the rest of the kingdoms against them if they did."

"The Tower isn't alone. They've clearly found an alliance with this new king and Elondria—"

"Which is one of the reasons Overlord Barl is holding this upcoming conclave with Briston and Keldor," Veldon said, leaning back in his seat as he slowly thumbed the flint hanging from his neck. "The Provincial Authority is the only way to legally block what the king is doing."

"If he's even willing to acknowledge that authority," Feoldor scoffed, proving once again that even with his generally pessimistic attitude, Feoldor could make a good point every now and then.

"I thought the king had to abide by the Provincial Authority's ruling?" Ty said, remembering what he'd been taught in school.

Orlyn chuckled. "In a perfect world, perhaps. I don't think this new High King will let little things like laws get in the way of him getting what he wants."

"How do we go about preparing?" Breen asked. "It's not like we have the numbers to defend against something like the White Tower."

"We hide," Gilly exclaimed, directly to Veldon's right.

Feoldor grunted. "That might work for you and the assassin down there, but that won't help the rest of us much. I can't turn myself invisible or live underwater like a fish."

Sheeva let her amber eyes do the talking for her as she glared down the table at Feoldor.

"Unfortunately," Ty's father said, "hiding is no longer an option. Not only does the Tower know we are here and protecting their prize, but the Sidaran Assembly knows there are wielders here as well. And they will be needing our help more than ever if the Tower does decide to attack."

"Barl was right to recall the lancers," Veldon said. "But if the Tower has been collecting wielders and training them, our small council won't be enough to stop them."

"I'd say we held our own," Feoldor said.

"And we lost two in the process," Ty's father added softly, his voice gruff. "How many more of those battles until we lose the rest?"

The table went quiet.

Ty's gaze drifted back to the empty chairs in the corner. He could feel the heat of his magic rising, the longer he stared. His magic seemed to live on the edge of his emotions. He wasn't sure which was harder to control.

"We were lucky this time," his father said. "They clearly hadn't expected resistance. The next time will be different."

Ty almost hoped they would come. At least then he would be guaranteed another run at Mangora.

Orlyn finished off the apple, core and all. "Kellen's right. Who knows how many of those bulradoer the Tower has? And those weapons. I've never seen anything like them. They far outmatched anything we have. How do we fight against something like that?"

"We didn't do too bad," Fraya said. "We survived."

"By luck. Pure. Simple. Luck."

"That staff of yours seemed to hold its own," Reloria said, nodding toward the large piece of wood resting behind Orlyn's seat.

"Yes. Well . . . that was an unexpected surprise, to be sure."

"What about Nyalis?" Adarra said, letting her quill hover over the notebook she'd been scribbling in. Ty had almost forgotten she was there. "Sure, they have the Tower, and the numbers, but we have a thousand-year-old wizard who was around before the Great Purge. I'm sure he can help."

All heads turned to Ty.

Why was he the one everyone looked to when it came to the wizard? Breen and Sheeva had been in Meerwood as well. Why didn't anyone look at them? "I didn't get the impression he intends to stick around and fight a battle right now. He has other things on his mind."

"Such as?" Veldon asked.

"Such as his wizard's keep." He wondered how much longer Nyalis would give him before he came looking. Ty was still uncertain as to whether he wanted to go traipsing off on some quest to find the hidden fortress when he could be spending that time looking for Mangora. "I think we should search Mangora's shop. There could be some valuable information in there on what the Tower is planning, or even how to stop them."

"There's a lot of dark stuff in there," Orlyn said. "It might be best if we stay clear for now. At least until we have an opportunity to carefully inventory the place."

Typical, Ty thought. *If it's something we don't understand, then ignore it.* How were they ever going to defeat the Tower if they didn't try to understand how the Tower thought? What better way to find a weakness than to see what kind of magic they were up against and how it worked? Or maybe it was something else. He looked across the table at Orlyn. Was there another reason he didn't want Ty searching the place?

Feoldor spun the bracelet on his wrist, rubbing the transferal crystal at its center with his thumb. "I say we just burn it all."

Ty's head shot up. "Are you crazy?! We can't just destroy it. There might be clues in there on how to stop them."

"It's not worth the risk," Orlyn said, unexpectedly backing Feoldor.

Ty could feel the heat burning in his chest. "How do you know?"

This time, his father turned to look at him. Even Adarra paused long enough to give him a curious look.

"Just because it's different doesn't make it bad." How could they think about destroying it all? He needed . . . wanted to look through the rest of those books. Why was everyone fighting him on this? "I'm different. Do you plan on burning me, too?"

"Are you all right?" Orlyn asked, a worried look on his face.

Ty looked at the others. Had he gone too far? The strange looks on their faces said he had. He took another deep breath, letting the fire inside him fade. "I'm just saying it seems like a waste to get rid of it all."

"I think at this point," his father said, "vigilance is our ally. I'd rather err on the side of caution than put us all in jeopardy by messing with things we don't understand." He looked at Ty. "I do agree, though, we don't need to simply destroy it. At least, not until the wizard has had a chance to go through it first and tell us what is safe and what isn't."

"Then what are we to do with it until then?" Reloria asked. She unwrapped a piece of candy and stuck it in her mouth. "We shouldn't just leave it there for anyone to get into."

"Agreed," Veldon said. "I say we inventory what is there, then box it up and find a safe place to store it until the wizard can go through it."

Ty wanted to ask how soon until they started, but that might raise unnecessary questions. One thing was for sure: He was going to need to act quickly if he planned on getting a peek at those books. The only problem was Orlyn's new protection spell. His fists tightened. He could strangle Nyalis for showing him that.

"In answer to Breen's earlier question of how to prepare," Ty's father said, "we should start by helping Barl plan for Sidara's defense."

"We also have another potential problem," Adarra said. "The Tallosians."

Yes, Ty thought, nibbling his lower lip. *The Northmen.* That was another group of people who needed to pay for his mother's death.

"How's that coming?" Orlyn asked. "Have you found any books on their language to help?"

Adarra shook her head. "Not much. And what I have found is too outdated to be of much use. The only way to decipher their language might be for me to talk with him."

"Are you sure that's wise?" Reloria asked. "Couldn't they find someone else, considering?"

Adarra passed a fleeting glance at Fraya before answering. "I'm afraid I'm the only one able in the time allotted."

No one seemed to envy Adarra having to face the savage again. Except maybe Ty.

He was more than anxious to talk with the prisoner. A nice, quiet conversation about where Mangora was hiding. Unfortunately, he had more important things to consider. Namely, his need to get into Mangora's shop before the council began boxing it up and secreting it off. If only he knew some way to get past that shield.

Chapter 48 | Ty

TY LAY QUIETLY ON his bed. His brother had been asleep for at least an hour, shifting positions every so often. The two beds were separated by a small table with a candle that Ty had relit with blue flame so he could see the empty pages of the book. The blue light was dimmer than a normal candle and less likely to wake his brother. It also made it a little harder to see the book. Not that it mattered. The pages were still empty.

Maybe he had just imagined the message in Mangora's shop. Maybe he had wanted it to hold some valuable piece of information so badly that he'd seen what he wanted to. Sure, it had warned him that Orlyn and Feoldor were coming, but that could have been anything. He could have heard something outside, or his magic picked up on theirs and subconsciously let him know that they were there.

"This is crazy," he said under his breath. There was nothing there. He turned over to blow out the candle when a slight buzzing stopped him, like the sound a sweat bee made when hovering close to his ear. He looked around but couldn't see anything.

It happened again. This time louder, as though the bee were in his head. His hand tingled from where he was holding the book. He opened to the first page and quickly sat up. Another message. It *was* real. He read it:

Search the shop.

Which shop? Mangora's? It had to be. Why would the book tell him to look anywhere else? Ty read the three words over and over again, too afraid to turn the page, in case they disappeared. Too afraid to even take his eyes off them.

After a few minutes with nothing more being revealed, Ty thumbed through the rest of the pages, waiting, hoping for more. But there was no more. Only the one message to search the shop. Three more times through the book and he finally closed it.

The book had proven to be quite the enigma, beginning with its title. *Hidden Perceptions.* What did that mean, anyway?

Adarra had said—quoting from a dictionary she had read years ago—that the word *perception* meant to see, hear, or become aware of something using the senses. It was also a way of interpreting something. The word *perception*, Ty understood. If he saw a trunk with branches and leaves, he perceived it to be a tree.

"But what if you were a hawk, or a beetle, or even a cloud?" Adarra had said. "What would you perceive that trunk, branches, and leaves to be then? Our perception of something can change depending on who or what is perceiving it."

That's when Ty had stopped the conversation. His sister had a way of making simple things complicated. A tree was a tree. It didn't suddenly become a table lamp just because someone else was looking at it. What he couldn't quite grasp was the first part of the title: *Hidden.* What was hidden? How do you hide a perception? Didn't Adarra say that the very definition of a perception was to become aware? If a person is aware, then how is it hidden? Does it mean that what they are aware of isn't quite what they think?

He could feel pressure building in his head once more, and he pressed his thumbs to his temples and rubbed. The book had been revealing things to him, not hiding them. But maybe that was the purpose. Maybe what it did was show perceptions that were hidden from everyone else.

Breen turned over on the bed next to him and Ty froze, waiting for the ropes under Breen's mattress to stop creaking. When they did, he slowly turned his head. His brother was facing the wall, with his back to Ty.

Ty felt another bit of buzzing, and he quickly reopened the book, turning to a random page somewhere in the middle. His eyes widened, heart pounding. Another message.

Go. Now.

There wasn't much in the way of a hidden perception there.

He closed the book and stared at the blue-lit candle. He knew he shouldn't go. The last thing he wanted to do was get dressed and ride all the way into town in the middle of the night. But if he didn't, he was afraid of missing out on something important.

Scooting to the edge of his bed, he quietly pulled on his clothes, then grabbed his boots and headed for the door, not wanting to put them on and risk making any noise. Creeping down the hall and into the main room, he sat down on his father's chair and pulled on his boots and knit hat and strapped on his dagger.

Once outside, he ran to the barn, saddled Waddle, and started for town.

It was a cloudless night. The stars were bright enough to urge Waddle into a fast trot, the cold night air pricking Ty's throat with every inhale. Crossing over the East Bridge, he listened to the river below. It seemed to call out to him, warning him against what he was attempting to do. Or maybe it was just his own conscience getting the better of him. Despite both, he kept Waddle moving.

The streets of Easthaven were empty, the windows dark and

shuttered. Waddle's hooves clopped along, echoing off the surrounding buildings and emphasizing the loneliness Ty felt. They made their way slowly through the south merchant district to the center of town. Ty had never ridden through Easthaven at night by himself. As much as he hated walking through the city with the streets crowded with people, he cared for this even less.

Turning right on Wood Lane, they passed four or five buildings before stopping in front of the spice shop. The narrow streetway between the spice shop and the fuller's was shrouded in darkness. Even the light from the streetlamp behind him seemed unwilling to reach any farther inside the passageway than the outer edge.

Ty nudged Waddle toward the alley, but the horse didn't move. Finally, Ty hopped off and grabbed the reins.

"Come on, coward. There's nothing to be frightened of."

Somewhere up the alley, a couple of cats hissed, and Ty yelped. He looked up at Waddle. "Sorry," he said, tightening his grip. "Not being a very good example, am I?"

Waddle nickered.

Ty felt for the book in his jacket as he started forward. His ears were pricked, half expecting to hear the screech of one of those spiders as it leaped out of the darkness for him. Quickly, he reached out with his magic, but instead of sensing the creatures, he was greeted with something else. A warm, tingling sensation rushed through him. It wasn't like the buzzing in his head he'd received from the book, more like an intense prickling across his entire body, deeper and more powerful. It felt like he'd just gotten over a good fright, where it took a minute or two to calm down. He held up his hand to see if it was shaking. It felt like his whole body was. He must be getting close to the barrier.

Waddle reared his head and pulled back, dragging Ty with him. Ty didn't bother trying to change his horse's mind. It was clear Waddle had enough good sense not to want to get too close.

Ty turned and waited for his eyes to adjust, but the moon hadn't risen high enough over the buildings to help. Closing his eyes, he reached for his magic. He didn't want to pull too much, so he concentrated on a small flame not much larger than the wick of a candle.

His magic responded, and a lick of blue fire ignited in the palm of his hand. Why was it always the palm? He released the flame and this time held up one finger, imagining the flame sitting on top. It immediately reappeared on the finger, from the first knuckle to just above the tip. Ty grinned with excitement at this new discovery. He'd have to show Adarra tomorrow. She always enjoyed seeing what he could do. And now that he had a little better control over it, he didn't have to worry about setting his sister on fire.

It needed to be bigger. He released a little more magic, the warmth running through his arm and out to his finger, and the flame doubled in size. "Much better." But he still needed more. He concentrated again, even harder this time as he focused on all five fingers. Sure enough, blue flame burst from the tip of each finger on his left hand.

Waddle leaned his neck over to inspect the light.

"What? You act like you've never seen blue fire before."

Ty lifted his hand, illuminating the street between himself and Mangora's shop. He couldn't see the barrier, but he knew it was close. He could feel it. The hairs on his arms rose in the same way they would during the spring storms when the lightning would reach all the way to the ground, setting trees aflame.

He took a step back, not wanting to touch the barrier in the event it somehow alerted Orlyn.

"Well, now what? I've gotten this far." He let go of Waddle's reins and removed the book from his jacket pocket and looked at the cover. "I don't know if this barrier would be considered a perception, but it's definitely hidden."

He snapped the clasp and flipped the book open to a random page. So far, the messages had appeared in different places. He didn't think he had to be on any one specific page for it to work. "You wanted me here.

Now what?" He felt silly talking to a book, but what other options did he have? "How do I take down a protection spell?"

Tares'ayden.

He shivered. Had the book heard him? He lowered it and cast a wary glance at the surrounding buildings. He suddenly felt as though he was being watched. If the book had heard him, what else had it heard? He'd been carrying it everywhere. Even the council meetings.

He didn't know anything about the book, really, but he didn't get the impression it was trying to do him harm. In fact, so far, it had been extremely helpful, showing him exactly what he needed. He took another deep breath and raised the book.

Memorizing the inscription, he cleared his throat. "Ter-rez—"

Another thought came to mind. Would releasing the barrier also trigger a warning to Orlyn? Or was that just in case someone tried breaking through it? He looked at the book, hoping for an answer, but other than the word that was already there, nothing else appeared. He hated not knowing, but he'd come this far. He couldn't stop now.

"Here goes nothing." He concentrated on the barrier. "Ter-rez Ayden."

Nothing happened. At least that he could see. He could still feel the tingling. "Why didn't that work?" He reread the word, this time using a different pronunciation. "Tairs Ay-den."

Still nothing.

He huffed and tried twice more.

Nothing.

"This is ridiculous. What's wrong with this book?" He gritted his teeth, tempted to burn the stupid thing to ash. Maybe it wasn't the book. Maybe it was him. What if he couldn't wield the magic necessary for this spell? It would be like the wizard to create something that only one person could wield. But if that was the case, then why did the book want him here? He was going to give it one last chance. If it didn't work, he was going home.

He read the word four times, trying to come up with a variation he hadn't already used. Finally, he closed the book and turned to face the shop, raising his hand as he had seen Nyalis do back in Meerwood. "Tare-ess-aye-den."

The ground beneath him shook, and the space between him and the shop sparkled a translucent gold. There it was. The barrier. It was as high as the rooftops, running only wide enough to cover the front of Mangora's shop and none of the others. It was very similar to the one he'd seen in Meerwood. As swiftly as the wall had appeared, it dropped straight into the cobbles and vanished. And the tingling was gone.

Ty's knees were shaking. He couldn't believe he'd just done that. It was the first time he'd used an incantation. So far, all he'd ever done was innate magic—magic that relied on elements in the physical world he could control. What other possibilities awaited him? He was anxious to find out.

Quickly, he guided Waddle up to the front of the shop and tied him off at the hitching post. "Don't go anywhere," he said, giving the horse a stern look.

Waddle gave him a blank stare.

Another buzz in the back of his mind had him quickly opening the book. He brought the blue flame a little closer. A new message:

Su-eth-ee-un Do-won-ite.

This time, the incantation had been written phonetically. A chill shot through him. The book was listening? How else would it have known the difficulty he'd had with the last pronunciation?

Ty stopped at the walkway in front of the shop and turned. He glanced at Waddle. He couldn't just leave him standing there. If he *had* alerted Orlyn, the first thing the apothecary would notice was Ty's horse standing out front. "Idiot," he said, berating himself for not thinking about it sooner.

Placing the book back in his pocket, he untied Waddle and started back up the side street, dousing his flames before reaching the end.

Turning right on Wood Lane, he crossed Lynden Street and took the next available alley on the right, where he tied Waddle to a fat pickle barrel. "Sorry about this, boy. I'll be back. I promise. Don't make any noise while I'm gone." He pulled out an apple he had intended to eat himself and left it on top of the barrel for Waddle to enjoy.

Back on Wood Lane, he scanned both sides of the street. Empty. He ran up the sidewalk, keeping to the shadows under the buildings' weather overhangs and cut back down the next opening leading to Mangora's.

Using his flame to see what he was doing, he pulled the book from his jacket and unhooked the clasp. Surprisingly, the same message that had shown up earlier was still there. He stopped at the front door and turned to look at the empty street.

Using the book's pronunciation, he called out the incantation. "*Suethian Duwanite.*"

The ground shook beneath him, and the barrier burst from the stones below, surrounding the shop before vanishing altogether. The strong tingling sensation was back, letting him know the barrier was in place.

Ty opened the door and stepped inside. He stared at the cluttered shelves, the blue light leaving eerie shadows across each, making their contents seem even more dangerous. "Where do I start?"

He shut the door and headed straight for the books on the right, the one place he knew that had something he was interested in. He barely made it to the second row when he felt the buzzing sensation again, letting him know the book was trying to get his attention.

He stopped a few feet from the shelf of tomes and opened the book. *Upstairs.*

Upstairs wasn't exactly on his list of places he wanted to see, but the book hadn't led him astray so far, so he left the books and headed toward the back of the shop, keeping his hand up to light the way. He slowed long enough to stare at the shrunken heads in the corner, then stepped around the counter to the closed door at the back. He pressed his ear against the wood to see if he could hear anything on the other side. He didn't. Steadying himself, he turned the knob and pushed.

The door creaked slowly open until coming to a stop when it hit the right wall. Ty raised his hand and pulled a little more magic, and the flames extending from his fingers grew.

Surprisingly, the back room was nearly empty. He would have expected the storeroom to have stored more stuff. A table and chair on the left wall, a couple of shelves on either side filled with more knickknacks and curios. There was a door at the back on the right. It had to lead up to the second floor.

He crossed the room, the floorboards groaning under his boots, leaving him with an uncertain feeling. He remembered how scared he had been the first time he'd stepped into the shop and met Mangora, and how nervous he'd been returning with Breen. But here he was, back again, this time completely alone and in the middle of the night.

Something about this book was rubbing off on him, giving him the strength to do things he'd never thought himself capable of. He felt stronger. Braver. He just knew he was going to find what he was looking for, the one thing that could lead him to Mangora, or better yet, the very thing that could destroy her.

He opened the door. Sure enough, there was a set of stairs leading up.

The stairs were so steep, he couldn't see the top, each step covered in a thick layer of dust at the sides. The centers were worn from use. He spared a quick glance back to the main room before heading up, leaving the door behind him open in case he needed to make a quick retreat if there was something up there that shouldn't be.

The creaking of the wood under his boots kept him on edge as he let the blue flames guide his way. He stopped and spun, lifting his hand. He thought he'd heard something on the stairs behind him. There was nothing there. His heart was drumming. Pounding, really. *Pull yourself together.* He turned and started back up the steps.

Finally reaching the top, he paused to get his bearings. The entire building groaned around him, the floors and joists shifting ever so slightly as the cold evening air tightened the supports. The smell of age was strong, like rotten wood infested with mildew.

He turned and started down the corridor. It seemed to run from one side of the shop to the other, three doors spaced evenly on the right side, every ten or so feet. The walls ahead were covered in dust and webs. Traffic had been kept to the center of the floor, as the sides were completely blanketed in the stuff.

Another buzzing, and he stopped and opened the book. "Which way?"

Third door.

"Third door it is." Ty continued until he reached the indicated room. It was shut like the others. Although, from the patterns in the dust on the floor around the door, and the semi-clean handle, it looked like it was the only room that had been used recently. He looked back down the hall, the blue light reaching as far as the stairwell. Empty. He took a deep breath and readied his flame in case he needed to use it. Tucking the book back in his pocket to free his hand, he opened the door.

It whined on its hinges, leaving behind another uneasy chill.

He raised his hand and peered inside. It was a bedchamber of sorts. Canopy bed on the right, dresser, large chifforobe in the corner, a desk littered with papers, and a standup shelf filled with even more oddities. There were two windows on the wall in front of him, thick draperies hanging from each.

The room, even though apparently more used than the others, still gave him the feeling of neglect. The dust wasn't quite as thick, but it was still there. The same musty smell clung to everything. He didn't want to be up there any longer than necessary. "What now?" He pulled out the book and opened it. Right on cue, the words appeared:

Top-right desk drawer.

He crossed the room, leaving a faint trail in the dust along the way. The desk, like everything else, was old and worn, the wood's color faded.

He grabbed the brass knob for the top-right drawer and pulled. It slid open. There was a box inside, pewter, with crisscrossing lines decorating each side. He lifted it out of the drawer and placed it on the desk. The lid wouldn't give. Either it had rusted shut or something else was holding it closed, like a spell.

He opened the book, this time to a different page.

Vera'Sintorum.

He looked at the box and concentrated, feeling the heat of his magic burn in his chest. "*Vera'Sintorum.*" The outer lip produced a faint green glow and was released with a soft *click*. He couldn't believe he'd gotten the pronunciation correct on the first try. He took a moment to stare at the box. It seemed harmless enough. What was the book trying to show him? He hesitated, but only for a second. He hadn't come all this way to stop now.

He opened the box slowly. Inside were three rows of rings, each one as unique as the next. Some were gold, some silver, some marble, stone, and even wood. *Odd thing for a witch to carry around,* he thought. She didn't seem the kind of woman who cared much for jewelry. Ty doubted the rings would have even fit her knobby fingers.

He raised the book. The spell was gone, replaced with a new message:

Second row, third from top.

Ty's brows lowered curiously, as that particular spot was the only one that didn't have a ring. He looked at the instruction once again. *Second row, third from top.*

He scanned the entire second row. "There's nothing here." He glanced at the page. The book's message never changed. Finally, he laid the book down on the desk and ran his finger down the second row. It hit something. "What's this?" He grabbed hold of whatever it was and lifted it out, holding it close to his flames.

It was a ring. One made completely of glass. He could see right through it. He felt the buzzing once again and glanced down at the open book on the desk.

Put it on.

He felt a tingling sensation in the back of his neck. This time it wasn't from the book or the barrier. It was his own common sense. "Why? What will it do?" He turned the ring over with his fingers. There were no markings of any kind, no indication as to what would happen to him if he put the ring on. He reached out with his magic to stroke the ring and received a minute tingling in return. It was clearly magical. He just had no way of knowing in what way.

Laying the ring down, he closed the box and placed it back in the desk and shut the drawer. He picked the ring back up. It was made for more petite fingers than his, but it looked like it might fit on his smallest. What did he have to lose? He'd come there looking for something to use against Mangora, and the book had led him to this ring. It hadn't lied to him so far, and at this point, he couldn't think of a good-enough excuse to not try. But still, there was something in the back of his mind that told him this might not be the best idea.

He huffed. Staring at the ring was getting him nowhere. He had to make a choice. "Here goes nothing."

Something scurried across the floorboards behind him, and he spun and threw a ball of fire. The flames hit the right side of the doorframe, leaving a large scorch mark in the paint. "What was that?"

The noise sounded again, this time near the bed. He raised his hand and spotted a rat running behind the bed stand. He almost laughed. The shop was getting to him. Shaking his head, he walked over and doused the cinders still burning on the wall he'd just attacked. He'd barely smothered the last of the flame when the book buzzed once more. He crossed the room to see what it wanted. Probably to demand he put the ring on.

They're coming.

"Who's coming?" Suddenly, he noticed the constant tingling from the barrier outside was gone. Quickly, he stuffed the book and the ring in his jacket pocket and left the room. He closed the door and headed down the hall for the stairs. With one last look over his shoulder, he started down.

Ty could feel the book buzzing, but he didn't have time to stop. He tripped and skidded down three steps before catching himself. He left the stairwell and dashed across the back room for the main part of the shop. He wanted to stop and grab a couple more books on the way out, but he didn't have time. Instead, he headed straight for the door. He grabbed the handle and stopped.

There were voices just outside.

He peeked through the shutter. It was Orlyn and Feoldor. *Blazes!* Lowering the barrier must have warned them after all. What was he going to do? There was no way to talk himself out of this one. He was clearly where he shouldn't be, and how could he ever explain getting past the barrier?

He looked around. There was nowhere to hide. Frantically, he ran for the back. The buzzing from the book was intensifying. He reached the storeroom and quickly opened the book, using his flame to read by. "Where can I hide?" He was half tempted to run upstairs and join the rat under Mangora's bed.

Trapdoor on your right. Quickly!

What trapdoor? The bell to the front door rang, and the voices grew louder as the two council members walked into the shop. He extinguished the flame as much as possible, keeping a single finger lit as he scurried across the floor. He could have kicked himself for not shutting the door leading out to the shop. *Where is it?* His hand found a groove between the boards right in front of the table, and he pulled. *Please don't make noise.*

He could hear footsteps crossing the shop, the muffled voices growing more distinct as they headed straight for him. He quickly pulled the hatch the rest of the way open and slipped in. Orlyn stopped outside the storeroom, and Ty lowered the trapdoor.

"There's no one here, Orlyn. You woke me for nothing."

"I'm telling you, I know what I felt. The barrier came down and then went back up. Someone was here. Or maybe still could be. Keep your eyes open."

"That'll be difficult," Feoldor grumbled with a yawn, "considering I'm still half-asleep,"

Ty twisted to find a more comfortable position, and one of the boards creaked.

"What was that?" Orlyn rushed into the room, his staff glowing a pale green in front of him. Ty could see the runes between the floorboards. Feoldor must have been carrying a lantern, because a sudden wash of amber light poured through the cracks.

Ty held his breath.

"There's nothing here, you old fossil. You woke me in the middle of the night for this?" Feoldor stepped directly on the trapdoor, the boards bending under his weight, raining dust down on Ty's head.

Ty pinched his nose.

Orlyn walked over to the shelf on the far wall and began rummaging through the curios. "To be honest, I was half expecting to find Ty in here. The way he's been acting lately, I wouldn't put it past him to try sneaking in here again."

Feoldor stepped off the trapdoor and walked over to join Orlyn in searching the shelves. "He has been acting a touch odd these days," he agreed, "but what boy wouldn't after losing his mother like that?"

Ty wasn't sure which to be more shocked at. The council members talking about him behind his back or the fact that it was Feoldor who stood up for him.

"Still," Orlyn said. "Something about the boy has changed. He's angrier. He would have never raised his voice the way he did during our last meeting. It's not like him to openly rebuke the council that way. I'm worried about him."

Ty balled his fists.

"He's in a dark place," Feoldor said. "With everything he's been through, I'm not surprised."

"True, but we can't afford to have him remain there. With powers like his, there's no telling what could happen."

Ty couldn't believe the way Orlyn was talking. He thought he had a special connection with the older man. It looked like he was wrong. *Goes to show you can't trust anyone.*

Orlyn started across the room. "Let's check upstairs."

Ty could hear the creaking of the steps as the two men headed up to the second floor.

He waited till he could hear them moving down the hall before opening the trapdoor. He crawled out and carefully closed it, listening to see if he could hear what the two were doing. He could hear them arguing but couldn't tell what about, so he rushed out the door and across the shop. He opened the front door just wide enough to slip through without catching the bell.

Orlyn's and Feoldor's horses were tied to the hitching rail outside. He was tempted to turn them loose and let the men walk home, but it would have definitely given away that someone was there. He glanced at the street beyond. Was the barrier still up? He couldn't feel the tingling. They must not have raised it when they entered.

Instead of heading straight out into the street and risking being spotted by either of the men from one of the upper windows, Ty made his way down the front of the shops. At the end of the walkway, he lifted his hood and stepped out of the shadows, heading for the main road. He didn't dare turn, in case someone was looking. Hopefully, all they'd see was a figure moving up the street.

As soon as he hit Wood Lane, he turned right and ran for the next building down past the fuller's and cut into the narrow passage on his right. Waddle was standing right where he'd left him. The apple was gone.

Ty was still shaking. He wasn't sure if it was from the fear of getting caught or from what he had heard. And they wondered why he was angry. The buzzing in his head was back, and he opened the book.

Use the ring. It will guide you.

Ty reached in his pocket and pulled out the ring. His previous apprehension was now gone, replaced with anger and disappointment. He'd come to the shop in the first place to find something to use against Mangora. This had to be it.

Putting aside any last vestige of warning, he slid it on.

Nothing seemed to happen. Then he felt a prickling in the tip of his small finger. And it grew. It rushed from one knuckle to the next until it reached his hand and spread outward from there, driving up his arm and eventually into his chest. His arm was as white as a three-day-old corpse. Whatever it was doing, he couldn't stop it. His entire body went cold. He'd never felt cold like this before. It was colder than what he'd felt the time he had been dared to jump into the East River in the middle of Zùl.

Ty grabbed the pickle barrel in front of Waddle to keep from pitching over on his face as the alley began to spin. A moment later, it stopped. The dizziness passed and the heat rushed back in. "What was that?" He lifted his hand. His fingers seemed back to normal. The slight distortion of his small finger when he looked directly at it let him know the ring was still there. If not looking for it, though, most would probably never see it.

He pulled out the book. He wanted answers.

"I'm here to help."

Ty jumped with a yelp, startling Waddle, who let out a harsh snort.

"Who's there?" Ty looked down the alley, at least as far as the streetlight would let him. He couldn't see anyone. "Show yourself."

"Open the book."

Ty spun around. There was no one there. The voice was strange, neither male nor female, somehow a mix of both. Distorted, but understandable.

He glanced at the open page on the book and read: *Open the book.*

His heart was pounding. Had the book just spoken to him? He swallowed. "Can you hear me?"

"*Yes,*" the voice said at the same time the word *Yes* appeared on the page.

His heart was pounding. He could hear the book, but not with his ears. It was more like a voice in the back of his mind. He lifted his hand. Was that what the ring was for?

"*Yes.*"

His eyes widened even farther. *You can hear my thoughts?*

"*Yes.*"

He gulped. *What are you?*

"*I'm a guide. I'm here to show you what you need, whether you know it or not.*"

"Is that what it meant by *hidden perceptions*?" He almost closed the book to look at the cover but changed his mind. He was afraid to shut it, in case the voice stopped.

"*In a way.*"

Ty bounced from one foot to the other, too excited to even know where to begin. This was exactly what he'd been looking for. He had so many questions.

"*All in good time,*" the book said. "*But for now, I think it's time we leave.*"

Ty felt the sudden tingling sensation of the barrier going back up. The book was right. He needed to get out of there before Orlyn and Feoldor spotted him.

Quickly, he stuffed the book back in his pocket, untied Waddle from the barrel, and swung onto the saddle. He flicked the reins and rode out of the alley, but instead of turning left toward River Street and taking the chance of passing Orlyn and Feoldor, he turned Waddle right and circled around another way.

He couldn't believe how close he'd come to being caught.

The farther he went, the more Orlyn and Feoldor's conversation nagged at him. Did the rest of the council distrust him as well? Which led him to wondering why they were so intent on keeping Mangora's shop out of his reach. Orlyn had looked more worried than surprised when he'd seen Ty and Breen in there the first time. Were they purposely hiding something from him? If so, what? And more importantly, why? He didn't like to think that the council was keeping secrets from him, but after what he'd seen and heard, what else was he to think?

"*Can you really trust them?*" the book asked.

It should have been an easy question to answer, but if he was being honest with himself, he wasn't sure. They'd been hiding things from him his entire life: who he was, where he'd come from, the Tower's desire to have him. His family hadn't even told him of their role in the wielder council until a couple of months back.

He had a lot of thinking to do. He spun the glass ring with his thumb. This time, he hoped to find some answers.

"*I told you, I'm always here to help.*"

Chapter 49 | Lenara

"WE'RE LOST . . . AGAIN," a Black Watch guard grumbled at the front as he reined in his horse. The rest of the guards pulled to a stop behind him, having come to the end of yet another trail that led to nowhere. This time, they found themselves at the base of the mountains.

Lenara groaned. The guards weren't the only ones frustrated by Sylas's apparent inability to track, or his obsessive need to remind everyone that he was in charge by demanding he be the one to determine which way they go. If he had simply let the Cylmaran trackers do their job, they would probably already be at Iraseth. Inside the Tower, he might have held a respected position, but out here, Sylas was proving to be less than useless.

"It's his fault," a second guard said, pointing at the inquisitor. Lenara thought the guard's name was Ensle. "He couldn't find his way out of bed in the morning. How's he going to find four people in the middle of Thornwood?"

Sylas's fingers tightened on his reins, his face reddening. "Are you questioning my judgment?"

"Unless they magically scaled this cliff with a toddler on their back, then yes, we're questioning your judgment."

Up until now, the guards had done their best to keep their complaints to themselves, but the harder Sylas pressed them, the angrier they grew. They'd been traveling for nearly two weeks with barely any sleep. Even Lenara was having a difficult time putting up with the inquisitor's bloated sense of self-regard.

"I'm the one the Archchancellor left in charge of this expedition. Not you!"

"And why is that?" Ensle asked. "Why would the Archchancellor place a know-nothing recruit like you in charge of something this important? Who are you?"

Everyone looked at Sylas.

Sylas smiled. "I'm the one who determines which of you my friend here will roast alive first," he said, gesturing at Lenara.

It took everything Lenara had not to set *him* on fire. She didn't appreciate being used like that, but for Joren's sake, she steeled her nerves and raised her hand, calling on her flames. The fire burst from her palm, and the men quieted. It was getting harder and harder to keep them in line. Sylas's arrogance was going to get Joren killed.

Ensle stared at her for a moment, plainly deciding whether he wanted to chance it. Finally, he exhaled. "Which way now?"

Sylas twisted in his saddle and pointed to the left. "That way."

Ensle snorted but obeyed, and the caravan of guards started back up again.

She waited until the rest of the Watch had ridden on ahead before turning to Sylas. "You need to let the trackers do their jobs."

"I have my *own* trackers."

"Then why did we end up riding straight into a mountain?"

Sylas looked up through the tops of the trees. "Because I haven't seen them in the last two days."

"You can't rely on the corax for everything. It wouldn't hurt to track from the ground as well. It's what they're getting paid to do."

Sylas grunted, keeping his eyes forward as he kicked his horse to catch up with the others.

She hoped he would heed her advice.

Sylas brought them to a stop a few hours later. The sun had already gone down, and the trail ahead was all but indistinguishable from the rest of the forest. After a quick meal of dried meat, cheese, and nuts, Lenara turned in for the night, hoping to catch as much sleep as she could. Her body ached from the amount of time spent in the saddle each day.

The fire did its best to cut the chill, but she still found herself pulling her blanket up to her nose. It didn't take long for the arms of sleep to wrap her in their loving embrace. She was exhausted.

Something shook her, and she jerked awake. She yanked the blanket down and found Sylas kneeling beside her.

"What is it?" she hissed.

"Sorry," Sylas said. "How long has it been?"

She sat up, wiping sleep from her eyes. "Joren?"

The young guard nodded with an endearing smile. "I hated waking you, you looked so peaceful."

"That's all right," she said with a yawn, trying unsuccessfully not to look tired. "I can think of worse reasons to be woken."

"Where are we now? Still hunting those same wielders?"

She nodded with a second yawn.

"I'm sorry," he said, looking ashamed. "I'll let you get back to sleep."

"No. It's fine. I'd only just dozed off," she lied.

"Are you sure?"

She smiled and nodded, and he sat down beside her.

"Are we getting closer? How long has it been since the last time I was here?"

She had to think about it. "Five days, I believe. Maybe six."

"Five days?" He released a slow, depressed sigh.

"We've been riding hard, barely sleeping," she said. "It's probably affecting your ability to take control."

"I guess. So, anything interesting happen so far?"

She shook her head. "Nothing. Just endless days surrounded by trees."

"Oh." Joren sat there a moment, looking at her. He seemed to be trying to think of something else to say. Surprisingly, she was having the same trouble. "The last time we talked, you mentioned that your sister was the reason you joined the Tower. Would it be acceptable for me to ask why?"

She crossed her legs, the blanket still covering her from the waist down. It had been years since she had thought about her sister; memories buried long ago hurt that much more when they resurfaced. These particular memories hadn't seen the light of day in quite some time. And for good reason. "Did I mention that my father would take Viena and me to the markets in Ecrin to sell hides each year?"

Joren nodded.

"We always looked forward to those trips: traveling with Father, seeing new places, meeting new people. Every year, Father would buy us each a dress at the shops in Ecrin. We didn't have shops that sold clothes like that in Erast, and by the time a new year had rolled around, we'd outgrown or outworn the previous dress." She smiled, remembering how their mother would make such a fuss over the new dresses when they returned, treating them to a party as though they were guests at the royal palace.

"It was during one of those trips that everything changed. I was fourteen, which made Viena . . ." She had to stop and think. It had been so long. "Eleven. We had only been in Ecrin for a day. Viena had asked Father to stop for a honey tart, one of her favorite things to eat. She always licked the honey off before eating the dough, which irritated

Father to no end because she'd usually get half of it on her face." The smile slid from her face. "I remember we had just left the vendor and were on our way to the dress shop when the fighting started.

"The Black Watch was chasing a man through the open market." She could see it coming to life in front of her. She could remember every detail—the smell of the blueberry tart in her hand; the sound of people shopping, bumping up against her as they passed; the warm sun on her face. She looked at Joren. "We just happened to be at the wrong place at the wrong time."

Joren's eyes narrowed as he listened, his expression making it clear that he knew where her story was going.

"We tried getting out of the way, but the man they were chasing grabbed Viena, using her as a shield. I remember he had a durma collar around his neck, which at the time meant nothing to me, but now I know it was why he had a knife pressed to Viena's throat instead of fighting back with magic. My father begged him to let her go, but the wielder didn't listen. The Watch demanded he release her, but he kept saying that if they didn't leave, he was going to kill her.

"They didn't leave." Lenara turned her head and wiped the unexpected tears from her cheeks. "That was the day I discovered my own magic. It was also the day I took my first life."

Joren raised his hand. "You don't need to—"

"Yes," she said, surprising herself. "I do."

She hadn't realized how much pain she had held inside, but now that it had broken free, she didn't want to hold it in any longer. She couldn't fight back the tears, so she let them come. "The man was cornered. He knew there was nowhere to run, so he made good on his word and slit Viena's throat and tossed her body in the street."

The memory of the look of horror on her sister's face was so vivid, it had Lenara squeezing her fists to the point that her nails dug into her palms. "The man was probably hoping to slow the guards down long enough to escape, but he didn't get the chance. Something broke inside me." She put her hand to her chest. "I remember the heat. It was like a fire burning from the inside out. Without even realizing what was happening, I screamed, and the man flew across the street and hit the side of one of the buildings. His head had been completely caved in, ribs poking through his chest. It was like I had smashed a bug."

She looked at Joren, afraid of what she might see in those brown eyes. But instead of disgust, she found sympathy, and instead of hatred, sorrow. It was a look she could have lived in, a look she hadn't received from another living soul since that day in Ecrin. She started to cry all over again, a burden somehow lifting off her shoulders.

Joren put his arm around her, and she found herself burying her head in his shoulder.

"I'm sorry that happened to you."

The tears finally stopped, but she didn't want to pull away from his embrace.

"I guess the guards took you with them?"

She lifted her head and wiped her eyes, taking a moment to compose herself. "I was in too much shock to realize what was happening. The only thing I remember was my father clutching Viena in his arms. In fact, I don't remember much of anything until arriving at the Tower."

Joren shook his head. "Your father lost two daughters in one day. I can't imagine." There was a moment's pause before he spoke again. "Have you ever gone back?"

She shook her head. There had been times when she had thought about going back. Wondered if her parents were still alive. Whether they had started a new family. Did she have other brothers or sisters out there that she didn't know about? She had always promised herself she'd go back one day, but she never did.

"How did you end up becoming . . ." Joren pointed at her black bulradoer robes.

A guard at one of the other fires turned over, and she scooted to the left, putting a little more distance between her and Joren. "I begged them to let me help them find wielders. Given my strength as a vanti, former Archchancellor Bezaleel allowed me to train with the other bulradoer."

"And you've been doing it ever since?"

She nodded, yawning once again. "I think I've had about as much emotion as I can take for one evening." She needed the sleep, and as much as she had come to enjoy her talks with Joren, she had to try keeping their reason for being out there in focus. She had a job to do. She couldn't let feelings—if she could even call them that—get in the way. Besides, she never knew when Sylas was going to reappear.

Joren nodded. "It might be a while before I'm back. Take care of yourself." He stood and walked back to his bedroll on the opposite side of the fire and lay down.

She'd never had anyone worry about her before. Other than her parents, of course. She watched Joren through the flames as he lay there staring at the stars, before finally crawling into her own blankets and closing her eyes.

She woke to the sound of shuffling feet and whispers.

It was still dark. Was it time to break camp? It took her a moment for her mind to come fully awake. A nervous tingling sensation had her pulling down her blanket, just far enough to peek out.

A small group of men were heading into the woods.

She threw her blanket off and sat up. The fire farthest from hers was empty. The one Ensle had been at. *Great,* she thought. *Now what is he up to?* She turned and looked across the fire, debating whether or not to wake Joren.

His bed was empty as well.

She hopped to her feet, heart racing. They'd come for him.

Quickly, she headed into the woods after them. She heard voices in the distance. All she could think was they were going to slit his throat just like her sister's. She ran, not caring whether she could see where she was going or not, the low-hanging branches cutting her face.

Someone screamed.

No! I'm too late!

Three or four more screams broke through the trees, followed by what sounded like barking or growling, then more screaming. *What in Aldor is going on?*

She burst into a small clearing and drew one of her ter'aks, its red flames searing the ground at her feet, lighting the horrific scene in front of her.

Joren stood in the middle of a small clearing. He wasn't moving. She didn't see any blood. On the right, four of the guards were being ripped apart by a pack of wolves. The last man standing managed to stab one, but a second used the distraction to leap up and sink its fangs into the man's neck. He went down gurgling.

Ensle was on the left side of the clearing, sword drawn, trying to fend off a mountain bear. He was backed against a tree. He only managed to clip the enormous grizzly in the side before it caught his arm in its powerful jaws and ripped it from his body.

Ensle screamed and went down. A single swipe from the grizzly's paw, and the screaming stopped.

Silence fell across the glen as the animals turned and headed back into the forest.

Heavy booted feet came crashing through the trees behind her as the rest of the guards charged in, swords drawn. They stopped at the edge of the clearing just as she had, no one daring to enter.

Sylas turned and looked at them. "Don't ever question my authority again," he said, then walked back into camp.

Chapter 50 | Ayrion

THE EARLY-MORNING SUN was shining, its light bringing with it a sense of hope.

After traveling from one small town to the next along the western side of Virn Run—a slow-moving river that snaked its way through the hillside—Ayrion was relieved to spend a day back inside the former rover camp. It was not filled with the sounds of music and dancing and stories as Tameel had said were typical of the colorfully clad nomads. Instead, the air was stale with a somber quietness as the plainly dressed wood folk from at least six outlying villages gathered around the firepits, sharing furtive glances and passing idle chatter as they waited for whatever was going to happen next.

Finding volunteers to join their cause had been easier than Ayrion anticipated, especially given their initial welcoming. Of course, the fact that their caravan carried with it the remaining survivors of Saeida helped spur people to action.

Shade whinnied from his pen on the left side of the camp, drawing

Ayrion's attention. Ayrion had been relieved when the warhorse had returned. He had opened the tavern door the next morning to see if the creatures had gone and found Shade standing there, waiting patiently for his apple. Zynora had managed to heal the deepest of the horse's wounds, letting the rest mend on their own.

As Ayrion passed through the camp on his way to talk to his old friend, he noticed new faces. More recruits were arriving every day. Most simply stared at his black leathers, twin swords, and grey eyes. The survivors from Saeida, however, nodded their heads or raised a glass to show their appreciation.

Belvin had apparently been the central city for this part of Sidara. It was surrounded by a network of towns and villages that stretched some forty miles north and south along the river. From Bek's description of Belvin and its size, it sounded as though they were going to need every able body they could find. Unfortunately, they didn't have time to wait for word to reach the farthest of the outlying communities, and the vulraaks had already taken those towns closest to Belvin.

Ayrion offered his giant friend one of the red apples he had stashed away in his jacket pocket. He rubbed Shade's ears and turned to take stock of their troops. *Not much to look at,* he thought. Most seemed dominated by either fear or anger, though both emotions, if nurtured correctly, could be useful in a fight.

Fear, although at times debilitating, kept people sharp, vigilant, watchful for an enemy they expected to arrive at any moment. Anger, on the other hand, was a little more dangerous to work with, as it tended to drive people to action without forethought. Either way, Ayrion knew he had his work cut out for him.

Ayrion left Shade and started for the back of the camp, where Bek was talking with Abiah. He wanted to see if the scouts Bek had sent out the previous night had returned.

"Gotcha!"

Ayrion turned to find Taylis kneeling beside the bottom half of a fallen tree. He was staring at something in the dirt. "What have you got there?"

The young rover boy flapped his arm at Ayrion. "No. Not there. Move over."

"What?"

"You're in my light." Taylis continued motioning, so Ayrion obliged by taking a couple of steps to the right. "There. Right there's fine," he said.

Ayrion stared at the small patch of ground Taylis was looking at. "What's going on? Are you testing those tracking skills Master Bek's been teaching you?"

"No," Taylis said without further explanation. He glanced over his shoulder at the position of the sun and then back at the small reflective object he held between his hands.

"What do you have there?"

"My crawly-killer."

"Your what?"

"My crawly-killer," he said with a hint of irritation.

"You don't say. And what exactly is a . . . crawly-killer?"

Taylis glared up at him with a look that said he couldn't believe Ayrion would ask such a silly question. "It kills crawlies, of course."

Ayrion knelt to get a better look. There was a small pile of black birch beetles lying off to the side, most of which seemed to be upside down, their legs unmoving. "And what did these crawlies do to deserve such an end?"

"They get into the flour," he said, "and the fruit. They'll even get in your bed if you aren't watching. Mama told me I should kill them wherever I find them."

"I guess that makes sense," Ayrion said, scratching his head. "So, how does it work?"

Taylis huffed. "Like this." He flipped the broken piece of glass over, and the reflection from the sun hit Ayrion in the face.

Ayrion raised his hand to protect his eyes, but not before he was seeing spots. "Sorry I asked." As sensitive as his eyes were, it took a moment for his vision to return.

Taylis angled his crawly-killer back toward one of the slow scurrying bugs and watched as the sun's light passed through the glass shard. The bug's thick shell began to smoke. Pretty soon, it too was on its back, legs in the air.

Ayrion wasn't sure if he should be impressed by the ingenuity or worried about the little boy's state of mind.

Behind him, a wagon door slammed shut, and he heard the patter of little feet rushing in his direction. "Ayrion."

Before he had a chance to fully turn, he was attacked by a flying creature with long brown hair and a bright yellow bow. Marissa's arms wrapped firmly around his waist.

Ayrion lifted the little rover girl the rest of the way into his arms. She smiled. Either she was surprisingly oblivious to the danger they were facing, or she had a remarkable gift for keeping a positive spirit. Ayrion only wished she had enough of that optimism to pass on to the rest of the encampment.

"You like my bow?" she asked, patting the top of her head and flattening the ribbon in the process.

Ayrion smiled. "I do," he said, fluffing one of the big loops. "It's a very beautiful bow, almost as beautiful as you." He finished by tapping the tip of her nose with his finger.

Her smile grew even wider as she puckered her lips and planted a soft peck on his cheek. "Eww!" She scrunched her face and wiped the front of her mouth. "Your hair is prickly."

Ayrion rubbed the sides of his face. "Hmm. I do need a shave, don't I?" Her head bobbed up and down. "I guess I better get to that, then. Can't be seen escorting such a pretty young lady with a scruffy face, now, can I?"

Her head shook in a resounding *no*.

Postponing his talk with Bek temporarily, Ayrion managed to get a quick shave in, with Marissa there to make sure he didn't miss any stray hairs. Once satisfied, she kissed his cheek and headed back to the wagon, leaving Ayrion free to meet with the others. He found the big trapper still on the outskirts of camp, talking with a couple of men who had apparently just ridden in.

Tameel stood off to the side, chatting with Abiah about something. Sounded like food supplies.

The scouts finished delivering their report to Bek and bowed deferentially to Ayrion as they walked by. One even went so far as to raise a fist to his chest in salute.

Rumors had spread quickly. The black warrior, atop his black steed, facing down an entire horde of white monsters. It was a story that seemed to grow with each new telling.

Ayrion didn't care for the attention and would have much preferred they stop, but Tameel and Zynora had convinced him otherwise, encouraging him to sell the pretense. "They're looking for someone to lead them," they said. "And you're it."

"What did our scouts have to say?" Ayrion asked, stopping alongside Abiah, who abruptly ended his conversation with Tameel to see what Bek had to say.

"It seems most everything this side of Belvin is fairly quiet. The city's been abandoned, at least during the day. The scouts couldn't find a soul. They checked a few of the outer residences before heading into the heart of the city. There was no sign of the vulraaks—"

"Apart from the destruction left in their wake," Abiah added, his arms resting atop his bulging midriff.

"We expected as much," Tameel said. "We know they don't care much for sunlight. No doubt they're holed up in some dark place, just waiting for night to arrive so they can proceed with their savaging."

"That would be the mines," Bek said. "Northeast of town. If I was looking for a dark place to make camp, that's where I'd be."

"Aye," Abiah concurred. "No place darker."

"Then that's where we'll look first," Ayrion said. "Strike the nest, hard and fast. Take out Argon as quickly as possible. Hopefully, us going in there and facing them head-on will be the last thing they'd expect."

"Yeppers," Tameel said, tugging on the sash at his waist. "I would say charging into a monster's stronghold with a band of untrained, unprepared, and barely armed townsfolk would most definitely be the last thing they would ever expect."

"Just hearing you say it aloud makes me question my own sanity," Abiah said with a groan.

Tameel glanced at the others. "How much longer do we wait?"

"We can't wait for long," Bek said, fingering a large knife. "Each day, they swallow a new town. The only benefit is that we've managed to stay ahead of their growth for now, helping people to clear out before the creatures arrive. But we can't keep this up forever. We already have more people displaced than we know what to do with. Even with the provisions they're bringing with them, it won't be enough to last, especially with the first snow looming."

"Aye," Abiah said, rubbing the thin patch of hair on top his head. "It gets mighty cold during the winter months. Without proper shelter, we're gonna start losing as many people to the weather as we do to those white monsters. Then again, with our ranks growing every day, the pragmatist in me wants to wait until we have a larger force before going toe to toe with whatever is waiting for us in Belvin."

Ayrion could understand the hesitance. He would much rather face Argon with a stronger force behind him as well, especially considering their army's lack of proper training. But Bek was right; they couldn't wait for long—the ground was already frosting at night, and he was sure snow was on its way.

Ayrion looked eastward. "I say we give it till the end of the week. Then, no matter what, we move on Belvin."

Chapter 51 | Amarysia

A MARYSIA BACKED AGAINST the wall. She took a deep breath before peeking around the corner. She knew that Dakaran had been looking for her earlier, and she tried to avoid him as best she could, but it wasn't always possible.

Being a lady-in-waiting to the Queen Mother had afforded her a certain amount of privilege when it came to moving about the palace, but ever since the deaths of King Rhydan and Ayrion, she had tried to keep that movement to a minimum. Most days she spent locked away in her chambers when she wasn't in direct service to the queen.

Ever since the Battle of Belbridge, Amarysia had become Ellise's confidante, if not surrogate daughter. It was a great comfort to know there was someone in the palace who could understand what she was going through, someone to lean on besides her brother and his floundering tribe of street rats.

In her hand, she held the piece of rolled parchment she'd received from one of the stable hands earlier that day. Ayrion had always said that if she needed to send messages outside the palace, Loren was the man to do it.

She stepped out from where she was hiding beside a low-hanging tapestry. Quietly, she made her way down the empty corridor toward the third-level stairwell that led directly to the main kitchens below. She hoped Loren was still waiting. Once inside the kitchen, she slipped behind some stacked barrels and grabbed one of the baskets off a nearby shelf. With her back to the wall, she moved along the outer wall, exiting through the servants' entrance and out to one of the lower courtyards on the east side of the palace grounds.

The sun was low on the horizon, and its rich colors cast long shadows at her back as she crossed the courtyard for the stables ahead. She kept her hood raised and her head lowered so as not to be seen by some of the white-uniformed guards she passed. A few stopped long enough to stare, forcing her to pick up her pace. These new Black Watch soldiers were a far cry from the kind of men Ayrion had trained.

Thankfully, other than a few lustful glares, no one bothered approaching. With her large wicker basket in hand, they probably assumed she was just another of the palace maids bringing some supper to one of the officers.

She breathed a little easier when she saw Loren standing just outside the west entrance. He was tall for his age and lanky, which worked well for maintaining eye contact with the horses. The young stableman waved when he saw her.

"I didn't think you were going to make it, miss," Loren said.

"To be honest, I wasn't all that sure myself." She handed him the basket. "I would have come earlier, but the queen needed me to help her prepare for another one of Dakaran's banquets this evening."

Loren shook his head. "Say no more. I have a mare all saddled and ready. How long do you expect to be gone?"

"I'm not sure," she said as she pulled on her gloves. She hadn't really thought that far ahead. "I need to be back in time for the banquet, I suppose."

Dakaran was holding a large feast that evening for those willing to genuflect to anything he said. He had been rather insistent that she attend. Amarysia couldn't think of anything she'd *less* rather do, but when the king demanded your presence, you showed up. Besides, she didn't like leaving the queen to attend on her own.

She followed Loren into the stables, where he had her horse waiting. He held the reins as she stepped up onto the mounting block and swung her leg up over the saddle. "Was the message hand-delivered?" she asked.

"Yes, missus. I was told to make sure that you received it unopened."

"Rest assured, the letter reached my hands unopened," she said. "Thank you."

"I knew Moira would make sure you got it all right." His eyes twinkled when he said her name.

Amarysia hadn't realized Loren had a relationship with the short, rosy-cheeked scullery girl. She was going to have to remember that in case she ever needed messages delivered in the future. She leaned forward and rubbed the mare's strong neck. "I'll try to have her back as soon as I can."

"Don't you worry none, missus. I'll be here when you do."

She gave the reins a slight pop, and the horse broke into a stable trot as they headed for the front gates and her awaiting rendezvous.

It took nearly a quarter of an hour to reach her destination. She'd turned down the wrong street the first time and had to backtrack. But soon enough, she was guiding her horse up the small carriage drive on the right side of the house. Only a single light was on, from what she could see, leaving her wondering if she had come at the wrong time or possibly even the wrong day. Leave it up to her to have read the message incorrectly.

She slid out of the saddle and pulled the parchment out from her cloak to reread it. No. It said the meeting was today.

Leaving her horse tied to what was no doubt the carriage house, she took the stone path around to the front porch. She took a moment to straighten her windblown hair back over her shoulders before brushing some of the wrinkles from the front of her dress. Satisfied that she didn't look a complete wreck, she knocked on the door.

A few moments later, it opened.

"Good evening, my dear, we were getting a bit worried you weren't going to make it." Commander Tolin towered over her, a warm smile on his face. From the light of the lantern he carried, she could see the grey in his hair was beginning to overpower the rest. His face looked tired but strong. He ushered her in before she had a chance to offer any reason for her late arrival, then stepped out onto the porch and scanned the grounds.

She had no idea why the former commander would want to see her. They had never been close. She had only met him once or twice with Ayrion. From those brief encounters, she thought Tolin a decent sort of man—firm but honest. Most importantly, Ayrion had believed in him.

Amarysia took a moment to glance around the room as the commander shut the door behind her. The walls were lined with crates and barrels and stacks of picture frames and furniture that looked like it had been moved from other rooms in the house.

"Don't mind the mess. You never realize how much stuff you have, or don't need, until you attempt to move."

"You're leaving?"

Tolin sighed. "I'm afraid I can't afford the place any longer with my loss of position, and I have a feeling that things might not go too well for me or my family here in Aramoor in the foreseeable future."

Amarysia didn't know what to say. "I hope you haven't been waiting long. The queen needed my help more than usual today."

"No bother. We've been enjoying the company."

"We?" She hadn't expected to be meeting with someone else.

"Yes, I have someone here who has been looking forward to seeing you again."

"Oh?" Unfortunately, the commander didn't say who it was; he simply led the way toward the back of the house. She hurried down the hall behind him, anxious to find out who was waiting.

"I hear the palace is quite busy tonight with another of Dakaran's lavish banquets." The words came out in a sneer.

"Indeed. He holds them more often than not these days."

Tolin nodded and opened a door on the left beside a stairwell that went to the second floor. Stepping back, he ushered her inside.

There was a warm fire in the hearth with a couple of seats gathered in front. Two men were seated there already. One stood rather quickly at their entrance.

"Amarysia!"

Amarysia froze. It couldn't be. He was dead.

"My, my," Barthol said with a satisfied grin. "You look as though you've seen a spirit."

"Haven't I?" She barely managed to take a single step when he swept across the room and lifted her off her feet with a tight squeeze. "You certainly hug like Barthol," she said, gasping for air.

The big man lowered her back to her feet.

The other man stood beside his chair, drink in hand. He didn't seem to want to interrupt Barthol's welcome. He was shorter than the other two but stout. His face was hard to forget with his long ducktail beard and eye patch.

"Amarysia, I'm not sure if you've been introduced to Overcaptain Asa yet," Tolin said. "He's been my right arm since . . ."

"Since you was old enough to stop wetting the bed." Asa snorted.

Tolin grunted. "Asa, this is Amarysia. She is a lady-in-waiting to the Queen Mother."

"Aye," Asa grunted. "I do believe I've seen you about the palace. Very happy to make your acquaintance." He offered her a nod and a deep smile, which she promptly returned.

"Thank you, Overcaptain. Ayrion spoke very highly of you, as well as the commander."

"Much obliged, ma'am."

She turned and looked at Barthol, still having a difficult time believing it was him. "What of Kensey and Arina? Do they know . . ."

"Yes, of course," Barthol said. "They were my first concern."

Amarysia released a small sigh of relief. She knew what his wife and daughter must have gone through: the same suffering she had experienced learning of Ayrion's . . . Then it hit her. If Barthol was still alive, then— "Is . . . Is Ayrion still . . ."

Barthol lowered his eyes and shook his head.

"Are you sure? They said you were dead as well. Maybe there's a chance—"

"I'm afraid not," he said, not leaving any room for doubt.

She could see it in his eyes. Ayrion was dead. But to have been given hope—even as short-lived as it was—and watch it dashed to pieces . . . she felt as though a mountain had been dropped on her chest. Tears blurred her vision, and she turned to look at the fire, not wanting them to see her cry.

She felt a hand on her shoulder. "Are you all right?" Tolin asked.

She wiped her eyes. "I don't know if I ever will be again."

"Please," he said, motioning to one of the empty seats.

She joined the others around the fire.

"Ayrion's death is part of the reason why we asked you here this evening," Tolin said as he poured a glass of wine for her.

She took a sip. It warmed the back of her throat but not as strongly as the emotions she was struggling to hold inside. She could feel the tears beginning to re-form and fought to hold them off. Leaning back in her chair, she let the warmth of the fire soothe her frayed nerves. "Why did you want to see me?" she asked. "And what does it have to do with Ayrion's death?"

The commander cleared his throat. "Like you, I was under the impression that our good captain here had been slain during the battle.

So, when he showed up on my doorstep in the middle of the night, my reaction wasn't much different than yours. And when he began to tell me of the circumstances surrounding his fictitious departure, I knew we were in a lot of trouble."

Amarysia thumbed the stem of her glass. "I don't understand. What circumstances?"

Tolin leaned forward in his seat. "The High King and Guardian Protector were not killed by hor'hounds. They were murdered by Dakaran."

Amarysia was struck speechless. Even if she had known what to say, she felt sure it would have caught in her throat. *Murdered?* She knew Dakaran was an arrogant pig, and a louse to boot, but she was having a hard time believing that he would outright murder his own father in cold blood.

"How?" she asked. "Dakaran's a decent swordsman, but I doubt he could have taken a veteran like his father, let alone Ayrion. Didn't anyone see it? Weren't there any witnesses?"

The commander crossed his legs. "I'll let Barthol be the one to tell it, seeing as how he was the one who was there."

Barthol described what had happened as best he could, starting from them killing off the rest of the hor'hounds, to Ayrion saving his life after kicking him over the side of a cliff, to waking up and finding everyone dead.

Tolin waved his glass at Barthol. "Dakaran told us that everyone had been killed by the hor'hounds and that they had respectfully laid what remained of Ayrion and Barthol's bodies to rest."

Barthol turned to Amarysia. "As you said, Dakaran could not have bettered his father even on his best day, and the notion of him even holding a candle to Ayrion would be absurd. No, the only way this was accomplished was with the help of the Tower's guards."

"Aye," Asa said, swallowing what remained in his glass in one swift gulp. "The same flaming whoresons as what's taken over everything around here." He looked as though he was about to spit, but after glancing around, he seemed to think better of it and swallowed. "The prince, or king, or whatever you want to call him, has done crawled in bed with the White Tower."

Barthol stared into his glass. "Maybe getting out while we still can isn't such a bad thing after all." He looked over at Tolin.

"You're planning on leaving Aramoor?" she asked, hoping that wasn't the case. Barthol and Tolin were about the only allies she had left besides Ellise.

Barthol didn't respond one way or the other.

Tolin laid his glass aside. "We thought you should know the truth about Ayrion's death. More importantly, we need the queen to know what happened to her husband. We were hoping you would be able to relay this information to her for us. She could be in danger. Dakaran has what he wants, his father's throne. And if he was willing to murder him for it, I doubt there's much he wouldn't do to keep it."

"The people still love and respect Ellise," Barthol said.

"Aye," Asa cut in, "and that loyalty might be enough for Dakaran to consider having someone slip something in her evening tea."

Tolin leaned forward, eyes serious. "Would you be willing to let the queen know what is going on?"

Amarysia nodded. "I also need to let the clans know that they won't be receiving any help from the throne concerning the kidnappings in the Warrens. Ayrion was the one overseeing it, and now that he . . ." She couldn't finish. "Well, they will need to be told."

"I had forgotten about them," Tolin said, the lines around his eyes tightening. "I was there when Ayrion asked the king for his help with the disappearances." He took a deep breath. "If you could set up a meeting with their chieftain, I'd be willing to take part."

Asa coughed, patting his chest as he leaned forward in his seat. "*You?* Meet with the clans?" He drew his dagger and pointed it at Tolin. "Who are you and what have you done with my friend?"

Tolin smiled. "I never thought to hear those words uttered from my lips either, but I'm not about to have this young woman face the clans alone. Besides, times are changing, and the lines between right and wrong are beginning to blur."

Amarysia smiled. "Thank you, Commander. I'll try to set something up as soon as possible, and I will send word through Loren when I do. But for now, I better be getting back before I'm missed. Dakaran was adamant about me attending his party this evening. And I don't want the queen going alone."

"Be careful with that one, young missy," Asa said. "He's a snake waiting to strike. Don't be in his line of sight when he does."

Chapter 52 | Amarysia

AMARYSIA HURRIED TO the gallery on the second floor, which was Dakaran's favored location for entertaining guests. On this particular evening, it appeared "guests" meant the entire Elondrian Senate, which seemed strange, since Dakaran had never shown the slightest interest in pandering to the ruling class before.

His lavish feasts had become quite the talk amongst the upper class. No expense spared. The leftovers from just one such dinner could have fed half their army. She never remembered his father hosting with such extravagance, but then again, Rhydan had been a man with at least a modicum of common sense.

Amarysia slowed as she rounded the final corner. White-clad sentries stood to either side of the gilded doors, seemingly oblivious to the sounds of merriment inside. She took a moment to compose herself. The skirt of her burgundy gown was rumpled, a consequence of her meeting with Commander Tolin. She'd barely had time to change clothes, let alone properly press and iron them. She reminded herself that she didn't have anyone to impress. In fact, quite the opposite.

She preferred to dress as simply as possible so as not to encourage attention. These new guards had neither the respect for women nor their station that the lancers trained under Commander Tolin had.

The guards opened the doors, leering as she passed. She pretended not to notice.

The banquet hall was as large as one of the outside courtyards—twice as long as it was wide. Heavily decorated tables lined the outer perimeter, leaving a wide, open area in the middle for the evening's entertainment. Glass-paned windows stretched up the walls on either side, allowing pale moonlight to mingle with the amber glow from the enormous chandeliers overhead.

It seemed every seat was filled. Apparently, no one dared turn down an invitation from the king, especially one that promised such frivolities as this. The guests were decked in their finest silks and laces, colorful as peacocks as they busied themselves in idle conversation while devouring the exorbitant amount of food on their plates.

The Queen Mother, who was seated next to Dakaran at the head table, smiled when she saw Amarysia and immediately motioned her over. The queen's smile looked more like relief than pleasure, leaving Amarysia to feel even more guilty about what she was required to do. How was she ever going to tell the queen what she had heard? How do you tell a mother that her son murdered his father?

Dakaran saw her as well; she did her best not to shudder at his smile. Like the others, he seemed dressed to the extreme with a gold shirt and azure cape with a white fur mantle. His crown sat high on his head as if he wanted to make sure everyone noticed.

Maybe staying in the palace wasn't the best idea. She could take Kira's advice and leave Aramoor. Grab her brother and never look back.

No. She needed to be there for the queen. Especially now, given what she knew.

Carefully, Amarysia wove her way through the army of attendants as they rushed from one table to the next, making sure the king's guests were afforded every available comfort. Some bowed as she passed; most just tried to keep from knocking her over.

She made her way up the steps to the platform at the front of the room and took the empty seat next to the queen.

"I was beginning to worry you weren't going to make it," Ellise said, having to lean in to be heard over the noise. "Were you able to finish your errand in town?"

Amarysia glanced at Dakaran to see if he was listening, but he seemed to be otherwise engaged with his counselor. "I was," she said, lifting her goblet and taking a small sip of the wine, enough to coat her dry throat and help calm her nerves.

Ellise looked her over. "Are you feeling well?"

"I am, Your Majesty," Amarysia said, attempting a smile. "I've received some troubling news, and I'm not sure what I need to do with it."

"Oh? Is it of a personal nature?"

Too personal, she thought. "It is, Your Majesty. To more than just myself."

Ellise laid her hand on top of Amarysia's and squeezed. "I'm sure you will do the right thing." The simple act was meant to be comforting, but Amarysia was already dreading what "the right thing" would mean for her.

"You look beautiful this evening," Dakaran said from his seat on the other side of his mother. He leaned forward to see her better, and his crown slid slightly to the side, forcing him to readjust it.

Beside him, Archchancellor Valtor offered a slight tilt of his head in acknowledgement.

"Thank you, Your Majesty. You're most kind."

"Not at all," he said, raising his goblet in salute and taking a deep swallow.

Thankfully, Dakaran's attention shifted back to the entertainment and away from her. There was plenty to be distracted with—musicians and dancers, troupes of acrobats, jugglers, fire blowers, and bards singing dramatic ballads. It seemed there would even be a contest of martial skill at some point, judging by the targets that had been set up on the far side of the room. The place was a circus, a dissonance of noise and movement meant to stimulate the digestion for the mountain of food the kitchens had been slaving over for the last four or five days.

Once the main course was cleared, Dakaran motioned the chamberlain over to his seat and whispered something in his ear. The short, pudgy man raised his staff and smacked it three times on the marble tile. "Hear ye! Hear ye! His Excellency, the High King of Elondria and ruler of the Provincial Authority, makes ready to speak."

The performers were quickly ushered out of the chamber as the servants continued their rounds, clearing the next set of half-empty dishes and ensuring the guests' wineglasses were filled to the brim.

Dakaran didn't bother to rise. "My dear friends." The slur in his voice was barely recognizable, but Amarysia was used to listening for it. "I trust the food and entertainment have been to your liking."

A chorus of hearty agreements echoed through the great room, accompanied by raised glasses, exuberant clapping, and a round of cheers.

"I have called you here this evening to discuss a rising concern of state."

Amarysia clenched a wad of dress under the table, fighting not to show the anger she was feeling. She could think of quite a few rising concerns. Chiefly, that Dakaran had killed his father and Ayrion in cold blood.

"It has come to my attention that our coffers are not what they once were. Gold is disappearing all over the place."

Gasps could be heard across the hall.

"Not to mention what was wasted in our recent and, if you ask me, unnecessary war with Cylmar."

A few raised their glasses at his sentiment, but most turned and looked at the queen, scandalized by this brazen slight against her husband's actions.

Ellise's hands tightened around the stem of her glass. Most wouldn't have noticed. But having spent every day for the last three years with the queen, Amarysia had learned to spot those subtle reactions.

The war effort had not been popular with the ruling class, considering the amount of revenue required to conduct the campaign, but a single glance at the epicurean excess that covered the tables in front of her, and one could easily see why the treasury had diminished.

"Our borders are expanding," Dakaran said, "and each day, more and more citizens are coming into Elondria, seeking a better way of life. We need to show them how benevolent we can be."

Claps of agreement filled the room.

"But it won't be cheap."

The praise quickly withered.

"And how does Your Majesty propose this happen?" one of the senators near the front asked.

"I have discussed this matter at length with my council." At that, every eye turned to the king's left, where Valtor sat watching their reactions. Amarysia noted the slight smirk on the Archchancellor's face. "We have decided to establish a new citizenry tax to be levied on all who live and work within the borders of Elondria."

Murmurs spread around the hall. There was more than one troubled face in the crowd.

"Son," the queen said softly, leaning forward to catch his eye, "your father spent his entire life fighting to lower the taxes on the people. Laying such an unexpected burden on them might cause an uprising."

Dakaran glanced briefly at Amarysia. He looked almost embarrassed, the same way any child did when reprimanded by their parents in front of their friends. He bit down on his lip and turned back to his guests. "Our people have grown soft and lazy. If they want to live off what we provide, then *just* compensation is in order. Protection isn't cheap, after all. I believe the tax should be levied by quantity. Those with more should pay more." He paused to judge the crowd's response.

It was all too apparent to Amarysia what the senators' sentiments were, as faces reddened and muffled whispers soon turned to angry shouts. But considering these were some of the wealthiest citizens in Aramoor, it was understandable.

"Perhaps we should consider cutting back on the amount of funding directed to the White Tower," one senator suggested, glaring at the Archchancellor. "Do we really need all these Black Watch? Why not reestablish the High Guard?"

Dakaran struck the top of the table with his goblet. "We are surrounded by potential enemies on three sides. Cylmar has shown us that already. And the High Guard already demonstrated their lack of usefulness when they let my father die."

Once more, Amarysia grabbed a thick wad of her dress under the table and squeezed, wanting to do the same to Dakaran's throat.

Dakaran leaned forward, the slur in his speech no longer present. "The High Guard is a thing of the past; the Black Watch is our future, and that future is looking bright." He raised his glass with a smile.

Valtor leaned forward in his seat. "Of course, the king is not suggesting that this burden should fall on the members of our illustrious senate."

Dakaran looked confused, but after a quick word with Valtor, his face brightened, and he addressed the room. "The Archchancellor is correct. You have enough to worry about keeping the kingdom running smoothly. There will be a waiver set in place for the senate."

The members quietly conversed amongst themselves, their earlier anger at the possibility of lost revenue quickly diminishing.

Dakaran, clearly not wanting to give them another chance to voice any further disagreements, turned to the chamberlain. "Bring in the next round of entertainment."

The chamberlain bowed and smacked his official staff against the floor. "Bring in the dancers!"

Amarysia watched the Archchancellor for a moment. He sat stiffly in his seat, his fingers tapping the top of the table in succession as he studied the senators. Eventually, he turned and whispered something in Dakaran's ear before rising from the table and leaving with a small contingent of white-robed guards.

She shuddered at the thought of how the citizens of Elondria would respond to this news. It almost appeared that Dakaran wanted some kind of open rebellion. Surely, he wasn't naïve enough to think that raising the taxes on the people was going to put him in good standing.

She needed to set up that meeting between Kira and Tolin soon.

Chapter 53 | Valtor

A FTER WATCHING THE overstuffed senators squirm, Valtor was content to leave the king to his sycophants. Pampering the senators was a necessary evil, but that didn't mean he had to sit around and watch them gloat.

There were times he wondered why he let this charade continue. But killing Dakaran now would only succeed in uniting the other kingdoms against him. For now, it was best to keep Dakaran on the throne and under his thumb.

He entered his chambers and uncovered the traveling mirror at the back. He spoke the name it was inscribed with, followed by that of its counterpart in the White Tower. "*Galaerion Sugethru. Nothleen Filaurel.*"

The glass rippled. Valtor waited for it to stop moving before he stepped through. On the other side, he made his way down through the White Tower's inner network of winding stairwells and empty corridors, enjoying the rare moment of solitude. He was seldom left alone to his own thoughts these days.

It was a respite from the chaos. His thoughts drifted to the future he saw for Aldor.

He dreamed of a day when wielders would reclaim their rightful place, no longer hiding on the fringes but instead holding power. The Creator had bequeathed that power to the ven'ae. That they had to fear the jun'ri just showed how completely upside down this world had become. He longed for the day when those with abilities would no longer have to hide. When people like his parents would no longer be able to cast their own aside. When the jun'ri would bend the knee to *them*.

But so many of the ven'ae were still unwilling to accept his vision. He didn't like killing wielders, but if they stood in the way of bringing this new era to pass, he didn't have much choice.

He realized he was hitting his staff against the floor harder than strictly necessary, so he slowed, making a conscious effort to control his anger. He was doing all of this for them. Why couldn't they see that?

He was close. Each day was another step in the right direction. Each day brought him closer to his vision of how the world should be. He paused at the bottom landing of a particularly long flight of steps to catch his breath.

Sure, he had suffered some setbacks. The faeling child and his protectors in Easthaven were proving to be more troublesome than expected, but he would be rid of them soon enough.

He reached the scrying room and raised his hand. *"Tares'ayden."*

The deadly wall of mist protecting the chamber dropped into the ground and disappeared. Stepping inside, he closed the door behind him and made his way between the pyres and up the steps to the center of the dais.

Aerodyne had promised him this. He knew the great wizard was the only one with enough power to bring his dream to pass, and because of this, Valtor worked night and day to put the pieces in play that would lead to the Dark Wizard's return.

The stone in his pocket warmed at his touch, and a single pyre burst to life with pale-green flame. A stocky, barrel-chested man appeared inside. He was much less formally attired than normal, wearing little more than a rumpled nightshirt.

"This had better be important, Valtor," the man snapped, rubbing his eyes with the back of his hand. "I was napping."

Valtor assumed that was the reason for the man's state of undress. "I am merely checking on your progress, Overlord."

"Progress? There is no progress. We don't meet until next week, you oaf." The man glanced down at the stone in his right hand and gave it a repulsed look. "You woke me to ask that?"

"I apologize for the interruption," Valtor said, realizing he needed to smooth the man's ruffled feathers. "I wanted you to be the first to know that the king has just announced a new source of revenue that will guarantee you payment for services rendered."

"And what of the other part of our arrangement?"

"As long as you continue to provide the throne with credible information, then the Crown will have no reason to operate within the boundaries of your kingdom." Valtor smiled. "Good allies are hard to find these days."

"Allies? Allies in what? You talk as though you are expecting a war."

"You can never be too careful. Just look at what happened with Cylmar. Nasty business, that was. Overlord Saryn should have known better than to test his might against Elondria."

The overlord lifted his hand to his neck. "Yes, nasty business indeed. Tell Dakaran he'll get his information." The overlord turned to walk away, then stopped. "Why is the throne so interested in Sidara? Not much there but woods."

"Let's just say, when three of the four remaining kingdoms hold a conclave where the throne is not in attendance, we tend to worry that the outcome will not be to Elondria's benefit. I would hate to think that the other overlords were conspiring against the High King. Those kinds of actions could have dire consequences."

The overlord was silent for a moment. "Just make sure your white riders stay clear of my kingdom."

"You uphold your end of the bargain, and I can guarantee it."

"Good." The man stifled another yawn. "If that's all, then I'm going back to bed. And judging by those dark circles," he said, pointing at Valtor, "you should do the same." With that, the green flames were snuffed out, and the pyre went dark once again.

"Insufferable fool." Valtor released the stone and started for the steps. He hated placating these buffoons. As much fun as it might have been, Valtor didn't have time to waste dreaming up new and creative ways to deal with the arrogant overlord. There would be plenty of time for that later. At the bottom of the steps, Valtor took a moment to stretch, fighting back the urge to yawn. He desperately wanted to crawl into bed, but there was still much that needed to be done.

Valtor shut the door to the scrying chamber and lifted the protection spell. He turned and yelped, startled to discover his apprentice standing behind him. The grotesque deformity on the side of Rowen's face made the young man look just short of evil.

"Rowen, what have I told you about sneaking up on me?"

Rowen smiled as if he had won some small victory. "Where are you headed?"

Valtor started back toward the staircase leading to the lower levels. "To check in on our recruits, if you must know."

Rowen grunted, then followed silently in Valtor's shadow.

After an unfortunate accident buckled the main support wall in one of the upper towers a few years back, causing the entire top three floors to collapse on those inside, they had decided to continue their training in a more structurally safe environment. The back half of the White Tower had been built straight into the side of the Razor Spine Mountains, creating an array of large vaulted chambers perfect for the use of educating new recruits in the art of magic without having to worry about their doing any serious damage to the main structures.

It would take considerably more than a few loose bolts of air to bring down the mountain.

Everywhere Valtor went, men in white uniforms snapped to attention. He passed a few of the black-robed bulradoer as they scurried down the halls. Their ranks were steadily increasing as well, which pleased him.

The Inquisition, with the help of the Black Watch, was doing a remarkable job in gathering information on new wielders. Given the choice between purging—which was normally a death sentence to the wielder—and joining, joining seemed to be the preferred option.

The new recruits wore the grey robes of a novice, which made them easy to spot. They were not allowed the black robes of the bulradoer until their training had been completed.

Valtor stopped beneath the archway leading out of the main keep and into the inner mountain chambers. Beyond lay an enormous room carved completely out of stone. Fluted pillars had been left scattered throughout as the main support for the mountain. Their size was incredible, each side measuring the span of two men standing side by side with arms outstretched. They had doubtless been built by wizard engineers during the Second Age. Braziers filled with flaming coals hung around each pillar, flooding the cavernous room with light.

A staircase wide enough to fit an entire company of lancers led from the arch down to the main floor of the cavern, where the wielders trained. Valtor descended slowly, Rowen remaining at least two steps behind.

One of the bulradoer spotted Valtor on the steps and rushed up to greet him.

"Your Eminence," the man bowed, trying to catch his breath. "How may I be of assistance?"

"I'm here to inspect your work. How goes the training?"

"Very well, Your Eminence. New recruits are being shipped in every month." The bulradoer turned and gestured to the open chamber beyond.

"As you can see, they are receiving a full course of instruction. If you'll follow me, I'll be happy to show you around."

Valtor followed the bulradoer down the steps, trying not to visibly lean on his staff. His legs were stiff, and his back ached from all the climbing.

The cavern had been divided into six stations, a single bulradoer overseeing a cluster of grey-robed novices at each. They stopped at the first station, which consisted of three rows of tables lined with recruits sitting on long benches, studying runes and incantations. Most stopped what they were doing when they saw him approach. After nodding his approval, the bulradoer continued on.

The second station was a series of desks covered with glass beakers, pewter mixing bowls, half-filled decanters, and cauldrons, as well as a variety of instruments used for teaching natural elements and the fundamentals of potion-making. This particular type of magic was one of Valtor's favorites. It required a healthy dose of patience, as the brewer had to determine not only the right ingredients but also the correct dosage and application. It was one of the reasons he spent so much time in his laboratory in the dungeons under the palace.

The next four stations were for battle magic—one for defensive and three for offensive.

The instruction Valtor had received from Nyalis before the wizard had walked away had proven invaluable when Valtor began to train his bulradoer. Most of his own apprenticeship with Nyalis had been spent studying the rudimentary elements of magic. Even after being sent away, Valtor had been able to take those elements and build on them, though some refinement by trial and error had been necessary.

Valtor's abilities, however, were mere child's play compared to the magic he had discovered within Aerodyne's grimoires, but that magic was for his eyes alone.

A high-pitched scream from the fifth station had Valtor skipping the other stations to see what had happened. By the time they pushed through the crowd, a young woman had been completely engulfed in flame. The bulradoer in charge of the station seemed unwilling to help and stood to the side, signaling to the others to stand back. It wasn't until the woman had fallen to the ground that the instructor conjured a blanket of air to quench the fire. The bulradoer called for a healer, and a young man pushed through the onlookers. He knelt beside the badly charred woman and laid his hand on her back. Her darkened skin slowly regained normal color.

"We make sure not to give aid too quickly," their guide said. He looked proud. "We find it forces our recruits to think before they act. Those who earn their robes will be worthy of them, I assure you."

"The principle is sound," Valtor said, "but we can't afford to lose any of our wielders. Make sure they have proper mastery of the basics. I don't want to find we have lost a quarter of our numbers due to negligence."

"Yes, Your Grace."

Valtor tapped his fingers on the head of his cane. "I can see you have things well in hand." He turned for the stairs. "How soon until this first batch might be ready for testing?"

The bulradoer thumbed his chin. "I'd say as early as spring, Your Grace."

Valtor stopped. "Not sooner?"

The man licked his lips nervously. "Well, no, Your Grace. There is a process involved in order to break them down so that they can be molded back the way that we need them to be. That takes time, I'm afraid. To hurry that along could result in creating bulradoer who, instead of following orders, might decide that thinking for themselves is more important."

Valtor nodded. "I'm sure their training will be put to the test soon enough."

"Of course, Your Eminence. We look forward to the challenge."

Valtor, feeling adequately impressed by their progress, left the bulradoer to his work and headed for his chambers and some much-needed rest. His vigilant apprentice trailed behind him in silence.

Chapter 54 | Ty

"I'M TELLING YOU, someone was in there," Orlyn said, leaning forward in his seat. He glanced around the table at the members of the council. Not all the members were present.

Ty noted Gilly was absent, as well as Reloria. She apparently hadn't had enough notice to find someone to watch her shop. Sheeva was also not in attendance. At least, Ty didn't think she was. With her, you never knew. He reached out with his magic to see if he could feel her presence, though he wasn't exactly sure what Sheeva's magic felt like. The only time he'd used his magic in that way was to search for Mangora and her spiders.

Breen was there, but Adarra had stayed behind to keep working her way through the books on the Tallosian language that Overlord Barl had found in his library.

"How do you know someone was there?" Veldon asked. He was in his usual seat at the head of the table, handkerchief clutched in his right hand. "I thought the wizard gave you a protection spell for the building.

How could someone get in?"

"I don't think it's made to keep people out. I think it's more to alert us of when someone goes in." He shrugged. "I don't know how it happened. I just know what I felt. The barrier came down, and a little while later, it went back up. That's when I got Feoldor to come help me take a look."

Feoldor yawned. "Don't remind me. I lost an entire night's sleep for nothing."

"Nothing?" Orlyn glared down the table.

"Yes, nothing. There was no one there."

Ty grinned but quickly wiped the expression from his face. He was still amazed at how he had managed to get into the witch's shop and back out without being spotted. If it hadn't been for the book, he wouldn't have made it through the front door. He spun the glass ring around his finger, making sure he kept his hand under the table so his father, who was sitting next to him, didn't see.

"Perhaps. Perhaps not," Orlyn said. "But one thing's for sure. Someone had been there, and recently."

"How do you know?" Ty's father asked. "Other than you believe the shield went down for a while."

Ty leaned forward. *Yes. How could they know?* He had been careful not to leave any clues. There were far too many footprints on those dusty floors to think they had been made by anyone recent. Had they seen him from one of the upper windows when he made a break down the alley?

"We could smell it," Orlyn said, causing Fraya, and even Breen, to chuckle.

"Smell it?" Veldon wiped his forehead with his kerchief.

"There was smoke. Something on the second floor had been burned."

Ty bit his tongue. *Idiot.*

"Don't worry. They won't know it's you."

Ty raised his head. "What?"

Orlyn turned and looked at him, drawing the others' attention as well.

"Did you have something to add?"

Ty winced. That stupid ring was going to get him caught. He was having a hard time telling what was real and what was in his head. "You said that something on the second floor had been burned. I was just wondering what."

"Part of the doorframe from one of the bedchambers was singed."

"How could you tell it was recent?" Breen asked. "Could it have been done before you set up the barrier?"

Feoldor grunted. "I think we can tell the difference between a week-old piece of charred wood and one cooked within the last few hours."

"Could the witch still be around?" Fraya asked, sounding nervous.

Orlyn glanced at Feoldor, and Feoldor glanced at Ty's father, who seemed in turn to be staring at the table.

"I hope not," Orlyn finally said.

Veldon leaned forward with a grunt. "One thing's for sure: We need to move her stuff out of that shop and somewhere safe. If she is still around, we don't want her getting her hands on anything she can use against us."

"Make sure you keep an eye on where they take it," the book said through the ring.

"I will," Ty mumbled.

Ty's father glanced his way briefly, then to Veldon. "We will be joining Barl this afternoon at the barracks. Adarra is going to attempt to communicate with our Northman prisoner."

"You need to be there," the book said.

This time, Ty didn't respond. *I will be.* He didn't know if the book could actually hear his thoughts, but it was worth a shot.

"Let us know how it goes," Veldon said. He glanced around the table. "If there's no other business—"

Ty cleared his throat. "When do you plan on moving the witch's stuff?"

Veldon looked at Orlyn, and Orlyn shrugged.

"I'm not sure," the apothecary said. "We still need to inventory the shop." He looked at Ty. "We'll let you know."

"He's lying," the book said.

Ty looked at Orlyn, and Orlyn offered an awkward smile. It was a smile Ty wasn't familiar with. Orlyn's smiles were usually so warm and friendly, almost affectionate. But this one was halfhearted at best. He spun the glass on his finger. The book was right.

They were lying.

Ty left the meeting feeling worse than when he'd arrived. What else were they keeping from him? It was a question he pondered all the way to the East Inn. His father decided to stop for lunch before meeting with Barl, and Fraya tagged along to spend more time with Breen.

"Are you feeling all right?" Ty's father asked him, slowly stirring the pieces of meat around in his bowl.

The stew wasn't quite as thick today, which Ty was grateful for. It meant it hadn't been sitting out for hours before being served. It did, however, have a strong peppered taste, which usually meant that Noreen Aboloff had been in charge of food preparations that morning instead of her husband. Strong or not, the heat rising from the bowl was a welcome relief from the chill outside.

"I'm fine," Ty said, sifting through his bowl for the long, stringy pieces of onion he didn't like to eat. He found another and dropped it on his plate.

His father slowly turned his cup. "You looked distracted during the meeting. Is it the witch?"

"Why does everyone want to keep me from knowing when they're moving her stuff?"

His father set his cup down. "No one wants to keep—"

"Every time I ask about it, someone changes the subject."

"Like Veldon said, they still need to inventory the place, and that could take a while. Besides, you heard Orlyn; they'll let us know when they're ready."

"Where are they taking it?" the book asked.

"I don't know," Ty mumbled under his breath. He looked up at his father. "Where do you think they'll take it?"

His father shook his head. "It hasn't been determined. You seem awful curious. Is there something we need to know?"

"Just wondering." He was going to need to keep his eye on the shop to make sure they didn't move what was inside without telling him. He really wanted to get his hands on those books.

After a few more minutes of uncomfortable silence, where everyone seemed to be doing nothing more than stirring the soup in their bowls, his father finally pushed his seat back from the table. "I think we've done about as much damage to this stew as we're going to." He stood, dropped a couple of coppers on the table, and headed for the door.

Ty stood to follow, but Breen grabbed his arm. "Wait a moment."

His brother whispered something to Fraya, and she left the two of them and followed their father out the door.

"What was that all about?" Breen asked.

Ty pulled his arm free. "What do you mean?"

"Why are you so interested in Mangora's shop?"

"I'm not."

"You're not? That's all you could talk about during the council meeting. And what's with that book?"

"What book?"

"The book in your jacket pocket. Don't think I don't notice you up reading it at all hours of the night." He glanced around the room, then leaned in. "I've even heard you . . . talking to it."

Ty chuckled nervously. "That's stupid. Why would I be talking to a book?"

"I don't know. You're not acting yourself." He glanced at Ty's coat. "What's it about, anyway?"

"It's not about anything. It's blank."

Breen stared at him a moment, then, with lightning speed, grabbed the front of Ty's coat.

Ty fought back, attempting to shove his brother's arm away, but it was like wrestling a bull. Breen's arms were twice the size of his, and despite how hard Ty struggled, his brother managed to pry the book free.

"Give it back, Breen!"

Breen ignored him and opened it.

A sharp pain lanced through Ty's head. What was that?

"Get the book!" the book commanded through the ring.

Ty lunged for it, but Breen held him off as he continued flipping through the pages.

"What is this? There's nothing here."

The pain in his head was growing more intense. "I told you. Now give it back. Give it to me!"

Breen closed the book and read the cover. *"Hidden Perceptions.* What does that mean?"

Ty finally managed to snatch the book from his brother's grip, and the aching subsided. By the time he managed to get it back in his pocket, he was panting. He took a deep breath and tried to calm down. Why did his brother care so much about the book?

"What's wrong with you?" Breen asked, looking at Ty like he'd lost his mind. "There's nothing there. Why in the world would you be up so late, reading an empty book? You need to get rid of that thing."

"I don't see you getting rid of your bow."

"You also don't see me talking to it, do you?"

Ty didn't bother responding. He turned and stormed out of the inn. Why was Breen so upset about the book?

"He wants me for himself."

Ty buttoned his jacket against the cold gust moving down the street.

He noticed Adarra waiting quietly on Thistle, her cloak pulled around her body. She must have just ridden over from Overlord Barl's estate, her satchel filled to the brim with books. She waved, and Ty nodded in return, trying to hide his anger as he untied Waddle from the post.

Ty swung into the saddle and pulled Waddle alongside his father as they waited for Breen and Fraya to say their goodbyes.

"Will I see you later this week?" she asked.

"Of course," his brother said, giving her a kiss on the cheek. "Give your father my best."

"I will." She climbed onto her horse and headed up the street.

"Time to go," Ty's father said, and none too soon. Ty's teeth were already beginning to chatter.

Ty kept alongside his father as they rode west toward the Sidaran barracks, still plagued with questions that needed answering.

Before he knew it, he was guiding Waddle through the barracks' north gate. He caught himself spinning the glass ring with his thumb. He wasn't used to wearing jewelry.

In front of him, his father steered Your Highness toward the main building. Adarra offered Thistle a gentle nudge, and the mare trotted along behind. Breen brought up the rear.

The barracks was swarming with activity. Green-and-gold uniforms filled the open yard, making it difficult to direct their horses. Near the south gate, Ty spotted groups of armed men training in pairs. They went through what appeared to be routine battle tactics with their swords and shields, and some with polearms. In the back was an archery range with a line of lancers waiting for a turn at the bow.

Breen was eyeing the range as well.

Ty dismounted in front of what looked like the main barracks building, taking a moment to tie Waddle to the rail. He was anxious to get inside and question the Northman.

Apparently, the only useful piece of information Overlord Barl had gathered from the big savage was his name: Jonas. Ty hadn't seen the

Tallosian during their battle—other than his unconscious body tied in the corner of their home during their fight with the spiders—but he had heard the story of how Adarra had gutted the man's comrade with one of their father's sickles.

No one had heard Tallosian speech for nearly a hundred years, and even with the smattering of ancient books on the topic, hidden within the dusty shops of Easthaven's booksellers, it would have taken years for someone to relearn. Well, it would have taken years for most people. Not his sister.

Still, there was only one piece of information that Ty wanted from the Tallosian: the whereabouts of Mangora.

He waited as his father helped Adarra unload her overflowing satchel from Thistle and carry it up the stairs to the front. Ty could see the tops of books peeking out from beneath the satchel's loose flaps.

The guards stationed at the door didn't move. Ty thought he saw them glance his way, but he wasn't sure. He patted the top of his head to make sure Orlyn's cap was still covering his white hair. It was.

"Ah, Kellen, thank you for coming." Overlord Barl stepped out from one of the back hallways to greet them.

"Happy to be of service, my lord."

"Barl," the overlord corrected. "Barl."

"Of course." Ty's father smiled. "Old habits."

The overlord turned to Adarra. "I see you brought our young scholar with you. Good."

Adarra smiled and curtsied.

"And Ty, it's always good to have your talents available," Barl added.

"Glad to be of service." Ty bowed. Enough with the niceties. It was time to talk to the Northman.

"We've barely gotten two words out him," Barl said. "He did allow us to see to his wounds but not much else. Other than his name, the only thing he's said that we could make sense of is something about a 'spotted warrior.' Apparently, he will speak with no one else."

For a brief moment, Ty wondered if he could have been referring to him, but Ty had kept his shirt sleeves down during the battle.

"Even if we knew who this person was, it's pretty unlikely they would have any better luck at understanding the savage than we did, which is unfortunate considering my upcoming meeting with the other overlords. I was hoping to have some information for them concerning this incident."

"We'll do our best," Ty's father said.

Barl looked at Adarra. "I'll be grateful for any assistance you can give. I know it won't be easy facing him again." He placed a hand on her shoulder. "You're a very brave young woman, my dear. You have your mother's determination. I know she would be very proud."

Adarra smiled. "Thank you."

"Have you been able to look through any of the books I sent you?"

"I have." Adarra kept her hands folded at her waist. "However, I've only made it through a couple of the tomes."

Only a couple? He thought his sister more capable than that. What had she been up to this whole time?

"The phrasing is old," she said, "and it's taking some time to translate. I only have a very basic knowledge at this point. Their form of communication is rather"—she pursed her lips—"different."

"Oh? How so?"

"Well, they don't rely entirely on verbal speech as we do. They incorporate their entire body into their communication. Hand gestures, facial expressions, indistinct noises, even the way they are standing could be used in portraying some deeper meaning behind what they are trying to communicate. It's kind of beautiful in its design."

"My, that sounds like a most difficult thing to learn. Wouldn't it be much easier to simply talk to each other?"

At this point, Ty didn't care. Why were they standing up there, discussing the Northman's language, when they could be putting it to good use?

"I'm sure they probably think the same thing about us, my lord. From what I can gather, their hand gestures can be used to communicate quite a bit. This, for example," she said, raising her right hand with fist clenched to her chest before opening it outward, palm up, and bowing in Barl's direction, "means that I am acknowledging that I am your inferior, that I have respect for your authority, that I will willingly lay my life in your hands."

Barl's eyes widened. "That one gesture meant all of that?"

"It does, and more, but right now, I'm not sure I understand all the nuances."

"Then let's find out," Ty said.

The overlord blew out his cheeks with a sigh. "Just do your best. We can't expect more than that." He turned and started toward the back. "This way."

Chapter 55 | Ty

THEY DESCENDED THREE flights of stairs, stopping on the bottom landing. The air was stale and cold, and Ty could feel his skin prickle. The warmth from the torches was hardly enough to break the chill, but it was better than the brisk winter gusts outside.

Ahead, the door leading into the prison had metal bars placed into the top half. A couple of armed guards sitting at a nearby table stood when they saw Overlord Barl.

The jailer stepped away from his desk to greet them, a heavy ring of keys hanging from one hand. He was average height, somewhere between Overlord Barl and Ty's father, with a round face, dark beard, and ears that stuck out rather noticeably. "Sir, I'm sorry, but before I let them pass," he said, gesturing at Ty's family, "I need to get everyone's name and reason for coming." The jailer looked almost embarrassed at having to make such a request in the overlord's presence, but Barl responded with a brisk nod.

"Quite right, Sergeant. I'm glad to see you have things well in order down here, especially considering who we have locked inside."

The jailer nodded. "Indeed, Your Lordship. We can't be too careful. I like to keep my men to the rules. Structure is key, I always say."

"Couldn't agree more."

Ty joined the others and gave his name and reason for being there, which seemed ridiculous since it was his family who had been responsible for capturing the prisoner in the first place. Once finished, the jailer unlocked the door, grabbed one of the torches from its bracket on the wall, and ushered them inside.

Finally, Ty thought as he followed the others through the inner maze of passages, first left, then right, then left again, coming to a stop outside a cell with a door made of tempered iron bars. The jailer held out his torch, revealing the big savage at the back lying on his side, face away from the door. He was still wearing his obscene cloak of human hair. As cold as it was down there, he probably needed it.

The jailer lit a couple of the torches on the wall between the cells, giving Ty and the others a clear view inside. "Will there be anything else, Your Lordship?"

"That'll be all, Sergeant."

The jailer saluted and started back up the corridor. "If you have need of anything, I'll have men posted at the end of the hall."

Barl waited for the jailer's steps to fade before turning back to the cell. "Jonas, we've come to talk."

They waited in silence. There was no response from the man inside the cell. Ty was starting to wonder if he'd died from his injuries after all. Adarra and his mother had not only opened his head with an iron skillet but had also shot him with an arrow.

Just my luck, Ty thought. He finally gets his chance to question someone who might know where Mangora was, and the man up and dies before he can get his first question out.

"Did you hear me?" Barl asked again, a little more forceful, as if it would make a difference. "I've brought some people here to talk to you."

There was a grunt from inside the cell, along with a couple of strange clicks. It sounded a lot like the way Ty's mother would click her tongue at him when she caught him sneaking an extra biscuit. The man said something Ty didn't understand, followed by two words he did: "spotted warrior."

Barl turned and shook his head. "Apart from finding this spotted warrior, I'm not sure what more we can do. Maybe you'll have better luck." He directed his last statement to Adarra.

"I'll see what I can do," she said as she lifted one of the books out of her sack.

The Northman turned over and, seeing her, stood. He started for the door, and Adarra quickly backed away. He still had some of the face paint left, mostly over his left eye.

Barl reached for his sword, forgetting they had relinquished them upon entry into the cells. "Guards!"

The Tallosian stopped when he heard the lancers running down the corridor in their direction. He looked at Barl, then at Adarra, and pointed to his face. "Spotted warrior."

"Wait!" Adarra held out her hand for the guards to stop and took a step forward. "He's trying to say something." She put three fingers to her mouth and then opened them toward the Northman, almost like blowing him a kiss. "Speak."

Jonas glanced around at the armed men before pointing at his face once more, then back at hers. "Spotted warrior."

"It's you, Adarra," Ty's father said.

"What?"

"It's you."

"Me? Why would he think—"

"Look at where he's pointing."

The Tallosian continued pushing his finger to his face.

"Your freckles," Breen finally said.

If Adarra's cheeks hadn't been red from the cold before, they were certainly glowing now.

The large Northman grunted with a nod and took another step forward. Ty hadn't noticed the nasty-looking burn running down the side of the man's face until now.

"It's fine," Barl said to the guards, waving them back. "We've got it under control." The two men turned and headed back down the hall.

Taking a moment to gain her composure, Adarra cleared her throat and started pulling the books from her carry sack, arranging them in piles on the floor. She took a seat in front of the cell and motioned for Jonas to do the same. "This might take a while," she said as she opened the first book. "You might want to get comfortable."

Ty huffed and walked to the other side of the corridor and looked in one of the empty cells. He hoped it wouldn't take too long. He wanted to question the man about Mangora. He turned and finally took a seat against the far wall where he could watch his sister work.

After what seemed like hours of back-and-forth hand signals, facial expressions, and complete gibberish, Ty's sister finally closed her books and turned. "So, what do you want me to ask him?"

"Ask him where Mangora is," Ty said, not giving the others a chance to even open their mouths.

Everyone turned to look at him. Even the Northman.

Barl grunted and then shifted his attention back to the prisoner. "Ask him what the Tallosians are doing back in Aldor, and why they chose to attack us."

Ty's face hardened.

"Calm yourself," the voice in his head said.

Ty thumbed the ring. "Why are they ignoring me?" he whispered.

"Because they don't want you to know the truth."

What truth?

"That they have no intention of looking for Mangora."

Why?

"You'll have to ask them."

Ty spun the ring even faster.

Adarra took a few moments to think and then started back up with her strange hand motions and prattle. Before long, Jonas replied. He appeared to be having difficulty understanding Adarra's attempt at his language, but the longer they spoke, the smoother it got. At least he didn't appear to be grunting and shaking his head quite as much.

"If I'm understanding him correctly," she said, "I believe his people had come to barter for food. Evidently, they've had a bad couple of years with their crops, and with winter coming, they didn't have enough to feed their families. He said that the one leading them—I'm guessing he's referring to the big Northman you killed, my lord—had been sent to make a trade, and they were promised supplies in exchange for their services as fighters." Adarra spared a glance at Jonas before turning back to the others. "It doesn't seem that they knew any of us personally or had a specific grudge."

Ty finally stood. His legs were growing numb from sitting so long. This was getting nowhere quickly.

"Go ahead," the book dared through the ring, *"ask them about Mangora, and see if they change the subject."*

Fine, he thought, and turned to Adarra. "Ask him where the witch is now. Where she's hiding. Was he supposed to meet her somewhere?"

"In a minute, Ty."

"See?" the book said. *"I told you."*

Ty's father stepped in. "We need to know if they are planning any future attacks. Will they be sending any more of their warriors to Sidara?"

"I just said they were here to barter for food," Adarra said. "Why would you think—"

"Because we just killed an entire Tallosian party. I doubt that goes unnoticed."

Barl thumbed his chin. "He has a point."

Adarra turned to the Tallosian and started up again.

Ty pressed his thumbs to the sides of his head. He wanted to scream.

After another lengthy back-and-forth with the prisoner, his sister turned to relay her findings. "The men we fought were from a single tribe, and not a very big one. Jonas says if he doesn't return, though, his people will send more." She looked up at Overlord Barl. "A lot more."

Who cares about more of these stupid savages coming over here? We'll just kill them, too. I want to know where Mangora is.

His father, Breen, and Barl conferred quietly off to the side, conveniently leaving him out of the conversation while his sister sat quietly looking through one of her books. Why was no one saying anything? For that matter, why was he even here? No one was listening to him. He walked over to Adarra. This was the perfect opportunity. "Ask him about the witch."

His sister huffed. "Fine," she said, and went to waving her hands.

After Jonas had offered his reply, with a few furtive glances in Ty's direction, Adarra turned and shrugged her shoulders. "He says he doesn't know."

"What do you mean, he doesn't know? Did you actually ask him?"

"Of course she didn't," the book said. *"I told you. They don't want you to know."*

Adarra gave him a funny look. "He's been locked away inside this cell since he woke up and doesn't know any more about where she is than we do."

Ty gritted his teeth. He was growing nauseous, his head pounding. "You didn't ask him, did you?"

Adarra stood, still clutching her book. "Yes, I did."

"No, she didn't."

Ty could feel the heat of his magic rising and took a deep breath. "Then he's lying," he said, pointing at the cell. "It's as plain as the scar on his face. Just look at him. He knows where Mangora is."

"Quit relying on her. Ask him yourself."

His chest felt as though it were on fire.

"Ty, he doesn't know any—"

"Then I'll ask him in the only language a savage like him can understand." Ty raised his hand and hit the Northman in the chest with a fist of air, throwing him across the cell and into the back wall. The big man wheezed as the air was ripped from his lungs. "Where's Mangora?" he shouted. "Tell me where she's hiding!"

"Ty, stop it!" Adarra said, dropping her book. "You're killing him."

"Son, stop! We need him alive."

"Ty!" Adarra grabbed his arm and spun him around.

He raised his hand, feeling the magic gather in his palm, and for a split second he almost released it, but got control of himself before he did. The look on her face had his magic withering inside him. She was frightened. Of *him*. He'd seen that look before in the woods behind their house when he had accidentally set her dress on fire. He looked down at his hand. What was he doing?

Breen pulled Adarra behind him, standing between her and Ty. "What's wrong with you? Have you completely lost it?"

Ty lowered his hand. "I . . . I'm sorry. I just wanted to know where Mangora was."

"I'm fine, Breen," Adarra said, placing a hand on his arm as she moved out from behind her older brother.

Ty was too embarrassed to even look at her. "I'm sorry. I don't know why I did that." He moved back against the far wall, keeping his distance.

Barl stared at him a moment, then took a step toward Jonas's cell. "I'll send someone down to look at his wounds. Best we leave for now."

Breen and his father helped gather Adarra's books. Ty was too shaken to do anything but lean against the far wall. Why had that happened? He'd almost killed an unarmed prisoner and, even worse, had nearly hurt his sister. Was he really that desperate to find the witch?

He followed a few steps behind the others as they silently made their way back through the dark corridors leading to the front of the prison. The jailer waiting on the other side unlocked the door and let them out.

Once back in the open lobby, Ty's father stopped to talk with the overlord, and Ty took the opportunity to walk outside with Waddle, the only one who hadn't borne witness to his shameful behavior. The cold air outside was refreshing, helping to soothe whatever was going on inside.

His father's conversation was brief, and soon enough, they were riding back out the south gate.

"Go on ahead," Ty's father said to Breen and Adarra. "We'll catch up."

Both Breen and Adarra looked at Ty, the same way they always did when he was about to get a good scolding.

"I wasn't much younger than you when my father left," Ty's father said, guiding Your Highness down the cobbled street at a slow trot. Ty kept Waddle at the same pace. "Your grandfather Azriel was a strong man, a hard worker, but when my mother died, he seemed to lose himself in his work. He'd spend days, sometimes weeks, away from home. Left me to fend for myself. Then, one day, he left, and I never saw him again. I spent a full month searching, tracking his usual trails through the forest from here to Crystal Lake, but I never found him."

Ty looked at his father, not quite sure why he was talking about this. It was the first time his father had mentioned anything significant about Ty's grandfather, other than he had one.

"Being abandoned in that way left me with a lot of anger. It also forced me to grow up faster than I should have. Didn't leave me with much of a childhood. Unlike you, I didn't have a brother and sister to depend on."

"Why are you—"

"I'm telling you this because I'm worried. I'm seeing the same pattern in you that I had. The anger, building just below the surface, eating you up inside. The difference is that I didn't have the magic in me that you do. I didn't have to worry about getting upset and accidentally killing someone." He looked at Ty. "You have to learn to control it."

Ty's grip tightened on his reins. It wasn't the same at all. Ty's mother hadn't run away; she'd been murdered in front of him, and he knew who was responsible.

"Your anger gives you strength," the book said. *"But don't let them see it. Don't let them use it against you."*

"Are you listening to me, Ty?" his father asked.

Ty didn't answer. He simply nodded.

Chapter 56 | Lenara

LENARA SWUNG DOWN FROM her horse, stretched, and stepped up onto the rickety wooden porch that fronted the small stone-block building. She was feeling more than thankful to be able to be off that insufferable animal. Her legs were so stiff, she was afraid she'd never be able to walk the same again. It was one thing to go on a simple jaunt but quite another to spend every day and night bouncing in the saddle. If she never saw another horse, it would be too soon.

The wind was cold, and she could see her breath floating upward with every exhalation. The sun had already set, and the stars were slowly blinking into existence. After the harsh rain they had traveled through a few nights back, the sky had remained clear, allowing for better light to travel with while hunting the Tower's escapees.

She waddled to the edge of the porch and peered around the corner at a dilapidated barn just behind the establishment. "Why are we here, Sylas? We could have found better accommodations sleeping in the woods."

"We're here because this is the last place they were seen," he said, moving past her to open the front door and step inside. She followed him in.

They had opted to leave their white uniforms and black robes tucked away in their saddlebags and don something a bit more common. They found that gathering information was easier when the people didn't run at the sight of you.

Inside, the tavern smelled of hard sweat, stale ale, and whatever poor animal had made the unfortunate mistake of getting caught by the proprietor. Most of the tables were filled. Dirty men with shifty eyes turned at the sound of the door swinging shut behind them.

The nameless town, if you could call it a town, reminded her of some of the smaller communities back in Cylmar. Same rundown buildings; loose boards patched where others had rotted through; chipped stone darkened by time and lack of cleaning; gruff people with hard faces and distrustful looks. It was a place you passed through and didn't stop.

Those seated around the tables studied the newcomers. Sylas first. She could see the cold, calculated stares as they determined how much effort it would take to slit his throat and make off with whatever they could find. With her, the looks shifted to something else as they let their eyes slowly move up and down her person. Getting answers from this lot was going to take more than a little persuasion. Then again, when looking for answers, who better to have as a travel companion than an inquisitor?

"What's your business here?" came a voice from the back. Lenara turned to see a short, solidly built woman standing in front of a set of swinging doors. A once-white apron covered her blouse and skirt. Her hair wasn't nearly as vibrant a red as Lenara's, but that was no doubt due to the grey lightening the natural color. The woman tucked a fallen strand behind one ear as she waited for an answer.

"Our business is our own," Sylas said, drawing nasty looks from a few of the local patrons. "We are seeking information."

"Information, ya say?" The stout woman took another step into the

445

room. "Hmm? Information isn't cheap. In fact, pretty much nothin' around these parts is these days, if ya know what I mean." The woman wiped her hands down the front of her discolored apron before sliding them inside the front pockets. Lenara spotted a butcher-knife-shaped bulge at the bottom.

Sylas smiled with Joren's boyish face. "Yes. Information can be rather costly, indeed. It is a most valuable commodity. I should know," he said, gesturing to himself. "It is my trade, after all."

"And what is it you do, might I ask?"

"A little of this. A little of that."

The woman waited for a straight answer, but when she didn't get it, she finally asked, "And what kind of information could have possibly sent ya all the way to the butt end of Elondria? Whatever it is, it must be very important." Lenara could see the wheels in the tavern owner's head spinning as she tried to determine how much that information might be worth. The poor woman had no idea what was coming her way.

"We're looking for a small party of travelers that might have passed this way in the last couple of days."

More than one set of eyes showed recognition, but no one spoke, probably waiting to see what the little woman at the back would do first.

"Travelers, ya say? Hmm, don't get many of those 'round these parts." The woman pursed her lips. "What do they look like?"

"Two men, a woman, and a little girl. One of the men is about this tall," Sylas said as he gestured a little above his own head, "broad in the shoulders, built like a smith, red hair. The other man's shorter, brown hair, and has a rather large nose. The woman traveling with them is short, olive-skinned, with cropped hair, and the little girl . . . well, she's a little girl."

The woman pinched her chin. "I must say, that's a pretty specific picture ya just painted. Sounds a mite personal, if ya ask me. What exactly ya wanting 'em for?"

"If I thought that was any of your business, I'd have shared it with you."

The woman's eyes narrowed, and some of the locals scooted their seats back. "So, what's it worth to ya?" She rubbed her fingers together. "How much ya willin' to pay for this information?"

"Pay?" Sylas held his smile. "Who said anything about paying?"

The woman looked confused. "Ya just said that this information was valuable. Ya don't expect us to make fair trade without being justly compensated, do ya?"

"Ah, I see you have misunderstood me, madam. I have no intention of paying for this information. I was merely being polite in offering you the opportunity to give us what we're looking for, before more unpleasant means of acquiring it become necessary."

The tavern owner stepped forward and bared her teeth. "You've definitely come to the wrong town to start laying down threats, mister."

All across the room, men stood, blades of all shapes and sizes appearing in their hands.

"Here's some free information for ya," the woman said with a nasty grin as she pulled the butcher knife from her apron. "Yer gonna wish ya'd never set foot in my establishment."

Idiot woman. She was going to force Lenara to get involved, something she had hoped to avoid. Killing townsfolk who didn't have the brains to keep their mouths shut was not part of her job description, at least not the part she enjoyed.

"Well?" the short woman said, raising her knife. "What are ya waiting for? Kill 'em both."

Lenara reached into her overcoat and pulled out a single steel rod laced in runes. It was a beautiful weapon. A weapon from an ancient time when wizards and sorceresses ruled the world.

One of the men in front took a step forward and smiled. "Apparently, you've come ill prepared," he said, and lifted his hatchet.

Lenara raised the silver rod and called its name in the ancient tongue, *"Cryora."*

A single braid of fire shot from the tip of her rod and draped across the floor, smoke rising from where it touched the wood.

No one moved.

For a brief moment, a single thought crossed her mind. She hoped Joren couldn't see what she was about to do.

She swung the whip overhead and with a loud *crack*, snapped it down across the man in front, who was already backing away. It entered from the top of his right shoulder and exited at the left hip. The two halves slid apart and landed on the floor between her and the rest of the tavern's patrons.

Some of the men near the front heaved at the sight; others froze.

Lenara shifted her feet, and all darkness broke loose as men scattered like rats for their cubbyholes, climbing over the top of each other as they fought to make for the back exit or side windows before the whip reached them. What they didn't know was that the rest of the Black Watch had surrounded the place with orders to round them up.

After the initial upheaval had finally died down and the men were huddling in groups along the back wall, awaiting whatever was coming, Sylas strolled across the room and tossed a few bodies aside that had piled up near the kitchen doors. Reaching underneath, he pulled the small tavern owner free. Her patrons had broken at least one of her legs and probably a few ribs after trampling over her to get out.

Sylas dragged her over to one of the few remaining usable seats and sat her down. She was trembling. Lenara wasn't sure if it was from the broken bones or what she saw in the inquisitor's eyes. "You wanted to know what I do for a living." He leaned in close. "I'm going to show you." He slid his finger down her bruised cheek. "This is going to be fun."

Lenara walked outside and shut the door before Sylas began. Hurting people because they deserved it was justifiable. Hurting people because you found it fun, that was something else entirely. She turned and walked down the street, not wanting to listen, hoping all the more that Joren was

unaware of what was happening.

Chapter 57 | Ayrion

T HE STARS WINKED OUT one by one as night released its grip.
The sky transformed from the color of pitch to stone grey, waiting
for the sun to rise and bring with it a new, more vivid arrangement of
colors.

Ayrion twisted in his saddle to get another look at the long caravan
of wagons behind him. It had been a slow march from their encampment
to the outskirts of Belvin, but he had pushed as much as he dared to give
them time to set up defenses while the vulraaks hid in their dark holes.

Their group had grown to somewhere around a hundred men and
women capable of wielding weapons.

There were still people arriving at the rover encampment every day,
but time was running out. They needed to strike before the creatures had
spread far enough that stopping them became impossible. He had given
Nell instructions to send their way those who showed up after they left,
in case they needed replacements. He hoped they wouldn't.

Ayrion rolled his shoulders, the weight of his swords a comforting feeling. He leaned forward in the saddle, the cold leather groaning under him as he stroked Shade's strong neck. The warhorse raised his head and snorted his appreciation. "Keep your eyes open, old friend. We can use all the help we can get."

Ayrion brought the caravan to a stop on the outskirts of the city. The vacant road ahead was littered with debris. Pieces of clothing and parchment scattered with every gust of wind. Two-story homes flanked both sides of the street, like an honor guard to welcome them in. The lower third of each dwelling was fieldstone, and the upper two-thirds, thick plaster framed with cedar. The windows were dark, shutters swinging back and forth as the wind blew down the street.

"This road will take us all the way in," Bek said next to Ayrion. The man was dressed from the top of his head to the bottom of his zabatas in brown leather and furs, making him appear even bigger than he already was. His hatchets swung loosely at his sides. "It winds back around and merges with three others at the center of town." He pointed to some unseen location ahead. "It's the largest area of open space in Belvin, and the Justice House sits directly at its center. If I were looking for a place to set camp, that would be it."

"Then the Justice House it is. If our attempt at taking their nest fails, we'll at least have a place to make a stand."

"Let's pray that won't be necessary," Tameel said, pulling the tinker wagon up beside him.

Sitting next to Tameel, Abiah removed his fur-lined cap to scratch the top of his head. "I'm not as familiar with Belvin as I should be. Are there any buildings near the Justice House large enough to stable the horses?"

"There's a few," Bek said, "but the back half of the Justice House should suffice. It's the largest building in town. It's also the most securely built."

"I like the sound of that," Abiah said.

Ayrion glanced over his shoulder to get a look at the small army of shopkeepers and farmers, merchants and vagrants, town officials and scholars, husbands and wives behind them—all there to fight for their homes, their friends, and their families. It was an emotional sight. He just wasn't sure which emotion to choose from—excitement at the prospect of leading such determined souls, or panic at the thought of going into battle backed by an army of recruits who had never swung a sword in earnest.

He was leaning toward the latter.

Bek motioned for those behind to follow as Ayrion nudged Shade, and the stallion started forward. He pulled back on the reins to keep from outpacing Bek as he scanned the surrounding buildings, watching for any sign of life as they entered the city limits.

There was an eerie sort of calm resting across the city. A window shutter slammed shut from the wind, and Ayrion reached for his sword.

"What was that?" he heard people behind him asking.

Each street they passed was devoid of life.

After a good ten minutes of riding, Bek signaled a stop at the next intersection, spotting a couple of riders on approach.

"The city's as quiet as a graveyard," one of the scouts said as he scratched his beard. "Probably not the most appropriate image, I guess, but pretty flaming accurate. It's a clear shot from here to the square. Not a living soul to be seen. Not even bodies. If I didn't know any better, I'd think the entire city had packed its bags and left."

The other scout bobbed his head in agreement.

Bek pointed to the adjoining street. "Take Foran and circle north. Meet us at the Justice House. We need to clear as many of the closer sections of the city as we can, to make sure we're not walking into an ambush." He looked at Ayrion. "Any thoughts?"

Ayrion shook his head. "Just keep your eyes open."

The two men took a moment to drink some water from their skins before they were off once again. Ayrion took a swallow from his as he watched them disappear around the bend. The sun was just beginning to peek over the rooftops. "Let's keep moving."

Bek nodded and motioned the wagons forward.

Continuing on, they passed one empty street after the next until finally crossing out of the residential district altogether. They moved off the main road and on to a stone pavilion that encircled a grassy area at the center of town. The emptiness felt even stronger here. The city square, surrounded by merchant shops and city offices with a few eateries interspersed between, should have been full of life, but it was nothing more than empty buildings. A city that seemed completely forgotten.

The Justice House stood near the center of the square. It was the only building Ayrion could see that had been constructed entirely from stone block.

"Let's get these wagons in place over there," Ayrion said, pointing to the front of the three-story building.

With Tameel leading the way, the other drivers pulled their teams around to line the wagons in a semicircle in front of the Justice House.

"Abiah, I'm putting you in charge of unloading the equipment and supplies. Place food stores near the back, weapons at the front."

"You can count on me, General," the stout man replied as he climbed down off the green-and-gold tinker wagon. Ayrion wasn't sure if he liked the idea of being labeled a general, but having been called far worse over the last several weeks, he let it slide.

"Willem! Where you at, boy?"

Willem stuck his head out of the back of the wagon. "Here, Pa!"

Abiah waved at him. "Hop down. We've got work to do."

The lanky boy leaped from the back and followed his father to the nearest wagon. Ayrion could hear the man barking orders and assigning duties as he marched down the row. He would have made a fair sergeant.

The Justice House suddenly disappeared, and Ayrion found himself standing in the front line of a group of soldiers, watching a short, stocky man with thick cheeks, an eye patch, and a ducktail beard march down the row, shouting orders to draw swords. Ayrion reached for his blade, and then, just as suddenly, he was back in front of the Justice House.

"You all right?" Zynora asked, her head sticking out of the back of the wagon.

Ayrion nodded. "Another memory."

"The battle again?"

Ayrion nodded once more. But he didn't believe it was the same battle. This one was different. He hadn't been wearing the black uniform but what looked like typical lancer garb, and instead of his twin blades, he'd been carrying a single sword at the waist. He shook his head. As much as he appreciated the possible return of his memories, having them appear at random was disorienting.

Ayrion dismounted and left Shade with Tameel's team. The stallion seemed to have bonded with the other two horses over the last few weeks of their journey.

He found Bek waiting for him on the stairs. "Let's take a look around while they set up the barricade."

The steps, like the rest of the building, were stone, and the doors at the top were tall and thick. "This was a good choice," Ayrion said. He didn't relish the idea of making a stand, but if it came to it, he much preferred this stone monstrosity to the tinderbox of a cabin they had fought from the last time.

Ayrion tried the door, but it was stuck. He put his shoulder to it and pushed. The door opened, and the overwhelming stench that greeted them had him gagging. Stepping inside, they stopped and let Bek's eyes adjust to the dim light. The building felt as cold and lonely as the streets outside. They tried forcing the door open farther, but it was blocked by broken pieces of furniture.

Bek tripped on a rolled-back rug and went down, catching himself on one knee. "I can't see a flaming thing in here," he growled.

Ayrion scanned the room, his Upakan eyes allowing him to see the wreckage that had been left. What light was available emanated from a couple of stained-glass windows above and behind them. The windows started on the second floor and worked their way up alongside an arcing staircase toward the third. "No windows on the first floor. Smart."

"I agree," Bek said, fumbling about looking for a torch. "But it doesn't help keep me from stubbing my toes."

Ayrion chuckled. This was one time Bek's zabatas hadn't been the best choice.

Bek pulled out a small tinderbox and lit one of the torches still sitting in its bracket on the wall. The light quickly scattered some of the shadows, revealing even more the state of disarray the room was in. It appeared all the wall hangings and furniture had been demolished and flung haphazardly across the floor. Chair legs and cabinet drawers, soft cushions, books, chandeliers, vases, portraits, and a few long draperies were strewn like carpet across the stone.

"I guess the vulraaks aren't all that big on embellishment," Bek said with a grunt as he handed Ayrion a second torch.

Ayrion held out the light, and they both started forward. "Embellishment? That's a big word for a trapper."

"Nell's the one who fancies all the book learning," Bek said, keeping his voice low. "Don't really have much call for it myself, but now that I know my letters, she enjoys it when I read a page or two to her in the evenings."

Ayrion smiled. "What we put ourselves through for the ones we love." Not that he could speak from firsthand knowledge.

"Ain't that the truth." Bek raised his torch to spread the light a little farther. "I think we found the source of the smell."

Ayrion maneuvered around an upturned table to get a better look. There was a pile of bones heaped together amidst all the clutter, meat still clinging to some. "Too little time for decay."

"No," Bek agreed. "Whoever they were, they were eaten. Maybe they don't turn everyone."

"Which means they need food to live." He stared at the bones, trying to determine by their sizes who it might have been. "I wonder how they choose who to turn and who to eat. Maybe they eat each other."

Bek shrugged. "Like any other rabid pack, I guess. Those too weak or too feeble get culled."

Ayrion shivered and raised his torch to take another look around the room, following the curve of the stairs up to the second and third balconies, searching for anything that might be watching. Not seeing anything, he pointed toward the back. "Any idea where those hallways lead to?"

Bek shook his head. "This is my first time inside the Justice House. Never had a reason to come in here before. It's a bit larger than I would have thought, judging from the outside."

"Guess there's only one way to find out, then," Ayrion said. "We'll need to organize a few teams to search the place while we set up camp."

"Aye," Bek said as he turned and headed back to the front. "There's nothing more annoying than unwelcome guests."

As if on cue, a pack of vulraaks charged from one of the halls and hit them before they had time to even draw their swords. Ayrion shouted as one of the creatures sank its teeth into his neck.

Everything spun, and suddenly he was back with his torch in hand, staring at an empty room. He threw the torch to the ground and drew both blades. "We're about to have company."

Chapter 58 | Ayrion

A T LEAST A DOZEN of the pale creatures poured out from the back of the Justice House, eyes as hungry as rabid dogs seeking their next meal.

"To arms! To arms!" Ayrion shouted as he kicked a fallen chair into the first of the creatures. The furniture brought down one of the vulraaks at the front, tripping those just behind. The creature skidded to a stop at Ayrion's feet, and he plunged his blade through its back. Yanking it back out, he opened the throat of the next.

Beside him, Bek roared as the first wave hit, his hatchets chopping apart creatures with every strike.

Ayrion's magic filled him as he entered his dance with death. His blades cut through the air as they sought new victims. He felt like a puppet on its strings as his magic seemed to take over, his visions helping him weave in and out of the creatures' attacks.

"Don't let them get their teeth in you!" he shouted at Bek.

"Don't need to tell me!" he shouted back.

Vulraaks fell at Ayrion's feet. Body parts covered the floor. He spun left as one lunged for his legs. With a single stroke, he took off the top of its head, painting the stone with blood. He sidestepped to the right and kicked the legs out from under another as he opened the fronts of two more with a swift backswing.

Behind him, he could hear Abiah hollering and the distinct echo of boots on stone as villagers charged across the rubble to their aid. Abiah's winter cap flew off his head as he lifted a large broadsword and swung at the closest creature.

By the time their reinforcements had arrived, Ayrion and Bek had all but finished off the assault. The fighters formed a circle and waited, weapons raised, as they stared at the dark corridors.

When nothing else came, men and women began clapping each other on the back and waving their swords.

Ayrion turned around. "What are you cheering for? You act like we've just won the battle. That was hardly enough to be considered a decent scouting party." He turned to Abiah. "Organize some men to do a thorough sweep of the building before we start bringing in the supplies. No fewer than five per group. We don't want any more surprises. Find out where those came from."

The stocky taverner wiped the top of his head and nodded. "Aye, General, I'll see to it right away."

"And quit calling me *general*."

"Yes, General," he said, this time with a salute and a smile as he marched across the debris, grabbing his winter cap on the way out. "Willem! Where are you, boy?"

Ayrion rolled his eyes. "And let's get these lit," he said, holding out a torch.

"I'll see to it," Tameel said as he and Zynora walked over to join them.

Ayrion turned to Bek. "We need to get a hunting party together and go look at those mines. How far outside the city would you say they are?"

"They're not."

"How's that?"

"The northeast section of the city is built around the main shaft. It's the oldest part of Belvin. The town started out as a mining camp. Lot of good men have lost their lives in there." Bek wiped the remaining blood from his hatchets and placed them back in their loops.

"I'd like to see it with my own eyes before we decide anything."

Bek nodded.

"Anyone wounded?" Zynora asked.

"I don't believe so," Bek said, looking around.

"Then Tameel and I will stay here and help Abiah organize the unloading. No need for us old people to go traipsing about the city."

Ayrion nodded. "Keep your eyes and ears open."

"Don't you worry about us," Tameel said, patting his crossbow. "Those creatures will think twice before messing with us." He took Ayrion by the arm and directed him away from the others. "Don't you think you might have been a little harsh back there?"

"No," Ayrion said, a little surprised by Tameel's reaction. "They need to take this seriously. They need to realize how dangerous this is."

"I understand that, but they're scared, and they need encouragement. A victory, no matter how small, is still a victory. They look up to you, Ayrion. Getting angry with them for taking pride in a win ain't the best way to build a relationship."

"I'm not here to build relationships. I'm here to keep them alive long enough to kill Argon. They should be scared. Blazes, Tameel. I'm scared."

Tameel glanced over his shoulder at the people scattered about the room, sifting through the mess. "Well, don't tell them that."

Chapter 59 | Ayrion

BEK BROUGHT THEIR small company to a halt on the outskirts of the original town. There were about thirty armed fighters on horseback, including Ayrion and Bek. Not their full force, but enough to make Ayrion feel safe about taking a quick look at the mine to see what they were up against.

In front of them lay the miners' community. Even though part of Belvin, it was clearly a separate entity of its own, resting inside a sunken valley. It looked as though it had at one time been home to a small lake that had long since dried up, leaving room for the antiquated town.

The community was nothing more than a large grouping of shanties, mining offices, and old warehouses where the ore was loaded and stored. On the east side of the warehouses were rickety-looking docks that led out to Virn Run.

Bek led them down the hill and into the maze of narrow one-lane streets that crisscrossed like a spider's web throughout the empty village. The dilapidated shacks were in varying states of disrepair, hardly worth living in.

On either side of the dirt path were rows of knee-high picket fencing, each made of little more than tree limbs haphazardly shoved into the ground and held together by horizontally spliced ones. They looked more like rows of unkempt teeth than fencing.

The wind howled through the streets, carrying with it the smell of death and lost hope. Ayrion had thought the smell had been coming from the shanties, but the closer they got to the mine, the more potent it became.

Once through the labyrinth of shanties, Bek brought them to a stop at the edge of one of the warehouses just in front of the mine. The entrance wasn't as large as Ayrion had expected, maybe nine feet tall and wide enough to fit three people at a time. The hole was dark enough that even Ayrion was having a difficult time seeing what was inside.

A cart rail stretched from the warehouse to the mine for hauling dirt, rock, and ore. Only one loading cart still stood upright on the metal beams. The others had been tipped over and their contents spilled out across the packed dirt. Scattered pieces of coal lay untouched beside the four-wheeled haulers, waiting for the miners to return to work.

"There's the smell," Bek said, pointing toward the front of the mine.

Just inside the entrance was a mound of discarded bodies, most too ravaged to recognize.

"I wonder how far in we'll have to go to reach their nest," Ayrion said, more to himself than expecting an answer.

"I've never been in there," Bek said, staring at the dark hole, "but they say it runs deep."

"Why not just collapse it?" one of the men behind them asked. "Bury them all and be done with it."

Ayrion turned. "Is there more than one way in?"

The man looked at the mine, then shrugged. "No idea."

"If there's more than one way in, then it wouldn't help us much to collapse it. We'd just be making it that much harder for us to reach their nest. And even if there were no other tunnels leading to the surface, I have a feeling that Argon wouldn't have all that much difficulty making one."

"What do you think?" Bek finally asked.

Ayrion sighed. "I think I'd rather be anywhere but here." He stared at the mine a moment longer, then turned his horse around. "Let's get back to the Justice House and muster the troops."

The early-afternoon sun was bright in the sky by the time they had managed to gather every able-bodied man and woman to march on the mine. Ayrion left a small contingent of guards behind—led by Tameel—to watch over the wagons, horses, and supplies. All the younger children had been left with Nell and a few other women back at the rover camp.

"Why not go in with a small scouting party first?" Abiah asked, constantly glancing over his shoulder at his son as if wanting to make sure the boy was still there. "You know. Find the nest before marching everyone inside?"

"I thought about that," Ayrion said, "but if we did take a small group in and were spotted, we would lose the only advantage we have. More importantly, how many have the training to make it in and out alive? Our army is made up of farmers, shopkeepers, and tradesmen. They aren't military. Other than Bek, I doubt we even have a handful of competent trackers. If those of us who are able went in there and were killed, what do you think the rest would do?"

"Run for the hills," Bek said with a snort.

"Could be right," Abiah said.

Ayrion nodded. "At this point, it's all or nothing. Our best shot is to go in with everything we have and try to find the nest."

Abiah winced. "Is it too late to change our minds and move to

Keldor?"

Bek chuckled.

Ayrion was too nervous to chuckle. Too nervous to do anything but focus on what lay ahead.

The ride from the Justice House to the old city took less time than Ayrion had hoped, and by the time he'd finally gotten his hands to quit shaking, they were once again outside the old shanty village. Even with their full force of a hundred strong present, it didn't give him much comfort, especially considering the frightened faces.

A silent tension fell across the ranks like a heavy mist, dampening their spirits as they quietly made their way through the ruins of the old mining community. The light chatter that had been a constant while walking through the main part of town had all but faded.

Ayrion brought the company to a halt just outside the last of the warehouses. On his left, Bek spun his two hatchets while performing a few practice swings. Behind him, with his winter cap pulled snug around his ears, Abiah chatted softly with Willem, who held a long dagger in one hand and an unlit torch in the other. The lanky boy stood a good head taller than his father and looked about ready to soil his trousers.

The smell of fear was in the air, maybe not as pungent as the half-chewed carcasses littering the opening of the mine beside them, but strong enough to make Ayrion wish he were anywhere else. Had he been this scared as the Guardian Protector? From the flashes of his previous life that had surfaced so far, he had led men into battle. Had losing his memories given him a different perspective, possibly robbing him of his courage? Or was this what it was always like?

Ayrion passed the word back to light the torches. All the way down the line, flames burst to life. Ayrion drew his swords. If he waited much longer, he was going to talk himself out of doing this. With a nod to Bek, he started in.

As expected, the mine was dark and damp, but it was also somehow familiar in a way he didn't understand. He wondered if it had to do with him being Upakan. Tameel and Zynora had told him that his people lived underground in the ruins of the Lost City. Was this similar?

The sound of feet crunching loose rock filled the tunnel, making it seem even smaller than it was. The smell of decay was strong enough to taste, lessened only by the burnt pitch from their torches.

The main shaft seemed to go on forever. Surprisingly enough, they encountered no resistance, no sign that there was even a single vulraak living there. The only clues as to the nature of the inhabitants were the scattered bones and the smell. Clearly, the creatures stayed well away from the entrance during the day.

Up ahead, the tunnel forked. One chute to the left, the other right. The thought of splitting their group didn't sit well with him, but he wasn't sure if there were enough hours of daylight left to check every dividing branch.

"Left," Bek said as he took a knee at the entrance to the tunnels and moved some of the loose soil and rock around with one of his hatchets.

"How can you tell?" Abiah asked, pushing forward to see what the big trapper was looking at.

"The amount of disturbance." Bek stared down the left tunnel. "They don't seem a bit worried with trying to hide their movements."

"That's because they don't expect someone as stupid as us to come traipsing in after them," Zynora said a few rows back.

Bek stood and wiped his knee. "One can hope. I definitely get the sense that Argon is a rather arrogant son of a faerie."

Ayrion smiled. "Gave you that impression, did he?" He took a moment to listen down both passageways, but other than the flicker of the torches and the constant echo of rocks shifting around them, he heard nothing. "Left it is."

Ayrion ordered a small contingent to stay behind to watch the second pass as the rest headed down the left fork. He hoped the nest wasn't too far in. From the smell alone, he'd thought they were already neck-deep in it.

The way forward was slow and tense as they followed the double rails farther into the mine's bowels. After having traveled awhile without the first trace of the creatures, Bek touched Ayrion's arm, and they came to a stop.

"What is it?" Abiah mumbled nervously as he scooted forward to see what was going on. "Do you see something?"

Bek held up his hand. "Quiet."

Everyone strained to hear what it was that Bek thought he heard. After a long moment of silence, the trapper lowered his hand. "Might be nothing." Without another word, the big fur-cloaked man dropped to his hands and knees. Ayrion lifted his weapons and scanned the dark shadows ahead, but even with the help of his Upakan eyes, he didn't see anything. He looked down at Bek, who was now prostrate on the ground with one ear pressed against the rail.

"Not exactly the ideal spot to be taking a nap," Abiah said.

"Quiet, I can't hear."

Ayrion looked at Abiah, and the taverner closed his mouth.

After a moment of complete silence, Bek stood and brushed the small pebbles from his knees as he scanned the darkness ahead. "They're not far. And they're coming fast."

Abiah grunted. "How could you possibly tell that from sticking your head in the dirt?"

"The rail. Metal carries vibrations."

"How would you—"

"My father was a miner."

"Oh, I, uh—"

Shouts rose from somewhere behind them.

"What was that?" Abiah said, raising his sword and pulling Willem close.

Ayrion gritted his teeth. "They must have been waiting farther down that second shaft. But how did they know we were coming?"

Bek looked at Ayrion. "What do we do? Fight our way forward or fight our way back?"

Ayrion had to make a spur-of-the-moment decision. If this was a trap, then pressing ahead wouldn't do them any good. For all they knew, the tunnel led to a dead end. And if they didn't get out of there now, they were going to be fighting a battle on two fronts, completely surrounded.

"Back!" he shouted to those behind them. "We go back!"

Ayrion's fighters turned and ran toward the fork. Ayrion and Bek brought up the rear, knowing that it was only a matter of time before they could be facing vulraaks from both sides.

The shouts and cries and clanging of steel grew fiercer as they neared the fork. Ayrion shuffled his feet to keep from stepping on some of their downed comrades, their bodies ripped apart by the creatures. Up ahead, his fighters were struggling to keep the vulraaks in the second tunnel. If he had taken a small scouting party instead of their entire group, they'd already be dead. But thankfully, the narrow tunnels and their numbers had managed to keep the vulraaks from surrounding them completely.

Before Ayrion and those near the end of the procession had made it back to the fork, the vulraaks tore out of the tunnel behind them.

Ayrion, Bek, and Abiah turned to meet the approaching horde.

"Come greet my hatchets, you white faeries!" Bek shouted. He didn't have to wait long. The vulraaks were hungry for blood, and they tore at each other, trying to be the first to sink their claws into them.

The creatures hit them like a wave against the side of a cliff. Ayrion's movements were sharp and precise, not wasting energy on flashy technique when a simple block-and-thrust would do. To the left, Bek shouted as he fought to keep from being completely overrun. Abiah remained surprisingly close-lipped, no doubt pouring all his energy into fending off those that got by the other two.

Ayrion swung, slicing a vulraak almost in two. Entrails poured out, cushioning its fall. He stabbed a second in the neck, using his other sword to keep its claws from reaching him.

As fast as he could kill them, more were there to take their place.

Every inch of retreat was a battle. One step at a time.

"On your left!" Ayrion shouted at Bek. The big trapper spun and buried his hatchet in a creature's skull.

"Thanks!" he said, and jerked it back out and chopped another down.

Ayrion cut the head from one while sweeping the legs out from two more. His leather jacket was helping stave off the worst of the vulraak's claws, those that made it past his steel.

"Willem! Where's that torch, boy?" Abiah shouted on Ayrion's right. His breathing was labored as he struggled to keep swinging. "Hold that thing up so I can see what I'm fighting!"

Ayrion pivoted to the right and hacked off the right arm of one and the left arm of another as they both lunged for him at the same time. He was about to slit their throats when a vulraak grabbed Bek's leg and pulled it out from under him.

Ayrion saw him go down out of the corner of his eye. Swinging wildly, he fought to reach him, cutting, stabbing, hacking at those in front, but the creatures' press was relentless. He didn't dare pull back to help, or they'd be overrun.

"Abiah! Get over—"

A pulse of energy knocked Ayrion to the side and sent the creatures on top of Bek flying backward. "Get him up!" Zynora shouted, already retreating toward the split in the tunnel.

Ayrion grabbed Bek and hauled him to his feet. Bek's thick furs must have saved him from any permanent damage. He shook himself off, grabbed his hatchets, and was back at the front alongside Ayrion.

The heat of Ayrion's magic poured through his arms, fueling his rage as he fought to hold the creatures off long enough for his fighters to make it past the split. He glanced over his shoulder every chance he got, which wasn't often. The last time he'd looked, the merging tunnels were within a stone's throw.

Behind him, his fighters were giving everything they had to keep from being completely flanked on both sides.

Finally, they broke through.

Ayrion was the last out of the forked tunnel. Bodies of men, women, and vulraaks lined the ground, making it hard to see where to step.

"Fall back! Fall back!" Ayrion shouted to those behind, grateful they weren't fighting the creatures from two sides any longer.

Abiah cried out on Ayrion's right and stumbled backward, his sword falling from his hands as a large vulraak raked his arm. He tried retrieving the weapon, but another clawed his leg, and he went down.

"Pa!" Willem leaped on the vulraak and sank his dagger into its back. He lit the second one on fire with his torch, but before he could pull his dagger free, a third vulraak punched him in the chest, knocking the torch from his hand.

Ayrion tried to reach him, but the vulraaks grabbed the boy's cloak and jerked him into their ranks before he could get there.

Willem screamed as he disappeared from view.

"Willem!" Abiah grabbed hold of the closest creature and sank his teeth into its neck and ripped out its throat. Spitting away the dark blood, the taverner grabbed his sword and pushed himself to his feet. "Willem, I'm coming!"

It was too late.

"Abiah, get out of there!" Bek cut the head off the vulraak he'd been fighting and grabbed Abiah by his jacket, yanking him off his feet and back into their own ranks.

"No! Willem!" Abiah shouted, swinging his fist at anyone trying to stop him. The big trapper smacked him across the face. "Keep fighting or we all die!"

Tears streamed down Abiah's face as he moved back into line and sunk his sword into the next creature.

The fighting seemed to last forever. Ayrion's hands were growing numb from gripping his swords. He wasn't going to be able to last much longer.

Without warning, the creatures suddenly pulled back. Confused,

Ayrion glanced over his shoulder and saw the light of the sun shining in from the mouth of the mine just behind him. They had somehow managed to fight their way back to the entrance.

Ayrion was the last one out, arms shaking as he struggled to catch his breath. This fight was far from over. They had just poked the hornet's nest, and all they could do now was wait for the swarm.

Chapter 60 | Ferrin

FERRIN GUIDED HIS MOUNT through the gates leading into Iraseth. The dry road shot puffs of dust into the air, marbling his horse's legs and underbelly. The dirt was eventually replaced by layered cobble as they neared the busier section of town.

Iraseth rested against the foothills of the Razor Spine Mountains, surrounded by Thornwood Forest on one side and Virn Run on the other. Being so far removed from Aramoor, Ferrin had expected to find a smaller township of simple mountain folk, but instead, he found a thriving city with varying degrees of culture.

The last time Ferrin had traveled this way had been from the back of a Black Watch prison wagon. After his attempted escape at Syrel, Captain Hatch had skirted Iraseth altogether to keep any more of his prisoners from following in Ferrin's footsteps. Needless to say, he'd never gotten the chance to actually see the city for himself.

Steering his horse to the right side of the road to make way for yet another set of heavily laden wagons, Ferrin eventually brought his weary band of runaways to a stop just inside what appeared to be Iraseth's main shopping district.

Myron made a rather dramatic show of swinging off his horse to stretch his aching muscles. "I need sleep," he grumbled, rubbing a finger under his dark-rimmed eyes. "You might be able to go on forever, smith, but these tired bones are nearing utter collapse."

Ferrin smiled. "Don't worry. I'll have us all a warm bed for the night, and by the look of you, a hot bath as well."

"You're one to talk," Myron jeered. "When was the last time you saw your own face? That bush hides all your pretty features, my friend."

Ferrin noticed Rae bobbed her head in agreement. "I guess I could use a shave, at that," he said, running a gloved hand down both sides of his face. "Although, I have to admit it's growing on me."

Rae turned her head, but not before she stuck her tongue out at the idea.

Ferrin smiled and twisted in the saddle to get a better look at the city proper. It was busy with people hurrying from one shop to the next, mothers watching their children play in a grassy area at the center of the square. He couldn't help but smile as he watched the kids toss around an old leather ball.

Suri eyed the scene with growing curiosity. For that matter, so did her mother. Neither had ever seen a real city before. Their eyes darted nervously back and forth as they took it all in.

"Are you at all familiar with Iraseth?" Ferrin asked Myron.

Myron didn't answer right away. He was too busy staring at a nearby bistro as the scent of fresh-cooked meat floated from its chimney stack. "Been here a time or two," he finally said.

"Know any good places to bed down for the night, somewhere off the beaten path?"

Myron smiled sheepishly. "I think I might know a place. It's right off the water. You'll like it." His smile brightened even further. "Best river-cat stew you'll find around these parts for sure, and rhubarb pie that'll make your mouth sing."

"Cat?" Ferrin had eaten quite a few types of meat before but never that.

"A river cat is a fish."

"Oh." Ferrin turned and looked at the shops, reading the signs lining both sides of the street. "We're going to need to restock while we're here. No telling how long it'll be till we reach another community large enough to buy from."

Myron stifled another yawn. "I also wouldn't mind laying my hands on a good map."

Ferrin nodded, smiling at Suri's giggles as she watched the children running around, shouting and laughing as they passed their ball up and down both sides of the open grass. Even Rae had a smile on her face as she watched, something Ferrin had rarely seen. It was a nice smile, and it lasted up until the point she caught him staring, then disappeared.

Myron mounted, and they left the shopping district and the children's games behind. The smell of fish grew stronger as they navigated the backstreets in the direction of the river. Passing the last of the dock warehouses, Ferrin spotted open water ahead and something he didn't expect. The city actually extended into the river, to a raised island that rested just offshore.

Veering back onto the main thoroughfare once again, Myron guided them across a stone bridge, its pilings rising at least twenty feet from the river's surface. The two- and three-story buildings lining the outer rim of the island were high enough to look out across the central parts of the city.

Some of the buildings, the ones that fronted the island's rocky edge, had long switchback staircases that led from the backs down to the piers below. From the bridge, Ferrin could see an assortment of fishermen hauling in the day's catch while longboatmen guided their flats toward the docks on the far side of the river.

Seeing all the water, Rae grabbed a tight hold of her reins, and Suri grabbed a tight hold on her.

Taking the first road to the left, Myron brought them to a stop in front of a three-story building that passed for a riverfront inn and tavern. The sign swinging from the front bore the faded image of a large fish leaping out of the water. It read THE SMELLY TROUT, and after taking a brief whiff, Ferrin agreed.

They dismounted and walked their horses around to the side, where there was a single-story stable. Standing on solid ground felt awkward after having spent so much time in the saddle. Ferrin's legs kept wanting to part as he walked.

After stabling the horses, they collected their gear and made their way through a side entrance. The main room was warm and well lit, and the smell of fish was even stronger inside, if that was possible, although Ferrin had to admit that whatever seasonings had been mixed in with the fish were making his mouth water.

There were a number of tables and chairs scattered across the room with a stone hearth on the side and a few benches lining the far wall.

"Can I help you folks?" an elderly man asked, walking out from the back with a stained apron that hung all the way to his knees. His grey hair was disheveled, and he had what looked like flour on his face.

Myron took the lead. "We're looking for a couple of rooms and a hot meal."

The old man smiled. "You've come to the right place, then." He walked across the room and held out his hand. "The name's Tibble."

Myron shook it. "I'm Myron." He turned to the others. "That's Ferrin, Rae, and Suri."

"Nice to meet you all," Tibble said with a bright smile. "Are you in for the winter festival?"

"Just traveling through, I'm afraid," Myron said.

"Too bad. It gets quite lively around here during the festivities." Tibble looked them over, stopping on Rae and Suri. "How many rooms do you need?"

"Three if possible, but we can make do with two if one of the rooms has a large-enough bed." Myron looked at Ferrin and smiled. "No offense, but you're smelling pretty ripe at the moment."

Ferrin chuckled. "Trust me, I'm not the only one."

"The washroom's on the first floor in the back," Tibble said. "I'll lay out some fresh towels and warm the water." He glanced at the stairs near the back leading up to the second floor. "I think we can manage three rooms."

"Wonderful," Myron said.

Ferrin agreed. It was worth the extra coin for the chance to sleep in a real bed.

Tibble stepped into the back for a moment, then returned with a set of keys. He led them up a flight of stairs, narrow enough that only one person could climb at a time. Ferrin had to duck to keep from scraping his head on the low rafters. At the top of the stairs was a hallway, not much wider than the staircase, with rooms interspersed.

"Here are your keys," Tibble said, unhooking them from the ring and handing all three to Myron. "Your rooms are on the end; numbers match the keys. The missus has a fresh batch of chowder on the fire and some dark rye in the oven. You look like you've seen some long hours today."

Myron grunted. "You have no idea, my friend, and I can't think of anything I'd rather do than sample some of that fine chowder I'm smelling. Well, apart from maybe sleeping for a week, that is."

The old man grinned. He was missing all but a few of his back teeth; Ferrin hoped that wasn't a sign of the strength of the stew.

Tibble turned to leave, but Myron caught his arm before he made it to the steps. "You wouldn't know if the cook will be serving rhubarb tonight, would you?"

"Aye," the old man said, smacking his gums. "Best pies in town." He took a moment to study Myron's face. "You sound as though you've been here before."

"I have, but it's been a couple of seasons. Last time I was here, I ate an entire pie myself. I haven't tasted anything that's come close to matching it since."

The old man beamed with pride. "No one can whip up a tastier pie than my Kyleen." He glanced at the others. "If you gents and ladies need anything, I'll be more than happy to help."

Ferrin watched the old man hobble back down the stairs before making his way toward their rooms. After unlocking Rae's room, he unloaded her and Suri's gear on the single bed in the corner. "I'll be in the next room if you need anything, and Myron is right across the hall."

He left Rae to her unpacking and went to check on his own room. The small chamber was a mirror image of Rae's. At the back was a single-shuttered window that opened out over the river. The bed was on the right side, and a small table near the door held a candle and a small washbasin with a drying cloth. In the left corner was an armoire for his clothes and a three-legged stand beside the bed with a lit reflector lamp sitting on top.

The rooms were a bit cramped, but for the luxury of being off the beaten path, and for the price, he could hardly complain. After taking the time to unpack, Ferrin waited for the others to finish washing before availing himself of the water and soap. It had been a long time since he'd enjoyed a warm bath. By the time he got out, his skin was wrinkled, and the water was cold and certainly too dirty to reuse. He shaved the thick whiskers from his face with a razor provided by Tibble and changed into a new shirt, one that wasn't quite so soiled. Afterward, he joined the others in the main room for some of that promised chowder and rhubarb pie. It was the best meal he'd eaten since leaving Rhowynn.

The last couple of months had been a blur, almost as if they had been nothing more than a bad dream, a nightmare he had endured but now had awakened from. It didn't feel real. He wanted to pinch himself and find he was still dreaming, that there was no one chasing him, that his sister was safe, and that he would be able to return to his little smithy as though nothing had ever happened.

Finishing his second helping of pie, Ferrin laid his fork across the empty platter in front of him. He was tempted to lick the plate clean as well. He couldn't remember the last time he'd enjoyed a normal meal, sitting around a table with friends, or in this case, a band of escaped convicts. The only thing keeping him from completely relaxing were the looks Rae, Suri, and even Myron kept throwing his way. Finally, he couldn't take it any longer.

"Is it really that bad?" he asked, rubbing his smooth chin.

Rae worked her pie to one side of her mouth in order to respond. "You look . . . different."

"Is that good or bad?"

She grunted with a shrug, which for Rae most likely meant good.

"You clean up well," Myron said, raising his glass in salute.

Out of the corner of his eye, Ferrin continued to catch Rae peeking at him when she thought he wasn't looking.

Ferrin waited until after Kyleen, the innkeeper's wife, had finished collecting their payment—along with praise from both Myron and Ferrin for the delicious meal—before addressing the others. "We need weapons. A pair of swords and a few belt daggers won't be enough to defend ourselves if we run into any real resistance."

"We could have used a few good crossbows during that wolf attack," Myron added, slowly sipping the rest of his ale. "And to bring down those corax that have been stalking us."

Ferrin nodded. "I'd like to get my hands on a good forge for the night. If I can forge us one or two of my blades, it would certainly help our odds in a confrontation."

"Magical blades?" Myron leaned forward, eagerness in his eyes. An impish grin spread from one corner of his mouth to the other. "I wouldn't mind getting my hands on one of those myself."

"Well, if you can take Rae and Suri with you and get the supplies, I'm going to start looking for a smithy who'll be willing to rent me his shop for the evening. I have a feeling it's not going to be as easy as it sounds."

Ferrin pushed his chair back from the table.

"Maybe we don't want to look for supplies," Rae said. "Maybe we would rather do something else."

Ferrin was a bit startled by the comment. Myron apparently was as well, as both men stood there staring, not knowing what to say. Sometimes he forgot about her previous situation at the White Tower and the abuse they had suffered. "I apologize. Was there something you wanted to do in particular?"

She thought for a moment, looked down at her plate, then thought some more. "No."

Ferrin waited. "So, you don't want to help Myron with the supplies?"

She stared at him. "I don't mind. I would just prefer to be asked." With that said, she stood from the table and headed for the side entrance, Suri right beside her.

Ferrin and Myron shared a glance. "Guess that's my cue," Myron said as he stood as well.

Ferrin followed him up. He handed Myron one of their smaller coin purses carrying only a few of the gold pieces he'd stolen during his escape. "Here, this should get us what we need for now. And find something nice if you can for the two of them."

Myron grimaced. "It's been years since I've purchased for a woman. I wouldn't know where to begin."

"Just take her and Suri around to some of the shops and see if anything catches their eye." He shrugged. "Shouldn't be that hard."

Myron gave him a look like he was crazy before hanging the coin pouch around his neck and walking out the door. Ferrin waited until they were gone before heading into the back to talk with Tibble. He hoped the old innkeeper could point him in the direction of a few good smithies.

Chapter 61 | Ferrin

S URPRISINGLY ENOUGH, with Tibble's suggestions, it didn't take Ferrin all that long to find a reputable smith willing to rent out his forge. All it took was a simple test of Ferrin's knowledge of how to work a forge and, more importantly, a down payment of six silver pieces, which was more money than any fair-priced smith in Rhowynn would have earned in half a month.

Ferrin not only paid for the man's forge and materials but also gave him enough coin to stipulate that he not be bothered by any unwanted intrusions.

The smith's wife didn't argue as she grabbed the silver from Ferrin's hand and pulled her husband out the door.

With the first part of his task completed, Ferrin decided to go into town and check on supplies. Tying his horse off in front of a cobbler on the main pavilion, he walked along the street that fronted the shops on the east side of the square. Up ahead, he saw the shop he had seen earlier that afternoon when they had arrived. The sign had a fresh coat of paint with a depiction of two crossed swords with blades pointing upward.

"Can I help you?" a large gentleman with a dark beard and gruff voice asked as Ferrin opened the door and stepped inside. The man was busy running a whetstone across one of his blades as he watched Ferrin shut the door.

"Just looking at the moment," he said as he studied some of the swords on the side wall. They seemed of good quality.

"Let me know if something catches your eye."

Ferrin nodded and started looking through the collection of blades, which ranged from boot daggers to falchions and even to two-handed swords. There was some beautiful craftsmanship here. No doubt the reason for the smithy's prime location in the city's main shopping district.

Ferrin particularly appreciated the assortment of grips the armorer used for the swords' handles. Besides the typical leather grip, there was wrought gold, silver, wood, even some smaller daggers with bone and antler. It was a fine collection that had him missing his own smithy back in Rhowynn. One thing that was missing from this man's work, though, was the detailing. The finishing designs on the blades were one of Ferrin's favorite things to add. The decorative engraving gave his work that extra cut above the other smiths.

There was a strict difference between a decorative sword and a functional one. The types of steel and forging techniques varied between the two. Just because a sword was beautiful didn't necessarily mean that it was strong and capable of standing up in battle. Most decorative swords used blades that were hard and brittle, while functional blades focused on forging strength into the steel.

Magical advantage or not, Ferrin prided himself on being able to create swords that were both.

It didn't take him long to find two swords of good stock that he could use in his forging. It was going to be much easier to start with an already-forged blade than to make one from scratch. He simply didn't have the time.

"One gold and four," the shopkeeper said as Ferrin laid the two blades on the desk.

The price was steep, but the swords were well made, and Ferrin didn't want to take the time to haggle with him. "Throw in a couple of solid sheaths and you've got yourself a deal."

The shopkeeper thought a moment, then nodded and grabbed a couple of medium-quality heavy leather sheaths under one of the tables, measuring to make sure they fit. He wrapped the items in a long piece of hunter-green cloth, and after taking Ferrin's coin, he handed him the package. "Pleasure doing business with you. You in town for the festival?"

"No. Just passing through." Ferrin started for the door but stopped when he noticed a couple of crossbows on the table to his left. Perfect for killing large reptilian-looking birds. "How much for these?"

The shopkeeper walked over to the table to take a look. He rubbed his chin. "I take it you'll want the quiver and quarrels as well?"

Ferrin smiled. "Not much good without something to shoot."

"I reckon not." The man looked over the items in question. "I can give them to you for no less than eight silvers."

Ferrin thought it a reasonable price, considering the good quality, and paid him. Picking up his haul, he bid the man a good day and opened the door.

"Come back and see me anytime," the shopkeeper said.

Ferrin left the swordsmith's shop and headed down the walkway to where he'd seen a sign depicting a cartographer. He spared a quick glance at the sound of children's laughter and spotted Rae on one of the benches by the park. Deciding to wait on the map until later, he started across the street, stopping long enough to let a wagon laden with furs pass.

The kids in the park were new, but the game was still the same— spread out and pass the ball. Ferrin stood behind Rae's bench for a moment and watched as Suri slowly inched her way out onto the grass to be closer to the other kids. Ferrin wasn't sure if she'd seen other children her age before. He hadn't noticed any kids running around the White Tower. She flailed her arms up and down excitedly as she mimicked their movements.

Seeing the little girl so enthralled with something as common as children playing nearly had him crying. He turned away to keep from embarrassing himself. The perimeter of the park was surrounded by groups of content parents as they chatted casually about the latest happenings. Ferrin wondered if that would ever be him one day.

He moved to the other side of the bench and plopped down beside Rae. She tried not to acknowledge his presence, but he could see her shoulders relax. Where she had been continually scanning the crowd of faces around her, she now focused solely on Suri and the games. He liked that she was starting to feel safe enough around him to lower her guard.

Suri squealed as one of the kids kicked the ball in her direction. She picked it up and looked at Rae, who smiled and motioned for her to throw it back. She turned and threw it, then jumped up and down like she'd just won the horseshoe toss at the city fair.

Ferrin chuckled and looked at Rae. "How was the shopping? Find anything of interest?"

She pulled a sweet stick out of her mouth and held it up.

"Oh. I guess that's interesting." Not exactly what he had in mind. "Anything else?"

"We only made it as far as the candy shop," Myron said, walking up behind them and stuffing a couple more packages into his saddlebags.

Rae smiled, as if finding some hidden pleasure in Myron's frustration.

Ferrin turned to look at him. "How are the supplies coming?"

"I think I've found most of what we need. Iraseth has plenty to choose from."

Ferrin looked down at his raggedy tunic and trousers and shook his head. "What we need is some new clothing."

"I saw a couple of shops down that street over there," Myron said, pointing to the other side of the square.

Ferrin stood. "Good. We don't need to linger too long in the open, anyway." He looked at the children playing. "Come on, Suri, time to go."

The little girl turned and frowned, not wanting to leave her new friends, but she ran over to join them anyway, hopping up into her mother's lap with a big smile. She was thoroughly enjoying herself.

"You ready?" Ferrin asked Rae.

Rae didn't say anything and took her time standing, just to let him know she was in control.

"I doubt anyone following has managed to keep up the pace you've set," Myron said with another brisk yawn. This time, he didn't bother with stifling it. "I say we pick up the rest of the supplies, catch an early supper, and hit our beds."

"Sleep would be nice," Ferrin said, adding a yawn of his own to the mix. "Just not for me."

Myron glanced back over his shoulder as they walked the horses down the street toward the clothing shops. "That's right. You're planning on forging tonight. Did you find a smithy willing to loan you his shop?"

"I did. But at a hefty price. It'll be worth it, though, if I can get the work done."

Myron smiled anxiously, clearly wanting to get his hands on one of Ferrin's swords. "This way," he said, leading them off the main road. He stopped about three shops down on the left and tied his horse to the hitching post out front.

Ferrin, who was walking both his horse and Rae's, did the same and followed the others inside. The shop was at least twice the size of the swordsmith's. In fact, he realized upon closer inspection, it was two shops connected by an opening in the right wall. The first shop held a wide selection of men's clothing—pants, tunics, cloaks, and boots— while the second carried women's.

Rae kept a tight grip on Suri's hand, as the little girl wanted to touch everything she saw and gazed in wonder at the racks and tables and shelves of clothing. Rae spotted the opening on the right leading into the women's section, and her eyes widened.

As badly as Ferrin wanted to shed his worn-out clothing, the look on Rae's face made him content to wait a little longer. "Come on," he said as he started for the other half of the shop.

She was close on his heels.

Normally, Ferrin would have been embarrassed walking through a women's shop, but to see the wonder on Rae's and Suri's faces was more than worth it. Even Myron followed them in just to watch, although he tried not to be too obvious about it as he casually hung by the door.

"May I help you?" a lady asked, walking over with what looked like women's undergarments hanging off her arm.

Ferrin flushed. "I, uh . . . We're looking for something for them," he said, nodding to Rae and Suri.

The shopkeeper smiled. She looked to be at least ten years older than Ferrin, closer to Myron's age. She was average height, with short chestnut hair that hung just above her shoulders, blue eyes, and an inviting smile. "Then you've come to the right place. We have the best selection in town." She looked at Rae. "What beautiful eyes you have, my dear." Rae's pale-green eyes were generally the first thing people noticed. A very uncommon trait for an islander with caramel skin and dark hair. "Let's see what we have to work with," she said as she proceeded to look Rae over. She stopped and frowned when she saw the trousers.

Women in this part of the kingdom were rarely seen wearing pants. It wasn't considered proper.

Rae rubbed her hand down the front of the loose-fitting legs. The trousers had come from one of the men they'd killed in the barn attack. Myron had done his best to cut and sew the legs and waist enough for her to wear, but it was plain as butter they didn't fit.

Ferrin lifted a sack of coins from around his neck. "We can pay," he said, hoping to draw the lady's attention away from Rae's outfit. "We've been on the road for some time, and as you can see, our clothes are a bit threadbare."

The lady's smile returned. "Of course. Do you have a preference?"

Ferrin looked at Rae, who was wearing a rather dumbfounded expression as she stared at some of the frilly gowns near the front. "Something durable," he said, unsure how to explain what they needed. The only time he'd ever purchased women's clothing was a scarf he'd gotten his sister on their birthday. "We still have a long road ahead of us, so we need something practical, if you know what I mean."

The lady looked at Rae once again, no doubt wondering why she didn't speak for herself. She probably thought Ferrin was some overbearing husband who demanded to make all the decisions for her. "I think we have just the thing," she said. "If you'll follow me." The shopkeeper started for the back.

Ferrin could hear Myron chuckling behind him, and he turned and gave him a sharp look, which only increased the snickers.

"Follow her," Ferrin said to Rae, hoping she would take the lead. The shopkeeper was halfway to the back, and Rae was still staring at the fancy dresses in the shop window.

She finally turned and started down the aisle, Suri trudging along beside her, running her hand across the material of each dress they passed. The styles of clothing in the back of the shop might not have been as flamboyant as those in the front, but they weren't exactly bland, either. Some were rather fetching.

They stopped about two rows from the back, which was fine, since the dresses on the back wall looked more like canvas potato sacks. The lady turned and pursed her lips, giving Rae a good looking-over before rifling through a nearby rack. She pulled a warm yellow dress from the group and held it up. "How about this?"

Rae wrinkled her nose.

"I guess not," she said, then went back to digging. "Ah, here we go. Something to complement those beautiful eyes of yours." The lady held up a light-green dress that was nearly a match for Rae's eyes. It had a thin white lace trim around the neck and some simple but tasteful embroidery that ran down the sleeves. It was a practical dress, but still, not hard on the eyes.

Rae didn't wrinkle her nose this time, which meant she must have liked it.

"Right," the shopkeeper said. "Let's see how it looks." Without giving Rae a chance to argue, the lady put her arm around her and directed her to the back corner of the shop where there was a privacy screen set up for changing.

Ferrin took Suri's hand. "You can wait with me while your mother tries on her new dress."

"I want one," Suri said, looking up at Ferrin with the same bright pale-green eyes as her mother's.

Ferrin smiled. "Don't worry. We won't leave here until—"

A loud slap followed by an even louder shriek had Ferrin spinning around to look at the dressing wall.

"Don't touch me!" Rae shouted.

"How am I going to change you if you won't let me touch you, girl?" the shopkeeper answered forcefully.

Ferrin shook his head and sighed.

"Maybe this wasn't such a good idea," Myron said, walking over to see what the fuss was.

"She'll have to learn sooner or later how things are done."

"Maybe we should have better explained how this works before bringing her in here."

"Too late now," Ferrin said.

"I said, don't touch me!" Rae's voice blurted out from behind the screen. "I can take my own clothes off and put them back on."

The shopkeeper finally exited from behind the wall. Her hair was ruffled and her necklace askew. "Well, I never. Act like you were raised in a barn." She stood to the side and waited.

Ferrin wondered how much extra Rae's obstinacy was going to cost. He made sure the shopkeeper didn't see his smile. Thankfully, Myron had enough sense not to laugh.

Ferrin was starting to wonder if he needed to go back there and help her himself when Rae finally stepped out from behind the dressing screen.

His breath caught for a second. She was lovely—even with her short-cropped hair. It was the first time he'd seen her in anything that wasn't half ripped apart or hanging so loose that she looked three times her normal size. For the first time, she actually looked like a woman. Ferrin could feel himself flushing and turned his head.

"My, my, my," Myron said admiringly. "Quite lovely, my dear."

Even the shopkeeper smiled, which looked a little funny with the right side of her face still bearing the imprint of Rae's hand.

Rae smiled at the compliment, then looked down at the dress, and finally at Ferrin.

He smiled awkwardly and nodded, trying not to look like he was staring. "We'll take it."

"My turn!" Suri shouted, tugging on Ferrin's arm.

Rae ran her hands slowly up and down the folds of the new material. There was a hint of a smile curling near the corners of her mouth.

Ferrin had to force himself to look away. "Yes, Suri. It's your turn."

The little girl jumped up and down, clapping her hands as she ran for the nearest rack of dresses.

An hour and a half later, they finally left the shop, each with a new set of clothes, their old ones wrapped in wax paper, which they carried out and placed in their saddlebags. Ferrin even went so far as to purchase new boots for himself and Myron and riding shoes for Rae and Suri, similar to the men's but with a cuff at the top and a buckle on the side.

On their way back, they made a quick stop by the cartographer, where Ferrin found a rather impressively detailed map of the five kingdoms, listing known landmarks, cities, and main thoroughfares connecting them. Also, an equally detailed map of Iraseth, certainly worth more than the eight silvers the man was asking. Ferrin purchased the maps and a carrier to keep them dry.

With the last of their shopping complete, the small group of weary travelers made their way back to the Smelly Trout. Supper was more of the same but served with a glass of wine if requested, and a loaf of white instead of the dark rye.

"Look," Suri said for the hundredth time as she spun around for the others to see her new dress. The folds of material swished as she twirled.

"My, don't you look pretty." Ferrin took a moment to admire one of the stitched roses on her right shoulder. "That's got to be the prettiest dress I've ever seen. What do you think?" Ferrin asked, turning to Myron.

"I couldn't agree more," he said as he laid his mug down. "No one more beautiful."

"Just like your mother," Ferrin added.

Rae choked on a small bite of stew she had just stuffed in her mouth. She kept her head lowered as she quietly continued to eat, clearly not wanting to draw attention to *her* new outfit. But every now and then, Ferrin would catch her moving her hand across her lap, letting the folds slide between her fingers.

"It's going to be a long night for me," Ferrin said as he pushed back from the table. He glanced around the room to make sure none of the other customers were close enough to hear, then leaned over to Rae. "I'll need to use the crystal tonight with my forging. Do you mind if I borrow it?" After being berated for not including her in the discussion the last time, he made sure not to repeat that mistake this time.

She took a moment to ponder the decision before finally removing the chain from around her neck and passing it under the table.

"Thank you," he said, then slipped it around his own neck and tucked it under his blue tunic. "It will probably take me the entire night to finish, so don't wait up for me."

"No arguments there," Myron said, stifling yet another yawn. "I could sleep for a month."

Ferrin was rather jealous of the thought of a full night's sleep, something he hadn't experienced since his capture and imprisonment. He stood from the table. "I better get a move on. Those swords aren't going to forge themselves." He stretched with a yawn. "It's been a while since I've done any forging. Hopefully, it'll come back easily enough."

"Before you go," Myron said, standing to join him, "I'd like you to take a look at that map of Iraseth with me. I want to make sure we have a clear route of escape mapped out."

Ferrin nodded. "Good idea. I'll meet you upstairs." He sighed and started up the narrow steps. It was going to be a long night.

Chapter 62 | Ayrion

"**G**IVE US A HAND," Ayrion shouted as he swung down off his horse. To his right, the sun was already beginning to lower.

"What happened?" Tameel rushed down the front steps of the Justice House to help them carry an injured Abiah inside. "We didn't expect you back so soon. Were you able to kill Argon? Did you find the nest?"

"It was an ambush," Bek said, spitting to the side. He had one arm around Abiah's waist for support. "I don't know how, but they knew we were coming."

"My boy. They took my boy." The taverner was in a daze as they helped him and the other injured into the stone building.

Tameel looked at Zynora, and she shook his head. There wasn't much they were going to be able to do for Abiah now. Ayrion couldn't imagine what he must be going through, knowing the fate that awaited his son.

Ayrion felt callous as he shoved thoughts of Willem aside. He needed to focus on the battle that was sure to come in the next few hours.

The sun was almost low enough to touch the tops of the buildings.

While Zynora and some of the women organized a healing station on the first floor, a few of the men stabled the horses in the back. Tameel, Bek, and Ayrion gathered around a long table on the second floor holding a detailed map of Belvin. One of the groups sent to sweep the building had found it hanging on a wall in an upper office, probably the city planner's.

"We are here," Ayrion said, circling with his finger the small section of the map that represented the Justice House. "The mining community and the entrance to the vulraaks' nest is here." Again, he circled another area at the top of the map where the sunken valley holding the old city was located. "We know they'll respond. Argon won't be able to let this go unchallenged.

"The question isn't *if* they are coming, or *when* they are coming, but *where*. Argon knows we have wounded. He also knows the sun is going down, and unless we want to risk getting caught in the open on the road back, we will most likely find a place like this to set up a defense. But to do that, we need to know where their point of attack will be." Ayrion looked at Bek. "This is your city. You know it better than anyone here. What do you think?"

Bek stared at the map. "The most direct route to us is by way of Dunleeth, here, the same direction we took earlier this afternoon. But," he said, leaning over to get a closer look, "they obviously know we'll expect that." His face tightened, the dirt from the mine gathering in the creases and wrinkles around his eyes. "If I were Argon, I might try taking the longer route around Gunner Branch"—he pointed at a section between the mines and the city square and drew an arc that circled around to the front of the square—"which would bring him up Lassiter, here, coming at us from the front." He shrugged in frustration. "That's just a guess, though. I have no idea how this creature really thinks. What about you, Ayrion? You fought him."

Ayrion nodded. "You'll be surprised how much you can learn about your opponent during combat." He scanned the faces around the table. "He's smart, and he wants you to know it."

Bek coughed. "Well, I'd say he's doing a flaming good job of it."

"Yes, and we'll use that to our advantage. We'll let him believe we really are that incompetent."

Tameel and Bek shared a look, but Ayrion chose to ignore it. "I believe that Argon will direct his creatures around to the front of the square. But I also believe he'll come at us from here," he said, jabbing at the map, "and here, and here." Ayrion pointed out every avenue available into or out of the center of town. "Argon isn't going to leave anything to chance. He'll send everything he has against us at once."

Bek studied the map. "I agree."

Tameel nodded. "It makes sense. After such a quick defeat, I doubt he believes us that much of a threat."

"My only concern is the Blind."

Tameel looked at Ayrion, his bushy eyebrows lowering slightly. "The what?"

"The Blind," he repeated, not quite sure himself where the term had come from. "In throwing everything our way, Argon will attempt to direct our focus where he wants and blind us to everything else."

The room disappeared, along with Tameel and Bek. The long table holding the map of Belvin was replaced by one half its size. The stone walls were now nothing but fabric, a tent of some sort. Ayrion was standing over a table with two men in uniform. The first held a bearing that demanded respect and eyes that spoke of experience; the second was as big as a bear. Before Ayrion could get a better look at the map on the table, everything shifted, and he was once again inside the Justice House.

Ayrion squeezed the table as he waited for everything to come back into focus. He wished there was some way to unlock the rest of those hidden secrets buried deep within his mind, if for no other reason than to keep these random memories from popping up at unexpected times. He glanced back down at the map, then turned and looked at the second-floor balcony windows at the front.

"What are you thinking?" Bek asked, turning to look at the windows as well. "You have that look on your face. The one that usually ends up landing me in a heap of trouble."

Ayrion smiled. "I have an idea."

Chapter 63 | Ayrion

T IME WAS RUNNING OUT. Ayrion worked as fast as he could to get their fortified wall of wagons built and ready before the sun went down. They lined the wagons with boxes, barrels, old tables and chairs, desks, cabinets, and any other loose item of size they could get their hands on.

Behind the blockade were buckets of pitch, two to a wagon. The same pitch Tameel was using to cover the pyres they had set up around the main pavilion in front of the Justice House.

The last of the day's light passed below the buildings on the far side of the square as men and women stood ready behind the makeshift wagon barrier, waiting for what they knew was coming. The front of the Justice House lay in silence. No one spoke, everyone listening for signs of the approaching enemy.

Ayrion stood at the top of the steps, the double doors at his back. Beside him, Bek rested his hands on the heads of his hatchets. Neither man spoke. The only sounds were those coming from the second-floor windows behind them as Abiah barked orders to fire only when they had a clear target.

"Was it wise to put him in charge of the bowmen?" Bek asked. "Losing his son like that would push most men over the edge."

Ayrion turned and looked up at the windows. They had removed the panes to give the archers plenty of room to shoot from. "Best he has something to keep his mind focused on, other than the grief."

"Do you trust his judgment?"

Ayrion turned back around. "I think he's angry enough at the moment that the only thing he cares about is killing vulraaks, which is exactly what we need."

Bek didn't say anything, but Ayrion could tell he wasn't exactly swayed.

Above them, the taverner continued shouting directions like a twenty-year veteran. Ayrion wanted to shake his head, knowing that before this week, the man had never seen a day of combat in his life. The closest he'd ever come to battle was the occasional tavern brawl.

"Almost wish they'd hurry up and get on with it," Bek said as he studied the empty square. "The waiting has me more on edge than the actual fight."

Ayrion nodded. He was feeling it as well, the calm before the storm. "It'll be here soon enough, and then we'll be wishing we were back to the waiting."

Bek grinned. "You're probably right."

"They're coming!" one of the lookouts on the far side of the square shouted.

In the distance, the vulraaks' screeching calls and guttural howls filled the night. They had no intention, or need, to mask their arrival. The half-human creatures poured into the square from every available route, like worker ants clambering out of their tunnels.

Shrieks, gasps, and calls for the Creator's mercy rose from those standing behind the barricades as they watched the vulraaks empty into the open square. They had no need to light the fires to see where to shoot. All they needed was to point their bows forward and they were bound to hit something.

Ayrion realized he was holding his breath and exhaled. He had expected a large force but not on the scale of what was looming before them.

"I take it back," Bek said. "I'd rather be waiting."

Ayrion drew his swords, the black blades singing as they slid from their sheaths. "No going back now." He turned around and looked up at the second-floor windows, where Abiah and his archers stood ready. "Light your arrows!"

Across the front of the building, like soldiers on the crenelated battlement of a great wall, archers lit their arrows. Abiah shouted at his men. "Aim for the pyres! The general wants light. So we give him light!"

Ayrion pointed his sword toward the massing army across the square. "Fire!"

"Fire!" Abiah echoed.

Ayrion watched the flaming shafts fly over their heads. One by one, the large piles of stacked wood and tar ignited, lighting the square and revealing the vulraaks' true numbers.

"Creator help us," Bek said solemnly. "We're not going to survive this."

The vulraaks cowered momentarily from the unexpected blaze but quickly regrouped and rushed the barricade.

From behind the wagons, archers on the ground fired off volley after volley, cutting down as many as they could. Most of those hit by arrows kept running. Beside the archers were men and women using long pikes to skewer the vulraaks as they tried to climb over the wagons.

His fighters held their ground. With swords and staves, axes and hammers, they fought, cutting down anything close enough to reach. They weren't warriors or trained soldiers, or even green recruits. They were farmers and merchants, husbands and wives, people who wanted nothing more than to live in peace but were willing to stand and fight for their freedom.

Ayrion admired their courage. If he *had* been a general, he couldn't imagine leading a braver band of fighters.

The creatures were beginning to mount the barricade. Some had managed to fight their way over the top and were opening up spots along the wall for others to follow. His people weren't going to hold much longer.

"Release the pitch!" Ayrion shouted.

His people pulled back from the wagons, giving those with the buckets of tar room to shower the wall and any vulraak still fighting to get over.

"Retreat!" Ayrion shouted, and the fighters scrambled up the steps.

Ayrion and a small group ran down the stairs, taking two at a time. Bek matched him step for step, his hatchets up and ready to kill. They pushed their way through the remaining pitch carriers to meet the vulraaks scrambling over the blockade.

Ayrion's heart slowed as he released his magic. Heat poured from his chest into his arms as he turned himself over to it. He didn't like the idea that he was finding it easier to relinquish control, but he could live with it if it kept them alive.

They reached the blockade, and his twin dragons cut down everything within reach, their steel glowing in the light of the flames. Creatures howled as they came for him, lunging but unable to penetrate his swords. Slowly, they worked their way back up the steps.

With a single swipe of his sword, he opened the fronts of two vulraaks as they tried to slip past him and grab those retreating farther up the stairs. Turning, he stabbed another in the neck as it rushed in from the side. Something hit his arm, and he turned to see a head rolling back down the steps from where Bek had stopped one of the creatures from getting in behind him.

The doors behind them were open, waiting for their fighters to make it back inside. Above him, he could hear Abiah shouting orders to fire into the oncoming horde. The front line of vulraaks fell under the barrage of arrows.

"Inside! All of you!" Bek shouted, nearing the top of the steps.

The rest of their people made a dash for the entrance. Ayrion followed them up, cutting down the creatures attacking from the sides.

"Hurry!" Bek shouted. "The doors are closing!"

Ayrion continued fighting; his movements were perfect, his strikes precise. The magic was invigorating. He used only enough force required for the kill and no more, conserving his energy. His blades flashed like streaks of lightning as they reflected the moon's beams with every strike.

He could hear Bek shouting somewhere behind him as he continued to back toward the shutting doors. White bodies littered the ground around his feet as he cut and stabbed and hacked them apart. The power was intoxicating.

"Get in here, you fool!" Zynora's voice rang out, pulling his focus away from his magic.

Ayrion turned, and his heart skipped. The doors were nearly shut. He'd waited too long. He released one last wild swing and ran, the vulraaks hot on his heels. He dove for the doors and barely squeezed through the small wedge of opening left, skidding across the floor as they reverberated shut behind him.

A massive wooden beam was dropped into place.

"Cutting it a bit close, wouldn't you say?" Bek said, helping Ayrion to his feet and clapping him on the shoulder. "Ah, yuck!" He flung black viscera from his hand.

Ayrion moved back into the room to get a look at the second-floor balcony. "Are we ready?" he shouted up to Abiah.

"Ready, General! Waiting for your orders!"

"Then fire!"

"Light 'em up, boys!" Abiah said as he spun back to the windows overlooking the square. "Light those white sons of faeries up!"

Ayrion stood in front of the heavy doors. If the fires didn't do their job, what they were about to attempt was going to be for nothing. He could hear the screeches and howls coming from the other side. "Positions!"

His fighters took up their places behind him. "Ready the doors!" Six men stood underneath the large wooden brackets and waited.

"Here goes nothing," Bek said beside him.

Ayrion could feel the pressure building within. It was all or nothing. *Come on, Abiah. Where's that signal?*

"Now!" Abiah shouted down to them.

Ayrion raised his sword. "Release!"

The heavy beam swung up and out of its brackets as men on both sides of the doors pulled—opening it only wide enough to allow one or two bodies through at a time. Ayrion could see the flames at the bottom of the steps had engulfed the entire barricade, separating the vulraaks that had made it over from the rest of their force, who were now pulling back from the inferno.

Ayrion squeezed his blades in triumph. It had worked. At least the first part.

Ayrion waited just inside the doors for the first of the white-skinned cannibals to breach the entrance. He had instructed his people to set up blockers on the backs of the doors so they would open only so far and no farther, forcing the vulraaks to funnel into a death trap.

As fast as he could swing, Ayrion cut them down. No creature for the first few moments made it past his blades. Pretty soon, the doors had been forced wide enough for more to get through, requiring him to move back or get overrun.

Bek and the rest of his fighters rushed in, hacking away at any that made it past. It didn't take long before the creatures had managed to pry the doors even further as they climbed over each other to get inside, but still it wasn't enough to overpower the determination of the people inside.

Ayrion's fighters slaughtered the creatures. The vulraaks' lust for blood overpowered any higher reasoning, and without the first thought or care about their own safety, they charged straight into the waiting armsmen. The bodies began to pile up, making it even more difficult for the ones behind to gain access.

Before long, the fight was over. All those between the barricades and the front doors had been utterly annihilated.

"Stack the bodies out front as quickly as you can. Those fires won't hold them back for long. Then shut those doors and get that bracer back in place." Ayrion left Bek in charge of the cleanup and headed for the stairwell to the second floor. He stopped at the foot of the stairs when he saw Zynora coming from the back, where the injured were being seen to.

"How are the wounded?"

"They'll survive."

"And you?"

Zynora didn't say anything at first. She took a moment to look him over. "We managed to stockpile some medicines and bandages we found in town, but there really isn't enough of me to go around."

Ayrion knew what she was referring to. He shouldn't count on one of her *impulso* blasts. "Save your strength. Only use it on the most dire, and only enough to keep them alive."

Zynora laid a gaunt hand on the side of his face. "Don't you worry about me, Grey Eyes. You worry about the rest of them. I can manage."

Ayrion smiled. He knew that no matter what he told her, she was going to do what she wanted to. He hoped her heart for others wouldn't be the end of her.

She patted his bloodstained cheek, then headed back toward the healing station.

Ayrion continued up the stairs and around the balcony to where Abiah was directing his men to ready the next assault.

"How's it going?" Ayrion asked as he stepped alongside the short taverner and stuck his head out the glassless windowpanes. Now that the flames were dying, the creatures were beginning to move near the wagons once more.

"For all that effort," Abiah said, looking out at the amassing force, "we didn't seem to do that much."

"It's not about winning," Ayrion said, hoping Abiah's defeatist attitude didn't spread to the others. "There's no way we could survive an all-out attack. The only way to beat a much larger force is to fight them a little at a time, which is exactly what we did, and quite successfully, I might add. Tonight is not about winning; it's about surviving until the sun comes back up."

Abiah stared out the window. "I'd say they won't wait much longer before ripping a hole through the wagons. And when they do, they'll have a right nasty surprise waiting on them."

Ayrion took a step closer to the window. "Looks like they're getting ready to break through now."

Abiah hopped up from his stoop and limped down the front stretch of windows. "Ready your barrels!"

Ayrion raced to the end of the balcony and shouted down to those inside. "Get those doors shut! They're coming!" He rejoined the bowmen at the windows and watched as the vulraaks pulled one of the wagons over, leaving a gaping hole in their barricade. White bodies poured through the opening and up the steps. A loud *thud* reverberated as the doors below shut and the heavy bracer was dropped into place.

The sound of the vulraaks beating against the doors sent a shiver up Ayrion's spine, but with no form of battering ram, he didn't see how they were going to do much damage.

"How sure are you that this stuff will light?" Ayrion asked.

Abiah grinned and pulled out a tin mug he had hidden behind some boxes he was sitting on. He dunked it in one of the casks and held it out to Ayrion. "Go ahead. Try it."

Everyone on the balcony turned to watch. Ayrion felt like he was about to be the butt of a joke. But not wanting to look weak in front of his men, he lifted the goblet and took a swallow. His first reaction was to inhale, but he'd somehow lost his breath. The liquid felt like it was melting his insides on its way down. His eyes watered, and he coughed so hard, he thought he'd spit out a lung.

Those watching laughed.

Abiah slapped him hard on the back. "Goes down smooth, doesn't it?"

"For the love of Aldor, what was that?" Ayrion asked, still trying to catch his breath. It was even stronger than the rovers' musca. If that was possible.

"That would be a Sidaran specialty—black briar. You like? It's distilled from the roots of a rare prickle plant that grows along the outer edges of Reed Marsh. Not many can afford such a luxury. I'd never be able to sell something like this in my tavern."

"Well, it's certainly flammable. Whatever you do, don't drop a torch in one of those barrels, or we won't have to wait for the vulraaks to kill us."

Abiah leaned his head back and roared. First bit of laughter Ayrion had heard from the man since the mines. It almost seemed unnatural, considering what he'd lost. But he figured everyone coped in different ways.

Ayrion turned to the men and women standing around. "And don't let me catch you helping yourselves to it, either. Last thing we need is a bunch of drunken archers shooting each other instead of the vulraaks."

Abiah saluted. "You have my word, General." He turned and limped back down the line of men. Ayrion could hear him mumbling under his breath as he went. "Hate to see such good stuff go to waste." At the end of the row, he finally turned. "Ready your barrels!"

Those standing on either side of the casks bent, ready to lift.

"Torches at the ready!"

Those standing at the windows held out their torches.

"Burn 'em alive!"

The men heaved with all their might as they tipped the ends of their barrels. The dark liquid cascaded like a waterfall over the creatures below. Those with torches dropped them out the windows and watched as the contents of the barrels transformed into liquid fire before reaching the ground. The creatures' screams were bloodcurdling as their bodies ignited into an inferno that lit the entire square. They tried to run, but there was nowhere to go.

Ayrion couldn't believe how well that had worked.

"Ready the next barrels!" Abiah yelled as he marched back down the row.

Bek joined Ayrion at one of the windows and looked out. "What in the name of Aldor is in those casks?" He walked over to one of the open barrels and looked inside, eyes wide. "Is that black briar?"

"That it be," Abiah said, joining them in front of the cask.

"They say it can make a grown man sweat."

Abiah glanced at Ayrion with a wicked grin, and Ayrion finally nodded. The taverner quickly produced the same mug he had offered Ayrion earlier and dipped it in, handing it to Bek.

Bek took a swallow, and his eyes bulged. He spit half back into the barrel, the other half across the floor. "Hot flaming—"

"Help! Vulraaks! They're inside the walls!"

Chapter 64 | Ayrion

EVERYONE ON THE SECOND floor rushed to the railing.

A young boy, blood running down the front of his tunic, stumbled into the main room from one of the back corridors. "Help! They killed my brother!" The boy's legs gave out, and he dropped to the floor.

"Keep that liquid flowing!" Ayrion yelled as he ran for the stairs. Bek was right behind him.

Abiah didn't need prodding. He was back to shouting out orders by the time Ayrion and Bek managed to make it down the stairs and push their way through the crowd of onlookers.

Zynora was there with the boy, hands glowing as she pushed some of her healing magic into him. A number of people scooted back, those not having been around long enough to know she was a wielder. The little boy's eyes opened.

"What happened?" Ayrion asked. "You said the vulraaks are here? Where are they?"

The boy pointed behind him in the direction of the east corridors.

"They're in the cellars. Father told me to run and get help."

Ayrion looked at Bek and Tameel. "Remember what I was saying about that Blind?" He ripped his blades from their sheaths and ran down the corridor. "On me!" Behind him, he could hear Bek shouting for more to follow. How had the vulraaks managed to get in? They had made a thorough sweep of the entire building. A few of the creatures must have found a place to hide when they had searched the first time.

Rounding the next corner, Ayrion could hear the sounds of battle ahead. Defenders were fighting their way out of a stairwell on the left.

"What's going on?" he shouted down the hall.

One of the men turned, blood running down his left arm. "They just came out of nowhere, sir. We were loading more of the casks for Master Abiah, and the next thing we know, we're being overrun."

"How many of you are there?"

"This is all that's left. The rest are dead."

Ayrion counted five men. "How many of the creatures are down there?" He pushed his way to the front of the steps and found his answer. He thrust his blade through the mouth of one creature that was working to get around the arm of one of his people. The creature squealed and fell backward into those coming up.

The entire staircase was covered in vulraaks. This wasn't just a few who'd been in hiding. This was an entire contingent.

"Get behind me!"

Bek and the fresh recruits pulled the five men back as they barricaded the cellar with their bodies, fighting to keep the creatures from entering the keep.

"Where are they coming from?" Ayrion drew his blade from one creature's chest and plunged it into another.

One of the men beside him was yanked right off his feet and pulled into the cellar stairwell before Ayrion could grab him.

"I don't know," Bek said, keeping his hatchets swinging, cutting off limbs as fast as they poked up out of the darkness below. "There must be some tunnels under the Justice House we didn't know about."

Ayrion dodged a set of claws aimed at his neck and cut the vulraak's arm off at the elbow. He kicked the rest of the body back into the others. "Fantastic! That might have been helpful to know before now."

"Don't look at me. I told you I've never been in here before." Bek spun around and lopped off the next vulraak's head with a single stroke, splattering the side of Ayrion's coat with blood.

Ayrion was getting winded, and his fighters looked ready to collapse. They had already fought several waves of the creatures, and the vulraaks were fresh. It was pure self-preservation alone that had kept them swinging their weapons.

He stabbed the legs of the next two and slit open the chest cavity of the third before shoving it back onto those still trying to reach the top. "We better think of something fast, because we're about to be overrun."

The vulraaks continued coming. Ayrion and his men were already being forced back into the main corridor and away from the open stairwell. They couldn't let them get a foothold. If they didn't manage to stop the creatures here, it was over.

"Move! Out of the way! Coming through!"

Behind him, Ayrion heard Tameel shout, "Get down! Get down!"

"I can't get down!" he said. "I'm up to my neck in vulraaks."

Ayrion was suddenly yanked backward off his feet and thrown to the ground by a pair of fur-covered arms. "What do you think you're—" Before he could finish, a gale of wind billowed over their heads, pinning them to the ground. It slammed into the vulraaks emerging from the cellars and threw their bodies like ragdolls down the corridor.

"Move! Clear a path!" Tameel shouted as he and a couple of men rolled three large casks toward the cellar entrance. Zynora pushed her way through to the top of the cellar stairs, her face pale and covered in sweat. She lifted her arms, reciting another one of her incantations, and another blast of air hammered the creatures on the steps, throwing them back into the darkness below. She collapsed into Tameel's arms, and a couple of the fighters carried her back down the hall.

Ayrion hoped she hadn't pushed herself too far.

"Roll them in!" Abiah ordered as he helped the men push the first of the barrels down the long staircase. One by one, the men shoved all three through the cellar door and down the stairs.

A single archer stood at the entrance with a lit shaft, waiting for Abiah's command.

Ayrion grabbed Abiah's arm. "Wait! Aren't the rest of the barrels down there?"

"Exactly," the taverner said with a wink. "Now run!"

By the time he turned, his fighters were already halfway down the hall. He spared a quick glance over his shoulder just as the archer released the flaming arrow down the stairs.

The man turned and ran. The walls and floor shook from the force of the exploding barrels. Behind them, the ceiling collapsed around the cellar entrance, taking a swath of the corridor with it. The archer leaped just in time to miss one of the walls tumbling in behind him. The force and loose debris knocked the man from his feet.

Ayrion and some of the others ran to help free him from the rubble. "What's your name?" Ayrion asked the archer as he helped him to his feet. Apart from an ugly cut on his forehead, the man was surprisingly unscathed.

"Taggert, sir."

"Well, Taggert, that was a brave thing you did back there. Don't believe I could have done better myself."

The man saluted with his fist to his chest. "Had to be done, sir."

Ayrion patted him on the back. "That it did." He turned and studied the damage behind them. He couldn't believe how much force those casks of black briar had produced. Dust filled the corridor, blinding everything around him. "We need to get back to the main room," he said, wiping the flumes of white powder from his eyes. "How many barrels of that stuff were down there?"

"Quite a few," Abiah said between fits of coughing. Once the cloud of debris began to settle, they could see that everything beyond that point had been completely encased in stone.

"I'm just glad to see that tunnel sealed," Ayrion said. "Now we know how Argon knew we were coming. His vulraaks have been right here with us the whole time."

Chapter 65 | Barthol

"IT'S GETTING LATE," Barthol said. "Do you still think she's coming?" He looked out the front window of Commander Tolin's home. The yard was dark, the moon barely casting enough light to see beyond the porch. He stared at the surrounding shadows, half expecting white-robed guards to come bursting out of the night to arrest them.

"She's the one who set up this meeting," Tolin said. "I say we give her a little more time." The words had barely escaped the commander's lips when there was a heavy knock at the door. He looked at Barthol. "Good timing." Tolin raised his lamp and crossed the room, sword bouncing in time against his leg.

Barthol took up a position on the opposite side of the door. One could never be too careful nowadays. His fingers tightened around the dagger at his waist as Tolin reached for the knob.

The door burst open. A large man grabbed the commander by the neck and pushed him back into the room. "Don't move or I'll slit your throat."

Barthol was so stunned, he never even pulled his dagger.

The light from Tolin's lamp reflected off a blade the man had pressed against the commander's neck. The fact that Tolin hadn't dropped the lamp in the scuffle spoke to the amount of combat he'd seen.

The attacker might have had Tolin overmatched in both size and shape, but not Barthol. Barthol drew his dagger, slipped out from behind the door, and pressed the tip against the small of the man's back. "I strongly suggest you rethink your position, friend. You seem to be at a disadvantage."

"Think again," a woman's voice said behind him. Before he could turn, Barthol felt the tip of a blade pressed against *his* back.

"What say we don't stand here in the doorway for all to see?" the mysterious woman said. "Might be kind of an awkward sight for the neighbors, don't you think?"

Barthol kept his blade pressed against the man in front of him, waiting to see who would move first. The knife at his back dug in.

"Kerson, move forward, you oaf, so I can shut the door." The man holding Tolin took two steps in, and Barthol quickly followed as they all paraded into Tolin's front room.

The door behind him shut. "Po, kindly relieve them of their weapons, will you?"

Barthol started to turn. *Who is she talking to?*

"My pleasure." A thin man with straight black hair stepped around to Barthol's side and held out his hand. Other than his scrawny size, there wasn't much about him that stood out. He was about as plain as a potato. *Po . . . potato.* Barthol tried not to smile. This was his chance.

Barthol spun away from the sharp point of the woman's knife and grabbed Po, jerking him backward and using him as a shield against the woman.

Just as soon as Kerson realized Barthol's blade was no longer there, he spun as well, taking Tolin with him. Everyone was now facing each other in a small circle: Kerson with his blade against Tolin's throat,

Barthol with his blade against the potato man's throat, and the mysterious woman—who turned out to be younger than Barthol would have expected and a good deal prettier—with her knife resting idly in her hand.

She wore a long leather overcoat that reminded him of the one Ayrion used to wear, except for the color. Hers was deep red. A single braid of raven hair hung down the middle of her back, swishing as she looked the two men over.

"Well, gentlemen." She was smiling as though it were all in good fun. "It appears as though we are at an impasse. I'm open to suggestions."

"I suggest we start with who you are and why you're in my home," Tolin said, appearing unaffected by the blade at his throat.

"Ah, the disgraced Commander Tolin, I take it." She glanced at Barthol. "Which would make you Barthol Respuel. Former captain of the disbanded High Guard and Ayrion's right arm.

"I'm Kira, Clan Chief of the Warren Council."

Barthol could see Tolin's demeanor slip as he bared his teeth and slowly reached for his sword.

"Ah," she said, pointing her knife at Tolin. "None of that, Commander."

Tolin lowered his hand.

"To my friends," she said, "I'm Red. To my enemies . . . well . . . best you not find out." She looked at Barthol, then back to Tolin. "For you, *Kira* will do nicely."

"So, that rabble of street whores, pickpockets, and murderers have elected a chief, have they?" Tolin said.

The man holding the knife to his throat tightened his grip, forcing Tolin to raise his head higher.

Tolin sneered. "By the looks of you, they chose well."

Kira leaned her head back and laughed. "You truly were Ayrion's mentor," she said. "You sound just like him." She laughed some more. "Tolin, I like you. Ayrion always was a good judge of character."

"Can't say as I reciprocate," Tolin interjected. "Now that introductions have been duly exchanged, how about you tell me what you're doing in my home?"

"I believe I can answer that, Commander," Amarysia said as she slid the front door open and stepped inside, her blonde hair hanging loose down her back. A robed individual stepped in behind her, their hood remaining up to conceal their face.

"Ah, and the hussy makes her grand entrance," Kira said, taking a step to the left to let Amarysia through. "Running a bit late, aren't we?"

Amarysia ignored the woman's snide remark and moved farther into the room. "Kira has a vested interest in what we discuss here tonight. She was also a close friend of Ayrion's. They grew up together on the streets."

Barthol looked at the young leather-clad chief. He thought it strange he'd never heard Ayrion mention her before. A character as colorful as she was would have come up in at least one conversation, surely. Then again, Ayrion had never been one to discuss much about his past.

Amarysia looked at the skinny man in Barthol's arms and smiled. "Po, it's nice to see you too," she said with a sly wink. "And with all your clothes on."

Barthol's eyes widened. *With all your clothes on?* He thought it best not to ask.

Amarysia closed the front door. "I see there's no need for introductions." She had an amused look on her face, not that he could blame her with everyone standing around holding knives to each other's throats. "Now if all the men are through hugging each other, I believe it's high time we got this meeting underway."

Barthol glared at Kerson, but they both eventually nodded and slowly lowered their blades.

As soon as Barthol's knife retreated, Po flew across the room to where Kira was standing.

Tolin, however, merely lifted his lamp to get a better look at everyone. "And who is that with you?" he asked, aiming the light in the direction of the robed individual near the door. "Will you ask them to kindly remove their hood? I have no desire to discuss matters of importance without knowing everyone in the room."

"A wise decision, Commander," came a soft voice from underneath the cowl. The voice was a woman's, and for some reason, recognizable, but it was muffled by the thick material. Two arms reached up and pulled back the hood. "Another firm reminder why my husband appointed you for the position."

Barthol froze, and Tolin dropped to one knee. "Your Majesty."

Barthol couldn't believe it. The Queen Mother was standing in Tolin's front room.

Tolin cleared his throat, and Barthol quickly dropped to his knee as well.

Kira and her entourage simply stood there. "You're prettier than I remember," the clan chief said matter-of-factly, not bothering to bow, or bend, or show any sign of overt respect.

Ellise smiled. "Thank you, my dear. You have grown into quite the woman." She gave the young chief a quick looking-over. Barthol spared a questioning glance at Tolin.

Tolin shrugged. But the look on his face said Barthol wasn't the only one surprised by the familiarity between the two.

"Yes, well, the last time you saw me, I was hiding under your bed."

That brought both men's heads up.

"And as I recall," the queen said, "Dakaran found you rather quickly. I told you, you should have used the quilt chest."

The two women chuckled.

"I never was as good at picking places to hide as Ayrion."

"I see why the clans chose you as their chief. You have fire. Make sure to brandish it well." The queen turned her attention back to Barthol and Tolin. "Please rise, gentlemen; there's no need for that. We are all friends here."

Barthol joined Tolin and stood, still feeling uncomfortable in the queen's presence. Apart from seeing her in the halls at the palace during his time in the High Guard, he had never actually been formally introduced or spoken so much as three words to her.

"I believe we will be more comfortable in the den," Tolin said. "If you'll follow me, Your Majesty." He led them down a hallway toward the back.

Barthol brought up the rear. He wanted to keep an eye on the others in case they had any ill intent toward the queen. Amarysia didn't seem to be bothered by the young chief, and if she was truly a friend of Ayrion's, she must be at least somewhat trustworthy. Barthol had never known Ayrion to associate with the wrong sort of people.

Once inside Tolin's study, the commander directed the queen and others to sit. The fire in the hearth was warm, and there were drinks waiting on them, although not enough. Tolin quickly pulled up a few more chairs and grabbed four more goblets from the cabinet. For the women, he had some wine, and for the men, something a bit stronger.

Kira demanded the stronger.

"Commander, I was told there was someone here who had news of my husband's death, but I take it that the formerly dead Captain Barthol here would be such a man?" She smiled at Barthol. "I see that word of your demise has been greatly exaggerated, Captain. It's good to see you alive and well." The queen leaned back in her cushioned seat, keeping her hands at the center of her lap, where they rested snugly around her goblet. Even masquerading in dark robes, she held a regal bearing.

"It's good to be seen, Your Majesty," Barthol said, still trying to wrap his head around the fact that he was sharing a drink with the queen.

"I must admit, I'm a bit shocked as to how such a mistake could have been made. Where have you been? And more importantly, why would they have reported you dead?"

Barthol squirmed. Hadn't Amarysia already passed this news on to the queen? She had promised them she would. He hadn't expected to convey the king's death directly to his wife, and he was suddenly at a loss for words. How could he tell her the truth, knowing her son was the one behind it?

Barthol cleared his throat. "Your Majesty, I'm not sure how much of my story Amarysia has already informed you of, but the fact that I'm sitting here is clear indication of its inaccuracy."

The queen's face remained emotionless, her hands still folded around her drink. "When Amarysia came to me and said that the accounting of events we had been led to believe concerning my husband's death had been purposely distorted, I demanded proof. When she told me there was a witness, I instructed her not to reveal anything else. I wanted to hear this knowledge directly from the source." She raised her hand. "So, please, leave nothing out."

Barthol nodded. "Thank you, Your Majesty. What I have to say will not be easy to hear, and I beg Your Majesty's forgiveness in advance." For the first time, the queen's face broke from its calm demeanor. Lines of concern formed over her lowered brows as he went on to explain in detail the events leading up to her husband's death.

"Are you saying my husband was still alive after these beasts were killed?"

"He was, Your Majesty. In fact, we were in the process of seeing to one of his injuries when Ayrion kicked me off the back of the rise."

The queen leaned forward. "He kicked you off the rise?"

"Are you saying he tried to kill you?" Kira butted in, skepticism on her face.

"No, I'm saying that in his last moments, Ayrion used what little time he had to save my life." Barthol went on to explain how he had seen bolts sticking from the back of the king's armor before clearing the rise, and how the only other people present at the time had been Dakaran, the Archchancellor, and a contingent of Black Watch.

"Why didn't he try saving the king instead?" Kira asked. "Or himself, for that matter?"

Barthol sighed, rubbing his hand through his hair. "Believe me, I've asked myself that question at least a thousand times. We all know Ayrion. He would have never tried to save himself at the expense of everyone else, let alone the king. But your husband," he said, directing his conversation back to the queen, "was too far from the edge of the rise for Ayrion to have forced him over, not to mention the added weight of his armor. And if Ayrion would have simply jumped in front of the king, stopping the bolts from reaching him, that would have left both Ayrion and myself dead and nothing there to stop the Black Watch from killing the king anyway."

Barthol paused a moment as the memories resurfaced. "I believe Ayrion knew what was about to happen, and his last thoughts were of Aldor. In that final moment, he knew the most important thing was to keep one of us alive to bear witness to this treachery. I believe that is why he kicked me over the side."

He finished by explaining how he had managed to land amongst a pile of rock, no doubt hiding him from those above. "By the time I woke and crawled back up the hillside, everyone was gone. And the rest you know. As soon as I made it back to Aramoor and saw that my family was safe, I came straight to the commander."

"Which answered a few nagging questions I had," Tolin said as he crossed his legs.

Ellise remained poised through it all, never touching her drink. "And what questions were those?"

"First of all, your son and the Archchancellor forbade any of my men from stepping foot on that rise after the battle. We were told that the king, the Guardian, and the High Guard had been killed by the hor'hounds. They were being hailed as heroes of Elondria, but because of the damage they had sustained by the creatures, the prince charged that their bodies be privately buried out of respect. All except for the king. We weren't even allowed to search for survivors."

Barthol could see Tolin's anger rising as his grip tightened on the arms of his chair.

"So, when Captain Barthol showed up on my doorstep in the middle of the night and told me what he had seen, it all began to make sense."

"Of course it makes sense!" Kira said. "That flaming coward saw his chance to get his hands on the crown and took it!"

Barthol choked on his drink.

"Dakaran hasn't changed a wink since we were kids! He was a weasel then, and he's a weasel now!"

The queen shook her head. "It can't be true. There must be an explanation."

Kira sighed. "I'm sorry, Your Queenness, you seem like a good sort, but even you have to admit your son is a bit of a monster."

Tolin's face tightened. "Watch your tongue. You're addressing the queen."

"Watch your own. If you lot ain't going to tell her what she needs to hear, I flaming will."

Ellise lowered her head. "Dakaran has his faults, but I . . . I can't believe he would go so far as to see his own father killed just for the right to sit on the throne. He was our only heir. The crown would have gone to him regardless."

Tolin leaned forward. "I overheard your husband make the statement that if Dakaran didn't straighten up his actions, he would revoke the Crown."

The queen looked up.

"Of course, I believe he was simply trying to urge your son to get more involved. I don't believe he meant it."

Ellise didn't say anything. Amarysia laid a hand on her arm, and she nodded to let her know she was all right.

"Most parents tend to want to see the best in their children," Kira said, her tone softening just a little. "They are blinded to their faults because of their love for them."

The queen shifted her attention from her drink to the fire. She quietly watched the flames dance across the burning logs.

Barthol wondered if maybe they had gone too far. Perhaps the queen wasn't ready to hear this much truth at once.

Tolin cleared his throat. "We don't believe that this was as simple as your son seeing an opportunity to claim the throne." He went on to tell the others about the wild claims the Cylmaran overlord had made concerning an alleged agreement between Cylmar and Dakaran prior to the battle. "Saryn wouldn't say what that agreement had been, and before I could question him further, the Archchancellor had the overlord and his men executed on Dakaran's orders."

"And now that Dakaran has disbanded the High Guard in favor of these White Tower goons," Barthol said, leaning forward and resting his elbows on his knees, "we're afraid of what could be coming next."

"And with this new citizen tax being levied to pay for all these new troops," Tolin added, "we can't help but wonder: does the throne still control the White Tower, or have those roles been reversed?"

Ellise remained quiet as she stared at the hearth.

"We weighed our options, Your Majesty," Tolin said. "We believed it important that you knew the truth. But we also feared that in telling you, we would be putting your life in danger."

The queen blinked as if coming out of a trance. "My life?"

"Yes, Your Majesty. If Dakaran were to find out that you knew the truth behind his father's death, I'm not sure how far he would go to keep such a secret."

The queen stared at the commander for a moment, then returned her gaze to the open flames.

Barthol shared a wary glance with the others. They appeared to be wondering the same thing. This might have been a mistake.

"Well," Kira said, "it's clear that the Warrens are on their own." She looked at the queen. "From what I could tell, your husband was an honorable man. He made a promise to help us with some difficulties we were facing, and up until his death, he had begun to make good on them.

So, for myself, I'm sad to see him go, especially considering who's taken his place. But my question is . . . now what? It's not like we five can march into the palace and demand the throne back." She chuckled. "Although it would be good sport to see the look on Dakaran's face if we did."

"Not without support, at least," Tolin said. "But building that kind of support will take time. I have some friends in the senate I trust. When we're ready, I can run some of this by them and see what options we might have."

"I thought you were leaving, Commander?" Amarysia said.

Tolin laid his drink aside. "Some things are more important. Unfortunately, I *will* have to find other accommodations, though. I have some savings, but without a regular salary, I have no way of keeping my family fed."

"You can stay with us," Barthol offered, not stopping to think what his wife might have to say about the issue. "Although I don't know for how long, since I too am without work, considering I'm dead."

"Your salaries will be taken care of," the queen said. "I'll see to it. But I believe you are correct in moving, Commander. If your intention is to find a way to subvert my son, remaining hidden would be a smart choice."

"Or I could just sneak into the palace and fix the problem myself," Kira said, flipping her dagger in her hand.

"No! No one touches my son."

Kira reluctantly slid the knife back into her jacket.

"Promise me," Ellise said, looking directly at the clan chief. "Promise you won't try killing him."

Kira sneered. "It's no better than he deserves."

"Maybe that's so. Maybe not. But I still want your word."

Kira looked at the others. She was clearly not happy about being cornered that way. "Fine. I promise to keep my distance . . . for now." She stood, and Kerson and Po followed her up. "I'm thankful for the invitation to join you this evening. If any of you find yourselves in need of safe harbor, you have but to mention my name. As the commander said, we are in for rough times. If I were you, I'd keep my head down."

She made her way to the door, the larger guard opening it as she approached. She stopped halfway through and turned to look at Amarysia. "You still have my ring?"

Amarysia nodded. "Yes."

"Good. Use it if you need to . . . hussy." She winked and disappeared out the door.

Amarysia was smiling when she turned to the queen. "Your Majesty, it might be best if we were heading back ourselves."

Ellise nodded with a heavy sigh as she let Amarysia help her to her feet. Barthol and Tolin rose as well. "I feel I should apologize to everyone for what has happened. And hope to beg your forgiveness for the actions of . . ." She didn't finish.

Tolin took a step forward. "Your Majesty, we hold you in no way responsible for Dakaran's actions. You and your husband have ever been our friends and allies. Our only concern is for your safety and well-being."

"I couldn't have asked for two more faithful guardians," she said, stepping forward to offer each a warm embrace.

Barthol was surprised by the strength of her grip.

"I have these for you." She took a step back and reached inside the folds of her cloak and produced two pouches. She handed one to Tolin and one to Barthol. "I had planned to offer them as a measure of repayment for your loss," she said to Tolin, "but consider it a down payment on future work if indeed you do decide to stay in Aramoor." She turned to Barthol. "That purse was intended for Overcaptain Asa, but since he wasn't able to make it tonight, take it with my blessing."

Barthol accepted the purse with a gracious bow.

"I wish I could do more, but—"

"You have done more than enough, Your Majesty," Barthol said, feeling almost ashamed by the queen's remorse.

The queen looked at Tolin. "I'll be sure to get you another for Overcaptain Asa. If you will be so kind as to make sure he gets it, along with my gratitude."

"Asa wanted to be here, Your Majesty," Tolin said, "but his nearing eviction hindered his attendance tonight."

"Be sure to tell him that I wish him well and I appreciate his exemplary service to Aramoor."

"I will, Your Majesty. And please, take our warning to heart. Aramoor is changing, and the palace is at the forefront of that change." Tolin looked at Amarysia. "Be sure to watch over her, and yourself."

Amarysia smiled and nodded.

"And if the need should arise, I would take the clan chief up on her word. There might come a time in the very near future when the Warrens will be the only safe place left in Aramoor."

Barthol shivered. "Creator help us all."

Chapter 66 | Kira

KIRA STEPPED OFF THE front porch and into the moonlight, her guards a step behind as they followed the walkway around to the carriage house and their awaiting horses. They walked the animals down the drive, stopping under a large oak that was growing at the front of the property, letting the shadow of its branches hide them from the streetlamp on the corner.

"Why didn't you say anything about what we found in the dungeons?" Po asked, keeping a tight rein on his skittish horse.

Kerson grunted, which mostly meant he agreed.

"What good would it have done?"

"You could have gotten Commander Tolin's help."

"Commander? He isn't the *commander* of anything. He's practically homeless. The only person in that room with any sway was the queen, and even she doesn't have much these days."

"Don't you think she deserves the right to know?" Po said. "Blazes, Kira! They're turning people into monsters down there."

"And how would a conversation like that go?" she asked, turning as if to address someone who wasn't there. "Oh, by the way, Your Queenness, did you know you have wielders living in your basement, performing all sorts of dark magic on the city's homeless?" She turned back to Po. "I'm sure that would have gone over well."

Po stiffened. "When you put it like that."

"How else would you put it? That's what happened." She punched her palm with her other fist. "We should have brought that body with us. Stupid of us to have left it there. We could have used it for proof. Let Tolin take that to the senators and see what their reaction is."

Po shivered.

"You couldn't pay me enough to touch that thing," Kerson said.

The man had a point. Kerson wasn't the sharpest tool in the pouch, but he tended to make good sense every now and then. Whatever it was they were doing down there was hideous.

Kira closed her eyes. She could see the transformed man begging for her to kill him, his one good eye pleading for death. She opened hers again. "It wouldn't have done any good to tell the queen. If we had and she went poking her nose around, she'd probably only succeed in getting it chopped off. Along with her head. Without Ayrion and the High Guard there for her protection, she's practically a prisoner in her own house. She just hasn't realized it yet."

"They'd kill her for sure," Kerson said, "and feed her body to the fishes."

"If they didn't try experimenting on her first," Po added, looking a bit pale.

They all shivered at that.

Kira mounted. "Best we leave them out of it for now." She looked at Po. "Head back to the Warrens and make sure those imbeciles haven't burned the place down in my absence."

"Where will you be?"

"I need to see an old friend."

Po frowned. He didn't like her wandering around Aramoor without him. In fact, he didn't much like her being anywhere without him, and he let her know in the manner in which he rode off—griping under his breath the whole way down the road.

Kira waited till he had turned on the first street heading south, then waited a little longer just to make sure he didn't try doubling back and following. She wouldn't have put it past him.

"What are we waiting for?" Kerson finally asked, staring up the empty street.

"Nothing, I guess."

Voices behind them signaled that the rest of the party had finally broken up and were leaving the commander's home.

"This way." She turned her horse opposite the direction Po had taken and nudged it with her boots. She groaned when it took off, the saddle slapping her backside until she could find a steady rhythm. She hated horses. But in a city this size, there wasn't much other choice.

They headed east, running parallel to King's Way, crossing the Tansian River just above the merchant district. The northeast quarter of the city wasn't nearly as affluent as the west, but it wasn't exactly Cheapside, either. The buildings were in good shape, not new but well maintained, and the streets were clean.

They passed the enormous cylindrical towers the tribal guild used for their meetings. Each tower was connected by a number of long covered walkways that looked out over a huge portion of the city. She wondered if the guild still had rooms there.

She had a lot of memories tied up with her time in the street tribes. A lot of memories she wished she could forget. Her eyes burned as her thoughts were once again drawn back to Ayri, the time they had spent as kids, the fights they'd had. He never let her get away with anything. She pinched her leg, trying to focus her thoughts.

Reaching the next street, she took them south. A quarter hour later, she turned off the main road and started east once again, heading toward the city wall. She could see the monolithic structure rising in the distance. They were getting close. She'd only been there a couple of times, and that was years back. On top of that, buildings tended to look different at night from how they did during the day. She hoped she recognized the place when she saw it.

Kira pulled her horse to a stop just outside a tall, somewhat older building on the left side of the road. Four stories, and every one of them filled. Two boys on the corner made a mad dash around the side. She didn't expect it would be too long before the welcoming party arrived.

"We'll leave the horses here," she said, gladly dismounting, adding, "They'll be safe enough," when she saw the troubled look in Kerson's eyes as he scanned the empty street.

"Where are we?"

The front door opened, and a very old man stepped out, his back bent with age, his white beard hanging down to his waist. He hobbled out to the front step and looked at them. "You just gonna stand there gawkin', or are you gonna tell me what you want?" His arm shook from the effort of balancing his weight on his cane.

Something about him seemed familiar.

"It's all right, Fentin," a voice behind the man said. Reevie limped out the front. "They're friends." He hobbled over to the front of the porch and looked down at Kira. "Correct?"

"You'd know it if we weren't." She turned and motioned for Kerson to follow, but Reevie raised his hand.

"The big man stays out here. He'd likely scare half the residents if he came inside."

Kira looked at Reevie for a moment, then finally nodded to Kerson. "Watch the horses."

"Didn't want to go in there, anyway," she heard him grumbling behind her.

She walked up the steps and onto the front porch. The old geezer blocking the doorway gave her a harsh look. Either that or his face was so wrinkled with age it had permanently formed that way. She tried not to stare as she went by, but there was something about him that she remembered.

Reevie looked at Fentin. "Kira here is—"

"I know exactly who she is," Fentin said, hobbling back inside and shutting the door behind them. "You've come a long way, young missy, since your time in the tribes."

She tried smiling. "Thank you."

He frowned. "It wasn't a compliment."

Reevie smiled. "Fentin, do you think you could get your wife to whip us up a couple of her famous sandwiches?"

Kira's head rose. Sandwiches. Now she knew where she'd seen him before. "You used to own that bookshop near the river."

Fentin smiled. "Aye. And if memory serves me correctly, it saved your skinny backside a time or two."

Kira nodded. "It did. I don't believe I ever thanked you for that."

"If you want to thank me, then leave us out of whatever scheming you have in mind. We have enough troubles of our own than to be adding the Warrens' mess on top of them." Fentin turned and grumbled all the way down the corridor toward the back.

"Pleasant fellow," she said.

Reevie smiled. "Orilla does make the most incredible sandwiches. Me and Ayrion used to call them her *mystery meat* sandwiches. She never would tell us what she used in them. Come to think of it, I still don't know." He shrugged. "But I'm sure you didn't come all this way to sample our fine cuisine." He pointed to a staircase on the other side of the front room. "This way."

They reached the second floor, then headed up an adjoining set of stairs to the third, all the while dodging kids. The place was crawling with them. Most stopped to stare at the strange woman in the red jacket; others, when they saw her, ran into the closest room to apparently spread the word about the visitor and returned with eight or nine more.

"Visitors usually mean the chance for an adoption," Reevie said over his shoulder.

She noticed a lot of the kids trying to flatten the wrinkles in their clothes or comb their hair with their hands; a couple of kids went so far as to lick their fingers and wipe the dirt off their faces. She tried not to notice, but it was difficult as they gathered in the halls to watch her go by.

Had she ever been that young? She couldn't remember.

"In here," Reevie said, opening a door at the end of the hall. The kids kept their distance from the room. He held the door open, and she walked in.

The room was quaint but tidy, with a bed positioned between two windows at the center, a dresser on the right, and a desk and chair in the corner. Griff lay in the bed.

A woman with thick blonde hair that hung halfway down her back turned from where she was sitting on the edge of the bed. She was holding a bowl of soup in one hand, spoon in the other. "I was wondering when you'd show up," she said, feeding Griff the soup. She looked at Kira. "You certainly haven't changed much. I see you're still wearing that gaudy coat."

"And I see that age hasn't bettered your manners any either, Sapphire," Kira said. "You always were a bit too stuck-up for your own good."

Sapphire laid the bowl down on the nightstand and stood. "Give me a sword and we'll see who gets *stuck*."

Kira pulled the dagger from her coat and spun it in the air, more for show than anything. Truth be told, she didn't have any desire to lock steel with the woman. Sapphire was probably the one person besides Ayri who might have actually been better with the sword than she was.

Reevie raised his hands and hobbled to the center of the room. "All right, enough's enough. I'm sure Kira didn't ride all this way just for the chance to insult you."

"Don't bet on it," Sapphire said, picking the bowl back up and sitting once more on the edge of the bed.

Reevie looked at Kira, as if waiting for her to agree.

She pointed to the bed. "I'm here to see Griff." She walked around to the opposite side and looked at the deep burns and scarring on the side of his body. The right side of his face had been burned as well, leaving a rather ugly patch of melted flesh. She couldn't help but wince when she saw him. "How bad is the pain?"

"Not too bad," he said, his throat raspy. "Whatever they're giving me is helping."

She looked at Reevie, who leaned against the railing at the foot of the bed. "Thank you for taking care of him."

"Least I could do for the ones who rescued me from a fate worse than death."

"You have no idea," she said, again thinking about that room where they had been experimenting on the homeless. She took a deep breath. "How's he doing?" she asked Reevie this time instead of Griff, who was trying to hold a brave face. From the slow slurps he took, she could see he was having a difficult time keeping it up.

"It's going to take time," he said, adjusting the blankets around Griff's feet. One foot was under the quilt, the partially burnt one on top. "The medicines are doing their job. It won't be an easy road back, but with time and some proper reconditioning, I suspect he'll make a full recovery." Reevie looked at Griff and smiled. "Might not be as pretty as you used to be, though."

Kira huffed. "A few good scars will do him some good." She looked at Griff. "Maybe now Gwen might pay you a little more attention."

Griff coughed, spilling some of the soup Sapphire had been feeding him.

She gave Kira a sharp look and wiped Griff's chin.

"I also came to say there's been some news concerning Ayrion's death."

Sapphire dropped the spoon in the bowl, and both she and Reevie turned to look at Kira. "What news?" she asked.

Kira spent the next couple of minutes retelling as best she could the information she'd gleaned from her meeting at Commander Tolin's house.

"I never liked Dakaran," Reevie said. "He was always a bad influence on . . ." He didn't say Ayrion's name, but everyone knew who he was referring to. "Even as kids, Dakaran always seemed to have a faerie in him. Troublemaker from the start."

"Is there anything else you can tell me of what happened to you in the dungeons?" Kira asked.

"Does he need to?" Sapphire said, setting the now empty bowl back on the nightstand. "He hasn't slept for days. Wakes half the orphanage up with his screaming."

Reevie's cheeks flushed.

"We need to know everything you saw. Even the smallest detail might be important."

"There's not much else to tell other than what you already know. They put bags over our eyes, loaded us on boats, and the next thing I knew, I was climbing a ladder and being hauled down a long corridor to those cages."

"How often did they bring new prisoners in? Did you know about the wielders? And what in flaming faerie fire were they doing to those people in that room?"

"All I can remember are the screams," he said, seemingly frozen in place, his eyes staring blankly at the wall behind the bed. "We never saw anything. People went in; no one came back out. At least, not the same way they had gone in. Mostly, the guards would carry out bags with what I can only imagine were body parts."

"That's enough," Sapphire said, raising her hand. "The last thing he needs is to relive that."

"It's all right," he said to Sapphire before turning to Kira. "To answer your question, no. I had no idea any of those people were wielders. In fact, the head of the White Tower was there on a regular basis—"

"The Archchancellor?" Kira asked. "Any idea what the Tower has to do with these atrocities?"

"Maybe they thought they were rounding up wielders."

"Not hardly," Kira hissed. "One way or another, we need to find out what's going on in there."

"That sounds like the perfect job for *you* to deal with," Sapphire said as she stood and crossed her arms. "But we have an orphanage to run. So, if you don't mind letting us get back to our work, there are kids that need putting to bed. Unless of course you'd like to stay and help give them their baths."

Kira took a step back. *Bathe the kids?* She had clearly overstayed her welcome. "Always a pleasure, Sapphire," she said with a smirk.

"You as well, Kira. I would say don't be a stranger, but . . ."

Kira held her smile until she left the room.

"That's about the friendliest I've seen you two in some time," Reevie said.

Kira rolled her eyes. She followed him down the stairs, where they met Fentin holding out a plate with a thick sandwich on top. "Don't mind if I do," she said with a wink as she relieved him of it.

He grumbled and walked off.

She had to admit it did smell good.

Reevie walked her to the door, and they stepped out on the front porch. Kerson was sitting on the top step, surrounded by four boys and a girl. They seemed to be in the middle of a staring contest. Kerson looked to be winning. She couldn't help but chuckle.

"Don't mind Sapphire," Reevie said, his breath misting in front of his face. Moonlight streaked the back of his head from a couple of holes in the porch roof. "She worries."

"Nothing wrong with that."

Reevie smiled. "Guess not."

Kira walked to the edge of the steps. "If you think of anything else, you know where I live."

"Yeah, the one place you'll never find me."

She laughed. "I'll be back to check on Griff. Is there anything you need me to bring? Herbs, food, better clothing?"

"All of it."

She smiled and headed down the porch steps, careful not to let the insides of her sandwich fall out as she climbed up into her saddle. "I'll see what I can do."

Chapter 67 | Breen

"TY'S NOT COMING?" Fraya asked, looking up at Breen from their side of the table. The meeting room was full. The only empty seat was Ty's. Even Gilly was there.

"Not this time," Breen said. He didn't like leaving his brother in the dark, but Ty had been acting more than a little strange the last couple of weeks.

"I heard about what happened in the prison," Fraya said, glancing briefly at Adarra on her left. Adarra kept her nose in her book, apparently not wanting to discuss it.

"What happened in the prison?" Feoldor asked, twisting the bracelet holding his transferal around on his wrist.

"It was nothing," Breen's father said, sitting directly to Breen's right. "Ty got a little overly ambitious when questioning the Tallosian prisoner."

"What does that mean?"

Breen's father cleared his throat. "He might have used some magic to throw him around the cell."

Feoldor smiled. "Flaming Northman deserves much worse, if you ask me."

Breen agreed. He wouldn't have minded a few minutes alone in the cell with the man either. But the problem wasn't the Tallosian. It was Ty. And not so much because he'd lost control and thrown the man around his cell, but because of the look in his eyes when he did it. It was like looking at a stranger. Breen couldn't help but think it might have something to do with that book Ty had taken from Mangora's shop. He had noticed the bulge in Ty's jacket where he seemed to be carrying it everywhere he went.

If it was the book, then maybe getting rid of his new bow might be the smart thing to do as well. He'd been practicing with it when no one was around and hadn't seen any ill effects, but he couldn't be sure. The thought of losing such an exquisite item turned his stomach. Perhaps it wasn't the book. Maybe Ty's recent near-death experience had made more of an impact than they realized. For all Breen knew, it could be some sort of residual effect of the spider's poison, or even the wizard's healing.

"Ty hasn't taken his mother's passing well," his father said, leaning forward far enough to see Fraya. "He blames himself. And it seems the only thing on his mind nowadays is Mangora." He clasped his hands together and sighed. "Best we leave Ty out of any further discussions that deal with the witch."

Feoldor huffed. "I wouldn't mind being left out of these discussions either. The two ventures I made into her shop were two too many for me. Place gives me the shivers."

"Why does Ty blame himself?" Reloria asked. "He fought just as hard as the rest of us."

"Ty blames himself because he is the one the Tower was after."

"Hogwash," Orlyn stated rather emphatically, the baggy sleeves of his robe resting on top of the table. "The Tower was coming for us regardless. They would like nothing more than to eradicate every last one of the wielder councils that oppose their agenda."

"Whatever that may be," Veldon said from the head of the table, kerchief clutched in one hand. "Other than rounding up every single ven'ae in the five kingdoms, we really have no idea what their overall goal is. The wizard says they want war. War with who? And why? More importantly, how does Ty fit into any of this? Sure, he's different. He has more than one gift, and if we are to believe Nyalis, he's part faerie. But is that really so important?"

"It is," Breen's father said, "if they plan on using him as a weapon."

Sheeva, who was sitting next to Breen's father, nodded in agreement, her amber eyes keeping a careful watch on everyone in the room.

"A weapon for what, though?" Breen asked. "Who do they expect him to fight?"

"Us," his father said, turning to look at him. "At least, that would be my guess." His father pulled his pipe from his inner jacket pocket and stuck it in his mouth. The stem had been replaced more times than Breen could count, from his father's nervous habit of chewing it off whenever he had some serious thinking to do.

"Don't like the sound of that," Feoldor said, tugging on his side whiskers. "Who knows what all that boy can do."

Reloria shook her head, then straightened the purple-and-gold bonnet on top.

Breen turned as Fraya took his hand in hers. He smiled, the tension easing slightly.

"Regardless of what the Tower's intentions are, we have more immediate problems to deal with," Breen's father said, bringing the conversation back around once again. The Easthaven Council had a tendency to chase jackrabbits. Everyone had their own concerns and opinions, making it difficult at times to keep meetings on track.

"Right you are," Veldon said, wiping the top of his head with his kerchief. "The witch's shop. Magical barrier or not, we can't have it simply sitting in the middle of town for anyone to accidentally stumble into—"

"More to the point," Orlyn said, "we don't want Mangora getting her hands on any of it. We have no idea where she went or if she'll be back. Best we keep what's inside good and hidden."

"And how do you plan to do that?" Feoldor asked. "Stuff it under your bed?" He smiled. "Or better yet, into one of those bottomless pockets in that robe of yours."

Breen chuckled at that.

"One thing's for sure," Feoldor continued, "I don't want any of her stuff in *my* house. Ow!" Feoldor looked at Reloria. "What was that for?"

"What?" Reloria asked, pretending she didn't know what he was talking about.

"Should we divide it up, or keep it all together?" Veldon asked.

"Doesn't really matter," Breen's father said, "as long as it remains hidden."

"What about here in the Harbor House?" Reloria said. "That way, we can all keep an eye on it."

Orlyn shook his head. "I think that would be a mistake. The temptation to trifle with some of it might prove dangerous even to us."

"That's right," Feoldor said adamantly. "I don't want that dark mess anywhere near me."

"What if we bury it?" Breen suggested. "There are places in the forest where I'm sure it could be kept safe."

Feoldor's brows lowered. "What, like dig a hole and toss it in?"

Breen nodded. "Why not?"

Feoldor shrugged. "Sounds good to me." He glanced at Veldon. "The sooner we're rid of it, the better."

Veldon fiddled with the piece of flint hanging around his neck. "Still sounds a bit unprotected, though."

"I can hide it," Gilly said in his usual playful voice.

Everyone turned to look at him.

"You believe you can hide her possessions, Gilly?" Veldon asked.

Gilly nodded energetically.

Feoldor laughed. "What are you going to do, toss them in the river?"

"No," Gilly said, raising his hand horizontally over the table and placing his transferal crystal below it. "I will hide them under it."

"How will you do that?" Fraya asked with a warm smile.

Gilly climbed down from his seat, his head not reaching much higher than the table. "Come. I'll show you." Before anyone could say anything, Gilly was out the door.

"I, uh . . . I guess this meeting is adjourned," Veldon said. "Or at least changing venues."

"I wonder where he's taking us," Fraya said, still holding Breen's hand.

Breen helped her up from her seat. "With Gilly, there's no telling." He followed his father and Sheeva out the door, across the cellar, and up the stairs to the Harbor House above. "Where are we going?" he asked the dwarf as the group gathered just inside the kitchen.

"The river," Gilly said, waiting on Eliab to lower his double crossbow and open the back door.

The Harbor House gatekeeper obliged and stepped out of the way.

"The docks?" Breen asked.

Gilly nodded and trotted down the back steps.

"We'll have to meet you there. Me and Fraya left our horses outside the East Inn."

"That's fine," Veldon said.

Breen and Fraya broke off from the rest of the group.

"We'll come with you," his father said, hurrying Adarra along to catch up. "We left ours in front of Orlyn's shop."

It didn't take them long to get from the Harbor House back to River Street. They stopped first at Orlyn's shop, where his father and Adarra had left Your Highness and Thistle, then headed north a couple of blocks to where Breen and Fraya had left their horses tied. Acorn looked happy to see him and snorted when he spotted Breen coming up the sidewalk.

"Sorry for leaving you here, boy," he said, rubbing the faint white spot just above Acorn's eyes. It was the only patch on the stallion that wasn't brown.

"Where did *that* bow come from?" his father asked, walking Your Highness around to the left side of Breen's horse. "I haven't seen it before."

Breen turned, and the breath caught in his throat. He'd forgotten to put the bow from Mangora's back in its hiding place in the barn. He'd been practicing with it earlier that day when they had gotten word about the council meeting, and in all the rush to keep Ty from knowing where they were going, he'd forgotten to replace it. "I, uh . . ."

What could he say? He couldn't tell him he'd found it amongst the Northmen bows. They'd already collected those, and none of them held a candle to this new one. He also couldn't tell him he'd gotten it in town. His father knew the artillator and would ask. "I bought if off a tinker earlier this week," he lied, nervously rubbing the back of his neck as he did. "The man was passing through Easthaven and had stopped at the inn for a drink." The more Breen lied, the tighter his stomach got. "He told me he had acquired some bows in Briston, and that Tallosian bow wasn't worth the wood it was made with."

His father lifted the black bow out of its holder on the front of the saddle. "You shouldn't be leaving something like this on your horse. It's a wonder it wasn't stolen." He tested the pull of the string. "Where did you say the tinker got it? This bow is exceptional."

"Uh. He didn't really say. Just somewhere in Briston."

"Did he have others?"

"None like this one. It's why I bought it. Cost me half my savings, but it was worth it."

"I'd say." His father held the bow up to study its markings. "Don't know if this is supposed to be a language or just decoration, but it's beautiful." He handed it back to Breen. "Take good care of it."

"I plan to," Breen said and placed it back in its holder. He wiped a sheen of sweat from his forehead. He hated lying to his father like that, but with all the talk of trying to secrete away the witch's belongings, he was too afraid to admit where he'd gotten it. "Best we get a move on," he said, trying to change the subject.

Adarra and Fraya were already mounted and waiting.

Breen swung up into the saddle, and they headed east toward the docks. The others were already there and waiting on the second pier from the end. Breen hopped down, grabbed his bow, and joined the others as they marched down the walkway.

"We were wondering if you'd gotten lost," Feoldor grumbled.

"We'll definitely need more than one boat," Orlyn said, looking at the group.

"That shouldn't be a problem," Veldon said, pointing to the left side of the dock. "Those two are available. Haven't rented them out in the last week, what with the colder weather coming in. Five in a boat." Which worked out evenly, since there were ten of them altogether.

"This is fun," Fraya said. She looked at Gilly. "Where are we going?"

Gilly placed a chubby finger to his lips. "Shh. It's a secret."

She winked in return.

Breen was the first to climb into the second boat. He helped Fraya and Adarra in after him, then grabbed one of the oars and waited for the others to board. The last time he'd been on the river, he'd been invisible, and Gilly had been at the helm, moving them so fast across the currents his eyes had watered. Being part of a community of wielders certainly had its advantages.

Breen sat on the left side, and his father the right. They raised the oars and loosed the mooring lines from the bow and stern. The water was cold but calm. The winds coming out of the north had slackened, and the sun was out, which helped against the chilly oncoming winter air. Working the oar might have been strenuous, but it kept his body warm.

Most of the regular seasonal traffic on the river had slowed, leaving

theirs the only boats on the river. After a good hour on the water, Gilly directed the boats toward the right bank and into a narrow canal that had been completely hidden by brush. If Gilly hadn't pointed it out, no one would have ever found it. Once through the brush, the stream took them away from the main branch of the river and was completely swallowed by the forest, blocking the late-afternoon sun from their boat and leaving Breen's teeth chattering.

"Kind of creepy in here," Fraya said, staring up at the low-hanging branches and vines that hovered from one side of the water to the other.

"I find it rather beautiful," Adarra said, closing her book and stuffing it inside her satchel. "A perfect getaway."

The top of the water was as calm as a sheet of ice.

The embankment on either side rose about fifteen feet off the water. From the front of the first boat, Gilly stood and pointed to something on the right. It appeared to be a small cottage peeking out from the heavy foliage on top of the rise. Was this Gilly's home? Breen knew the little man lived on the river, but he hadn't expected it to be quite so isolated. As far as hiding places went, this was certainly a good one.

Breen helped his father angle the boat toward the bank, where a small dock waited that ran from the water to a set of stairs that scaled the cliffside.

"We're here," Gilly said, hopping out of the first boat onto the rickety wooden slip. He tied the rope to one of the pilings and started climbing up the switchback staircase to the top.

Breen climbed out of the boat and finished securing it before helping the others out. "For someone who prefers to be alone, this place seems ideal."

"Clearly a good spot to keep the witch's belongings hidden," his father said as he walked Adarra down the loose planks of the dock to the stairs. Breen was the last one up, directly behind Fraya.

Gilly stood at the top, waiting patiently for the rest to make it up. As soon as Breen stepped off the stairs, he was moving again. "Come. This way."

Instead of taking them into the house, he guided them around the back, where they took a small trail leading even deeper into the forest. Breen, his father, and Orlyn had to duck on more than one occasion to keep from getting their heads caught in the overhead brush.

"Here we are," Gilly said, stepping into a small clearing and walking around to the other side of a large hole, probably eight feet in diameter.

Breen joined the others around the hole, staring down at the murky water that started about two feet down from the top.

"What's this?" Veldon asked.

Gilly smiled. "My hidey-hole."

"It's got water in it," Feoldor said. "We might as well just toss her stuff in the river, for all the good that'll do."

Gilly shook his head and laughed. "Jump!"

Feoldor huffed. "What do you mean, *jump*? You jump. I'm not throwing myself into a freezing bog hole." He looked at the others. "This was clearly a waste of time."

"No!" Gilly shouted, his stout finger pointing straight at Feoldor. It was the first time Breen had ever seen the little man angry. "You jump!"

Feoldor crossed his arms and took a step back.

This is getting ridiculous, Breen thought.

Suddenly, someone flew off the ledge. It was Adarra, satchel and all. But instead of plunging beneath the icy depths into whatever was down there, she landed softly on top of the water.

Gilly jumped up and down, clapping with excitement. "See! See!"

Everyone gawked in wonder as Adarra walked across the top of the water from one side of the hole to the other.

"Here goes nothing," Breen said, and stepped off the ledge. His feet hit the water, and just like his sister, he didn't go under. The bottom of his boots sloshed as though walking through a shallow puddle, but other than that, the rest of him remained dry. He looked up at the others and shrugged. "Seems safe."

One by one, the other members hopped down into the hole, chatting excitedly about the new experience.

Gilly was the last one in, after waiting for Feoldor to gather the nerve to jump himself. As soon as the dwarf was in, he pushed his way to the center. "Down."

The floor of water suddenly began to sink, lowering everyone into the hole.

"Whoa, what's going on?" Feoldor asked.

"I told you. Down."

"I can see we're going down. But down where?"

"You'll see. It's nice."

Breen kept his arm around Fraya as they continued to sink farther into the ground. He watched the hole above them shrink as the wind faded and everything grew silent. They had to be at least thirty feet underground. It was amazing. Pretty soon, the water slowed and then stopped altogether, revealing a stone tunnel behind them that headed back in the general direction of Gilly's house.

"This way," Gilly said as he stepped off the water and into the tunnel.

Feoldor quickly hopped in behind him, obviously wanting to get on solid ground as soon as possible.

A spark ignited near the front of the group, and a small blaze erupted in Veldon's hand, lighting the way ahead. He released the piece of flint hanging from his neck and held up the flame.

Breen's father was the last one off the platform. As soon as he stepped into the tunnel behind him, the water shot straight up into the air, filling the hole they had just come down.

A couple of the members gasped. Feoldor yelped and stumbled back, probably expecting the water to come crashing in and fill the tunnel they were in.

"We are safe," Gilly said, walking over to the wall of water blocking the tunnel. "See." He pushed against the liquid, and it didn't move.

Breen walked over and did the same. *Amazing!* It was cold and wet to the touch, like pushing against a large block of ice. He wondered what it must have been like living in Aldor back when magic had been so prevalent. The wonders they must have seen and accomplished. With a heavy sigh, he finally wiped his hand on his pants and took his place in line as the group followed Gilly, two by two, down the passageway.

The rock surrounding them was moist and smelled of mildew. Drops of water landed on his head and shoulders as they passed. The tunnel rose about seven or eight feet, so he didn't have to worry about bumping his head. It twisted and turned, eventually opening into a large cavern with shelves of rock lining the outer walls. A pool of water rested at the center of the cavern, clear enough to see that the bottom wasn't too far down.

Crystals growing from somewhere in the water produced a bluish light, bright enough to keep them from tripping on the protruding rock formations.

A few odds and ends had been left on one of the shelves near the entrance, most of which looked like children's toys: some carved animals, a wooden puppet, a couple of pinwheels in the shape of flower petals, a top with the string still attached, and a beautifully carved boat about the size of Breen's hand. Probably Gilly's collectibles. He was certainly a strange one.

"What is this place?" Orlyn asked. "It's quite lovely." He walked over to the right wall and laid his hand on the shelf, and a spray of winter lilies bloomed to either side. "The soil between the rock is rich."

Gilly clapped at the flowers.

"This is quite the hiding place, Gilly," Reloria said with a smile, releasing Feoldor's arm long enough to walk over and take a look at Orlyn's work. "No one would find the witch's stuff down here."

Veldon kept his flame raised as he circled the cavern. "Yes. But it's certainly going to take more work on our part."

"The extra effort will be worth it," Breen's father said, stopping beside the pool to look inside, "if it means keeping her stuff out of the wrong hands."

Veldon nodded.

Fraya tugged on Breen's arm, indicating she wanted to get closer to the water. So, he helped her to the edge, then knelt and stuck his hand in. It was freezing. "Where's the water coming from? Does this lead back to the river?"

"Yes," Gilly said, walking over and dropping a rock into the pool. It started to sink, but then hit some kind of unseen current and disappeared.

"Whatever you do, don't fall in," his father said half-jokingly.

Feoldor took a step back from the edge.

Everyone stood quietly around the pool. Everyone except Sheeva, who maintained her silent vigil near the exit as she kept an eye on the tunnel behind them.

The cavern was silent, peaceful, with nothing but the flicker of Veldon's flame and the lap of the water to be heard. Breen took a deep breath and slowly let it out, enjoying the moment.

"Best we be getting back," Veldon finally said, taking a step back. "Starting tomorrow night, we have our work cut out for us."

One by one, the members left the water and headed for the tunnel.

Breen wasn't exactly looking forward to spending his nights hauling Mangora's wares upriver, especially when it meant having to lie to his brother to keep it secret. He wished there was something he could do to help Ty, but his brother seemed bent on refusing to let him.

Chapter 68 | Ty

"WHERE ARE YOU GOING?" Ty asked Breen as his brother passed him on the way to the door. Breen was carrying his satchel over his shoulder, something he didn't normally take unless he was planning on going hunting.

"I'm going into town."

"At this time of evening?" Ty lifted his head from the sofa and looked out the front window. "The sun's almost down. It'll be dark before you get there."

Breen stopped, his hand on the door. "I'm . . . I'm meeting Fraya at the East Inn."

Ty lay back down, his head propped on the armrest. "When's Father and Adarra going to be back? Weren't they meeting with Barl?"

"Father was," Breen said, turning the handle and opening the front door. "You know Adarra, though. Any chance to spend time with Aiden." Breen chuckled, but it sounded forced. "Don't burn the house down while I'm gone." With that, his brother walked outside and let the door shut behind him.

"See. I told you, you couldn't trust him," the book said.

Ty spun the glass ring on his finger. "He said he was meeting Fraya."

"And you believe him?"

He shrugged as though someone were there to see. "He's my brother."

"A brother who's jealous of what you can do. Of what you'll become."

"You don't know what you're talking about."

The distorted voice laughed. *"I know much more than you realize."*

Ty closed his eyes. "Oh?"

"The knowledge I hold in my pages goes back millennia. I was created by wizards, breathed on by dragons. You couldn't begin to understand the depths of the information I possess. Unless of course you . . ." There was a moment's pause. *"Never mind."*

"What?" Ty asked, sitting up. "What were you going to say?"

"No. It's too dangerous. You're too young. Too inexperienced."

Ty scooted to the edge of his seat and raised his hand to look at the ring. "I'm not too young! Tell me."

"Very well. There is one way to access my knowledge. But it requires a blending."

"A blending?" Ty's heart was racing. He might not have to go to Aero'set after all. Why risk his life to bring back some mythical wizard's keep when everything he needed to defeat Mangora could be right here? Was Nyalis simply using him to get what *he* wanted?

"It's a joining of the minds. My mind and yours."

"How does it work?"

"You would have to open your mind, free your thoughts, and release your magic into me."

"How do I do that?"

"You would start by holding the book in your hands and thinking about my pages. Blank. Nothing there but emptiness waiting to be filled.

Your mind should be the same. Once you've freed your mind of all thoughts, then you'd release your magic into me, and I would do the rest."

"Does it hurt?"

"I won't lie. It's a tricky spell. Conjuring it can be dangerous. Sometimes fatal."

Ty sighed and plopped back in the seat.

The book chuckled. *"But if it were to work . . . oh, the power you could have. I could teach you what it really means to be a faeling. Why the Tower wants you. I could even help you find your father."*

Ty's head shot up. "My father?"

"Your real father."

"You mean the faerie?"

"You didn't think he simply vanished into thin air, did you? I can show you how to track him."

Ty wasn't sure if he wanted to know where his father was or not. But his head was certainly swimming with other possibilities. The things he could do with such knowledge. He wouldn't need Nyalis after all. He could find Mangora himself. Kill her. Make her pay for what she took from him. Then he could visit the Tallosians and put a stop to whatever it was they had planned. He could protect his family in a way he hadn't been able to before. He stopped and took a breath. He needed to think. As tempting as this sounded, the potential of what this joining could do was a little intimidating, if not terrifying, especially considering the book's warning that it could be fatal. "I'll think about it."

"What is there to think about, boy? I'm offering you the wisdom of the ages."

"You just said that it could be—"

The sound of hoofbeats caught his attention. He stood and walked to the window and looked out. He watched Breen ride down the drive toward the road.

"Go on. You know you want to follow him. And when you see that

I'm telling you the truth about him having secrets, will you consider the blending?"

Ty took a moment to think about it. "Maybe."

"Then what are you waiting for?"

What *was* he waiting for? Ty took off for his room and threw on his boots and coat. As fast as he could, he ran out the door and headed for the barn. He didn't even give Waddle time enough to finish his feed before he had him out of the stall, saddled, and walking outside.

Waddle blew out his lips in aggravation.

"Fine. Here's an apple to make up for it." Ty held out the piece of fruit, and Waddle gratefully accepted. The horse barely had time to chomp it down, though, before Ty was in the saddle and snapping the reins. "Let's go."

The sun had completely set by the time he reached the main road leading north toward Easthaven. And since the moon had barely had time to rise, Ty was forced to keep Waddle to a slow trot. He kicked himself for not thinking to grab a lantern; then again, it might have just drawn unwanted attention.

A mile or two up the road, Ty spotted Breen. His brother had just crested the East Bridge, heading into the city proper. Breen didn't look to be in much of a hurry, which was surprising, considering he was on his way to see Fraya. Ty slowed even further as he entered the shopping district, not wanting to be spotted if his brother happened to look behind him. He knew where Breen was going, so it wasn't like he needed to rush.

River Street was fairly empty this time of night. Most of the windows in the surrounding buildings were shuttered, with light seeping through the cracks. Supper was over, and children were no doubt being tucked into bed.

Ty kept to the edge of the street, letting the lamps guide his horse's steps. The sound of Waddle's hooves on the worn cobbles echoed off the front of the shops they passed, leaving him with an uncomfortable feeling. Mostly guilt for the sneaking around he was doing. Was he really so paranoid about his brother hiding something from him that he had to be spying on him in the middle of the night?

He almost stopped and turned around, but there was a nagging feeling in the back of his mind that kept him going. What if the book was right? Anyway, it wasn't much farther. He'd come this far; he might as well see it through. Once he proved the book wrong, he could go home and crawl into bed. The thought of sliding under his thick quilt had him yawning.

Ty caught his first glimpse of the inn ahead and pulled back on the reins. He waited in the shadows of a building a couple of shops up from Orlyn's apothecary. Ahead, Breen had stopped Acorn at the hitching rail in front of the inn but hadn't climbed down. What was he doing? There were a number of other horses tied off, which meant the inn was busy tonight.

This is getting ridiculous, he thought as he held up his hands to blow some warmth back into them. Was all this really worth it? Not only had he not brought a lantern, but in his mad rush to leave the house, he'd forgotten his gloves as well. Thankful his cap was in his jacket pocket, he quickly put it on. Besides keeping his head warm, he needed to keep his white hair covered while in town.

Ty heard the faint sound of another horse approaching from the other side of the inn, and a lone rider rode out of the darkness. Ty was too far away to see the person's face, but he could tell it was a woman.

By the time she pulled her horse alongside Breen's, there was no doubt. It was Fraya. She was wearing another one of those colorful ribbons in her hair, something she generally wore whenever Breen was around. Ty shook his head. "See? I told you Breen wasn't lying."

"Oh? Then why aren't they going inside?"

Ty's eyes widened as his brother and Fraya turned their horses and headed straight for him.

Quickly, he jerked Waddle to the right into a narrow alley stacked with old barrels, barely managing to squeeze between them. He lowered himself on Waddle and held his breath, waiting for them to pass. Fortunately, Breen was too focused on Fraya to notice Waddle's backside sticking partway out of the alley.

"Where are they going?"

"How should I know? One thing's for sure: it certainly isn't where he said."

"Actually," Ty corrected, sticking up for his brother, "Breen said he was *meeting* Fraya at the inn. He didn't say they were going inside."

He could almost hear the book rolling its eyes. He didn't believe it either. He didn't know what hurt worse: admitting he might be wrong, or the reason for it.

Quietly, Ty backed Waddle out of the alley and started after his brother. The farther they got from the inn, the angrier he became. Had his brother lied to him? By the time he reached the city square, Breen and Fraya were nowhere to be seen. Where had they gone?

Frantically, he moved Waddle out from around the corner and spotted them on Wood Lane, heading east. He pulled to a stop, hoping they didn't turn. Ty could only think of one reason why Breen would be heading down that side of Wood Lane. *Surely, he isn't . . .*

His brother stopped just between the spice shop and the fuller's.

"Why is he taking her there?" His stomach tightened as his brother directed Fraya into the all-too-familiar side street beside the spice shop.

"I told you they were up to something."

Ty didn't respond. He kicked Waddle, and they crossed Wood Lane, heading back in the direction of the East Bridge. He couldn't leave his horse to be spotted, so he rode until he found an alley to hide him in, one large enough for Waddle to actually fit.

He hopped down and grabbed the reins.

Waddle jerked his head.

"Come on. Quit being so difficult. I'll be back." He pulled Waddle deep enough into the alley that the streetlamps couldn't reach him and tied him to a half-filled barrel of what looked like milled flour. He wasn't sure why the chandler wasn't storing it in his cellar as opposed to the alley, but from the rancid smell, he thought he could guess.

Ty released a little magic and connected with his horse. He could feel Waddle's unease. Waddle didn't like being stuck in such a confined space. He also didn't appreciate the smell. "Sorry, boy," he said, feeling bad for leaving him tied to something that stank so bad. "Can't be helped."

Ty took a moment to make sure no one was coming before stepping out from between the buildings and scurrying down the walkway. He stopped at the corner of Wood Lane, his breath misting in front of his face as he peered around the edge of the building. The street was empty. Perfect. Keeping to the shadows at the front of the buildings, he worked his way down the street.

As soon as he reached the spice merchant's shop, he stopped and listened. He could hear voices. He thought he recognized Orlyn's. But why would—

Then it hit him. They were moving Mangora's stuff without him. Even after they told him they would be sure to let him know. His fists clenched tight enough for his nails to dig into his palms. *They lied.*

"I don't know why you're surprised. I keep telling you, but you don't listen. They've been lying to you from the start. They have no intention of letting you anywhere near her magic. My guess is they plan to destroy it. You need to stop them before they do."

"And how exactly am I going to stop them?"

"Blend with me and I'll show you."

"I told you, no."

"What about the books? They're going to take them as well. Do you really want to lose the wealth of information they hold?"

Ty's head was pounding. He did want those books, especially the one concerning the hidden magic of the Fae. He wanted to know more about his heritage. Where he came from. What his people were really like. He had never admitted it, but there had always been a part of him that longed to know who he was, and ever since finding out about his Fae lineage, that desire had only grown.

"Do something before it's too late."

He peeked around the corner. There was a wagon just outside her shop, and it was packed to the brim. He didn't see Breen or Fraya, but he did spot Orlyn standing to the side, leaning on his staff. Feoldor was in the bed of the wagon, stacking crates of items that the others brought out to him.

Someone else was leaving the shop with an armload of stuff. Ty craned his neck to see who it was. By the size, it looked like Breen. He dropped the load in the back and turned. Ty gasped.

It was his father.

Ty couldn't believe it. His father had lied to him as well.

"I'm sorry you had to find out like this, but it's better you see it now than later. You're not like the rest of them. You're not even human. The faeries enslaved this world when they came. Nearly destroyed it. Do you think they're going to trust a half-faerie with something as powerful as the witch's belongings?"

Ty's face was red. "How can I stop them?"

"Blend with me."

Ty shook his head. "It's too dangerous. There's got to be another way. Surely with all that wealth of knowledge, you can help me get those books."

"It's not that simple. The spells and conjuring you might need take time to learn. It would be much easier for me to just give it to you all at once."

"I . . ."

The sound of reins popping pulled Ty from the conversation in time to see the wagon laden with Mangora's wares heading up the narrow street in his direction.

"Blazes!" He turned and ran back up Wood Lane for the first opening he could find to hide in. He'd barely started to squeeze between two buildings when the horses pulled out onto the road. Feoldor held the reins and turned the team to the right and away from Ty. He watched as the entire entourage made its way east down Wood Lane. Feoldor and Orlyn rode together in the front seat while Sheeva sat in the back with the merchandise. Behind the wagon, Fraya, Veldon, and his father kept their horses in single file.

He had seen Mistress Reloria at one point during the loading, but she wasn't riding with them. And where was Adarra? More importantly, where were they taking the wagon? He had hoped they would take it to the Harbor House—at least then he could sneak in and take a look through the stuff—but they were going in the opposite direction.

Ty stepped out from his hiding spot and followed, trying not to get too close but not letting them get so far ahead that he lost them. The wagon turned left down Lynden, which ran parallel to River Street just behind the shopping district. Where were they going?

About three streets up, Feoldor turned the wagon east toward the docks.

Were they going to toss her stuff in the river? Surely not. Ty picked up his pace. He stopped at the corner of the street they'd taken and peeked around the side of the three-story home he was pressed against.

Sure enough, they were heading straight for the docks. Keeping to the shadows wasn't very difficult, since there was no lamp on this street to guide his way. The lack of light slowed his progress as he felt his way along the sides of the buildings, trying not to trip over loose crates and piles of trash sitting just outside the doors. He stopped and waited against the last house on the left and watched as Feoldor and Orlyn pulled the wagon around in front of the second pier. The two men crawled into the bed of the wagon and started handing stuff down to the others.

Ty's hands were shaking. He couldn't let them just throw it all in the river. There was a wealth of untold things there that could be used to help him fight the Tower. He had to stop them. He stepped out from the shadows, then stopped when he noticed someone standing in one of the boats. It was Gilly. Why was he—

His father had the first armload, but instead of chucking it in the water, he handed it down to Gilly, who promptly dropped it in the bow of the boat. Ty stepped back in the alleyway and waited as the council members unloaded the wagon, stacking what was in it into three separate skiffs, leaving only just enough room for the members to sit. Ty watched as the three boats parted from the dock and started north up the river.

"Well, what are you waiting for? Follow them."

Ty ran down the gravel embankment to the boardwalk leading to the docks. A couple of flatboats and a few small sculls and dinghies were tied to the piers. Spotting one small enough for a single rower, he hopped in and released the rope from the dock shoe. Locking the oars into place, he started rowing.

By now, the moon had risen above the trees, casting its pale glow across the water, leaving a sparkle across the top like millions of tiny glowing fish swimming just below the surface. The water was calm, which meant he didn't have to fight too hard against the current, something his arms were grateful for.

Up ahead, the river cut back into the Sidaran Forest, leaving Ty straining to see where he was going. Somehow, he'd lost sight of the other boats. He stopped rowing altogether, afraid of catching up to them without realizing it. Cocking his head, he listened for the sound of their oars. Other than the water, he heard nothing.

Ty wanted to throw the oar in the water, or at least hit the boat with it. "I can't see anything," he said.

"Which is why you need to blend with me, so I can help you."

Ty was tempted to say yes just to shut the book up. Instead, he rowed all the harder. After what felt like an hour but was probably only a quarter of that, he stopped again, still not having spotted the three boats. They couldn't have gotten that far ahead. Could they? "Give me something."

"I've already told you how to get it."

Ty huffed and started rowing once again. He needed to do something. He'd lost them, and even with the available moonlight, there was enough brush lining the embankments that they could have stowed their boats and he'd never know it. He might have already passed them. Frustrated, he released the oars and let the boat drift in the current. "What good are you if you can't help me find them? I can't see anything out here."

"You're trying my patience, child."

Ty gritted his teeth. "I'm not a child."

"Then prove me wrong and do what needs to be done."

"You're the one who said how dangerous it was. *Fatal,* I believe, is the word you used."

"Yes, well, I might have overstated the risk. For a non-wielder it would be fatal. For a ven'ae whose abilities have not been strengthened through practice and training, it can prove extremely dangerous. But for you, a half-faerie who has clearly seen extensive use of his gifts, I don't see any lasting problems. But if you are too frightened to try, then there might be one thing I can give you."

"What is that?" Ty huffed, his patience running thin. He didn't like being called a coward, or a child, and was about two shakes of a horse's tail away from tossing the ring and the book in the river and being done with it.

"Repeat what I say. Exactly. Ru'kasha Kor. *"*

Ty waited for more. "Is that it?"

"Say it exactly as I did."

Ty took a deep breath. "*Ru'kasha Kor.*" Nothing happened. What was supposed to happen? "I don't feel anything. Did it work?"

"No. You didn't use any magic, and you pronounced it incorrectly. It's not Ru *as in* rug*. It's* Ru*, as in your skills are rudimentary."*

Ty gritted his teeth. "Fine. I'll try again." This time, he opened himself up to his magic, letting the warmth of it fill him before speaking. "Here goes nothing." He took another deep breath. "*Ru'kasha Kor.*"

Chapter 69 | Ty

THE WORLD BRIGHTENED. He could see everything. The river, the trees, even the brush along the embankments. It was amazing. It wasn't like seeing things in the bright of day, more like a grey dawn where the sun hadn't risen high enough for the colors to be seen. The moon was still the natural source of light, but its luminance was much stronger. In a way, it reminded him of the effects of Sheeva's invisibility, where everything seemed a little washed out.

"What happened?" he asked, holding up his hand and noticing he could even see the glass ring.

"This is but a minute amount of knowledge I can bestow once you agree to the blending. You now have the ability to see in the dark like an Upakan."

"How long does it last?"

"Until you decide to stop it."

"And how do I do that?"

"By repeating this: Ru'kasha Sve.*"*

"*Ru'kasha Sve.*" The world dimmed, and he found himself in the dark once more, barely able to see the shoreline. "*Ru'kasha Kor.*" The world brightened. His earlier hesitancy about the blending was fast dissolving. If this was just a sample of what he could gain, why was he saying no? He shook his head. Now wasn't the time to do anything drastic, though. He needed to find those boats. Grabbing the oars, he put his back into it.

Another quarter hour passed, and his arms were beginning to burn, but there was still no sign of the council members. They couldn't have gotten that far ahead. He rowed around the next bend.

Something moved just ahead on his right. *What was that?*

He thought he had seen the back of one of the boats sliding into the brush a few hundred feet upriver, but he wasn't sure. Angling his boat closer to the right shore, he kept rowing until he reached the spot where he thought it went in.

There was nothing but undergrowth stretching from the trees down the embankment and into the water. He poked his way along the shore with one of the oars, pushing branches and low-hanging moss aside as he went. About twenty feet up, his oar hit a section of limbs that spread when he pushed. They weren't connected to anything.

This had to be it.

Pushing the branches aside with his oar, he guided the boat inside. The brush slid back into place behind him as soon as he made it through. *Clever,* he thought. Even with the aid of this new magic, he would have never found this place if he hadn't seen the other boat. He released a short sigh of relief, then started rowing, his nerves tingling the farther he went. He was almost afraid of what he might find.

Unlike the main branch of the river, the water here seemed calm, at least on the surface, almost the way he felt inside at the moment. There was no telling how deep it went. He looked over the edge of the boat, but it was too murky to see much more than his reflection. The trees overshadowed the waterway, blocking the moon's light. If it wasn't for this new night sight, he'd be sitting in total darkness.

He slowed when he heard voices ahead, relying on just a single oar instead of two. A sharp curve in the waterway kept him from seeing what was going on. Quietly, he edged his boat closer to the right shoreline as he neared the bend. The embankment on either side of the water rose probably twenty feet—as though the river had sliced straight through the middle of a hillside—making it more than a little difficult to reach the top without a rope and a good pair of climbing boots.

Scooting to the front of the boat, he worked his way along the edge of the mud and rock and peeked around the corner.

There they were. His heart was racing, each beat pulling him closer to a confrontation he wasn't looking forward to having.

All three boats were tied to a small dock that was attached to a winding set of stairs, leading up to the top of the rise. An old cabin stood just back from the ledge, watching the water below like a sentinel. Was this where Gilly lived? Admittedly, it seemed a good place to store the items if the goal was to keep them out of the wrong hands. He just couldn't believe that those hands had been *his*.

He waited and watched as the council members each took an armload and started for the stairs. He figured he better get comfortable, because this was going to take all night. However, before they reached the head of the dock, Gilly ran up the stairs and shouted something down to those at the bottom before lowering a large basin over the side, attached to some kind of makeshift pulley.

As soon as the basin hit the dock, the members began filling it with the cargo from the boats. It took about seven loads, but they managed to get it all to the top of the rise.

As Ty waited, he mulled over what he could possibly say when he faced them. He had originally intended to remain hidden, to not let them know he had discovered their plotting, but the more he thought about it, the more he wanted them to know they hadn't gotten away with anything. Every member of the council had lied to him, gone behind his back, and purposely hid what they were doing. His own family had betrayed his trust, which hurt more than anything. What's worse was that he had no idea why they'd done it.

"Quit feeling sorry for yourself, and go find out what they're doing with those books. You can't let them be destroyed."

The book was right. Now wasn't the time to be wallowing in self-pity. Before he confronted them, he needed to find out what they were up to and make sure they didn't destroy the very things that might tell him who he was.

As soon as the dock and ramp were empty and the last of the members had left the edge, he guided the boat around the bend and started for the pier. He tied the boat with a very loose knot in case he needed to make a quick escape, then made his way up the rickety switchback staircase.

He stopped before reaching the top and peered up over the edge. There was no one there. All the windows in the house were dark, and he couldn't hear any noises coming from inside. He did hear something from around the back of the house, though, farther in the woods. He climbed off the step and quietly moved through the brush around the side of the house.

The back was empty. He was starting to get tired of this cat-and-mouse hunt.

He noticed a narrow path leading from the back of the house into the woods, and not seeing any other reasonable explanation as to where they had gone, he took it.

He slowed when he heard voices ahead, stopping before reaching what appeared to be a small clearing in the trees. He moved into the brush on the side of the path and crawled forward. He couldn't make out what they were saying, but he did recognize Gilly's voice. He wanted to peek through the brush, but he was too afraid they'd spot him. What were they doing out there? Burying it?

Ty wasn't sure, but it sounded as though the voices were growing

fainter. *They must be on the move again.* He stood and headed back for the path, stopping just outside the clearing where he spotted the hole. *They* are *burying it.* He ground his teeth and started for the hole but stopped and dropped to his stomach when he heard voices coming from inside.

Quickly, he crawled to the edge of the pit and peeked in. He couldn't hear the voices any longer. Where'd they go? Then he heard something else. It sounded like water, and it was getting louder.

Ty jumped back, landing on his backside as a wave of water shot straight up the hole. He waited for it to blow out over the top and soak him, but not a single drop made it above the lip. He crawled back to the edge and looked inside. The water had stopped about two feet from the top.

He wanted to scream. Now how was he going to get those books? He doubted he could swim down. He had no idea how far it went. He stared at the water, and finding he didn't care anymore, he leaned back and yelled at the top of his lungs.

"You see. This is what you get when you don't listen."

"Shut up!" Ty said, staring at the hole.

The book groaned. *"Is this truly what I have been relegated to? I was created for the use of wizards, and now I find myself in the hands of a child too afraid of disappointing the very people who have lied to him to do what's necessary. Do you really want to put your life in the hands of liars? Or do you want the ability to protect yourself? With the knowledge I hold in my pages, I can not only get you down there, but I can help you become what you were created to be. You'll never have to depend on anyone ever again."*

Ty's knuckles were white. Why was he still fighting this? Even if a fraction of what the book had said was true, wouldn't it be worth it to try?

"Make your decision, child . . ."

An image of his mother being feasted on by the spiders flooded his

thoughts. He had been too weak to stop it then.

" . . . *before it's too late.*"

"Fine!" He pulled the book out from his pocket and cleared his mind. He let go of his anxiety, his anger, his fear. He shut out the images of his mother, of the council, of the water just below him, and concentrated on nothing but the blank pages of the book. He closed his eyes.

He was ready.

"*Good. Now release your magic into me.*"

Ty obeyed, and the magic poured from him like it had during his fight with Mangora. He could feel the burning in his arm where the mark was undoubtedly growing. He wanted to open his eyes, but he was too afraid of breaking his concentration.

"*Yes. More. Release it all.*"

Ty didn't hold back. He shattered every dam and let the floodgates of his magic surge into the book until he had nothing left to give. The heat was gone, and he felt nothing but cold and numb. There was no pain. In fact, he felt nothing at all: not the wind on his face, the book in his hands, or the clothes on his back. He couldn't even feel the ground under his feet. He felt . . . *nothing*!

"*What happened?*" Ty tried asking, but nothing came out. Had it worked? He didn't feel smarter. Something wasn't right. "*Hello? Are you still there?*" He tried opening his eyes, but he couldn't. He was left alone to the darkness.

"Of course I'm here," the book said, but somehow with Ty's voice. "And let me say, it feels wonderful."

"*Wait. Why do I hear you speaking and not me? What's happening?*"

Ty's eyes opened involuntarily. He was still standing near the edge of the hole. He tried moving his arms, but like his eyes, they wouldn't obey him. "*Something's wrong.*"

"On the contrary, my little faeling. Everything is exactly as it should be. Thank you so much for the loan of your body. It's quite something."

"You did this on purpose?"

"Ever since you first walked into my store all those weeks ago, I could have never in my wildest dreams imagined we would be connected in such a way."

The book cackled, and this time, even hearing it through his own voice, Ty recognized it immediately. *"Mangora?"*

She laughed. "And he finally catches on."

"How?"

"You didn't think I'd just up and leave without some sort of assurance that my task would be completed, did you? I'm the last of the Ahvari witches. My bloodline runs all the way back to Pinnella Ahvari herself."

"But how could you have known I'd take the book?"

"I saw your fascination with them the first time, so I spelled it to call to you. Simple spell, really, but one that has produced overwhelming results."

He wanted to heave, but he couldn't even do that. The very person he'd been trying to find a way to kill had been with him all along, listening to his thoughts, feeding his emotions and desires. He wanted to punch himself in the face for being so stupid, or at least throw himself in the pit and let the water take him. Every inch of his skin crawled.

How could he have been so blind? She was right. He was a child. An ignorant, petulant, goat-sucking child. And now, she had taken everything.

Ty concentrated as hard as he could to move a leg, an arm, a single finger.

But nothing happening.

"I'd forgotten how good it feels to be young," she said as she ran his hands down his chest. She hopped up and down, then ran in a circle around the hole. Twice. "To be able to move like this is wonderful." She raised his left hand, and blue flames burst from his palm.

He could feel a small tingling in his arms from the release, but nothing more.

"Oh, my. I can feel it. You are powerful." Both hands rose this time, aiming at the trees to either side of the hole. Mangora mumbled something under her breath, and a torrent of fire burst from his palms, burning everything around him. It was more powerful than anything he'd ever accomplished before. The tingling sensation in his arm grew. His arm felt much the same as waking in the middle of the night to discover he'd been lying on it, and it had gone to sleep.

Releasing Ty's fire, she lowered his hands and shook his head. "Such a waste. Oh well." She walked over to the hole and looked in. "Now to get my stuff back."

"What are you going to do?"

"I'm going to finish what I started." She leaped from the edge of the hole and Ty yelped.

He was even more surprised when she landed on top of the water without sinking in.

"Your voda is more talented than I gave him credit for."

"You mean Gilly?" Ty's heart was pounding; at least, he thought it was his heart. Maybe it was just his imagination. He tried to determine what to do. He'd rather die than allow her to use his magic to kill everyone he cared about.

"Aquaria Lavidia," Mangora said, and the water they were standing on began to lower.

The opening to the hole grew smaller as they descended into the pit.

"Please, I'll do anything you want. Just don't hurt them." It turned his stomach to beg, especially to her. But at this point he was too desperate to care. She had all the control.

"You'll do anything I want either way."

Water ran down the mud-slicked sides of the pit as they lowered into the darkness beyond. Ty tried looking up to see how small the hole had gotten to estimate how far down they'd gone, but he couldn't get his head to work. He was resigned to looking down at his feet and the shelf of water he was miraculously standing on.

He tried everything he could to take control back, focusing as hard as he could to move. He had to reclaim his body before they reached the bottom and she made him do something he'd never forgive himself for.

The water slowed, stopping altogether as they reached the entrance of a tunnel. Ty breathed a small sigh of relief when he realized no one was there. Again, he willed his legs to stand in place, but no matter how hard he tried, he had no control.

"Interesting," Mangora said as she stepped off the platform and into the tunnel. She spared a quick glance over her shoulder. The water remained where it was. "Who would have ever thought your little council was so resourceful?"

"They're smarter than you think."

"I doubt that," she said as she started down the tunnel. It seemed to be heading back in the direction of the river.

"They defeated your army of bulradoer and Black Watch."

Mangora laughed, but softly. "That was hardly an army. One single contingent of Black Watch and what? Four bulradoer?"

"Five," Ty corrected.

"Oh, forgive me. Five." She raised Ty's hands and studied them. "You'll find that things have changed considerably."

"If you hurt them, I'll kill you! You hear me?"

"I can't help but hear you, boy," Mangora gruffed. "An unfortunate side effect of this magic."

They continued forward slowly. Mangora remained vigilant, carefully checking the way ahead as if expecting it to be laced with traps. Ty wondered how much time he had to stop her before they reached his family.

His heart sank when he heard voices ahead.

A couple of rocks skidded around the corner and stopped a few feet from where they were standing. Someone was coming.

Mangora quickly moved up against the left wall and waited.

Ty tried to shout. To warn them. He fought to move, to make some noise, to do anything. He was as useless as he'd been the day his mother died.

Gilly waddled around the corner, and Mangora grabbed him by the neck and shoved him up against the side of the tunnel, Ty's hand pressed against his mouth. The little man jumped up and down, trying to break free, but Mangora's grip was firm. There was confusion in his eyes as he saw who had him, and for a brief moment, he stopped struggling. That's when Mangora slammed his head up against the stone wall. He cried out, but his scream was muffled by Ty's hand.

"Stop! You're going to kill him!" Blood seeped down the side of Gilly's face where it had hit one of the rocks jutting from the wall.

"Don't move, midget," she said. "Don't even whimper, or I'll turn your insides out and let you play with them before you die."

Gilly went limp in Ty's arms. The confusion on his face burned Ty to the core. Ty tried looking away so he didn't have to see the hurt in the man's eyes, but it was no use. He was forced to watch it all.

Mangora shoved Gilly forward, using him as a shield as she marched him toward the voices.

The tunnel opened into a small cavern with a pool of water at its center. Natural shelves of rock protruded from the wall, each lined with rows of items from her shop as the members unloaded the crates they'd carted down.

"Well, isn't this quite the handy little hideaway," Mangora said, stepping out of the tunnel with Gilly in front. "Glad to see you've made such good use of my stuff."

Everyone turned.

"Ty?" His father stepped away from one of the shelves at the back and started forward. "What are you . . . How did you find this place?" He stopped in back of the pool and looked at Gilly, then at Ty. His brows lowered with the same confused look that Gilly had when Mangora had pinned him against the wall. "Gilly, are you all right?"

Gilly didn't move.

"He will be as soon as you tell me what you think you're doing here."

"Look, Ty, I'm sorry we didn't tell you, but with everything you've been through lately, I thought it best we didn't add to your troubles." He took a step forward. "Mangora seems to be growing into an obsession. And we can all see it's affecting you."

"It's not me!" Ty shouted, but no one heard him.

"Just let Gilly go, son," his father said, moving a little closer.

"Don't take another step," Mangora threatened, raising Ty's hand and calling on his magic. Blue flames rose from his palm.

His father's expression shifted from confusion to concern, and he froze, glancing at the others. "Why are you acting like this, Ty?"

Ty fought to break free. *He* was in control, he told himself. He concentrated on a single action: moving his hand away from Gilly's neck. He tried to remember what it felt like for his elbow to bend, his fingers to curl, his shoulder to turn.

Nothing. He wanted to cry. This couldn't be happening. Not again.

"Ty, what are you're doing?" Breen asked, stepping away from the right wall, keeping Fraya protectively hidden behind him. "Have you completely lost your mind? Let Gilly—"

"Stop!" Mangora shouted, pointing at Breen. "I said don't take another step."

Breen froze. "It's that book, isn't it?"

Mangora pushed Gilly farther into the chamber, closer to where the others were now standing. "Not so thick-headed after all."

Ty's father looked at Breen. "What book?"

"What do you want?" Ty yelled at Mangora. *"If you want your stuff, then let me talk to them. I can persuade them."*

Mangora laughed. "Nice try."

"The boy's gone daft," Feoldor said on the left, holding one half of a chest while Orlyn held the other.

"You got brain rot, boy?" Orlyn asked, slowly lowering the container and reaching for his staff.

"Ah! Don't you think about it."

"Please," Ty finally begged, realizing his threats were as hollow as the cave they were standing in. *"Please, don't hurt them."*

The tension in the room was as sharp as a knife. One little spark would set the whole thing—

Gilly raised his hand.

Ty froze. *No!*

A column of water rose from the center of the pool and flew straight back at them. But before it hit, Mangora muttered something under her breath and sent it careening into the wall behind them, sending rocks flying in all directions as it shook the cavern.

Mangora kicked Gilly's short legs out from under him. "I told you not to move."

"NO!" Ty fought with everything in him to take control. To stop her. But his hand lowered nonetheless, blue flames licking at his palm. He could feel the magic swelling once again as she turned and sent the fire down into the little man.

Gilly ignited in a ball of blue light, the heat so intense he couldn't even scream.

Ty reacted on instinct. This time, instead of reaching for his body, he dove for the one thing he could still feel. His magic.

For a split second it obeyed, and the flames disappeared.

"What?" Mangora looked at Ty's hand. "That's not suppos—"

Something hit him from behind, and Ty flew forward across the rock and directly for the pool.

Mangora screamed as they hit the surface of the water and went in. She turned, and Ty spotted Sheeva's amber eyes staring down at them just before something grabbed them and sucked them down.

It was a current. A strong one.

Mangora was still screaming as they were dragged by the water through the underground tunnel. Her screams might not have been audible underwater, but he could certainly hear them in his head.

This was bad. Had she taken a breath before they went in? At this point, Ty almost didn't care. He'd just killed one of the nicest, most innocent people in all of Aldor. He hoped they both drowned. *Wait. Will Mangora drown? She isn't even here*. This was Ty's body. He fought to move, but he still didn't have control. He couldn't die. Not like this. Not to her. He struggled to keep his mind alive. He'd managed to regain at least part of his magic for that split moment before being thrown into the water. Maybe he could do it again?

He was having a hard time concentrating. He was surrounded by darkness. Or was it just the fact that they were in an underground cavern about to drown? His legs and arms had gone completely limp. He wasn't moving at all, other than bouncing off the walls as the current swept him along. Why wasn't he moving? Was Mangora gone? He was having a hard time concentrating.

This must be what it's like to die.

Suddenly, the current stopped, and he was no longer being pulled along. Instead, he seemed to be floating. He didn't know if he was floating up or down or simply in place. His body spasmed as it gasped for air. He was drowning. This couldn't be the end. This couldn't—

His mouth opened unexpectedly, and he took a huge gulp of air. His eyes opened as well, blurry at first, but then clearing enough to see that his head was resting just above the water. On his left was the dock, all four boats still tied in place.

The current had pulled him all the way back to the river.

Chapter 70 | Breen

"WHAT DID YOU DO?" Breen shouted at Sheeva as he ran for the water, ready to jump in.

Fraya grabbed his arm and pulled him back before he could.

"I did what was necessary," Sheeva said, backing away.

"You killed him. You killed Ty."

"Whoever that was," Feoldor said, shuffling down to the water to take a look for himself, "it wasn't Ty."

"Fraya, quick. He's still breathing."

Breen turned. His father was kneeling beside Gilly, whose body was severely charred. Breen couldn't believe the little man was still alive.

Fraya released Breen's jacket and ran to help.

As soon as she let go, Breen dropped to his knees beside the water's edge. He knew he should be more worried about Gilly, but all he could think about was his brother being sucked underwater and out of sight. Was he drowning? Or possibly already dead? He couldn't lose another member of his family. Not like this.

"Give me some room, please," Fraya said as the rest of the council crowded around.

Over his shoulder, Breen could see her hands glowing. He said a quick prayer for the little man and turned back to the pool. What if Ty was stuck just under the surface? What if there was a way to save him?

"That would be a bad idea."

A hand rested on Breen's shoulder. He looked up to find Veldon standing beside him, kerchief hanging from his other hand.

"No telling where that water goes," the portmaster said, looking over the side. He released Breen's shoulder and headed to the front of the cavern where the rest of the council were gathered around Fraya. "What say we see how Gilly's doing, aye?"

Breen squeezed his fists as tight as he could, knuckles turning white. He needed to leave the pool. The more he thought about it, the more he wanted to jump in or weep. Or both.

"Breen, come help Fraya," his father said.

Breen pulled himself away from the water's edge and walked over to where Fraya was leaning against his father, her head lolling to the side, evidently too weak to lift it. Gilly, too, lay there. He wasn't quite as disfigured as before—the skin was no longer melted shut around his eyes, nose, and mouth—but he still looked like meat that had been left on the spit for too long. The areas that had blackened were now a fiery red. Thankfully, his chest was continuing to rise and fall.

"Can you get me one of the apples from my satchel?" Fraya asked.

"I've got one here," Orlyn said, digging into one of the inner pockets of his robe. He pulled out a bright yellow apple and handed it to her. "I promise you won't taste a finer fruit."

She smiled her thanks and bit into it, juices beading at the corner of her mouth. Breen leaned over and picked her up. He carried her to the side and propped her against one of the shelves of rock beside the entrance.

Sheeva, who had been guarding the tunnel, moved to the other side of the opening to give them room. Feoldor joined her, making sure to keep his distance as he glanced nervously into the dark passageway beyond.

Breen tucked a blanket under Fraya's head. "How's that?"

Fraya nodded. "Better. The apple's helping."

"Will he live?" Veldon asked, kneeling to get a better look at Gilly's wounds.

"Yes. But he'll be in a lot of pain when he wakes, at least until I can recover enough to finish the job."

"I'm so sorry, my friend," Veldon said, reaching out to touch the little man but seeming to think better of it.

"I can help with the pain." Orlyn dug through the pockets of his baggy robe. He removed a small vial holding a greenish liquid. "When he wakes, I'll be sure to give him some of this. Special tincture I make from tellareen mushrooms."

Breen's father turned. "Aren't those supposed to . . ."

Orlyn smiled. "I might have sampled a few too many in my younger years, but I assure you, this particular tincture isn't habitual."

Breen's father raised his brow.

"I say it's time we leave," Feoldor grumbled over by the entrance. "What if Ty comes back? We're stuck in here like jackrabbits in a cage."

"We can't move Gilly," Veldon said, glancing at Fraya. "Can we?"

She shook her head. "I wouldn't."

"How far do you think we're going to get?" Breen's father said, pointing down the tunnel. "Gilly's the only one who can get us out."

"Flaming faeries!" Feoldor said in a panic. "I hadn't even thought of that. What if he doesn't make it?" He turned and looked at Gilly. "We'll starve down here. No one knows where we are."

"Why does the glass always have to be half empty with you?" Breen's father said, giving Feoldor a stern look. "Gilly's going to make it." He turned and looked at Breen. "Now, what is all this about a book?

Whoever that was back there, it wasn't my son."

Breen bit his tongue. This was a conversation he wasn't looking forward to. "Ty found a book in Mangora's shop a few weeks back, back before we had decided what to do with everything." He shrugged. "Seemed harmless enough. The book was empty."

"There was nothing written in it?"

Breen shook his head.

"Then why did you think the book was the problem?"

Breen sighed. How was he going to explain this? "Because he . . . he talks to it."

"He what?" Feoldor said, tugging his whiskers.

"I've seen him talking to it in bed when he thinks I'm asleep."

"And you didn't think that odd?"

"After what Ty's been through, I find it odd he's even walking around."

Orlyn leaned on his staff. "Did you ever hear it . . ." He sighed. "I can't believe I'm about to ask this. Did you ever hear it talk back?"

Breen looked at the man like he was crazy. "No, I never heard it talk back. What kind of question was that?"

Orlyn shrugged. "Just wondering. If it came from that dark den Mangora calls a shop, one can never be too careful."

The muscles in Breen's neck tensed. "Honestly, I don't really know if the book is the problem; all I know is what I've seen. And I'd rather think this transformation was due to dark magic than to think my brother has suddenly lost all reason and wants to kill us all."

"Did the book have a name?" Fraya asked.

"*Hidden Perceptions*, I think. But other than that, I don't know much more. And honestly," he said, standing, "I don't really care, because my brother is probably dead right now, floating in some underground pocket of water, and none of it matters."

"It's called a *numori*."

Breen spun on his heels and reached for his bow, forgetting he'd laid it down on the other side of the cavern to help Fraya. He grabbed a dagger instead.

Someone in a grey robe shuffled into the cavern, Sheeva standing directly behind them. "And if Ty has gotten his hands on one, we're in greater danger than you know." The man removed his hood.

"Nyalis!" Breen's father was the first across the cavern to greet the old wizard.

Breen lifted Fraya and chased after them.

"How did you find us?" his father asked.

"I'm a wizard," Nyalis said, as if that explained everything. "I've been waiting on Ty to return so he could begin his quest, but after weeks with no word, I started to get worried." He looked around. "Apparently, for good reason."

"Your timing's off once again, you old codger," Feoldor grumbled. "We could have used your assistance an hour ago when that boy was trying to kill us all. As it is, he cooked our friend over there like a roast pig."

Orlyn nudged Feoldor in the side with his elbow. "Show some respect."

"Well, it's true. And if it wasn't for our little white-haired wonder behind you, we'd all be charred crispies for sure."

"Where is he?" Nyalis asked.

Feoldor pointed to the water. "Sheeva sent him headfirst into there."

Nyalis walked to the edge of the pool and raised his hand out over the water. After a minute, he lowered it. "He's alive."

"How do you know?" Breen asked, walking down to the water, Fraya still in his arms.

"The water here flows out to the river just below the cabin I saw on my way here. I don't sense him in the water."

"Great!" Feoldor said, glancing back at the tunnel entrance. "He's probably on his way back to finish the job."

Before Nyalis could turn around, Breen held Fraya out for him to inspect. "Will she be all right?"

Nyalis felt her forehead, looked in one ear, then pinched her nose and winked. "She'll be fine." He left the pool and headed across the rock to where Gilly was lying up against a rock shelf. "I see you still have that staff handy," he said to Orlyn as he passed. "Good."

Orlyn nodded. "More for my legs than anything."

Nyalis knelt beside the dwarf and studied the burns. "You've done a nice job so far," he said to Fraya. "But you still have much to learn." He held his hands over Gilly's chest and closed his eyes. As he mumbled something, his hands began to glow a bright gold, much brighter than Fraya's had been. Breen watched in awe as Gilly's skin knitted back together, leaving a healed but naked dwarf in the process. The little man opened his eyes.

"It's good to see you back with us," Veldon said, standing to the side.

Gilly smiled when he saw him, then looked down and squealed.

Breen's father quickly draped a blanket they had used to wrap some of the more breakable items around him, then helped Nyalis to his feet, leaving Gilly to rest.

"So, tell me more about Ty," Nyalis said, walking over and sitting on a nearby shelf, low enough to crawl up on. "Start from the beginning and don't leave anything out. Even the smallest detail could be important."

Since Breen was the one who'd been with his brother from the beginning, he was the one to tell the story, starting with their inspection of Mangora's shop, Ty's decision to take the book, the council's decision to relocate her stuff, Ty's arrival in the cavern, his attack on Gilly, and finally his exit through the underground aquifer.

"What exactly is happening to my son?" Breen's father asked before Breen got the chance. "More importantly, how can we help him?" Breen noticed his father didn't ask the question of whether Ty *could* be helped, but simply how they were going to do it.

"A *numori* is a bit difficult to explain," Nyalis said. "It's a type of magic that, if used in the wrong way, can be very dangerous. It allows for control."

"What kind of control?" Breen asked.

"If a wielder uses the spell properly, they can gain control over the object that is spelled. Take a book, for example. I could use a *numori* spell on a book I'm reading that would give me the ability to turn its pages without me having to physically reach out with my hand and flip them. It's as though, for a time, I'm part of the book, or the book is a part of me. Like the pages are my fingers. Flipping a page would be just as easy as moving a finger."

"Sounds like a useful piece of magic," Orlyn said. "I can think of some ways that would be helpful around my shop."

"It's a fairly harmless spell, unless used on a living creature, especially a human, then it can be very dangerous. Only fifth-year apprentices were allowed to use such magic. The wielder would have to be gifted. Not to mention, the subject would have to be a willing participant."

"That's impossible," Breen said. "Ty would never allow someone to control him."

Nyalis nodded. "I didn't say the subject had to understand what was happening, only that they be a willing participant. There's no telling what Ty thought he was getting himself into when he agreed. Whoever is doing this has a good understanding of this spell and their own capabilities." He tugged lightly on his beard in thought. "And if someone has managed to trick Ty into giving up control, we are in a lot of danger. Even untapped as it is, his power is far greater than anyone's here, including my own."

Chapter 71 | Ferrin

T HE EARLY-MORNING LIGHT forced its way through the split
shutters as Ferrin brought his hammer down across the smooth
steel once again. Amber sparks scattered in every direction. He loved the
heat, the familiar smell of the coals and wrought iron, the melodic ringing
of the sledge as it struck the anvil, the feel of its balanced weight in his
hands. It was intoxicating, especially now that he was melding his own
magic within the folded layers of the newly reforged blades.

His sweat-soaked arms glistened in the firelight, and his muscles
ached. It was an ache that left him with a feeling of accomplishment, an
ache that brought a proud smile to his face as he held up the second blade
with his tongs. He'd forgotten how much he loved his work, watching
the steel as it formed to the image in his mind. It almost seemed like
another life. He hardly recognized the one he was living now—sleep
deprived, saddle sore, constantly looking over his shoulder for fear the
Tower would be there waiting.

He dipped the blade inside the cooling tank and watched the bubbles rise to the top. Ferrin had spent the entire night working on the two swords. The first was resting snugly in its sheath on the post to his right, while the second still needed to have its crossguard and hilt attached.

After finishing the pairing, Ferrin raised the sword and inspected his work. Running his thumb down the blade, he used his magic to infuse it with durability so that its edge would never dull, something he had learned to do years before when first experimenting with his gift.

He leveled the sword against a thick piece of wood, raised it over his head, then swung. The top half of the wood tilted and fell, landing at his feet with a *thump*. He raised the blade again to check the edge—not so much as a scuff mark.

"Ah, my dear smith, it's so good to see you again."

Ferrin froze. He'd been so busy with his work, he hadn't heard anyone enter.

He kept his back turned, hoping that whoever it was thought he was the owner of the smithy and needed some work done. "Is there something I can help you with?" he asked, keeping a tight grip on his sword.

"I see the Archchancellor was right about your talents. Your work is exquisite, but I would expect nothing less from a man with such dedication to his craft."

Ferrin's breath caught in his throat. It couldn't be. Cheeks was dead. Rae had killed him. He'd watched the last trace of the sadistic inquisitor's life drain from his eyes. But still, there was something about the way this man spoke that had Ferrin's hands shaking.

"Oh, let's not play coy, my dear smith; it doesn't suit you."

Ferrin turned slowly, keeping the blade at his side.

Two people stood just inside the doorway. The man was of average build, maybe early to midtwenties, with shoulder-length brown hair, and eyes to match. He had a kind face, except for the eyes. Something about the eyes made Ferrin squirm.

The woman, on the other hand, was more Ferrin's age, midthirties, fairly attractive with frizzy red hair and . . . strawberry-colored eyes with gold flecks that seemed to glow when she faced the hearth.

"What kind of way is that to greet an old friend?" The young man stretched his arms wide and beamed. "Do I look so different?" He tilted his head and laughed. "I guess I do, at that."

"What is this?" Ferrin asked, pointing his sword at the man. "Who are you?"

"Come now, I know you recognize me. Look me in the eyes and tell me you don't see."

Ferrin stared at the man. It sounded like Cheeks. But how had he managed to come back from the dead, let alone look like someone else? Had he taken someone else's body, or was this all some kind of elaborate ruse to catch him off guard? If so, it was working.

"I watched you die," Ferrin said, feeling all the muscles in his body tense.

The man smiled. "Guess I missed your company so much, I had to come all the way back from the underworld for more."

"So, who's the poor soul that got saddled with you inside? Somehow I doubt it was voluntary."

The woman beside Cheeks shifted.

"Yes, it is quite the specimen," the man said, turning to the woman on his left. "Don't you think, Lenara?"

"Shut up, Sylas, and get on with it."

Ferrin took a step back. He had to get out of there and warn the others. Then again, this might be his one chance to put an end to the inquisitor once and for all. He looked at the door behind them. Cheeks wasn't stupid. He wouldn't have come alone. There was probably an entire contingent of Black Watch right outside the door.

There was a window on Ferrin's right. If he could make it out, perhaps he could lose the guards in the backstreets.

Ferrin tightened his grip. "What now?"

"Now we take you back to the Tower where you belong. The Archchancellor has great plans for you, my dear smith, and I've missed our little chats, our witty repartee. I just know we will have many, many years of grand conversations together."

"Over my dead body. Or better yet . . . yours."

"Well, that was rather hurtful." The man folded his arms, pouting in mock rejection. It looked even more perverse coming from the young man's body. "I have no desire to see either one of us hurt. In fact, I was given explicit instruction to keep you intact. But," he said, raising his hand in warning, "make no mistake. If forced, I have no problem having them cut off a leg or two. Doubt you need those to work your magic."

Ferrin didn't move, but his hands were visibly trembling.

"But why all the hostility? Why not make this easier on yourself?" The man's smile darkened, and for the first time, Ferrin caught a glimpse of the true spirit living within.

Ferrin sneered. "When have you ever known me to do anything the easy way?"

Cheeks laughed.

"How did you find me? I haven't seen those corax things in a couple of days."

"Ah, I see our good captain has been giving out our secrets. Rather gifted creatures, the corax. Their eyes are just as good at night as they are during the day. They had no problem finding you. The same way they had no problem finding your companions."

Ferrin felt the floor beneath him vanish. "You're lying," he spat.

"Am I? How else would I be here? How else in all this city would I know the one place where you would be?"

Ferrin looked Cheeks in the eyes. He couldn't tell if the man was bluffing. Not that it mattered. If he couldn't make it past the guards, there wasn't anything he could do anyway. He had but one choice—fight. At least this time he had something to fight with.

Ferrin raised his sword.

Cheeks took a quick look around the room, his smug expression fading when he noticed the plethora of metal objects within Ferrin's reach. He took a step toward the door, and the woman beside him lifted one of the metal rods hanging from her waist.

"I don't have any grievance with you," Ferrin said to her. "But I will defend myself. Please step aside and let me pass. There's no point in anyone dying here today."

The woman didn't budge.

"Don't say I didn't warn you."

The woman mumbled something under her breath, and a fiery lash extended from the end of the rod in her hand.

Ferrin's eyes widened. She was a bulradoer.

Chapter 72 | Ferrin

FERRIN TOOK A STEP BACK. And just in time.

The woman swung her whip and cut the bracer post beside him in half, causing part of the ceiling to collapse.

He grabbed his other sword from the peg and leaped to the side, dodging most of the wood and debris as it fell. "Are you crazy? You're going to bring the whole roof down on our heads." He couldn't believe the power her weapon had. How was he going to stand against something like that?

Ferrin rolled to his feet, the sheathed sword and scabbard in one hand and open blade in the other. Cheeks was nowhere to be seen. Ferrin glanced over his shoulder at the window and his heart sank. It was blocked by a pile of fallen rubble. There was now only one way in and one way out.

The woman started for him, moving cautiously around the right side of the room.

Ferrin moved as well, backing farther away from the door in the hopes of drawing her in. He held the black blade out in front of him as though it were going to stop a weapon made of fire that could cut through a beam the size of his leg. Reaching the stone wall at the back of the smithy, he worked his way left.

She moved to cut him off, her whip burning a path through the dirt as she came. She brought it up and swung once more. The whip made a loud *crack* and hissed as it struck just to his right, splitting another of the support beams and causing more of the ceiling to collapse. Ferrin dove out of the way, just missing being pinned by a section of wood planks. She seemed to be herding him. He was back on his feet before she had a chance to reset her whip. Clearly, she wasn't trying to kill him, at least not yet. Maybe he could use that.

The woman moved toward the center of the room, keeping herself between him and the exit. She raised her whip again. He was running out of room to move. She swung, and he spun to the left. The whip struck the forge behind him, splitting the cooling tank in two. Water hissed and shot into the air, splashing the right side of his body.

He circled left, keeping his eye on her whip as he headed for the only section of the smithy left intact. His payment certainly wasn't going to cover replacing the man's entire shop, but he didn't have time to feel guilty about it. There was only about eight feet of open space between him and the wall, with a single post in the middle. He couldn't let her cut through another bracer, or the whole place was likely to come down on their heads. Then again, maybe that's what she wanted. For all he knew, she had some way to protect herself. She was a bulradoer, after all.

He stood in front of the last remaining post on the right side of the building and braced for the attack. She whipped the fiery brand back around and sent it flying for a spot about two feet above his head. He raised his sword, and the whip wrapped around the black blade and stuck. He wasn't sure who was more surprised, him or the bulradoer.

The whip's fire was hot, but he was a smith and used to heat. He yanked his sword backward with all his might, pulling the whip right out of her hand.

The flames immediately disappeared as the rod flew across the room and landed beside one of the split beams.

She gasped and raised her hand, but before she could open her mouth, he lunged for her neck. She yelped and dove out of the way, landing in a pile of shingles and collapsed thatching on the right.

Ferrin ran for the door and out into the street in front of the smithy. He stopped when he spotted the white robes. Cheeks was standing in front, his mouth gaping.

The guards looked just as stunned, undoubtedly expecting Ferrin to be in chains and collared.

Ferrin bolted down the alley next to the smithy.

"Stop him!" Cheeks shouted. "Stop him, you fools!"

Ferrin cut right at the next street and ran as fast as his legs would carry him. He was already weak from having spent the entire night slaving over a hot forge, but his fear of being taken back to the Tower was more than enough to keep him moving.

He could hear the horses' hooves behind him as the guards scrambled to catch up. He cut down another street, then right at the next intersection, which happened to be a main thoroughfare. Crossing the road, he rushed past a couple of unopened shops before ducking between two more, hoping to make it into the small jetty before the others spotted which direction he'd taken.

He had to get to the Smelly Trout. He had to make sure the others were still alive. If Cheeks was to be believed, it might already be too late.

Taking a northerly approach, he came out just upriver from the bridge. Fog lined the streets, coming in off the water, limiting his sight. He scanned the stone walkway for any sign of white riders, then slung the scabbards over his shoulder and charged across the bridge spanning the channel. He could see a few fishermen in the docks below, getting an early start on the day. There were surprisingly few people on the roads at that hour.

Once across the bridge, he turned left at the first street and skidded to a stop. He could hear horses ahead, but the fog on the island was thicker, and he couldn't tell who it was. Quickly, he ducked into the closest building and waited for them to pass. He found himself standing in what appeared to be another small tavern. He could smell breakfast being cooked somewhere in the back. It didn't smell anywhere near as good as Kyleen's.

Peeking through the crack in the door, he watched as another group of Black Watch rode by. He scanned each rider as they passed, looking for familiar faces. What if Cheeks had been telling the truth and his companions had been captured? What would he do then? Would he be willing to risk his sister's safety by going after them? He'd already been down that road before. The first time they'd captured him, he'd managed to free every prisoner in his wagon except himself. He couldn't do that again.

The final rider trotted by, and he breathed a heavy sigh of relief. He hadn't seen Myron, Rae, or Suri. Quietly, he slipped out the door and made his way down the narrow street to the Smelly Trout. The inn was quiet, no lights in the windows, so he worked his way around to the stables on the side.

Their horses were missing.

The sky was slate grey, too early yet for the sun, but late enough that his friends should be waking for breakfast. The fact that their horses were gone was troubling. He moved toward the door at the side leading into the dining room.

He couldn't help but notice the lack of smell coming from inside. Odd. Tibble had said that he and Kyleen were up every morning before dawn preparing breakfast.

Cautiously, he placed his ear to the door. He couldn't hear anything, but that didn't mean there weren't soldiers waiting inside. Holding his sword at the ready, he pushed his magic into the open room beyond to see if he could detect any hint of additional steel. He might not have been able to manipulate the metal without touching it, but he could at least tell what was there. Apart from the tin mugs, plates, and occasional lantern, it seemed empty.

He couldn't just stand there waiting for something to happen, so he inched open the door and slipped inside. The place was in ruin. There were tables overturned, chairs piled up, dishes broken and scattered across the floor.

Ferrin ran across the room and up the stairs to the second floor. All down the narrow hall, doors stood ajar. Each room looked like it had been tossed. Ferrin glanced in Rae and Suri's room, but there was no sign of them. The bed was on its side and the dresser drawers were strewn across the floor.

His room was much the same. His gear was gone.

Panic was already setting in as he paced between rooms. What should he do? He wrung his hands. What *could* he do? He knew Cheeks wouldn't leave without him, which meant as long as he could keep from getting himself captured, he at least stood a chance. But a chance for what? The only option he had was to try finding the Black Watch camp. At least then he could determine whether or not his friends had been captured. Of course, he could cut his losses and keep going. He doubted Cheeks would be willing to kill Rae. She was too valuable a tool for his interrogations. And he'd probably find a way to make use of Suri's gift as well. Myron was another story. He'd torture him as long as he could.

Ferrin punched the wall, managing to crack one of the boards and send a lance of searing pain running through his fingers. He rubbed the ache out as he headed back down the stairs.

A bowl clanged in the kitchen, and Ferrin froze. Keeping as quiet as possible, he navigated around the loose debris toward the back. He waited a moment. Not hearing anything, he inched open the kitchen door and peered through.

His stomach tightened to the point of not being able to breathe. He wasn't at all prepared for what he saw. There was blood everywhere.

Tibble lay on his back. There were unusual puncture wounds all up and down his body. His eyes and mouth were open as if trying to scream, and his hand clasped the folds of his wife's skirt. Beside him, Kyleen sat slumped against a cabinet, a large bowl of her famous rhubarb mix in her lap. Like Tibble, her body was riddled with strange holes. Her eyes appeared to be missing.

He took a deep breath, trying to swallow down the bile rising in the back of his throat. He was going to kill every last one of those guards, rip them limb from limb. Only the most inhuman of monsters could do something like this. He might not have known the old couple all that well, but no one had treated him kinder.

Just inside the door to his right, a loud, throaty caw broke the silence as two of the black winged creatures that had been tracking them hopped into sight and once again took up their feasting.

Ferrin's rage boiled to the surface as every muscle in his body tightened.

The creatures were even more terrifying up close. They were three times the size of a normal bird. Instead of feathers, they had a type of thin, flaky skin that stretched across the bones that made up their wings. Their hides looked more like the skin of a black viper than a bird, but the basic shape of their head was much like an oversized raven, apart from the small spiky protrusions that ran down the backs of their necks.

Besides wanting to make sure he kept these creatures from being able to continue tracking him, Ferrin wasn't leaving until this poor couple had been avenged.

Gently, he raised his sword, keeping the second sheathed. There wasn't much room in the kitchen, certainly not enough to be swinging two swords. He could use the second to hold the winged creatures back as he struck with the first. Tightening his grip, he readied himself. He had to be quick. He couldn't let them escape and tell the others where he was.

He lowered his shoulder against the door and threw it open, hollering as loudly as he could. The creatures were taken by surprise. The first lifted itself about knee-high into the air before meeting Ferrin's sword on the downswing. The bird screeched and hissed as it split in two, its wings still beating hard on the ground after landing.

The second creature had more time to prepare, but instead of retreating, it came straight at him. "Blazes!" Ferrin tried to get his sword up in time, but the corax was too quick, and the creature hit him in the chest. He lost his breath for a moment, its considerable size nearly knocking him from his feet as it dug its claws into his forearm.

Ferrin cried out in pain and dropped the sword. He stumbled back into a shelf as he swung his arm to break the creature's grip. He punched the bird in the chest, and it released its claws and flew backward. Blood was running down his arm as he inspected the damage. He could still move his fingers.

The corax positioned itself over Ferrin's discarded sword, almost taunting him.

Ferrin cradled the injured arm, trying not to think of the pain as he turned to get a better look at the kitchen. A large oven and hearth took up a good portion of the back wall. The right side was lined with counters and tables for chopping and mixing. The left side, where he was, had rows of shelves standing about six feet in height, along with an open window in the corner. The corax seemed to notice it as well and flew into the air, making a clear dive for the opening.

"No you don't!" Ferrin leaped in front of the creature and grabbed it by the wing. Spinning it around, he flung the corax back across the room, where it slammed into a row of pots on the far counter and fell to the floor. Ferrin shut the window and bolted it back into place. "Looks like it's just you and me now, birdy," he said, starting forward.

The creature watched him with one eye, its head cocked to the side. There was hunger in its glare as it opened a bloody beak and cawed.

The shelves on his side of the kitchen were too close together to swing a sword, so he grabbed a skillet from its place on the rack.

"Nothing like a hot piece of roasted fowl to start the day, don't you think?"

The corax released another ear-piercing cry and attacked. It was fast, faster than he had expected. He managed to get a swing in with the skillet but merely nicked the side of one of its wings as it flew above him.

Ferrin spun out of the way and used part of the shelf beside him to block his side. The large bird flew back around and came at him again. There just wasn't room to maneuver. He dove forward and rolled underneath the creature's talons, landing on top of Tibble in the process. He grabbed Kyleen's large pot of rhubarb filling and threw it in the air. The doughy substance splattered across the corax, completely covering its head and blinding it.

It beat its wings in fury, cawing ferociously as it collided with the cabinets and stove, trying to fly free. Ferrin grabbed his sword and hopped back to his feet, swinging at the creature as it flew by. The blade severed one of its wings.

The corax fell. It tried to use its remaining wing to get off the ground, but Ferrin didn't give it the chance. He stepped on its back, pinning it in place. "This is for Tibble and Kyleen." The corax released one final caw, and Ferrin chopped off its head.

He left it there to jerk and flop as he respectfully closed Tibble's eyes and lay Kyleen down beside him. Ferrin regretted not having enough time to give the two a proper burial, but he needed to get away before the others came back. He wrapped his arm with one of Kyleen's towels and started for the door.

He stopped when he heard voices on the other side.

"They've got to be here. Find them!"

Them? Did that mean Cheeks had lied when he said he had captured his friends? Not that it mattered. He was trapped inside the kitchen with the Black Watch between him and the exit.

He ran to the back of the kitchen and unbarred the window. It made a slight squeak, but he didn't have much of a choice. He opened it and looked out. Apparently, the Smelly Trout fronted a cliff face that dropped all the way to the waters of Virn Run below. A rickety-looking staircase led from a door at the back of the inn down to the docks, probably for bringing up supplies from the boats. Unfortunately, there was at least ten feet of rock between him and the stairs, and it was a long drop down.

He pulled a string from a sack of flour and tied it around the hilt of each sword, then slung them over his shoulder. Ducking, he shimmied out the window, wincing when his injured arm hit the side. He had to hurry. They could be coming through the kitchen door at any moment. He lowered himself from the sill, sliding the window shut as he did. He hoped none of them bothered looking through it.

He worked his way carefully along the rocky ledge, hand over hand, worrying with every new grip that his injured arm would give out. He was nearing the point of exhaustion, and the loss of blood wasn't helping. With one last heave, he swung from the rocks onto the rickety staircase at the side. He grunted when he hit, one of the swords digging into his side.

He scrambled to his feet, using the railing to pull himself up. The wooden stairs wound down to the awaiting docks. As far as he could tell, he hadn't been spotted.

Reaching the docks below, he looked up at the inn, but his vision was blocked by part of the cliff face and the overhanging fog. He glanced around to see if anyone was watching before helping himself to the first available skiff that had an oar. The way the Tower guards were still searching, he didn't believe they had found the others yet, but it still left him with the problem of not knowing where they were. He tried putting himself in Myron's shoes.

The captain wouldn't be able to just wander the streets with Rae and Suri in tow. They would be too easy to spot. He didn't know how well Myron knew the city's inhabitants. He might have been able to find someone willing to hide them, but that seemed unlikely, since he had never mentioned it before. The white riders would be watching all the roads in and out of Iraseth, which only left one other option.

Ferrin turned his boat and headed upriver. He needed to make his way to the mountain passes.

Chapter 73 | Breen

"I FOUND HIM!" Breen shouted as he ran out of the woods. He crossed over the little creek behind their house and headed straight for the barn, where his father was chatting with two men on horseback.

The council had been searching for Ty ever since his attack in the cave under Gilly's house, but with little luck.

Breen hadn't been able to sleep. He kept waking with nightmares of his brother being sucked into the underground river. Even with the wizard's assurances that Ty hadn't drowned, it still weighed heavy on him.

He slowed when he realized the two men talking with his father weren't men after all.

"We have company," his father said, about the time Lyessa turned and looked his way. Her long blonde hair was tucked up under the brim of her hat.

Breen gritted his teeth. She couldn't have picked a worse time to show up for a visit. He'd just found Ty, and they needed to go after him.

"Who have you found?" she asked. "Ty? I've been looking everywhere for him."

Breen didn't respond. They hadn't told her yet about Ty's situation. The uneasy look on his father's face said he was just as conflicted. Lyessa had proven herself an ally, and if there was to be any future relationship between her and his brother, they were going to need to be more inclusive. But, unfortunately, with her father being the overlord of Sidara, it made the choice precarious, since the council didn't want the overlord privy to every detail of their operations.

Lyessa's skill with a sword had proven invaluable during their battle with the Northmen, and Breen thought she deserved to be more involved. She certainly wasn't the dainty young woman Ty had always claimed her to be. She was quite the force of nature and no doubt exactly what Ty needed to keep him in line.

Breen opened his mouth to answer when Lyessa's riding companion leaned forward far enough for him to see her face. *Fraya?*

She seemed different. More confident. She also appeared to be wearing men's apparel, including a pair of trousers and an overcoat. If it hadn't been for the face and hair, he could have easily mistaken her for a boy, albeit a very pretty one. He had never seen her in pants before. Lyessa was clearly rubbing off on her, and he couldn't help but like it.

He walked over to help the two women from their mounts. The sooner they chatted, the sooner they would leave. He offered Fraya his hand, but she ignored it and swung her leg around and hopped off. Breen lowered his hand, disappointed, then turned to help Lyessa.

"Here's another lesson for you, Fraya," Lyessa said. "When a man like Breen offers to help you from your horse, you let him." She held out her arms and let Breen lift her by the waist and help her down. "See how I did that?" She cast a glance over her shoulder to make sure Fraya was paying attention. "Not only does it make him feel good about himself, but in turn you get the thrill of his hands around your waist."

Too embarrassed to even mention how much he liked Fraya's outfit,

Breen blushed and grabbed the horses' reins from his father. "I'll just stable them, shall I?" Without waiting for an answer, he headed into the barn. He couldn't help but notice the smirk on his father's face as he passed. "Having a good laugh, are we?"

"I think those two could charm a snake out of its hole," his father said, shifting his weight against the barn door. His father rested one foot on a pitchfork whose prongs were buried quarter-deep in the dirt. "Enjoy it while you can, son. Don't take a moment of it for granted." His father might have been smiling, but Breen could hear the heartache in his voice.

Breen maneuvered the horses into their stalls, then poured some feed from the old hogshead barrel into their troughs.

After making sure they had plenty of water, he joined the others outside, pulling his coat tight as his breath steamed in front of his face. The days were getting colder. It wouldn't be long before the first of the snows reached them, making travel through the forest more difficult.

"If there's anything that you or your family need, Father and I would be only too happy to help."

"Thank you, Lady Lyessa," Breen's father said. "That's very kind of you, but I believe we are managing for now. Breen's helping me with the work, and Adarra has taken on her mother's responsibilities as best she can."

"We left Adarra in town," Fraya said, rubbing her hands together. "She said she wanted to spend more time with the Tallosian. She's been working hard to learn his language. I think she's attempting to teach him ours as well."

Breen's father smiled. "That's my Adarra, ever the studious one. She'd probably go without eating if we didn't drag her away from those books of hers."

Breen noticed that Lyessa's gaze kept wandering about the yard when she thought no one was looking. He knew who she was searching for. Unfortunately, it wasn't going to do her much good.

Breen was getting more restless by the minute. He needed to tell his father about Ty, but he didn't want to say anything with Lyessa there.

"Is Ty here?" she finally asked. "We actually came to see him."

Fraya looked at Breen and raised an eyebrow. Evidently, she'd been careful not to tell Lyessa either.

"We haven't seen much of him lately," his father said. "I figure he's grieving in his own way."

Lyessa nodded. "I guess I can understand. I remember how it felt when I lost my mother. I didn't leave my room for days."

Breen shifted from one foot to the next. He didn't care about Lyessa's personal experiences with loss. They needed to go after Ty, but he couldn't think of a polite way of asking her to leave while at the same time keeping Fraya around in case they needed her gift of healing. Hang it! He didn't have a choice. "The truth is," he said, "Ty isn't exactly *Ty* anymore."

"Breen." His father shook his head.

"She's going to find out eventually if we can't stop this. And we can't keep sitting here gossiping when I know where he is."

His father took a step forward. "You know where he is?"

"Yes. If we don't hurry, he'll be gone before we get there."

"Gone from where?" Lyessa asked, looking at the two of them. "Will someone please tell me what's going on?"

Breen took a deep breath. "We don't exactly know all the details ourselves, but Ty seems to have been possessed by a book."

She looked at him like he had three heads. "What?"

He explained the situation as best he could, leaving out the part with the underground cavern, and simply told her that Ty had attacked them while they were cleaning out the witch's shop.

"And you know where he is?" she asked.

He nodded. "At least as of a half hour ago. It's a spot in the woods I followed him to a few years back. He tends to go there when he wants to be alone."

"Then why are we just standing here?" she asked.

His father laid the pitchfork up against the barn wall and started for the house. "Let's get the gear."

Breen followed just behind.

"We're coming as well," Lyessa said, not giving anyone a chance to argue. "I didn't ride all the way out here for nothing."

"Besides," Fraya added, "we have our swords."

Breen stopped and turned around. "Since when did you start carrying a sword?" He hadn't even noticed the weapon until now.

"Since, I . . ." She glanced at Lyessa sheepishly. "Since I started learning how to fight. Lyessa has been teaching us."

Breen noticed the slight discoloration around Fraya's cheek. He had seen it earlier but had assumed it was some of Lyessa's face powder. "What's this?" he asked, walking over and gently cupping the side of her face to get a better look.

"It's nothing. I told you, Lyessa's training us how to fight."

"What do you mean . . . *us*?"

"She's training me and . . . and Adarra."

"What? You've got my sister mixed up in this as well? It's bad enough that you would subject yourself to that," he said, glancing once again at her powder-covered bruises, "but Adarra's not like you. She'll get hurt."

Fraya crossed her arms. "Are you saying that because we are women, we can't protect ourselves?"

"No. I . . . I just think that's why I'm here. To protect you."

Fraya laid her hand on his arm. "Breen, if there's anything I've learned from our fight with the bulradoer and the Black Watch, it's that I can't rely on others to be there to save me."

Breen knew how much Saleena's death weighed on Fraya. Having someone sacrifice their life for you put things into perspective.

"You were miles away, fighting your own battle," she continued, "and I almost lost my life because I had no idea how to even hold a sword. The closest I've ever come to using a weapon is swinging an axe to chop firewood, and the wood wasn't trying to kill me when I did."

Her tone softened. "The point is, as nice as it is knowing that I have someone like you to protect me, you won't always be there, and when that happens, I need to know how to protect myself."

Breen exhaled slowly. He hated being wrong. Worse, he hated other people pointing it out in such an obvious way. "You're right. I'm sorry." He scooted a little closer to keep from being overheard by Lyessa. "I just don't want you to get to the point that you feel like you don't need me anymore."

Fraya smiled and wrapped her arms around him. "Are you kidding? You're my giant protector. I'll always need you. Besides," she said, pulling away and tapping the hilt of her sword, "I'm not very good yet."

"That will change," Lyessa said with a grin, apparently eavesdropping after all. "Now go get your gear so we can find Ty."

It didn't take Breen or his father long to pack and the group to be on their way. With his new bow and quiver over his shoulder, sword at his waist, and brace of knives under his coat, Breen felt like they were about to go to war. Then again, with the kind of power his brother possessed, it could be a war.

Breen guided them down a deer trail that led into the denser part of the forest. The farther in they went, the antsier he became. There was a burnt smell in the air. One that hadn't been present the first time he'd been through there. He kept his eyes peeled for signs of movement. Where there were normally traces of life—the song of the birds, the playful skittering of the tree-rats, cottontails hopping from one hole to the next—there was nothing.

The forest was eerily silent.

The hairs on the back of his neck pricked. It was the same feeling he'd gotten when tracking down that arachnobe with Ty. He remembered the fear all too well.

After a good half hour of trekking northeast through dense forest in the general direction of Reed Marsh, Breen slowed. "It should be over the next rise," he whispered to the others.

Cautiously, they worked their way up the hill, skirting trees and brush as they climbed. The smell of burnt wood was now suffocating, and small flakes of ash rained down on them, covering their hair and clothing. They crested the rise and stopped, all four staring in bewilderment at the silent valley below.

"This is where he goes to think?" Lyessa asked, her face wrinkling in disgust.

"It didn't used to be like this," Breen whispered as he scanned the clearing.

Everything was covered in ash, like a fresh layer of fallen snow. Everything was dead. Every bush, briar, and patch of grass had been burned away. Most of the trees had lost their leaves already, anticipating winter's approach, but even the evergreens were bare and lifeless. Not even the wind dared blow. The place seemed nothing more than a hollow tomb.

Ty was seated at the center of the lifeless sanctuary, his white hair blending in with his surroundings, almost making him appear headless.

Breen wasn't sure if Ty hadn't noticed their arrival or was simply ignoring it.

"I see the book," Fraya whispered.

Ty was holding it in his lap. He appeared to be reading it as he rocked slowly back and forth.

Lyessa held out her hand and let a couple of pieces of ash land in her palm. "What did he do to this place?"

"We need to get that book," his father said.

"And how do you propose we do that?" she asked.

"I'll talk to him," Breen said, taking a step forward.

His father grabbed his arm. "No. I'll go. You stay with them."

Breen nodded reluctantly. He didn't like the idea of his father going down there alone, but he liked the idea of disobeying him even less. Besides, when it came to his brother, his father was better at keeping his calm than Breen. So, he watched as his father made his way down the shallow incline toward the ash-covered valley below.

Ty never moved. If he heard his father's approach, he wasn't showing it.

Breen still couldn't understand how a simple book could allow someone to use Ty in such a way. Did his brother really have no control? Was he even aware of what he was doing? After nearly killing Gilly, he hated to think he was. Come to think of it, why was his brother even here? This was Ty's hiding spot. How would the one controlling him know to come here?

Breen's father reached the bottom of the clearing and slowly made his way out to the middle where Ty remained seated. "Ty?"

Breen held his breath.

His brother didn't move, other than to continue rocking. His father stopped a few steps back, not wanting to startle him.

"Ty, are you all right? We were worried about you." Even from the top of the rise, Breen could still hear his father's voice.

Still no answer.

"Are you hungry? Have you eaten?"

Breen huffed. *What kind of question is that? Ty or not, who cares if he's hungry? Grab the book.*

His father waited for a reply, but none came. "What are you reading, son?"

Ty stopped rocking. Slowly, he stood and turned around.

Breen grabbed his bow, getting ready to pull an arrow if needed.

Ty's face was twisted in rage. "I'm not your *son*." In one swift move, he raised his hand, and their father lifted into the air.

Breen grabbed an arrow and charged down the slope. He barely had time to nock it before his father was suddenly thrown across the meadow, landing with a hard *thud* on the far side.

"Ty!" Breen shouted, half running, half stumbling the rest of the way down the hill. His father wasn't moving. He ran to the outer edge of the glade and yanked the bowstring, but Ty was gone. The valley was completely empty.

"Is he alive?" Lyessa asked as she and Fraya rushed in behind him, swords drawn.

Breen lowered his bow and ran to his father and knelt beside him. He wasn't moving. There was a slight wheeze, letting them know he was at least still alive.

"Here, let me through," Fraya said.

Breen moved out of the way, giving her plenty of room to work her magic. She ran her hands across his chest and closed her eyes. Her palms began to glow. The light from her hands seeped through his shirt and down into his father's chest.

"It's not as bad as it could have been," she said. "He has a couple of broken ribs, and he hit his head, which has left him unconscious. Probably a good thing. He won't feel the pain." Fraya smiled up at him reassuringly. "He'll be fine, Breen."

"Where did he go?" Lyessa asked.

Breen turned to find her walking out onto the ash-covered floor of the glen.

"He was here just a moment ago."

Breen followed her out. He walked to the center and studied the tracks. Other than the single set leading to where his father had been standing and the round indention where his brother had been seated, there was no sign of anyone else coming or going. He scanned the tree line on either side. "I have no idea. He just . . . vanished."

"Is that something he's capable of doing?"

"At this point, there's no telling what he's capable of."

Breen started back to where Fraya was helping his father, who was now awake, to a sitting position.

"Your brother packs quite the punch," his father said, taking a moment to look around the empty clearing. "Where is he?"

"I don't know," Breen said. "He was there one minute and gone the next. Whoever is controlling him is plainly well versed in magic."

"How can we find him?" Lyessa asked. "Did the wizard say what to do when we did?"

"No," Breen admitted. "But I'm guessing we need to get that book away from him."

"Ty couldn't have picked a worse time to go completely insane," Lyessa said. "What was he thinking?"

"He's not thinking," Breen's father said. "He's reacting. His anger and guilt have driven him to this."

Lyessa clicked her tongue. "The overlords are already here. The conclave is scheduled for tomorrow. The last thing we need is for Ty to be running around Easthaven in his condition."

Behind them, a twig snapped.

Chapter 74 | Dakaran

DAKARAN WASHED THE SOAP from his face and stared into the mirror. He smiled. "What do you think, Fernon?"

The head groom cleared his throat as he dabbed the remaining soap from Dakaran's neck with his towel. "Regal, Your Majesty. You have a bearing that demands respect."

Dakaran couldn't tell if Fernon was being sincere or simply pandering. The man had a face like a statue, completely emotionless. A character trait ingrained into every royal attendant from birth, it would seem. Dakaran had attempted numerous pranks on the older man over the years, hoping to get a rise out of him, but sadly, to no avail. He'd even gone so far as to leave a snake in the man's bed. Fernon hadn't even flinched.

"Most amusing," the groom had said before sliding the serpent onto the floor and placing a bucket over it.

Regardless of whether Fernon was capable of emotion or not, he was certainly proficient with a straight razor and snippers. Dakaran turned his head to the side, admiring the new look. He had always hated the idea of hair on his face hiding his features. But he had to admit, it did make him appear more commanding. More kingly.

He had requested Fernon trim it in the same style Ayrion had always worn—thin along the jaw and widening out to a slight goatee. He held his head up and admired the man's work. Hopefully, Amarysia would notice.

"Fernon, my clothes."

"Yes, Your Majesty." Fernon clapped his hands, and three attendants who had been standing quietly at the back of the room quickly rushed forward to be of assistance.

Much like Fernon, the three attendants were dressed in their formal palace uniforms: a deep-crimson doublet with gold lining over a white tunic. The sleeves were affixed with ribbon ties at the shoulder joints for easy removal. Along with the uniform, they wore matching caps with gold crests attached to the side.

The attendants held out a variety of outfits from Dakaran's closets for him to inspect, each as regal as the next. It was a difficult choice, but he finally settled on the forest green with white lace and gold trim. It was one of three that came with its own cape. He knew Amarysia had a fondness for capes. At least, he thought he remembered her saying something to that effect.

Lastly, Fernon positioned the crown on Dakaran's head, letting it rest in place just over his brow. It was the finishing touch, the icing on the cake.

Dakaran strode over to the full standing mirror beside his chifforobe and examined the end result. "Very nice," he said with a satisfied nod, fiddling with the crown. He shifted his bangs to the side to keep them from getting in his eyes.

Content with the way he looked, he left his chambers and made his way to the throne room. It was that time of week again, and from what he'd heard, the crowd was extensive, the line wrapping clear down the hall, across the foyer, and into the upper courtyard outside. He never remembered there being such a turnout while his father sat on the throne. Most of his father's sessions had been finished in time for lunch.

Dakaran decided to take the west wing today, not wanting to face the swarming throngs coming in from the east. He'd made the mistake the last time of entering from the front, barely making it down the hall as people pressed him with their concerns and desires before he'd even had a chance to get inside. The only reason he'd attempted it was to please Amarysia, who had suggested spending more time amongst them as opposed to sitting up on his throne.

That had been a mistake.

The white-clad guards standing outside the back entrance to the throne room opened the doors at his approach. They didn't bother saluting or bowing as he passed. In fact, very few of these new guards Valtor had assigned showed any modicum of respect. At least, not in the way the High Guard had with his father. He gritted his teeth at the thought. Just another thing on the long list of differences between his rule and his father's.

Once inside, his eyes went straight to the platform. It was empty. He took a moment to glance around the room, but he didn't see either his mother or Amarysia amongst the servants at the side. *Running late as usual, it seems.*

With a frustrated sigh, he climbed the stairs and took his seat. At least his servants had stacked the pillows this time. He eased himself down on top of them, needing to shift only one.

By the time he'd found a comfortable position, his cupbearer was halfway up the steps with his favorite goblet. He was carrying a tray with two pitchers. "Red or white, Your Majesty?"

It was still early, but Dakaran found it helped dull the boredom and the constant aching of his head. "Red."

The servant bowed and, with one hand balancing the tray, managed to fill the goblet without spilling. The servant bowed once more, then made his way back down to the bottom.

Dakaran lifted the goblet, took a whiff to get the full effect, then downed his first swallow of the day. It was lightly spiced, filling him with warm tingles as it coated his throat. He moaned softly and eased back in his seat, waiting for the proceedings to start. His mother had better hurry if she wanted to make it before they opened the doors.

Looking around, he noticed his advisor wasn't present either. Where was everyone? He had no intention of sitting there all day by himself, listening to people whine on and on about their problems. About the time he raised his glass for another swallow, the chamberlain walked out to the center of the room and smacked his ceremonial staff on the marble floor.

It couldn't be time to start already, could it? Where were his mother and Amarysia? Where was Valtor? The pressure in his head was building, and he took another swallow.

The guards at the far end of the hall released the latch and pulled open the double doors, allowing those in the hall to begin filing in. The entire corridor outside was filled.

He pressed his thumb to the side of his head. This was not what he had bargained for. The chamberlain stood at the front of the line, which the guards kept about ten feet from the steps leading up to the throne, taking names in order to offer proper introductions before allowing them to speak.

"Master Grimshorn of South Avis, Your Majesty," the chamberlain said, following each name with the street they resided on. It allowed Dakaran to get a better idea of the person's situation by knowing what part of the city they lived in.

The situation of people from South Avis, however, was a little harder to ascertain, considering the street ran from the merchant district at the center of Aramoor all the way down to the old city. What part of South Avis Master Grimshorn lived on could be the difference between a respectable middle-class merchant or someone living in the slums of

Cheapside.

Either way, Dakaran was sure to be anything but pleased with whatever the man had to say, since few of his citizens came to these assemblies bearing joyful tidings. In fact, he couldn't think of any who had.

Dakaran waved the man forward.

Master Grimshorn bowed nervously, hat in hand, as he took a couple of steps closer to the platform steps. He stopped and bowed once more, as if that were going to make his complaints any more palatable. "I represent a small consortium of spice merchants on the upper west side, Your Majesty," he said, head lowered and voice shaking. "We ask the king for a stay on the increased taxes. It's driving us to raise the cost of our goods to the point we are no longer able to compete. Three of our group have already lost their businesses, and the rest are soon to follow if we can't find a way to lower this new burden."

Dakaran balled his fist. Another complaint about the new citizen tax. He was growing weary of fielding one criticism after another concerning his decision to refill the royal coffers. "Do you enjoy living in Aramoor?"

The man looked up, seemingly shocked by the question. "Yes . . . Your Majesty?" His response came off sounding more like a question than a statement.

"And do you enjoy walking to work every day without the fear of getting beaten and robbed?" Of course, depending where on South Avis he lived, that might have been a moot question, so Dakaran followed it with another. "Do you enjoy the safety this city affords with its grand walls and trained soldiers?"

"Of course, Your Majesty," Grimshorn said, sounding a little more certain than the last time.

"Do you think those benefits come without a price?"

The man didn't respond, but he did tilt his head up far enough to see Dakaran.

"In order to protect Aramoor from its enemies, we need soldiers, we need ships, we need armament. Those don't come cheap. The citizens of Aramoor have the privilege of living in the grandest city in the five kingdoms. Is it not fair to seek just compensation for such a right?"

"I . . . uh. I guess so, Your Majesty. But . . ." The man took a deep gulp. "We've lived this long without such a tax. Why is it being enforced now?"

Others down the line chimed in, voicing their own concerns over the new citizen tax. In fact, by the reaction, it seemed as though the majority of those in line were all there for the same reason.

Dakaran squeezed the stem of his goblet. *Because I said so!* was what he wanted to say. Instead, he waited for the chamberlain to quiet the crowd. "The reason for implementing a new tax is because our battle with Cylmar depleted the Elondrian treasury. My father raided our coffers in order to pay for his war, then lost half our army in the process, forcing me to rebuild. And that can't be done without gold."

Dakaran's jaw tightened. Why was he having to explain himself? He was the king.

"But how are we to make a profit with such a high expense?" another man farther back in line shouted.

"That's not my problem," Dakaran said angrily. "If you can't run a business in the most luxurious city in the world, then I recommend you move somewhere you can. Might I suggest Gnarr, or Erast? I hear southern Cylmar is quite lovely this time of year." Dakaran stood and the people quieted. Without saying a word, he walked down the stairs and left through the back door. He could hear some of the people behind him asking if he was coming back.

That was one of the worst experiences he'd ever been forced to endure. He had no intention of ever holding another assembly again.

The servants in the halls moved to get out of his way. A wise decision. He stormed into his room and threw his crown across the chamber, shattering the mirror on the other side and bringing Fernon running. "Why weren't they there?" he shouted.

"Who, Your Majesty?" Fernon asked as he rushed to get a broom for the glass.

Not only had his mother and Amarysia not shown as they had promised, but his own advisor had disappeared as well. How could they have left him there alone? And after he'd spent such an effort on his grooming. He rubbed the thickening hair on his chin, then shouted once more at the top of his lungs.

"Fernon! Wine!"

The old groomsman rushed back into the personal attendants' room, which was attached to Dakaran's personal chambers, and returned with a pitcher and goblet, careful not to step on the pile of glass as he followed Dakaran into his sleeping quarters.

Dakaran sat on the edge of his canopy bed and waited for the man to hand him his drink. He drained it in a single gulp and held it out to be refilled.

Fernon wisely didn't argue.

"Send someone to my mother's quarters and find out why she didn't attend the assembly this morning. Hurry!"

Fernon set the pitcher on the table beside the bed and rushed to the door. Dakaran could hear the man ordering one of the guards outside to make the inquiry.

Dakaran lay back on the bed, taking a deep breath. His headache was getting worse. This was what he got for trying to please a woman. He closed his eyes, hoping the pain would lessen.

A knock on the door had him sitting back up. "Come!"

The door opened, but instead of one of the guards returning with a good explanation as to his mother and Amarysia's absence, Valtor strolled in, shutting the door behind him and motioning for Fernon to leave.

Fernon glanced at Dakaran for final assurance, and Dakaran nodded. He did appreciate the old man's loyalty. Fernon skirted around Valtor on his way out the door.

"I hear you made quite the exit during your assembly this morning," he said with a wry smile. "I believe there are people still standing in line, wondering whether you will return."

"And where were you?" Dakaran asked, taking another gulp of his drink. The lingering ache in his head suddenly eased, and he looked in his glass. He'd have to remember to use more of the red wine in the morning, apparently.

"I apologize, Your Majesty," his advisor said as he crossed the room, "but I had pressing business in town."

"More pressing than serving at your king's behest?"

Valtor smiled, offering a deep bow. "I would not have missed it otherwise, Your Majesty."

There was another knock on the door.

Dakaran leaned to see past his advisor. "Come."

Fernon stuck his head in, and Dakaran motioned for him to enter, one of the guards following his attendant in.

"Well?" Dakaran asked. "What did my mother have to say?"

The guard cleared his throat. "The Queen Mother sends her apologies, Your Majesty, but appears to be suffering from a bout of dizziness."

"Dizziness? I suffer from that every day, but you don't see me shirking my duties." He wanted to throw his goblet, but he hadn't finished what was inside yet. He also didn't want to listen to another scolding from his advisor. "Fine. Let my mother know I hope the spell is short-lived."

He hoped she suffered extensively and passed it along to Amarysia.

Fernon bowed and ushered the guard out the door, closing it behind him.

Dakaran looked at Valtor. "You look like you have something to say, and that I'm not going to like it."

Valtor smirked. "How very perceptive of you, Your Majesty. As it happens, I do have news. It appears as though the overlord of Sidara has

issued a summons to convene a council of the Provincial Authority."

"I've received no such summons."

"Apparently, the topic of conversation is you."

"How could they be meeting without my knowledge?"

"It appears to be a *secret* council."

"Then how did you find out about it?"

"I have my ways," he said. "From what I gather, they are upset with your decision to bring Cylmar under Elondrian rule."

"I don't care what they're upset about. I'm the king. I don't need their permission."

Valtor shifted his feet, resting his weight on that ugly wolf-head staff of his. "All the same. I warned you there would be repercussions for such a bold action."

Dakaran waved it off. "Even in its depleted state, we still have the largest army in the five kingdoms. I don't think we have much to worry about."

Valtor's lips tightened. "There is always something to worry about. That's part of what being a leader is. We might have the largest army of any single kingdom, but not if those kingdoms decide to join forces."

Dakaran pursed his lips. That was a troubling thought. He took another sip from his cup, and his head felt clearer. "Then how should we respond?"

"Swiftly, Your Majesty. Which is why I have taken the liberty of putting something into place that will assure us a favorable outcome."

Chapter 75 | Ayrion

NEVER HAD THE DREARY grey of a coming dawn taken so long to arrive.

Ayrion watched from the second-floor battlement as the last of the vulraaks retreated toward the mines. Thankfully, the creatures' assault against the doors had been unsuccessful. With a heavy sigh of relief, he headed across the balcony to study the map of Belvin once more. Bek, Tameel, and Abiah soon joined him.

"We won't last another night," Bek said.

"I'm surprised we've lasted this long," Ayrion said, shading his eyes. The first rays of dawn were now poking through the windows and hitting him in the face.

"Many of us didn't," Tameel said, limping back to the railing behind them and looking down at the healing station below. Tameel had taken a bad tumble down the stairs earlier that evening, and since Zynora couldn't afford to waste any magic on less-severe injuries, he had to make do with a simple wrap.

"Our numbers are dwindling fast, General," Abiah said, holding a cloth to a cut on his arm just below the shoulder.

"Aye," Bek agreed. "The number of dead and injured have tripled after last night."

Ayrion joined Tameel at the rail and stared down at the rows of covered bodies below. The battle had taken a lot out of them. Even though they were behind stone walls, Ayrion and his fighters had spent the rest of the night at the second-floor windows, repelling ladders the vulraaks had brought with them from the mines.

It had been sheer determination, or perhaps desperation, that had kept them alive and fighting as long as they had. Bek was right: there was no way they would survive another night.

All eyes were on Ayrion, awaiting direction from their fearless leader.

Ayrion, however, had plenty of fears. He feared that what they were attempting was a hopeless cause. He feared he had let his friends down, and that all these good people he had persuaded to take up arms and fight were going to die for nothing. He was also afraid of what would happen to the rest of Aldor if Argon were free to continue spreading his plague. It was this fear, above all else, that kept his mind racing, fighting to come up with an answer, a solution that could bring about a tipping point.

But nothing came.

Ayrion pushed back the flaps of his black coat and leaned over the table, squinting at the harsh sunlight flooding the room. "I won't lie. I don't have an answer. We tried a direct approach on the mines and failed, losing good men and women in the process. We managed to hold out the night against impossible odds, but short of an act from the Creator, I don't see that repeating itself."

"What are you saying?" Abiah asked, his voice tinged with anger. "Are you suggesting we give up? I'm not leaving until every last one of these faerie-spawned creatures is sent back to the abyss. My Willem *will* be avenged."

Ayrion straightened. "What I'm saying is I only see three options here. Either we fall back to the encampment and spend the next month trying to raise another force, or we cut our losses and encourage people to resettle somewhere else, which seems an almost-wasted effort, since there will be nowhere left to hide when Argon spreads this disease across all of Aldor."

"And the third?" Bek said, taking a step to the right to block the sun from Ayrion's face.

"We keep fighting."

Abiah looked at the others. "Well, I'm not leaving. I don't care if I have to storm that flaming mine on my own. I'll chase this Argon creature into the Pits of Aran'gal if I have to."

Tameel patted Abiah on the shoulder. "None of us are planning on giving up."

"But I also don't want to throw our lives away, either," Ayrion said. "We need a plan. We need some kind of leverage."

"Riders!" a watchman called from the balcony.

Everyone turned. The watchman walked to the railing. "Riders approaching from the east, General!"

Abiah reached for his sword.

Ayrion raised his hand. "Calm yourself. We know they aren't vulraaks."

"How can you be sure?"

"Because, other than the fact that the sun is up, vulraaks *eat* horses; they don't ride them." He called down to those guarding the entrance. "Open a door."

"You couldn't have asked for a timelier arrival," Tameel said with a wide grin.

Ayrion left the table and headed down the stairs to the main floor. Riders filed into the town square. It looked like there were at least twenty or thirty in the group. Nell must have sent them straight from the encampment, for which he was grateful.

Sunlight streamed through the open door and reflected off the polished head of one of Bek's hatchets, hitting Ayrion square in the eyes. He tried moving out of the way, but every time he moved, Bek shifted too.

"For pity's sake, Bek! Will you stop moving!" Ayrion laughed as he managed to find a safe spot to stand.

A thought struck him.

"And there it is," Tameel said, pointing at Ayrion.

"There what is?" Abiah asked.

"*The Look.*"

Bek turned. "What look?"

"The look that says we are about to get tossed out of the frying pan and straight into the flames."

Ayrion smiled. "You're right. I do have an idea." He took a deep breath. Was he seriously considering this? "And it's completely insane."

"The best ones usually are," Bek said with a wary smile.

"Well?" Abiah asked. "What's your idea?"

"We're going after the nest."

"That's not an idea," Abiah grumbled. "That's lunacy."

Tameel flung his arms in the air. "You're right. You are insane! The last time you attempted that, you barely made it out alive!"

"Yes, but that's because the last time, we didn't have our secret weapon."

Bek rested his hand on the top of one of his hatchets. "And what the blazes would that be?"

Ayrion couldn't help but laugh. "Gentlemen, we are going to make a *crawly-killer.*"

Chapter 76 | Ayrion

"A LITTLE MORE TO the right. No, your other right, you daft fool! Are you trying to get us all killed?" Abiah glared at the man holding the mirror until the man, with a sheepish expression, finally turned. As soon as he did, the glass caught the sun's rays and burned a hole into the darkness of the mine shaft.

The mine seemed to Ayrion to be a giant sand orm, waiting to swallow them whole. At least now they could see where the monstrous throat would take them.

Ayrion shaded his eyes as he looked up at the intermittent clouds. The sun warmed his face. "Hope it holds out," he said, more to himself than for the benefit of those nearby.

Bek smiled. "This plan is too ridiculous not to work."

"What happens if the clouds cover the sun?" Zynora asked, calmly inspecting her two daggers. With this being their one and only chance to destroy the creature's nest, every man and woman capable of holding a weapon was there, apart from a select few who had been left to tend to the wounded.

Tameel had reluctantly volunteered to stay behind. He had been less than enthused at the idea of his wife facing the vulraaks without him, but with the injury to his leg, he couldn't very well argue the point.

"If we lose the sun," Bek said, "then we fight with torch and blade." He stared at his reflection in the polished steel of his hatchet and bared his teeth.

"And if all else fails," Ayrion said, placing an arm around Zynora's bony shoulders, "we have you."

"If that's the case, Grey Eyes, I reckon we're all out of luck."

Another blinding flash of light caught Ayrion in the face, and he moved to the side to get out of the way. Large pieces of reflective glass that they had been able to scavenge from town were interspersed throughout the ragtag band of fighters, as well as polished bronze, copper, and even steel plating. Each reflected light across the entirety of the cave's open face and surrounding warehouses.

"I just hope we don't run out of reflectors," Abiah said as he counted down the line.

Ayrion drew his swords. "Let's move while we still have the sun."

The company of fighters pressed to the left wall as best they could to allow the reflected light to make its way down the first leg of their journey. Ahead, the sun sparkled off veins of ore still buried in the walls, revealing the first turn in the tunnel.

The light flickered periodically as the person holding the mirror behind them shifted positions to move with the sun. Once or twice it went out altogether, leaving them in darkness. At those times, they were forced to rely on the torches, which barely gave off enough light to see the next ten feet ahead.

Ayrion wasn't much of a praying man—at least he didn't think he was—but he found himself desperate enough to ask the Creator to keep the light strong.

The air was damp and cold, and the smell of death was pervasive, drowning out everything else. Breathing from the mouth only did so much.

It didn't take long before they reached the fork in the tunnel where they had been ambushed before. This time, instead of a single mirror to reflect the light, Ayrion had them tie off two mirrors in a broad V shape with the tip pointed into the light from the previous mirror. The beam split, casting a stream of light against each opposing side of the tunnel, where they set two more mirrors to direct that light down both shafts.

Loud shrieks filled the right passageway as scores of hidden vulraaks were suddenly drowned in sunlight. Many fled into the darker recesses of the mine, but those unable to do so lined the packed dirt and rock with their white bodies.

It was nice to have the upper hand for a change.

After the first time, Ayrion was surprised Argon had attempted the ambush again. Surely, he knew they would expect it. Argon didn't seem to care about the lives of his vulraaks. Perhaps because there were always more where they came from.

"What is that?" some of the fighters asked as they stared down the right fork at the black mist swirling around the tunnel.

"It's the plague being forced from their bodies," Zynora said as the black cloud floated upward and dissipated.

Ayrion wondered if once the plague left their bodies, they would return to normal like Nell had, but he didn't have time to wait around and find out. After leaving a small contingent to stay behind and protect the mirrors, he waved them forward, taking the left passageway, the same one they had traveled the day before.

So far, the left tunnel seemed to be empty. More than once, Bek stopped to put his ear to the rail, each time shaking his head. "Does anyone but me think this has been a little too easy?" he asked.

Ayrion was thinking the same thing. But other than giving up and turning around, they only had one option. *Keep going.*

Chapter 77 | Breen

THE MORNING WAS COLDER than usual. Breen and his father, along with Fraya and Lyessa, had spent the entire night trying to track Ty through the forest. Whoever, or whatever, was controlling his brother had been able to move about without leaving any sign of passing. Finally, as the time for the overlords' meeting neared, they returned to town.

Breen followed his father and Lyessa down River Street, keeping Acorn abreast of Fraya's horse as they went. The white dome of the Sidaran Assembly was just coming into view. He bit off a small piece of dried meat he had laid aside for breakfast and offered Fraya the rest. She devoured the entire thing, apparently not caring about appearing ladylike.

"I'm not exactly dressed for the occasion," Fraya said, looking down at her dirty jacket and pants.

Lyessa smiled. "I'm not in any better shape than you, and I'm the overlord's daughter." She had dark circles under her eyes, and strands of hair had pulled loose from under her hat.

They stopped at the assembly building and Breen dismounted, then helped Fraya down from her horse. Her straight black hair clung to her face, like gloved hands cupping her cheeks, giving her an almost-gaunt look. They were all tired.

Breen would have helped Lyessa as well, but she had already dismounted by the time he got around to her horse, no doubt anxious to get inside.

They tied their horses on the first open rail they could find and started up the front steps. Once inside, they followed Lyessa down the right corridor, stopping just outside the third room on the left.

"They aren't meeting in the assembly room?" Breen asked.

Lyessa shook her head. "The conclave between the overlords isn't open to the full assembly."

"And you're sure your father wants us there?" Breen's father asked. "From what I gathered, the meeting was to discuss the king dismantling Cylmar. Hardly a reason for the wielder council to be in attendance."

"I believe he intends to share the recent attack on Easthaven by the White Tower."

Breen's nerves had him tightening his grip on his belt. It was one thing to stand in front of the Sidaran Assembly and discuss magic, but quite another to do so with three of the most powerful men in Aldor.

The guards opened the doors when they saw Lyessa and raised their fists in salute.

The room Overlord Barl had chosen for this particular meeting was half the size of the assembly chamber and felt less intimidating, which Breen appreciated. Instead of the cold white marble, it held a rich array of wood, all native to the Sidaran Forest. An enormous hearth took up the center of the right wall, with a long table for the overlords directly in front.

"I didn't expect there to be this many in attendance," Breen said, staring at the packed room.

Lyessa smiled. "It's a conclave of the Provincial Authority. Everyone wants to be here."

"Yes, but I figured they would keep it to a minimum for security reasons."

"Which is why they're here," she said, pointing to the host of lancers lining the perimeter of the room, each decked in their finest green-and-gold livery, each holding a ceremonial halberd.

The room was filled with chatter, and from the anxious looks on the faces of those gathered, it appeared the proceedings were about to get underway.

"Over there," Fraya said, pointing to the other side of the room, where Orlyn was standing, waving them over. Apparently, the wielder council had saved them some seats.

As they moved around the back of the audience, Breen couldn't help but notice how underdressed he was. He was still wearing his thick leather riding gear from the previous day, along with a heavy cloak to keep the selection of weaponry he had tucked underneath away from prying eyes. Like his father, he'd opted to leave his bow and quiver with his horse. The guards might not have allowed them in so heavily armed, and with all the added security, they didn't feel the need to worry about thieves roaming around in front of the Sidaran Assembly Hall.

"Well?" Feoldor asked. "Any sign of him?"

Breen's father shook his head. "We'll have to keep looking tomorrow. Maybe Nyalis will find him."

They barely had time to sit before three clacks from the chamberlain's staff on the floor signaled the meeting's commencement, and Overlord Barl stood to address the crowd.

"I would like to welcome Overlord Agnar of Keldor and Overlord Meyrose of Briston to Easthaven," he said, gesturing in both men's direction, "and hope you find your stay a pleasant one."

Each overlord acknowledged this welcome with a slight nod, though Breen thought they didn't seem too pleased to be there. Or perhaps this was simply the way overlords behaved when in each other's company—no one wanting to appear any more eager than their counterparts.

Barl took his seat as Overlord Agnar stood and cleared his throat. "On behalf of the peoples of Keldor, I would like to extend my appreciation to Overlord Barl and the great city of Easthaven for their generous hospitality." Sweeping back the gold-trimmed cape from his dress uniform, he offered a bow from the hip toward the head of the table and retook his seat.

Agnar was the tallest of the three overlords. His face was thin but hard, accented by his square jaw and angular nose. His sharp eyes and crisp actions gave him the appearance of someone with military training.

Overlord Meyrose, on the other hand, didn't bother rising. "I, too, would like to extend my kingdom's sincerest thanks for your generosity," he said, lifting his half-empty glass in salute, "during these most difficult of times." The overlord's cheeks looked flushed, whether due to the man's size or, perhaps, the extent of his drinking, Breen wasn't sure.

Sheeva, who was sitting on the other side of Breen's father, focused her attention on the back of Overlord Meyrose's head. Breen noticed she had one hand around her knife. He had almost forgotten that Meyrose had once employed her and had since put a bounty on her head.

Sheeva must have sensed him staring, because she turned and looked directly at him. He smiled and turned back around.

Those amber eyes were unnerving.

Even with the time they'd spent in Meerwood while the wizard worked on Ty, Breen still felt like he didn't know much about her.

Lyessa spoke softly to his father, and Breen leaned in as she briefly explained how the proceedings would go. Between the audience and the overlords were three desks. Each kingdom was allowed a single scrivener to record the proceedings. The scrivener on the right wore robes with the Sidaran green and gold, while the one in the middle wore Briston's blue and white, and the far left had Keldor's orange and gold.

Along with three separate scriveners, there were also three individual sections of seating for those in attendance, mostly consisting of the overlords' personal entourages, along with a few members of their respective governance. Breen noted the wide, empty aisle between each section, wide enough that those sitting on the outsides could not reach each other.

Barl's section held ten members of the Sidaran Assembly, including the very outspoken Cirian. The overlord had also invited the Easthaven Wielder Council—a risky move on his part—along with a number of other faces Breen didn't recognize.

Barl cleared his throat. "Before we officially open this assembly, are there any grievances that need airing?"

The three overlords took a moment to glance at one another from across the table.

Agnar was the first to speak. "The kingdom of Keldor has no grievance to air with any here at this time."

"The kingdom of Briston also has no grievances at this time," Meyrose said, still clinging to his goblet.

Barl released a small sigh of relief. "Sidara concurs and makes a motion to proceed. All in favor?"

All three echoed, "Aye."

Breen rolled his eyes. Could this get any more boring? He needed to be looking for Ty, not sitting here watching three men take entirely too long to establish that no one wanted to fight the other. The official formalities of this meeting seemed utterly ridiculous. He wondered if anyone would notice if he were to slip out.

"Excellent." Barl folded his hands. "Now concerning the matters at hand."

About time, Breen thought.

"I would be lying if I didn't state that I find the reasons for this meeting, and the fact that we have two empty seats at the table, most disturbing."

"Highly unconventional, to say the least," Meyrose added with a small burp that had Breen shaking his head at the man's lack of decorum. Having just finished what was in his glass, Meyrose held it out to the side, and one of his butlers rushed over to refill it, pouring from a crystal decanter.

"I'm afraid it can't be helped," Barl said.

"I agree," Agnar said forcefully, his own goblet untouched. "Since the time of Torrin, not one of the kingdoms has been in subjection to another. This sets a concerning precedent, especially considering Keldor now shares unimpeded borders with Elondria."

Breen thought Agnar made a good point. Sidara at least had the Razor Spine Mountains as a barrier between it and Elondria. Keldor didn't.

"Dakaran is not his father," Barl said. "He has no respect for the old covenants. He seems to care more for power than he does the rule of law."

Meyrose took another sip of his drink. "Surely you don't hold Elondria to blame for the defense of its people?"

"Of course not. Any one of us would have done the same, and rightly so. No, what I blame is what followed—the complete overthrow of Cylmar and the unprecedented usurping of power by the throne."

"Aye," Agnar said, tugging on the greying whiskers of his ducktail beard. "However, this isn't merely a single overlord that has overstepped his bounds. We are talking about the High King."

"Yes," Barl said. "But it was for this very reason that High King Torrin divided Aldor into the five Provincial Authorities in the first place. To prevent the rise of a single dictator."

"There's no need for a history lesson, Barl," Meyrose said.

Breen hated to agree with the slovenly overlord, but Meyrose was right. Barl needed to get to the point. The sooner they were able to figure out a solution, the sooner he could go look for Ty.

"We wouldn't be here if we didn't already see the need. What I want to know is what can be done about it."

"Yes," Agnar agreed. "Elondria now possesses the largest force of armsmen in Aldor. We need to be careful how we approach this."

"My thoughts exactly," Meyrose said as he held out his empty goblet once more, and once more the same skinny butler hopped from his seat to fill it.

Barl sighed. "And I agree with you. We need to be careful. But we also need to be judicious, which is why I've asked one of our historians of the law to apprise us of what rights we hold under the Aldoran Acts of Alliance."

From the back of the room, an elderly woman stood and made her way to the front. White hair cupped her angular face and draped across her shoulders like a winter's cloak. It looked long enough to sit on. In her arms she cradled a large leather tome, carrying it much like one would a child.

"Gentlemen," Barl said, motioning to the approaching historian. "I give you Alberta Trendall, our Keeper of Books and Historian of Provincial Law."

Alberta bowed.

Breen thought the older woman was going to fall over, but she managed to right herself and make her way to a podium at the opposite end of the table. She opened the book, pulled the long curtain of hair back from her face, and began to read.

Breen quickly discovered he couldn't easily keep up with the highly complex legal jargon. In some places, he felt like he understood what was being read, but in others, it was as though the woman were speaking a completely different language. The overlords didn't appear to be too bothered, though, occasionally nodding at the passages.

Breen's eyes were glazing over as the historian spent more than a quarter hour reading from the large tome in one of the most monotonous voices Breen had ever heard. Finally, the old woman came across a few statutes that Breen did understand.

"The voting majority of the Provincial Authority has the right to suspend or nullify any edict or action not agreed upon by the voting majority of the Provincial Authority. The Provincial Authority is thereby granted the power to reverse any ruling set forth by the High King, provided that ruling is deemed not to be in the best interest of any kingdom other than Elondria, over which the king has complete authority."

Simply put, from what Breen could tell, if the king made an edict that affected more than just the kingdom of Elondria, and the remaining overlords unanimously voted to reject it for their kingdoms, the edict could be reversed. Why hadn't she just said that in the first place and saved them all the headache?

"It appears we do have the rule of law on our side," Agnar said, sitting stiffly in his seat. "But what good does it do if those who are duty-bound to uphold the law not only disregard it but also hold it in blatant contempt?"

All eyes were on the old historian as she stuck her sharp nose back in the pages of her book. She ran her finger across several heavy vellum pages. "Ah!" she said finally. "It says here on page four hundred and thirty-two, section eight, that the Provincial Authority, when by unanimous vote, and having been able to clearly prove that there has been an infringement of those statutes written herein, is granted the right to . . ." Alberta lifted her head from the book and glanced across the table at Barl, her face worried.

Breen held his breath, anxious to hear the verdict.

"Well, go on," Agnar said, sitting on the edge of his seat. "What does it say?"

"They are granted the right to . . . to unseat the reigning king."

Chapter 78 | Breen

THE ROOM WENT SILENT as Alberta left the podium and carried her tome back to her seat.

Surprisingly enough, the first to open his mouth was Meyrose, as he burst into a fit of laughter. "Yes, I can see it now as we walk into the throne room and demand Dakaran give up his crown." The obese overlord laughed some more. "We would be toting our newly severed heads in our laps on the way back out."

Breen almost laughed himself. The thought of any king being willing to give up his throne was preposterous, let alone Dakaran. Breen didn't know much about the man other than rumor, but from what he'd heard, Dakaran would be about the last person to ever give up his seat.

"Yes, well, I hardly think we will be approaching the matter quite in that way," Agnar replied, lifting his hand to rub his neck.

"No," Barl agreed, "but there needs to be an official response. We cannot let this go unanswered. That would only further weaken our position as the Provincial Authority."

"Which is what Dakaran has already done by his own actions," Agnar said. "We should strike now while we still have the ability. With Sidara and Briston standing beside Keldor, we could put an end to this."

Barl leaned forward, resting his arms on the table. Breen wondered if it would come to that. A war of the kingdoms. There hadn't been a war like that in . . . well, he wasn't sure.

"War could be a likely outcome," Barl said. "But I, for one, would rather see a diplomatic solution reached first, if possible. A list of formal grievances should be drawn up and sent to the king to see if he will concede, one of those being to restore Cylmar to its rightful place as one of the five provinces of Aldor."

"That's all well and good," Agnar said, "but we all know what the response will be. Our only option is to start preparing for more aggressive action."

Barl leaned back in his seat. Breen noticed that he didn't argue with Agnar's statement. Probably because the overlord was right.

Breen's stomach tightened at the thought of going to war with Elondria. Didn't they already have enough to worry about? Again, his thoughts shifted back to his brother. They had more pressing matters that needed fixing than the king.

The whole world seemed to be spinning out of control. First, they found out the Tower was hunting them, then they were set upon by a Tallosian war party and a dark witch with her horde of giant spiders, and just when they thought they might make it through, Ty goes and gets himself possessed, and now there was talk of a possible war between the five kingdoms.

Barl tapped his fingers on the arm of his chair. "A more direct action is a possibility we should consider, but—"

"It's more than a possibility," Agnar stated, looking puzzled by Barl's reluctance. "It's a reality."

Barl reached for his goblet but didn't drink. "If we are to consider such actions, we will also need to discuss another growing concern, one that might be the reason behind our new king's rash decisions."

Breen leaned forward anxiously. Lyessa had hinted that her father might address his newly acquired position on magic during the meeting, but Breen was hoping he'd forgotten. The last thing they needed were more eyes on them.

"You are referring to the White Tower, I take it?" Agnar finished the rest of his drink and wiped his mouth. "This new Archchancellor has me concerned. He has more than quadrupled the Tower's size and influence in the short time he's held the position."

Breen noticed Overlord Meyrose fidgeting in his seat at the mention of the White Tower and its Archchancellor.

Agnar pushed his goblet aside. "I don't know how it is here in Sidara, but their presence is growing throughout my kingdom. There's hardly a city or township that hasn't been visited by the white riders. Honestly, I'm beginning to feel that the Black Watch are more of a nuisance than the wielders they hunt."

"Death to all those with magic, I say." Meyrose tilted his head and finished another long pull from his drink and wiped his face with the back of his hand. "Magic is a plague on this land. The sooner it's destroyed, the safer we'll be."

Breen clenched his fists. If there was any justice in the world, Meyrose would choke on his drink. People's willful ignorance never ceased to astound him. Apparently, being an overlord was no exception to such ignorance.

"I hardly think magic is to blame for all of Aldor's problems," Barl said with a quick glance in the wielder council's direction.

Breen took a deep breath. This was it.

"In fact, I have recently had my eyes opened concerning the plight of the ven'ae."

"The *plight* of the ven'ae?" Agnar scooted forward in his seat, eyebrows drawn together. Even Meyrose lowered his drink long enough to listen.

"I can assure you that what I'm about to say is not something I have taken lightly, considering my audience. Agnar, you mentioned earlier that Keldor was being inundated with white riders. Unfortunately, it has been the same here, and worse."

Agnar cocked his head. "Worse?"

"Not three weeks ago, Easthaven came under attack, and I found myself fighting for my very life. If it hadn't been for the intervention of a group of local wielders, I wouldn't be here today."

"Wielders?" Meyrose stiffened, his face reddening even more than normal.

"Yes," Barl said. "We were attacked by a Tallosian war party."

Agnar grunted. "Tallosians? Is this a joke? The Northmen haven't stepped foot on these shores in at least a hundred years."

Barl leaned forward, his expression serious. "They're kind of hard to miss. We managed to capture one and are currently holding him for questioning. But that wasn't the worst of it," he said, his expression growing even more solemn, if that was possible. "What was really disturbing was that they were led by a representative of the White Tower . . . a sorceress."

Meyrose spit his drink. "Don't be absurd, Barl. The White Tower doesn't hire wielders; it kills them."

"The witch called herself Mangora. Not only did she have great power at her fingertips, she also commanded a horde of arachnobes."

Agnar didn't respond. He had appeared skeptical before, but now he looked to be doing his best to keep from laughing. "Far be it for me to ever agree with Meyrose. But even I'm having a hard time believing such a story." Agnar dropped back into his seat with a heavy sigh. "Perhaps we need to call you a physicker."

Meyrose waved his goblet. "Barl, you've gone completely mad."

Barl didn't say anything. He simply leaned back and folded his arms.

Breen knew what was coming, and he tapped his foot anxiously as he waited. Even Cirian, the head speaker for the Sidaran Assembly, was leaning forward in his seat.

Barl twisted around and motioned toward the entrance. The doors opened and a handful of lancers carried in a large wrapped package.

"What's this?" Agnar demanded as the five men positioned themselves on the other end of the table.

"For the love of Aldor, Barl, what in blazes is that flaming awful smell?" Meyrose started to choke as he pinched his nose and waved his hand in front of his face.

With a heave, the armed guards swung the wrapped item up onto the table, leaving Meyrose to quickly snatch his goblet before it overturned.

"Here, let me show you." Barl stood and walked around to the other end of the table and grabbed the cloth. Not waiting for his lancers to finish untying it, he took a deep breath and ripped back the material. The spider's legs came flopping out.

Agnar leaped from his seat and grabbed his sword as he stumbled backward. Meyrose, on the other hand, didn't even make it out of his chair. He squealed as it overturned with him still stuck inside. All of his attendants but one—the man who had been refilling his drink—left him on the floor as they ran in the opposite direction.

Breen laughed out loud before covering his mouth with his hand.

Men and women from the other sections flew from their seats, screaming. There was a stampede for the doors. Not one person took into account the fact that the creature wasn't moving. Those still seated in Barl's section tried their best not to look too amused as they watched the mayhem.

"There's nothing to fear," Barl shouted. With the lancers' help, he managed to calm the people down enough to coax them back to their seats. "The creature is dead." He even went so far as to order one of the soldiers to poke it with a halberd. Once the assembly realized the threat wasn't as dire as it had seemed, they grew more inquisitive and began to crowd around the overlords to get a closer look at the once-ferocious eight-legged creature.

Meyrose's attendants finally righted his seat. The front of his silk vest and velvet overcoat were covered in red wine.

On Barl's command, the lancers rewrapped the spider and carried it back out of the meeting room.

Barl took his seat and waited as the overlords conversed with their advisors before returning to the table. Clearly, the shock of witnessing such a mythical creature had put them in a more open frame of mind.

"I could take you to the site where we burned and buried the bodies of the Tallosian warriors and the rest of the arachnobes, but I figure if this little demonstration isn't enough to convince you that what I say is true, then there's no hope of me ever accomplishing it."

"You've got *my* attention," Agnar said, sharing a stern glance across the table with Meyrose.

Meyrose, still flushed from his embarrassing tumble, merely nodded, his jowls wobbling with the effort.

Barl smiled and clapped his hands together. "Good. Then I believe we—"

A commotion broke out in the corridor outside the meeting room. Shouts could be heard from the other side of the double doors, along with the sharp ring of steel.

"What's this?" Agnar demanded, standing once more.

Meyrose, still wielding his goblet, struggled to his feet with the help of one of his aides and turned around. "What's going on, Barl? I demand an explanation."

There was a loud crack, like lightning striking a tree, and the doors ripped from their hinges and flew across the room, scattering men and women in their wake. The entire assembly erupted once more into a panicked stampede, with members clawing over one another as they tried to reach the far side of the room. Many screamed that the spider had woken to eat them.

Breen's father leaped from his seat and charged headfirst into the terrified throng of people. "Breen! Protect the girls!" he shouted back over his shoulder. "I've got to get to Barl."

Chapter 79 | Breen

"**I** DON'T NEED PROTECTION," Lyessa said as she whipped out her sword and stood next to Breen.

Fraya stood just behind Lyessa, her sword also in hand, albeit somewhat shakily. Breen didn't think he'd ever get used to seeing her like that.

"We've got them," Orlyn said as he and Feoldor moved up beside them. The apothecary held his rune-covered staff in front of him. "Go help your father."

Breen attempted to fight his way through the crowd, but the mass of bodies pressing against each other overwhelmed him. Sheeva, on the other hand seemed to have no problem weaving in and out of the hysteria. Her white head bobbed up and down, disappearing in one place and reappearing in another as she worked her way toward his father.

On Breen's right, Overlord Meyrose tried his best to fend off the mob that was rushing straight for him. When panic took over, it seemed all civilized behavior and social niceties—like titles, wealth, and prestige—

disappeared. Meyrose managed to upend his cup on a woman trying to push by, splashing what remained of its contents in her face and down her dress, while at the same time using it as a bludgeon to crack another man across the side of his head as he attempted to throw the overlord out of the way. The man turned and punched Meyrose full in the face, knocking him clean off his feet.

Breen didn't have time to laugh as he focused on keeping from getting hit himself. By the time he reached Barl's seat, the overlord was nowhere to be seen. His father was standing on the overlord's chair, trying to get a better look. Sheeva stood in front, fighting back those attempting to push the chair aside.

"What do you see?" Breen asked.

"Not much. But knowing Barl, he's probably on his way toward the fighting."

"Kellen!"

His father turned. Feoldor and Veldon were just coming into view as they worked through the sea of faces.

"What's going on?" the dockmaster asked. "You don't think the White Tower has sent a squad of bulradoer to assassinate the overlord council, do you?"

"I almost hope it is," his father said. "But I have a sinking feeling we might have just found Ty."

"Or he found us," Breen added, hoping he was wrong.

Feoldor held up both hands and pushed a wedge of air in front of them that split what remained of the crowd in two. The five of them passed through, with Sheeva in the lead.

"Why in the flaming Pits would Ty be attacking the Provincial Authority?" Feoldor asked.

"'Cause it ain't Ty doing it," Breen said. "Whoever's controlling him is."

"Well, that's a real problem for us, don't you think?" Feoldor said, continuing to push people aside with the hardened air. "He's a faeling, for pity's sake. How are we going to stop him?"

"I'm going to try talking to him," Breen's father said.

"Talking? The last time we tried talking to him, he set Gilly on fire." As if on cue, two lancers flew past the door, screaming. Their bodies had been set ablaze.

The fire was blue.

"It's Ty," Breen said, almost wishing it had been the bulradoer.

They found Barl standing with his men in the doorway.

"We need to get your men back," Breen's father said.

Barl turned, his sword in hand. "It's Dakaran! He's sent assassins to kill the overlords."

"It's not Dakaran," Breen's father said. "It's worse. You need to pull your men back and protect the people. We'll deal with this."

Barl hesitated, but the look on Breen's father's face was apparently enough to convince him. "Captain, order a retreat!"

The Sidaran captain rushed back up the hall, shouting for the lancers to retreat.

Breen's father turned to the others. "Feoldor, we're going to need you to try setting up a shield. Veldon, if that doesn't work, we might need your fire. But do your best not to hurt him if you can."

"I'll try, Kellen, but I can't promise much."

"Hurt who?" Barl asked. "Who are you talking about? Do you know what's going on?"

The lancers were getting closer, slowly retreating in their direction.

"Ty has been possessed by some sort of dark magic," Breen's father said. "Please keep your men back. We're going to attempt to set up a blockade in the corridor. When we do, we need you to get these people out of here. They're going to be like rats in a trap if they stay in this room."

Barl nodded and stepped into the meeting room, ordering his lancers to start herding the frightened people toward the entrance, a difficult task, considering they were all pressed against each other on the opposite side of the room.

Breen scanned the hallway. All the council members who had attended the meeting seemed to be accounted for, except Sheeva. She was nowhere to be seen, but that didn't mean she wasn't close by. Breen only hoped she didn't do anything stupid, like go after his brother on her own.

The floor was layered with lancers, some struggling to rise, others working to help those unable to move. The lancers were now only a couple of doors away.

Shouts rang out and a few of the men in front were thrown backward over the others. Breen watched their bodies hit the ground. They didn't move.

The captain continued shouting for his men to retreat.

Breen and the rest of the council moved against the walls to let them pass. Behind him, Breen could hear Barl issuing orders, directing his men to escort those inside to safety.

Another line of lancers passed, and Breen caught his first glimpse of Ty. His brother stood in the center of the corridor, having stopped about twenty feet from where they were. He seemed to be waiting on something.

As soon as the last of the guards passed, Breen's father shouted at Feoldor, who raised a barrier of hardened air between them and Ty. It wasn't enough to cover the entire hallway, but it was enough to protect the council. The four of them walked out to the center of the corridor and waited. Orlyn, Reloria, and Fraya stayed behind to help with the injured lancers.

Ty remained where he was, white hair tucked behind his ears, the tan overcoat their mother had made for him hanging open at the front. There was something else as well. Something off. A disturbing sort of unnatural grin on his face. Breen shivered. The features were Ty's, but his eyes were anything but. Was there any part of his brother still left? *Fight it, Ty.*

"I don't see it," Breen said.

"See what?" Veldon asked.

"The book."

"It's probably in his jacket," his father said.

Ty took a small step forward, more adjusting his feet than anything. "I heard there was a meeting today, and I didn't want to miss it. Looks like I got here just in time." Ty appeared relaxed, as though he knew he had nothing to fear from the four of them.

Breen's father took a step forward as well, only able to go so far with Feoldor's wall blocking their way. "We're not here to fight you, Ty. We're here to help you."

Breen wondered if Ty could even hear them. Or if his brother was even still in there.

Ty cocked his head. "Help me?" He laughed.

"Ty, can't you see you're acting like a lunatic?" someone said on the right.

Breen leaned forward. It was Lyessa. She passed Veldon, working her way up the wall until she reached the barrier. She knew it wasn't Ty. She'd seen the way he'd attacked his father in the woods. What was she doing?

Surprisingly, Ty didn't do anything but stand there. Perhaps there was still a part of him that had control? Maybe she could reach him.

"Ty, no one here wants to hurt you. Look at me," she said, raising both arms out and doing a complete spin on her heels to let him see she was unarmed. "I'm not a wielder. I don't have any great powers. You could squash me like a bug if you wanted."

Breen's heart was thumping in his ears. Lyessa seemed to be the first person Ty was responding to.

"You know I wouldn't do anything to hurt you. I care about you. And even though you act like a stubborn two-headed donkey sometimes, I know you care about me." She waited for him to say something. "Are you listening to me?"

Feoldor muttered something under his breath concerning her two-headed-donkey comment, and Veldon shook his head. But Breen, for the first time, saw a ray of hope. Ty did actually seem to be listening, his focus solely on her. The disturbing grin he'd been wearing a moment ago was gone. Breen had no idea how much was Ty and how much was the book, but something was working.

"Give her a chance," Breen's father whispered, and Feoldor lowered part of the barrier, just enough to let her slip by.

"Shut up, boy," Ty suddenly said, and Lyessa stopped, not quite sure what to do. "Or I'll make it slow."

She glanced back at the council members, then back at Ty. "I know you care about me, Ty," she continued, her voice noticeably shaking. She took two steps forward and held out her hand. "Please, just give me the book."

Ty's eyes hardened, and the smile returned.

Breen's breath caught in his throat. If he didn't do something, Ty was going to kill her. "Who are you?" he asked, taking a step forward.

Ty turned. "What a silly question. I'm your brother." Ty's smile was enough to send chill bumps down Breen's arms.

"My brother would never threaten his family. He would certainly never try to murder a friend." From the corner of his eye, Breen could see Lyessa slowly easing back toward Feoldor's shield. He needed to keep Ty talking.

"So, the midget made it, did he? How unexpected. Guess I'll have to be more thorough next time."

"There won't be a next time," Breen's father said, having picked up on what Breen was trying to do. "Now, my son asked you a question. Who are you?"

Ty released a loud cackle. "I thought it would have been obvious by now, Master Huntsman. My spiders might not have feasted on your flesh, but that doesn't mean I can't finish what they started."

Breen pulled two daggers from his coat. "Mangora."

Mangora's smile faded as she slowly turned her head and looked at Lyessa. "Now, where do you think *you're* going?"

Chapter 80 | Breen

MANGORA RAISED TY'S HAND and threw a ball of blue flames straight at Lyessa.

There was nothing Breen could do but watch as Lyessa screamed, arms raised to block the flames.

The fire turned a few feet from her face and slammed into the wall, scattering debris across the floor and leaving a dark, smoldering stain where it hit the white stone.

"I've got her!" Feoldor shouted, having deflected the attack by extending his shield.

Lyessa tripped on her own feet and nearly went down as she scrambled to get behind the others.

Ty snarled, blue flames rising from both palms as the light scored his face with deep, threatening shadows. *It's not Ty,* Breen kept telling himself. *It's not Ty.*

Breen's father took a step back to give Feoldor some room and collided with Barl, who was trying to collect his daughter, but Lyessa was having none of it. She drew her sword and stood with the others.

Ty turned his attention back to the wielder council.

Breen stared at his brother, still having trouble believing what he was seeing. There had to be a way to reach him. "Ty, you don't want to do this."

"Waste of breath at this point, son," Veldon said on the other side of Feoldor, his flint in hand, ready to strike.

Of course, he was right. It wasn't Ty they were talking to. Still, Breen couldn't help himself. "Ty, can you hear me? If you're still in there, you need to fight!" He balled his fists. He wanted to scream at how utterly useless he felt. He didn't even have his bow. Not that he would have used it on his brother, but at least he would have felt better prepared.

Feoldor barely had time to brace himself when Ty raised his hand and sent a wave of fire against his shield, strong enough to push him back a step. Intense heat leaked through the shield. Sweat ran down Breen's face as the stone around them baked like an oven. It was hard to breathe, the air coming only in shallow spurts.

Veldon countered with his own flames as Feoldor opened small pockets in the shield for him.

Ty responded with shields of his own, deflecting each attack. The shields were like pieces of glass; if you looked at them directly, you could see through them, but at an angle, it made what was on the other side seem distorted.

"I can't get around her," Veldon said. "She's blocking me at every turn."

"Keep trying!" Feoldor's face was red. He kept his hands in motion as he blocked one volley of blue flame after another, deflecting them into the floor, walls, and ceiling, chipping stone and cracking marble.

Veldon unleashed a wide swath of flame as well, trying to cut through Ty's defenses, managing to force Ty back a step or two.

"We're not trying to kill him," Breen said, worried they were pushing too hard.

Veldon finally let the fire die. "He's too strong!"

"What can I do?" Lyessa asked, sword drawn.

"Nothing we can do," Feoldor yelled back over his shoulder. He turned to angle his shield, and his foot slipped on a piece of loose rubble.

Ty seized the opportunity and flung a single ball of fire through the opening before Feoldor could right himself. Breen's father was standing directly in its path, and Breen was too far away to reach him.

"Look out!" he shouted.

His father turned and started to raise his hands but was suddenly lifted off his feet and thrown through the air, the flames missing him by a handbreadth.

Breen ran to help. He reached down to grab his father's arm, but his hand hit something else.

The air distorted, and Sheeva appeared.

His father looked up at the white-haired assassin and smiled. "Lucky you were there."

She crawled off his chest. "You have all the reflexes of a gopher turtle."

Breen yanked his father back to his feet.

"We can't hold him much longer, Kellen!" Veldon shouted from the front, sending another burst of flame against Ty's shield, trying to distract the witch controlling him long enough for Feoldor to catch his breath.

Ty smothered Veldon's flames, then turned and threw a pulse of energy at the left wall, shattering the marble and leaving the floor covered in its pieces.

"What's he do—" Breen didn't get a chance to finish.

Ty lifted his hands and, muttering something, sent a thin layer of air to lift the rubble.

"Feoldor, the shield!" his father shouted, but it was too late. The witch hurled the rubble straight at them.

Feoldor sent the glassy barrier racing across the hall, but he wasn't fast enough to catch everything. A couple of pieces tore through and hit the guards standing in front of Barl, killing both. One hit Barl in the arm, and he went down, and one ricocheted off the wall and hit Breen in the leg. He fell.

Breen gritted his teeth and looked down, afraid to see how badly he was injured. The piece must have been small; it seemed to have passed straight through his thigh. His father ripped a tunic from one of the fallen soldiers and quickly tied off the wound. Breen cried out as soon as his father slipped the knot and the material tightened around the hole.

"It's clean," his father said. "You'll live."

Breen hobbled back in line behind the others, everyone packed tight behind Feoldor and Veldon to keep from having that happen again.

Feoldor's shield was growing smaller. He didn't have enough strength to hold one wide enough to encompass the entire hall, at least not anymore. It was taking everything he had just to block the witch's fireballs.

Ty was still trading volleys with Veldon, blue fire colliding with orange. If it hadn't been so terrifying, it would have been rather beautiful. The walls shook with the impact as each volley collided with their shields.

Ty moved to the side and hurled another ball, except this time he used one of his own shields to cause the flame to ricochet back around behind them.

Feoldor stood there gaping, with nothing he could do as the blue flames flew around his shield and drove straight for Breen's father once again.

This time, Breen *was* close enough. He jumped in front of his father, knocking him out of the way. He closed his eyes, and in that moment an image of his mother appeared, her straight brunette hair, her kind eyes, her warm smile as she stood there with arms raised, beckoning for him. He would be glad to see her again.

"What are you doing, just standing there?"

What? He was still alive? Breen peeked through his lids. Ty's blue inferno was floating right in front of him. Breen yelped and stumbled backward, wincing as he put weight on his injured leg. The ball of fire twisted and spun in the air as though alive, hungry for the kill. Soon, the flames withered and snuffed out. He turned to find Orlyn walking up behind them, his staff raised and pointed in their direction. The runes were glowing. It was the first time Breen had seen the old apothecary wield it.

"Thanks" was about all Breen managed to get out. "I didn't know you could do that."

Orlyn shrugged. "I didn't either." He looked at the staff. "It was almost instinctual." He started to say more, but another wave of attacks had the old man rushing forward to help the others.

Breen shook his head. He had to do something. Something besides standing there bleeding.

For the moment, with Orlyn's help, the three council members were holding their own, actually forcing Ty back toward the rotunda. But Breen could see they weren't going to last long. Ty was simply too strong to handle, and it had been a number of years since Veldon, Feoldor, or Orlyn had been in their prime.

Breen marveled at his brother's strength. He didn't remember him having such control over his abilities during their battle with the Tallosians. If something as simple as a single book could twist Ty's mind to the point of wanting to kill his own family, what would happen if the White Tower were to get their hands on him?

Something cold slithered up his leg, and he nearly jumped. He turned to find Fraya standing beside him, her hand glowing as she held it over his wound. It was the first time he'd experienced her magic. The pain eased, then subsided altogether, leaving him with a rather pleasant numbing feeling.

He kissed her. He didn't figure a simple thank-you would suffice. "Stay behind me," he said, moving to shield her, but she pushed him to

the side and drew her own sword. He grunted but moved.

The council's momentum was slowing. All three men looked on the verge of passing out, especially Feoldor. If they fell, there was nothing to stop Mangora. Ty was nearing the end of the corridor, and the council's attempt to push him out into the open had faltered, grinding to a halt.

Breen looked around. He had the same gift as his father, but what good was having perfect aim when facing someone who could literally stop anything you tried to throw at them? Then it occurred to him. Why not borrow one of the witch's tricks?

He reached into his pocket and grabbed one of the marbles he used for target practice when he got bored. He studied the witch's shield, the way she blocked Veldon's attacks. She was good, deflecting, parrying. Every attempt diverted.

Breen found his center, releasing his magic to help anticipate the throw. Everything came into focus, allowing him to see exactly what it would take for the marble to reach its destination: the force of the throw, the direction it should take, the angle of the hit to make it around the shields. It was all there. Taking a deep breath, he pulled his arm as far back as he could and waited for an opening in Feoldor's shield.

There it was. He took a deep breath, and the ground under him split, floor tiles snapping as an enormous root tore through and grabbed him by the leg, the same one Fraya had just healed.

"What in faerie fire!" Breen tried to pull his sword, but the root had pinned it to his side. He cried out as it tightened. He grabbed one of the daggers from under his coat and sank it into the wood. The root recoiled and jerked but maintained its grip.

Fraya screamed and lunged, her sword narrowly missing his arm as she swung wildly at the piece of root. She cleaved it in two with a single chop, and it sank back into the ground, only to have three more burst through farther down.

Lyessa and Barl were there in an instant, spinning and cutting, dodging and hacking at the long vines and thick roots as fast as they appeared.

"Orlyn!" Breen's father shouted. "Get back here!"

Orlyn turned and raised his staff in the air, runes glowing. "Begone!"

The roots curled up and immediately pulled back into the ground.

From the front, Ty released another heavy barrage of blue fire against what was left of their shield. Feoldor was about to collapse.

Breen turned, surprised to find the marble still clutched in his hand. He refocused himself and released his magic. He couldn't wait, and as soon as the shield opened for Veldon, Breen responded. He threw the marble, his fingers releasing at the exact moment needed to send it barreling toward the floor.

The marble flew through a hole in Feoldor's shield, sparking blue and orange as it reflected the fires coming from both sides. It hit the floor four feet from the right wall, just missing a piece of broken tile that had been splintered in an earlier attack. The glass ball ricocheted off the ground and hit the right wall, where it bounced once again, slipping just behind Mangora's shield.

The marble clipped Ty's head, and he stumbled to the side, shrieking as his fire was extinguished and shield dissolved. He grabbed his head. The strike had been hard enough to disorient him but not enough to do any permanent damage.

At least, Breen hoped not.

"Now, Feoldor! Hit her now!"

Feoldor didn't look like he could have hit the floor had he fallen, which is what it looked like he was about to do, but somehow he managed to gather one last volley of air and send it straight at Ty.

Ty's body flew through the air and into the foyer, sliding to a stop near the center. Slowly, he lifted his hand to his head, and it came away with blood on it.

Breen gasped. Had they gone too far?

Before they managed to get into the atrium, Ty was back on his feet, his hand glowing as he pressed it to his head.

"That was quite the throw," Breen's father said to him as they ran into the open foyer. Fraya was standing behind Feoldor, her hand glowing as she pushed her magic into him. His face was still pale.

The atrium's vaulted ceiling and wide-open space forced Feoldor to expand his shield even further to keep everyone protected. His arms and legs were shaking as they stopped and took up position about ten feet from where Ty stood.

"This way," Breen's father said as he and Sheeva broke away from the others and headed left around the back of the pillars that lined the outer wall. "We need to get behind him."

Breen ran to catch up, blood pumping as he ignored the pain in his leg from where the roots had wrapped him.

They passed the third pillar and headed for the fourth when his father stopped. Breen skidded into him as someone stepped out from behind the column.

"You're going to need this," Nyalis said, tossing Breen his black bow and quiver. "I found that outside, tied to a horse. Can you believe it? One of the lost magical bows of the Sol Ghati just sitting there for anyone to take."

"Magical?" Breen asked, looking at the runes.

"Created to fight faeries. We'll discuss how you ended up with it later. For now, what in the flaming tongues of Oriffon is going on around here?"

"We found Ty," Breen said, still perplexed about how Nyalis had known he was the one who had left the bow.

Nyalis turned and started for the next pillar. "I can see that for myself. But why here?"

"Barl called for a conclave of the Provincial Authority," Breen's father said as they chased after him. "My guess is she's here to kill them."

"She?"

Breen sneered. "It's Mangora."

Feoldor shouted, and everyone stopped. His shield had given out completely this time. Veldon had his arm around him, holding him on his feet. The rest of the council, along with Barl and Lyessa, were standing behind them with nothing between them and Ty but their clothes and a prayer.

Ty billowed with excitement and hit them with a blast of energy, scattering the group like leaves in a strong wind. Most flew back down the corridor, a couple landed against the walls of the atrium, and Orlyn smacked into one of the pillars and fell. He didn't move.

Fraya struggled to her feet and rushed to help, desperately pushing strands of purple light into the most injured.

Ty raised his hand, and blue flames ignited again in his palm.

Breen didn't stop to think. He grabbed another marble from his pocket and ran out into the center of the atrium. He released his magic and threw the glass ball straight for the side of Ty's chest. He didn't want to risk hitting his brother in the head again.

The marble stopped mere inches away and dropped to the floor.

His heart sank. Ty was shielding his sides as well.

Ty turned and smiled. "You didn't think I'd fall for that twice, did you?" He reached out as if grabbing an invisible object and muttered something under his breath.

Breen's eyes widened, and he clutched his throat. He couldn't breathe. Why couldn't he breathe? The witch had somehow closed off the air. He gasped and dropped to his knees.

"Stop!" His father flew past him, daggers flying from both hands, downward toward Ty's legs. Both the daggers and his father slammed into an invisible barrier and fell backward. His father would have hit the ground if Sheeva hadn't been there to catch him and pull him behind one of the pillars.

Breen tried to speak, but it came out half garbled as he fought for breath. "Ty! Fight it! Please!" His heart pounded in his ears, each beat faster than the one before. His body convulsed. Someone was shouting.

He couldn't tell who it was or what they were saying. What was that stupid wizard waiting—

A blinding stream of golden light flew over his head and slammed into Ty's shield, throwing him off his feet, sending him careening across the floor.

Breen's throat was released, and he sucked in a gulp of air. His head felt like it was going to explode as he sucked in another. He tried to stand, but his father and Sheeva were there, grabbing his arms and pulling him toward one of the pillars.

On the other side of the room, Ty was back on his feet, blood running from the side of his mouth. He hurled a line of blue fire directly at them before they could make it behind the pillar.

Nyalis stepped out and raised his staff. The fire exploded in a cloud of smoke and flew out the front doors.

"It's good to see you again, my boy," the wizard said, walking toward him as though they had merely met on the street. "What have you managed to get yourself into this time?"

"You!" Ty raised his hand and sent a lance of fire directly at him.

Nyalis raised his staff and conjured a hollowed-out shield that curved backward in a half circle and sent Ty's flames straight back at him.

Ty was forced to block his own fire.

Nyalis raised one hand and sent what looked like gold lightning barreling across the room. Ty's eyes bulged as he raised both his hands with a howl, and blue lightning connected with the gold, ricocheting off the walls and ceiling and floor, sending pieces of white granite and debris everywhere.

Claps of thunder shook the hall. The entire foyer was popping and buzzing. Sparks shot in all directions, bouncing off the walls and pillars, finally coming to rest on the tile below.

Every hair on Breen's body stood on end. Was the wizard trying to kill his brother?

"Impressive!" Nyalis shouted over the buzz and hiss of their connecting magic. "Your power is growing."

Breen couldn't tell if he was addressing Ty or Mangora, but he could see sweat beading on the old man's forehead. Nyalis had told them that Ty was more powerful than all of them, including the wizard. What if Nyalis wasn't strong enough to stop Ty, either? The thought hadn't occurred to him until now.

Mangora also seemed to be having difficulty. Ty's arms were shaking under the strain. With a look of desperation, the witch broke off her attack and wrapped Ty in a shield. "You're too late, wizard. I'll kill the faeling before I let you have him."

Nyalis released his attack, and the gold strands of light disappeared.

"Kill?" Breen started to step out from behind the pillar, but Nyalis waved him off. What was the wizard waiting for? Mangora had completely shielded Ty. How were they going to get to the book now? Breen peered around the column. He could see the bulge in Ty's left jacket pocket where he kept the *numori*.

"Your master won't be too pleased to hear you killed his prize," Nyalis said, taking a step forward.

"Stay back, wizard, or I'll suffocate the faeling with his own shield."

Nyalis stopped. He seemed to be pondering her threat.

Breen peeked around the pillar once again. Ty was bent over. He looked like he was having a hard time breathing. Could she really suffocate him?

Breen frantically unhooked his bow. He wasn't going to just stand there and watch his brother die. He looked down at the runes. Nyalis said it was magical. But what kind of magic? If it was created to use against faeries, it had to be powerful. Maybe powerful enough to pierce her shield. He had no idea, but he was desperate enough to try.

"Release him, Mangora," Nyalis said, his voice sounding almost worried. "He's no good to you dead."

Breen's hands were shaking as he pulled one of the black shafts and nocked it. This was crazy. Even if the arrow managed to make it through

Ty's shield—a shield that not even Nyalis's lightning could pierce—he was going to have to shoot a target that was not only a few inches thick but was resting directly over his brother's heart. He wasn't sure that even *his* magic was that accurate.

He glanced around the pillar. Ty was down on one knee, his face pale, lips blue. Breen couldn't wait any longer. Taking a deep breath, he stepped out from behind the column and lifted the bow. He released his magic, and the runes flared to life. His brother turned, fear flashing in his eyes.

Breen concentrated on the bulge over his brother's heart. He pulled the string, but only partially, his eyes never leaving the book. This was an impossible shot.

Mangora evidently saw what he was planning and reached for the book, but Breen was already deep within his magic and his aim locked.

Please don't let me shoot too far, he prayed, then released the arrow.

The string buzzed, and the arrow flew off the bow.

Ty tried to dive out of the way, but the arrow punched through the shield and pierced the book before he could.

Mangora screamed as Ty went down. The shield dissolved.

His brother wasn't moving.

Breen's breath caught in his throat. "No!" He'd shot too far.

Ty suddenly jerked, and Breen exhaled. *He's not dead.*

"Get that book!" Nyalis shouted.

Breen ran past the wizard, his father meeting him halfway.

Ty was writhing on the ground by the time they reached him, his body curled and shaking as he continued to scream.

"Hold his arm," Breen told his father as he bent over and yanked the arrow out and threw it behind him. He reached into Ty's pocket and grabbed the book.

Ty's eyes opened and locked on Breen. There was nothing in them but hatred.

Breen didn't even have time to open his mouth before Ty hit him in the chest with something that sent Breen and the book straight into the air. He was halfway to the ceiling before he realized what had happened, the impact so strong that he had nothing inside to even scream with as he started back down.

Nyalis raised his staff, and Breen hit an invisible wall and slid sideways at least twenty feet safely to the floor. His knees were shaking by the time he reached solid ground.

"Drop it!" Nyalis said.

It took Breen a moment to catch his breath. He quickly threw the book to the floor and backed away. The wizard unleashed a single strand of his golden lightning, and the *numori* burst into flames.

Ty screamed once more, convulsing so strongly that Breen's father was thrown to the side.

Breen hobbled back to his brother and knelt to pick him up.

"Stop!" Nyalis said. "Don't touch him. I need to purge the darkness from his mind." The urgency in the wizard's voice held Breen back. Nyalis leaned on his staff and stiffly knelt beside Ty's limp body.

"Will he live?" Breen asked.

Nyalis laid his staff on the floor beside him and stretched his hands over the top of Ty's head. "I believe so. However, the effects of such a twisting can only be healed with time and patience."

Breen glanced over his shoulder. Fraya was helping Orlyn to his feet, her hands still glowing as she infused the old apothecary with her magic. She looked pale herself.

Lyessa and her father, along with the other members of the council, limped over to join them as they gathered to watch the wizard perform his magic, being sure to keep a safe distance.

"I believe I can reverse the damage," Nyalis said. He started chanting softly, so softly Breen couldn't make out the words.

Breen breathed a heavy sigh of relief, though, when his brother's body seemed to relax, his chest rising and falling in a slow rhythmic fashion. "As long as there is hope."

Nyalis looked up and smiled. "There is always hope."

Chapter 81 | Ferrin

ERRIN URGED THE HORSE faster through the mountain pass. He had stolen the animal in town, not something he was proud of, but when being chased by an inquisitor and his bulradoer, desperate times sometimes called for unscrupulous decisions.

The walls of the pass were steep and jagged. Loose rock lined both sides of the narrow trail, forcing him to stay near the center of the winding passage. The wind whipping down through the rocks from the snowcaps above was so cold, it burned his skin like a hot poker.

Ferrin pushed on, knowing all too well that Cheeks wouldn't be too far behind. He didn't have to hear or see the corax to know they were there. He could feel them in the small hairs on the back of his neck.

He prayed his friends had made it out. The thought of what the inquisitor would do to them, especially to Rae, sent a chill through him that threatened to overpower even the icy gusts.

He rounded the next bend and kicked his horse into a full gallop when he saw travelers up ahead. Could it be—

They turned at the sound of his horse, and Ferrin almost started to cry when he saw their faces. They'd made it out.

Myron looked relieved, Suri waved enthusiastically, and even Rae had a small grin for him, until she saw the blood on his arm.

Ferrin pulled alongside Rae, and she held out her hand. He shook his head, not understanding what she wanted.

"My crystal."

"What, no warm welcome? No 'it's great to see you're alive, Ferrin'?" He removed the chain holding her transferal from his neck and handed it to her. She grabbed it, wrapped it around her neck, then leaned over and stuck her hand through his torn sleeve. The familiar icy burn worked its way into his arm, followed by a soothing numbness.

Ferrin lifted his arm to inspect her work. Good as new.

"Well, I'm glad to see you," Myron said. "We feared the worst when you didn't show up this morning."

"How did you know—"

"It was Suri. She heard those creatures again, so we packed the gear and headed for the passes. We left your horse and saddle in case you needed them." He glanced at Ferrin's tired mount. "But apparently, you didn't. We also left word with Tibble and Kyleen that if they were to see you, they should let you know where we went."

"I'm afraid they didn't get the chance."

"What do you mean?"

"By the time I made it back to the inn, the place had been ransacked. Two of those bird creatures were . . ." He glanced at Suri and decided not to finish. "They just didn't make it."

Myron shook his head, and Rae put her arm around Suri.

"I would have been here sooner," Ferrin said, "but I had a run-in with the hunting party who's been tracking us. I barely escaped. And that's not the worst of it." He glanced at Rae. "Sylas is back."

Rae's face went blank.

"Inquisitor Sylas?" Myron asked. "How's that possible? I thought you said you killed him."

"I did. Or . . . that is, Rae did. He's not the same, though. He's been . . . changed."

"Changed?"

Ferrin explained what had happened to him since Cheeks's arrival at the smithy. How he was traveling with a bulradoer, one with red hair and strangely colored eyes.

"Lenara," Rae said under her breath. "Her name is Lenara."

"You know her?"

Rae nodded.

"I've seen her around," Myron said. "She works for the Archchancellor."

"She's dangerous, I'll say that," Ferrin said. "If it hadn't been for these blades, I wouldn't be here now."

Myron glanced excitedly at the two swords strapped to Ferrin's waist. "They stood up to a bulradoer?"

Ferrin nodded, and Myron's eyes lit up.

Ferrin went on to describe the fight between him and Lenara as well as his battle with the corax and the narrow escape down the side of the cliff.

"Someone up there's watching out for you," Myron said. "Best we get out—"

Suri gasped and everyone turned. She grabbed Rae's arm and pointed back the way they had just come. Twisting in his saddle, Ferrin could just make out the two dark winged shapes heading their way.

"It appears our time has just run out," Myron said.

Ferrin looked at Rae. "You and Suri head for the bridge. We'll catch up."

"Why? What are you going to do?" Rae didn't appear eager to take off without them.

"Do I detect a hint of concern?" Ferrin asked, swinging down from his horse.

Rae scowled. "Concerned you two will lose our supplies."

"How very thoughtful of you," Ferrin said, then smacked the back of her horse and sent it galloping. "We'll be right behind you!"

Myron had already grabbed one of the crossbows from his saddle and handed the second to Ferrin. "I've had just about enough of these black-winged pigeons." Swinging down off his horse, the former captain loaded his bow.

"You took the words right out of my mouth," Ferrin said as he slid a wide-tipped bolt onto his. Both men moved their horses out of the open and behind some of the larger boulders at the side. Myron took up a position on the opposite wall as they waited for the corax to get within shooting range.

"Whatever you do," Ferrin said, "don't miss. This is our one chance to make a clean break without them knowing where we're going."

"So, no pressure, then."

Ferrin chuckled, then focused, watching the corax slowly head their way.

Their wingspan was quite impressive, reminding Ferrin of the great wood owls he used to see at night in the forests near Rhowynn, nearly five feet from tip to tip. The birds closed the distance, their heads shifting right to left as they scanned the empty chasm below. The one on the left released a loud caw as they came within range.

The two creatures suddenly broke away, realizing they were being targeted.

Ferrin cursed, and the two men stepped out from behind the boulder and took aim.

Ferrin hit the release, and the bowstring thrummed. He heard Myron do the same. He held his breath and craned his neck to see if he'd hit anything. His bird shrieked and faltered as it slowly spun downward. Myron's didn't make a sound; it simply went stiff and fell.

"Yes!" Myron shouted.

Ferrin turned, and the two men started laughing. It had been a long time since they'd had a victory. If they could get through the pass, they could very well give those hunting them the slip.

"Blazes!" Myron pointed up at the sky.

Ferrin turned. The creature he'd hit had somehow righted itself and was flying off in the opposite direction. It was too far away to shoot now.

Ferrin wanted to throw his bow. He looked at Myron. "At least you killed yours. Remind me to find some time to practice with these stupid things."

"I'm afraid time is the one thing we don't have."

Neither bothered reloading.

Ferrin swung back onto his horse and handed Myron the bow. "Hurry. Now that we've been spotted, it won't take the corax long to report our whereabouts." Ferrin dug his boots into his horse's sides and took off.

Myron was right behind him.

"If we can make it across the bridge," he shouted, "I might be able to use my sword to stop the Black Watch from following!"

"How do you plan on doing that?" Myron shouted back over the sound of the wind and horses' hooves.

"By destroying it behind us."

Both men leaned low across their horses' necks, urging the animals on. Ferrin's tired steed was having a hard time keeping pace. "Come on, old boy, hang in there," he said, rubbing the animal's neck. His hand came away wet with lather. "Hold on; it can't be much farther."

The pass continued to twist and turn as they went farther in, the tunnel of rock snaking toward Virn Run. If they could reach the other side before their pursuers caught up, he could try cutting away the bridge's supports to keep Cheeks and the bulradoer from crossing.

Ferrin cut his horse sharply around the next bend and yanked back on his reins to keep from colliding with Myron. The captain had stopped in the middle of the trail to keep from running over Rae and Suri, who were staring at the embankment ahead.

"What are you waiting . . ." Then he saw it.

The bridge was gone.

Chapter 82 | Ayrion

H ALFWAY DOWN THE next tunnel, their light disappeared again, but this time, it didn't seem to be coming back as quickly.

Whenever the darkness took over, Ayrion could feel the tension escalate, those around him jumping at every little thing, prayers coming from some, curses from others. "We're getting close," he said. The thunderous sound of water ahead was coming from around the next bend.

If not for their light going out, they probably wouldn't have noticed the faint teal glow filtering in from the connecting passageway ahead. They moved forward to get a better look, stopping where their tunnel opened into a large cavern.

No one entered the chamber until the next reflector was in place. As soon as the light bounced off the standing mirror and into the cavern beyond, Ayrion waved them forward, making sure he was the first out of the tunnel.

The cavern was enormous. It was one of the most impressive things he'd ever seen, or at least that he could remember seeing. Along the walls, strange crystals jutted out from random outcroppings of rock. The crystals were clearly the source for the teal glow they had seen earlier, lighting the cavern to the point of them not needing their torches.

On the right wall, a waterfall cascaded down an open face of dark rock from a higher ledge above, pooling at the bottom, where it formed a small underground river that flowed across the entire length of the cavern, reaching the far-left wall. From there, it wound into a tunnel and disappeared beyond. Halfway between the waterfall and where the river disappeared into the left tunnel, a bridge spanned the water, allowing passage to the back half of the cavern.

"This place smells like rot and . . . and wet dog," Abiah said, wrinkling his nose. "We're clearly heading in the right direction."

"That would be my guess." Bek pointed at the array of bones scattered across the open rock between them and the river about thirty feet ahead. Some still had fresh pieces of flesh attached.

Ayrion scanned the empty room. Where were the vulraaks? Were they hiding in one of the other tunnels behind them, waiting for them to get trapped in this chamber before attacking? "Let's set up another couple of mirrors here and here," he said, pointing to two spots just outside the tunnel entrance. "I want to be able to aim that light in more than one direction at a time."

Abiah worked with those holding the reflectors while Bek organized two groups to start a thorough search of the cavern.

Zynora was one of the last out of the tunnel, her daggers at the ready. They appeared almost natural in her hands. He wondered how many times she'd been forced to use them before now. Her Rhivanni arm cuffs gave her the appearance of an ancient warrior, battle hardened and ready for anything.

"Any sign of where they went?" she asked.

He shook his head.

Zynora looked around the cavern, studying the river as it moved from one side of the open chamber to the other. "Normally, I would say that's a good thing, but we need to find them before the sun goes down."

"I agree." Ayrion headed for the bridge. It spanned one of the narrowest regions of the river, at least fifteen feet. The bridge was barely wide enough to fit three, shoulder to shoulder, but the wood was solid with no give at all as he walked across. He stopped about halfway and leaned over the railing, kicking a piece of rock into the quick-moving water below. He wondered how deep it was.

"I don't understand," Zynora said as she and Abiah joined him. "Where are they? They should have been here."

"Perhaps we should have taken the other fork," Abiah suggested.

"No," Ayrion said, walking back to their side of the cavern and following the water back toward the pool at the bottom of the falls. "This is the most logical spot—fresh water, plenty of room, and by the size of those piles of carcasses back there, we've clearly found the nest." Ayrion stared up at the rocky ledge, watching the water pour over the shelf in heavy sheets. "I don't know why they're not here."

The spray from the waterfall felt cool on his face, his leather coat shimmering from the moisture building on the outer layer.

"We've searched every inch," Abiah said, speaking loudly to be heard over the water. He pointed back toward the entrance. "The only way in is the way we came."

"That's not entirely true." Ayrion pointed his sword in the direction of the waterfall. "We haven't looked there."

"Behind the falls?"

Ayrion nodded.

A group of villagers were already nearing the falls from the other side of the river, having made a partial sweep of the back half of the cavern. Ayrion waved at them and pointed in the direction of the water. They must have understood, because they immediately started climbing up the rock to a small shelf about ten or twelve feet off the main floor, which ran the entire length of the falls.

They worked their way along the back edge, weapons at the ready, until they were right up against the water. One of the men in front slipped and would have fallen headfirst into the pool below if not for the woman beside him grabbing hold of his clothing and pulling him back against the rock face.

Abiah huffed. "That was a close—"

The entire cavern suddenly went dark as the light from the reflectors behind them disappeared, leaving the chamber awash in the crystals' light.

Abiah lifted his sword. "Makes my skin crawl every time it does that."

Ayrion stepped forward to wave the searchers back, but before he could, the man at the front who'd almost fallen a moment ago was suddenly ripped off his feet and dragged into the cascading water. The lady beside him grabbed for his legs but only managed to hold on to his boot as she was thrown off the edge and into the pool below.

There was a short burst of horrific screaming from somewhere behind the falls, and then the water ran red as what was left of the man's body was flung out of the spillway. The corpse almost landed on the woman in the pool. She screamed and swam as fast as she could to reach the far side, where Ayrion and others were standing.

Ayrion hopped down on the rocks leading to the pool and helped her out, handing her up to Abiah and some of the others who'd rushed over to see what was happening.

Up on the ledge, the search party nearly threw each other off as they fled back across the stone walkway and started climbing back down. They'd only made it about halfway when white bodies poured out from the falls behind them.

Ayrion's heart nearly stopped.

One look at the vulraaks, and those still on the ledge threw themselves off without waiting for those in front to finish their climb. By the time they had all reached the bottom, more than half needed help just to walk, having sprained, twisted, or broken arms or legs in the process.

A few managed to jump far enough to land in the pool, but most had landed on the cavern floor.

Bek and a second party of searchers were already running across the back half of the chamber toward the falls to help.

"On me!" Ayrion shouted as he hopped up from the pool and raced for the bridge.

The rest of their fighters ran to join him.

Bek and his team quickly grabbed those of the injured they could before the vulraaks descended on them, then ran for the bridge. Those left behind cried out for help, attempting to drag themselves to the water, hoping to throw themselves in before the creatures got them.

Ayrion hit the other side of the bridge at a full run, blades drawn. Abiah, Zynora, and their fighters were only a few steps behind. "Where is that flaming light?"

The vulraaks had no problem leaping from the ledge down to the main floor of the cavern. Their bodies were stronger, more agile, and their lust for blood overpowered all other instincts.

Bek, with his long legs, was the first to reach Ayrion. He handed the injured woman he was carrying off to another villager behind them, grabbed his hatchets, and turned to catch up. Wrapped from head to toe in thick furs, and lips curled back like a rabid dog, the big trapper looked more frightening than the vulraaks.

Ayrion pushed out with his senses and let his magic take over as he lifted his swords and tore into the white creatures.

The vulraaks screeched and hissed as they reached for him with their claws. By the time his momentum had stopped, he was at least six or seven deep into their ranks. He cut down everything moving. His entire body became a weapon, its only purpose to kill vulraaks. Heads rolled, arms dropped, insides burst wide. Yet they kept coming.

It took a moment for the rest of his fighters to reach him. Bek made it the closest. Ayrion could hear the man growling as he chopped down one creature after another.

Above them, an enormous bellow rang out, echoing across the open rock. Out of the corner of his eye, Ayrion saw Argon raise his massive wedge of steel and leap from the ledge, cutting down three of Ayrion's men with one swing.

"Retreat!" Ayrion shouted. "Get to the bridge!"

Argon swung his enormous blade through their ranks like a scythe to a row of wheat, reaping bodies with every pass. Those who didn't die immediately, he crushed underfoot.

Ayrion fought near the front, holding as many of the creatures back as he could, giving his people a little more time. If they could just make it back into the tunnel on the other side, the narrow passage would give them at least a small chance at holding their enemy at bay.

Argon howled as he swung left and right, killing human and vulraak alike to reach Ayrion. Anything that got in his way died.

Where is that light?

Argon kicked a handful of vulraaks out of the way and swung his massive blade down at Ayrion's head. The swords connected, sparks flying. The force of Argon's swing should have driven Ayrion straight into the rock, but the magic of his blades absorbed it, leaving him with only a minimal tingling in his arms.

The ten-foot-tall creature seemed to have all the advantage. It took both of Ayrion's weapons and all his concentration to keep Argon's steel from chopping him in half. Dancing to the left, he barely escaped as the steel struck the rock where he'd been standing, throwing debris into the air. Ayrion ducked and spun right, clipping Argon in the leg but not enough to bring him down.

Diving to the right, Ayrion rolled onto the bridge. His people were already on the other side. He deflected another swing, and Argon's steel sliced straight through the railing on the left side, splintering it into pieces and leaving half of it hanging in the water.

Back and forth they fought, blade against blade, the rest of the creatures pulling back to give their master plenty of room.

In one of the few moments Ayrion got the chance to look behind him, he could see Bek and Abiah standing at the far edge of the wooden slats, ready to run to his aid if he called them.

The bridge, like a small stage to a badly performed drama, shook under the force of Argon's weight, both sides watching from their respective banks as their champion fought for the victory.

Ducking low, Ayrion felt the rush of air from Argon's blade fly overhead. He spun and managed to land a sharp cut to Argon's arm as he righted himself for the creature's backswing. Ayrion's arms felt as heavy as tree trunks; each breath was a battle in itself. Even with the aid of his magic, Argon's size and strength were forcing Ayrion back, one step at a time. Before he knew it, his feet were no longer scraping against wooden planks but bare stone.

Bek and Abiah stood at the forefront of their fighters behind him, watching as the vulraaks slowly descended on the bridge. The white creatures were now crossing over behind Argon, hoping to get a foothold on the other side.

"Get to the tunnels!" he shouted.

Ayrion fought to keep the ancient general from advancing, but Argon was too powerful. Deflecting another overhead blow, Ayrion rolled to the side and swung for Argon's legs once again. Having already taken more than one cut from Ayrion's steel, Argon wasn't willing to be caught unprepared again. He sidestepped and blocked, then kicked Ayrion, sending him backward a good five feet, where he landed and rolled, the wind knocked out of him.

He was back on his feet, swords up, still struggling to catch his breath, when white bodies poured from the bridge.

"Get down!"

Ayrion recognized the voice and immediately dropped to the cavern floor as a thunderous blast of energy drove over him and straight into the right side of the creatures' ranks.

The shock wave shook the cavern and sent vulraaks flying through the air in all directions. Argon, seeing what was coming, had dropped to the ground as well, only receiving a partial blast that sent him rolling a few feet toward the river. He stopped himself at the edge before going in.

Ayrion was back on his feet and running for the exit. "Into the tunnel! We need to protect the reflectors!"

They had lost at least a quarter of their fighters in the initial barrage, leaving those who were left nearly too petrified to continue. The vulraaks, however, had lost at least a third of theirs, many of which ended up floating off in the river's current.

"A lot of flaming good those stupid things have done us!" Abiah barked as he helped Bek carry Zynora back inside the tunnel's entrance, trying not to trip over the upright mirrors behind him.

No one argued the point, least of all Ayrion. His reflectors had led them into this death trap and had done precious little to aid them in their fight.

"Something must have happened back up the line," Bek said. "Maybe the creatures managed to kill some of our holders. It only takes one to put an end to the entire thing."

Ayrion pointed at a small group of fighters cowering near the right wall. "Go see if you can find out what's happening with our light."

They took off running, eager to be away from the vulraak-infested cavern in front of them.

"We left as many people as we thought we could spare to protect them," Abiah said. "What else could we do?"

Bek spun his hatchets. "It was a good idea. We just lack the luck needed to pull it off."

Abiah grunted. "No doubt we used it all trying to survive last night."

Inside the cavern, the remaining vulraaks spread out in front of Argon. Their numbers were staggering. They extended halfway across the entire front of the underground river, and more were still crossing from the other side.

Ayrion sighed. This was going to be a short fight.

"I wonder why the big one is staying back this time," Abiah said, nodding toward Argon.

"Because these tunnels are too small for something as big as him to maneuver in," Ayrion said. "We would have too much of an advantage."

Bek smacked his lips. "I could really use another one of those shots of black briar right about now."

Abiah smiled. "Aye. Can't think of a better way to go."

Argon roared from the back of his army, signaling them to charge.

"Well, gentlemen, it's been an honor," Ayrion said as he tightened his grip on his blood-soaked blades.

"I'll be seeing my son soon enough," Abiah said.

Ayrion closed his eyes as the vulraaks neared, releasing what magic he had left. He could feel the weight of their charge through his boots. He opened his eyes and raised his blades.

Abiah was the first to bellow out a high-pitched battle cry as the creatures tore into the tunnel and hit their line.

Bek roared like a bear on Ayrion's left.

Ayrion didn't bother. He let his blades speak for him as they tore into the vulraaks with a fury that set his blood on fire. He cut and slashed, lunged and thrust. With every swing of his blades, another vulraak lost its life.

On his right, Abiah kept his sword moving, rage driving him for vengeance. He hit the side wall but pushed his way back while stabbing at the guts of every white belly he saw, spitting insults the entire way.

The tunnel might have kept them from being surrounded but not from being overrun, as they were outnumbered at least three to one.

Ayrion didn't know what to do except keep his blades moving. He felt a sharp pain in his arm and kicked the creature that had clawed him in the knee, then took off the top of its head. Bone, blood, and viscera splattered the creatures behind. With his left sword, he severed an arm, and letting the momentum continue, he chopped off the same creature's leg halfway down its thigh.

From the corner of his eye, Ayrion could see Bek's hatchets swinging but not the man himself. He was completely surrounded.

Ayrion could taste the creatures' blood in his mouth. It covered his face. He shook his head to fling the drops from his eyes. He cried out as another creature broke through and raked the side of his leg with its claws.

He kicked it in the face and drove his sword down through its skull and out of its mouth before the vulraak could get its teeth in him.

Ayrion was in the middle of offering one final prayer for salvation when he heard what sounded like another horde of creatures coming from the tunnels directly behind.

His heart sank. He didn't finish his prayer. His pleas were evidently falling on deaf ears. With what little strength he had left, he poured all his hatred into his black steel and waited for the end.

Suddenly, the tunnel filled with light as a small wave of fighters behind them, led by a crazy white-haired tinker with bronze cuffs on his forearms and a long dagger in each hand, tore around the bend.

"We fixed the lights!" Tameel shouted, half limping, half hopping his way to the front.

The vulraaks quickly retreated back toward the cavern, shrieking.

"Get those mirrors up!" Ayrion shouted, grabbing one of them himself and running after the fleeing creatures. He hit the entrance and spun, angling the mirror and watching with glee as the sunlight tore across the front of the river and into the vulraaks' ranks.

They screamed in terror. Everywhere the blinding light hit, the creatures were stopped in their tracks, white bodies writhing across the stone as the sun's rays ripped the darkness from them. Like a surgeon, the light cut its way through their flesh and released the plague underneath. Dark clouds of mist enveloped the cavern as the pandemic gathered in the air.

Abiah grabbed another mirror and doubled the assault. "Take that, you flaming white faeries! I'll roast every last one of you!" He bellowed out a hard laugh as he chased vulraaks all across the chamber with the light.

Ayrion spun the mirror around and hit Argon with a direct beam, but nothing happened. The enormous creature laughed as he tore across the bridge. Those vulraaks on the other side of the river joined him as they made a swift retreat back to the waterfall.

This wasn't over.

Chapter 83 | Ferrin

HE RIVER WASN'T TOO far of a drop below them—maybe ten feet—but the bank on the other side was too steep to climb.

"What are we going to do?" Rae had to shout to be heard over the force of the river's current. She clutched Suri's hand to keep the little girl from getting too close to the edge.

"Even if we were to climb down there," Myron said, "we'd never be able to swim to the other side. The water's too strong."

"Where's that map?" Ferrin headed for the horses. "Are there any other routes out of here? Maybe we can double back and take one of them."

Myron pulled the map from one of the saddlebags and held it out for the two to study.

"There," Ferrin said, pointing to a small trail that forked off the main pass not far from where they were. "I remember seeing it on the way in. Hardly large enough for a single rider, but we don't have much of an option."

The captain nodded, rolling the vellum and stowing it in the bag before mounting.

"Hurry," Ferrin said, helping Rae and Suri onto their horse, then climbing onto his own. He snapped the reins, and the four rode hard back the way they'd come. He realized he was holding his breath at every new turn, expecting to see white riders heading their way.

Up ahead, Ferrin recognized some of the outcroppings from the long straightaway where they had attempted to shoot the corax. "Come on, you poor old animal, don't fail me now." The narrow trail they were racing to lay at the back end of the corridor, just before the next curve. He spurred his horse even faster. By the sound of its heavy breathing, Ferrin was afraid the old animal was going to collapse underneath him.

They raced down the straightaway. Ferrin could see the small turn ahead. "There!" he shouted, pointing off to the right. He'd barely gotten the words out when riders rounded the corner ahead. Riders with white uniforms.

"No!" Ferrin yanked back on the reins, but it took his horse a few strides to stop. There was no way they could reach the turnoff before the Tower's guards had them, and even if they did, it wouldn't matter. The whole point was to get away without the Watch knowing where they'd gone. If only he'd managed to kill that second corax.

"Back!" Ferrin yelled, spinning his poor horse around and kicking it into a full gallop. "Back to the river!"

The Tower guards picked up speed when they saw them, the sound of their horses' hooves sending chills up Ferrin's spine as he urged his tired horse to go faster. They reached the end of the straightaway and cut to the left, then back to the right, then right again as they followed the snaking passage back to the river.

"What do you have against me?" Ferrin shouted up at whoever might be listening. Azriel's voice came back to him. *We all have a purpose. You must find yours.*

Ferrin growled. Even out here, he couldn't seem to escape his cellmate's preaching.

He glanced over his shoulder at the next straightaway. The Tower's guards were catching up.

Rounding the last corner, Ferrin leaped off his horse and raced to the edge of the small rise where the bridge had once been. Never had freedom been so close and yet so far away.

"Well, do something!" Rae shouted.

"Like what? We have nowhere to go." He glanced up the stone face, but the rock was sheer and smooth, no foot- or handholds of any kind. Not that they could have scaled the mountain with Suri in tow anyway. "Get the weapons."

They quickly unpacked their bags and grabbed anything they could fight with. Side by side, they stood waiting, swords at their waists and crossbows in hand. Myron took a few moments to show Rae how to use the weapon. He'd already loaded the bolt, so all that remained was to aim and snap the trigger. Ferrin doubted she'd hit anything, but it couldn't hurt to have one more shot in the mix.

Suri remained behind Rae, holding tight to the folds of her mother's new dress.

Ferrin could feel the horses before he heard them, the ground shaking as the Black Watch rounded the bend. Ferrin lifted his bow.

"Don't waste your shot," Myron said. "We'll only get the one. Make it count."

Cheeks was one of the last around the corner.

"I've got the—"

Rae's bolt flew from its bow before Ferrin could finish. The arrow flew directly at Cheeks, then veered up and over his head as the redheaded bulradoer waved her arm to the side.

Rae threw the bow on the ground, screaming at having missed.

The riders reined in when they saw the crossbows. They clearly hadn't expected to see the four of them standing in the middle of the pass, waiting for them.

Myron fired next, aiming for the bulradoer.

While she was busy keeping herself from getting hit, Ferrin quickly shifted his aim and fired. A man in the front slumped over and fell from his mount. Ferrin let his bow drop and drew one of his newly forged blades.

"This is flaming worthless!" Myron said as he tossed his bow to the side and drew Ferrin's other sword from his belt, balancing it in his hands. "Oh, I like this."

Rae grabbed the short sword Myron had given her and stood ready. "Stay behind me," she said to Suri, who looked on the verge of crying.

Cheeks smiled from atop his horse. And why wouldn't he? He had them exactly where he wanted them. The man was as lucky as a three-handed Delgan in a wrestling match. He couldn't even die without cheating death.

"My dear smith, we need to quit meeting like this. All this hostility's not good for the digestion."

"Well, if anyone would know something about digestion, it would be you," Ferrin spat.

The inquisitor laughed. "Yes," he said, patting his now-thin frame. "I guess you're right. Looks like I have a new body to reshape." He looked at Rae. "And how do you like my new body, my dear?"

She raised her sword in answer.

"I see you've taken care of my little Suri." He waved at his daughter. "Do you want to come give your papa a big kiss?"

The little girl ducked behind Rae, shaking her head no.

Cheeks looked at Myron. "I see the traitorous captain is still hanging around. I figured you would've made a break for it the first chance you got. Glad to be proven wrong. I will enjoy my time with you on the rack. I promise to make it slow and painful."

When Myron didn't give him the satisfaction of a response, Cheeks turned to Ferrin. "I must admit I wouldn't mind getting my hands on one of those swords myself."

"Come a little closer and I'll oblige that request."

Cheeks grinned and wagged his finger. "Ah, ah, ahh. I want you alive." He turned to the bulradoer, then pointed at Rae and Suri. "Bring them to me."

The cloaked wielder raised her hands and mumbled something under her breath.

Ferrin tensed. He didn't like where this was going. He turned to pull Rae and Suri behind him, but his hand hit an invisible wall. He pushed on it, but it wouldn't move. He punched it, and nearly broke his fingers. Finally, he tried using his sword, and the blade struck the edge and bounced off.

Rae beat her fist against the back of the barrier, trying to break free as it slowly pulled her and Suri in the guards' direction. Myron swung at the wall as well, his sword faring no better than Ferrin's.

Rae turned and looked at him, tears in her eyes. She knew what she was about to lose. She knew what being captured meant for her and Suri.

Ferrin's heart sank, his mind racing as he racked his brain for something he could do. But there was nothing. What good was being a metallurgist if he couldn't use it?

He turned to take one last swing at the wall when Suri stepped out from behind her mother's dress and pointed at the guards' horses. "Go away!"

All of the horses' heads snapped to attention. All but Cheeks's.

The horses bolted back down the trail, tossing half of their riders to the ground. Those who managed to stay seated were carried off with them, including the bulradoer, who was clinging to her horse's neck to keep from being thrown.

Cheeks sat calmly, his horse the only one impervious to Suri's command. He stared at the little girl with a greedy smile on his face that had Ferrin cringing.

Ferrin reached out and found the bulradoer's shield was gone. "Run!" he cried, slamming his sword into its sheath and scooping Suri up in the process.

Rae quickly caught up.

Myron grabbed three of their gear bags and dashed for the ledge. He dove off just in front of them.

"No!" Cheeks shouted behind him. "Get them, you fools!"

"Hold your nose," Ferrin told Suri. He snatched the last bag and leaped over the edge.

The water stung like a thousand needles as they went in. He fought his way back to the top, breaking free of the surface just in time to see Rae hitting the water behind him. He held Suri's head above the waves as she screamed for her mother.

Downriver, Myron's head bobbed up and down as he fought against the current.

Turning, Ferrin caught a quick glimpse of Cheeks standing at the edge of the embankment. Even over the rush of the water, Ferrin could still hear the inquisitor shouting at the top of his lungs.

"This isn't over, smith! I *will* find you!"

The current pulled Ferrin around the next bend as he fought to keep Suri's head above the water. He was a good swimmer. He'd spent years fishing on Lake Baeron, and when the fish weren't biting and the summer sun was hot, he'd strip and dive in. There were places around the northwest edge of the lake that were so clear, he could see the bottom. But the placid waters of the lake were a far cry from the raging torrent of Virn Run as it sped through the mountain passes.

By himself, he might have been able to make it. But not only did he have to worry about making sure Suri could breathe, he was also holding on to the precious little supplies they had just purchased in town.

Something grabbed his shoulder and pulled him under. He choked on the water, fighting to keep Suri above it. Kicking his legs as hard as he could, he resurfaced, gasping for breath.

"Help! I can't swim!" Rae screeched, clawing her way up Ferrin's back.

"Get off!" he yelled, spitting water with every breath. "You're going to kill us all!" He couldn't carry everyone, plus their supplies, and hope to remain above water. He wasn't sure which travel bag he was carrying. It could have been nothing more than extra blankets, or it could have been their food, or worse, their gold. His fingers were growing numb. Pretty soon, he wouldn't be able to carry anything.

They rounded another bend and smacked against the rock on the far side, shaking Rae loose for a brief moment. She paddled instinctively like a dog to keep above water, but no matter how hard she tried, her head kept going back under. Ferrin grabbed her and pulled her up, treading as hard and as fast as he could to keep himself and Suri from going under.

He knew he had to make a choice. "Use your legs!" he shouted, but Rae was too frightened to understand. She went down again and this time didn't come back up. He released the bag and swam for her. He dove under the water, taking Suri with him as he blindly swung his arms. His hand grabbed hold of a wad of material and he kicked upward, pulling them all back to the surface.

Rae and Suri both had too much water in them to even cry, but not enough to keep them from trying to mount his shoulders. "No! Stop fighting! Hold still or I can't carry you." Rae ignored him and kept climbing, forcing Ferrin to throw her off. He grabbed her head and dunked her underwater. She came up screaming. "Now stop!"

Her head bobbed up and down as she gasped for air, but she finally relaxed enough for Ferrin to reach around her neck and up under one arm to pull her to him. With Suri still around his neck and one arm taken up with Rae, it took everything he had to keep afloat. He used his legs to tread and his one arm to guide away from the larger rocks.

The water was freezing, and his body was already numb, which meant he wasn't going to be able to keep his legs and arms moving much longer. They rounded another turn, and he spotted a downed tree on the right side, half in the water. It was their only chance.

He kicked and paddled as hard as he could, and they were still only halfway across. A submerged rock clipped his leg, and pain shot through him as they veered off course, but he didn't stop kicking and somehow managed to turn them back around. Rae spat and choked as he tried to keep her head above the current. The tree was coming up on the right.

As strong as he was, he could see they weren't going to make it, but he didn't stop. Pulling them through the water like a man possessed, he screamed as he dug in the last few strokes, reaching as far as he could to grab the tree.

He missed.

All hope fled, and he was ready to go with it, to let go and give in to the fates. They clearly wanted him dead, anyway, so what was the use of fighting it?

"Catch!"

A rope landed on his head and Suri grabbed it. Ferrin, latching on to what little spark of faith he had left, wrapped his arm around it as well, and it went taut, dragging them against the current. Through the water, Ferrin could see Myron clinging to the other side of the downed tree.

"Hold on!" Myron shouted as he began to pull.

Ferrin clung to the rope with everything he had. He could no longer feel his fingers; he simply willed them to keep gripping. The current swung them like a pendulum up against the rocky embankment on the far side, where the water wasn't quite so strong, giving Myron the chance to pull them in.

"Thought I'd lost you for sure," Myron said, grabbing Suri and placing her up the tree a little, where she clung to the bark and didn't move.

Rae was next. Ferrin helped push her up until Myron could pull her the rest of the way. As soon as she was out, she scurried up to Suri and practically lay on top of her.

"You're next, smith. Give me your hand."

Myron pulled until Ferrin was half out of the water, barely able to move.

His entire body shook, his teeth chattering so fast that if he stuck his tongue out, he'd probably bite it off. He laid his head against the soft bark. "I could die right here, and it would be all right."

"You've got too much to live for," Myron said, grabbing the travel sacks he'd been carrying and moving up to where Rae and Suri were still lying prostrate across the face of the tree. "What say we not tempt fate any longer and get back on dry ground? If we don't get a fire started soon, we're all going to die from the cold."

The sun was already down below the rock line, and before long, it would be too dark to see. With a painful grunt, Ferrin pulled himself to his hands and knees and started climbing. Myron moved on ahead and tossed the bags up into the narrow pass where the tree had fallen, then came back down to help the others.

It took them about ten minutes to scale the tree and make it back to dry ground, and another ten minutes to peel enough bark and twigs off to get a small fire going. Not worrying about proper decorum, they quickly peeled off their soaked clothing and huddled around the flames, leaving on only the smallest amount for simple modesty.

Slowly, the warmth began to permeate their bodies. Ferrin felt his skin prickle as his blood began to thaw, allowing his fingers to bend once again. It was a long time before he stopped shaking and the heat set in.

"Well," Myron said, looking back over the river, "we're alive."

"Barely," Ferrin added, still trying to get his fingers working. "I lost one of our travel bags, I'm afraid." He glanced at Rae, but she ignored him and kept her eyes on the fire. "And I'm not sure which one it was."

"Food, I'm afraid," Myron said.

"What about the gold?" Ferrin asked. "The bags from my horse had the gold."

"Then it's a good thing I grabbed those first," Myron said with a smile.

Ferrin released a heavy sigh. "Thankful for that, at least."

"We have much to be thankful for," Myron said. "Not only did we escape Sylas, the Black Watch, and a bulradoer, but we survived the raging waters of Virn Run and managed to land on the very side we were trying to get to all along."

Ferrin turned and looked down at the river behind them. He hadn't thought about that till now. He smiled. They had made it to the other side after all.

Chapter 84 | Ayrion

A YRION SHOOK HIS HEAD, throwing wet strands of black hair from his face as he stepped through to the other side of the falls. He held his swords up, bracing for an attack that never came.

The tunnel was shrouded in darkness, making it difficult to see, even for one with Upakan eyes. He stood to the side and waited for the rest of his fighters to make it through, maybe forty strong, less than half of what they had started with, including those Tameel had brought with him from the Justice House.

Tameel stayed behind, along with those too injured to continue, and kept an eye on the unconscious creatures.

Abiah had spent as much time as he could sifting through the bodies, looking for Willem. If his son was still alive, he should have still been recognizable. He'd only been taken the day before, and as far as Ayrion could tell, a full transformation took several days.

The search had proven fruitless.

Ayrion took a few more steps inside the dark passageway, keeping to the balls of his feet, ready to spring into action. The stench of decay was more pervasive here than in the open chamber on the other side of the falls.

"Oy, I'm gonna be sick," Abiah said as he stepped through the water and took his first big whiff. He turned toward the wall and emptied his stomach. His retching quickly elicited responses from others.

Bek unwrapped the thick strips of cloth they'd tied to keep the torches dry and ignited the pitch with a striker. He passed one back and joined Ayrion at the front. The way ahead wasn't much larger than the mining tunnels leading out. Ayrion could see a glimmer of light coming from what looked like another open chamber ahead.

"Interesting," Bek said as he lifted the torch to get a better look.

"Yes," Ayrion said. "It's quite the hideaway."

Abiah moved up beside them, wiping his mouth. "I can think of a few better places." His face was pale.

Once the rest of their small band of brave citizens had made it through the water, Ayrion started them forward, careful to keep from stepping on the litter of human remains at their feet.

"I believe we have finally found the nest," Bek said as he spun his hatchet around in one hand, looking eager to sink it into something.

Ayrion kept his eyes on the tunnel ahead. "I can see why Argon chose it. It's highly defensible. Absolutely no chance of sunlight breaking through."

"And if one could ignore the rather distasteful décor of entrails," Zynora said, keeping a few steps behind as she leaned heavily on one of the villagers, "the place has a certain kind of natural beauty to it."

Ayrion was surprised Zynora was still on her feet. Tameel had force-fed her two apples, a cut of meat, and three pieces of strong cheese before she managed to make it up to the falls. Even then, it took the help of three men to get her there. She was as determined as the rest to see this through.

Ayrion brought them to a halt at the end of the passageway. The open

chamber ahead was nowhere near the size of the one they'd just left with its waterfall and winding canal. It was closer to the size of the entryway at the Justice House.

"Welcome," Argon said, his booming voice filling the cavern.

On the far side of the room against the back wall, an outcropping of rock rose halfway to the ceiling. A set of stone steps built into the side led all the way to the top, where a large piece of granite, which had been chiseled out to form a monolithic seat, sat near the front.

Ayrion wondered if this place had been here all along, or if Argon had built it since his release.

Argon greeted them with outstretched arms, reclining comfortably in a rather kingly fashion. The chamber felt like the throne room from some obscure palace, which undeniably fit Argon's inflated sense of self-worth. All that was missing was his crown.

"Ah, and I see you brought dinner," Argon said with a wicked grin.

Ayrion scanned the surrounding rock, looking for the vulraaks he had seen following Argon through the water. They were nowhere to be seen. There was, however, a rather large firepit just below the shelf of rock Argon was sitting on, lighting the entire chamber with its flames. Piles of bones and carcasses lay scattered around the edges.

"Your army has been thwarted," Ayrion said, daring a few steps into the cavern. "Whatever plans you had for Aldor end here."

Argon threw back his head and roared. His laughter shook the surrounding rock, encouraging some of Ayrion's own men to scurry back into the darker recess of the tunnel behind them.

"You think your short-lived victory over those pathetic wretches constitutes my surrender? Then you have no idea who I am or what I'm capable of. When I'm through, I will have raised an army that envelops all of Aldor." Argon leaned forward in his stone seat, veins as dark as the crystal that hung from his neck, bulging through his white skin. "I have seen this generation's fear of magic. You have grown weak and complacent. A thousand years of fear has ripened you for conquest.

Aldor needs a leader, one that can bring back the glories it once possessed and the power it once held."

"And you believe yourself to be such a person?"

Argon's red eyes shone bright. "Who better? It was I, and those ven'ae like me, who helped throw back our faerie oppressors, who gave rise to the great Wizard Council, who brought freedom and enlightenment to the peoples of Aldor." His face suddenly darkened. "Look how they repaid us! They hunted us down. Forced us into hiding. They used those cursed faerie collars to control us. With the durmas around our necks, we were no more than slaves to their will. Can you blame us for fighting back?"

"That's not quite the way I heard it told," Zynora said, stepping out to join Ayrion in the light. "It was the wizards, or at least a faction of them, who were the aggressors. They began to believe themselves more than human. Believed that because of their gifts, they were above the law. It was you and your kind's lust for power that prodded your delving into darker magics like necromancy, twisting it into something perverse." Zynora sneered. "It was you and your master's desire for domination that led to the Wizard Wars."

Argon glared at the old Rhivanni healer. "I see history has once again been written by the victors. But that will soon change."

"You speak of uniting Aldor, of bringing back some former age of glory." Ayrion pointed his sword at the piles of bodies covering the cavern floor. "Is this your vision, then? Feeding on the helpless, molding humans into some twisted image of yourself? If so, I see why they locked you away for the last millennium."

Argon shrugged. "Every war has its casualties. Only a true leader is willing to make the sacrifices necessary to accomplish his goal. I can see in your eyes you are a man who knows this all too well."

Ayrion took another step forward, moving completely out of the shadows of the tunnel. "And only a *true* leader is willing to put the people under his charge above himself." Ayrion pointed a sword toward the rise.

"You are no leader, Argon. You're a coward and a bully, a parasite that feeds off the lives of others."

Argon stood, his lips parting in a harsh sneer. "Bring them!"

Out from behind the large throne-shaped rock, five vulraaks emerged from a crevice in the rock, each dragging at least one unturned person with them. Most were children.

A shield for a coward, Ayrion thought, feeling sick.

"I like my meat young and fresh," Argon said. "Much softer to chew before they are turned."

"Willem! It's my Willem!" Abiah pushed his way to the front, but Bek grabbed the desperate man by the shoulders and pulled him back.

Willem shouted as soon as he caught sight of his father, but the creature holding his leash backhanded him across the face and pushed him forward to stand with the rest at the edge of the shelf.

"Let go of me!" Abiah roared. "That's my son up there!"

"Yes," Bek said, "and the last thing he needs is for you to go running out there like a madman and get him killed."

Abiah offered a reluctant nod, but Ayrion could see in his eyes that if it wasn't for Bek's strong grip, the man wouldn't still be standing there.

"Well, what's it to be, warrior? You leave now, and I'll let these young ones go, untouched. Or shall we see how much *you* are willing to sacrifice?"

The children were shaking, most openly crying. Even Willem had tears in his eyes as the vulraaks pressed their sharp claws against their captives' throats.

"Better yet," Argon said, sliding to the edge of his seat, "shall we test your steel against mine? You speak of sacrifice. Let's see how far you're willing to go."

"Give me a moment to consider." Ayrion turned to those behind him.

"I'm not considering anything," Abiah said.

"Neither am I," Ayrion countered, keeping is voice lowered. "Now, how many of you think you could hit those vulraaks from here with an arrow?"

"I can," Abiah said, shrugging out of Bek's grip. "Give me a crossbow. I can hit them from here."

"Good. Find four more who can as well. As soon as I draw Argon away from the rise, take the shot."

"And what are you going to do?" Zynora asked.

"Whatever I have to." Ayrion turned around and strode farther into the chamber, gripping his swords, feeling the smooth curves of the dragon crossguards pressing against the backs of his fingers. *Here goes nothing.*

Argon's clawed toes gripped the edge of the rock as he sneered down at him from the top of the ledge.

"You wanted to know what I'd be willing to risk. Well, here I am," Ayrion said, lifting his arms out to the sides. "As you can see, I'm willing to put *my* life on the line. How about *you*?"

The creature chuckled. "Oh, I'm more than willing to put *your* life on the line as well." With a powerful push of his legs, Argon leaped into the air and landed on Ayrion's left, just out of sword-reach. Aerodyne's former general rose to full height, towering over Ayrion. "It will be my pleasure to cut you into pieces and cook you over the fire."

Ayrion raised his blades. "You'll find no pleasure here."

Argon glanced over Ayrion's shoulder, back toward the entrance. "Keep your people back, or I'll let them watch the children get fed upon."

"Stay back!" Ayrion shouted over his shoulder, not looking away.

Argon raised his sword. "This is going to be a short fight."

"Good," Ayrion said with a cold grin. "You made me miss my dinner."

Argon's meaty lips curled back to reveal a full set of sharp fangs. "You *are* dinner," he said, then charged.

Chapter 85 | Ayrion

A YRION SAW THE ATTACK before it happened and deflected Argon's blade. He sidestepped and readied himself for the backswing he knew was coming. He ducked, and Argon's blade sheared off a piece of granite behind him as thick as Ayrion's chest.

He retreated slowly toward the left side of the room, drawing Argon away from the tunnel. He had to give his fighters the chance to reach the vulraaks.

Their steel rang through the cavern, sparks spitting with every clash. Ayrion leaped to the side just in time to keep from getting split in two as Argon's blade plowed into the rock, sending a tremor up Ayrion's legs. But it wasn't just Argon's blade he needed to worry about; he also had to watch the massive dagger-like claws on each hand.

The fire behind them sent their shadows dancing across the stone walls as they fought for the very control of Aldor. Argon was immensely powerful and faster than anything that size had a right to be. Even with Ayrion's ability to foresee the creature's movements, it was still all he could do to keep up with him.

Argon's strength and speed seemed to flow from a bottomless reserve. He never slowed and never faltered, while Ayrion lost ground with every new swing. He danced back and forth, struggling to keep up. Whatever magic the creature was using, Ayrion wished he had some of it. His breathing grew labored, and his body ached from the abuse.

They approached the far side of the chamber. Argon beat back another of Ayrion's advances and then swung at his head. Ayrion dove to the side, aiming for Argon's leg as he passed, but the vulraak was too quick.

Rolling back to his feet, Ayrion spared a passing glance back at the tunnel. He could see Abiah, Bek, and a few others lifting crossbows. *Please, don't let them miss.* Ayrion attacked, trying to keep Argon focused on him. He lashed out with both blades, angling to break through Argon's guard and deliver that fatal blow, but the enormous creature managed to turn them aside.

Ayrion spun and ducked underneath another attempt at his midsection and heard the snap of crossbows. Shrieks from the top of the rise followed. He attacked again, trying to keep the huge vulraak from turning, but Argon sidestepped with a quick backswing of his sword, forcing Ayrion to leap out of the way or be cut down.

Using the momentary break, Argon turned to see what had happened. Across the room, Ayrion's fighters were charging the rise, Abiah leading the way as they mounted the steps for the hostages.

"Attack!" Argon roared.

White bodies poured out from behind the throne on top of the shelf. There must have been a passageway hidden behind the rock.

Ayrion and Argon continued to circle one another as they were momentarily distracted by the battle, each keeping one eye on the other.

By the time Willem had grabbed the other kids and made it to the steps, Ayrion's fighters crested the rise and hit the vulraaks' front line. Ayrion could see Bek's hatchets swinging through the air, sending up

ribbons of dark blood with every pass.

Argon lunged.

Ayrion was so distracted by the battle that he barely missed being skewered by the enormous blade. He managed to get his swords up just in time to deflect the attack, sidestepping to the left as Argon barreled straight through. His escape was temporary, though, as he ended up with his back against the cavern wall.

Argon roared and swung with everything he had. Ayrion ducked, and the steel bit into the wall, the impact so strong, it shook some of the larger boulders above them free, and they came raining down on top of them.

Ayrion ran, using his visions to dodge the hail of rock, each one shaking the ground as they hit.

Argon wasn't quite as lucky, taking one to the back and another that grazed the side of his head.

"Retreat! Retreat!" Bek shouted from the rise as the villagers fought their way slowly back down the steps.

Ayrion turned. The creatures were already leaping from the sides of the rise and moving around to flank his fighters.

They were trapped.

Ayrion lifted his blades to run and help but dove to the right instead as a rock larger than his head flew by and slammed into the rise. His fighters were completely surrounded, boxed in from both sides of the steps. They needed his help.

He steeled his emotions. As much as he wanted to save them, he was there for one purpose and one purpose only. If he had to spend all their lives to accomplish it, that was the price he would pay. It was the price they had all resigned to pay.

He raised his swords and turned back around, giving himself in to his magic, holding nothing back. Heat pulsed through his body as he stared into the vulraak's bloodred eyes. "One way or the other, this ends today."

Argon swung, but instead of blocking or dodging, or simply doing whatever he could to stay clear of the deadly weapon, Ayrion dove *into* the attack. With all the speed he could muster, he threw one of the swords and rolled through the creature's legs before Argon had made it halfway through his swing.

The sword buried itself in Argon's upper chest.

The ancient general roared as he stumbled backward, and with a lucky swing, he hit Ayrion in the side with the back of his hand, sending him through the air. Ayrion bounced off a boulder about ten feet away and landed on his hands and knees, coughing blood. He knew his ribs were cracked.

The enormous creature yanked Ayrion's sword from his chest and tossed it into the firepit.

Ayrion smiled as he struggled to his feet, fighting back the pain in his chest. He'd finally managed to inflict a serious blow against Aerodyne's general. Up until that very moment, he had begun to wonder if it was even possible. "So, you bleed after all."

The leader of the vulraak released a booming howl and charged.

Ayrion braced for the impact, his legs already trembling.

Argon raised his sword, but a shock wave tore through the room, sending him to his knees. The creature skidded to a stop as white bodies flew through the air in all directions. The cavern was raining vulraaks.

Ayrion dove to the left to miss getting hit by one as it came down beside him. It squealed and went still. Quickly, he crawled to his feet, turning to look at the steps. Zynora had managed to clear their path down, but they were still fighting the ones from the top. Ayrion lifted his remaining sword and turned to face Argon, but he wasn't there.

Ayrion spun back around to see Argon racing past the firepit toward the stairs.

"No!" Ayrion took off running. "Behind you! Behind you!" He barely had time to get the words out before Argon tore into the back of their ranks.

Every swing of Argon's blade sent pieces of townsfolk in all

directions. In a panic, the people turned and charged the vulraaks at the top, cutting them down in a mad frenzy to get away from Argon. By the time they reached the pinnacle, what few vulraaks were left were leaping from the sides of the rise to escape.

Ayrion tore up the steps behind them, Argon cresting the rise just ahead. His people were left with nowhere to go. Unlike the vulraaks, if they attempted jumping from that height, it would mean immediate death.

"Argon, you coward!" Ayrion shouted as he charged up the steps. By the time he reached the top, his fighters were struggling to make it into the small opening behind Argon's throne. Bek, Abiah, and a few of the other men were standing in a line out front, desperately trying to hold the monster back.

The taverner deflected Argon's blade with his own, but the strike ripped the old sword from his hands and sent him bouncing off the wall behind him.

Ayrion reached the summit in time to see Zynora stumble to the front of the group and raise her arms. Argon stopped his attack and braced himself, but nothing happened. The panic on her face said she had nothing left. Ayrion raced across the rise to reach her, but not before Argon had turned and kicked Zynora sideways. Ayrion could hear the bones snapping as she crashed into the side of Argon's throne and collapsed.

Ayrion dove for Argon's legs, but the vulraak leaped over him and back toward the edge. Dark blood was still seeping from the wound on the creature's chest, covering half his white torso.

Ayrion started for the front of the rise, pain so intense it overwhelmed everything but his need to kill this creature. He pushed all other worries aside. Too many people had given their lives for him to give up now.

He lunged, but Argon deflected and countered with a wide swing of his own. With only one blade, Ayrion was having a difficult time blocking both Argon's steel and his claws at the same time. He swung to the right, temporarily diverting the enormous sword but leaving himself open in the process.

Ayrion screamed as a single claw raked his chest. His black coat might as well have been made of silk, for all the good it did. All the air was forced from his lungs as he skidded across the ground, back toward the steps. Ayrion rolled to his side and caught a glimpse of Zynora's motionless body. It didn't look like she was breathing.

He could hardly breathe himself. Blood filled his mouth. He spat it across the stone and forced his shaky arms to push himself up. He was barely able to make it to his knees before Argon started across the rise for him. The former general didn't seem to be in a hurry, probably wanting to savor his victory.

Ayrion attempted to stand but stumbled back to one knee, still dazed by the blow. Argon grinned as he raised his weapon. Ayrion barely got his sword up in time to stop the blow, the force of it sending him to both knees. Argon twisted to try from the other side, but not before Bek attacked from behind. The big trapper swung his hatchets with the speed of a cat, burying them in Argon's back while he was turned.

The monstrous vulraak roared as he spun and backhanded Bek. The trapper's body went limp as he hit the edge of the rise and fell off.

"No!" Ayrion screamed, tears burning his eyes. He forced himself the rest of the way to his feet, using his remaining sword for balance. He stumbled forward. His legs were shaking. He could feel the blood dripping from his chin. He coughed, and it nearly brought him to his knees all over again. He knew his insides were broken.

Argon limped over to his throne. "I'm going to save you for last, warrior," he sneered over his shoulder. "I want you to watch as I kill your friends one by one, knowing there's nothing you can do to save them." Argon stopped at the side of the granite seat. "And I think I'll start with this meddlesome old hag," he said, nudging Zynora with his foot. The movement brought her out of unconsciousness, and she started to move.

No! Ayrion stumbled forward. "Take me instead. I'm right here." His words were nearly the only weapon he had left to fight with as he stumbled to one knee, barely catching himself with his hand to keep from going down completely. He didn't think he had enough strength to parry a single strike.

Argon raised his foot over one of Zynora's legs and looked at Ayrion. He grinned, then stepped down. Ayrion could hear the brittle bones snap.

Zynora screamed.

Ayrion dug deep, pulling every last drop of magic he had, gathering what small amount of life he still clung to, and bottled it for one final attack. He got to his feet and lifted his sword. This was it. All or nothing. He'd managed to take a single step when Zynora suddenly sat up and grabbed Argon's leg. Purple light tore into the vulraak's ankle, and he reared his head back and roared, the wedge of steel in his hand dropping to clang on the stone below. The creature couldn't seem to move as the magic ripped through him. His screams shook the cavern.

Zynora was giving Ayrion his chance. How she was even still conscious under such pain, Ayrion couldn't guess, but he wasn't going to waste her effort.

With a deep breath, he raised his sword over his head. "Guide my aim," he prayed, then lunged forward and threw his blade. It made two rotations, end over end. He could almost feel the impact as it punched through Argon's chest, sending the creature reeling to his back, still paralyzed by the hold of Zynora's magic.

Ayrion stumbled forward.

"Hurry!" Zynora mumbled. "I can't hold him much . . ." The glow from her hands disappeared, and her eyes rolled up in the back of her head as she dropped.

Ayrion yanked the blade from Argon's chest, and before the creature had a chance to recover, he swung for the vulraak's neck.

Argon's head rolled toward the ledge, where Abiah sent it the rest of the way over with a good kick, watching as it dropped into the fire below.

"Back to the flaming Pits of Aran'gal for you!" he said, then hocked up a wet glob and sent it over the edge for good measure. Willem was there, trying to hold his father on his feet.

Ayrion watched as the pillar of black smoke rose from Argon's corpse, much thicker and larger than any he'd seen before. The smoke rose above them, blocking the top of the cavern from view. Ayrion stared up at the menacing cloud. Why wasn't it dissipating? All the others had dispersed within seconds, but Argon's wasn't. In fact, it seemed to be coalescing as it circled the upper platform.

By the time Ayrion realized something was wrong, the cloud struck. Ayrion had nowhere to go. It pinned him to the ground, leaving him unable to move.

Something was terribly wrong.

He could feel the smoke working its way into his mouth and eyes and ears, like a red-hot poker searing everything it touched as it pushed further inside him. He could feel Argon's presence, his thoughts, his desires, his hatred. Ayrion struggled to move, but he was no longer in control. He could see the others standing there watching him. From the dumbfounded looks on their faces, they didn't know what to do any more than he did. It was like peering through a hole in the wall, watching what was taking place in the next room, but not being able to interact with it.

"Your body is a perfect fit, warrior," Argon said, using Ayrion's voice as he raised Ayrion's arms and moved them about to test their motion. "So kind of you to share it."

Ayrion shouted, but no one heard him.

A flash of something out of the corner of his eye had Argon turning. Ayrion wasn't sure who was more surprised, Argon or himself, as they watched a man in thick furs clear the top steps and race across the platform. He was carrying one of Ayrion's dragon blades in his hand.

"No!" Argon jumped to his feet and chased after him, giving Ayrion no other option but to watch in stunned silence as Argon tried to reach the fur-clad trapper. But Bek had too much of a lead for Argon to catch up in Ayrion's body.

Bek dove through the air and landed on the ground beside the headless creature, bringing Ayrion's black steel down across the rocks.

What in the name of the Creator is that lunatic doing with my sword?

Suddenly, Ayrion's body convulsed, and he skidded to his knees, pain shooting through him as he and Argon screamed at the same time. What was happening?

Again, Bek lifted his blade and struck the hard stone, and *again* Ayrion's body jerked and twisted and eventually staggered to the ground, where he curled into a fetal position facing Bek. That's when he saw it. The crystal Argon had been wearing around his neck. It was lying beside the creature's body. Bek struck it once more, and the gem shattered.

Ayrion fell flat on his back. He couldn't move. He could, however, hear Argon's voice screaming something in an unknown tongue. He watched as the dark cloud of Argon's essence poured from his mouth and rose into the air.

Those gathered to witness Ayrion's transformation ran for the hole in the wall behind Argon's throne, undoubtedly afraid he'd come for them next. However, this time, the dark, angry column of smoke didn't attack. Instead, it floated upward, eventually disintegrating as it hit the farthest reaches of the rock over their heads.

Finally, Ayrion was able to breathe on his own. Tears flooded his eyes. Tears of joy as he realized it was finally over. The pain of his broken body washed over him, and he was thankful for it. It meant he was still alive.

Bek dragged Ayrion over to Zynora's side as Abiah attempted to wrap her ruined leg. "Don't you worry about me, Grey Eyes," she said as she tried to hold a brave face. "I've seen worse." Her voice was shaking, but it didn't stop her from laying a hand on the top of his chest.

He could feel her magic trickle into him. He was surprised she had any left. He finally grabbed her hand and pulled it away. "Stop. You've already used too much as it is. I'll be fine."

"You'll be fine when I say you're fine," she said, and laid her hand back on him, but before she could continue feeding him her magic, a couple of men lifted her up and carried her back toward the stairs leading off the rise. She complained the whole way down.

Ayrion turned over and smiled at the sight of Willem with his arms wrapped around his father's barrel chest, tight enough to make the taverner wince.

"Give me your arm," Bek said, helping Ayrion to his feet. Even with the healing Zynora had managed to give him, Ayrion's legs were too wobbly to stand on their own.

"Oh, I found this lying halfway out of the fire. Crazy thing wasn't even warm."

Ayrion grinned when he saw the dragon blade resting in Bek's hand.

"Wouldn't mind a couple of these myself," Bek said. He placed the sword in its sheath on Ayrion's back.

"Apparently, you don't need any weapons at all," Ayrion said.

Bek cocked his head with a confused look.

"Well, one moment, you're tumbling to your death over the side of the rise, and the next, you're back up here like nothing happened, saving the day." Ayrion studied the big trapper's face. "Is there something you want to confess? A secret gift for wielding that we don't know about?"

Bek clapped Ayrion on the back and laughed. Ayrion didn't find it too funny, as Bek's hand sent a sheer jolt of pain down his spine. "No, no magic here. It was all providence. After going over the side, I managed to land on a pile of vulraaks that had been thrown off during Zynora's last blast."

Ayrion and Bek walked over to the edge of the rise and looked down.

"It appears the plague died with him," Bek said, pointing to the remaining vulraaks who'd managed to survive the battle. Their bodies were already changing, their skin reddening, their claws and fangs receding.

"Recovery is going to be a long road for them," Ayrion said.

Bek nodded. "Even if they managed to completely revert, I'm afraid Belvin will never be the same."

"No, I doubt it will." Ayrion placed his arm around Bek's shoulders. "What say we get these people home?"

Chapter 86 | Breen

BREEN HELPED HIS FATHER carry Ty into a private study near the back of the Sidaran Assembly Hall.

"What do I tell the overlords?" Barl asked, pacing in front of the sofa where they had laid Ty's unconscious body.

"Tell them the truth," Nyalis said as he warmed his hands in front of the fire. "You tell them that this was an overt attack by the White Tower to drive a wedge between the overlords in the hopes of putting an end to these talks. They cannot risk the kingdoms forming an alliance."

Breen knelt beside the sofa, joining Lyessa and Fraya as they watched the slow rise and fall of Ty's chest. He couldn't believe how much the witch had put his brother through. First the spider's bite, then the *numori*. What was it going to take to get rid of her?

"And as far as the overlords go," Nyalis continued, "you said that neither saw who the guards were fighting, correct?"

Barl crossed his arms. "They were ushered out of the building through the northwest corridors. They were never within eyeshot of the front."

"Good. Then the situation is easily rectified. In fact, you can probably use this to your advantage."

Barl nodded, but slowly, as if not entirely convinced.

"And in truth," Nyalis said, "this was indeed an attack by the White Tower, if in an indirect sort of way. It shouldn't be taken lightly."

"And what exactly are those plans?" Breen's father asked.

Breen wanted an answer to that as well. He stood and stretched his legs, which were going numb from kneeling beside the sofa.

"What is it that they want with my son? You show up here, drop off a baby, and tell us to protect him because he's important, but you never tell us why."

The wizard sighed and gave his long beard a couple of brisk tugs. "Truthfully, I'm not sure how our young Ty plays a role in the events to come. I believe the Archchancellor seeks the fulfillment of ancient prophecies written down after the fall of the Defiler. Some of the prophetic texts discuss, in the vaguest sense, a possible returning."

"Returning?" Feoldor shifted his feet when Reloria leaned against his shoulder. "Returning of what?"

"Not *what*, but *who*."

Veldon rubbed his kerchief nervously across the top of his head. "You're not saying that you believe the Dark Wizard will return, are you?"

Nyalis stared at an empty section of the burgundy-and-gold-striped carpet as if he would find an answer woven into the finely stitched edging. "Yes, that is precisely what I'm saying."

The room fell silent.

Breen forgot about his legs. Was Nyalis serious? Did he really believe that Aerodyne was going to return?

"How is that possible?" Orlyn asked. "He's locked inside Taerin nu'Cyllian."

"If there's one thing I have learned over the centuries, it's that if there is a way in, there is always a way out. Nothing built by man or faerie, no matter how powerful, can last forever. Aerodyne's penitentiary inside the Pits of Aran'gal is crumbling. The containment spells are failing, and when they do, we had better be ready."

Again, silence.

Barl cleared his throat. "I can't believe I'm about to ask this, but how long do we have?"

"There's no telling, really. It might be next week. It might not happen in your lifetimes."

"So, you can't be sure?"

"No, I can't."

Breen found himself breathing a small sigh of relief.

"From what I've seen, though, I believe it will be sooner rather than later."

Breen's relief was short-lived.

"Great," Feoldor said, throwing his arms up. "Not only do we have to worry about the White Tower trying to kill us, but now we have to worry about some all-powerful dark mystic coming back from the dead to wipe out all life as we know it. And the news just keeps getting better and better." Reloria patted his arm, but it didn't seem to help.

"Yes, well, every door has two sides," Nyalis said. "There is another prophecy that predates that of even the Wizard Order. 'A savior will always be given to the race of man whenever their darkest hour is at hand.'"

Feoldor chuckled. "Sounds like a poorly written verse from 'Bart the Fool.'"

"You'd be surprised how many of the old children's rhymes are based off of prophecy," Nyalis said. "How do you think the prophets made sure their work was passed down? You should recognize this one:

When hope is all but lost,

And light has turned to dark.

There will a sign be given,

The rising of the Marked."

More than a few eyebrows were raised at that one. Breen's parents had taught that to him when he was younger. "Is that what's growing down his arm?" Ty had mentioned that Nyalis had spoken of the Marked Ones, but Breen wanted to hear it for himself.

"Yes. That particular pattern symbolizes strength."

Lyessa lifted Ty's shirt to get a look.

"The stronger he becomes, the further it will grow. But putting that aside, the White Tower believes that Ty is somehow the key to Aerodyne's release, which is why it's time for him to leave."

"Leave?" Lyessa released Ty's shirt and turned. "Leave where?"

"As long as Ty remains in Easthaven, it will be more dangerous for the people here, which is why I'm sending him to bring back the lost Keep of Aero'set." He looked at Breen. "Did you not mention this to them?"

"We did. But with everything that happened . . ."

Nyalis nodded.

"So, Aero'set is real?" Orlyn asked, using his staff for support.

"Very real, I assure you. It will be the only truly safe place left in Aldor if the White Tower's influence continues to spread. But what's important now is to see to our young faeling's well-being." Nyalis left the others and walked over to where Breen was standing at the head of the sofa. "I also want a look at that bow."

Breen had hoped the old wizard had forgotten about it. The last thing he wanted was to be called out on the lie he'd told his father. Reluctantly, he unhooked it from his shoulder and handed it to him.

The wizard took a moment to examine it, carefully studying the markings along both sides. "It is certainly one of the Sol Ghati bows. Where did you get it?"

Breen gulped. "I might have misled some people to believe I had purchased it from a traveling peddler," he said, passing a nervous glance to his father, "but—"

"But you found this in Mangora's shop," Nyalis said.

Breen looked at his father and, with another gulp, reluctantly nodded.

"Lucky for you it was a Sol Ghati bow. These bows can't be spelled."

Breen wilted under his father's hard glare. He wasn't feeling so lucky now.

"As it happens, fortune favored your thievery. If it wasn't for the bow, we might not have been able to stop Mangora."

"What is a Sol Ghati? And how did my arrow pierce her shield?"

"The Sol Ghati were a group of wardens that protected the Westlands almost two thousand years ago. It was said their arrows could cut through most forms of magic. The glyphs on the sides of the bow are their oath to protect their land." He handed Breen back the bow. "A rare find. Guard it well."

Breen nodded, careful not to look at his father again. He was going to have to apologize later, which was sure to mean a doubling-up on chores for the next month or two.

"What more can we do for him?" Fraya asked from her seat at the foot of the sofa, clearly wanting to help.

"There's not much more we can do, I'm afraid. The rest is up to him."

Breen watched as his brother slept. So much rested on those shoulders. How was Ty going to survive what was coming?

"He will need your help," the old wizard said, as if reading Breen's mind.

Breen lifted his head. "And he will always have it."

The End of

Book Two of
The Aldoran Chronicles

Dear Reader,

I HOPE YOU enjoyed this second book in the Aldoran Chronicles series. If you found the story entertaining and would like to see more, then please consider helping me reach that goal by leaving a quick review on Amazon.

Reviews are very important. They help encourage other readers to try the book while at the same time showing Amazon that the book is worth promoting. Reviews don't need to be long or involved, just a sentence or two that tells people what you liked about the book in order to help readers know why they might like it too.

Thank you in advance!

Love fantasy merchandise? Stop by the **Aramoor Market** and take a look at the new Aldoran store.

<<www.store.michaelwisehart.com>>

Author Note

YOU CAN LEARN more about the World of Aldor on my website. If you haven't taken the time to peruse, I believe you'll find it both educational and entertaining. Don't forget to read the *History of Aldor* while you're there. It will give you a better understanding behind the internal struggles and conflicts taking place between those with magic and those without.

Stop by and say hello!
« michaelwisehart.com »
« facebook.com/MichaelWisehart.author »

Acknowledgements

I THANK GOD for the doors and windows He's allowed to open in order for me to reach this point.

I want to thank my parents, *Mickey and Julie Wisehart,* for their unending loyalty, encouragement, and support over the years. None of this would be possible without you. Love you both.

I want to thank my Author Team, whose endless talent, time, and dedication have made this project possible:

AUTHOR TEAM

I want to thank my cover illustrator and sister, whose imagination and talent have given us our first glimpse of Ayrion's swords—*Janelle Wisehart*

I want to thank my cartographer, who patiently worked with me and my continual need to tweak things, and still managed to produce one incredible map for the capital city of Easthaven—*Elwira Pawlikowska*

I want to thank my cartographer, who managed to take a maze of jumbled ideas and turn them into the capital city of Aramoor—*RenflowerGrapx*

I want to thank my illustrator, who managed to capture the essence of a faerie crystal—*Jack Adams*

I want to thank my content editor, who has spent countless hours advising me on the proper structure of my thoughts—*Nathan Hall*

I want to thank my line editor, who managed to take a floundering script and turn it into something readable—*Danae Smith*

I want to thank my copy editors, whose careful eyes have made my book shine—*Tammy Salyer, Richard Shealy, Crystal Watanabe*

I want to thank my *Beta Team,* who took precious time out of their busy schedule to suffer through the first and second drafts in order to leave such valuable feedback as to help me make this book worth reading.

About the Author

MICHAEL WISEHART graduated with a bachelor's degree in business before going back to school for film and starting his own production company. As much as he enjoyed film work, the call of writing a novel got the better of him, and on April 14, 2014, he started typing the first words of what would become two epic fantasy series: The Aldoran Chronicles and the Street Rats of Aramoor.

He currently lives and writes in South Georgia.

Character Glossary

Abbet Lydale [*ă -bit/lĭ-del*] Easthaven Fuller. Town drunk.

Acorn [*ā -corn*] Breen's horse.

Adarra [*uh-dar-uh*] Sister of Ty and Breen. Daughter of Kellen and Nilla.

Aerodyne [*air-o-dine*] The founder of the first Wizard Order. Known as the Dark One.

Agnar [*ag-nar*] Overlord of Keldor.

Aiden Raycrest [*aye-den/ray-crest*] Son of wealthy millworks owner in Highcrest. Lyessa's fiancé.

Amarysia [*am-uh-ree-see-uh*] Lady in Waiting to High Queen Ellise.

Arina Respuel [*uh-ree-nuh/res-pee-ule*] Overcaptain Barthol's daughter.

Arnoni [*ar-non-ee*] Night Walker whom Kellen's great, great grandfather saved and received a moonstone for his generosity.

Arnst [*arn-st*] Elondrian scout.

Asa [*ace-uh*] Overcaptain under Tolin.

Ayrion [*air-ee-un*] Known as Death's Shadow. Guardian Protector of the High King. Upakan heritage.

Azriel [*az-ree-el*] Seer inside of the White Tower. Ferrin's roommate.

Baeldor [*bay-el-dor*] Leader of Tallosian war party.

Barl [*barl*] Overlord of Sidara. Father of Lyessa.

Barthol Respuel [*bar-thol/res-pee-ule*] Captain of High Guard under Ayrion.

Bartimus [*bar-tĭ-mus*] Fool who went in search for a wife and had a song written about his experience.

Bashan [*bay-shun*] Undercaptain in charge of the Elondrian foot soldiers under Captain Janus.

Basil Kilburn [*bace-le/kill-bern*] Cooper's son. Local bully who went to school with Ty. Dared him to jump into East River.

Bayle [*bay-ul*] Elondrian scout, partner to Merrick. Seafaring accent. Wields a battle-axe.

Belkor [*bel-kor*] Ambassador to Cylmar.

Bellar [*bel-ar*] Bulradoer from Elondria.

Bellos [*bel-lō-ce*] Captain in charge of Elondrian crossbowmen.

Bezaleel [*bez-uh-leel*] Former Archchancellor.

Black Watch [*black/watch*] Group of mercenaries sent to round up magic wielders.

Breen [*breen*] Brother of Ty.

Bue Aboloff [*a-bo-loff*] Husband of Noreen. Innkeeper. Chef.

Calina Tirfing [*cuh-lee-nuh*] Class beauty. Justice Tirfing's only daughter.

Cheeks/Sylas [*sī -lus*] Sadistic inquisitor in the White Tower.

Clye Durran [*klī/dir-an*] Former Easthaven cooper and storyteller.

Dak [*dak*] Bully in Easthaven. Tried dunking Ty in a pickle barrel.

Dakaran [*duh-kar-un*] High Prince of Elondria. Son of Rhydan and Ellise.

Damar [*duh-mar*] Mercenary hired by Baeldor and Mangora to fight Ty's family.

Darryk [*dare-ick*] Lyessa's martial trainer in weapons and combat.

Derryk Lahorn [*dare-ick/luh-horn*] Tal Lahorn's oldest son. Died from a brain fever.

Dorbin [*dor-bin*] Old hermit living outside of Easthaven.

Eliab [*ee-lie-ub*] Gatekeeper for the Easthaven Harbor House.

Elior [*el-ee-or*] Head of Elondrian war-runners.

Ellise [*el-leece*] High Queen of Elondria.

Ellson [*el-son*] Elondrian scout, partner to Terris.

Ethen [*ee-thin*] Local carpenter.

Felina [*fel-ee-nuh*] Citizen of Easthaven. Friend of Helene.

Feoldor [*fay-ol-dor*] Member of Easthaven Wielder Council. Glassblower. Vanti.

Ferrin [*fare-in*] Rhowynn weaponsmith. Imprisoned in the White Tower.

Forel [*for-el*] Member of Tallosian war party.

Fraya Lahorn [*fray-uh/luh-horn*] Daughter of Tal Lahorn. Member of Easthaven Wielder Council. Healer.

Furgus McKesh [*fer-gus/mc-kesh*] Easthaven blacksmith.

Gilly [*gil-ee*] Member of Easthaven Wielder Council. Dwarf. Voda.

Gina [*gee-nuh*] Nanny to Lady Lyessa.

Gunther Mezard [*gun-ther/mez-ard*] Chandler in Easthaven.

Gyin [*guy-in*] Ambassador to Briston.

Hatch [*hach*] Captain of Black Watch riders.

Heglith [*heg-lith*] Black Watch rider under Captain Hatch.

Helene Tunsfield [*hel-een/tuns-field*] Citizen of Easthaven. Friend of Felina.

Heleyna [*huh-lee-nuh*] Mother of Lyessa. Deceased.

Horvah [*hor-vuh*] Weasily bulradoer in charge of the Tower's recruitment.

Janus [*jan-us*] Captain of Elondrian foot soldiers.

Jaylen [*jay-len*] Black Watch rider under Captain Hatch.

Jonas [*joe-nus*] Member of the Tallosian war party.

Josten [*joss-ten*] Mill owner in Easthaven.

Kassyna Lahorn [*kuh-see-nuh/luh-horn*] Wife of Tal Lahorn. Deceased.

Kellen [*kel-en*] Adoptive father of Ty, gamekeeper.

Kensey Respuel [*kin-zee/res-pee-ule*] Overcaptain Barthol Respuel's wife

Kerson [*kir-son*] Warren clansman who challenges the Right of Oktar.

Kira [*keir-ruh*] Street Tribe chief Ayrion grew up with. Head of the Warren clans.

Lanmiere [*lan-meer*] Ambassador to Sidara.

Lenara [*len-ar-uh*] Bulradoer from Cylmar.

Lerra [*lare-uh*] The name of Tameel's wagon.

Loren [*lor-en*] High Guard ostler.

Luc Kilburn [*luke*] Town cooper.

Lugar [*loo-gar*] Head of the Harbor House in Duport. Trusted friend of Veldon.

Lyessa [*lee-es-uh*] Daughter of Overlord Barl and Lady Heleyna.

Mangora [*man-gor-uh*] Dark Witch in Easthaven.

Marta [*mar-tuh*] Legate Superior at the White Tower.

Medarin [*meh-dar-in*] Bulradoer. Outspoken against Valtor's rise to Archchancellor.

Merrick [*mare-ick*] Elondrian scout. Husband of Taleen.

Meyrose [*may-rose*] Overlord of Briston.

Myriah [*mer-eye-uh*] Sister to Ferrin. Lives in Rhowynn.

Nadeer [*nuh-deer*] In charge of the Elondrian longbowmen.

Narri Lahorn [*nar-ee/luh-horn*] Youngest son of Tal.

Nierdon [*nee-air-dun*] Ambassador to Keldor.

Nilla [*nee-luh*] Adoptive mother of Ty. Wife of Kellen.

Nora [*nor-uh*] Orlyn's dead wife.

Noreen Aboloff [*nor-een*] Wife of Bue. Runs the East Inn.

Nyalis [*nee-al-is*] Last of the Aerodyne Wizards.

Old Man Wyker [*wick-er*] Owns a distillery in Easthaven.

Orlyn [*or-lin*] Member of the Easthaven Wielder Council. Apothecary. Floratide.

Peyla [*pee-luh*] Easthaven baker's wife.

Piel [*pee-el*] Head butler to Overlord Barl.

Pinon [*pĭ-non*] Peddler that Ferrin is sold to as a child by his uncle. Former captain in the Keldoran army.

Po [*poe*] Street kid Ayrion gew up with. Second in command under Kira.

Rae [*ray-uh*] Healer in the White Tower. Mother of Suri.

Raguel [*rah-gool*] Master painter who after the death of his wife turned to morbid depictions of humanity.

Reevie [*ree-vee*] Childhood best friend of Ayrion.

Reloria [*reh-lor-ee-uh*] Member of the Easthaven Wielder Council. Telasaro. Owns the Easthaven Sweet Shop.

Rhydan [*rī-dun*] High King of Elondria.

Roan [*rone*] Elondrian scout.

Rowen [*roe-win*] Apprentice to Valtor. Has an ugly deformity on the side of his face.

Rukar [roo-kar] Bulradoer. Well built. Dark skin with strong face. Always seen with a handful of weapons.

Saleena [*suh-lee-nuh*] Physicker captured near Reed Marsh by the Black Watch.

Saryn [*sar-in*] Overlord of Cylmar. Wages war against Elondria.

Sedgewick [*sej-wik*] Younger brother of Amarysia. Nickname is Sedge or Howler. Aramoor street tribe chief.

Selma [sell-muh] Bulradoer. Tall with straight brown hair and a long face. She has a nervous twitch in her left eye.

Shade [*shade*] Ayrion's black warhorse.

Sheeva [*shee-vuh*] New member of Easthaven Wielder Council. From Duport. Short cut blonde hair. Night Walker. Invisibility. Assassin.

Sil'foren [*sil-for-in*] Factory owner in Aramoor who uses street urchins as forced labor.

Soren [*sor-en*] Black Watch rider under Captain Hatch.

Sorna Blaudell [*sor-nuh/blah-dell*] Widow who has had her sights set on Orlyn for the last twenty years.

Suri [*sir-ee*] Daughter of Rae.

Syglara [*sig-lar-uh*] Queen of the Spiders.

Tal Lahorn [*tall/luh-horn*] Father of Fraya. Easthaven farmer.

Taleen [*tuh-leen*] Wife of Merrick who longed to live in the city.

Tameel [*tuh-meel*] Tinker. Husband of Zynora. Part of the Dar'Rhivanni.

Tate [*tayt*] Young street kid that Valtor's henchmen kidnap.

Terris [*tare-iss*] Elondrian scout with scraggy hairy and beard. Broadsword. Slight country accent.

Tess Lahorn [*tess/luh-horn*] Youngest Daughter of Tal.

Thistle [*thiss-le*] Adarra's mare.

Tirana [*tir-ah-nuh*] Wife of Commander Tolin.

Tolin [*tol-in*] Commander of the Elondrian Forces under King Rhydan.

Tolvin [*tol-vin*] Bulradoer from Elondria.

Topin [*toe-pin*] Bulradoer.

Trepin Odel [*trep-in/o-del*] Town cobbler.

Tulvik [*tul-vik*] Wealthy lord who owns an estate north of the Tansian River.

Ty [*tī*] Bearer of The Mark, adopted son of Kellen and Nilla. Brother to Breen and Adarra. Faeling.

Valtor [*val-tor*] Birth name is Milo. [*my-lo*] Archchancellor of the White Tower.

Veldon [*vel-dun*] Portmaster for Easthaven. Leader of Easthaven Wielder

Council. Incidi.

Waddle [*wŏd-le*] Ty's horse.

Widow Windel [*win-dul*] Crazy woman who dressed her pony in her husband's suit and tried to marry him.

Your Highness [*hi-ness*] Kellen's horse, a bit high spirited, chestnut in color.

Zynora [*zin-or-uh*] Wife of Tameel. Tinker. Part of the Dar'Rhivanni.

Stop by and visit:
www.michaelwisehart.com

Made in the USA
Coppell, TX
23 September 2021

62857219R00418